THE MINOR FALL

First published in Ireland by Kayla M. Martell.

Copyright © 2025 by Kayla M. Martell
All rights reserved.
www.kaylammartell.com
hello@kaylammartell.com

Cover Art
Victoria Georgieva
@veryberrydraws

Very Berry

Back artwork
@incendiosketches

ISBN PAPERBACK: 978-1-0369-1310-6
ISBN HARDCOVER: 978-1-0369-1309-0

Published by Kayla M. Martell

Follow the story of Ruhaven

WWW.THEMINORFALL.COM

KAYLA M. MARTELL

THE MINOR FALL

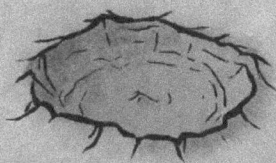

To my sister, Rachelle,
for all the times I was so terrible to you.

Nothing is so startling as truth to human beings—in a canvas too.
— Charles Hawthorne

CHAPTER 1

Girl from the North Country

I had two reasons for accepting this job in Ireland—the first *a lot* more sensible than the second—but neither included dying on the dilapidated roof of Hotel Naruka, where an ambulance wouldn't have a chance of making it up the Kerry mountains.

I winced as my knee banged off the rain-soaked tiles.

"Ah, Jayzus, Roe!" James yelled from below. "Ye come down right now or ye'll be blown straight off, so ye will."

"I'm fine," I said quickly, rising to my feet. "But if I leave the roof like this, your friend might end up with a pond in his old guest room." I turned to face the ocean view from Naruka, hoping James wouldn't notice me massaging my knee. Despite the blustery Atlantic wind, the real storm was still hovering miles away over velvet hills.

"Luckily," James drawled, "Bryn isn't coming here for the room."

"Just the thrill of chance electrocution then?" I returned with a wry grin, having explained to James just yesterday the unfortunate state of his hotel's wiring.

He tucked two thumbs under corduroy suspenders. "Ye forget who owns this place?"

"Time?"

His lips twitched. "If it was, I'd have a word or two with her."

"Make sure you ask her what happened to the fuse box."

His eyes twinkled. "I've a fair idea. Now, will ye come down so she doesn't take me old frail Irish heart?"

Snorting, I glanced at the man who couldn't be much older than thirty-five. Fine-featured and unintimidatingly pretty, James had such an easygoing nature that at first, I'd worried some quick-fingered guest would steal his hotel's silverware. But hidden under that befuddling charm and a pair of foggy glasses, was a man who didn't miss much.

I started tucking a coil of wire back in my toolbelt. "You know that accent will only work on me for so long," I lied.

"Ye should hear me after a pint."

"I've heard you after ten, and I think you lost fifty bucks when I did."

"Forty, and t'was on a fine horse race."

I tucked my tongue in my cheek. "James, it was a *replay*." And I'd only barely won his money back over a game of pool.

He coughed to hide either his laugh or his regret, then tugged off his flat cap so inky-black hair sprang as loose and free as the greenery crawling over Naruka. "Listen, I'll have Bryn stay in another room, so I will, if it means ye'll not end up a corpse in me raspberry bushes."

Which would be a shame, since he used them to make drool-worthy scones each morning.

I tugged my braid over my shoulder and scooted toward the ladder. "I promise not to sue for the insurance or anything."

James gawked behind his glasses and leaned forward. "Ye think they'd give me insurance on *this* bloody place?" he said, jerking his thumb at the hotel's greenhouse, currently growing from her side like a hot glass wart. "Sure, if it all burned down it'd be just as well for me. Though me mammy would be spinning in her grave."

I paused mid-rung of the ladder to admire the place.

He might have a point; Naruka in 1992 didn't look that much different than the 1500s. Her massive stone staircase ascended to a blood-orange door framed by ivory pillars and rose-blooming vines. Ethereal, historical, and unabashedly devoid of good maintenance— like a woman who knew her worth and wasn't going to cover it up with cheap makeup. Twelve chimneys protruded at almost comical angles, most with a tree or shrub growing from them that I'd enjoy pulling out, and twin orange urns sat on either side of the staircase—one overflowing with hydrangeas, the other barren.

The cleanest thing she could claim was the wire I'd installed, now pinned to her side. But there was an undeniable character I'd loved from the first glance. Like she'd grown out of the bogs and mountains behind her, formed by Ireland herself, making my wire seem like an unwanted intrusion.

"When are you expecting Bryn again?" I asked when my boots sank into the squishy underbelly of Ireland. I might have been joking about the pond, but there was probably a good amount of water damage I'd need to patch up before he arrived.

James glanced at his watch like it had the days on it—maybe it did. The set of exposed gears glinted a wet gold along with the ring on his right hand. "Two weeks, when he's to host a wee ceremony for me," James replied, drawing a cigarette from the breast pocket of his tweed jacket.

Ceremony? Like a wedding? "Is he a priest?"

James chuckled lightly. "A priest? *Bryn?* He is in me hole. No, sure, he's an artist, and done most of the oil portraits ye've seen in our library, and some of the repairs as well, but..." James caught my look just as his cigarette lit. "Ye'd better practice now if yer to have any hope of convincin' him when he's here," he warned.

I schooled my face. "I thought the paintings were very nice."

When James leaned in, the scent of tobacco wafted enticingly under my nose. "Listen now, there's not one of us who claims to know much about good art," he said seriously, "but ye'd best pretend for all of our sakes."

Squeezing my lips together to hide my smile, I nodded, and James gestured for me to follow him around the hotel, through the uncut grass he pretended was a meadow. "Now about this ceremony. We've an old tradition up in the mountains—it's a special thing, and not many go through it."

I scratched at my ear. "Why's that?"

He took his time answering, brushing his fingers over the unkept rosemary, plucking the head of a fading daffodil that had managed to bloom well past the spring.

The grass soaked my jeans to the knees as I followed him, the taller stems stamping dark tattoos on my calves. But I enjoyed it, each step a reminder that I wasn't in Canada anymore, that I'd left those twenty-six years behind. To start fresh, to figure out why I'd been the half that survived, to be someone my twin would have been proud of.

And all that was the *first*, very sensible reason I'd taken this job.

"It's a rite of passage," James said when the unruly grass brushed up against a wire fence. "Or 'tis the closest thing ye could call it."

I propped an elbow on the top of a wooden post, and the overgrown ivy pricked through my denim sleeve with ease.

God, the look of this place, the *feel* of it. The mist tickling my lips with its odd taste of worms and soil, still just new enough to enjoy. And everything burst and crawled and sprung and dangled, reveling in the forever damp like a mangy dog after a swim, shimmering in its wet coat whenever the sun peeked over the hills of West Kerry.

Which was decidedly not today.

"And Bryn's coming here specifically to host this ceremony?" I clarified, tearing my gaze from the wild, wicked ruin of the fields.

James blinked droplets of mist away, nodded. "We take turns every year, and this is his. He'll take one guest up the mountains, and if they're lucky, they'll come back a new person."

"Then I hope we get someone checking in soon," I offered, frowning at the cliffs behind us, only jutting gray masses beneath the fog. "What happens at this ceremony, exactly?"

Now, James grinned. "Oh, Bryn'll say a few Irish blessings from a teacup, sprinkle some fairy dust, and the like."

"So a regular Friday night at the pub," I said, then smirked at him. "Will you be breaking into song again too?"

James puffed out his cheeks. "T'was *one* time."

It was three times—in one night. "You have a very pretty voice, James." He blushed, then rolled his eyes. "And guests pay for this ceremony experience?"

"Aye, but few can afford the cost." He turned, folding his arms over the top of a fence post so we mirrored each other, then glanced back at the hotel. "Did I ever tell ye what *Naruka* means?"

He waited until I shook my head.

"*Memory*," he said. "It means memory."

"Irish?"

"No, another language. It came from a ledger they found in the bogs out back, not far from where Bryn will lead the ceremony. That's how it started centuries ago, when..."

The sudden drumbeat of hooves had James drifting into silence.

I lifted my cheek from my fist, my ears tracking the familiar *thud-thud-thud* that sprinted over the land. Already, my pulse quickened in anticipation, my heart *whomp-whomping* in my chest like the blades of a fan on a hot Canadian night.

As fog clawed back from the fields, the sun peeked through the clouds, shying away from the storm that stood as a dark smudge not too far behind. But in any weather, under any light, Ireland was still beautiful.

Then, my second reason galloped through the fog.

Tye's burnt-coffee hair clung to the base of his neck, slick with sweat and mist and exhilaration. He perched slightly off the western saddle, muscled thighs tensing in soaked jeans as he moved with the horse. His cheeks were flushed with the thrill of racing across the hills—or maybe the insanity of doing it on a morning with a weather warning in place.

Someone looking for their own kind of freedom, as my twin would have said.

Would this be mine? Here in Ireland, fixing hotels? I wanted it to be—wanted to have something like Tye did, like my sister had.

"Ye know that saddle cost me a hundred quid?" James remarked with a chuckle. "Said he wouldn't ride none of that fancy English shite."

I smiled to myself. "You should have heard him arguing with the horse school back home in L'Ardoise. After six months, they were probably happy to see him go," I said dryly, watching as Tye thundered across the field, spraying ribbons of mud.

"'Twas a long sabbatical, and I can't say I'm not glad to have him back." James tucked his thumbs into his suspenders and eyed me through lashes beaded with dew. "Glad he brought ye with him too."

Something swelled in my throat—Hope? Chance? That thrumming anticipation for the new—no, the *unknown.*

My reply was swallowed by thundering hooves as Tye blew past. He didn't glance at us, his attention fixed on the fog, his arms drawn taut from bracing the reins. His full lips moved, damp with rain as he murmured to the horse, whatever he said drowned out by the storm moving in.

Then he was past us, a silhouette against a wall of gray trees.

⚙☀

It rained on Tuesday, sprinkled on Wednesday, misted on Thursday, and spat at me by the time Friday rolled around. Even today, in broad daylight when the sky was completely cloudless, Ireland had the supernatural ability to coat Naruka with its grievances.

But I never minded overmuch, as there was always plenty to fix inside the house, which meant I was now on a first-name basis with the hardware shop owner—and his sons and sixteen cousins. But this paled in comparison to my budding relationship with the postman and his wife, who would ask me about the weather (poor), how James and I met (through Tye), then how Tye was enjoying being back (great, he's busy wrestling milk out of the beast James calls a cow), if Naruka had any new guests (no), and again, a comment on the weather.

Despite having a seemingly photographic memory of the recorded date of every death in town, the postman had never heard of this ceremony Bryn was conducting. It might be for the best though, if it didn't happen, because while Bryn's old room wasn't exactly a pond yet, we certainly wouldn't be winning the West Kerry hotel award.

Plop. Splat.

I backed away from the dripping ceiling, nearly bumping into James, who stood staring aghast at the puddle in guest room three.

"Sorry, Roe, ye warned me there might be a leak, but I'd only just found the room's key." He held it up with a sheepish grin before tucking it tidily into his breast pocket.

I watched the leak drip like weak filtered coffee into a pair of Oxford shoes. "Those his?"

"Aye," James said, peeling back the linen curtains. "And he's a picky bastard."

"About his things, or the room?"

James looked at me for a long moment, his eyes flicking down my overalls. "About everything," he decided, shifting away from the window. "Now, what do ye think?"

"That the shoes are a goner." I set my toolbox on a desk still littered with papers. "I can patch up the ceiling easily enough, but you might need a new—"

I stopped when James's hands started swatting at invisible cobwebs. "Not the roof, sure, the *room*," he emphasized. "What do ye make of it?"

The room? It wasn't much different than my own, though this one was bigger, with a sense of someone who knew how he liked things— clean, tidy, particular—and it smelled kind of like clean laundry hung out to dry in winter.

I paused my scan when dark, hooded eyes blinked back at me from a rusty mirror, reflecting my full upper lip, the dent in my chin, and my flat, freckled nose. Like James's Asian complexion, my First Nations bronze was an oddity around here.

"Besides the ceiling," I answered, "the room's in pretty good condition, a few cracks down the—"

"Ah, never mind," James said briskly.

I frowned at his tone. "Is everything alright?"

"Of course, sure. Ye can start with the leak while I tidy a wee bit."

Did he want me to compliment the decor? I tried a few more times, mentioning the beautiful old hope chest currently eating the sleeve of a sweater, the bookcase bending from the weight of medical texts and leather journals, the curtains tangled around a four-poster bed, but none of my comments cheered James overmuch.

"Are these Bryn's things?" I asked when the *tick-tick* of three clocks filled the silence.

James inclined his head. "He left them here some years ago now."

"He didn't want his stuff?"

"Yera, he wanted a clean break from the place."

That piqued my interest. A clean break? "Did something happen?"

James paused in the middle of shuffling papers together and glanced out the window, where the Kerry mountains ascended to blue ridges, then wilted under smoky clouds. "He made a mistake," he said at length.

Oh. Well. "I guess Bryn's coming back for his things, too, then," I deduced.

"No, he's coming back because it's his duty to."

Duty? "For the ceremony? What does—"

"Ah!" James exclaimed, grasping a torn piece of paper in his hands, a bewildered smile playing on his thin lips. "I didn't know he drew her—isn't she pretty?" he murmured to himself.

I eyed the rough sketch of a woman with spiraling horns that James all but beamed at. Under the gray light, the brown of his eyes glowed nearly purple, a deep, velvet indigo from some reflection I couldn't see.

Then it was gone.

Setting the sketch aside, James tugged open the desk drawer, revealing a stack of polaroids weighed down with a single golden ring.

A lot of things to leave behind—because Bryn had to? Because there'd been some emergency? A death in the family, maybe, but why not send for your stuff? A "mistake," James had said, but still…

I paced the room, eyes skimming the model boat bookend, the maps stowed on the shelves. Why leave this here for *years*? You get rid of it, if you're James, at least sell it or something, unless you thought Bryn would be coming back. For a ceremony? Was it that important for Bryn to lead it?

"Roe, do ye want to see him?" James asked.

"Who?"

In answer, he motioned me over with three quick flicks of his hand.

When my shoulder brushed his, James tilted a Polaroid toward me. In it, a grainy photo of a man stood with his arm around our one current and long-term guest, Kazie, who lived in the room beside mine.

"Is this Bryn?"

James inclined his head. "Aye, some years ago."

He was still a boy, really, young enough that his jaw had a soft delicateness to it, but his eyes were a haunting blue, his skin snowmelt white. He looked like he had all the answers, a little secret, a piece of something he'd found and *hey*, wouldn't you like to have it too?

James packed the rest of the photos away, all except the sketch of the horned woman—that he folded and stowed in his breast pocket and, whistling, continued his sweep of the room.

I stood for a moment, staring after him. He hadn't been what I expected, certainly not the typical boss I'd gotten back home. Nothing ever rattled him, not even our lack of guests, and any job I did—big or small—only pleased James more. So if he wanted me to prepare Naruka for Bryn to lead some Irish ceremony, I was game.

By the time he had mopped the floors, I'd managed to wrestle the leak into submission, and he'd left only when I assured him I wouldn't slip off the ladder.

I hummed an old song under my breath. Something my sister had played for her tutor over and over on the piano, then eventually something she'd taught me, but—

A low rumble slid under the cracked window.

I glanced over. Not James's car, that's for sure; I could hear that decrepit beast two miles away.

Stowing my plaster scraper, I crossed the room, my boots echoing dully on the oak floors. Was Bryn early? Or was this the guest he'd lead a ceremony for?

The radiator warmed my jaw as I drew back the curtain, its heat a welcome contrast to the cool draft sliding under the window. Rain beaded on the glass, and a moth smacked into the misty surface over and over and over, its powdered wings turning deathly translucent.

Thump. Thump. Thump.

And there, coming to a smooth stop in the shadow of Naruka, its left tire crushing James's raspberries, was a blood-red Mercedes.

CHAPTER 2

Cowboy Like Me

T he carpet runner muffled my boots as I made my way downstairs, circling the L-shaped staircase around a wide pillar that speared through the heart of Naruka. The plush rugs, dull wood floors, and fireplace boasted of a character that couldn't be bought—could barely be maintained, if my own bill was any proof.

When I reached the bottom, I peeked into the kitchen to tell James about the car outside. But it was empty, oddly silent, and missing the usual *tick-tick* of clocks that sounded like the hum of insects. Beside one of those clocks—a half-eaten apple with a smiling worm—hung a calendar with June's new priest. He stood legs apart, wearing only his clerical collar and baring his midsummer night's dream. A long, very impressive dream that—

"Hey, darlin'."

I nearly jumped at the voice. At that slow, rangy drawl carrying the same Southern heat it had the day he'd walked into my dad's shop, asking if I knew how to fix trucks.

When I turned, I got an eyeful of Tye Cannon striding through Naruka's double doors. A crisp, salty breeze followed, stirring a needlework tapestry of indigo skies before the doors slammed shut behind him.

"Ya keep oglin' that calendar, a man's gonna start to get jealous." A ruinous dimple popped in his left cheek. "Though I can't say I got much to offer in the way of priesthood," Tye drawled, slinging his jacket over a sculpture of a one-legged bird.

"I don't know," I said. "I heard you got pretty religious when Montana lost."

"Would've made my ma blush." He chuckled, running a hand through his damp hair before plopping his ball cap back down and squeezing a wave out of those burnt locks. It cast a shadow over his heavy brow, the bump in his nose that some horse might have caused— or maybe it'd been a bar fight. With the plaid shirt and faded blue jeans, he looked like pure warmth, like the sun stroking your back and the grass tickling your knees on a summer's day.

Just then I realized I was still wearing my damn headlight. I yanked it off, rubbing at the itchy patch it left as I shifted past Tye.

"Friends of yours?" I asked, peering out one of the two church-style windows. Outside, the Mercedes purred into reverse, flattening a new trail through the raspberry bushes—not a guest, then.

"Who?" He glanced over his shoulder, frowned. "Oh. That's James's aunt. I ran into her in Capolinn and she gave me a ride. Nice woman."

I let the curtain fall back into place. "She lives nearby?"

"Visits," Tye corrected, "from time to time."

James had never mentioned an aunt, which was odd when he'd given me the postman's complete family history. "Is she coming for the ceremony?"

"Naw, she's already gone through it." Tye reached up to grab an overhead rafter, stretching out his neck as he hung from it. A half-dragon, half-human tattoo flexed around the tanned muscle of his forearm. "Woman used to run this place with James's mom before she brought me here." He scratched at the faint stubble on his jaw. "Six years ago now."

Tye let go of the rafter to swipe a crystal glass off a low-lit bar, followed by a whiskey so expensive it would make James's eyes water. With a groan, he dropped onto the sofa and stretched out his legs, a sunburned hand kneading his thigh.

"About this ceremony…You knew Bryn, right?"

"Stornoway?" Tye's brows flew up into his dark hair, pausing there in time with the whiskey at his lips. "Suppose so, though I don't think many ever *really* knew him. Why ya askin'?"

I waited until he swallowed another healthy dose, then explained the leftover things in Bryn's room.

Tye huffed a dark laugh. "Stornoway left in a hurry after James had me kick his ass out. Not that I didn't give him time to pack, but the man's a little…" Tye twirled a finger around his ear, whistled. "James felt a little guilty about the whole thing, ya ask me. Might be why he's askin' him back now, but we don't need him. And from what I'm hearin', James is havin' some trouble gettin' hold of the man."

Then what made James think he'd travel from... "Where *is* Bryn?"

"Norway, last I heard."

Travel from *Norway*, then, to host a ceremony for a man who'd supposedly kicked him out? "Why did James ask him to leave?"

Tye twirled his finger again. "Crazy, like I said."

Then why invite him back? Why hold on to his things? James *was* sentimental—he kept all the Irish knickknacks that Kazie gave him, even the ridiculous leprechaun apron. So maybe it wasn't much of a stretch to keep Bryn's things too.

"I got ya somethin' in town today."

My thoughts scattered. "I— You did?"

"In the pocket." Tye pointed at his jacket, the one still clinging to a marble beak. "I was thinkin' of ya earlier at the racetrack when I was in the parade ring, tryin' to figure out what horse I was gonna bet on."

Curious and a little surprised, I moved toward the statue. "And what, one of the horses was called 'Mediocre Electrician'?" I joked, searching through his jacket that still smelled of beer and cigarette smoke from the pub last night. My hand curled around a small box. "This it?"

"Yup. So I'm standin' there at the fence..." He rolled back his sleeves as if to demonstrate. "Watchin' this mare's rotten teeth grind a bucket of slop, and I thought, 'Hey, that gruel looks a lot like what Roe tried to feed me after Montana lost.'"

"It wasn't *that* bad."

"You kiddin'? It was the worst thing I'd eaten since you dared me to try cat food that night we got piss-faced."

Laughing now, I peeled back the box's cardboard lid to find a marshmallow cupcake. "So you thought you'd buy the opposite?" Tenderly, I lifted it from the box, held it in my palm.

Tye leaned forward until his glittering green eyes met mine. "No, hun, I remembered it was your birthday."

I froze.

Remembered it was your birthday. My birthday. Mine—except it wasn't.

My chest hollowed as I stared at the perfect sugared marshmallow. It was embarrassing to feel like this, to feel somehow cheated when my sister and I had always celebrated it on the same day anyway.

"I was gonna offer to take ya up the mountain on the horses, but James wanted to wait."

My fingers tightened around the wrapping. "Thanks Tye, I—" The cupcake tilted in my palm, the weight of the icing dragging it to the left, to the right.

No, no, no!

Like a baby with a gigantic head, it plunged out of my grasp, smacking icing-side down on the hairy rug. *Great.*

Tye chuckled. "Next time I'll just get the cheesecake."

"Sorry, it's—" I rushed to scoop up my victim. "It's fine." I yanked a hair from the icing. "The cake part is fine," I amended.

Tye sucked in his lips, let them out. "Somethin' wrong besides the cupcake? Ain't you turnin' twenty-seven today?"

"No, I am," I lied. "I'm just surprised you knew. My sister and I were born minutes apart around midnight, but we always celebrated it on the same day."

He paused with the whiskey at his lips, frowned. "That so?"

"It doesn't matter, sorry. Thanks for the offer with the horses, but I'd just fall off."

Tye lifted the brim of his hat. "If a little horse scares ya, you ain't gonna last long around here."

⚙✳⚙

With only a week to go before Bryn arrived, and all my plaster used on his ceiling, I took James's beat up old Ford and drove into Capolinn.

The streets swam with tourists, locals, and those still recovering from last night's drinks, looking bleary-eyed and half-surprised to see what Ireland mistook for sunshine. The townhouses were cheerful, the streets cobbled, and even the drizzle of rain couldn't dampen the joy of one very dedicated pipe player. Surprisingly for such a tiny town, Capolinn boasted three churches, fifteen pubs, and one very old—

"When did ye say ye came to Naruka?"

Post office.

I dragged my gaze from the window and glanced at the woman behind an oak desk, currently eyeing me over a cup of steaming tea that left a faint sheen on her weathered cheeks.

"A few months back," I answered, handing her my hastily scrawled postcard.

She grimaced at my writing, staring at it so long and hard I worried I'd forgotten my own address. "Didn't take ye for a Yank," she declared, despite the giant letters spelling '*CANADA.*' "A few months, ye said? And this is the first time yer writing to yer folks?"

I shifted under her stare. "No, I wrote before," I lied—and poorly by her expression.

She looked so far down her nose that her cat-eye glasses slid an inch to catch on the crooked tip. "I've never seen ye in here before," she decided, setting her milky tea on a doily. "Me own daughter is living in France. Did James tell ye? No? She calls me every Sunday whether I want her to or not. Good girl." She nodded to herself, needing no prompting to continue.

Even when she double-dipped her biscuit into the tea, the steady stream of her daughter's accomplishments, prizes, and feats didn't cease. By the end of it, I was certain she'd have given my twin some stiff competition. "And yer gettin' on well, are ye so, at Naruka?"

I shifted my hardware bag to my other arm to nudge the coins for the postcard toward her. "Yeah, James has been great—"

"Good lad," she said with another brisk nod. "Took over for his mammy, God rest her soul. Not easy running a place like that."

"Yeah, it needs some work," I agreed. "Is it two dollars for the post card?" Maybe I'd gotten the change wrong.

"Two quid, aye. Work?" she echoed.

"Naruka's fine," I corrected, in case she warned potential guests off. "Just a few things—sockets…" Fire hazards, overloaded circuits, frayed wires, melted insulation. All of which, I recently learned, Bryn had contributed to, which was why artists probably shouldn't rewire houses. "Nothing too important."

She made a little cough in the back of her throat as she straightened a stack of envelopes and continued to ignore my change. "Well, I don't see many people staying at Naruka, but when I do, it seems there's only two kinds. The first," she said, leaning forward far enough that her floral perfume drowned out the smell of wood cleaner, "is always in a hurry when they leave."

My eyes met her clear blue ones. "A hurry?"

"*Sure*," she said, dragging out the word. "Not a year ago, James had a woman—a *guest*—staying with him. She was there only two months—much like yerself—before she comes in one morning, mascara running, eyes as red as I've ever seen, raving about some vision she'd had. Pure nonsense, so it was! I've never heard the like. Gears in the bloody sky." She waved this away quickly, as if she'd lose my rapt attention. "The girl was on the drink. Then James comes in—good lad," she added, lifting her thin chin as if daring me to say otherwise.

"He's great," I quickly agreed.

"Looking for yer wan, and it wasn't a week later I find out she's gone and left one of the local boys high and dry. Seems they were a thing.

Not that I mind. I keep me nose where it belongs—on me face." She pointed a bony finger at the wart on hers. "I had only pity for James, what with her takin' off like that half mad. Bad for business. And a young woman no less?" This seemed the biggest grievance of all. "*Well*," she huffed, her gaze roving over my work boots, then my cheap overalls and damp braid.

But the woman—*Mary*, I saw now—was too much of a goldmine for me to be insulted. "And the second type?" I prompted. "Of guest?"

"Long termers," she stated. "They'll stay *years* at Hotel Naruka. Now, if I had that kind of money, ye wouldn't see me working here, no ye wouldn't. Sure, I'd be in France with me daughter."

I took a shot in the dark. "You wouldn't have known a man who used to live at Naruka? From Norway?"

What was left of her eyebrows lifted, her face tilted, her cheeks positively glowed. "Bryn?" Her voice took on the high-pitched coo of a mother talking about her favorite son. "Sure, I knew him, so I did. A good lad, a *very* good lad. Maybe not in the same way as James, if ye know what I mean."

Even the drunks outside would know what she meant. "I think I'm following."

She leaned so far over the desk that her breasts smothered both my change and the postcard. "When he arrived at Naruka, I was worried about a few of the girls here. Such silly things." She wrinkled her nose. "But then he didn't show much interest. Might have a girl himself. Though if he did, *I* never saw her."

And for the second time in five minutes, I realized I shouldn't have waited months to send a postcard. I'd have gotten the town lore that much earlier and easier.

"Bryn rarely came into Capolinn, but there was always a word or two for folks when he did, like meself. He was a good lad," she repeated sagely. The highest praise, I was beginning to understand.

"Any reason he'd be coming back for a ceremony?"

"*Ceremony?*" she said incredulously. "What ceremony? A wedding?"

"No, something that Naruka hosts for guests."

"Well, if there is, I don't know anything of it," she said with the deepest affront, and collected my change. "When ye go back, ye'll tell James to come in, won't ye? Might be I'll ask him about this ceremony."

Not wanting to give up just yet, I tried a few more angles, hoping to tease out more information, but I ended up leaving with only the hardware store bag.

CHAPTER 3

Hares on the Mountain

With three days until Bryn was supposed to arrive, I had nothing to do but the remaining repairs—which should have kept me occupied, but I spent most of my time pondering the reason for James inviting Bryn, beyond some ceremony.

I began cataloging what I'd seen in Bryn's room, like the answer to James's insistence on him returning would be found among the medical books or the sailing paraphernalia I'd noticed he collected during my second inspection.

Finally, over a brunch stomaching fried mushrooms, it hit me: not the mushrooms, though I hadn't yet told James that funguses should be treated and never eaten, but the obvious answer. I'd ask our long-term guest, which was why I was currently pacing in the shadowy woods behind Naruka, hoping to catch Kazie after her morning hike.

"Roe?" she called, spotting me at last, lowering the hood of a jacket that could only be described as the color of an electrified pumpkin. Dew beaded on skin like purple velvet and clung to her round nose, pouty lips, and springy curls of hair. Her mouth curved into a wide smile.

I glanced over her shoulder. "Oh, I thought Tye was—"

Without missing a beat, she looped her elbow through mine, the gesture so familiar, so much like my sister, that I stumbled the first few steps. Then she was tugging me along, through the opening in the woods where the loch crept toward the stables.

"—with you," I finished, our boots *plop-plopping* in the wet.

"He was. He took another way back. Were you waiting for him?"

I eyed the water, the rippling teardrops on its blue surface. Waiting for Tye would have made a lot more sense. "Yeah," I lied. "I wanted to ask him if he needed anything done for the ceremony."

"Ceremony?" she repeated around a mouthful of gum.

"The one Bryn's conducting."

"*Oh*. I can't *wait* to see him," she said, a smile lighting her face. "You know, he was the one who brought me here from Malawi, like, three years ago? *That's* in Africa," she added matter-of-factly, which I appreciated because I had no clue where Malawi was. "He was working at this bike repair shop where I lived. I thought he was the freaking devil at first. Never saw anyone with blue eyes before." *Pop*. Her gum burst on a blown bubble. "He's, like, the nicest guy ever. So sweet. I just adore him."

That didn't seem to be Tye's take.

"Thanks for fixing my birdcage, by the way," Kazie added as she pulled me along beside the loch, "on behalf of my budgies."

I kicked away the curling rosemary that huddled over the dirt trail. "No problem. It was an easy fix," I said, keeping to her right, because I knew what it was to sink down into that mucky lake. Far enough that the putrid yellow shifted to a shadowy green, then to nothing at all—no light, no sound. Until, at eight years old, my sister had pulled me out—and promptly punched the boy who'd thrown me in.

"Do you know what happened between Bryn and James?" I asked. "That caused James to ask him to leave?"

Her face puckered. "James overreacted," she said stiffly. "Bryn just made a teeny, tiny mistake." She indicated the size by pinching her thumb and forefinger together.

Despite their seeming friendship, Kazie hadn't left with Bryn; instead, she'd stayed here with James. Yet I'd never seen her work, never seen her do anything besides these morning walks. How could she afford a hotel for years? Had I missed something here?

"Kazie, you're not..."

Her eyes slid to me, and suddenly, those whimsical mannerisms transformed into cunning. "Not what?"

"Uh—*with* James?"

She blinked, and just like that, the childlike amusement returned. "*With* James?" She clapped her hands, dragging me to the left. "He's *married*."

Married? I looked around like his spouse would come strolling though the fields. "Where's his wife?"

"In Ruhaven," she said promptly.

Ruhaven? Did that mean she'd left him? Divorce wasn't legal in Ireland, but Kazie hadn't said *separated*.

Before I could ask, she Tinkerbell'd her way into the tack room, leaving me standing outside, my hands in my pockets, eyeing the hotel thoughtfully.

Something was just a little odd about Naruka—and not just the eavestrough hanging by a thread.

Then again, this was Ireland. Everything was a little odd, including the postman, who knew way too much about my family by this point. What did it matter that James kept some guy's things if he had ten other rooms to spare? He was generous, which is probably why he'd let Kazie stay so long. She did help out with the cooking, cleaning, and sometimes—when I couldn't stop her—the repairs.

Yet a churning feeling lingered in my gut, that same budding anticipation I'd felt when I first arrived. As if I were standing on the edge of a cliff with my hands in my pockets, tilting back on my heels as a frightening wind buffeted my shoulders.

I inhaled a gulp of Ireland's wet air.

For a moment, I swore I could almost hear my sister playing the piano in Naruka's music room, her fingers sprinting over the keys. The imagined notes hovered in the air, just a whispered, beckoning call of a song I once knew.

Then it was gone.

⚙✺

T his was a stupid idea.

And I mean *really* stupid.

Even moving to Ireland partly because some guy with good muscle tone had offered you a job was less stupid than this by a wide degree. But because I rarely got a chance to be alone with Tye, I'd jumped at his offer to take me up the mountain before realizing he meant *on a horse*.

"Here now," Tye coaxed, holding the reins as James puttered around the stable. "Ya just step your foot over. She ain't gonna bite."

"Of course not," I said quickly, eyeing the rotten teeth dripping with green juice. "She looks *really* nice…"

"Just don't risk me favorite electrician," James warned. He grasped the halter of my mare, patting her snout. "Yer going to be fine, love," he said to either me or the horse. "The trails are well marked and should make for an easy enough ride."

I eyed the violet mountains just visible under the barn's overhang. Maybe the horse would find it easy, but staying on top of the Gypsy Cob would be an exercise in not embarrassing myself. I already had images of Tye watching me thrown from the saddle, landing face down and butt up in a pile of moss. But he'd gone to the effort of packing a lunch for the both of us, and I'd wanted to see the view up top before things got too busy with the ceremony.

To distract myself, I asked James, "When is Bryn due in?"

"The guy ain't comin' back," Tye answered instead, "and we're all better off for it."

"He's only a wee bit delayed," James insisted, selecting a helmet off the stack.

Delayed? But James had been prepping the house for weeks for Bryn's visit. "Can someone else lead the ceremony?"

James looked at Tye. "Aye, but by Bryn's own rules, he'd have to come." He strode around the horse, its tail flicking.

"*Old* rules," Tye corrected, "and I'd say he's pretty damn happy in Norway right now."

The words drew James's mouth into a tight line—distracting him, so that he didn't see the mare's eyes pivot, its back leg lifting.

With a shout, I lunged for James. My fingers clutched the soft tweed of his sleeve, yanking him toward me just as a hoof whizzed past. I felt the air shift over my cheek, the stiff tail flick my hands. My pulse thumped so loud I didn't hear James's sputtering words.

Then he pulled away from me, lifted a stern finger to the back of the horse, and shouted, "If ye bloody try that again, I'll be sending ye out with the cow, so I will!"

Even I shuddered at the threat—only Tye seemed to be able to coax that beast into milking. Twice, she'd nearly taken my knee out.

"James, how many times I gotta tell ya not to walk behind a horse?" Tye said, patting the mare's neck sympathetically before motioning to the mounting block. "C'mon, kid, up ya go."

It took me a second to realize he was talking to me.

After I made sure James hadn't caught a stray hoof, Tye's dimple gave me the shot of courage I needed to swing my leg over—too far— and he grabbed my calf with a warm, calloused hand.

"Ya got long legs," Tye said, sliding my heel out so he could adjust the length of the stirrup. "Didn't ya say ya used to ride?"

I squeezed the reins he handed me. "My sister used to, and she won a few competitions too." Before she'd given it up for the piano.

"Twins, right? Probably transfers over or something." Tye glanced at James, who blanked his face.

I wish. "Unfortunately not."

Once we were in the open, wet fields, Tye ran us through a few different strides. The trot was the equivalent of trying to ride a jackhammer, and the canter almost dislodged me altogether. He looked a little disappointed that I was stuck with the walk, but after another round where cantering was firmly ruled out, we broke into a fast stride to the woods.

I glanced over my shoulder before the forest swallowed us up. James stood in the middle of the field, the drizzle dampening his black hair to a glistening blue, his hands in the pockets of his slacks, a strange look darkening his handsome face.

As the cold canopy blocked him out, I twisted in my saddle to face Tye. He didn't use a crop as I'd seen my sister do, and didn't wear a helmet like the one now itching the top of my head. The heels of his leather boots dug firmly into the horse's sides, urging both our mounts up and up and up the forested trail. He was too far ahead to talk easily, so I settled into the rhythm, enjoying the hum of birds, the sound of our horses' heavy breathing, and the impossibly green woods.

And the green crawled over *everything*.

Ivy dangled from branches, moss spread over rocks and fallen logs, and even the soil seemed alive with snails cracking under hooves. A viridian world filled to the brim, where everything the rain touched flourished. The air was heavier, too, weighed down with the thick mixture of peat and worms and the ever-present *pitter-patter* of rain from last night's storm, the uneven sound like fistfuls of rice tossed from the sky.

"Roe, I gotta question for ya," Tye said, as our horses drew even. He lit his cigarette and, lifting off the saddle, jammed the lighter in his back pocket. "Why'd ya take this job? Hm?" Smoke billowed between the pricked ears of his horse. "Ya didn't have to. Ya could've stayed workin' at your daddy's shop."

"Maybe I was desperate for a redhead," I joked.

"Hun, ain't no one that desperate," he said with a short laugh. "But no, I'm bein' serious now. When I said you could work for James for a while, told ya about the job, you were interested from the get-go. Might even say ya jumped at it, and not two days later, you were on the phone with James." He sucked on the cigarette as the horses' hooves splashed in the mucky trail. "Why's that?"

Two days? No, I'd called James the next morning, listened to him explain in the accent I still found charming about a hotel he needed a live-in repairwoman for, that Tye would be working there, too, on the farm, so I'd have a friendly face. That evening, I'd spoken to my dad, and a part of me had hoped he'd be upset about the lack of help with the shop, but he'd been all too eager to see me go.

"Got nothin'?" Tye said when I remained silent. "Well, I guess I've just been thinkin' recently, 'bout these moments my ma used to call 'the before and after.'" He took a long drag of his cigarette that had the end shooting orange. "I ever told ya I had a brother?"

I shook my head, my thoughts still in the shop with my dad, then I clued in. "Had?"

"That's right. Good kid, stayed in school, had some smarts on him, a lot more than me. But one weekend he's with some boys up north, they're out at night on snowmobiles on the frozen lake. Didn't see the tree." He sighed smoke out his nose. "They said his skull was split in two."

"Tye, I—I'm sorry that—"

"Past is past. But that used to be mine—the before and after." He dug his heels in. "C'mon, just up here now."

I frowned at the back of his jacket, my horse following his when the dirt trail turned into stone steps, its sweat a musty scent under my nose. Had Tye ever spoken of his family before? His mom a little, his dad never—but what made him think of his brother now? He was too far away to ask, to do more than swallow the ache in my gut that was selfishly as much for my own loss as his.

When the ground leveled out again, Tye settled back in the saddle, tilting his head so mist gathered on the dorsal hump of his nose. The trees began to give way, the sky peeking through thinning leaves, and soon what was left of the brambles dissolved into a serene meadow.

I'd never seen real wildflowers before—well, maybe the odd buttercup, but not the pinks dotting the meadow, or the bluebells surrounding it, or the purple foxgloves that cozied up to the ancient oaks. Tall grass and spawning bulbs swayed in a wave, except for a spot in the middle, where the green had been flattened to dirt.

At the edge of the mountain, the sheer vastness of County Kerry looked like the postcard my parents hadn't answered. Deep-purple hues where the clouds blocked the sun, then blazing green from the pockets of light that escaped, so the walled hills looked like a patchwork of bruises.

"Roe?"

I glanced down to where Tye waited, heavy-lidded eyes watching me, his warm hand bracing my thigh.

He said nothing as he helped me off the horse, as he went to tie them up and I removed the itchy helmet.

"It must be nice to be back at work after your months in L'Ardoise," I pried. In a land my town could never compete with, not in a million years, just like my sister had always said.

"It ain't work if ya love it, hun."

Maybe that was why I'd felt every second of every minute working in my dad's shop, heard the pen dent the page with each receipt drawn. Felt the sting of fresh-cut pine in my nostrils.

And all that was bullshit. At any point I could have saved my money and gone back to college, could have worked somewhere else, could have left with my sister like she'd wanted to.

I kicked at the long stalks of the pretty wildflowers she'd have loved to see. "It was a knock."

Tye turned from the horses. The sun beat down on his face, the shadow of his deep brow hiding his eyes. "A knock?"

"The before and after, like you were saying." I threaded my fingers into my pockets. "I didn't know when Willow died." Hadn't felt the aneurysm that killed her. Hadn't felt *anything*. My twin, my sister— what did that make *me*? "They said it was sometime around three in the morning, on her way home after celebrating her last recital, but I didn't know until a cop knocked at the door. Didn't know what it meant for him to be there, but my mom did. She started crying before he'd said anything."

Three years ago, and I could still smell the lemon wood cleaner she'd used that morning in the hallway, could still feel the way she'd *looked* at me.

Like the cop had gotten the wrong twin.

"So, is this the picnic spot?" I asked, jerking my head toward the knapsack Tye had laid on the flattened grass.

Sun at his back, shadows at his feet, he looked at me, gentle green crinkling under thick eyelashes. "Yeah, this is the spot."

I blew out a breath as I settled on the cool grass, the stems tickling my ankles. My spine molded to all the little lumps of the forest, the hard acorns buried under soft dirt, the dried leaves from last fall that brushed the pads of my fingertips.

I puffed away a strand of hair that caught my lips, listening to the sound of Tye unpacking the metal canister James had filled, the crinkle of paper around the sandwiches. A cold shadow tickled my legs before Tye settled quietly beside me.

"Ya deserve to be here, ya know," he said, his arm brushing my side. "To see this, even if Willow couldn't."

No, I didn't. But I was what was left, and I was here, and that had to be enough.

His fingers threaded through mine, squeezed. Warm, rough, solid, and my pulse sped up before I could rein in my surprise.

Tye smiled when I glanced over, not enough to bring out the dimple. Sad, almost. Like the one I'd seen my mom give before she told the cashier my sister had died.

"Ya know, I woulda asked ya out before now, but James wouldn't have been too happy 'bout it."

My mouth went dry. I hadn't thought that working here meant we couldn't be together, and maybe I should have. Maybe that was my mistake.

My eyes flicked to our joined hands. "But things are different now?"

Tye pushed back a strand of my hair that caught my lips. "That'll depend," he murmured, but when I started to sit up, he tugged me back down.

"Tye?"

"Let's just lay here a while, alright?"

After a moment, I relaxed again, but he didn't take his hand away. As he spoke—some story about a horse—I tried not to hyper-focus on the fact that he was still holding my hand. Or think about how the skin under the collar of his shirt had looked so mouth-wateringly bronze, I could almost feel the heat from the sun that'd tanned it. Maybe that's why I'd liked him from the beginning—not just because of his looks, but the *comfort* of him. Kind of like apple pie, or a dusty baseball game in summer, the smell of a new leather glove, the leftover smoke of a campfire on a plaid shirt. I drifted on the thought, my body melting into the earth.

But when I tried to rouse myself, something soft and warm brushed my jaw.

"Eyes closed," Tye murmured when I struggled to open them. But I couldn't, because suddenly everything inside me felt heavy and faintly numb, like I'd fallen asleep without realizing it.

Then he shifted, and I felt his lips brush my cheek, his hand tangling in my hair, whispering words I couldn't make out. His mouth was like summer's dappled heat, trailing back and forth along my ear as I sank a little further.

This was Tye. *Tye.* I wanted to commit him to perfect memory, to remember how each touch felt, but I was still floating.

His breath whispered over my skin, my fingers curling into the grass, the cold shadows of leaves dancing over my face. He wasn't like the guys in L'Ardoise—not quick, groping hands in the back of a pickup, then on to the next woman, or the next thing.

My thoughts grew heavier and heavier, a sack of flour with a hole in it, seeping into dirt. I was sinking and floating at the same time. Rising and falling. Was he still kissing my neck? Holding my hand? Did he say something…maybe. A hot whisper in my ear, a silky promise, but it was lost in the sinking nothingness. Gone was the salty taste of the Atlantic, the breeze that had fluttered my eyelashes.

It felt like I was slipping on clothes I hadn't worn in years. A little tight, loose in unexpected areas, but comfortably broken in and invariably mine all the same.

And then…

Then I wasn't me.

I was a cork bobbing in the waves. Lost, floating, drifting. A million miles from shore. Somewhere there were no stars, no lighthouses, no…anything.

Just me, lost in an endless night.

Was I asleep? No, couldn't be. But I struggled to rouse myself, my limbs slow and dense as thick molasses.

My mouth might have opened, then clamped shut. Had I done that? It opened again, my tongue flicking out of its own volition to swallow the taste of something foreign—smoked honey, and…amber?

New sounds began to fill my ears.

The calls of birds and distant waves were replaced by a heavy grinding, louder than the automated machines in the factory lines I used to work at—picking up one part, swiveling, and dropping it with a clatter on the conveyer belt.

What the hell was…

I tried to squint, to lift a hand and block the blinding indigo light, but my muscles didn't obey. So I lay there, unblinking, unmoving, as my vision cleared and each minuscule detail magnified itself tenfold.

And I saw…

Clocks?

No, no—not clocks, *gears*.

Thousands of gears spinning in an indigo sky, grinding in my very *bones*. The sound was some terrible kind of music. Notes that didn't exist in any octave, for any ears, with any instrument, in any world.

A dream.

The cogs continued to turn around the vines growing between their centers, suspending the gears from a floating mechanical forest.

My chest hurt. My brain was ripping itself apart at the *seams*. Everything in me revolted, denied, begged.

"Let me out!" I begged, screamed, but only in my mind. *Let me out, let me out, let me out…*

CHAPTER 4

Color Me In

Dirt, socks, diesel. *Ireland.*

Still screaming, I broke from the dream into sickening pastel greens. The oaks spun, the sky whirled, birds wailed at an ear-splitting volume, and somewhere far away, the horses we'd tied up nickered.

Rolling over, I crawled to the edge of the meadow, sucked in the largest mouthful of air I'd ever take, then emptied my entire breakfast of James's raspberry pancakes onto a hawthorn tree.

I dug my fingers into waterlogged moss. Earth. Life. Not dead, not floating. No gears. No forest in the sky. Alive. I was alive.

"You're alright, Roe. Deep breaths, now."

Oh God—Tye.

Hot humiliation rolled in to replace the nausea. This couldn't be happening. It couldn't. But it *was.*

I'd fallen asleep with Tye *kissing* me, and he was now staring at my vomit. Willow would have laughed herself silly, except she wouldn't, not ever again.

"I—I don't know what happened," I managed.

Tye bent and tugged my hands from my face. "Hun, don't worry," he said, pulling me against him in a fierce hug. At least he wasn't staring at my burning face, or smelling my breath, or seeing what tasted like snot dripping over my lip. "You're okay. You're fine. But ya need to drink somethin'." He peeled back far enough to reach for his bag and pulled out a canister, handing it to me.

I drank a throat-scorching gulp, choked. "This isn't water."

Tye grinned, and the simple sight of his dimple brought me some relief. "The Irish might disagree. Ya need somethin' strong." He grabbed the tree beside me, sliding down its faded pink bark until he rested on the ground with one knee bent.

"Tye, I'm—I'm sorry," I said pathetically.

His lips tightened around a cigarette, released, and a breeze blew the puffs of gray haze away before they had time to settle between us. "No, Roe, I'm sorry," he said softly. "But not about that. 'Bout what I'm about to tell ya."

Tell me? God, what else had I done?

Tye peeled off his hat, rubbed at the indent it left on his forehead. A bit of sweat curled the hair that clung to his temples. "It's the first time I've done this," he admitted, draping his arms over his knees. "It's normally James who takes people on up here and shows 'em the Gate."

I glanced around. What gate?

"He wanted to wait for Bryn," Tye continued in that same monotone. "I suppose I needed the time anyway, to find the right way to go about this so you'd believe me."

My stomach jittered a little, at the tone more than the words. Gone was the drawl, the easy sway that warned you a joke would follow. "Believe you about what, Tye?"

He rose, pulling himself up with the polished branch of a birch before coming to stand at the edge of the mountain, a twig snapping under his boot. "Christ, darlin', what'd ya just see?"

A teeny, tiny alarm bell started to go off inside my head before I smothered it. "See?"

He chucked his cigarette in the grass. "How 'bout that whole world? Ya know, the one with the gears in the sky? Ring any bells?"

A bird tweeted. I closed my gaping mouth. Didn't realize it'd dried out entirely until my tongue wet it again. Had I hit my head when I passed out? I started to get up, swayed against the tree. Maybe. Must have.

"Look, honey, this is a bit harder than I thought," Tye continued while my stomach bottomed out. "But, well, maybe hard and fast is better, huh?" His dimple winked. "Or maybe it ain't the time for that joke."

I started to feel my scalp for a lump. Then Tye was there, gripping my shoulders, turning me to face him, smelling of tobacco and firewood.

"I think I need to lie down."

His thumbs brushed circles over my shoulders, his face a mass of consternation I could barely focus on.

"Roe, it ain't no accident that we met in Canada," he said. "James sent me to find ya."

I was going to vomit again, like the dream had left some residue I couldn't shake. I swallowed deeply, trying to focus on the bit of stubble on Tye's neck, anything but the crimson-checkered shirt he wore that wouldn't stop spinning.

"To find an electrician?"

"No, to find *you*."

The beard blurred, shifting in and out of focus as my headache worsened. *Me?* "Did someone recommend me? My dad?" My heart lifted at the idea, but I didn't think James knew him.

"No." Tye let go, stepped back. "Smoke?"

It took me a moment, then I saw he was handing me a cigarette from his pack.

"I…sure," I said, but my fingers trembled when I reached for it. "Who recommended me?"

Tye lit his second one, then mine, waving the match in the air until only a faint whiff of burning remained. "Ain't no one recommended you. It's not about that, okay? Ya see, what James and I do is, well, we find people like us, and we show 'em the Gate."

What was with this *gate*? "Tye, I think I'd better head home. Maybe you can tell me about this later."

When I started to turn, he grabbed me. "Roe, I need ya to believe what I showed ya, okay?" he said quickly. "That memory ya saw, it's real, or it was, but it's why I brought ya here, what I'm tryin' to tell ya. I need ya to take a breather now. Don't need ya keelin' over on my first ever recruitin' job or James'll fry my hide."

How often did he recruit electricians? Why was he telling me all this *now*? "I—I'm going to find James."

"I wouldn't do that, not when you're still recoverin' from the Gate."

I lurched toward the path, horses forgotten. I'd walk home without them, use the time to get rid of this pounding ache between my temples. When my stomach seized, I braced a hand on a mossy trunk and sucked in cold, damp air through my nostrils.

"Ain't ya been wonderin' what that ceremony is? Why we ain't got no guests? Why Bryn was comin' back?" Yes, yes, *yes*. "Why I had James make up this job for ya?"

My heart gave two painful thumps. "Why are you saying you…" I trailed off at the look on his face, the one I'd seen so many times before—the no-nonsense tight line of his lips, the furrowed brow.

The chiming warning bell in my head grew louder, and I stumbled, the overgrown brambles tugging at my hair.

Tye stopped feet from me. "Ya know why ya came here, Roe? It ain't 'cause ya had a little crush on me. It's 'cause ya couldn't stomach who ya were without Willow. I know the feelin' of not likin' who ya are, to find that deep down"—he touched a hand to his chest—"there ain't nothin' there. So I gave ya this chance, Roe, so ya could be more than just a reminder to your parents of what was left."

Confused, tears threatening, I shoved away from the brambles. He didn't stop me when I scrambled over a moss-ridden log that crumpled under my boot, or when my feet finally found that muddy path.

He kept talking, kept speaking so quietly about that chance—but he didn't stop me.

So I ran.

⚙️✳️

By the time I crossed the river, breath was wheezing out my lungs. It'd been too long since I'd run like this, too long since my sister died, and my veins strained for the oxygen that my heart couldn't pump fast enough.

I chased the overgrown bank as dew soaked my jeans, my footsteps echoing a disjointed tempo, crunching what should have been left undisturbed. But I was fast—I'd spent every summer running through Canada's rough forests with my sister, and even in this freakishly green land, I dodged rotted logs and shaky rocks with the muscle memory of years.

When my feet slapped a hard trail, I crossed the back lawn, trampling the foxgloves, and careened through Naruka's tack room and into the kitchen.

Bang.

I slapped the door closed, then stood there, shuddering with my back against it. Clocks ticked in unison around me, watching, waiting. My breaths panted out in a painful, stuttering rhythm.

Outside, the winds tested themselves against the kitchen's bay window. Wood groaned, glass protested. But the kitchen looked normal with its bright yellow tea towels, the bench covered in sheepskin rugs, that damn naked priest calendar revealing it was now July.

I peeled my sticky back from the door. Maybe I'd hallucinated. Not just the gears in the sky, but the whole thing. Maybe I'd picked up something, some Irish bug, or—

"*James.*"

He stepped into the kitchen, his glasses smeared with flour, his hair gray with it. His zigzag wool sweater belonged in a 1930s circus, but the sight of it caused the sharp edge of my panic to subside.

"Roe?" His eyes searched mine. "Where's Tye?"

I dragged a hand down my sweaty face. "He's still—still in the woods," I stuttered, "with the horses."

James moistened his lower lip. "Is he so?"

I nodded, my throat parched, every breath like knives in my chest.

He stepped into the warmer light. "Ye know, Roe, 'tis not the first time I've seen that look in someone's eyes."

My pulse ratcheted up. "What?"

"The look of someone who's seen our memories for the first time." *Tick. Tick-tock.*

Something was wrong with him, with Naruka, something that put a wild look on James's face as he stepped closer. The same look I'd seen in the eyes of a photo in guest room three. "Ye've gone through the ceremony," he said quietly. "Won't ye let me answer yer questions?"

I fumbled behind me. "James, I…"

"Yes, Roe?"

My fingers curled around the keys at last. "I'm going for a drive."

"Are ye so? In me own bloody car?"

I sucked in a breath, and threw open the door.

CHAPTER 5

The Great Escape

I n seconds, I was out and careening through the tack room.
I kicked over a bucket in my scramble, sending thick, black hoof
oil spreading over the cement floor before I slammed through the
barn door. My shoulder sang from the impact, but I didn't stop. Cackling
birds took off in fright as I charged through the front garden toward the
old Ford twenty feet away, ten feet away, five, the keys locked in my
fist.

Behind me, the long creak of a door made my limbs go rigid with
fear.

I peeked over my shoulder.

James burst from the tack room, gripping his flat cap against the
brewing storm, his jacket flapping in the wind. "Roe, love, would ye
just—"

My thighs quaked so hard I nearly collided with the driver's door.
Knees throbbing, my fingers like swollen sausages, I fumbled with the
latch before I finally wrenched the damn thing open.

James shouted something as the ignition jackhammered in my palm,
the spark plugs firing a *rat-a-tat-tat*.

Bang.

The engine spluttered to life, diesel fumes pluming in a black cloud
out the exhaust.

Stomach-curling relief shuddered through me, but it did little to help
my focus. I'd have one chance at this—*one*. Get to the road, then don't
stop until I made it to the airport, and only when I was on the plane

would I consider what the hell was going on. I'd have to call the cops, or whatever they called them here, and—

"Roe, just give me a chance to explain!"

That was one thing I wouldn't do.

Grinding the clutch, I reversed just as James hurtled himself at the Ford's hood. The shock of the impact, of the sound of his belt buckle cracking against the metal, startled me before I recovered and slapped the gas.

James held on. "Roe, sure this is me bloody job, like!" he cried, banging on the windshield. "To find ye, to bring ye here."

His *job*? The hell it was. I wouldn't be any part of what he had going on here—smuggling, trafficking, kidnapping.

I slammed the brake, threw the car into first. Not for the first time, Willow's insistence on teaching me to drive manual saved me.

James skidded off the hood, taking the right windshield wiper with him so he clenched it like a sword in his fist. "Ye think I want to go through this every time?" he shouted. "Ye think I want to lie to ye—lie to others—just to bring them here? Kazie was like yerself, Roe."

So this was some kind of cult.

I stomped the gas, my sweaty grip slipping on the steering wheel as I swung the Ford around and toward the line of trees. Rocks flew up, causing James to yelp when one pinged off his knee.

Wouldn't feel guilty. I wouldn't feel guilty.

The car seesawed down the driveway, over potholes and under twisted oaks, with Naruka glowering in the rearview mirror, her windows flashing as the rain pounded them. The front tire dipped, snapping my jaw shut and rattling my brain, so I stomped harder on the gas, shouting at James to back off, *back the hell off!*

In the driver's side mirror, James pumped his arms harder, sprinting to keep up, his jacket cracking like a whip behind him. God, he might just catch me. The end of the road seemed impossibly far, the distant hum of traffic pure imagination in my ears. And even now, a part of me couldn't believe what was happening, was convinced that the glasses jumping up and down on James's nose couldn't belong to a madman.

Focus.

I whipped the car around a rocky bend, my stomach whooshing as the nose dipped down, then up. Bushes whacked the side of the car, each thump like thunder in my roaring ears.

This shouldn't be happening to me. I'd wanted to find something I was good at, figure out who I was without my sister, not *this*.

I swiped the steering wheel left to avoid another pothole that would have disabled the car—

Oh god!

I sucked in a breath, slamming the brakes to avoid colliding with the man standing in the middle of the road, my forehead cracking off the steering wheel.

My vision swam, my head throbbing like it was split in two, or three, or four. Tears sparked in my eyes—from the panic or the pain, I didn't know. I blinked rapidly, trying to bring into focus the figure obscured by the hood's billowing smoke, and my stomach sank.

So he'd come after all.

Standing in the beam of the headlights, his hands tucked into the pockets of his rich coat, was Bryn. Older than in the photograph, his jaw firm where it'd been softer before. But him, unforgettably.

Hands shaking, I tried to restart the car.

His eyes flashed, a blue warning in the glow of the headlights.

"Roe!" James's voice broke through the dull roar in my ears. "Jayzus, Roe, are ye alright?"

No, I wasn't alright. Hadn't been in three long years.

But Bryn's expression never changed. His lips remained in a wide, firm line, his eyes wary and unreadable, and even when he began to fade like the car's steam dissipating in the air, he only offered that unrelating stare.

Then he was gone.

And I was alone, the woods empty, the air still.

I was going crazy. My gut clenched at the hallucination I'd just witnessed, some by-product of whatever had happened up in the woods. A concussion, maybe, and the idea brought me some brief relief before I spotted James in the driver-side mirror.

His heavy panting carried through my open window, then he ducked inside, cursing me, cursing Tye, as he yanked out the keys.

I couldn't seem to move.

Something was *wrong*—with me? With Naruka? I couldn't be sure, and that uncertainty was worse than the hallucination.

Then James was gripping my hands, prying my stiff fingers off the steering wheel and folding them in my lap. He pressed two fingers to my temple, my forehead, the back of my head as I sat there, numb, my bottom lip trembling and tasting of snot.

"Jayzus, ye really got yerself good," James huffed, straightening his glasses over a sheen of sweat. He shouted over his shoulder, "Tye, would ye bring some ice?"

The man who'd been kissing my cheek only an hour ago slid into sight in the rearview mirror. "Hey, darlin'," he drawled, flashing a dimple and a salute.

I could smell the sweat pooling in my armpits.

James reached into his pocket and drew out a pack of smokes, offered one. "No? Ah well," he said, sliding it between his lips. "Ye know it wasn't supposed to be like this. 'Twas supposed to be Bryn who showed ye the Gate, who explained things."

I didn't care about Bryn, didn't care about any of it anymore—I wanted to scrub every piece of Naruka from my brain.

I quickly motioned for the cigarette I'd turned away and stuffed it between my lips. I'd have a smoke before I died, or before my mind sank into the next illusion.

James flicked the lighter, and I inhaled the lung-searing heat with trembling relief.

"The truth of it is," he continued, "what ye saw up there in the Gate, on top o' the mountain—it's a memory. *Yours.* As real as yerself or I right here."

This was it. My body would be found years from now under the bluebells by some tourist. My bones rotten. My parents oblivious to what had happened. I'd never be buried next to my sister in the grave at the church on the hill.

"What do you want?" I managed. And what the hell did I have to offer?

"Want?" James rubbed a chin that never grew any stubble. "I want to tell ye where yer from, where *we're* from. I want to share with ye the history of that place, and why…" He lifted a brow. "Suppose first I want ye to stop looking at me like I'm stark raving mad." His lips stretched into a grin. "For I'm only a wee bit. But Roe, yer not the first to come through and ye won't be the last." He stabbed his cigarette on the dashboard and flicked it away. "I'll prove to ye 'twas no dream, because I'm going to tell ye exactly what ye saw, and then yer going to believe me."

No, then I was going to swallow my last mouthful of air and scream until my lungs were shriveled grapes.

James took the smoke from my shaking fingers. "So here's how it went," he began. "Ye were lying in the Gate—that's what we call it— when ye slowly started to sink into the earth before ye woke up to the strangest scent, a bit like smoked vanilla, and yer eyes were so thick and heavy ye might have thought ye were underwater. But when they did open, ye saw a sky the color of burnt indigo, and a million cogs turning among the stars, with a forest growing through them, where the vines drag down and trail on the earth.

"And when ye breathed, ye tasted the air in yer lungs rather than yer throat, and they filled up with the stuff 'til ye almost thought ye were drowning. Then ye held it in ye, the taste of our world, until ye thought ye might burst from the weight, before ye exhaled at last."

My breath was coming in quick, harsh gasps now.

"It was terrifying. Not what ye saw in the memories," he mused, "but what ye'd left behind for a tiny moment. That's why when ye woke, ye weren't scared right away. No, ye felt like a mother who's lost her child, a terrifying longing, like something vital was ripped from yer soul."

James laid his hand over my clammy one.

"Roe, love, come back to the house with me. We'll have a cuppa, and ye can hear me out, see what I've got to show ye."

The leaves whinnied in the quickening winds. "I want to go home," I said weakly.

James leaned closer and murmured, "Roe? I am taking ye home. To Ruhaven."

⊗✦

James wrenched open the car door, waited. Gripping the window for support, I rose slowly, carefully. He gestured to the lane that led to Naruka, the hotel watching the unfolding scene in silence. I started toward her. Stopped. Pivoted.

Bolted.

I didn't know how I had any strength left, but I got my legs under me, even if they felt like bags of lead. I'd take my chances with—

Arms locked around my waist, yanking me back. "Roe, would ye feckin' just let me—"

James swore as we fell into a tangled mess, pebbles digging into my spine. He reeked of cinnamon and flour and yeast—a lie, when he should have smelled like the traitorous wet of this place. Not a new start for me at all, but the end.

I rolled over, kicking at his legs. He grasped my arms again. Firm, but not painful. Not yet.

"Let *go*!" Panic blurred my vision—for the pain to come, for the person I'd never be, for the desperate, horrifying relief that soon I'd see my sister.

Two cowboy boots *clunk-clunked* at my shoulder. I stopped fighting James long enough to look up, over the muddy knees and the leather jacket bulging at the breast pocket with a pack of cigarettes.

Tye blew out a long trail of smoke. "Darlin', ya can do this the easy way or the hard way. But ya best remember I've broken horses 'bout ten times your weight. So it won't bother me none to toss ya on over my shoulder and drag ya back to that hotel." He hiked up his jeans, crouched. "I might even enjoy it a little. Now, which way do you wanna have it?"

I could barely look at his face, at the crinkles forming around his lips when he smirked at me.

James pulled himself off me to glower at Tye. "Yer making a bloody bollocks of this, ye know?"

"*I* am?" Tye replied, eyebrows flying into his hairline. "Ain't you supposed to stop her at the house, not let her steal your damn car?"

James peeled off an apron still coated in flour. "Yera, Kazie was talking me ear off about the usual shite, and ye were taking so bloody long I nearly fell asleep from it. Ye know she was trying to convince me to turn the gate lodge into a giant birdcage? Made it seem so reasonable that I—ah, sorry, Roe." He turned to me with his hand extended. *Lunatic.* "Ye wanna do this yerself or no?"

I'd be better off making another attempt at the road, but I'd never outrun Tye, not when—

"*The easy way,*" I hissed when he bent to grab me.

Tye held up his hands. "Alright."

They waited until I started moving toward the hotel, then Tye took up the rear with James leading. I felt like a prisoner on death row, and could only hope it all ended quickly, preferably without me knowing when the blow was coming.

What would Kazie think when she saw them leading me back? James had said I used to be like her—did that mean she was in on it? How many others were involved? Would I be allowed to live like her, or would I be…

Would I be like Bryn? Exiled. Except…except that wasn't what happened to him, was it?

I sucked in a sharp breath, felt all the blood drain from my face.

James glanced over his shoulder, brow furrowing. "What in the name of Mary are ye on about now?"

"Did you—is he dead?" I coughed out. "*Bryn.*"

"Why in the bloody hell would I be trying to get a dead man to show ye the Gate?"

Tye stopped to grin at me. "Stornoway, dead? Oh, darlin', don't be sayin' things that'll just get me excited." He put a hand on my back, guiding me up Naruka's crumbling steps until the castle door loomed tall and bloody. "In ya go."

The foyer was dark but for a low-lit chandelier. The bird sculpture by the door cast a wicked silhouette before Tye tossed his jacket over it.

"I can't believe ye think I'd be killin' people, like," James muttered, aiming toward the library door on his left. "Bryn *is* in Norway, and he's——"

"——fine," Tye finished, slamming the main entrance shut, and I shuddered in the firewood heat of the foyer. "Buck up, kid." He gripped my shoulders, thumbs massaging the tight knots there.

I whipped around. "Don't *touch* me."

"Whoa." Tye lifted his hands. "That ain't what ya said an hour ago."

Despite everything, my cheeks scorched at the reminder.

"Tye, what the feck did ye do?" James demanded.

Tye angled his gaze over my shoulder. "She was gettin' up and I needed her to lie down. Ya know, for the Gate to take her."

So even the brief fantasy had been a lie. That shouldn't bother me. Not when I was about to be something the mushrooms would feast on in Naruka's cellar.

James stomped his foot. "*No* romantic stuff when yer recruitin', like. I know I bloody well told ye that."

Tye winked at me. "No regrets. Now you go on and listen to James. He's got a nice ol' speech planned that he's been practicing all week."

"*Tye!*" It was James's turn to look indignant now. "Ye can be the brute ye are and wait out here. Guard the door since me knee is banjaxed." He cast Tye a studying look. "I can see why Bryn didn't take too kindly to ye now."

Tye bared his teeth.

Scowling, James ushered me inside before closing the door with a *thud* behind us, the sound vibrating up through my toes.

Just a library, I reminded myself. Ancient, massive, and surreal. No torture contraptions, no chains, just the same library where I'd hung Bryn's paintings a week ago on the burgundy wall.

James brushed past me to sweep back a velvet curtain as tall as the intricately molded ceilings. When he did, storm light filtered into a room that smelled of the grassy tang of old books, rows and rows of them climbing to the ceiling. When they weren't stuffed into the wall, they cuddled in freestanding bookshelves lined up like church pews, the boards curved from the weight of the tomes.

"Take a seat, Roe. Ye've nothing to do but listen to an Irishman's tales for the next hour."

I remained standing, even as my adrenaline bottomed out. "Is this what you wanted to show me? Ruhaven?"

James scrunched his eyebrows. "Roe, this is the library," he stated, sounding a little miffed that I didn't know the difference.

I was about to toss something back at him, but if he was relaxed enough, trusting enough that I'd sit here, maybe I'd be able to surprise him.

On shaky legs, I lowered into the weathered springs of a teacup chair, tracking James's movement as he wove between labeled bookcases. Looking for something to bludgeon me with? That bronze horse statue would do the job. And worse, Tye probably knew whatever race the beast had won.

But James moved on, past aisles with handwritten labels reading *1500–1600: Lacontiz, Azekiel*, then the next row, *1700–1800: Originals in Box A0F: Mavante, Iskamastin*. And the next: *1900–2000*.

He stopped at a desk with hundreds of drawers, all decorated with different colors and patterns. He opened the smallest, a deep purple with a hand-painted knob, and pulled out a key twice the size of the library's, then made his way toward an enormous fireplace opposite the bay windows, and stopped.

I followed his gaze above the mantelpiece. Nailed to the wall was a maple cabinet as polished and wide as the fireplace with two doors of pristine glass. Flickering light reflected off its surface, obscuring what I hadn't bothered to notice before.

James slid the key into its lock, turned.

Click.

The doors opened with a quiet *whoosh*. This had to be the only hinge in Naruka James kept oiled. He stood there a moment, staring at something deep within the cabinet.

Then he stepped back and revealed the largest book I'd ever seen.

It stood nearly four feet high and, with its pages spread, spanned five feet wide. Irish bog, weeds, and dirt caked the book's rotted parchment, and chunks of soil clung to the edges, devouring the rows of scrawled text. Though the pages were shrunken and furrowed, the glittering bronze script remained pristine, as if it had been written in some god's blood.

Had James stolen it? Maybe he was a smuggler of old artifacts and wanted my help. The idea sounded a lot better than my murder.

"Come have a look, Roe."

"No, no, I'm fine," I croaked. "It's better from a distance." Especially with the door only ten feet to my right.

"Love, I'm not going to bloody hurt ye. I just want ye to see this. 'Tis over two thousand years old, ye know."

Jesus. He'd go to prison for years. But as James beckoned, I rose and stepped closer, navigating around sunken chairs and stacks of books until a strange smell hit me, like vanilla and jasmine blooming at night—smoky, sweet.

"*This* is the *Ledger*," James announced reverently. He clasped his hands behind his back, staring at the book—the *Ledger*—with its shimmering text reflected in his eyes. "'Tis the answer to the reason we're here, Roe, and why ye saw what ye did in the Gate."

Again, that word: *Gate*. A clue to whatever illegal thing they were up to.

"I can see why you're fascinated by it," I said. Reasonable, comforting, like prey pretending it wasn't snared in a hunter's net when I could all but see the ground spinning beneath me.

James tucked his tongue in his cheek. "Ye think I'm a wee bit mad, Roe. I know, as I've explained this to people far more stuck in their ways than yerself, like Tye, ye see."

I didn't see, not at all, even when my nose was inches from the ancient book, the paper grainy and thicker than stretched animal hide. It was open to page 241, but only the left sheet still bore a number; the right had disintegrated under the bog. A two-inch border of symbols framed rows and rows of golden writing, mostly numbers interspersed with a few words in another language.

"It was this book that led me to ye," James explained, tapping the glass so the sharp *tick-tick* of his nail matched the clocks. I gazed fleetingly at the line under his finger's cast shadow.

7 Iúil 1965 23:58 45.740234, -61.137997

He read the line aloud, breath thick with excitement in my ear. "What ye saw today wasn't a dream, but a *memory*. This line, Roe, this is why ye could see what ye did at the Gate. Day. Month. Year. Time. Coordinates. Iúil, sure that's Irish for July."

"What does that have to do with…" Then I saw—I *really* saw, but not what James had intended, not what had led him to drag me into this room. My throat went dry, my armpits damp. "You—you think this is my birthday."

"Roe, it *is* yer birthday."

I almost laughed, except it came out more as a croaking sob. Because of course it wasn't. Even in this hoax of a book, *my* birthdate wouldn't be written.

"—yer listed right here, and the row above yers is Bryn's," James continued, pointing at the line.

7 Iúil 1965 23:56 63.519469, 9.090167

"Two minutes before ye. Then ye've got this one here."

8 Iúil 1965 00:02 47.8344143, -110.6582699

"That's Tye, four minutes after. Different coordinates, as ye see, but when ye take into account the time it took yer souls to travel, it means ye crossed together." He nudged me and hovered a finger over 23:58. "This, Roe, is the time ye were born."

I shook my head, backing away, because it wasn't *my* birthdate—it was Willow's.

James grabbed me by the collar of my jacket. "No, don't ye lose it on me yet. Ye see this last number? I said, do ye see these last two numbers?"

When he gave my jacket a rough shake, cold sweat broke out along my spine, but I glanced at where he pointed.

45.740234, -61.137997

Bullshit. This was bullshit. "Let go of me."

James's eyes darkened with the fervor of the devoted. "That's the exact coordinates of yer birth, love."

No.

I gripped James's wrist, tried to pry it off. "Let me go," I repeated, weakly now.

"Roe, I tell ye someone knew ye'd be born on this day, at this time, in a wee First Nations village on the coast of Cape Breton, and they knew it almost two thousand years ago."

I licked my lips, my pulse jittering a sloppy double-time beat. This was all wrong, horribly wrong. Did I admit the truth? What would he do if he knew it wasn't me listed in the book he believed in? He'd kidnapped me, faked a job, lied about the hotel, pretended to care—all for a lie.

"This is some hoax, James—"

It was the wrong thing to say.

"A hoax!" James yelled. "Roe, this may be the only real truth in this whole feckin' world. Ye want to tell Kazie she's a forgery?"

"Look at line 1021," James demanded, pushing me into the cabinet. His body bracketed mine until my cheek was pressed against the cold glass and my shallow breathing fogged the words beneath.

21 Aibreán 1965 05:23 13.9738825, 33.8276906

"That's Kazie. Me own recording is four rows above, in 1953, where ye'll find the coordinates for a town in Thailand me mammy adopted me from. I'm not lying to ye. This is the feckin' truth, Roe."

When he released me, I teetered back into the wall, chest heaving. Kazie? Tye?

I slid a hand along the sticky wallpaper. "Tye believes in this?" No one was steadier, more grounded. He didn't even read books.

"We all do." Breathing heavily, James locked the cabinet again. "We're all in the *Ledger*."

I slid down the wall, landing on the echoey floor as the room swam. "You find these people, then." But he couldn't, because there were hundreds—no, *thousands*—of rows in the *Ledger*. He'd never be able to bring that many here and...and...

I stared in horror at the bookcases: *1301–1400, 1401–1500, 1501–1600*.

Not books, but *journals*.

I pressed a hand to my trembling lips, biting my knuckle to keep back the rising hysteria.

I was so completely fucked.

James circled the library, breathing in the journals like oxygen. "Now, I'll tell ye what it means to be in the *Ledger*." He stopped before a window, the curtains framing him like a mad king's cape. "Ye see, almost eight hundred years ago, we lived in a different land, and when we died, our souls were reborn here. But someone made this book so we could return to that exact spot ye were today. It lets us relive the memories of who we were before we died. That's what ye saw." James watched me, hope shimmering on his face before it crumpled. "Ah, Roe!"

He rushed across the room, dropping to his knees and taking my hands. His were soft and warm against my calloused palms.

"Don't cry, love. I'm sorry I've got to tell ye all this, and I know 'tis hard to understand." He thumbed away the tears spilling freely over my cheeks.

I'd never escape this, escape whatever Naruka was, whatever he believed. I'd never escape Willow.

"'Tis my job to find those in the *Ledger*, to show them the Gate as someone wanted me to. It's what me family does, what me mam did and hers before." He dug into his pocket, then held up a dinner napkin, pressed it to my nose.

Swiping it from him, I blew the rest of my dignity onto chicken-patterned cotton.

"What can I do to make ye believe me, Roe?"

I looked into his smoky, determined gaze, and took a breath. "I do believe you, James." Believed that if anyone would be written into his book, it would be Willow. That if anyone was worth remembering, it was her.

He searched my face, looking for something that could never be. Then he whisked the napkin from me, unbothered that it was soaked with tears and snot. "Well, it looks like I'll just have to show ye. Again."

I didn't fight when Tye and James dragged me up the mountain. When James let Tye return to Naruka after. When he forced me to my knees, ordering me to close my eyes and wait. It was late afternoon now, the tree trunks nearly red against a sun shining parallel with the land.

"There ye are now, Roe, go on…" James said when I squeezed my eyes shut and prayed for this to end.

Of course, nothing happened.

Birds rustled in the trees, chirping so innocently no one would ever believe what I'd been dragged through today.

I cracked open an eye when James started humming.

"Ah, keep them closed!" he said happily. "Or ye'll just end up hearing me entire rendition of 'The Fields of Athenry.'"

When I shut them again, James's low tune replaced the birds and the wind tickling my ears. Not being able to carry a tune had never stopped him from belting one in the pub after a few nudges from Tye. When James had been nothing but my boss, and Naruka nothing but a hotel in desperate need of repairs. When I'd been nothing but a repair woman from L'Ardoise. Nothing but the sister who survived.

Then I felt it.

CHAPTER 6

If We Were Vampires

I should have died next to my twin. Should be lying in a grave in the church cemetery where we'd watched the town at night and drunk boxed wine. It should have been her standing at the podium of my funeral, surrounded by soft stares and the reek of lilies, fumbling over a eulogy. Except she wouldn't have fumbled, and she wouldn't have broken down into hiccupping sobs that had people looking away and my parents' lips thinning with what we both knew was true.

But it wasn't me who died that day.

This time, when the phosphorescent forest came into focus, I didn't fight it. I was too exhausted, too broken, too tired with myself and every decision I'd never made. Maybe that's what this place was: some purple purgatory, the sky painted like someone had spilled a bucket of glow-in-the-dark indigo.

A memory, James had said. Another world. Another land. But no place like this could exist in the universe, because no forest could have grown to such wild, wicked ruin.

Forest.

I almost laughed—couldn't, because I had no control of the dream. Not my breath, languid and long; not my eyes, zooming like I wore binoculars; not my neck tilting too far to the side.

So I could only watch as my feet—*claws*—tiptoed through not sand or dirt, but white, jelly-like pearls. They oozed between my toes, and even that felt different, because my skin was not only silver, but thicker and taut.

And the *colors*. What did I even call *that* one? A new primary color, it had to be. Neither blue nor red nor yellow nor anything in between, and from it grew a new flood of mixtures.

The plants glowed in mesmerizing lavenders, phthalo blues, and glittering emeralds. Rocks grew in clusters of crystals. Dew floated up in tiny, sparkling diamonds. Purple light oozed between mammoth leaves, dripping over the long-haired trunks that I wouldn't be able to fit my arms around, pooling like water.

Somewhere deep inside me, in the place that was still *Roe*, horror and wonder melded into a sticky mix. But I couldn't *feel* that here.

My eyeballs didn't obey what should have turned them left or right, and my arms felt heavier and longer, like my entire nervous system had been rewired and plugged into all the wrong sockets. It was like I was inside one of those giant team mascots at baseball games, strolling around a forest in a remote-control suit. Except I glided more than walked, my silver arm stretching out to brush aside a furred polka-dotted tree with swaying feathers.

A path stretched ahead, just a dent in the pearly ground like a bowling alley's gutter, but I followed it while a new sense tingled my eardrums.

Music—but not played by instruments. Instead, it was like the land itself was singing. I heard the air whistling through holes in a tree trunk, the pearls shifting under my feet in a soft wave, the crackling bass note of some distant animal. And every few minutes, it would all stop. Then deafening silence would replace it, and the forest floor would rise a few feet, until, with an exhale, the music resumed.

As if the world were alive.

When a hanging green tentacle blocked my path, I jumped over it with more dexterity than I knew I possessed. I took another step forward, feeling the warmth ooze between my toes—

Something grabbed me from behind.

The force yanked me back, slapping me against a wall of solid heat. It was so startling, I jiggled in the dream for a moment before my vision cleared and my senses returned.

A sound like wood chimes escaped my throat. But not a sound I'd chosen to make.

I glanced down and nearly screamed at the thing wrapped around my waist. Burnt tattoos covered a male's golden forearm, one with muscles that made Tye's look like a young boy's. Claws replaced fingernails. Pulsing veins pumped with dark bronze blood.

A demon.

Breath whispered over my neck, sending shivers down a spine I still thankfully had.

The hold around me tightened, so much that I felt his muscles tense against my back, his deep inhale dragging me closer.

We waited like that, suspended as the world moved around us—leaves the size of small cars swaying, purple light like tiny beads floating down, flowers opening and closing their teeth.

What was that?

I tilted my head—no, no, *she* tilted her head—and a low rumble filled my ear, something that might be played on the lower notes of a piano. Was it him? Was he speaking?

Before I could react, could prepare myself, it—he—*jumped*.

Oh god.

Wings the color of storm clouds shot out around me, pushing at air thicker than water. Leaves blurred, furry branches cracked, bubbly dew burst against my face. Trees shuddered out of the way as the squid-like vegetation thinned to blinding violet. The demon braced a hand over my head—blocking the worst of it, I would realize later.

Please don't drop me, please don't...

We flew faster, harder, wings beating the air in a thunderous drumming, my legs dangling uselessly, his arms pinning me to his chest.

Then we burst through, and I saw the sky.

Oh, oh god. *It was real.*

Gears hung from the stars.

I wanted to weep, I wanted to pray, I wanted to beg a god I thought I didn't believe in.

This was impossible.

They glittered in the atmosphere—a beautiful, mechanical forest of slowly turning gears. Some were the size of Ferris wheels, others no bigger than a clock. They all spun as one, the sound like icebergs colliding underwater—low, deep, a baritone that promised something impossible.

But the dream looked away, tearing my watering eyes from the horrifying beauty floating in the sky.

I was still mourning the loss when the demon banked left, gliding us over glow-in-the-dark trees that lit up the gears. *Flying.*

God, I was flying, with the cold wind stirring the tips of my ears—higher up than they should be, but I didn't care. Not now, not here, not with the world tumbling below me, with this wild exhilaration filling my belly.

I threw out my arms, the glide of crisp freedom sliding between my fingertips. Tears blurred my eyes from the sting of the wind, but as

quickly as they came, they were wiped away by a golden fingertip—
his.

I'd never been so free. So weightless. So impossibly infinite.

And that's when I felt a tug on my hand.

My hand. Not this body I inhabited, but *me*. Like even lost here
among the whirling gears, someone remembered who I was. But maybe
I didn't want to remember, didn't want to be what waited as only a
distant memory.

In this vision, this world, this dream, I heard James's low chuckle.
Then a soft tugging on my hands as though he still held them in the
clearing, telling me to let go. Let go and follow him out.

The firm grip tightened, and my world blackened bit by bit. Music
dissolved. Scents disintegrated in my nostrils.

The demon evaporated.

No, no, no.

Then there was nothing but darkness. Cold brushed my naked skin,
but I couldn't *see* myself.

"James?" I whispered, breath rising on a curling fog.

The last notes of the song disappeared into the darkness, until only
an echoing hollowness remained. Until I was nothing.

But I felt that tug on my hand again—gentle, kind, a mother guiding
a child on their first bike ride. This time, I let him lead me out, tiptoeing
through the cool waters, through the darkness where light was a myth.

I could smell him already, as warm and comforting as my mother's
kitchen on a Sunday morning. Before she'd thrown me out. Before my
sister had died. Before everything.

And then James lifted me up.

⚙☀

"James, *James*."

His name became an embarrassing, burbling fountain on my lips.
I lost all sense of dignity, forgot that he'd dragged me up here, forgot
that only minutes—hours? Days?—ago, he'd pressed me against a glass
cabinet and demanded I read the *Ledger*.

But James didn't hesitate, simply wrapped his arms around me and
held. It took everything I had not to dissolve into a puddle against him.

"It's not me," I cried. "It's not me. It's not *me*."

"Of course it is. 'Tis just another version," he cooed, stroking my
hair. "I've got ye now."

I squeezed him tighter, grasping for that solidness of the here and
now, the warmth that only another person could offer.

~ 44 ~

I *missed* it. The dream. That world. Something in my chest was breaking like it had when my twin died. Because god, what if I never saw it again?

A terrifying part of me wanted to *believe*, wanted to know that every piece of that dream had somehow been real. To believe that there was more to this world, to everything I'd known, that everything James had told me had been dipped in some bit of truth, even if it wasn't *my* truth.

The sun dropped into the ocean, the moon winked into a fading sky, the birds lowered their chirping to soft whispers, but still, James held on.

Then other smells returned slowly. Not the rich honey of that dream, but diesel, socks, the vague burning that drifted from farmers' chimneys, the crisp, salty air.

I'd seen another world. I'd *lived* it as a three-fingered creature. I'd watched a dream come to life while my own reality crumbled like the Japanese knotweed eating through Naruka's foundation.

Up was down. Down was a portal in Naruka. Naruka was a gate to another world.

I pulled back from James, my eyes burning like they'd been scrubbed raw with sandpaper.

"Ye want to talk about it?" he asked, peering at me from under girly eyelashes.

I wiped my nose on my shoulder. "I don't know." And that was the goddamn truth—because I'd seen something meant for someone else, meant for Willow, and worse, I'd wanted it.

"Then I'll explain it to ye," he said calmly, handing me a cup. "Have some of this first. 'Tis hot whiskey and lemon and will help with the nerves. Now, I'll start with the easy thing. Ye know something of Bryn. 'Twas supposed to be him who showed ye the Gate, that's why I wanted him back. He's a special connection with the Gate that would have made this easier. But he's having none of me anymore, not since we forced him out."

I lowered the cup, the whiskey already numbing me. "Why did you? What's the *truth*?"

Guilt, or something very like it, flickered over James's pretty face. "Some can get lost in that world, ye know?"

I stared at the cup clasped in my hands, at the ripples forming from the rain dripping off the leaves. Yes, yes, I could understand perfectly how someone could get lost in that dream. Hadn't I done the same? I'd wanted to stay in those skies, flying above the glittering trees. I'd never have come back if James hadn't insisted.

"I felt you," I said softly, "in the—the dream, calling me back."

James took the empty cup from my shaking fingers. "And so I did. We always need someone to be here to anchor us."

"Because we might not want to come back?"

James dug in his knapsack. "No, because ye can't. There's no way to lift yerself from that world without someone here calling ye. Here ye are, now," he said, sliding a fingerless glove over my left hand, then the right. "Ye were only in for a few minutes, but yer cold from the shock of it."

I flexed my fingers. The last person to take care of me like this had been Willow. "Minutes? It felt longer."

"Time moves a wee bit different," James explained, sitting back on his haunches with his arms draped over his knees. Dew sparkled in the blackness of his hair, and a wet piece of it clung to the hollow of his left cheek.

"Who *are* you?" I murmured.

A slow grin spread from ear to ear, lighting up James's features. "'Tis true this is me hotel, but 'tis not a place for humans. I took over Naruka from me mammy after her aneurysm, and all the responsibility that comes with it."

But only one word registered. "I didn't know your mother died from an *aneurysm*." *Like Willow.*

His eyes flickered. "Aye, she did. Now, 'tis my duty to guard the *Ledger*, to find those listed, to bring them here to show them exactly what I just did. So they can remember. So they can dream."

I let his words wash over me, a wave that flowed into one ear, circling and cooling around and around in my brain, until I could almost believe that someone had wanted Willow to see this.

"James, what is it, exactly? The—the dream."

He grasped the hand I'd been trailing through dirt, rubbed it between his. A gesture of utter and complete comfort.

"'Tis Ruhaven," James answered, voice solemn and low, and he continued with a little less of his accent. "It's the land we're from before our souls are reborn here. Up here in this wee meadow above Naruka, it's the place me mammy's ancestors once found the *Ledger*. They learned that those listed in its pages can return where the *Ledger* was and witness the life they once had. But 'tis only a memory, Roe, a memory of that other life." He tugged a box of cigarettes from his front pocket, and there was a touch of sadness when he said, "Now yer seeing that life replaying, like a movie."

He squeezed a smoke between his lips, then stuck another between mine.

"Ye feel what she feels, ye go where she goes. Yer memory, I mean. But ye can't change or control it. Yer just watching." He paused to crank his hands like we were playing charades. "But there's no pausing, and it keeps playing whether yer in the Gate or not."

Like a movie playing in another room, and I just stepped in to watch small bits of it.

I swallowed my doubt, my common sense, everything that kept me grounded. All of it lodged in my throat until it was a struggle to form words. "So it's a replay of my—my—my—"

"Past life," James finished.

"And it's playing—"

"Has played. It's already happened so, about eight hundred years ago. Yer memory's dead now. She was reborn here as yerself when she died."

I inhaled deeply on the smoke. It mixed with the whiskey to form a sticky coating in my gut. Ireland moved around me, from the distant ferry gliding toward Capolinn's port, to the sheep strolling in an overgrown field, to our deranged cow whose belching I could hear even from this height.

"If the memory *is* playing," I began, "then where does it start? When does it end? Has it been playing for eight hundred years and I'm just sneaking in now?" Like some latecomer at a movie. *Pardon me, there's my seat.*

"Naw, it took about that long for yer soul to pass from Tallah—that's the realm we're originally from—to here."

"*Realm?*"

"Yera, it sure didn't look like Earth, did it?" He chuckled to himself. "There's two countries on Tallah—Ruhaven and Drachaut. We're all from Ruhaven, and when yer reborn here, the memories start playing. So ye've missed twenty-seven years of them."

Just how many had James witnessed? How long did it take before someone forced you from Naruka like he did Bryn?

"Were you there now?" I asked. "Did you enter…" *The memories? Your past life? The reason I'd be insane within a week?*

"The Gate," James said helpfully and with no small amount of humor. "And no, I didn't go with ye, as I had to pull ye out."

Needing to move, I rose and walked toward the opening in the trees.

Magic—that's what we were talking about—and the child in me wanted to think it was possible that Ruhaven could exist, and the dream was some memory. But that girl had died with my twin. Long before, if I was being honest, back when I'd dropped out of music college, back when I'd started working a real job at my dad's shop. And in that world, there was no magic.

James came to stand beside me and gazed out at the smoky sea. Maybe something in the misty hills of Ireland made it easier to believe. It didn't seem so foolish up here, with the light flickering off the dewy leaves and the brilliant greens lit up, that something *more* might exist.

"What are ye thinking, Roe?"

I blew out smoke. "I'm thinking about how I can possibility rationalize magic."

This earned me a coughing laugh of mostly smoke. "Magic?" James cried. "Magic is just the name for questions we're not yet able to answer, and ye'll find I have quite a few explanations for just what allows us to witness these memories."

What did explanations matter when I knew that if I lay in that shadowy patch again, I'd see just what had awaited me before—the spinning gears, the world that was as much a dream as alive? Even now, I felt the invisible pull of it, as if the swaying stalks of the meadow were daring me to return. Maybe I wanted to. Maybe that's why I was willing to throw every ounce of reasonable precaution to the wind, every piece of grounding reality I'd clung to, and just *dream*. Even if the dream wasn't mine.

I shoved the cigarette back in my mouth. "Let's start with this," I said around it. "Why am I in the *Ledger*?"

"Because yer one of the few who made the crossing. Not all Ruhavens are reborn here, but our souls escaped the natural way of things, and so I have to believe someone wanted us to be found. The time between births in the *Ledger* tells us how close ye were to crossing together."

"And the ones that don't make it to the *Ledger*?"

Something came and went in his smoky eyes. "They died in Ruhaven, having never made the crossing here." After a heartbeat, James finished the smoke.

"How is it possible, though?"

"Being reborn? Simple. In Ruhaven our souls are energy, and the first rule of the conservation of energy is—"

"It can't be created or destroyed," I finished.

"Exactly—barring entropy, it's conserved. So ye see, our souls are preserved like any other energy, except ours were sent here. Why? That's another question, one I'm trying to figure out."

We stood there like that, shoulder to shoulder, him answering my questions, until most of the daylight gathered on the horizon like the lid of a smoking pot. By the time I finished the second glass of whiskey James handed me, magic didn't seem quite so insane.

"There was this, um, demon thing," I said, "in the—the Gate, as you called it. Could he be you? You said others are witnessing their memories, so I wondered…"

James's eyes flickered. "Demon? Had he purple skin?"

My eyebrows flew up. "Gold."

"Then no, as I've purple meself. But aye, he could be. There's a good chance we knew those who made the crossing, especially for those born close together."

I handed him the smoke when he gestured for it. "James," I said quietly, "what is it you really want from me?"

"Want?" He inhaled until the end sparked red. "That's up to yerself. Ye can leave today if ye like, but I'd miss ye, as yer fierce handy to have around Naruka." When I looked over, he was grinning again.

"But why stay here? Why witness these memories? Why live like *this*?"

The grin floated away. "Why? Roe, if ye can't answer that, maybe 'tis best ye don't stay after all."

He turned away from me, the sunlight flickering off the suspenders of his corduroy pants, and repacked the bag he'd brought for us.

As I watched him—something I found oddly comforting—I inhaled a long drag, needing the burn of it in my lungs. The last time I'd smoked like this, I'd been sitting on a sidewalk in L'Ardoise, the sun baking me in its heat while my parents inspected waxy coffins in the funeral home.

CHAPTER 7

Einstein's Idea

One month later

Like everything I'd ever known, time also seemed to lose all meaning. It was only thanks to the naked priest calendar that I knew we were somewhere in August.

I hadn't left Naruka.

No, wait, that wasn't quite true. After James showed me the Gate— a day after? Two?—I'd decided I was definitely going insane. That those mushrooms Willow had given me back in college had finally caught up with me.

I'd gotten all the way to Limerick before I turned the car around. James said I got one look at the city and drove back in horror, but I think that was just some Irish joke.

I didn't know why exactly I came back. Somewhere along the way, when the rugged heather of County Kerry had given way to the springy grass of Limerick, the fear of just being *me* again was worse than the fear of being someone else. Or maybe I'd just felt guilty for stealing James's car—again.

When I drove back, James was waiting for me on Naruka's steps, a cup of tea in his hand, a romance novel in the other. "How far did ye get?" he'd asked, as if this were all perfectly expected. Instead of insisting I give him the keys, or come inside with him, he'd simply climbed into the passenger seat and said, "Well, I might as well show ye a bit of Kerry."

We'd driven up, around, and down roads that would struggle to fit two horses, never mind the beat-up old Ford, and James had answered every question I'd thrown at him.

How is it possible to witness the memories here?

There's a connection between our worlds that goes back centuries, formed intentionally, and souls have been traveling here for years. It's why our lands share so many things.

I didn't think we shared gears in the sky, but didn't mention it.

What happens if someone visits the Gate who isn't a Ruhaven?

There's nothing to happen but a little snooze in a meadow if they're not—and few are, aye, few are.

But that couldn't be true, because the Gate had allowed *me* through.

Me. An electrician, a tradeswoman, without even a college degree to my name.

I kept asking questions, and after four hours of hearing the hedges demolish the side of James's tiny car, we drove back to Naruka.

Tye had tried to talk to me a few times, but I'd pushed him away. Not because I was still upset he'd lied, but because I was embarrassed with myself—in so many ways.

James was still taking care of me: making breakfast, carrying a tray of stew up to my room when the shock of Ruhaven meant I couldn't get out of bed. Whatever Ruhaven was, whatever the truth of the Gate may be, James believed it. And he treated me so well because he believed *I* was a part of that world, the history of this place, written in the *Ledger*.

But I wasn't.

That shame was enough to keep me up at night as much as the dreams of flying through the gears.

I'd never done anything to deserve this. Never. It wasn't my birthdate written in the *Ledger*, not me the book wanted, not Roe from L'Ardoise whose biggest achievement was being a half-decent plumber. I wasn't a prodigy on the piano, I hadn't won any awards in high school, I hadn't graduated college on the dean's list, I hadn't graduated college at all.

I hadn't been there when my sister died. Hadn't felt it.

So no, it wasn't me listed on row 1274 of a centuries-old book, my name inked on ancient parchment by Irish monks. Wasn't me written in precise, golden handwriting, as much as James wanted it to be. As much as he looked at me like I was something special.

All the work he'd gone to, all the hope he'd had, all for a doppelgänger.

What might have been worse was how much, sometimes, I wouldn't mind being that lie. Had wanted so *badly* for it to be me written in the

Ledger that I'd stayed weeks after I should have left. Now, there was a ball of pitiable envy and *want* in my gut that was slowly eating me from the inside, that begged me to reach out and claim this thing that wasn't even mine.

Because then I would mean something, be someone, and I might eventually believe that who and what I was could matter in the universe, that someone out there was waiting for me. So much that they'd look down and give me this.

But they hadn't.

⚙✺

In one of Capolinn's smoky pubs, Tye's fist slapped down hard on the table, jittering the empty pint glasses James had left to replenish. "So that's it, then," he said as Kazie folded herself onto the stool beside him, ignoring me entirely, as she'd done for weeks. "I spend six months draggin' your ass to Ireland, to show ya what a lot of others would kill to see, and you're just leavin'?"

The stare he leveled at me could have peeled layers off an onion. But I couldn't answer him, not with the truth, not without them knowing they'd confessed all the secrets of Naruka to a fraud. Which was why I had to leave.

I licked my lips, curled my fingers, wishing for that fresh pint that couldn't come fast enough.

Kazie had wrangled us a snug in the back after a couple men in sweater vests rose to offer us their table, maybe out of manners, or maybe because the girl asking them if they were done with it was wearing a jacket made out of glittery seagull feathers. A veritable Dr. Seuss book hung on the pub's walls—cracked photos, fishing reels, fiddles, and figs, and the owner's family tree with every cousin, grandmother, and dog for at least eight generations.

Other people stood or sat on church pews crammed against yellow wallpaper, and the whole space was so narrow, the parish priest would have declared us all standing in sin—if he wasn't busy ordering a pint at the bar beside James.

"I'm sorry," I repeated roughly. "Sorry for the time it took to bring me here. Sorry that you had to pretend."

Tye's eyes narrowed. "Pretend?"

I shouldn't have said that, especially not with the note of bitterness Tye had homed in on. "To be someone else," I amended, "in L'Ardoise."

He leaned forward on his stool, loose hair coming to rest at his shoulders. I could still feel it sliding between my fingers, his groan humming against my throat.

"Ya listen to me now," Tye said, voice like gravel. "Things between us may not have been what ya thought, but that don't mean it was a lie, ya hear? It don't mean I don't care for ya, Roe."

I stared hard at the stained carpet under my feet, memorizing the patterns of the old weave as I struggled to form words that wouldn't give away how badly I'd wanted to mean more, a lot more. To exist for something more than the empty apartment with my sister's dreams strung on the walls.

"I wanna know why you're goin' back," he pressed.

That, I couldn't tell him. "It's home," I hedged.

"*Home*," Tye repeated, nodding slowly as he leaned back again, lifting a smoke to his lips. "Ya know, Roe, I learned a lot about ya when I needed to convince you to come here, so I know what ya were to people in that town you say is home." He braced an elbow on the table, the light of the candle brushing his flexed jaw. "You know what they called ya?"

"I—"

"*Willow's sister*," he finished on a sneer. "And that's what you wanna go back to? Let me tell ya, Roe, maybe ya should. 'Cause Ruhaven ain't got time for folks who wanna be *nothin'*."

I dug my fingernails into my thigh.

Willow's sister. Maybe it was my biggest achievement. And maybe, if he and James had come to L'Ardoise three years earlier, they'd have found the one they wanted.

"Jayzus, that took too long," James said, unloading the pints between us. "Bloody Colm stopped me at the bar."

Grateful for the reprieve, I glanced over, following Tye's gaze to a man with cropped hair, beady eyes, and a stout clenched in his fist. "Who's he?"

In answer, Kazie lifted her shoulders, letting them dangle by her feather earrings as the fiddles finished their jig, struck up the next.

Tye turned back around, reached for his pint. "Used to date a girl at Naruka, but when we showed her the Gate, she damn up and left like you're about to, and now he's got it in his stupid head we did somethin' to her." He bared his teeth. "You ain't datin' someone in town that's gonna cause me trouble too, are ya?"

I stared right back. "Worried they'll whisk me away to the Gate for a kiss, too?"

"Darlin', if ya think that was a kiss, ya got bigger problems than Ruhaven."

James thrust my pint between us. "For the love of Mary, me nerves can't take the two of ya goin' at it. Now, I know yer of a mind to leave," he said, straddling a stool, "and maybe that's me own fault for letting Tye show ye the Gate as he did. Still, as much as most *do* want to live in Ruhaven, to know who they once were, I know 'tis not for everyone. But in this yer unique, Roe, as I've brought ye here for two reasons. I need to tell ye about—"

Tye rose abruptly, sending the stool flying back. "Ya got no business droppin' this on her when she's goin'," he said, grabbing his coat and turning to me. "And as much as I like ya, kid, you don't got any business with us anymore. With me," he added.

The words landed hard enough that I was cooling my aching throat with the pint by the time Tye hit the door.

I'd never had any business with them—he was right about that. All his work to get me to move here had been for nothing.

James laid a hand over mine, nearly as comforting as the pint, which only increased my guilt. "He's wrong, Roe. Whatever ye choose, ye can talk to me, and ye can come back and visit Naruka too, should ye change yer mind."

I should have blurted out the truth right then, confessed everything, and damn the consequences.

"But I've something ye need to know, something ye might not find easy. It's about Willow."

My mind stilled, my hand freezing around the glass, so that it hovered in mid-air until cold liquid spilled onto my jeans, jolting me. "I—sorry, I—" *He'd found me out already.* Why had I thought he wouldn't check? He and Tye had known enough about me to know where I worked, to convince me to move here. They'd known I had a twin, would've checked her birthdate too.

"—that's why we think yer twin's death is related to Ruhaven," James finished over the roar in my ears.

"You know that I—I'm— Wait, *what*?" The room yawned open, ripe with cigarette smoke. Had he said her death was—

"Willow died from an aneurysm," James said calmly, like there wasn't a ping-pong ball bouncing around my brain. "Like me mother, and others before her, all Ruhavens in the *Ledger*, who've suffered some—some disease, we think, coming from the Gate. I've not all the information on it, but I think Willow's death is related—even if she's not in the *Ledger*."

I swallowed the dregs of my beer; my mouth had gone bone dry.

"You're the only twins ever in the *Ledger*," Kazie said, and it took me a moment to realize it was her speaking. "Maybe the infection that causes the aneurysms in Ruhavens can jump between you and Willow."

Willow, dying in the hospital when I hadn't even known what an aneurysm was. Something I'd worried would prevent her from playing the piano, something I'd help her recover from—together, always.

"An infection?" I said at last, then repeated James's words. "You have a list?"

"I've twenty-seven cases of Ruhavens dead from aneurysms this century," James repeated softly, "and most were under thirty, like yer sister. 'Tis rare, Roe, ye know yerself. Too rare for so many of us to die from it."

My ears rang with the deadened mayhem of the bar, the squeaking fiddles a muffled whisper, the whistle an imperceptible whine.

James flattened his palms on the table. "I can't absolutely swear to ye the disease is behind yer sister's aneurysm. I'm not the person who'd know."

"But we have a couple ideas," Kazie added, my sister and me suddenly interesting to her for the first time. "Tye and I think there's something that happens in the memories that causes the disease to infect us here. Something we did, right, or someone we spoke to. I dunno why Willow was infected, but I gotta believe it's because there was that transference."

"A transference," I repeated slowly.

She continued, missing the edge in my voice. "Yeah, yeah, I'm always reading about twins and stuff, especially when we found you, and I'm thinking your connection probably transferred. I don't think you gotta be in the Gate to be infected. James, remember that woman from India?"

"Kazie, I don't think Roe wants to hear that," he said, picking up on the chill in the air.

"Well, whatever, anyway. She never went to the Gate, died on recruitment. So maybe that's what happened to Willow, right, and she, like, picked up something through their twin bond."

"Kazie."

"But the point is," she steamrolled over James with a finger in the air, "Roe can live the memories, can figure out what might have caused the infection back then. Maybe it's always in us. But if you went in the Gate, Roe, with your special connection to Willow, you might—"

I shot up from the bench, the pint shaking in my fist. Kazie blinked at me.

She didn't talk to me for a month and *now* she wanted to pretend to care about my sister? Only because it could benefit her, could benefit Ruhaven, the only thing anyone at Naruka really cared about. Not me, and not Willow, not who she'd been.

I set the glass down with a crack that sent beer spilling over my fingers. "Willow and I *did* have a connection, and it had nothing to do with whatever was going on in Naruka. She is—I mean, she *was* my—"

Fuck.

I swore, looked away, at the dog behind the bar, then at the old woman falling asleep on her accordion.

When I was sure my voice wouldn't break, I said, "She was the only person who ever knew me. And she didn't die because of a disease from Ruhaven. She died because her brain exploded when I wasn't there."

Face burning, I bent and fumbled for my coat.

Kazie watched me, eyes wide. "Roe, I swear it's the truth that we're really dying of this thing. I'm so sorry about Willow, but—"

"No, you're not, or you wouldn't bring any of this up. You didn't see her dead in the hospital, didn't look at what happened to her brain, and you *definitely* don't have any evidence it was from this disease."

I tried to shove my arm through the suddenly minuscule hole in Willow's old jean jacket.

"But there are others who've died of the infection, who suffered an aneurysm and—"

"Maybe they were just sudden deaths and you're confused. You said yourself, James, that your mother was older. But my twin's death isn't some science experiment for you to pick apart."

James put a hand on Kazie's arm, lifting eyes full of sympathy to me. "We didn't mean to upset ye, Roe."

Hadn't they?

"No, you just wanted to make up something to keep me here."

Hurt clouded James's eyes. "Ye think I'd lie about me own mother?"

"You? Lie? Yeah, why would I think that?" I spun on my heel, nearly knocking over a table. "I'll see you at the *hotel*."

"But Roe, we *do* have proof," Kazie called behind me. "There's someone who—"

I shoved through the pub, the taps too bright in the dingy dark. Then I was out the door and sucking back night air like a fish thrown overboard.

Lights flared as cars rumbled over the road, the loose cobblestones clacking like thunder. A horse came next, followed by ten men bellowing an off-key Irish tune.

I turned left, stomping through puddles in my search for a cab in the tiny, fifteen-pub town of Capolinn.

"Roe! I'm sorry—wait!"

Ignoring Kazie's shouts, I hustled toward a taxi driver who'd just switched on his sign. Crimson breaklights shone in zigzag patterns.

I rapped on the cabbie's window, then coughed when it opened and smoke billowed out.

"Where ye goin', love?" he asked, a grizzled man of at least fifty years, with rainy blue eyes and a beard gone yellow.

"Naruka," I was forced to admit. "Just up the road, not ten minutes past—"

"Forty years I've lived here. Ye think I don't know where it is? Bloody Yanks. In ye go, so."

I stepped to the back, pried open the passenger door—

Kazie slapped it closed.

She kept her hand braced on the door, frizzy hair shining midnight black with the rain. Spots of color stained a face normally a pristine, dusty purple. "So that's, like, just it?" she panted. "You're just going to floof off back home? You won't even look into this?"

I whipped up my hood as the rain thundered down. "*This*?" I repeated. "*This* isn't anything. *This* is barely even a disease. *This* is just a convenient way to force me to stay." To force me to live a life that wasn't mine, and it was only a matter of time until they found out. Keeping my voice low, I added, "To witness whatever messed-up movie is playing a mile above Naruka."

I shouldered her aside, wrenching open the door. Kazie threw her weight against it, the *crack* reverberating through the street. Horns blared.

"*Convenient?*" she seethed. "So you think us being killed by a disease is convenient? I *knew* people who have died. Ruhavens who'd have given anything to live in that 'messed-up movie.' The one you're *throwing away*."

Because it was terrifying how much I wanted to keep it.

I swatted at the finger she drilled into my chest. "Convenient, because I was about to leave when you and James dumped this on me."

"Because James wanted to *help* you. Though I don't know why. You're selfish, and you don't deserve Ruhaven." She paced in a tight circle, pinprick heels clacking off stone and in danger of snagging in the crevices. "I'd give my freaking life to her, to Ruhaven, and you're actually just going home."

"Yeah, and when I get there, I'm spending all the money James paid me on a bottle of 1947 scotch and sinking into a stupor so deep and dark that when I wake up, I'll forget all about this."

"Love, I'd like nothing more than the same meself!" the cabbie shouted.

In answer, Kazie grabbed my shoulders and slammed me against the cab—hard, despite being a foot shorter. "So that's all you care about?" she demanded, face a mask of barely contained fury. "Going home? Drinking? Why don't you think of someone else, Roe? You could save the next person. You might have saved Bryn from the disease."

"The man James kicked out of Naruka? Where is Bryn, anyway? Here for the *ceremony*?" I sneered, and god, I could only be grateful there wasn't another person here to witness my—

She slapped me. A quick, hard blow that left my cheek stinging from this—this pixie sprout of a girl.

"Bryn *survived*, you ungrateful cow." With my collar in her grip, she yanked me down to eye level, wrenching open the cab door. "He was the only one who did, the only one who has answers for you. Think about *that*."

I barely avoided whacking my head on the roof before my butt hit the cigarette-burned seat.

"If Bryn suffered an aneurysm, then why's he still alive?"

She grinned, a blinding row of teeth, not the least bit amused. "What do you care, huh? He's nobody, just another lunatic who wanted to find you, to show you all this, just so you could skedaddle back to *L'Ar-freaking-Doise*. And I'm oh-so-sure your sister's aneurysm was just a coincidence too." She kicked my knee in, slammed the door. "Bye-bye!" she yelled, then slapped the hood of the car. "Naruka!"

I cranked down the window. "Kazie, wait, I—ah!"

Tires squealed, rolling over the cobblestone roads hard enough to make my brain rattle.

CHAPTER 8

Anatomy

The stove in Naruka's kitchen was just a vague wisp of applewood by the time I returned.

I thought I'd put Willow's death behind me when I moved here. After months of crying myself to sleep, waking up to remember she wasn't there, and listening to recordings of her playing the piano, I had finally accepted it. Accepted what the doctors had tried to explain—that a sudden aneurysm could kill without warning. Accepted that I had no control over it, and nothing could have prevented what happened. Accepted that the only place she was still alive was in this hollow ache below my heart.

And now?

I'd never know if her death was due to an unexplainable aneurysm or if it was because of the Gate. James didn't really know either—he admitted as much—and Kazie assumed everything was about Ruhaven. But this was Willow's life, and this was all I had left of her.

Shaking, I gripped the edge of the counter, concrete digging into my fingers, and stared out the window at that jagged cliff where James had explained, so hopefully, how I was a Ruhaven. But I wasn't, couldn't be. Not me, the electrician, but Willow, the prodigy. Willow who might have died because *she* was the Ruhaven the *Ledger* had wanted.

I circled the kitchen until my left knee ached, then switched directions.

If there *was* a disease from the Gate, had she been born with it? Were there any signs, symptoms? *Your soul isn't yours, but a woman's from centuries ago, and here's something she picked up along the way?*

Willow had never mentioned any health problems before she died. There'd been no trips to the doctor, no sudden headaches, no flu or fever. She'd been the pride and joy of L'Ardoise, about to join the national orchestra and get out of the town she'd never loved.

But what about Bryn? Was there some symptom he hadn't noticed? And what did it matter if Willow died because of a natural aneurysm here, or one caused by the Gate?

I shook my head. It *did* matter—of course it did—and so far, only Bryn might know the truth.

If he *had* been infected and survived, wouldn't he have wanted to know *why?* Wouldn't he have spent every waking moment trying to find those answers for himself and James? Instead, James had exiled him, and he'd had no answers to…

I stopped pacing to look up, seeing through the crown molding and stucco ceiling, the glass beads Kazie had strung across the kitchen.

The *books*.

Rows and rows of textbooks and journals had bowed the shelves in Bryn's room to near collapse. Was that why James had asked what I thought of the room? Because he'd expected me to recognize the obvious evidence of Bryn's old research?

Blood racing, I hurried out the kitchen and up the stairs. Portraits of Ruhavens long dead, or maybe those who'd left, glared at me under the rays of candlelight as I barreled down the hallway and shoved open the door to Bryn's room.

Curtains billowed in purple hues around the bed, then drooped to stillness. When I flicked on the lamp, gold chased away the violet night.

My breath came in hard, desperate pants, filling the silence. Only Naruka could be this quiet. No crickets, no howling coyotes, no noisy bin tossed over by raccoons. Utter, deafening silence—except for the clocks, and those I barely noticed anymore.

I took one breath. Two. Then stepped to the bookcase and read each title—*carefully*, this time.

James must have wondered how I could stand here, oblivious to someone's obvious obsession with what had killed my own sister.

I yanked the first book out. *Anatomy of the Brain.*

Grabbed another. *Neurology of Brain Hemorrhages.*

Infections of the Spine.

The Central Nervous System.

And on and on it went, until a pile of fifteen books lay scattered at my feet.

Was it possible? Some *reason* for her death? Not a freak aneurysm, but something inherited because of who she was?

Or had been.

I grabbed for the Polaroids James had stowed in the desk, flipping through until I found Bryn. I didn't know why I needed to see it, but my fingers trembled on the photo, gripping it like it was my last lifeline to Willow. Some tenuous connection between this man and a disease that might have infected my twin.

Impossible. Stupid. But…

Headlights flashed through the window, briefly illuminating Bryn's startling cobalt eyes. My hallucination had gotten that much right.

It should have been *Willow* who'd survived. Willow, who'd never made a mistake in her life, who'd been impossibly gifted at the piano from the moment she was born, who'd deserved a chance to see who she'd have become. It should have been Willow who lived long enough for James to find and bring her here, so she could look at the book with her birth written in it.

I owed her answers.

When I heard the door downstairs creak open, I stuffed the photo back with the rest of them. But I left the books, stepping over their ominous covers like they were proof of *something*, and hustled downstairs.

"What the bleeding hell happened out there?" James yelled as I entered the kitchen. He wrung his soaked flat cap in the sink before slapping it on the coat hook. "Ye left, fair enough, then next I see yerself and Kaz in a near brawl right in the middle of Capolinn! Yer doing nothing to help Naruka keep a low profile when yer feckin' screaming yer heads off and——"

"I want to talk to him," I interrupted, tugging out the table's bench.

"*Who*?" James asked, aghast. "For everyone in bleedin' Capolinn has surely heard ye tarnish the reputation of what was previously this *hotel*."

As annoyed as I'd ever seen him, he stomped to the woodstove, tossed four logs into it before he seemed to remember he'd run out of matches this morning.

At the table, I reached for a glass and poured the whiskey, needing it for my next admission. "Bryn," I said, "I need to talk to Bryn."

James rose, dusting soot off his knees. "Bryn? What the hell do ye—" He goggled at me. Wait, no—not *me*, the bottle on the table. "Is that me thirty-year-aged whiskey?"

I smacked my lips together. "You tell me."

James spluttered, shuddered, then slumped into the stool across from me. "Well, go on so, give me some. I need it, for I'll be years explaining away the likes of Ruhaven and all the rest of our baggage ye've left in the middle of the road."

I winced, but filled a glass and pushed it at him. "Kazie said Bryn survived this disease?"

Calmer now, James adjusted his spectacles. "Survived, yes."

I leaned forward, the sheepskin rug shifting under me. "Then why didn't he continue researching it? I found the books you must have wanted me to notice, but why did he leave them?"

The rim of James's glass dug into his bottom lip as he seemed to decide how to answer. "He didn't want the reminder."

"Of the disease?"

"Of Ruhaven." James set the whiskey down without drinking. "Do ye not understand what it'd do to someone to live in that world every day, to have friends, lovers, then to be denied it?" He shook his head. "It's me own fault he wants no contact anymore. I'm sorry."

I shook my head automatically. Whatever James's reasons for exiling Bryn, I knew they were warranted, but I still needed answers.

"I just—I need to know, James. Need to know for certain that what happened to Willow was because of the Gate." I shuffled the whiskey from hand to hand. "Maybe I'll call him and see if there were any signs."

"Ye think I haven't tried that? He'll not speak to any of us."

"And nothing in his notes told you if there were any symptoms?"

"They didn't, no. He focused only on the memories of those killed. But yer right, ye do need answers, even if he's not wanting to give them. So I was planning to visit him meself in Norway."

This was new. "When?"

"After I showed ye Ruhaven, got ye settled." He opened his hands, folded them again. "But now yer leaving. So I've less work than I thought."

I wouldn't feel guilty. But goddamn it, I *did* feel guilty—on so many levels. Still, I couldn't admit the truth to him, couldn't tell James how much time he'd wasted. But maybe—maybe I could make it mean *something*.

I sat back with the whiskey, letting the burn of it smooth all the rough edges of the night. And all the while, the clocks *tick-tick-tick*ed, louder in the silence.

"Let me come with you," I said at last.

James frowned. "I'm not sure that's such a good idea."

"What? Why not?"

"Do ye even know where Oslo is?"

"No, but I'm guessing I don't have to fly the plane." Why was James resisting? Didn't he and Kazie want me to help them find answers? "What's this really about?"

"Ye were wantin' to leave, swearin' off Ruhaven, and now ye want to see Bryn?"

I crossed my arms. I could play hardball. Had until I was ten. "You shouldn't have told me if you didn't want me to get answers. Why did you?" I leaned forward, drilling my finger into the table. "Why *did* you?" I repeated when I sensed the guilt, the hesitancy, both convincing me I needed to see Bryn, to find out what James was hiding. "When was Bryn infected?"

James stared out the window, the moonlight reflecting off his glasses and the whiskey stain on his lips. Was he staring up at Ruhaven? Imagining he was there?

"December last year."

Yet he'd been exiled from Naruka two years ago. Why would he have been researching the disease so extensively before he was infected? A passing interest? But the research had been stored in his bookcase, not the library, as if it'd been the first thing he wanted to see when he woke.

"Was Bryn close to someone who was infected?"

A shadow passed behind James's eyes. "He didn't know anyone."

Was that an answer, or a subtle evasion? "Then why was he researching—"

"Roe," James cut me off, turning away from the window. "Bryn's a private person, and I don't have all the answers ye need because of it. But I don't know that you seeing him is the right way to get them. Let me go for ye."

If Bryn could tell me the truth behind Willow's death, then nothing would stop me from going to Oslo. "You owe me, James."

His eyes lit. "Owe *you*, do I?"

"You kidnapped me."

He lifted the whiskey again. "*Wee* bit of a stretch."

"Sending Tye?"

"Duty?" His lips twitched.

"I really don't like you," I said, wishing it was the truth.

James let out a long, weary sigh. "Aye, but ye'll like Oslo."

CHAPTER 9

The Man Who Fell to Earth

I did like Oslo.

Begrudgingly so, like admitting your cousin was a lot more beautiful than you. James and I had arrived a week later to a sparse but cozy bed and breakfast by the port. In our twin guest room, we unpacked the few days' worth of clothes we'd brought. James took up the entire bathroom with his moisturizers, hair products, brushes, and whatever else had the man looking at least ten years younger than he should.

When I'd told Tye about our plan to speak to Bryn, he was even more disappointed than when I'd wanted to leave. Why was this worse? Because Bryn was a "*fucking lunatic*" about Ruhaven, according to Tye.

I believed him. Anyone who'd spent years visiting that Gate would have to be a bit crazy. Living as someone else. *Being* someone else.

So why didn't the idea scare me as much as it should have?

I glanced over at James as we navigated the streets of Oslo. His eyes were still a bit sleepy from our early start, but he looked otherwise content in a city that was too...*clean*. Suspiciously clean—no cans in the ditches, no cigarette butts fallen between the sidewalk cracks, no litter blocking the sewage grates. I could practically eat off these streets.

I'd spent a good thirty minutes walking around with an empty coffee cup before I realized the bins were actually the twisted iron rectangles I'd mistaken as sculptures. They sat in the manicured parks between bubbling fountains and twisted trees—imported, according to the proudly displayed sign.

"When did you first see the Gate?" I asked James as we passed a café whose wafting buttery scent had lured me for a block.

"Ruhaven? When I was five, sure."

"*Five?*"

He chuckled lightly. "Maggie, me mam, knew when I was coming because of the *Ledger*. When she saw that I was up for adoption, she had an opportunity to bring the first child to Naruka. I went to school during the day and into Ruhaven in the evenings. Not such a bad life."

Considering it, I sipped my second coffee of the day. Wouldn't it be weird to have a life here, then be living another in the Gate? "Were you a child in the memory as well? Did you have friends? Or...demons?"

"Ruhavens. I was, and I did. When I was only but eight, I met a young female named Essie, another Ruhaven. She was me mate."

I lifted my coffee cup. "And what's that?"

"Kind of like a wife, I suppose."

Splshhhh. Dark liquid spat out my mouth, smearing the perfect marble sidewalk, much to the disgust of the suit walking past, whose briefcase barely escaped becoming a victim too.

I hastily wiped my mouth. "You have a *wife*?" I repeated as James laughed. Wait—was *that* what Kazie had meant? "In *Ruhaven*?"

"Yera, ye'll find a mate's something a bit more intense."

I certainly hoped I didn't. But I darted a glance at the band on his right hand, then up to the shimmering laughter in his eyes. "And you got married when you were...*eight*," I repeated slowly.

He crossed the road. "Jayzus, ye think me mam would let me get married in Ruhaven when I was but only a wee lad? No, sure, that was all later. Too many years ago now."

James had a *wife* in Ruhaven. I hadn't even considered the relationships that might form in another world, the ones you could only witness.

"Do you...?"

He lifted a brow. "Do I what?"

I cleared my throat. "I mean, *can* they?"

"Yera, I've not a clue what yer to be meaning, Roe."

Heat crept into my cheeks. "Never mind," I mumbled—none of this mattered now.

"Why Roe, are ye a wee bit embarrassed about asking if I've had an ol' Ruhaven snog?" he teased, reading me perfectly. "Yera, we have sex and the like, if that's what ye want to know."

I tossed my cup of coffee—which was just causing my nerves to jitter—into the now identifiable trash. "I was just curious." Morbidly, ashamedly curious, and I had no right to be.

"Sure, ye can ask me anything ye like. Essie has always been a lot more to me than just what yer blushing at. Ye might say I got bullied a wee bit in school, and Essie was like a...a salvation. I couldn't talk to her, as 'twas only a memory, but it was enough to be near her. And in some ways, a relief not to need to control anything, be anything, make any decisions, ye know?"

Maybe I did. Maybe Willow had been a bit like that for me.

It wasn't until she was gone that I'd realized I didn't really have anything that wasn't hers. Our shared friends weren't mine at all, and when she died, they stopped calling, stopped inviting me to New Year's parties. We'd been dating two brothers, and even that had withered, as if without Willow, I had started to disappear as well. As if there wasn't enough of me left to hold on to when she was gone.

"But James, Essie's not real, just a memory."

He pulled a smoke from his pack. "Roe, I don't know that Essie is any less real than you and I right now. She's real to me. Aye, she is, and that's enough."

Could it be, though? Just seeing a woman, talking to her, in a memory you couldn't control?

"Now, about Bryn," James said as we rounded a corner. "I want ye to mind yerself when yer around him. Keep yer questions about the disease, about Willow. Don't mention Ruhaven."

"Why?"

"Because he's gone to some trouble to move on, it seems, and it'll likely upset him. No one likes to have their dreams taken away."

"Is that what you think you did to him?"

"Yera, it *is* what I did to him." James sighed, long and deep. "There's another reason, as well, for ye to be careful of what ye say around him. I haven't told ye about Marks, yet. It wasn't necessary, as ye were leaving, but I don't want ye to be surprised should ye see it."

I scratched at my cheek. "Marks?" Was Bryn scarred in some way?

"In Ruhaven, our Marks are our species, each one signifying the race ye belong to. Like how a cat has claws, except I can bond with a spirit. But ye need to know, as sometimes our Marks can drift over here if we're particularly close to the Gate."

Great. "And what's Bryn's?"

James took a second to answer. "Light," he said at last.

"Light," I repeated. "So if he starts glowing, I should run?"

James hiccupped into his tea. "Not exactly, but ye might see him look a wee bit strange. 'Tis nothing to worry too much of. He won't hurt ye, but ye might get a fright. So it's best not to mention Ruhaven because of it."

My questions would be about Willow, anyway. "Did you know Bryn, in the Gate?"

James tossed his tea in a bin. "Bryn? No."

Had *my* past life and James's met? What would it be like to find someone else to share all that with? "What do you look like? In the— the memories, I mean? What's your Mark?"

He lifted the map, angled us along the port boardwalk. "I've all the basics—arms and legs and such. If ye'd stayed in the Gate longer, we'd find out what ye look like too."

I grumbled a response.

"As for me Mark, I'm a *Kalista*, which means I can share the powers of the spirit I choose to bond with—and it so happens that Essie's me spirit and me mate."

"Share the powers...?"

"Aye, Essie's a female carved from a type of clay in Ruhaven, and so I've a bit of a green thumb."

Before I could unpack that, James veered toward a set of stone steps leading away from the port. They spiraled up through picturesque townhouses, each with a window box stuffed with flowers I couldn't identify, but James bent to sniff. Two fishing rods leaned against the buttermilk house on my left, their orange bobbers bright spots in the sun. Beside them, water beaded on the lid of a Styrofoam tub of worms.

"Which is his?" I asked as my thighs begged me to stop.

James panted a breath, in even worse shape than me despite his slim body. "One more now, the little white one."

I limped up another ten steps—no wonder Europeans are so fit— until I could read the house's hand-painted address. Unlike its neighbors, the flower box boasted only dry, baked dirt, and moss grew in the spaces between the wainscoting. Above the door's porthole hung a silver coin that would have been stolen within minutes back home.

When James's labored breathing finally echoed in my ear, he moved to straighten my cardigan, redoing buttons that hadn't been wrong in the first place. I frowned down at myself, at the fingers that shook on the pearly buttons, at the glinting gold band he wore on the ring finger of his right hand.

"It'll be okay, James," I said softly, earning a brisk nod.

But where to begin when that door opened? How did I explain to the man inside that I needed answers about what I'd willingly given up— the very thing he'd been exiled from?

Tension bracketed James's mouth. He tugged my braid over my cardigan, letting the black weave hang down my chest. "Ye look well."

I probably smelled like that bucket of worms. At least I felt like it, with the sun heating a sticky trail along my spine.

"Think that'll help?"

He faced the door, lifted a fist. "Couldn't hurt, like."

Knock-knock-knock.

This was it. Pure desperation would probably be written all over my face when he opened that door.

I curled my hands in my pockets. Desperate, pathetic—it didn't matter. I wasn't doing this for me; I was doing this for my twin, and I could be a lot of things for her.

Feet *click-clicked* across the floor. Stopped. A chain rattled. Locks slid.

Thunk.

When the door inched open at last, James's eyes widened.

A *woman* stepped out. And all I could think was that her features were in such stark contrast to mine, James could have stuck us on opposite sides of a coin and flipped it.

Short, soft hair the color of white wine brushed her shoulders, and pearl earrings dotted each lobe, matching the strand resting on a slim collarbone. Her skin was Norwegian white, her eyes an enviable blue, and her polite, restrained smile and salmon-orange suit might have hinted that she was about to leave for work—but the tapping black heel said it a hell of a lot louder.

I smiled hesitantly, waiting for James to apologize that he'd gotten the wrong house, but he said, "Ah, sorry, is there any chance Bryn is here?"

"Brynjar?" she repeated in a heavy accent, and his name went from sounding like the ping of a guitar strum to an exotic Viking caress. *Brynyar*, with the first "r" rolled in a way I'd never manage.

"Sorry, this is the last address I've had for him," James said, stepping a leg up in case she closed the door. Bolder than I gave him credit for. "We're old friends. Do ye know him?"

By the way she smoothed her tongue over her teeth, I'd say she knew him very well. "Brynjar moved out six months ago. He's at work now, I think. He accepted a job in the university." She folded her arms as if it were cold with the door open.

I stepped a little more into view. "Which university?"

The woman tilted her head, voice taking on a frigid tone. "You— your accent. Where are you from?"

"L'Ardoise."

Her waif-thin body bristled, fuchsia fingernails puncturing the leather purse at her hip. "I am not a map."

James laid a hand on my tensed shoulder. "We've enough to find him, I think—"

"Nova Scotia, Cape Breton—Canada," I said quickly, because some perverse part of me had to know what put that look on her face.

"*Canada*," she repeated, emotions flying high. Fury? Embarrassment? Jealousy? Eyes like chipped glass scanned all five feet nine inches of me, and measured each one. Her glossy mouth soured. "I suppose you thought to come here, to my home, to rub my nose in what you have stolen?"

I blinked. "Me? *Stolen*?" Bewildered, I looked around. One worm had escaped the fisherman's container and now lay shriveled in the sun next to a cigarette butt. "We've never met." I didn't even know her name.

But when I glanced at James, his face was carefully blank. "Yera, we're sorry to have bothered ye. We won't—"

She cut him off with a look that must have been the reason the flowers had died. "Be sure you do not. If Brynjar has sent you here to find my forgiveness, you can tell him there is none to give. Neither I, nor my family, shall *ever* offer that."

Her hair swayed as she spun around, and James barely dodged the slamming door. Back and forth went the wooden sign as locks slid shut.

We both stood there for a moment, stunned, pigeons feeding beside us on breadcrumbs thrown out by the neighbor who'd needed an excuse to listen in. Now, she made a show of rolling out laundry on the second floor. A pair of cotton undies waved between townhouses.

What had Bryn *done* to this woman? How had he managed to piss off seemingly everyone he came into contact with? Kazie had spoken well of him, but I wasn't sure that was a good thing.

Grabbing my elbow, James led us down the stairs and back to the port, his face so acutely distressed that I waited until the smell of dead fish greeted us again to say anything.

"How does Bryn's roommate know me?"

James let go of me to lift his wrist, studying the twirling gears beneath the ticking minute hand of his watch. "I don't know." It was said flatly, no lilt, no playful up-and-down roll.

"Is she a Ruhaven?"

He chewed on his thumbnail. "No."

Turning, he stuffed his hands in his pockets, huddling against the wind as he strode briskly along the boardwalk and wound between pedestrians.

"Wait, James!" I hurried to keep up, cardigan flapping around my hips, the rusty air stinging my nostrils. "Where are you going?"

"University of Oslo," he said, all business. "It closes in an hour."

So Bryn worked in the city. "What about that woman who—"

"Maybe it's not yerself," James said shortly. "Maybe 'tis another Canadian she knew, and nothing to do with ye."

I drew alongside him, considering it. That could be right—she hadn't said my name, hadn't known me. Just some woman from Canada. Or someone with my accent. I was no one.

The knot in my gut lessened. "Right. You're right."

I peppered James with questions as he crossed the road. Twice, he stopped for directions before finding a woman in a green blazer who spoke English.

"And if Bryn has some vendetta against Canadians like his roommate?" I asked again after she pointed us down a tiny side street. "Maybe we should make an appointment."

James lifted a hand to the changing sky. "An appointment! Sure, I recruited him meself, and now I'm to make an appointment?" he muttered under his breath. "No, we'll go on up to his department and ask for a blond-headed eejit who won't return me calls."

My stomach took a nosedive as I hurried to keep up. *So James was Bryn's recruiter.* "How did you convince him to come to Naruka?"

James flashed me a shameless grin. "As our Bryn isn't nearly as handy as yerself, I commissioned him to do all our portraits, so I did." Please, let him never do mine. "Here we are, Roe."

Distracted, I tripped on the stone sidewalk. "What? Where?"

Oh.

Wow.

Limestone towers, three massive wooden doors, a staircase missing only the red carpet—but with giant rings waiting should it make an appearance. Over a marble arch with the school's gilded name, the Norwegian flag snapped in the wind.

"No chance Bryn's the bell tower oiler?" I asked as James ambled up the university's royal path.

He smirked over his shoulder. "Not a one, love."

Vaguely nauseous, I plodded after him, over the tiled courtyard arranged in a sundial of the school's crimson colors, up the steps where copper statues of war heroes glared at the tissue I pulled from my pocket. I quickly tucked it away again.

James caught the door when students ambled out. God, the smell of the place. Money. Fresh books. Coffee. Absolutely *nothing* like my brief stint in music college with Willow, where squealing saxophones assaulted the ears and the ripe smell of clarinet oil stung your nose.

Except for the tiny practice rooms. There, other smells had lingered, but even remembering it seemed blasphemous in this regal space.

Yet as I stood in the grand entrance, eyeing the dual staircases, the polished banisters ending in carved swans, the chandeliers pinging yellow lights off the marble floor, that old longing still threatened to strangle me. Not for the practice rooms, but for the beginning of it all. Hadn't that been why I'd followed Willow to music school? Hoping to find that *calling* like she had, as though by sharing the same biology I could obtain it too.

"Roe? 'Tis this way," James said, whistling an Irish tune that drew more than a few glances. I followed a careful five feet behind.

As we climbed the next set of stairs—oiled, gleaming, with a carpet runner vacuumed to within an inch of its life—it was all painfully quiet. Too quiet for a university. People spoke in hushed whispers, paper fluttered, a photocopier let out a tentative *beep-beep*. A chair groaned, a man heaved a long sigh, lights flickered. But there was no laughter, no giggling, no cursing at that exam or the teacher who'd given it.

"Sorry," I mumbled when I bumped into a swinging briefcase. But the man stopped, and I glanced up at him.

Curly midnight hair, a dusting of a beard, and a dimple in each cheek when he smiled at me. "Do you know who you're looking for?" he asked in English, his voice a rich baritone.

"Art history," James replied behind me.

Twisting on polished black shoes, the man strode ten feet to our left with a wave of his hand. He pushed open a door and it, too, swung on silent hinges. I had a second to admire the wood carving of an angel on it before James pushed me through.

"One flight up," the man said, and turned and left.

James wiggled his eyebrows at me, then angled us up the carpeted stairs, only slowing when we passed a corkboard. He scanned the pinned list, brows furrowed into kissing caterpillars, then murmured, "Alright, I've been thinking on the way here, and 'tis best if ye talk to Bryn first."

"What?" I balked. "I thought we were doing this together?"

"Oh, now she hesitates?"

"But James, if you would just—"

He held a finger to his lips, pointed down the hall. "Number three."

I craned my neck to look. Two rooms lined up on the left, four on the right. Each door was closed, except one. From that open doorway, a shaft of gold light spilled into the corridor, crisscrossing the awards displayed in glass cabinets.

I tucked a stand of hair behind my ear. "Are you sure it's—"

"*Yes*," he said in the same hushed whisper. "Go on, so, and get this over with."

I should have rehearsed some speech before, should have practiced in front of that rusty mirror in the bed and breakfast. Because I hadn't, everything I was about to say, about to ask, sounded idiotic, even in my head.

Slowly, I stepped toward the office, my steel-toed boots eating into what was likely a piece of artwork. What if Bryn wasn't there? Gone out for coffee? A walk? Moved up north? I shivered at the thought—I'd seen those snow-capped peaks on the flight in, and the fjords that looked like some god had dragged their claws through the landscape. It should have seemed surreally beautiful, but compared to Ruhaven…

My nose twitched when cold tingled my nostrils, like the memory of that Norwegian frost was more than just my imagination.

I took out a napkin, blew my nose softly in the hallway, and just as I was tucking it into my pocket—

I saw him.

CHAPTER 10

Blue is the Eye

Amongst humans, James stood out like an exotic neighbor, a Ruhaven amongst the mundane and the ordinary.

But Bryn could never be mistaken.

He was something bred in and of Ruhaven. Mythical, like the gears churning in the sky, or the silky long-haired trees gliding through my fingertips.

In the doorway of his office, I could do nothing but stare. The photograph really hadn't done him justice, but my imagination that day on the road had been painfully accurate.

Bryn stood in front of a stained-glass window, the bright colors of it playing rainbow hues over his crisp linen shirt. Hands made for the piano flicked through a stack of stapled papers, maybe exams. On the corner of his gleaming desk, a black coffee cup sat next to a wilted vase of roses—from a lover? Admirer?

Bryn probably didn't lack for either.

His skin was white as milk, a kind of impossible porcelain that explained why, as Willow had once told me, women used to take arsenic. Whipped, golden moonlight—I couldn't think of another color for his hair—fell in short waves to his ears. Angel-wing cheekbones swept to a wide, sculpted mouth of pale rose. His bottom lip glistened under the window light like he'd been biting it while marking papers.

Delicate, bone-china features and a firm, angular jaw gave him an aristocratic look. He was someone who suited this office, this university, someone probably well-accustomed to the length of his own nose.

Meanwhile, I felt like something the office cat had dragged in.

It was all the worse because I was still standing here in his doorway, spying on the man I needed answers from, breathing in a snowy scent that was either from him or the room.

I was lifting my hand, preparing for the most awkward knock of my life, when he froze. Stilled.

Stopped.

Knuckles whitened as he flattened his palm on the exams. A ripple rolled over his shoulders, shuddering down a body as tall and whip lean as a willow tree. He had to be at least six three, maybe four. Taller than Tye.

"Bryn?"

His nostrils flared, once, twice, and for the first time in my life, I think I regretted not wearing perfume.

Then his head snapped up.

I took a fumbling step back.

The papers on his desk fluttered, like they, too, could feel it. A pencil rolled with a clatter that seemed piercingly loud until it *plopped* onto the carpet.

His *eyes*. They were like the lake back home—depthless and cold. Empty. Aching.

"*Rowan?*"

I shivered at his voice, at the otherness of him, at the memory of how far I'd sunk before my twin had dragged me out. How the stinging cold felt wrapped around my ankles, how the water had been black and lightless. How I'd imagined all the leeches gathering at my toes, yet felt nothing. "I—yes?"

"Come inside, Rowan."

His brisk tone snapped me out of it, and I glanced down the hallway towards James, but the corridor was empty. So he wasn't going to help me.

Don't mention Ruhaven, that's what he'd said. But how could I talk about Willow without bringing up the Gate?

Still standing in the doorway, I asked a simpler question, "How do you know me?" Though Bryn seemed like the kind of man who *would* know, someone Ruhaven would have plucked out to be all hers—so opposite of me in every way. I tried to picture him next to Willow, and that image suited a lot more.

"I know all Ruhavens in the *Ledger*." Or he thought he did.

Avoiding his eyes, I stepped inside.

The office was like an overcast beach, all sandy beiges and gray blues and seaweed greens. The only bright color in the entire space was a mustard yellow—and that was in a cabinet of *dead moths*. Even the binders on the desk were boring, empty, the dividers in clear plastic with white labels and black marker. Sterile, like hospital tiles that *click-clicked* under black shoes.

Busts of some Roman emperor, or maybe it was Greek—my sister would have known—sat next to a rocking chair. Certificates hung in dreary but likely expensive frames. An award for portraiture, for oil, the latest from three years ago for something called *Plein Air* in Ireland.

Before he'd been exiled.

I stopped feet from his desk.

Stiff and tall, he stood at attention behind it, one hand bunched in a fist at his side, the other still pressing into the stack of papers. The collar of his blazer, a striking royal blue, brushed his tensed jaw.

Definitely six four.

"I did not expect to see you here," Bryn said in an accent coated with musical German. "In my office."

"Sorry," I said immediately, shivering from him or the lifeless room. "I can make an appointment. It *is* Bryn, right? Bryn Stornoway?"

The corners of his lips tugged upward, like maybe I'd mispronounced his name. Probably butchered it with my accent. But the movement revealed his only flaw—a mouth just a bit too wide for the face.

"Do you wish to sit?"

I eyed the hard, wooden rocking chair and the breakable art pieces beside it. "No, but thank you."

A clock *tick-ticked* on the wall behind him. Air whistled through an ancient heater. Traffic puttered along the street below.

I cleared my throat. "Bryn, I'm here about my sister, about Willow."

His face betrayed nothing. No flicker of recognition of what had once been my entire world.

"I take it you have seen Ruhaven?" he asked instead.

"I—yes. Tye showed me." He stiffened at the name of my recruiter. "James told me about the infection that's been spreading to Ruhavens," I said, lowering my voice. "I saw your research, the books in your old room in Naruka. James said you might have more answers, ones that he couldn't give me. And—" he waited in that utter stillness, "—and James said you'd been infected once as well. That you survived, unlike the others." Unlike my sister.

His eyebrow rose so slowly, I expected to look up and find a stage manager lifting it. "You are here because of my encounter?"

Encounter? That was an odd way to describe a disease. Maybe he meant to add "*with death*" at the end. "Yes, that and your research, your notes, anything you can tell me."

"Why?"

Silence hung as heavy as the thick drapery.

How could I move on without knowing the truth behind Willow's death? Was it an aneurysm like the doctors claimed, or had something from the Gate infected her? If she'd never visited Ruhaven, how could a connection to the Gate cause her death miles away in L'Ardoise?

I took a breath. "Because my twin died three years ago." I hated that word. *Died*. One syllable. Clean and painfully to the point, when her death had been anything but.

"Your sister died from an aneurysm," Bryn stated, not a question.

I answered anyway. "Yes, in L'Ardoise." Long before she'd had a chance for James to recruit her.

He reached for something behind his desk. "Yet your twin is not Ruhaven, should not have been... *infected*, as you say."

If I admitted what I knew, that it wasn't me in the *Ledger*, he'd tell James. Then what?

"James doesn't know enough about the disease to tell me either way. Doesn't know if there are any symptoms, any signs, that might indicate it's connected," I said, wetting my lips. His eyes tracked the movement. "So when I discovered you were not only researching the disease, but *survived*—no, were the *only* one to survive—I thought maybe you could tell me if there was something to look for—tell me if..."

I trailed off when I saw what he'd been reaching for.

A cane.

I dropped my eyes as Bryn limped around the desk.

"I take it, by your reaction," Bryn drawled, "that James did not inform you of the result of my *infection*."

I stared at the cane. "No," I managed. "He never said—he said you survived, but...I didn't know."

The three clocks in the room *ticked* in unison, so hauntingly familiar to the constant drone at Naruka.

As Bryn moved past me, a hint of snow followed, though he made not a sound until he gripped the door I'd come through and closed it with a soft *click*.

His pants were ironed to knife-edge pleats, his linen shirt tucked in at a cinched waist. But the cane was even higher quality than the clothes, with symbols carved from the staff's curved handle to the end biting into a plush rug.

Tick. Tick-tock.

Bryn turned with all the slowness of a minute hand.

I didn't meet his eyes, but I felt them all the same—a wintery shimmer that raked down and over my cardigan, lingering on each loose thread and embroidered patch, sweeping a path to my work boots, to where my toes curled inside.

Inspection complete, his eyes found my face again—my nose tingling where they landed. "Tell me, Rowan, what do you know of Ruhaven?"

How to answer? "Just what James explained to me," I said vaguely, noting the single trail of dirt marring his creamy carpet from where I'd entered.

"I am asking of your own experience."

James's warning *dinged* in my head, so loud I wondered if his power didn't extend beyond Ruhaven to more than just scones.

"I've only been through the Gate a few times," I admitted. "At first, not voluntarily. How would I know if the aneurysm killed—"

Bryn straightened off the door. "Voluntarily?"

"Yes. I was wondering if there are symptoms or—"

"No. What was involuntary?"

"It doesn't matter. About Willow—"

"Rowan," he said with all the false calm of a tidal wave approaching shore. "I am aware that James is, even now, slinking outside this office. That he has likely warned you against mentioning Ruhaven, or anything that may reference Naruka and the Gate that lies there. Am I correct?"

I might have wondered how he knew that if the answer wasn't written all over him, in every inch that said—no, *screamed*—that Bryn wasn't part of this world.

I nodded.

Bryn took a step closer. "Answer my question. Was it Tye that showed you the Gate *involuntarily*?"

Heat crept up my neck until I was sure, even with my bronze skin, my face burned. "Yes."

As if in confirmation, his eyes flickered over my cheeks, then up again. "And the other time?" he asked coldly.

I forced away the image of Tye. "The second time, when I still wasn't convinced of Ruhaven, James forced me in again. Then I believed."

Bryn circled the room, his cane padding softly into the beige carpet. "Yet you are here, looking for answers for your sister, instead of experiencing the Gate, when at these early stages, it is important to visit frequently. To build up a tolerance, else you shall not be able to witness the memories for more than a few minutes."

Her memories.

"I don't need to. I'm not going back."

He stopped, and the look he aimed my way could have boiled molasses. "Not going back? Why? Where are you going?"

"Home," I said, hugging my cardigan against the sudden chill. "To L'Ardoise."

Bryn took another step forward. "You are leaving to pack, then? So you may return to Naruka?"

Why was he looking at me like that? "No," I said slowly, deliberately. "I'm moving back home—permanently."

His shoulders went rigid before he turned in a slow circle, forcing me to pivot. "You would so easily turn away from what is, in every sense, an honor and duty that is afforded a rare few?" His perfect lips tightened in disapproval. "Why?"

I scanned the award-studded office. Of course he'd been enthralled by Ruhaven—with the idea of someone wanting *him* to be found, wanting *him* to witness what awaited up in Naruka's mountains.

"Because Ruhaven isn't real," I offered at last, mixing half-truths and lies. "It's just memories. But it's not here, not reality, it's some…anomaly. A fantasy for someone else." Even if I wanted it to be mine.

He blinked at me, thick, golden eyelashes shuttering over painfully blue eyes, and this close, I could see the faintest smattering of golden freckles over his nose, barely visible. I counted the imperfections like they were a currency I could exchange for my own fragile ego.

"An *anomaly*?" Bryn repeated, voice going dark, and I blinked at the sudden change. "A hallucination? A fickle story? Or perhaps a sickness that has spread to your mind?"

"No, I—"

"Then is Ruhaven a cult? A raving religion, a vision, a fairytale for the Irish?" he whispered in a low rapid-fire until he was all but standing over me. Until my neck hurt from staring up into a face that was no longer amused, no longer patient. "A bedtime story for children, a madman's ramblings, a fever dream?"

I stumbled back, nearly falling over a marble bust before righting myself on Caesar's nose.

"Well, which is it, Rowan?" Bryn demanded. "Since you have come here to disrupt my life for a thing of which you do not even believe."

My heart beat wildly in my chest. Fear, anticipation, nerves. I wanted to throw up. "Whichever."

Bryn's eyes solidified to steel. "Get out," he said softly.

What?

Disgust curled his upper lip before he turned away from me and circled his desk.

My breath came out in embarrassingly harsh gasps. I hadn't done anything to deserve that. "I'll go if you tell me whether there were any symptoms—"

"Why?" Bryn cut me off.

"Why?" I repeated, throat dry.

He flicked through the papers on his desk with quick, jerky movements. "Yes. Why do you care whether Willow was targeted with a disease from Ruhaven?"

Why? *Why?*

Because I should have felt the aneurysm that killed Willow. Should have felt it right *here* in this space below my heart that was now empty, and hungry, and hollow.

But I hadn't.

Despite being my twin, my mirror, the closest person I'd ever known or would know, I'd slept soundlessly while she died. We were supposed to have a connection. Something that would wake me. Something that would tell me my own twin was *dead*.

"Because she's my sister. My twin." The best of both of us.

Behind the crossbars of the window, the sun wilted into the clouds. "I fail to understand why you would seek answers for a thing you do not believe in. That despite having no belief at all in Ruhaven, you have chosen to travel here to interrogate me about a disease born of Naruka's Gate."

Slow rain began to pound the window.

"To ask that I provide you, a stranger, with intricate details of a terrifying moment of my life, so that you may discern whether this part of the fairy tale concerns you. Am I correct?"

It wasn't true, but it wasn't entirely a lie either. "Bryn, I'm sorry about what happened to you, but—"

"You cannot be, as you do not possess any true concept of what *did* happen to me, Rowan." His eyes flickered once. "Or what I have chosen to give up."

Despite the dismissal in his voice, I latched on to that one word—*chosen*. Chosen, not forced? Not exiled?

Bryn continued to say nothing, looking like he could exist in this void long after my bones had withered to dirt.

"What did you give up?"

His eyes roamed over me—not like the men at construction sites I'd worked on, but not brotherly like James either. It had the frightening quality of an owl sizing up the chain locking it to its handler. "We do not know each other well enough for me to answer that," Bryn said, dismissing me. "Nor for me to answer questions about what has left me a cripple."

He pointed to the door.

My heart hammered against my ribs. Maybe I'd messed this up. Maybe. But I owed this to Willow, owed everything good I'd ever had to her.

So I steeled my spine, planted my hands on his desk, and tried a different tack. "How does your roommate know me?"

For the first time, I'd surprised him. Not in a good way.

His eyes went to crystal slits. "You should *not* have spoken to Abby."

"You should have answered James's calls."

Bryn's hand curled on the desk. "Yes, I see I have chosen unwisely, as not doing so has brought you to my place of work. However, you are mistaken about Abby. She does not know you, and I do not appreciate James interrogating those in my life."

"Then tell me if there's any sign of this disease."

"Attack."

Attack?

"Wait, what? What do you mean? Do you think you were—were targeted with it?"

He stared down at me, dwarfing my height. "Not in the way you mean."

"Bryn, if it—"

"— *they*—"

"—killed my sister, and you know something, I'm not—well, I'm not leaving your office."

There. Let him throw me out. Though he could probably manage it, even with the leg.

His eyes flickered to simmering fire before banking. "You should leave—*now*, Rowan."

"It's Roe."

Bang.

CHAPTER 11

Somebody Desperate

B ryn didn't look toward the intruder. Didn't so much as blink. It was me who turned when the office door swung open so hard, it slapped a smile onto James's pretty face.

"Bryn, how ye? Love the haircut."

Haircut? Who *cared* about some damn haircut, other than the fact it was possible on a man carved from limestone.

But the fresh blast of air and James's quick wink had my shoulders relaxing a fraction. This had all gone to hell just as he'd predicted. Because I should never have come here. "James, you should try talking to—"

"My office is not the town *piazza* for your enjoyment."

"—since he won't tell me about the disease," I finished.

"Attack." Bryn.

"I warned ye he's a wee bit touchy on the subject." James peeled off his jacket, tossing it over a sculpture with a small penis before sinking into a rocking chair. He yanked out a textbook with a wince. "Recovery going well?"

Bryn sucked in his cheeks, which only made his sweeping cheekbones more devastating, and eyed the phone on his desk, as if weighing up which button dialed security. "You know I did not want to become involved again," he warned in a low voice. "And yet you traveled here despite my wishes. And far worse, you have brought Rowan."

I shrank under the words, knowing he could probably sense the fraud I was hiding behind.

"I cannot help you," he said to me without sympathy. "You should leave, and quickly."

"Oh no, I think we'll be in town for a good while, right, Roe?" James said merrily as I blinked at him. God, I hoped not.

He pushed the rocker back. "Maybe I didn't come for ye at all, Bryn. I hear there's a Turner exhibit in town." James picked up a miniature statue, pretending to examine it before setting it back down. "Might be I'll drop by for the local artwork."

"Turner is most certainly not *local artwork,*" Bryn said with a voice like warmed ice. "And if I recall, the last exhibit we visited, you departed after successfully finding the entire subset of naked women. As Turner is known for his landscapes, I am sure you will be disappointed."

As Turner is known for his landscapes.

"Rowan, while you may believe that is a close imitation of my accent, you are sorely mistaken."

I jolted. Had I said that aloud?

James pursed his lips. "Sure, a man doesn't want to be looking at trees all day, and ye can't blame me when all I have is me sweet Essie."

All he had was Essie? His wife—no, his *mate.* But surely James dated here, was *with* women here—wasn't he? He couldn't be that committed to a memory, to a dream.

"Rowan, your mouth is open."

I clamped it shut at Bryn's dry comment.

"I take it," he drawled, "that you share as much disdain for Ruhaven's law of mates as you do for Ruhaven."

Law of mates? "You mean, marriage laws?"

Bryn curled his lip. "No, those are not equivalent."

James saw me glancing to his right hand and held it up. "Ah, ye've been wondering about this?" The gold band winked under the colourful stain glass light. "The symbol itself came from Ruhaven. I wear this for Essie, it's a token for mates in Tallah, and one that found its way here as well. But sometimes, something gets a bit mixed up along the way. For it's Drachaut—the other country—who wear it on the left hand, and Ruhaven who wear it on the right."

How could James be so devoted to a memory? There was no way a guy from L'Ardoise would be caught dead wearing a symbol from a dream. And when the memories finished—when James's past life died—wouldn't Essie die as well? He'd never be able to talk to this woman again, in any life. She'd cease to exist, and then she really would be just a memory.

Maybe one like Willow, slowly fading each time James touched it.

Then my gaze darted to Bryn's empty hand. In this one case, at least, maybe James was crazier. "It's just hard to believe you have a wife," I said at length.

James looked perplexed. "Why? I make a sound husband."

He probably did. "But she's not, um," I said, a blush creeping in, "not a *real* wife."

Amusement danced in James's brown eyes. He tucked in his chin, clucked his tongue. "Why, Roe, what would ye be meaning by that?"

I don't know why I'd said anything. "You know what I mean, James."

"Pray tell us, Rowan," Bryn said dryly, "what *do* you mean?"

I kept my mouth shut.

James's grin was wide, brilliant, and utterly amused. "Now, ye wouldn't think it, as I'm only too charming, but I am indeed entirely and completely faithful to me sweet Essie."

God. That couldn't be possible, could it?

"Essie is a spirit of rock," Bryn stated. "I assume you have not met, as you have been in the Gate so little. But it is common for mates to be as committed here as they are in Ruhaven."

So if my past life found a boyfriend, I'd have to give up men? "Just another reason I'm going home," I said to annoy him.

"Indeed." Bryn turned back to James, dismissing me. "Though, now that I reflect on Essie's spirit trait, I feel this does explain your fascination with Stephan Winding's exhibition of sculptures from the nineteenth century."

James scowled. "Are we going to spend all afternoon talking of me love for me sweet Essie, or settle this at the bar?"

"I see no reason I should accompany either of you to the bar or otherwise."

James slowed the rocking chair. "It may be," he began, voice thickening with his Irish brogue, "that I've a mind to reconsider yer exile from Naruka."

Bryn stilled. "You assume I wish to return?"

Oh, I'd say he did. So why didn't he come back before?

The two men eyed each other, and somehow, James held his own under a look that had almost brought me to my knees at the door.

"I know ye do," James said smoothly, then rubbed his hands together. "Ye know if the Jeger pub is still around? Or did we drink it dry three summers ago?"

The Jeger pub had not been drunken dry after all—far from it. From every wall, stuffed reindeer, white foxes, and grizzlies eyed the diners' plates with bared teeth. A shark skeleton swam from suspended wires, its bones glowing in the atmospheric din. A musician strummed a simpering guitar next to a rack of harpoons, and behind him, a skewered pig rotated in the kitchen. Juice sluiced off the hog, its honeyed scent drifting through the pub.

Bryn, James, and I had walked here in stony silence, with Bryn's cane thumping behind us the only clue he was following.

"Can you at least tell me if you think the infection—?" But the words were no sooner out of my mouth than the waitress decided to tap over on needle-thin heels.

Across from me, under the soft light of our window booth, Bryn lowered the menu. "*Attack*. What are you having, Rowan?"

Having? "Oh, I…" I glanced at the Norwegian menu I couldn't read, then pointed at something random. "It's only that if there is some sign, besides an aneurysm, that—"

"*Hallo*," Bryn said, twisting toward the waitress.

I looked up.

She was young, about the same age as Willow when she'd died, with curly red hair fastened at her nape. She offered Bryn a shy smile before exchanging a rapid back and forth that sounded a lot like German yodeling.

James lifted a smoke to his lips. "Bryn'll tell ye when he's ready," he murmured of the disease.

Except ready might be a day, a month, a year from now, or never, and my sister deserved better.

"Tell me something, Rowan," Bryn began when the waitress clicked away, "what is this special charm L'Ardoise holds which makes Ruhaven so terribly boring to you?"

"That wasn't what I said."

"Bryn, would ye leave it alone," James warned.

Bryn shifted, his cane or leg bumping my foot before he settled. "I am only wondering what could possibly maintain more interest in such a tiny town than the lived memories of a fantastical realm," Bryn replied blandly. Behind him, a lady dressed for church started in her seat. "Perhaps she has a man waiting at home?"

My reflection frowned back at me in the glass, and I started to regret not just telling him the truth.

"Leave it be, ye git," James warned again.

Bryn brushed him off. "No? Surely there is some sticky-fingered boy running the L'Ardoise movie theatre who has caught Rowan's eye, a childhood sweetheart who took her to a prom at the farmers' community center, or perhaps it is a man from the Midwest whom she favors—"

"*Bryn*," James fumed as my face burned. "Jayzus, Mary, and Joseph, what the feck has gotten in to ye?"

Yet he'd been mortifyingly close to the mark. Not only did Bryn seem to know about Tye, but he'd also guessed at every parking lot where I'd endured fumbling hands and sloppy kisses, in a town so puny it must have embarrassed him to ever hear about.

Was that part of his *Mark*? Knowing someone's history? Or, maybe, just being able to read people really—

"Me?" Bryn repeated mercilessly. "I believe it is *you*, James, who has let the standards for recruiting Ruhavens slip so low."

The words landed like an open-palm slap. And he didn't even have the decency to look at me when it did, as if James were to blame for Bryn needing to call out his recruiting mistake.

A mistake. Because I was a stupid repair woman, with no dreams, no ambitions, and nothing to show for it but a dead sister and a lie on row 1274 in the *Ledger*.

I shoved up from the bench at the same time James's fist came down on the table.

"What are ye bloody on about?" James demanded as heads swiveled our way, the church lady clutching her oversized baubles. "No, Roe, ye sit down while I deal with this ejit. *Sit*," he ordered in a voice James had never once used before.

When I did, he moved the ashtray aside, elbows pressing into the plastic menu. "If ye've a problem with how I recruit people," he warned Bryn, "ye'll bloody say it to me in private and not be insulting a woman who—after what ye did—has more right to Ruhaven than yerself."

I didn't know if Bryn had deserved his exile, but in that moment, James's faith in me nearly had me reconsidering my trip home. And he wasn't even done.

Bryn let James rip into him—a true spectacle, with enough Irish lingo that while half of it may not have landed, it did cause people to gawk openly. He was just winding down when the waitress reappeared, saving Bryn.

James leaned back with a huff of exasperation, but the tall stout she set in front of him seemed to drain the last of his ire.

While the waitress unloaded the drinks, passing a pale wine to Bryn, he spoke to her in rapid, quiet Norwegian. She looked a little perplexed as she toyed with the heart-shaped necklace at her collarbone, but eventually nodded.

"Let's just take a wee breather here," James said when she'd left. "I don't know where all of this came from. Maybe 'tis that pig over there that's got us all worked up."

I glanced at the sizzling hog. What did the pig have to do with anything?

"But Roe, should he ever speak to ye like that again," James continued, digging another smoke from the pocket of his tweed jacket. He blew off a fleck of lint. "Ye've only to remind the man of his shoddy work that ye've been fixing in Naruka for months."

The wineglass hovered an inch from Bryn's lips. "Excuse me?"

I covered my smile with my pint, remembering just what non-waterproof sealant did to a kitchen pipe. "To be fair," I said to James, "I never knew there were so many uses for hot glue."

"While I do not proclaim to possess any expertise in repair work," Bryn said archly, "I am certain that stopping a leak is more important than the manner in which it is done."

The manner in which it is done. Boarding school, without a doubt.

"I don't know," James said, taking another long drag before waving the cigarette at Bryn. "Wood glue for caulking, exposed wires because ye didn't use electrical tape, and what was it ye said, Roe?"

I crossed my arms. "That the wall he tried to knock down in the music room was load-bearing?"

James waved the cigarette and, for a moment, thick smoke obscured Bryn's face into a blur of disbelief. "No, no, not that, though aye, 'tis true enough. I think ye said, *'He's too pretty for repair work,'* that was it."

I felt my cheeks flame and reached for my cold pint. Kazie had a big mouth. Huge. Enormous. And that was the last time I ever confided in her.

Bryn lifted a cornsilk eyebrow at me, and I braced for the insult. Then his mouth quirked up, just a little at one end. "Some, I imagine," Bryn said quietly, "might say the same of you, Rowan."

I quickly looked away.

Over the next fifteen minutes, James peppered Bryn with questions on Oslo, on adapting to "regular life," and his job at the university, his accent traveling up and down so much we could have been driving over the Kerry hills. Bryn answered each question automatically, with as little detail as possible. Was he thinking about Ruhaven? What would it be like to visit those memories every day for years, then to be forced to slot yourself back into life in Oslo?

By the time the food arrived, I'd switched to a stout dense enough to withstand a few rounds with whatever nightmare James had ordered.

He gawked at the bowl the waitress set before him. I couldn't blame him—he'd ordered something that looked like shrunken intestines with fries.

As the waitress unloaded more food, Bryn handed me a plate, then another, and another. Sausages, potatoes, and food I couldn't identify slid in tiny dishes until I was surrounded like royalty.

"Bryn, can you tell her I didn't order…" I trailed off as he slid over a plate of braised beef dripping with juice. My stomach kicked me square between the ribs. Or maybe that was anxiety.

But Bryn said nothing and the waitress walked away.

So he'd done this on purpose. To embarrass me? A little punishment for showing up at his office, for asking questions about his infection, for denying Ruhaven.

Well, it'd worked, because I was absolutely sweating. "I *didn't* order this," I repeated. Or had I pointed to some family-size menu item?

His face didn't change. "I know. I did, Rowan." He passed me a final plate of crisp broccoli. "I did not think you would enjoy your appetizer of boknafisk soup—stockfish, rehydrated cod—so I ordered additional selections. The sooner our dinner is over, the sooner you may return home and forget about Ruhaven, or is that not what you want?"

The last thing he knew was what I wanted. "I want the soup."

Bryn's brow lifted on a slow wave. "Do you?"

Not only couldn't I afford all this, but I didn't want food—I wanted answers about Willow, and I didn't need Bryn substituting that with honey-glazed chicken.

I tugged the bowl toward me. "Yes." But my nose twitched at the smell of ripe fish. "This is what I ordered, because this is what I want."

Even if it was floating in little chunks.

Didn't matter. I'd eaten plenty of Willow's cooking before, and something even worse—my own. My stomach was fortified steel.

So I spooned up a generous portion and ignored the reek of rehydrated fish—*what the hell was rehydrated fish?* Swallowed.

Maybe my stomach was more like tinfoil than steel, but I got it down.

"Enjoying that?" Bryn asked drolly.

I picked up the plate of braised beef. "So much so that I'm not going to be able to touch any of this. Why don't you eat—"

Bryn recoiled like I'd dangled a live snake.

Cursing, James ushered my beef and me away, bad children at the grown-up's table.

"Roe, we can't eat meat," James explained while Bryn stuck his nose in the wine like the smell could wipe away his near-death encounter.

"It's the Gate. Ruhavens don't eat meat and I suppose it rubs off after a while. We can get quite sick from it, actually."

I stared at him, aghast. "You mention the Marks but not *this*?"

"It's not so bad like."

I looked pointedly at Bryn, whose blown-glass cheeks hollowed on deliberate exhales. "I have never fully recovered from my time in Ruhaven," he said carefully, holding James's gaze a second before lowering his wine. *I'll say.*

"I know it like," James said softly. "And 'tis why I want ye to come back now. I never liked how we ended things."

If he did return, it'd only be one more reason to avoid Naruka.

Bryn stabbed a cherry tomato. "Why? Although Tye may have enforced it, I recall it was *you,* James, who exiled me." The tone was mild, but his look could have sliced my medium-rare beef.

"Ah, come off it. 'Tis yerself who stopped answering me calls after yer leg," James reminded him. "I used to be able to talk to ye at least, and ye bloody well know I didn't force ye out forever. Ye needed a break. So ye took it and ye got some perspective." James paused, a frown playing around the corners of his lips as he worried his ring. "And *a lot* of it, or so I hear."

Bryn's careful mask *snapped.*

His nostrils flared, his lips snarled over pink gums, and—for a shattering heartbeat—a monster sat before me, more terrifying than anything I'd seen in Ruhaven.

I dropped my fork, my pulse ping-ponging in my ribs. Then I blinked, and Bryn's features rearranged themselves into smooth limestone.

Sweat trickled between my shoulder blades.

I glanced around the restaurant, expecting faces to be frozen in horror, but laughter carried over the booth, glasses clinked, steak was carved and served. A lady with a rose on her blazer did stare at Bryn—except it wasn't fear but blatant interest in her hazel eyes. At the opposite end of the pub—obviously, chosen intentionally—the pig rotated on its skewer, mouth gaping, fat bubbling from its seared flesh.

"Rowan."

I whirled at Bryn's low voice.

"I apologize for startling you."

I swallowed heavily. "Is that your—your—"

James bumped my elbow. "I warned ye, just a glimmer of his *Mark* is all. A good reminder not to stay in the memories too long, else ye'll end up like this freak." He shoveled a fry through mayonnaise. "Don't ye worry though; Bryn's bark is worse than his bite."

His bark seemed bad enough. "James said your Mark is light."

Before Bryn could answer, James said, "In Ruhaven, he wiggles around like a wee little fish." James mimicked the motion with his hands while Bryn rolled his eyes.

A surprised laugh escaped me. "Really?"

"Aye. Now, Bryn, if yer done scaring Roe, I want to talk to ye about Willow," James said, and I felt my eardrums lift and revolve in my head, the *glimmer* forgotten. "If ye've anything to tell us about the infection——"

"Attack."

James lifted an eyebrow. "Attack then, if ye believe it."

"I do."

"Then let us see yer research on it."

I held my breath as Bryn replied, "You assume I have continued my research?"

"I know ye have," James corrected.

Instead of answering, Bryn looked across the bar at the lady with the rose, the pretty one who'd been staring at him, and— But no, he wasn't looking at her. He was looking at the paintings—pictures of the sea, of pirate ships and churning black water with clouds divided between storms and light. Of a narrow bolt of lightning warming the ocean.

James scratched at his eyebrow with a cigarette, bringing it so close, his hairline sizzled. "Ye know I thought things would be different for ye now. Maybe I didn't understand."

I didn't understand either—didn't understand what would make James reconsider this man's exile.

"Perhaps you did not," Bryn agreed, shoving up so abruptly that his head narrowly missed the rainbow lampshade. "I believe it is my round. James?" He reached for his cane.

As Bryn limped to the bar, James on his heels, I gripped the dessert menu I wouldn't order from.

Coming here had been a mistake. But it was exactly what Willow would have done. If there'd been any chance of finding out the truth of why *I'd* died, she'd have stopped at nothing, torn apart the world to find those answers, interrogating every Ruhaven or human, living or dead.

Why did Bryn think he'd been targeted with the disease? And if he knew anything about the symptoms, why wouldn't he just tell me? Then we could leave and he could return to his nudeless Turner exhibits.

My gaze drifted over to the bar. Bryn spoke rapidly to James, cheeks flushed with faint color as James flung out a hand, nearly knocking over the pint the bartender sat before him. Oh, to be an ear on that stuffed reindeer right now.

Whatever James said next had Bryn leaning in closer, brow wedged in a tight knot.

How had his Mark materialized like that? Could it happen to me after just one trip to the Gate? Could I be sitting here, enjoying dehydrated fish soup, then suddenly scare a small child?

I shifted in my seat, turning away from both of them to stare out the window.

It should have been Willow and I here together, exploring Europe, like she'd always wanted. Watching the smokers huddled against the rain under café roofs, gazing in the windows of fancy shops whose clothes we'd never afford, slipping into a smoky pub to join the musicians in the back.

My lips twitched at the memory of when we'd done just that, when she'd sat down at an old piano and earned a hundred dollars in tips.

Outside our window, a woman slowed, paused, like she'd experienced the same longing I'd just felt. Oblivious, people swarmed past on the sidewalk, but there was something about the set of her shoulders that...

Then she lifted her eyes, twin blue storms, so impossibly familiar that I jerked back.

The sweep of her pixie chin and heart-shaped face was softer, paler, and more beautiful than mine. Freckles streaked across her cheeks like stars and gathered on the tip of her nose, that dyed-blonde hair she'd once hated now drenched and swaying in the rain.

My heart clogged when she lifted a sandy-skinned hand and waved, her lips twitching into a wild, mischievous smile.

She'd flashed the same one after punching that boy from eighth grade.

I bolted upright, slamming my knee into the table. Pints rolled, shattering against the stone tiles. Heads swiveled on skewers toward the mess.

I squeezed the top of the leather booth as if it'd wring sanity into my mind. What if Ruhaven had brought her back? What if this was why I was here, right now, in this place and time?

For a moment, everything made sense—Ruhaven, Naruka and its forgotten Gate, the memories.

She wasn't dead—she'd always been larger than life, impossibly full of everything I wasn't. The prodigy. The pianist. The cheerleader. And here she was, standing in a street in Oslo. Waiting.

"Willow?" I croaked.

CHAPTER 12

Please Forgive Me

I whirled.

I'm coming, Willow, don't move, don't move, I chanted, sprinting past plates of burgers and bewildered glances, ignoring the shouted warnings. A waitress dodged out of my way, dumping a full glass of pinot grigio on a woman's lap. She let out a strangled cry, her husband flying out of his seat in outrage. But I was already past the mess when I snagged the exit door at last and sucked in a blast of salty air.

I yelled Willow's name as I rounded the doorway. I'd forgotten my sweater, but despite my thin shirt and the rain, I barely felt the cold as I barreled down the sidewalk.

She hadn't disappeared.

There was no mistaking my sister—no mistaking the cocky gait, the over-plucked eyebrow she'd laughed at, the freckles that matched my own.

My eyes burned. "*Willow*?" I called, voice breaking.

She stepped away, her lips curling with that old mischief. Grief wrapped around my throat and squeezed.

I didn't care why. I didn't care how. But my twin had come back from the dead.

And I'd tell her I was so very sorry—sorry I hadn't been with her that night, sorry I'd left her recital, sorry that it was me in Ireland and not her, sorry that she'd died before Ruhaven ever had a chance to pick her, sorry that I hadn't felt when she'd died, and—

A force struck me from behind.

"*Nooooo!*"

Willow darted away, vanishing into the crowd.

I plowed headfirst into the boulevard, my palms tearing open as I slid over cement, glass, and prickly weeds. Pain throbbed in my knee, but it was all secondary to the voice screaming inside me to *get up, get up, get up*!

Someone panted in my ear. Tires squealed, and a wave of icy rainwater drenched my jeans, sending a bone-chilling shiver through me. I shifted onto my elbows, saw that I'd torn a hole in both knees and blood was oozing from one. It didn't matter. Willow was here, frightened but alive.

As I struggled to push up, a weight pressed between my shoulder blades, shoving me down. My chin hit the ground with a *clack* that rattled my jaw. I would lose Willow again—already had lost her, because I'd tripped into a sidewalk. Why had she run? Why hadn't she—

"*Rowan*." Bryn?

Bryn.

That son of a *bitch*.

With renewed energy, I fought to get my hands under me, swore.

"It is an illusion," he snapped. "You must ignore it." I hated that no-nonsense tone, the command in it that sliced like a slow-motion whip.

He'd tackled me, frightening Willow away, and after refusing to explain anything about the disease. The traffic light flooded the sidewalk red, or maybe that was my vision.

"*You*," I growled, and tossed an elbow behind me. His satisfying grunt barely registered over the adrenaline pumping in my ears, but the weight was gone, the way clear.

I started to get up—I'd chase Willow all over Oslo if I had to, jump on a Viking ship if she decided on it. That'd be just like her too. She was made for this country, for the port and the boats and the adventure of it all. She was made for Ruhaven.

Strong hands gripped my shoulders, flipping me into a freezing puddle that muffled my hearing.

"Get off me," I growled.

"No." Bryn pinned me, blocking out the sky as he watched me through irises carved from a Norwegian glacier. There was no warmth there. No remorse for the chance that was slipping away with each minute. "Do you believe I would permit them to harm you as they did me?"

Them? Harm? The man was as delusional as the colorless spiral artwork in his office.

We fought a brief, almost childlike battle, with me yanking on his arms and him batting my attempts away. Rain soaked through my shirt until I could see the outline of my bra. My braid resembled a rat's tail dragged from the sewer. And meanwhile, Willow was getting away.

Bryn slid a knee over my gut, applying enough pressure that I had to curse him or breathe. I went with the former. "You can go fu—"

"What you are witnessing is not *real*," he panted, breathless.

Good. At least I'd landed some of my punches.

"Willow!" I screamed. "Willow!"

As I fought with Bryn's knee, James slid out of the pub, tossing apologies behind him like he was fielding a football. He skidded to a halt at the sight of us, eyes widening behind glasses askew on his nose. "Bryn, what's going on? Did ye feckin' do this?" He grabbed Bryn by his shoulders, wrenched him off me, and I had never been more grateful. "Roe's bruised and bleeding—have ye lost yer goddamn mind?" he shouted, fisting Bryn's collar.

I grunted in agreement. "James, it's Willow, she was here and…and then…"

Wait, what was I *saying*? Willow was dead. *Dead*.

Lying in an open coffin with a face so much like mine, but done up with caked makeup when she'd never worn any. Buried with her hair in ugly blonde ringlets, lotuses clasped in her rigid hands. *Dead*.

"Rowan?" Bryn's voice cut through the memory as James slowly released him. I stared at Bryn's pale face, his shadowed eyes, and steadied.

"I mean," I said, swallowing hard. "I mean, I thought I saw someone who looked like her. Then Bryn tackled me. For no reason."

With a grunt, Bryn planted his cane, bent, and gripped my bruised elbow. I winced as he pulled me up. "You may lie to James," Bryn warned, his cool breath washing over my face, "but never to me. I know what you saw."

I withered under twin jewels that belonged somewhere deep in the Mariana Trench. "And what did I see?"

"An Inquitate."

"An *Inquitate*?"

"That is what they are called, Rowan."

My breath stalled. "They?"

His eyes glinted. "Your *disease*."

❈

"**W**hat is an *Inquitate*?" I repeated when we were back at the bed and breakfast.

Saying nothing, Bryn brushed back the curtain of the room James and I had rented and squinted into the dark waters off the port. He'd hung up his cashmere sweater on the heater's slotted surface, and now wore only a collared shirt, looking more like a Viking professor than an artist.

Our room in the converted-farmhouse-turned-bed-and-breakfast was one of four, with wallpaper the color of Bryn's sweater—in that it had none—and a kitchenette, where James was currently busying himself to distraction with tea. He'd changed into an embroidered sweater with a patchy bluebird over the heart.

"Why do you think I saw my sister?"

Still, nothing.

In Willow's old college sweater, I crossed my arms against the cold, my fingertips grazing the worn felt of a faded treble clef on the breast. My knees had stopped bleeding on the way here, but my palms needed Band-Aids I didn't have, so I'd stuffed them into a pair of James's fingerless gloves for now.

Whatever Bryn claimed, it'd been Willow who'd stood on a street in Oslo, alive for a brief moment with that wild smile and the mole below her right eye that she swore was a freckle. I should have left faster instead of standing there, staring at her through the pub window, debating how much of my sanity I was willing to part with.

But why had she run away?

"Roe, would ye sit down?" James chided me, "Either the carpet will have a hole from yer pacing, or Bryn's head'll have a hole in it."

I shot him a parting glare before selecting one of the twin chairs opposite the bed, my fingers grazing the raised pattern of ugly roses on its armrest. Beside it, an end table sported two magazines on interior design—James's—and a glass lamp.

Bryn glanced over his shoulder, his gaze sweeping my puddle-soaked hair and landing on my unpainted toes. His frown deepened.

I sucked in my cheeks, worked all my annoyance into the stare I leveled back at him. This morning, I might have gone back to L'Ardoise, might have resigned myself to never knowing the truth of Willow's death—but now?

"Rowan, I must inform you that as we are not in Ruhaven, your act of staring me down shall do absolutely nothing to further your objective."

I could only imagine what my Mark would let me do, and briefly hoped we'd meet in the memories so I could find out.

James faced Bryn with the whistling teapot in a white-knuckled hand. "How long have ye known?" he asked softly, but not nearly as composed as I'd thought. It'd been his mother, after all, who'd suffered like Willow had.

Port lights flickered over Bryn's face—reds, greens, yellows, all playing in the hollows of his cheekbones. "Since I was first attacked."

James set the pot down with a clatter that had the pewter teaspoons jumping. "And yet ye didn't think to tell me? To warn me?"

Bryn ran a hand over his jaw. "I did not think they would target..." His eyes flicked to me.

"A repair woman?" I finished for him, ignoring the twisting in my gut that wasn't at all the steel I imagined.

He didn't bat an eye. "Precisely."

"And what about James's mother," I pushed, "did you think she'd be spared, too?"

James shook his head at Bryn, then he crossed to me with the tray of tea, set it down on the doily over the coffee table, and started filling me a cup before I'd asked. I tugged up the suspender he hadn't noticed had slipped over his shoulder.

"Thanks, Roe," he murmured, handing me the teacup. "Black, is it?"

"Yes, I—" The cup and saucer rattled in my palm, my cut hand burning through the thin glove. I was going to drop the damn tea right in my lap and I'd really—

In less than a second, Bryn plucked it from my grasp, setting it on the side table's doily in such a smooth motion, the tea barely rippled.

I sat there, hands still in the air, palms still stinging, with my heart thundering a staccato rhythm as loud as the heater. Fast, he was so fast. *How*? His Mark again? The speed of *light* was a thing, but that sounded ridiculous.

"I apologize for injuring you, Rowan," Bryn said, folding himself into the opposite chair and crossing his legs. I flexed my fingers, willing them onto the armrests until my pulse dipped. "I panicked when you chased after the Inquitate and reacted poorly."

That was right. He'd been fast then, too, hadn't he? Fast enough to tackle me at a run, though I'd been in a dead sprint when I left the bar.

I glanced at the cane resting beside his leather satchel. "How did you catch up with me so fast?"

"I was near the exit when you ran. You caused quite a commotion."

Liar.

He'd been at the bar with James, over twenty feet from the door, *with a cane*. "Are you sure it wasn't another..." I glanced at James, who came to sit heavily on the end of the bed. "Glimmer?"

"Hardly." Bryn's lips tightened under the lamplight.

But James had had enough.

"Bryn, what the feck happened out there today? Yer flying out the pub, Roe thinks she saw Willow, and the only thing I know for sure—besides that it's raining in Kerry—is that we'll never be allowed back at that pub again."

Bryn stretched out his leg, and in the tiny guest room, it bumped against the foot of the bed. "It was an illusion, as I have said. The Inquitate are able to create them to lure Ruhavens, and should you acquiesce, you shall find yourself dead. Because the cause of our sudden aneurysms was never a disease but a creature like us, born and bred of the Gate. They are sentient, highly aware, and their illusions are the beginning of the attack."

The faded wallpaper swam in my vision. A creature? Not a disease Willow had been infected with, but something that had intentionally targeted her. For what reason?

And what did it want with me?

"A *creature*," James repeated. "Yer telling me, ye think me mammy was killed by some creature from the Gate! How the bloody hell would ye know that?"

"In my research, I have read journals written by Ruhavens which describe such a creature as one that is neither Ruhaven, nor Drachaut. That can wear the skins of others, a creature which—when attacking—causes a brain bleed, even in Ruhavens. I must assume that the Inquitate have somehow escaped the Gate and now hunt us here as well."

Hunt us? Then this was on purpose? They'd attacked Willow on *purpose*? Not only my sister, but the others, like James's mom.

"You knew what's been killing Ruhavens and you've said *nothing*?" I accused. "If James had known, my sister might not be *dead*."

Bryn started to speak, but James cut him off. "She's feckin' right, ye know." His mouth opened, shut, fury radiating out of him. "What are ye *thinking*? Another bloody creature of the Gate, and not even in the *Ledger*? Yet ye say nothing." Seeming to need a minute, he braced on his knees and rose from the bed. "Do ye not know how much I've worried of this? Yet ye've suspected we've been targeted all along? Me own mother deserves some feckin' peace, like. I can't be recruiting Ruhavens if this is true."

Bryn looked at him sharply. "You will." An order.

James lifted his finger, drilled it at Bryn. "Don't ye sit there and look at *me* like that. 'Tis *yerself* who's responsible for yer exile, and if ye hadn't done what ye did, ye'd still be recruiting."

Bryn's eyes flashed, a thunder strike in a cloudless sky, then he seemed to reel himself in, smothering even that brief emotion.

I looked between him and James, my sympathies lying entirely and completely with the Irishman. Whatever Bryn had done to be exiled— and his current actions seemed bad enough—I could be sure that he'd deserved it.

Face stony, Bryn rose and moved to stand by the window again, where the boats bobbed in a purple-hued night and the dripping vertical streaks of the port lights illuminated the waters. He cracked the window, and the sounds of lapping water rushed in.

If Bryn wasn't going to explain why he'd kept everything to himself, I'd figure it out for Willow.

"James, you told me the disease causes an aneurysm," I began.

He lifted his tea, hands nearly shaking. "That's right."

"But not in Bryn? Why?"

James looked at the Norwegian peering out the window, the boats docking beyond. "I don't know. Maybe that's another thing he's keeping from us."

I rose from my seat, leaving behind the tea I hadn't touched. My palms burned where the glass had torn, my knees ached from Bryn's tackle to the pavement, but I paced the tiny room again, walking from the washroom to the twin chairs facing the beds and back.

Because things weren't adding up.

"If it's supposed to cause an aneurysm, then how does Bryn know it's the disease at all that caused…" I didn't need to gesture at his leg.

"That's for Bryn to answer, but I've no doubt meself." James tucked in his knees as I passed. "Roe, yer making me bloody dizzy."

"Has *anyone* else survived the Inquitate?"

"No. Just Bryn sure."

Exactly. It didn't make sense. How could he be the only one to survive? And who knew if he'd been attacked by the Inquitate at all? It was only his word that said he'd been a victim. But…

I stared at the leg he kept bent, supported by the strength of the cane.

Maybe he was lying about that too. After all, he'd chased me out of the pub, hadn't he? He'd tackled me to the ground, stopped me from pursuing Willow, then he—*he* said she was an illusion.

But what if she wasn't? What if she really had come back, just like our Marks could appear here?

My pulse started to pick up, and a little trickle of sweat slid down the back of my neck. Bryn could be lying about the entire thing.

"Maybe you weren't attacked or infected," I said softly.

"Excuse me?" The curtain swayed to a stop as Bryn turned, disbelief coating his carved features.

James murmured under his breath. "*Roe…*"

I hesitated. But James was too nice, too trusting, and Bryn could be inventing a story about the Inquitate to get back into Ruhaven.

"You were kicked out of Naruka," I began, and his lips thinned. "Forced to give up the memories. Exiled for over two years. When did you say he was infected, James?"

"Roe, ye've not the right way of it—"

"*When*?" I insisted.

"Six months ago," Bryn answered in a voice like dry ice.

I swung back to him as James protested. "Yet you don't tell me anything about the disease when I flew across countries to ask about my own sister. You don't tell me the symptoms. Why?"

Bryn's entire body settled into eerie stillness. "Because you should not be here, because it should not have targeted you."

A cold weight settled over my shoulders. He knew then—knew it wasn't me.

"Here's what I think," I said, pushing away the hollowness in my belly. "You were obsessed with the memories of Ruhaven, and James forced you out because of it, but like any addict, you needed to find a way back. You didn't know that James was—only recently—trying to reach you."

Cold leaked from Bryn, as black and dark and depthless as the sea. Light? No, that he wasn't.

James laid a hand on my arm. "Roe, ye don't know what yer—"

"You could have just told me what happened to you," I pushed, addressing Bryn. "But you didn't. Maybe because you *can't*."

"You have no idea of what you speak," Bryn said, voice low, dark.

"I know exactly *what I speak*. You wanted—*needed*—to find a way back to Naruka," I continued unabated. "So you decided to blame your accident on this disease. Except that wasn't enough to convince James to let you back, you needed it to be deliberate—an *attack*. So James would feel guilty enough to lift your exile."

"So I *crippled* myself?" Bryn seethed, and I could have sliced my hands again on the sharp edge in his voice. "Rowan, should I wish to return to Naruka, I assure you I would find better ways than permanent injury."

As if he didn't want to return, as if every fiber in his body wasn't humming with that otherworldly need.

James started to stand. "Can we just try to calm down a wee bit and—"

"Sit down, James," Bryn said, voice going to steel. My entire body wilted under the command in it, like he could funnel some strength from the Gate even here.

James sank quietly onto the squeaky bed, as affected as I was.

Then Bryn turned his burning stare on me. "Well, Rowan, let us hear the rest of your inflammatory theory."

I swallowed the thickness in my throat, forced myself to weather the coldness beating at me from across the room.

What if I was supposed to see Willow today? Maybe it wasn't an illusion but some—some ghost of her created from the Gate, and I was supposed to talk to her.

And yet Bryn had stopped me. Maybe—well, maybe before Willow could tell me something.

"I think you're a liar," I accused, my voice surprisingly steady. "You ran out of the pub on a leg you say is crippled, to stop me from speaking to my sister—or some ghost of her. You make up that she's an Inquitate—a disease that caused an aneurysm in everyone except you. You lied about why your roommate knows me, or someone like me. So I don't believe you, Bryn, and I think I should go back out and look for whatever it was that tried to—to—that tried…"

He didn't say a word. Didn't need to when the room dropped two degrees and cold heat pumped off him. My knees shook like a weed shriveling in an unexpected frost as he shoved away from the window and crossed the room in slow, deliberate steps.

I took one step back before my spine decided to reappear. Then I planted my feet, squared my shoulders. He wouldn't hurt me, would he? Not in front of James, not…

"A *liar*?" Bryn whispered, brushing past James, who didn't seem the least bit concerned. "It is *you* who traveled here, Rowan, *you* who disturbed me at my place of work. Do you recall that I was exiled? Perhaps you might consider the effort it took for me to move on from what you continually disabuse."

He never raised his voice, never so much as lifted it above a whisper, and I trembled all the more because of it.

"I just needed to know about Willow, about the aneurysm," I insisted. "You could have told me or—"

The back of my knees hit the chair, knocking me into a seat still warm from where Bryn had sat. His briefcase tumbled off the armrest, scattering papers, pencils, and binder clips.

But still, he advanced on me like a wave spilling on the sand before the icy cold washes over your ankles. On the wallpaper behind his unmoving face, winged horses galloped into the sky, their veins throbbing, sweat glistening on their necks, tendons straining against the bit that yanked them back.

"You enter my office, uninvited, and demand that I tell you every detail of what has been my personal nightmare these last six months," he said in a low voice. "Not because you wish to help James resolve this affliction, but because you wish to verify that of which is so obviously true—that your sister died by the hand of the Inquitate." He bent over me, bracing a hand on one armrest at a time, deliberately, slowly, his fingers clenching the rose-patterned fabric. The cane fell to the side. "And once you have extracted this information, you tell me you shall go home, shall abandon what I was forbidden to see."

I shrank into the cushions as his breath whispered over my face. He was like a frozen lake at night when it was the most terrifying—a black mass, endless and opaque.

"And in doing so," he continued, relentless, unforgiving, but still in that same breath of calm dispassion, "you spit on a world I have given my life to. You sneer at what is *mine*. And when I prevent the Inquitate from destroying you as well, you call me a liar. Because you did not come here to find the truth, you came to find the lie. To shove your thumb in the eye of Ruhaven." He inhaled through his nostrils. "So look, Rowan, and see what a liar I am."

When he pulled away, I sucked in a shuddering breath.

"*Look*, Rowan," Bryn repeated coldly.

Look? I could barely take my eyes from his face. What did he...

And then I saw that he was pulling up his pant leg.

I dropped my gaze.

Oh. Oh, god.

Dark veins flooded up his calf, spilling into stained puddles under his otherwise perfect skin, like the blood had oozed out and found nowhere to go. Bones. I could see his *bones*. Or his, his ligaments, like his skin was a black nylon pulled over the inside of his leg.

I doubled over, nearly retching, the carpet blurring for a second.

He dropped his pant leg again, covering the deadly evidence.

"Well, Rowan? Is it a *liar* I am?" he asked in a whisper.

"No," I murmured, staring at the sketches on the carpet, the ones that had spilled out of his bag. Of eyes too large to be human, of scaled beasts and twisted ears, of eggs that grew instead of leaves.

All—*all* were of Ruhaven. Even now, years later. Even after what the Inquitate had done to him, even after how long he'd waited.

Bryn bent and scooped the lot into a pile, shoving them into his satchel. "Are you quite satisfied with my humiliation, Rowan? Or do you wish to look through more of what exiling has done to me?"

"You've made your point," I said thickly.

"I am glad to hear it."

He picked up his cane, took the seat I'd previously been sitting in, lifted my tea that must have gone cold, sipped.

My insides felt like they'd been ripped out and returned in all the wrong places. I tried to gather myself, running my hands over my thighs to warm them, but I wanted out of this room, away from *him*.

James loosed a breath, having not moved from his spot on the bed. "Jayzus, yer one scary langer. Ye didn't need to frighten Roe to make yer point."

"I'm not..." But it was a lie, and I didn't have the heart to make it a good one. But I didn't need to stay here, either, with the shame and humiliation and guilt that was all but suffocating.

"Where are you going?" Bryn demanded when I rose.

I shoved an arm through the sleeve of my jacket. "I'm taking a walk."

"No, you are not," Bryn said calmly. "Sit down, *Rowan*."

Ignoring him, I strode down the thin hallway, past the bathroom with a claw-footed tub and the rows of flower paintings. I reached for the doorknob—

A hand gripped my elbow.

I spun around, nearly colliding with Bryn's chest as I ripped my arm from his grasp. "I'm not—"

"You are," Bryn said firmly, planting a hand on the door and boxing me in. The fear he'd summoned paled next to my own humiliation now. "You will stay inside, as the Inquitate are likely still nearby waiting for one of us to leave, and I will not have your death be on James's conscience."

Behind him, James offered a hesitant smile from the bed, one that had my shoulders slumping in defeat.

James had warned me about Bryn, and I should have known I couldn't get my answers with a quick trip to Norway and a few questions. Instead, I'd tried to resolve Willow and her aneurysm like Bryn had rewired the fuse box—by carelessly shoving everything into whatever fit.

Sensing the change, Bryn lifted his hand, moved aside.

Ashamed, and with little dignity left, I dragged myself to the chair again, tucking my knees to my chest and resting my cheek on them. I was so tired, so goddamn tired of all this. Of me.

James cleared his throat. "Well, suppose we might get answers, at least, to what ye know of the Inquitate. Attacked, ye say?"

I closed my eyes, hearing Bryn take his seat again. I shouldn't have come here. That'd been my first mistake—wanting Willow's death to mean something. Or worse, maybe *I'd* just wanted to mean something.

"Yes, I believe so," Bryn replied. "Because, like Rowan, I also saw an illusion that was sentient. And until today, I believed there was a reason it targeted those it did. I no longer do. Rowan does not fit the pattern."

No, I didn't. I wasn't a Ruhaven. I shouldn't be involved in any of this.

"Are ye gonna tell us yer theory or no?" There was a brief silence, then James sighed. "Well, are ye at least going to come back and help me figure this out? I don't want another Ruhaven to suffer. And I've never seen it so bad, attack or no. Both yerself and Roe in a year? 'Tis unheard of. What if they come here again?"

They. James already believed Bryn's theory that it wasn't an infection.

"If they return, then it appears that the way to prevent an attack is to break the illusion they present. If Rowan had persisted, she would be dead. But I did not see the projected version of Willow today, I saw nothing, so they must only be able to deceive one person."

Then how did he know what I saw? *You cannot lie to me*, he'd said afterwards. So had he seen *something*?

"...so if we remain close, it shall be more difficult to fall victim," Bryn finished.

"And yet ye want to stay here, in Oslo? Alone?"

"I…" Bryn hesitated for the first time.

"Ye've not seen them here before and not told me?" Concern darkened James's voice.

"I have not."

Another long pause. Then James said, more forcefully, "Ye need to come back to Naruka. As ye said yerself, yer safer with other Ruhavens around."

At least I wouldn't be there, but how long was Bryn going to stay in this room? It was taking everything in me not to fall apart on this chair and there wasn't much left.

"And what of Tye?" Bryn asked.

"He'll not stop ye from visiting the Gate. Though, I don't expect that to be a problem now, do you?"

Bryn said nothing for a moment. "It is not Tye's reluctance to see me visit the Gate to which I am referring."

The bed creaked, blankets rustled. "Ye mean what ye accused me of at the bar? Well, I don't think ye've the right way of it. He wouldn't have. Didn't, as far as I know."

I hugged my knees tighter. Just go. *Go.*

But Bryn replied, "Tye rang me before I moved from my old apartment. He was very, *very* clear, James."

Clear about *what*? This must be how dogs felt.

"Maybe he wanted to be sure ye stayed gone. Ye did a feckin' number on him after yer stunt in the Gate."

Leave. Just leave. It was too late to be here, nearly midnight. I wanted to face-plant in my bed and forget today. Forget all of this.

I flinched when Bryn suddenly spoke from above me. "Tye is aware of the rules, James."

"Not everyone lives by Ruhaven's," James replied evenly.

He'd never mentioned any rules from Ruhaven, but then, I hadn't stayed long enough to find out.

"Rowan, where are your socks?" Bryn asked.

When his hand brushed my freezing toes, I yanked them under me. "When are you leaving?" I said instead.

He tucked his hand into the pocket of his beige slacks. "I will stay here tonight, in case the Inquitate return."

I yanked my head up, quick enough to catch the barest hint of amusement in his eyes before it was wiped away. Stay here? *The hell you will.*

Do you truly find me so unpleasant?

"Why?" James asked, and relief flooded me. "Do ye not have roommates?"

What did that have to do with it?

Bryn studied me as he answered James. "No, but even if I did, it is only fellow Ruhavens who can interfere should an Inquitate return."

Oh. *Oh.* He was afraid it'd come back for him, finish what it had started with his leg—the blackened skin, the poisoned veins. I should have thought of that. He'd avoided Naruka since the attack—because he was hiding from the Inquitate? What if, somehow, I'd brought them here with me? What if I'd somehow brought them to L'Ardoise? To my sister?

Shame had me reconsidering. "It's fine, James. Bryn can have my bed." I wouldn't be able to sleep anyway.

James rose with a huff. "Don't ye take pity on him, Roe. I've seen him pass out drunk in Naruka's kitchen chair."

I made a small choking sound.

"Rowan," Bryn drawled, "I was not raised so poorly as to force a woman out of her own bed. I shall sleep on the chair."

Before I could demonstrate my own good manners—namely, not forcing a six-foot-four cripple to sleep on a decrepit chair—he settled into the old thing and propped his leg on the stool.

After murmuring a few half-hearted protests about him having the bed, all of which he again declined, I uncurled and rose, keeping my head down so Bryn didn't see the puddle he'd reduced me to.

At least he'd be gone in the morning.

If I'd been thinking clearer, I'd have dragged in a pillow and blanket and slept in the tub just to avoid having to face him again.

So I gave myself time to settle, brushing my teeth until they hurt, trying out James's face moisturizers and serums, and rebraiding my hair the way Willow had taught me.

By the time I finished, James was snoring under the comforter, his hair growing over the pillow like a black weed. Bryn sat in his chair, reading in silence under the lamp, face calm in thought.

I inched past him and slid under the crisp cotton sheets, pulling the quilt to my chin.

A minute later, Bryn folded his book with a snap and clicked off the light. "Good night, Rowan," he murmured.

I pulled the blanket tighter like I could cocoon myself off from him. And much later, long after James's snoring filled the room and my cheek warmed the cool pillow, Bryn's blue eyes still winked in the night.

And I swore I could hear his pulse, as thick and slow as Ruhaven.

Thump.

Thump.

Thump.

CHAPTER 13

I Only Ever Loved Your Ghost

I fought my way out of sleep like a swimmer rising from a great depth.

Willow had once tried scuba diving off the coast of L'Ardoise—she'd wanted to explore a shipwreck before they explained that was only for advanced divers—but she'd told me you have to ascend slowly because of the pressure change, that your body needs time to adjust.

Willow.

I shifted under rough sheets. The fabric was hot, starchy, the pillow too soft and fluffy, not the hard sack of flour I slept on in Naruka.

Where was I?

Home, in L'Ardoise? Maybe in my roommate's apartment, or the college dorm I'd shared with Willow before I'd dropped out.

Slowly, I peeled open my eyes.

A tasseled light hung from a faded-pink ceiling. Sunlight beamed across it in a blinding tangerine that could never come from Ireland. The *cawing* of seagulls snuck in under a cracked window, followed by a crisp breeze that tickled my nose.

This wasn't Naruka, wasn't L'Ardoise. What had I dreamed? Images and memories tangled in my head.

Willow, waving at me on a rainy street, her face shining with dew, blonde hair in droopy ringlets. Why would she have dyed her hair like that again? She wouldn't have, so maybe she— Wait, I'd seen Willow?

My lungs strained from the sudden effort of breathing, flexing muscles I hadn't used in years.

Willow. Alive.

God, alive and *here*.

I flung the sheets off me, swung my legs over the bed. I needed to find her, to tell Willow—I don't know, but *something*, before the relief of the dream wore off and I forgot what it was to lose her.

My bare feet slapped onto a crusty rug as I shoved off the mattress, shielding my eyes from a glittering sea light. Where was I? And what was—

"*Ahhhhhh!*" The scream burst from me on a gasping wail.

No. No. No, no!

In a tall portrait mirror, an angel lifted an elegant eyebrow, his long fingers pausing around the knot of a beige tie, blond hair combed tidily to the side. Willow had wanted hands like that so she could reach wider than an octave.

"Does the sight of someone properly dressed always send you into such shock, Rowan?" Bryn's voice brought reality crashing down.

Willow was dead.

"Holy, Mary, and Joseph," James cried, sitting up in bed and wincing from the sun. "It's bloody seven in the morning." He fumbled for his glasses on the nightstand.

"Nine," Bryn corrected.

Willow. Dead. Not alive.

I pressed a hand to my belly. Oh no, not in front of—

Sucking in a breath, I scrambled to the washroom, half-tripping over Bryn's cane before I shoved open the door and my knees smacked into the tiles with a thud, bruises protesting the impact as I gripped the rim of the toilet and heaved.

Bile soured the back of my throat. Breath wheezed in, out. But I didn't throw up, was at least spared that indignity.

The bathroom door creaked open wider, and when imaginary snowflakes flickered over the back of my neck, I knew it was Bryn.

"Rowan, I must admit, this is not the usual reaction women have to me in a suit."

I just bet, but I was too ashamed with how I'd spoken to him yesterday to answer, too ashamed that I'd accused a cripple of lying about his leg—and a little scared, too, of that *thing* he'd been.

When the worst passed, I brushed back the hair that had come loose from my braid and shakily rose.

Bryn was half-dressed in a cream shirt tucked at his trim waist and cinched with a chocolate leather belt. A matching tie draped loosely around his neck. He'd shaved whatever beard had tried to escape the night to a fine 220-grit sandpaper, so clean I could eat off him.

But there was no sign of the man who had crept into my nightmares, only bored curiosity in those cool Norwegian eyes.

As we stared at each other, James called from the other room, "Since when did they need ye all fancy at work? Aren't ye supposed to be an artist?"

He couldn't be farther from the image. No color, no fun, no loose appreciation for the wild and ironic.

Bryn's gaze dropped to my left shoulder, where my shirt had slipped off. I jerked it up, covering a pale birthmark.

"Was," he said shortly. "I *was* an artist. Now I am instructing on the history of art." Bryn continued to study me as he spoke to James. "I let myself out at five this morning for a change of clothes—rather easy with your snoring for cover. I must speak to the dean if I am to return to Naruka."

So he'd decided to take James up on his offer after all, which brought me a surprising measure of relief. However much Bryn disliked me, he seemed to feel a responsibility to James, one that would hopefully keep the Irishman safe when I was gone.

There was a beat of silence in the other room, then James let out a relieved groan. "I'm glad of it, so I am," he said.

I held Bryn's stare, let him see just what I thought about the answers he still kept from me. Behind Bryn's eyes, fire simmered and banked like a flame in the night, causing each tiny hair on my neck to stand up.

"But I have conditions," he added.

"Conditions?" James parroted.

"Indeed. Rowan, when you are ready, come into the room so we may negotiate properly."

I started after him, then quietly shut the bathroom door. He probably wanted to ensure I never returned to Ruhaven, a world I'd dreamed of nearly every night since I'd seen it.

I shook myself. Not *mine*. My world would be in L'Ardoise, where I could drive Willow's truck up to her gravestone at the church, under the old town wall we used to drink on for our birthday. I'd tell her about Naruka, about James and Ruhaven, maybe complain about Bryn. She'd like that, like to hear whatever was a bit outrageous.

On autopilot, I showered, changed into my other jeans before pulling on the now-dry cardigan I'd worn yesterday, brushed my teeth, toothpaste stinging my cut palms, and swung my hair into a ponytail that brushed the small of my back.

Thinking of Willow, I stepped into the wallpapered hallway.

And paused as something shimmered up my spine.

A painted blue teapot hung as crookedly as the paintings at Naruka, but otherwise, there was nothing but the sound of James flipping through paper.

After a moment, I shook off the feeling and followed the smell of coffee into the bedroom.

James sat upright against the headboard, a mug in one hand with the paper spread before him on the quilted bedspread. Glasses rested on the tip of his slightly crooked nose. What I wouldn't give for a cup of that—

"Coffee?"

I caught myself an instant before knocking the offering out of Bryn's outstretched hand.

"Are you always so unobservant, Rowan?" the Norwegian drawled while I righted myself on the coat stand.

"No, thanks," I said when he offered the mug again.

The corners of his mouth wilted. "Do you prefer tea?"

"No, thank you."

James grimaced at the newspaper. "Yer not off to a great start, lad."

"Indeed." Bryn set the steaming cup on the corner of the kitchenette, picking up his cane instead. "Rowan, we shall need to work together to determine why the Inquitate are targeting us, and by extension, your sister. So I would suggest you overcome your disapproval of me."

How could I when he might be responsible for— Wait, what did he mean by *work together*?

God, that coffee smelled good.

"Work together?" What would he want with a non-Ruhaven?

Bryn slipped past me. "Yes, Rowan, for you are the only one who has lost a twin to the Inquitate and therefore, are more likely to find a connection." He scooped up his leather bag, movements deft and purposeful as he flipped through the contents. "It is clear I cannot avoid the Inquitate here, and my previous suppositions as to why they targeted me appear decidedly incorrect."

"And yer not going to tell us what yer theory was?" James vocalized my own questions.

"No. But I believe the answers may lie with Rowan and her twin." Bryn snapped his satchel closed. "Willow had never been to Naruka, never seen Ruhaven, yet she was attacked in her hometown. Perhaps something she did, or someone she met, triggered it. Or perhaps it is a connection—through Rowan—to something that occurred in the memories—in Ruhaven."

My stomach flip-flopped. Why didn't he just say it was because it was Willow that Ruhaven wanted? And besides, had he really proven *anything* yet? I might have stuck my ample foot in my mouth last night, but that didn't mean it was a creature from the Gate causing aneurysms.

"How do you know it wasn't just an aneurysm?"

His eyes swept me, measuring, assessing. Deciding. "There are a number of coincidences with your sister's death and the others that cannot be overlooked," he said at last. "First, of course, the cause. A brain bleed in the frontal lobe." He tapped the area of the skull that the doctors had explained very calmly, very rationally, had been the cause of Willow's death. A pale finger pointing to the scan, nails brittle from all the sanitizer. "I viewed her medical records."

"You *what*—"

"In my research, as she was a potential candidate for Inquitate targeting," he said smoothly, and bottled insult rose in my chest. He'd known all along, he'd even researched her, and he'd said *nothing* to me. "Though Willow had not visited Ruhaven like the others, and there has never been a Ruhaven born with a twin before."

Never? After centuries of Ruhavens born, not one was a twin?

"Secondly, for the Inquitate to attack and approach both her and I in the same town cannot be a coincidence."

The same *town*? I looked at James incredulously. "What's he talking about?"

James only lifted his coffee, sipped. "Ask him."

Bryn looped the satchel over one shoulder, tightened the strap. "I take it you are unaware that it was, in fact, myself who was sent to recruit you initially."

I blinked at him. *Bryn*? Bryn was sent to recruit me? In L'Ardoise? "You? I've never met you before. It was Tye who—"

"Who took over for me," Bryn finished. "Because I was attacked while on recruitment in L'Ardoise. So you see, Rowan, it is highly unlikely for your sister's aneurysm to be unrelated to the Inquitate when they came upon me only a few years later in the same location."

He'd been in L'Ardoise. Before Tye, before James. Had we met? No, no. I'd never forget his face, the *alienness* of him. Yet he'd known, even back then, that the Inquitate had likely killed Willow and he'd said nothing to me. What kind of person did that make him? Maybe my accusations hadn't been so far off the mark. I'd never leave someone to grieve like that, not knowing the truth of what happened.

"This leads me into my conditions," Bryn said.

I jerked my head up. "Conditions?"

"Indeed, for you are going to assist me, Rowan." He reached for his coat, a knee-length wool that was brushed to smooth coal. "Willow is the outlier—never before has a relation of a Ruhaven been targeted. And now, even stranger, her twin is targeted as well. Why? I have a number of lines to investigate."

"Which are?"

His bottom lip puckered. "The state of things has changed. I did not expect the Inquitate to target you. However, now that they have, we must determine the cause before others are similarly affected.

"First, because your sister has neither visited Ruhaven, nor been written into the *Ledger*, her death may be related to an interaction she had on Earth. Perhaps she met an Inquitate who crossed from the Gate? We must track her movements in the year before her death."

But he knew it was Willow meant for the *Ledger*. Wasn't that the simple answer? That the Inquitate—if that's what they were—had targeted her for that reason? But then why had they been here in Oslo as an illusion of Willow? Why would they target *me*? I was nothing to them, unless there was more Bryn wasn't telling me.

"Second, there is a reason some Ruhavens are meeting the Inquitate in the Gate. Did they know something in their past lives? Find something? What attracts the Inquitate to them? For this, you can assist, Rowan."

I lifted my chin. "Assist *how* exactly? Yesterday, you wanted nothing to do with Willow or I."

"Do you not wish to determine why your twin was killed?" He wrapped a soft, cotton scarf around his neck, tucked it under the collar's marble button. "Or was I under the mistaken belief that when you stormed into my office yesterday, it was because she was important to you?"

"What? Yes, of course, I just—"

"Good, then you, Rowan, shall have no issue providing me the material I require, such as friends you shared, places you have visited, anywhere Willow went outside of your town. The Inquitate appear to be targeting Ruhavens due to something that occurred in the memories, or an interaction, event, or other such incident here. We must pursue both paths."

Something fluttered in my chest, so foreign, so strange, that I barely recognized it.

I tried to smother the spark of hope. "Okay. I'll need time to sort through her things." To figure out how to convince my parents to see me again, to let me go through Willow's things, her diary, calendar, whatever I couldn't remember. "Then I'll write to James in a few weeks with what I find. If you tell me what you're looking for, I can—"

"You misunderstand me, Rowan," Bryn interrupted, long fingers slipping pearl buttons through slits. "You cannot go back to L'Ardoise.

You must return with James and I to Naruka. You can compile your list there." He straightened his collar.

Return to Naruka? Why would he ask that when he knew what I wasn't?

When I glanced at James, he sipped his coffee, a glint in his eyes. I opened my mouth, shut it. "But Willow's things are in L'Ardoise," I said, making up an excuse, because the alternative would be facing Willow's past life.

"If you do not return to Naruka, how will you visit Ruhaven?" Bryn said, limping toward the door with the satchel thumping his thigh.

I stared after him. "Visit Ruhaven?" I repeated dumbly. Why would he want that? Wouldn't that be an insult to him?

"Yes, indeed, Rowan. Our past lives must have encountered these Inquitate, and something they have done will lead to the reason our lives were attempted upon here. Why your sister was executed. Perhaps, the insult was so egregious as to need to eliminate the bloodline entirely."

Something bubbled up inside me, hot and ripe. "*Nothing* my sister did would ever—"

"And so I ask you," Bryn barreled over me, "how you shall possibly uncover the grievance our past lives inflicted if you do not relive the memories?" He stopped with a hand on the doorknob, glanced over his shoulder. The window light seemed to stretch across the room to play tenderly with his hair. "Do you have some other prerogative in L'Ardoise?"

Prerogative? "No, I—"

"We have already determined there is no community popcorn maker for you to return to, have we not?"

I pulled on my collar. "No, there's no one." No boyfriend. No friends after Willow's death. No sister.

His eyes flickered. "And your job, I understand you are unemployed now? That your father does not wish for you to resume working for him?"

The blow landed like he'd intended, though how he knew, I didn't know. "Yes," I said quietly.

"And you are pursuing no other higher education?"

This time, I said nothing.

"You are not developing some unique hobby, are you? Perhaps longing to join the L'Ardoise marching band? Training for the hammer-throwing contest? Well, Rowan?" he pushed.

I couldn't even look at James now. "No."

"Then this is my condition. You return with me, visit Ruhaven regularly, and I will continue my research, with which you will assist.

And perhaps, if we are lucky, we shall discover why your twin was attacked." Bryn swept open the door, striding out with the cane leading. "Now, let us hope the dean is more amenable to me than yourself, Rowan, as taking a sabbatical this early in one's tenure is rather frowned upon."

The door whisked shut behind him.

There was nothing in L'Ardoise waiting for me. That much was true. Everything I'd wanted, planned for, all of it was more of a dream now than Ruhaven had ever been.

Willow and I would never buy a house together. I'd never make that maid of honor speech I'd been running through my head since her first date. I'd never watch when she played for the national orchestra. We'd never drink wine on the church wall overlooking L'Ardoise, or laugh at the pigeon lady at Port Michaud beach again.

When I returned to Ruhaven, I'd be doing what I'd always done— chasing Willow's dreams.

"What do you think of Oslo?" Bryn asked.

In the hallway of the bed and breakfast, I shifted my knapsack to my other shoulder before releasing a long breath. I pressed my lips together, half to smother the thoughts that swarmed like bees, half to suppress the taste of apple perfume trailing the woman who passed, heels *click-clicking* down the sunlit hall.

It'd taken Bryn only a few days to pack his entire life into the striped leather suitcase he gripped—a life that appeared to consist of ten matching shirts and four pairs of pants in the same color.

"It's very clean," I said when the woman turned the corner.

Bryn's shoulder brushed mine as he angled toward me in the narrow hall. I kept my eyes fixed on the tops of his shoes, the embroidered leather glistening a chocolate orange in soft contrast to the oatmeal cuffs of his slacks. No man had ever worn anything so nice in L'Ardoise— and these were Bryn's *traveling* clothes.

"I thought you may have wished to see the fjords," he said.

Yes, ever since I'd flown overhead and seen those grooves clawing through the landscape—yet I could never afford the tour prices. "I'm sure they're nice," I offered.

"Yes, in the same way that Ruhaven is *nice*, I am sure."

I probably deserved that after accusing him of lying about being crippled—and when he'd been attacked trying to recruit *me*.

"Did we ever meet?" I asked quietly.

"Meet?"

He knew what I meant, but I said it anyway. "In L'Ardoise."

His heel tapped the carpet runner three times. "You do not remember?"

The words drew me up short. Did I? I peeked at him from under my braid. His face was set in stone, his smooth jaw clenched, his slicing cheekbones turning those blue eyes into severe pops of ice under his shadowed brow. A face no one would forget.

"I guess not," I said at length.

"Then I guess it does not matter. *James*," Bryn said deftly when the door opened. "Will we leave now? Or do you wish to steal more of the shampoo?"

"Nope, got it all," he assured us, and whistled through the hallway.

We walked to the train station while James filled Bryn in. "Kazie will be happy to see ye," he said.

Bryn's lips twitched in a rare warm smile.

James warned him about Kazie's latest hobby—crocheting. "And she'll make ye wear the feckin' things too," he lamented as we followed a sign for platform sixteen. "Mary from the post office asked me why I was wearing an ice cream cone on me head."

I lost them briefly in the crowd at the station, but Bryn's tall form provided an easy beacon.

"I take it you are not much of a traveler, Rowan," Bryn commented when I at last found my seat across from him.

I crossed my legs, careful not to knock his cane. "I prefer to drive."

James shook his head and took out *The Kerryman* newspaper, the same he'd read on the flight here. Even when the train whistled under a tunnel and the darkness left little room for reading, he merely turned a page about a builder not wanting to cut down a tree.

When the light came back, I asked him why.

"Ah, because 'tis a hawthorn tree and we're a superstitious lot."

"But it's just a tree."

James looked at me, the towns of Oslo disappearing into a blur behind him. "And it's just a dream," he reminded me, and returned to his paper.

As the train picked up steam, Bryn asked James about Essie, and for anyone who might have overheard, they'd think she really was James's wife. I hadn't considered how it would feel to leave these people he knew in the Gate, to not be able to hold a photo of them, certainly not to call, for days or weeks on end.

What if someone discovered the Gate and stopped him from visiting? Actually, how were people not storming the West Irish countryside and bottling whatever magical element grew a mile up?

"Because 'tis not exactly advertised, Roe," James said when I asked him. The train rumbled as we careened through tunnel after tunnel, not short underpasses like in Nova Scotia, but mile-long monstrosities that carved through mountains. "And the Gate being in Ireland is a blessing, for if any tales do come out, we can fob it off on more Yank nonsense and play up the whole thing."

He wasn't going to get off that easy. "But what if someone you showed Ruhaven to told someone?"

James signaled when a woman pushed a cart over. "Black with a wee drop of milk," he said, handing her change. "Ah a bit more, go on sure, a bit…there ye are," he finished when his tea was white. "We did have someone once, ye remember, Bryn?"

He turned a page of his novel—a weighty thing about Greek love stories. "It was Aushin, I recall, who went on to write a rather extravagant book that would have been better literature should she have remained in Ruhaven." He eyed me pointedly. "Regardless, it was published and now resides in the fantasy section of some unfortunate library."

I think it was a joke, but Bryn's eyes drifted back to his page.

James smirked. "That's it. So ye see, Roe, even if people do tell a tale, there's not many who will believe 'tis more than a story. And if they do, sure it's lost in all the other fables the Yanks invent."

"And if they go up to the Gate and investigate?" I pushed.

James shrugged and sipped his milk. "They'll see nothing, as 'tis only Ruhavens who can experience the memories."

Only Ruhavens? But did he really know for sure? There was another country, wasn't there—*Drachaut*—that's what he'd told me, so what about them?

"Are you sure?"

"Of course, Rowan," Bryn replied to his spread novel. "If someone did not once exist in Ruhaven, there is no past life to witness."

Unless Kazie had been right about a twin connection, and enough of the Gate recognized me as Willow.

We plunged into another tunnel, darkness consuming the train so long that Bryn sighed and folded the novel on his lap. When he looked at me, his brittle blue eyes reflected the steady beat of passing lights.

"Roe," James said, and I glanced away. "I want to ask a favor of ye before we arrive in Naruka." He planted his elbows on his knees. "About Tye." I kept my face neutral. "I know that yer close, and yer going to want to tell him what happened, but…" He steepled his hands. "Well, I'd prefer if ye didn't. So I'm asking ye not to, for me."

I peeked at Bryn, but his face betrayed nothing. "For *you*, James?"

"For me," James agreed, in a way that said we both knew it wasn't. "I know Tye'll worry about ye if he finds out the Inquitate have approached."

I caught my bottom lip between my teeth. Why didn't Bryn want Tye to know the Inquitate had been in Oslo? Because that's what this was about—not some misplaced concern for me.

I shifted on the carpeted seat. "But I'll be researching Willow's connection. How am I going to explain that?"

Bryn spoke now, one finger tapping his knee. "This is simple, Rowan. You can explain your research of the Inquitate because Willow was killed by them. You do not need to mention they approached you in Oslo."

While the train rumbled side to side, Bryn barely moved.

"Why do you want me to lie to my recruiter?"

The hand on Bryn's knee stopped its tapping. "Is that what he is to you, Rowan?"

He couldn't possibly know what I felt for Tye. "What exactly are you trying to say?"

"I think you understand me perfectly," Bryn replied, holding my gaze for a knowing beat. "But should you proceed to tell him, I will not assist with the Inquitate," Bryn threatened. "And my second condition," he continued in the same even tone, "is that you remain with myself, James, or another Ruhaven at all times."

"*What?* Why?"

James winced as heads turned our way.

Bryn arched one elegant eyebrow. "I had thought it obvious, Rowan. You are now a target of the Inquitate, and therefore, should take precautions to ensure that there is a Ruhaven near you who will break any illusion."

"Like when you tackled me to the sidewalk?"

His eyes flicked to my knee, then my hands where they curled on my lap. "Perhaps with more finesse, but yes."

James crossed a leg over his knee. "Roe, he's right, so he is. Until we know why the Inquitate have come after yerself and Willow—"

"And Bryn," I interjected.

"Aye, and Bryn," James agreed. "We should be sure to stick together. *All* of us."

CHAPTER 14

Meet Me in the Woods

The flight that should have taken me home instead crawled over the mountain ranges of Norway, the flat and barren highlands of Scotland, the Isle of Skye—pointed out by James—wrapped in mist. Then, the patchwork of Ireland flew into view with its golden rapeseed fields, pale-mint greens, and washed-out lavenders. The land resembled my nanny's quilt blanket—that's what I'd first thought all those months ago.

But here we landed, on the west coast of Ireland at Shannon Airport. Not the dirt runway of L'Ardoise where Willow and I had watched the planes take off a lifetime ago.

Hitching my backpack over a shoulder, I squeezed between a stroller and a teenager walking with her nose in a novel, and scanned the crowd.

A man with a thatch of sandy hair clenched the saddest bunch of roses I'd ever seen, a hopeful smile dotting his chapped lips. But my eyes slid to the man next to him, and our gazes connected.

Tye's lips pulled into a tight, restrained smile, but not a flicker of surprise lit his shadowed eyes. So James had told him then, that I'd changed my mind, and what would Tye make of that? I was coming back, but not for the right reasons, not to dream in a world that wasn't mine, but to encounter an Inquitate in the life that belonged to Willow. To hope that when I did, I'd know why it'd targeted her.

But where did that leave Tye and I?

I searched his face, looking for some sign. The toothpick between his lips bopped up and down in a face so tanned, even Ireland couldn't get rid of it, like that homey warmth was a part of him.

I hadn't said goodbye, had never once thanked him once for spending six months in L'Ardoise trying to bring me here. It wasn't Tye's fault he'd grabbed the wrong person.

Something in those August-green eyes shifted as I approached. "*Darlin'.*"

That one word, just that one word, loosened something inside me. "I—you don't look surprised to see me."

He straightened off the pillar. "You ain't the first woman to change her mind on me."

Then his dimple winked. Before I could think better of it, Tye was yanking me to him in a tight hug.

God, he smelled good, like a broken-in baseball glove—leather and salt and sweat. His hand smoothed my hair, his mouth a whisper of summer at my ear. "It's gonna be okay, hun," he said as I clung to him, clung to what I'd known. "I know all of this is scary, I know it ain't easy, but ya did the right thing. You're gonna get the hang of it too."

Because I'd be visiting the Gate like the rest of them, living that other life, pretending it was mine. But maybe it didn't matter that it wasn't. It was just a dream, after all, a memory, and I wasn't hurting anyone by watching it. Or was that just an excuse to justify the desperate desire already curling in my gut to see that world again?

When Tye released me at last, I noticed he held the *second* saddest bunch of roses in this airport. He angled them under the overhead lights. "Got these for James. Guy goes sweet on me every time I buy him flowers." Tye fanned himself with the bunch. "Man's weak for 'em."

He grinned when I laughed again, and handed me the bouquet. I pretended to smell them, then got an unexpected whiff of cigarette smoke and the back end of a convenience store.

"We all square, hun?" Tye asked.

I lowered them again, met his now-cautious eyes. "Only if you don't spring another magical world on me."

His lips tugged up as a sly look came over his face. "What, James didn't tell ya about the *Alice in Wonderland* hole in the garage?" He slipped my backpack off my shoulders and swung the leather stirrup over his. "Right under the table saw. Ya slip right through."

"Must be buried under all the Christmas decorations he keeps there."

Tye chuckled. "It's pretty good to have ya back."

"Oh yeah?"

"Sure, the electricity went out twice." He flicked my ball cap, but the playful light in his eyes faded to serious green. "Now, ya wanna tell me what ya found out 'bout your sister?"

While Tye dug out the airplane food I hadn't eaten, I told him what Bryn suspected of the Inquitate and their involvement in Willow's death, that he believed it was an attack, and the possible overlap between my sister's life and the others who'd died. I left out all mention of their appearance in Oslo.

"So Stornoway thinks this disease ain't a thing but a *who*," Tye said when the corn cobbler was almost gone. "Seems a little far-fetched. Ya sure James believes it?"

I didn't admit that I'd seen them myself. "Bryn saw them in L'Ardoise before he was injured."

Tye gave me a tight nod. "Yeah, James said as much when he called me."

"Why didn't you tell me Bryn was there before you?"

"Didn't see much point in complicatin' things, ya know? Besides, he wasn't nothin' to ya anyway."

I guess not. "So you're not going back to Montana on me?" I pried. "You know, now that I'm officially staying."

"What, and leave all this?" Tye gestured with the cobbler to the sheet of rain blurring the window. "Naw, I'm here for the long haul. Maybe hang up my recruiting hat and let Kazie take the next one."

Relief washed over me, and a little of something else too. "Bryn wants me to keep visiting the Gate," I admitted. "He thinks it's related to what happened to—"

Bang.

I jumped out of the way as a suitcase—no, *my* suitcase—nearly landed on my foot.

"Speak of the blond devil," Tye said, lighting a cigarette as Bryn stepped into view.

"Your luggage, Rowan. Though, generally, they prefer that one collect it. Tye," he said, voice clipped.

Tye tilted his head back, blew out a puff of smoke. "*Romeo*," he replied smoothly. *Romeo*? Few people on the face of this earth could less fit the image.

Bryn shook his head before limping for the exit.

Tye draped an arm across my shoulders. "This is a proud moment, Roe."

I looked up at him. "What?"

"Stornoway seems to like ya even less than he likes me." Tye wiped a mock tear from his eye. "Now tell me why, and don't spare a single gruesome detail."

I didn't.

J ames was trying to kill me.

Well, either myself or the car, but one of us wasn't getting to Naruka alive.

The 1972 Ford Granada sailed over a speed bump, teetering on the edge of a potholed road designed for a doll's house, while brambles *thwack-thwack-thwacked* against its metal side.

In the backseat, I gripped the Jesus handle, trying to focus as James explained everything he and Bryn had discussed about the Inquitate. Tye nodded along, but I could tell he wasn't convinced the aneurysm wasn't from a disease. And truthfully, the farther from Oslo we got, the more the whole day seemed like a dream.

Ireland was sort of like that, too, the land bathed in the foggy beauty that lent itself to the whimsical. Mist swelled on hills of eye-watering viridian, all framing ancient ruins and abandoned churches.

Opposite me, Tye cracked his window, tapping his smoke in the wind as Ireland flooded in—a wet, peaty fog that mixed with the taste of tobacco and coated the back of my throat.

The first time I'd seen the west of Ireland, I'd been struck stupid by the glowing fields, the ruins that would have been made into theme parks in North America. Then, in the smoky hills above Naruka, the Gate had made it all insignificant.

I pressed my forehead to the cold glass. Was I ready to see that again? To live and love as someone else? To *be* someone else? Someone at the mercy of a memory, with no control of their own actions, of what they touched, heard, or saw. What if I had a spouse, like James? Family? *Kids?*

When I asked as much, it was Bryn who drawled from the seat in front of me, "If the possibility of motherhood concerns you, then on this, at least, you need not worry. Ruhavens do not procreate as humans do."

But I thought that James...? "They don't have *sex*?" I blurted, then blushed.

Tye guffawed. "Hun, ya really think I'd live in a world where a man and woman can't do what god intended?"

The blush spread to my neck, but it was Bryn who saved me. "That is not what I said, Rowan," he answered like we were talking about the weather. "I said that is not how they procreate."

Because I didn't want to know how they did it otherwise, I vowed not to speak again for the rest of the car ride.

Tye made up for my silence, giving everyone a complete rundown of Ireland's racehorse breeding schedule. While he did, the soft hills of Limerick gave way to the rugged terrain of County Kerry. Here, the grass was thicker, rougher, and buoyed like a trampoline when you strode across. Wildflowers as hearty as the landscape thrust their way from rocks and sand, so purple and yellow flowers dotted the banks of the beaches we drove past.

There were few sidewalks, no curbs. Roads that had been relatively recently expanded for cars fought for space with the ash and birch trees, and anyone who was brave enough to walk got a two-finger wave from James. Tye's cigarette smoke had slowly built up inside the car, and combined with James's driving, my stomach didn't stand a chance.

The moody weather switched from rain to hail to glittering, gorgeous sun, then—as we lurched up another mountain—to clementine rays that lit up the clouds like a flashlight shone through a thin blanket.

"Close that damn window, Stornoway," Tye admonished as we bumped from a small gravel road to an even smaller dirt one—the one that would wind its way to Naruka.

I leaned forward in the seat, gulping that worm-laden air and squinting at the *No Vacancies* sign for a hotel that never was. It flapped in the wind, the fierce crack of its chains a built-in warning sign for the brewing storm, as were the leaves upturned to the sky, their white bellies marking the wind's change in direction.

Hotel Naruka—but only for Ruhavens. How long had that moss-ridden sign marked the entrance road, a harbinger of half-truths and myths for those recruited like me?

The car ambled on, ducking the oaks whose acorns *pinged* off the roof, creeping around puddles that had only deepened since we left.

Then finally, finally, like a princess at a ball, Naruka made her entrance.

It was a punch in the gut as much as the first time. The old hunting lodge that looked more like an enchanted castle, the glinting windows that seemed alive in the purplish evening light, the sweat steaming inside the rose house awkwardly installed on its left side, the foxgloves holding on to the end of summer.

But there, in the gravel beside the stable, was a familiar blood-red Mercedes.

"Bryn, I've kept the room as ye left it," James said quietly in the front.

The one with the sailboats, the medieval bed, the photos in the drawer.

Bird calls replaced the car's rumble as James pulled to a stop outside the barn and cranked the parking brake. The odd baying of sheep carried from the fields surrounding the manor, and further yet yawned the Atlantic Ocean, the bruised water dividing Ireland from L'Ardoise.

After climbing out, Bryn opened my door as he passed, his cane squelching in the long-haired grass.

"Well, kid," Tye said, patting my leg. "Guess you're about to do this, huh?" He climbed out, the car lurching to the side with the weight before I followed with the flowers.

Not only would I need to visit Ruhaven, but I'd also have to work with Bryn to find the details of my twin's life that mattered. To sift through concerts and travel plans, retracing her steps in the last few months of her life. What if we found a connection between her and—

The door of Naruka burst open.

Kazie leapt from the house, bounding down the stone steps like a dancer in search of a stage. Had she died her hair *blue*? The twisting curls bounced around her shoulders with each step of her ballet slippers. Beneath the setting sun and mist, her skin shone like wet velvet. She dashed through the untamed weeds of the front yard, yelling Bryn's name.

He'd barely gotten his luggage from the car before she launched herself at his torso. He fell backward, adding a new dent to the rear door, but still managed to catch all hundred pounds of her.

She grinned up at him, barely reaching his chest. "Bryn, oh-my-god-I've-missed-you," she squealed, the words coming in one long jumble.

He laughed—actually, genuinely laughed—the sound like a deep bell. His eyes softened, too, all the tightness in his face melting away until, for the first time, he actually looked my age. Then he murmured something in her ear, patted the blue curls back from her face, and set her on those prancing toes.

"Oh, I can't wait to tell you *everything*," she enthused, pirouetting in the mud. Then, as if noticing me for the first time, she added, "So I guess you came to your senses."

Rain pelted the ground between us so entrails of mud ran under the car's smoking engine. "I guess so."

Her tightened lips relaxed. "That's good. You can come with me to the Gate now. I'll anchor you. Maybe you'll meet Kazmira."

"Who?"

She rolled eyes that I noticed were lined with a color to match her hair. "*Me*. Kazmira. Kazie. James is Jamellian."

It took me a moment. Then another. They actually went by their *Ruhaven* names.

I shot a glance at Tye. "You're not…?"

"Tyrellius?" He wiggled his eyebrows. "Naw, hun, just Tye. Ya don't gotta change your name like these freaks."

Speaking of… "And Bryn?"

"To *you*," he said without even a glance to indicate the *'you'* part, "I am Bryn."

James hoisted the luggage with a grunt. "Why don't ye all make yerselves useful and help this freak with dinner? I'm bloody starving, like."

"I'm not much of a—" I broke off when Naruka's door groaned open, and another woman stepped out.

Tye dropped the bags he'd been unloading.

Polished crimson heels sidestepped the weeds and divots eating away Naruka's entrance. The woman wore stockings beneath a trim pencil skirt and a blazer in the same matching color of the shoes. Her brows were colored in with military precision. With her silver hair drawn into a tight bun, she looked like a Russian ballerina—poised, pretentious, her lips pressed to a smooth, bloody line.

I felt Tye behind me, his warm cinnamon scent smothering the sudden chill.

James stepped forward, bags in hand. "Auntie Carmen. I hope Kazie didn't drive ye too mad while I was away."

So this was the woman who'd recruited Tye.

Aunt, James had said, yet there wasn't a line on that stern, beautiful face that would have even hinted at fifty. Was that because she was Ruhaven? Was her Mark youth?

"Not at all," she said in a faint, British accent.

"Carmen looks after Naruka when I'm away," James explained after he'd kissed each of her pale, waxy cheeks.

Because they needed someone to anchor?

Carmen's lips pulled out and up, so the red line had two ticks at the end. "I only worry how you shall manage when I leave for the château in France next week. But I see, at least, that Norway was successful?"

James clapped Bryn on the shoulder as the Norwegian only stood there, staring at Carmen with a look that could have finished off the roses I held. A typical Bryn welcome, I assumed.

"Bryn's agreed to continue his research on the aneurysms." I held my breath, waiting for James to explain the rest—the Inquitate, the illusions—but he only said, "With some of our help, of course."

Carmen made a non-committal noise as she surveyed Bryn. "I only worry, like Maggie did, that you shall grow too close to the Gate again." So he'd known Maggie, James's mom.

The skies darkened behind him. "Of that, you need not worry."

Carmen's gaze flicked to me. "Indeed."

James said quickly, "Was there any trouble while we were gone?"

She looked back at him. "There was something. This imbecile came by on Saturday, asking about a— What was her name?—*Lana*, I think. Yes, Lana."

"Colm," James said sagely. "I've not been able to get rid of the lad after his girlfriend left." He spoke to me now. "She didn't much care for Ruhaven and took off."

"Well," Carmen continued briskly, "you should deal with him, lest he bring the Gardaí here and they wonder why there are so many foreigners."

"Speakin' of the foreign rabble." Tye gripped my shoulder. "This is Roe."

She extended a hand that looked as brittle as a Christmas wafer, but was strong and firm when she shook mine. "Rowan, of course. I was Tye's recruiter, as he is now yours."

She dropped my hand to greet Tye, and this time, the kiss lingered, her wine-red lips brushing the hard line of his jaw.

His *recruiter*. Had she shown him the Gate all those years ago like he did me? Just how deep did a connection go between recruiter and recruitee?

Tye took Carmen's elbow, tipped the hat he'd stolen back from me, and said, "Why don't we catch up before ya head on back to France?"

She patted his offered arm with crimson nails. "I would love that. James? Kazie? You do still have that Shiraz I left last time?"

James picked up our bags with an easy smile. "If I'd drunk it, ye can be sure I'd pretend otherwise."

The wind pressed against their backs as they followed the winding path to Naruka's entrance. Tye kept Carmen's arm in his, the worn jeans stretching over his muscled calves as he walked, his legs toned from years in the saddle—

In one deft movement, Bryn grabbed the roses from me and tossed them into the weeds.

"Hey!"

"They are *dead*, Rowan," he said when I protested. "Leave them be."

I fished them from the lawn, though most of the petals had been flung off by his throw. "Don't throw my things away," I said, swearing as a nettle pricked my wrist. "I'm going to help with the research, to find the overlap between Willow and the others, but that doesn't give you the right to—" I glanced over my shoulder. "Bryn?"

But he wasn't looking at me, wasn't even listening.

Mist wetting his pale cheeks, Bryn stared at the jutting cliff rising over the hotel. His eyes all but glowed, two visions of Neptune in a face as surreal as the Gate.

They swirled with emotion. Not tepid waters, but a churning sea of longing, guilt, and—and *hunger*.

I shivered at the blatant desire simmering in a face that had forgotten about me, about Naruka, about the decomposing roses.

He slid the satchel off his shoulder. The leather smacked into the mud at his feet, strap flopping into grass before raindrops beaded and ran in veiny rivers down its weathered surface.

Leaving the bag, Bryn took one step with the cane, then another.

Not toward the hotel but to the woods, where the trail was a faint patch of shadow on the edge of Naruka. The rain came harder, protesting at the choice, soaking his hair until it was closer to muddy blond than pale gold. Until it was glued to the pulsing vein in his neck.

The trail would be impossible with the loose stones and churned soil, the banks of the mountain slippery and unforgiving.

Impossible with a cane.

But he limped forward, never looking back, and didn't pause until he stood at the cusp of Naruka, where the winding trail led up the mountain and to Ruhaven.

Then he stopped, turned slowly.

Across Naruka's sprawling gardens, the weight of his gaze landed like a blow, a heat that zinged down my neck.

It was only an instant, then he looked away again.

I shall see you in the Gate, Rowan.

And started the climb.

CHAPTER 15

All You Never Say

C armen left the next day. I'd barely had a chance to speak with James's aunt before Tye was suddenly driving her to the airport. Did she not want to stay and watch the memories like him? When I asked, Tye said only that Carmen had known Ruhaven for long enough.

But with her gone, it was one less Ruhaven I'd have to lie to.

"Roe?"

At the Gate, James waited as I inhaled a last breath of dirt and worms, then joined him where he bent, unloading a knapsack. It'd be my first time seeing Ruhaven since I returned, and my stomach fluttered between nerves and sweet anticipation. Like a drug addict—was that what I'd eventually become? Someone like Bryn, who was so addicted, James had exiled him from Naruka.

"You're sure it's safe?" I asked. Safe for someone who wasn't in the *Ledger*? Maybe the last few times were a fluke.

"Aye, of course," James replied gamely, unraveling a wool blanket that had seen the turn of the century. "I'll only leave ye in for a few minutes or so, as ye need time to get used to the transition."

Sweat cooled in the small of my back. I was really going to do this, going to try to live Willow's life. "How long can *you* stay in?"

"Perhaps ninety minutes, though I try to keep meself to an hour." He patted his flat stomach. "Ye can get a bit nauseous if ye push it." He rifled through his knapsack before taking out a canister of tea, two wooden cups, and a banana. "For when ye wake," he explained, arranging them so well that any passerby—though there'd be none up here—would think we'd set out for a romantic picnic. "Ye need to keep yer blood sugar up, especially when ye eventually stay in longer."

"What am I looking for?" My toes brushed the edge of the blanket. "Bryn didn't explain what the Inquitate looked like." Hadn't said more than two words to me this last week, and those had been, "*coffee?*" and "*gate*".

"Ye won't be in long enough to see much of anything right now," James said, grabbing another blanket as I laid down. Blades of grass nipped at my calves. "But ye can start building up the ol' tolerance now."

"What about side effects?" I asked. "Should I stop eating meat?"

James kneeled beside me, one shoelace untied and dragging in mud. "It'll be a while yet before it comes to that." Above his head, a lantern swung on a creeping rope suspended between trees. Rusted hooks were screwed into two of them for the canopy James hung up when it rained.

"What about that *glimmer*, as you called it, that piece of Bryn's Mark I saw?"

James wiggled his fingers. "What, now yer worried ye'll get superpowers?"

It hadn't looked so much like a superpower as a curse. "I'm worried it'll change me."

Behind dew-soaked glasses, his eyes smoked to coal. "Of that, I've no doubt."

I exhaled a slow breath, willing my body to calm, to relax. "And what if—I don't know—something happens?" Like Ruhaven exorcising me from Willow's life.

"Ye can feel pain, love, and all the rest, but I'll be watching ye here. Yer body will react if there's anything amiss and I'll pull ye out," James repeated, then patted my hand. "Now, last thing. When we move between Naruka and the memories, there's a space ye'll enter we call the *Prayama*. 'Tis only temporary, but it looks a wee bit different for all of us. It's just a cushion yer mind makes for ye to accept what's to come. Mine looks like an auld kitchen, and sure I don't even know where it's from."

I think I'd already seen mine—that empty room with the trickling water.

So I folded one hand over my stomach and tried to relax, to let the Gate take me again, praying that if it did reject me, it wasn't too painful.

After five unsuccessful minutes, I was shaking, feeling every bumpy ridge, every washed-out divot beneath the blanket, every twig that'd blown into the clearing since the last storm.

Then I felt it.

A sharp yank on the inside of my ribs like hell had thrown a harpoon through the dirt.

I opened my eyes.

Except I didn't. Couldn't.

And then...

Then I started the fall.

⚙☀

I exhaled a slow breath.

It rose in a glittering cloud, like mist on a winter's day in L'Ardoise, except the tiny particles sparkled under Ruhaven's indigo light.

How my memory must have shivered at the intrusion, knowing I was just some thieving toad crouching in a mind that didn't belong to me, witnessing events I had no business seeing. My own skin all but crawled with the feeling.

I breathed out, in, and again felt that *wrongness* when my chest expanded to twice its normal capacity, tasting every fleck of jasmine floating in the honeyed air as though my lungs had tastebuds.

I was still in the wild forest. Still walking on the pearly dirt, the beads swelling between my toes. Still ducking massive foliage that seemed more mammal than plant, thick enough for its protruding veins to carry blood through furry stems.

If I'd been in my own body, my palms would have been sweaty, that old anxiety would squeeze my chest. But I felt none of that here, the mind and body entirely separate from each other.

Our skirt shifted around our legs as we walked, but her arms were longer—my fingertips brushing farther down my thighs than they should have. Even my touch felt different, the sensation of skin on skin softer than velvet.

I was her and she was me.

And right now, she was searching for something.

My clawed hand peeled back a slimy stem. Was she looking for food? I hadn't experienced her eating yet, and at this point, just hoped we had a mouth.

Something shot out of the bushes.

I jumped back as a foot-tall toothy sprite buzzed in front of me. No, not a sprite, a *creature,* like me, like the demon whose arm I'd seen before. Except besides the teeth, this one wasn't nearly as intimidating. Burgundy hair stood at all angles, like she'd been woken with the worst case of bed hair I'd ever seen. Massive bug eyes consumed half her face as she glared at me.

Ouch.

I grasped the cheek she flicked with her wing. We had a quick back and forth that started with me apologizing, and ended with my memory threatening to saw her wings from the sprite's body if the dagger I now held was any indication.

But eventually, she zoomed off, emitting a litany of snorts as she disappeared into the woods.

Weird. Absolutely, impossibly *weird*.

But she hadn't been what I'd been searching for.

We moved on, the long-haired trees replaced by lizard-looking ones with giant squid arms. No suction cups. Its skin was smooth and cool as a frog's belly when we pushed it aside and stepped under the shade of the tree.

She peered around a tentacle, tilted her head back, then squinted at something above.

Suddenly, our vision shot forward, propelled on an imaginary slingshot. We zoomed through the leaves, phosphorescent foliage a blur of color, eyes flickering over the tiniest speckle of dust. Our sight dove through a shimmering crack in the trees to find the gears turning slowly, mesmerizing in the atmosphere, but she dwelled on them as much as I bothered with clouds.

Searching for something else.

When her claws tightened on the tentacle, it jerked as if in pain. She murmured softly and our vocal cords *ping-pinged* like a harp in my throat. Apologizing? It *felt* like it. But the words were tinkering bells.

With a laugh—more bells—she tilted her head back, continued zooming through the trees.

There.

A shadow passed behind the glowing canopy of flowers and vines and mushrooms that made up the foliage. Something hunting us? Or were we hunting it?

My body throbbed with awareness, with an extra sense I couldn't identify that told her exactly who or what this was.

The same creature, I think, that we'd encountered before Oslo. The one with the tattooed arm that had grabbed her and flung us into the skies.

Her eyes tracked its movement, following the male to where the foliage thinned. The pulse at her throat hiccuped, then dived into a racing heartbeat that finally reached the tempo of a human's.

I caught a flash of feathers, then a glimmer of gold, and—

Something tugged on my wrists.

My vision blurred.

No, no, not *now*. Let me just see what was—

But James yanked again, harder, and my mind spun out of the memory, into the room with the emptiness and the trickling water.

James sat back, arms draped over his knees, a hangdog smile on his face. "Well? Wasn't so bad, right?"

It was better than I remembered, better than I'd dreamed. "I forgot how *real* it all is, but it seemed short?"

"I left ye in for seven minutes like we agreed. Any longer, ye'd be sick." James helped me up, then quickly rolled up the blanket he'd laid out and extinguished the candle. "When I first went in as a child, it took me a while to build up some stamina too. Funnily enough, I always thought I'd find what I saw in Ruhaven here, and when I couldn't, 'twas a bit like finding out Santa wasn't real." He stuffed his hands into his pockets with a sheepish expression.

And how I could picture him as that young boy for a heartbeat. "Can we live in the Gate?"

Dried leaves from last autumn crinkled under our feet. Wild foxgloves sprung up along a ruined fence, so bursts of deep violet added color to the green.

"Ye mean for days? Not really, only as long as it takes for us to need to eat, drink, and all the other necessities. It doesn't count for sleep either, as we're fully awake, even if our bodies are lying in the Gate. Ye want more tea?" he asked, offering me the canister.

"No, I'm fine, thanks."

"Sandwich? I've some packed in this bag."

I shook my head.

"Ah, I see I'm worse than me own mammy."

"James, you said before that each of us has a Mark, that yours is a spirit handler. "

"Aye, that's right. In Ruhaven, it's called a Kalista. We can bond with things." He plucked an ash leaf off the tree. "Like this."

I looked at the sodden leaf doubtfully. "You can bond with a *leaf*?"

He chuckled, low and deep. "Yera, could be anything really. If it was a leaf, I might fall in love with a tree."

"You're joking."

"Only a wee bit. I'd more likely have an affinity for sunlight, be able to photosynthesize, produce oxygen, and so on." He let it flutter into the muck. "But as Essie is me bonded spirit, and she's a female grown from a type of rock, I've a good ability to sense the mineral levels in soil. Even here, I find I've quite the green thumb."

"Grown," I repeated slowly, "from a type of *rock*."

"Sure, the spirit ye bond with may be a blade of grass, a memory, an animal, or a song! Though in me own case, because me mate is me spirit as well, I'd not be so happy if she was a tune."

No, no, I suppose not.

He clapped my shoulder. "Maybe 'tis too soon for all this. We'll have to see what yer own Mark is."

Curiosity burned a tiny hole in my gut. "Do you think it could be zooming vision? She can see really far away and—"

James laughed. "Ah, no, we can all do that so."

Oh.

I kicked back a thorny, twisting bramble from our path. I wouldn't mind being bonded to a blackberry bush. Maybe I'd always smell like blackberries if I did, or I'd have a scone recipe to rival James's.

"So Essie's your bonded spirit, something you only get because you're a Kalista Mark. But I thought you said she was your mate?"

"Aye, she's both for me, as it happens. That's not unusual for Kalistas, for the spirit ye bond with to be close, but I suppose I am glad she's a woman and not that leaf."

It was so ridiculous, I burst out laughing.

By the time we crossed the river and James tightened his grip on mine, I was well and truly committed to a bonding with blackberries as long as they didn't end up being my mate.

"So ye didn't see anyone else? Besides the sprite...?" James prompted.

When I shook my head, he looked almost disappointed.

"Is everything alright?" I asked, stepping into the tack room that led to the kitchen.

He patted my hand absently, and said, "I'm just glad ye decided to stay."

I was now at ten minutes. Ten. Whole. Minutes.

Not long enough to catch sight of more than a few tiny creatures, but long enough for Bryn to ask me about it. I had very little to tell him, and a part of me wondered if he just asked to make me confess how little I'd seen. Woods, a white lake, more forest. A butterfly humanoid-looking thing, a male with deer legs, with the latter more shocking until the butterfly had pulled back its gums and revealed rows of glittering teeth.

But with such a poor endurance in the Gate and no sign of my Mark yet, I had no lack of time for studying how the memories worked.

If it was the preservation of energy that allowed our souls to be reborn, then the process was scientific, not magical. Science—that I could deal with. Magic—less so.

If the Inquitate were sentient, then they'd come through the Gate like us. But they weren't Ruhaven, and Drachaut didn't make the crossing, and why was that? Weren't their souls preserved too?

Something to ask James.

If it was science, maybe they were a side effect of the crossing. Chemical reactions released energy—that was how combustion engines ran. Fuel was injected into a carburetor, the narrow passage forcing it through quickly, and then a spark ignited.

Pop. The piston fired.

What if there was something in our crossing that released a similar energy? What if it—

"Roe!"

A baseball slapped into my glove, inches from my nose.

"Damn, girl," Tye admonished. "You used to be able to catch. Ruhaven's got your head in the clouds."

Or in the gears that grew there. I scrubbed at my face, wincing at the salty sweat of the glove. I was terrible at baseball, but it was an excuse to be with Tye now that he spent most of his weekdays exercising the horses at a farm in town.

Lying on a blanket between Tye and I, James snored loudly in the Gate. But since Tye couldn't sit still when he anchored, and I was visiting the Gate after James, he'd asked me to throw the ball with him over the Irishman's unconscious body.

And my aim wasn't good.

"When do you think Bryn is going to find something I can use about the Inquitate?"

Tye arched a long brow. "Hun, that guy is catching up on two years out of Ruhaven. He ain't gonna be doing much else except visiting the Gate and rejoicing with all the females in there."

I nearly missed the ball again. Was *that* why he'd wanted to return so badly? To be with women in Ruhaven?

I threw the ball back with more force than necessary, the smack of it in Tye's glove echoing in the woods. "You don't know each other in the Gate, do you?" Like James and Kazie did.

Would I ever meet them? It'd be weird knowing they were witnessing everything my memory said and did.

"No, praise Jesus, I do not."

I nodded in understanding.

"You gonna throw that?" When I did, Tye dove and snagged it with an ice cream cone catch. "Ha!" Sweat glistened on his brow from the number of times he'd dived for my throw, his lungs puffing with exhilaration.

"Do Ruhavens breathe oxygen?" I asked. "It seems thicker."

"Dunno."

"Gravity?"

Tye drew his brows together, motioned for the ball. "Hun, I really am just a Montana farmer, so I ain't gonna be able to explain gravity and space memory travel to ya. What I do know is this..." He caught the ball. "We died. We crossed. We were reborn. Now we got these memories. It's that simple."

"But why us? Why not the people from the other country, Drachaut?"

"Not everyone makes this crossing when they die," he said simply.

"Why not?"

"'Cause they didn't drink the magic potion?"

I felt my lips twitch. But for the next twenty minutes, Tye let me ping him with questions, some that sounded intelligent only until they rolled off my tongue and he burst into laughter. Still, he made the whole thing easy, as if we were discussing farming techniques or horseback riding.

"Do you think we'll ever meet in Ruhaven?"

The wind picked up, tossing Tye's now-curly locks across his forehead. "Yeah, 'course we'll meet. How we gonna eventually make the crossing so close together and not meet? Could be years though."

"How will I recognize you? I mean, are you a man or a woman or...?"

Tye cocked a slow eyebrow. "Me? A woman? Honey, there ain't no life I ever lived that didn't bless me with what would make other men jealous and you blush." His dimple made an appearance when I did just that.

Whatever Tye looked like in the Gate, it couldn't be better than him here, with his dark eyelashes framing eyes greener than Ireland.

This time, I caught the ball with a hair's breadth to spare.

"So how does that work if—"

A sudden low moan cut me off. *James?*

Feet away, still asleep at the Gate with his arms and legs in an almost comical sprawl, he whimpered again.

Concerned, I tossed off the baseball glove, stepped toward him.

Sweat beaded on his temples as color blossomed up his neck and cheeks. He flinched, his fingers curling in on themselves as a sudden fear struck me.

"Tye, you've got to wake him," I said quickly, hurrying to James's side. His forehead was hot and sticky against the back of my hand, his breathing ragged.

"Huh? Why?" Tye replied, tossing the ball away.

The wind picked up, stirring dead leaves that gathered on the edges of the worn blanket. "He warned me about this," I explained as Tye strode over. "That if something happened in the Gate, he'd feel it here." I called his name, shaking him by the shoulders. How *did* you wake someone from the Gate? "Tye, please."

When Tye said nothing, I looked up to find an amused smirk curling his lips. "Oh, I'd say he's feeling it alright."

"Can you be serious for *once*?"

Laughter crinkled his emerald eyes now. "Darling—and I do so regret to say this—I am."

"You're..." Then I caught his meaning.

With deliberate slowness, I peeled my gaze from Tye, forced it back to James, looked down...

I dropped his hand and scrambled back so hard, I landed in a pile of stinging nettles.

Tye absolutely hooted with laughter.

I ran my hands down my face, massaging the image out of my eyeballs. Then tore them away again, wiping both vigorously on my thighs while Tye burst into a fresh round of cackling laughter. And still, it wasn't enough to wake James.

"I'm going," I muttered, rising to my feet. Ears burning, throat itchy, the hot embarrassment of it all had me sweating in the autumn chill.

"Hell no," Tye said, catching my arm. "You're goin' in the Gate when he's done."

James punctuated Tye's words with a breathy moan.

I tried to yank loose, but he held on. "Just—just wake him early. *Please*."

"What, right at the good part?" Tye released me to swing his arms at James in a gesture of male solidarity. "You got any idea how long he's probably waited for—"

A long, low groan thundered through the clearing, burning my cheeks to cinders.

"I'm. Begging. You."

Tye patted an invisible laundry pile. "Alright, alright, but only 'cause you're such a prude. Though I'll warn ya, he ain't gonna be happy."

Crouching, Tye bent and braced a hand on James's shoulder.

I inched closer, careful to keep Tye blocking the worst of it from view. Was he grasping his hand? For a moment, there was no movement at all, no moans, no breathy gasps, not even bird calls. Then Tye spoke quietly, calmly, and James's left leg kicked out. His right hand bunched into a fist and released as he—

"What the bleedin' hell are ye trying to do to me!" James swore, scattering crows. "Do ye not feckin' see I'm a *wee* bit busy in here? And yet here ye are, yanking me away from me mate."

Both heads turned in my direction—Tye's amused, James's in comical frustration.

"Sorry, James," I muttered, stuffing my hands in my pockets, and maybe I did feel a little guilty. "It's weird."

He patted his cheeks. "Yer the absolute devil woman, ye know that? I've a mind to wait until yer in the throes yerself and rip ye out at the bloody peak."

My cheeks burned another degree. That wasn't possible, was it? Surely, nothing I'd encountered so far could even be capable of sex. I pictured the walking mushroom with antennas and shuddered.

Tye winked at me. "Don't worry, I'll leave ya in like a gentleman."

"Please don't."

James exhaled a long sigh before getting up *with* the blanket over him—thank god—and stumbling to a knapsack. He gulped back whiskey like his life depended on it, then said, "Tye, ye can head back now. There's some leftovers in the fridge."

Just the thought of food had Tye perking up, then he frowned. "It ain't the casserole, is it?"

"No one made you eat it," I retorted, a bit put out.

He grinned at me. "Well then, if you ain't gonna be puttin' on such an entertaining performance as James, I'm gonna find my way back home." He tapped his cap, then sauntered off with a whistle.

I watched him go, the jeans pulling tight over the backs of his thighs—

"Ye ready, Roe?"

I bit my bottom lip as I caught the flicker of amusement on James's face, and something else too.

He pointed to the rumpled blanket he'd been lying on. "I've not got cooties. Just lay down."

Probably true. Still, it felt weird.

"And I'll be hoping ye stumble upon a little fun yerself so I can repay ye."

My horror must have shown because James rolled his eyes. "Ye've nothing to worry about yet." And just how would he know?

"You don't know me in Ruhaven, do you?" I asked warily, kneeling on the blanket, still warm from where he'd lain.

He scratched at his temple. "I don't know. Ye've not told me enough of yer memories to know who or what ye are."

I slipped off my boots—I could never get comfortable with them on—and wiggled my sock feet in the crisp air. "James, when we returned after Norway, and you went in the house, I saw Bryn start into the woods, toward the Gate." Burning blue eyes, face a mask of simmering restraint, the heat that punched through me.

"Yeah, and what about it?" James asked, unwrapping a sandwich from a cheesecloth.

"Well, I thought you said everyone needed an anchor. But Bryn didn't have anyone with him when he left for the Gate. So how does he wake from the memories?"

James pursed his lips, all signs of his earlier annoyance vanishing in the first bite of his cheese and onion sandwich. "Ah, 'tis true what I told ye—don't ye *ever* come here without an anchor—but Bryn's always been an exception. He's a connection to the Gate that even me mum didn't understand, and there wasn't much she didn't know."

Yes—Bryn the golden child, the PhD, and I couldn't wait to see him walk on water too.

CHAPTER 16

Painters

September came and went, and though Bryn never walked on water, I did learn other things about him.

He took his coffee black, his lunch to go, and spent a majority of his time either in the Gate or the library.

He dressed in the same outfit every day—a long-sleeved collared shirt, trousers, and Oxford shoes—unless he was visiting the Gate—then he switched them for brushed leather boots. I never once saw Bryn in a T-shirt, even when the kitchen was stuffy with thick heat from the woodstove and I had to open the adjoining tack room door. Never jeans, and certainly never, ever shorts.

On Fridays, he joined us for our weekly trip to the market, loading an easel and a box of paints into the back of the Ford. He never stayed with us or bought a single thing, instead choosing to disappear with his paints for hours at a time.

Last Monday, during one of those trips to Capolinn, I'd shaken Kazie off in search for Bryn. After twenty minutes of striding up and down the narrow cobblestone streets and slippery stone stairs, I'd found him standing by the mouth of the port, the sunrise coating his hair in burnt golds, painting some of the worst boats I'd ever seen.

Rowan, he'd said, lips tightening in that vague disapproval, *you should not be alone with the Inquitate about.*

So I'd sat on the port wall watching him finish the painting, and experienced an almost euphoric rush of knowing he was this bad at something.

But like me, he wrote no letters, made no calls. It was as if he existed only in the Gate.

Meanwhile, I couldn't manage more than twelve minutes. And when you included the five it took to transition through the Prayama, then the time to get adjusted, it meant I barely saw anything.

Especially because I was never in control.

But it was almost better that way. I didn't need to think or worry, didn't need to feel that hollow emptiness of missing Willow. Didn't need to battle the constant worry the Gate would recognize me for the fraud I was.

But each time I slipped through, it never protested, only showed me that empty room before I transitioned into the world, like now, when the memories opened to a white swamp.

It sprawled in all directions, flowing around freckled lavender trees and floating squid plants. Sparkles played off the surface, bubbles burst with creamy liquid, and all of it—from the leaves, to the milk, to the beach—reflected our star's purple light.

I waited on the shoreline, toes curling in sand softer than a spilled bag of flour, while a crisp breeze tickled ears that ended at the wrong length.

She scanned the waters, searching with eyes that zoomed like an eagle's might soar above the lakes of L'Ardoise, picking out the slightest ripple of fish in water. Except the water here was an opaque, creamy white and tasted like burnt honey.

Bubbles the size of my fist pushed at the surface, bursting through, the milk dripping off their glowing spheres as they floated up, up, up.

Across the swamp, something flickered.

My eyes—her eyes—latched on to it, zooming with that impossible speed that wasn't my Mark, but felt like a superpower anyway.

Then she stopped, her gaze landing on a creature I'd never seen.

Wild awareness flooded my senses—mine? Hers? I *should* have been terrified.

The male's eyes were two enormous eight balls in a skull with translucent skin. Coal-black bones shimmered through it like stars at night, revealing a skull fused in the wrong places.

I recoiled when it grinned in a two-step process, lips peeling up and back, teeth retreating inwards.

A smile. Had to be.

As it stood, white liquid dripped off a body as long and angular as the face, with skin the color of squashed blueberries. A sopping cloth draped over narrow hips, ending at corded thighs showing yet more bone. Hair as black as its bones sprouted in a thick rope from its skull. Coarse and strong enough to grab hold of and swing on.

Behind him, another followed in his shadow.

She was—kind of beautiful. With marbled skin carved from a bucket of pink and black paint swirled together, like the tiger tail ice cream Willow had loved. Creamy and soft, it wasn't translucent like the male's, and her face was rounder, almost a complete circle that gave her childlike cheeks and a bubble nose with four nostrils.

I itched to reach up and check my own nose.

With the same weird smile on his face, the male extended a four-jointed hand toward her. Their fingers linked, locked. He brushed back her sphere of curls, murmured in a round ear that elicited a quick giggle from her white lips, the sound like jumping crickets, and twin dimples popped into her rosy cheeks.

Then the male spoke—or was it singing?

A series of notes pitched up and down at different intervals—somehow, impossibly, more than what could fit in a single octave. She answered in the same musical anomaly, so rhythmical, I wanted to sway to the beat of it. A sound that no instrument could ever capture.

So I listened, to the words, to the music, marveling at all the hidden notes, and when the call home finally came, I was as reluctant to leave as before. Each anchor felt different when they pulled me back. Kazie was like a sprinkle of fairy dust. Tye, a lasso around the waist.

But this, a warm and familiar hand grasping mine, was undoubtedly James.

"James, I saw another one, big this time," I gasped as soon as the world stopped spinning.

"Easy now," he murmured, face wavering in and out of focus. A lock of mist-dampened hair curled into his eyebrow. "Breathe."

"He had these arms that were— And these eyes that—"

"*Breathe*," James repeated, firmer. "Ye can tell me all about it, just get a breath now, and ye need to drink something, eat. Yer blood sugar's low."

Under the low glow of dawn, I tilted my head back, letting the soft mist of rain dampen my skin under a creamsicle sky. I smiled, still hearing the musical speech and wondering if it was their Mark.

"Well, I'm glad ye liked it, so I am," James said when I lowered my chin at last. Under the hood of his rain jacket, honey-brown eyes took my measure.

I worked the smile from my cheeks. "How long this time?"

James shoved back the sleeve of his jacket. "About thirteen minutes."

I took a bite of the apple he handed me. "Rounding up?"

He bit his bottom lip. "Might be, but yer doing well. And here I thought ye didn't want to be in the Gate?" James teased.

I rolled the fruit in my hands. It wasn't that I didn't want to be in the Gate, but that the Gate didn't want me. "If I'm going to figure out why Willow was targeted, I need to be in longer."

"Ah, but yer exhausted." His two friendly slaps on my back sent me lurching toward the hawthorn tree. "Ye see? Ye need to build endurance."

I stood, stabbing my feet back into my boots. "And what if I can't?" What if the reason I was struggling was because I wasn't meant to make this trip?

James rose with me. "Roe, of course ye can. It takes time. Everyone goes through this period. Kazie did, Tye did, and now ye are as well." We started down the steps toward Naruka, with James asking me what happened.

I explained the white swamp, then the creatures I'd seen, the translucent skin pulled over black bones and elongated ears like the sketches I'd once seen in Bryn's room.

We shifted to single file over a mucky path that muffled our footsteps. Rocks wore the moss as olive-green wigs, and the way the bare branches caught the evening light made them look like lightning rods in the woods.

But the more I rambled, the slower James walked, and his face seemed to lose color with each step.

"James? What is it? What's wrong?" Were they dangerous? Wait. "Are they *Inquitate*?"

He stopped, ground the heels of his hands into his eyes. His shoulders lifted on an inhale and shook on his exhale, looking ready to collapse.

I reached out a hand for him, didn't know where to touch, and ended up patting his back awkwardly. "What is it?" I asked again.

He pulled his hands from his face, and his bloodshot eyes blinked rapidly.

Fear rippled down my spine. I grabbed his elbows firmly. "James, tell me what it is. Are you in trouble? Is it the Gate? Is it—"

But he yanked his arms from my grasp and swung away.

"James!"

He shoved a branch out of his way, choked on a sobbing curse, then broke into a run, backpack bobbing through the trees that swallowed him.

My mind went entirely blank.

Never had James been anything but steady. He'd watched me drive off with his own car after Tye showed me the Gate, with nothing more than a smirk and a few Irish idioms. He'd carried tea and fresh scones to my room every morning after. He'd listened to my raging disbelief of the Gate with patience. And when he told me of the disease, that Bryn might have the answers, he'd accompanied me to Oslo to help me get them.

"James!"

I sprinted after him.

Cold fear crept into my blood—for him, for me, for the Inquitate that Bryn had warned might still be following us.

I dove after him. It was like the first time I'd run from Tye, shoving through brambles and brush, except I knew my way now. Knew how the ground dipped and swerved, the loose stones on the makeshift steps that I'd once tripped over.

James was fast—freakishly fast—his slim form slipping through trees like quiet butter, making my subsequent stampede almost offensive. His wool jacket became smaller and smaller, the leaves eating it up, the sound of snapping branches growing distant.

What had I told him that would cause this? We'd spoken about different creatures before. Did he think they were Inquitate? If so, why run away from *me*?

The trees quivered as a gust of wind tore through thin branches, stirring up pine cones and growling pained yelps.

And there, by the bank of the river, with his hands in his pockets and the ferns brushing his thighs, stood James.

The water rushed in front of him, curling into foamy rapids that gathered like the spittle of a hungry beast. His eyes seemed to glow in his face, either from the rain or the Irish air, but they felt like night come to life. Like the space between a million tiny stars.

I slowed my pace, breathing ragged, and stalked through the brush for him. A twist of thorns snagged my sweater, forcing me to yank a few stitches out to free it.

James turned at the sound.

His nostrils flared in a face pale but for the reddened eyes. He squeezed them shut, opened them. "I've no right to feel like this," he said quietly, curling his hand into a fist and banging it on his thigh. "I've no *right*, Roe."

"No right to what?" Worry gripped me as I stood helpless in the mucky trail, watching the spray of the river soak James's boots, watching him shiver in his shiny rain jacket. "Is there something wrong with what I saw?"

His face caved in. "Aye, in a way."

Mud squished around my boots as I stepped toward him, my fingertips brushing the wet tips of wild greens.

He murmured something the rapids ate up, then said louder, "Roe, yer a *Kalista*. That's yer Mark."

I slowed, stopped. A Kalista? I was *his* Mark? My heart started to speed up. "Is it bad to share a Mark?"

He glanced down the river, where the light eked through the thinning leaves. "No. No, 'tis not bad."

Then what put that *look* on his face? Like he'd seen death.

If I was a Kalista, then I'd be bonded to something too. "Is my spirit something bad?"

He tried on a smile that was more a wet grimace. "No, as it is, ye aren't bonded to anything. Ye haven't gone through the rite yet. It's what ye need to do to activate yer Mark. A test ye need to pass."

I frowned as something occurred to me. He *knew* me in the Gate, or knew the woman I was. That's how he knew I wasn't bonded to a spirit, didn't have any ability, wouldn't be able to fly, wouldn't have a leaf or blackberry bush.

Didn't matter.

"James, I'm sorry, I don't understand what's—"

"*Rowan*."

I yelped, the sudden musical voice causing me to snag my foot on a log. I hopped, stumbled, then flailed my arms like a crane about to soar over the river. *Oh, Jesus.* I was going to slip right in. *You can swim, you can swim, there's nothing below, it's just—*

An arm snagged my waist, yanked me back.

I slapped into something hard before my knees hit the ground and mud oozed between my fingers.

Light? No, he was definitely a ghost.

But there Bryn stood, hovering over me, cool rain unable to loosen his stiff shirt, his trousers—nothing that nice could be called pants— ironed and perfectly clean amongst the blooming forest. He opened the top button of his collar, revealing the hollow of his long, pale throat. His cane gleamed in the rain.

I ignored his offered hand and lurched to my feet.

His eyes left mine to find James. "You were not to leave her alone," Bryn stated.

James scrubbed at his face. "I wasn't thinking."

"No, don't apologize," I said quickly.

He turned to Bryn. "Ye were right."

"What's wrong with James?" I asked Bryn, because he knew everything about the Gate. "Did I break a law? Is there something bad about a Kalista without a spirit yet?"

His mouth tightened into a pale line, but any sign of the cold fury I'd witnessed in Oslo had been carefully locked away since we returned. "It is not what you are, but who you are *not*."

Willow. I wasn't Willow.

And James had figured it out. Had figured out I'd been lying to him from the beginning, posing as this—this *thing*.

I took a breath, my chest heaving. "I—I—James, I'm sorry if—"

"*Stop*." James's voice echoed through the woods, silencing me. He pinched the bridge of his nose before releasing a weary sigh. "Bloody hell. I've no business being like this, no business at all." He motioned to pass Bryn, who stood blocking the path.

After a brief hesitation, Bryn stepped out of the way.

I braced myself.

James lifted his gaze, met mine, and opened his arms. "God, come here, Roe. I'm sorry. I'm…'twas just a shock. I've had a shock. I'm not meself. I just…"

I walked toward him in a daze, then my arms were around his waist, hugging his slim, shaking body to me. He smelled like my mom's kitchen—cinnamon, honey, warmth, comfort. I squeezed my eyes shut, my pulse pounding against my ribcage. "How did you figure it out?" I whispered.

"When ye told me who ye saw, I…" James trailed off, squeezing me so hard my lungs shrank a size. I sucked for air just as Bryn took a step toward us. "I recognized who ye were looking at. It told me who ye were in the Gate."

I stiffened. "What?"

Then James said, "Yer name's Nereida."

My mind went blank. Nereida?

Bryn laid a hand on James's shoulder, pulling him slightly away, and my ribs relaxed again. "James has always known who you are. Though he has not wanted to accept it."

James held me at arm's length, eyes red-rimmed and watery. A smile wavered on his lips. "Roe," he said, "you're Nereida. And I'm—I'm yer brother."

"My—my *brother*?" I repeated numbly.

James wiped away freshly brimming tears. "Aye, your brother. 'Tis me ye described in the memory. And Essie," he added on a hiccup. "But I'm—I'm so glad 'tis yerself, Roe. So glad yer here."

This couldn't be happening. God, this couldn't be happening.

"You think I'm you're—you're—"

"Sister, aye." He squeezed me to him, his warm body offering comfort to a lie. Over his shoulder, Bryn watched me knowingly, as if he was waiting for me to confess.

I should. I should tell James right now before this got any worse.

I squeezed my eyes shut, knowing I couldn't handle that rejection. It was wrong, so wrong to use this connection, to use his own belief to keep him here with me, but I couldn't let go.

Not yet.

CHAPTER 17

Between Me & You

T he translucent-skinned, black-boned creature had been James, and the bubble-faced female his mate, Essie.

And he was my brother.

James tried to explain it to me—siblings in Ruhaven—how they worked, what they were, but I couldn't hear him over the buzzing in my ears. Couldn't handle the watering sincerity and belief and hope ringing in his eyes that made my gut want to eat itself alive.

It was one thing to lie to myself, to live the memories of a woman who couldn't possibly be me. Stealing her life, pretending it'd been mine, posing as this memory. My thievery was never supposed to affect James.

But now?

For James to look at me as he did, to call me *sister*? To be so convinced that the woman he'd known—Nereida, that's what he'd called her, what he'd called me—was finally returned to him.

I wanted to claw my own skin off.

"Roe, watch out!"

Breath left me on a *whoosh* as Simona, Naruka's unwieldy cow, bowled me into a mound of hot mud—maybe dung—then warmed my face with a sour exhale.

Yeah, this was about what I deserved.

"C'mon, Roe, get up!" Kazie shouted, launching herself at Simona's broad neck, but with a bony shrug, the beast bumped Kazie off again, splattering her feet away from my disgrace.

She laughed at my expression. "It's not that bad."

"I think you have dung on your chin." Not to mention on her pink overalls where a previously glittering unicorn was pinned to the breast pocket.

She wrinkled her nose, wiped it with a ruined sleeve, then shrugged. "So, how's your research on the Inquitate going?"

"Not good. I'm starting to worry about Bryn," I said, hunting for a branch while Kaz tossed another rope over Simona's neck, "it's been a month and he still hasn't given me any details about the other deaths."

She lifted her hand to slap Simona. "He's working on it, Roe—oh dear Lord!" she exclaimed, barely missing bringing her palm down on diarrhea. "I hate this cow."

In that, at least, we were in complete agreement. "You don't think Bryn should have something by now?"

"What do ya think he's doing in his room after the Gate?"

"Recovering?" I hazarded. "He visits Ruhaven for *six hours* every day." *Six hours in Ruhaven.* I could only imagine what I'd be able to see in that time.

She *tsk*-ed me as I located a branch at last. "It's totally fine," Kazie insisted, mistaking my envy for annoyance. "What'd you get up to yesterday?"

"Rode an eight-legged llama through the woods."

She goggled.

"I know," I said, "it was a little ridi—"

"*You rode a Dinkleamu?*"

Now it was my turn to goggle. "A *Dinkleamu*?" I laughed. "You're messing with me." With that, I lifted the stick, brought it down on Simona's backside. The cow belched. Moaned. Bayed. But at last, she trodded onward, farting the entire way to the barn while Kazie quizzed me on *Dimkleamus*.

The gray sky dimmed to faded black when we clomped under the tin roof, the sweet vegetable scent of hoof oil replacing the wormy damp outside.

I yanked on the pull cord of the nearest stall's light bulb. Warmth flowed over the fresh hay piled high for a cow who definitely didn't deserve it or the waiting oats. But I led her in, fastened the rope to the hook, and prepared to hunt up a clean bucket for Kazie to milk her.

"So, think you'll find a spirit soon?" Kazie asked, watching me. "Since you're a Kalista."

"James says I don't get one until I complete some rite. I guess my Mark doesn't really mean anything until I find one."

"Yeah, it's the same for all Marks to activate. You haven't seen me yet, though, have you? I see Nereida now and then."

I shook my head. "Horns, is that what I'm looking out for?"

"And dark skin, yup." Then her eyes softened. "Heard James told you he's your brother."

A sinking feeling started up again in the pit of my gut. "Yeah. I'm not—I'm not something to you, too, am I?" I hadn't even considered it and I should have. Another sister, maybe a *mother* for all I knew, but—

"Naw, you're just a friend." That was a small mercy. "You don't seem, like, all that excited about the brother situation, though."

I hated that it was so obvious. Especially when, under normal circumstances, I'd be happy to have James as a brother. "No, I am. I mean, I'm grateful to James, and he's—" *The kindest man I'd ever met,* "—real nice. I don't want to—*Ah!*"

My heart tripped over itself at the sight of *him*.

Tall and lean, Bryn stood next to the saddle rack, cane tucked under one arm, a leather satchel on his shoulder.

In the unforgiving light of the barn, with dung covering my jeans, I couldn't look much better than the cow. Bryn, on the other hand, looked like he'd escaped a Norwegian fashion magazine on the season of beige.

"Hello, Rowan," he said smoothly.

As I frowned, Kazie hurried from the stall with a muttered, "See ya in the Gate later!"

"Wait, Kazie, what about—" But the barn door swung shut behind her. "Simona," I finished lamely.

Bryn unlatched the stall, limped in.

With the end of his cane, he nudged away the stick I'd swatted her with, and in a low voice, clucked at Simona, using soft noises that had her tail swaying. She flicked bored, cataract eyes at him before returning to munching hay.

"Sometimes, Rowan, a softer touch will do better." He took the bucket I'd found, then lowered onto an upturned crate beside the cow and tapped Simona's belly with the flat of his palm.

I gripped the top of the stall. "Are you enjoying Ruhaven now that you're back?"

"*Enjoying?*" He seemed to taste the word. "That is not how I would describe it."

"So you haven't encountered any Inquitate in the Gate?"

"Surely, Rowan, I would tell you if I had."

You'd think, but it'd taken for me to be targeted in Oslo for him to tell James the truth. "What about the list of other deaths?"

"I have been compiling my research, as I said to you last week."

Milk began to trickle into the bucket. "But it's been nearly a month."

He started to roll his sleeves up, stopped. "I assume you wish me to be thorough? If not, I would have delivered you my summary on the very first day."

I picked up the shovel, stabbed it into the steaming pile Simona had left. "And I suppose the delay has nothing to do with the fairy women you're with?" I asked, impatience getting the better of me.

His eyebrow cocked up. "Has visiting the Gate been so torturous to you? James tells me you have been *enjoying* the memories."

Of course I was, and that was exactly the problem. Because I wanted it so much I was already willing to pretend to be James's sister. Was willing to use his affection, his trust, and his own belief, to find a reason for Willow's death— Or was it just for me?

I dumped the shovel's contents shakily into the bin. "Is that what you wanted? For me to enjoy it?"

"It is what I expected," Bryn said, keeping his head down, silky hair brushing Simona's coral-pink belly.

"Why?" I asked quietly. "Why are you doing this to me?" Was it some kind of punishment?

His hands stilled, and when he lifted his head, those crystal-blue eyes clouded. "To you, Rowan?"

"You know what I mean."

"No, in fact, I am entirely at a loss." He rose slowly, coming toward me as I stood, nearly shaking, outside the stall. He curled one hand over the top, his jaw tight. "I do not know what it is you believe I am doing to you, nor do I know why I am being labeled a roving fairy lover in Ruhaven. Is this what you think of me?"

"It's what Tye said."

"It is obviously ridiculous." The left side of his mouth lifted. "There are no fairies in Ruhaven."

Maybe Tye had simplified. "You said you'd help me if I went into the Gate," I reminded him, gathering my dignity and starting toward the exit. "You broke your promise."

His eyes lit, then died. "Rowan, wait."

"I'm going to fix the washing machine."

"You fixed it yesterday."

"The fuse box then." *After the crime you committed on it.*

"*Rowan.*" His voice was a growl of impatience.

I felt my shoulders hunch, already giving in before I turned and walked back to him.

He shifted, bending down so his head briefly dipped below the stall. When he rose, he reached over the door and dropped a thick notebook into my baffled hands. "Here."

The cover was battered leather, old and ancient, with cracks forming like a farmer's sun-aged skin. Probably some book on the different types of Ruhaven fauna.

With a frown, I peeled it open. It gave with barely a sound, the leather tired and worn and well-used, but I recognized his writing immediately—a garden of curving letters that bloomed on every page. Names, places, detailed notes, a history of each Ruhaven's life, where they'd lived, who they'd known, their friends and family, there was even a genealogy chart for a few of them. Each death was listed in precise detail. Time, medical notes taped to the page, the person who'd found them, letters written and signed in James's loose scrawl.

Leather bookmarks divided the notebook by decades of deaths, with the most recent being...*Willow*.

My throat closed when I saw the photo he'd taped to her page. She sat at the piano, hands raised, a grin curving her lips as she stared at the photographer—at me. Here was her life, written in delicate handwriting from the school we'd attended, to the college I'd dropped out of, to the awards she'd graduated with. All of it listed with such careful dedication, I could only hope someone would remember me with the same detail.

"As I said, Rowan," Bryn murmured, and I flinched, half-forgetting he was there. "Sometimes, a softer touch is preferred."

I spent the next week poring over Bryn's notes, and if I felt some guilt for accusing him of taking his time, I pushed that aside, shoved it into the place where I kept the guilt over James, Ruhaven, and Willow.

Since meeting James in the Gate, I'd yet to meet an Inquitate, but I had seen two other creatures—one with three legs, the third used as a rudder, and a mermaid in the milk swamp, except its face was two feet long and only an inch wide, like it'd been pressed through a crevice in a rock and what was left emerged as this creature.

But Nereida didn't speak to either, and only passed them with a pulse of energy that served as a Ruhaven greeting. She was still searching for something, or someone, but her thoughts were as confusing as the world.

If the answers were in the Gate, it could be years before I met an Inquitate. I had a much better chance of finding some connection between Willow and them here.

Which was why I was sitting in the library now, pouring over writing nicer than my mother's Christmas cards. Bryn had spared no detail, having included every possible connection to an Inquitate, even if they were missing but not dead. He must have read through countless journals between visits to the Gate.

Guilt pecked me right in the temple. I flicked it away and picked up where I'd left off with his notes on Ben.

17 November 1961—Ben Einhart, New York, USA. Found dead outside a bodega. Collapsed at thirty-two due to an aneurysm.

His parents were listed below, their birthdates, and where they were born. A copy of the medical report was included as well. No wonder this took a month.

But I needed a general sense of each of the most recent deaths before diving in too deeply, so I flipped to the next page, then the next, until a milky sun glided through the library window, highlighting the history of Patrick Dubois.

In 1981, Patrick worked as a tradesman in the port of Marseille. He maintained a residence on Rue de Saint-Jean and wrote regularly to Naruka. He was recruited the same year, and stayed at Naruka between 1981 and 1987, but in 1987, with the Fall only months away, he returned to his home in Marseille.

That same year, Patrick was found dead by the Gendarmerie Nationale at the Calanques de Marseille, a cliff hiking spot. Later, James discovered he had died from a brain bleed. His next of kin, an ex-wife, was informed but was unaware of his ties to Naruka. When Patrick did not return our letters, James traveled to Marseille to visit him.

The inky writing, almost musical, ended on a smudge. I could hear Bryn in the words, the soft yet formal lilt of his voice that was hard to shake.

Willow had visited Paris once on a school music trip. What if they'd interacted in France? Maybe something could transfer between Ruhavens. After all, something *had* transferred from Willow to me if I could live her memories.

I moved to the next person.

Levi Lopez. Missing since 1986. Last known address 140291 Calle Ignacio, Oaxaca, Mexico.

Bryn had added a note to his list: *We presume Levi may be another victim of the Inquitate, but with no secondary contact for him, we were unable to determine.*

So he might have gone home and lost contact, or he might have been attacked as well. But he wasn't visiting the Gate anymore, so what did the Inquitate care if he was living out his human life here?

Maybe, for the same reason they'd cared about Willow. Which begged the question—what could her past life have possibly done to warrant an execution here?

I took out the notepad, scribbled a few ideas on my page.

Levi—why did he leave Naruka? When did they lose contact?

Patrick—how far is Marseille from Paris?

The Fall—what is this? What does it mean to be months away?

James called us to dinner at five by banging the cowbell he should have kept on Simona. Bryn didn't join, and Tye was busy working on the farm next door, so it was James, Kazie, and I who scooped up his vegetarian soup, a ginger-carrot combination that wasn't bad.

How long did I have before I couldn't eat meat either?

"James," I said, pulling out my notebook. "How far is Marseille from Paris?"

He sipped a French wine. "I thought I told ye no Inquitate at the table."

"It's geography," I corrected.

"Five hours," Kazie answered, then prodded James with her fork. "Stop being such a stickler. So, Roe, it looks like Bryn finished that research after all."

I stabbed a cherry tomato, nodded into my soup.

"Well, that's good, because we're all going to the Gate tonight—Bryn too," she proclaimed. "You'll come, won't you, Roe?"

"Actually, I wanted to go over these notes and—"

James wagged a finger at me. "Ah no, yerself and Bryn aren't to be alone after the attack. Ye'll have to come with us." Last week, Bryn had filled Kazie in when she'd caught him pulling old journals in the library. Luckily for Bryn, Tye was busy most days helping a farmer down the road, and too tired to take much note of what he was up to.

⚙ ☀

My memory—*Nereida*—was combing her fingers through strands of silver jelly hair when I opened my eyes.

I'd never get used to this. The world—no, the *planet*—and its heavy scent of blooming vanilla-jasmine, or the way she slurped in the air like water.

Nereida. I was in Nereida's body, but wouldn't some part of her know I was here—listening, watching, feeling all that had happened some eight hundred years ago?

Maybe. Or maybe it was just a movie, an echo, and no more intimate than plopping down at a cinema and expecting the movie to care that you were there.

But if that were true, then how could Bryn embody that glimmer I'd seen? Surely, there must be some connection between then and now. Whatever that was might be responsible for the Inquitate.

I waited for my eyes to adjust, for the fog to clear, and when it did— *Holy god.*

If it could, my head would have rotated on a pivot and never stopped. As it was, I fought to rein in my wildly beating thoughts, because trying to force Nereida to look, to *stare,* to soak in every shiny scale of the twenty or thirty creatures milling around us strained something inside me.

The scales, the feathers, the sizes! The necks that curled and twisted, the dinosaur spikes growing from the ridges of their spines, the plants that grew out of their *ears.* They walked and hummed and sang and danced and trailed and traced and even *flew.*

And it was strange to be amongst them. Trapped, almost, in a body that couldn't respond with the hiccuping surprise and exhilaration I should have felt, that was instead constrained to a memory whose pulse beat like a lumbering bear settling into hibernation.

So I absorbed what I could, storing it away in case I woke up and never saw this again.

Look at that guy! *Nereida, turn your head, just a little…*ah! She craned her neck so far back, we ended up staring at the massive jaw of a giant. He scratched at a beard that was the size and color of a grizzly bear, then bent low enough to speak to a woman with two deer legs and curling horns. His breath sent her mane blowing back over her freckled shoulders. Then Nereida proceeded onward, passing a scaled man a few feet shorter with a round belly, and then—*James.*

He and Essie stood at the edge of a cliff. He drew back a bow with four-jointed fingers—that had to be handy. She giggled at him, her smile taking up half her face, but it was endearing rather than creepy.

Puffing out his purple chest, James let the arrow fly.

She lifted her hand, and with a flick of a finger, shifted the rock he'd been aiming for. It skirted to the left before the arrow *thudded* into it.

Rock spirit, indeed.

But we moved on, Nereida's gait more glide than walk as she browsed the myriad stalls. Eventually, she selected one owned by a female with a mushroom growing on her head.

I tried not to stare, then realized it didn't matter.

The roots of the mushroom grew from her skull, curling over the side of her jaw and down her long, long neck. Blue blood pulsed in the stem before it disappeared under an extravagant gown. The top was a laced vest pulled snugly over a chest that bloomed with thorns. Intricate lace decorated every seam and stitch. It all ended at feet that—*Jesus Christ*—grew into the ground.

I looked down when the fungus woman held out her hand. In her thorny palm, she cradled a patch of spotted weeds, soft as a hatched chicken. "Daringa!" the woman shouted at me, grinning a row of thorns.

Daringa? What was that word again? James had been practicing with me in the kitchen. It was...*eat*! Ah, that was it. It'd be great to tell James I could translate my first—

Wait? Eat *what*?

Oh, no.

I groaned inwardly, but couldn't stop Nereida's clawed fingers from lifting the offering to our mouth. She bit into the soft moss and squishy bits as I tried to spit out the vile taste of mushrooms. *Bad, Nereida, very, very bad.*

But she swallowed every shimmering weed, and seemed to enjoy it so much that she started browsing more of the fungus woman's wares, including an assortment of petals, rocks, and chunks of bark to sample—each more intimidating than the last.

What about that candy bowling ball I'd eaten weeks ago, did she have any of those? They weren't so bad compared to the—

Oh. God.

Sudden, bone-splitting pain thundered through my body. Then Nereida screamed. No, no—*I* screamed.

Because something was breaking *inside* me.

I couldn't see what attacked us as I fell, only the indigo sky swirling above like a demented painting.

A male with tangled hair swam into my blurred vision, desperate eyes searching my face as he fluttered skeleton fingers over my forehead, a moth bouncing around the light. Nereida tried to speak, but the sound died on the liquid bubbling from our lips.

Then he came into focus. Jamellian. *James.*

Could he lift me out? *Please, James, pull me home.* I tried to feel his hand in mine, the easy comfort that always dragged me out of this world, but my arm was cold. Everything was cold.

Because Tye was anchoring, not James. God, the *pain*, I could barely *think*.

I was burning alive.

Dying? Maybe. Had to be. The end of the memories. And I'd suffer every searing bit of it. Never to see Ruhaven again, never to eat the mushroom moss, never to breathe the spiced honey air.

Or had Ruhaven finally realized who I was? Like antibodies attacking an infection it hadn't known was there.

Something flickered at my neck. Not more pain, but a pinprick coolness that didn't belong to this world. *Tye*? No, he felt different.

As I tried to reach for it, Jamellian's panicked fluttering stopped, his hairy ears twitched. Was he calling me home? Or telling Tye to? Could he do that?

But instead he looked up, purple eyes rotating back in enormous sockets. Because a massive shadow had just blanketed the burning sky.

The pain in my chest lessened, just a fraction, and I all but sagged with relief. It felt like invisible fingers were rubbing over each bone in my rib cage, caressing Nereida's spine and organs until the burning inside me simmered to a low flame—enough to see clearly again.

Still, the shadow careened toward us, roaring its fury now.

All around us, creatures—males, females, animals, some towering above the indigo trees—began backing away. I wanted to scream at them to stay, to help me, but the market emptied until only Jamellian and I remained.

And then I saw why they'd all scattered like ants from a fire. I saw the monster.

Boom.

It smacked into Ruhaven, rattling the leaves and shaking the stalls, breathing a throaty growl that promised if the pain didn't kill Nereida, it would.

Its skin was shimmering gold, its waist-length hair blackened at the tips. A cloth draped over its chest, hanging to its muscled thighs, and the upper half of its body was covered in demonic markings.

James squeezed my shoulder before sprinting for cover. If I made it out of here, I'd tell him exactly how much of a coward his past life was, but for now, my eyes remained transfixed on my executioner.

Behind the beast, something fluttered, moved.

Feathered wings shot out of his back like dark thunderclouds, rippling in both directions, spanning at least twenty meters.

My thoughts stuttered at the sight. It was—*neolithic.* Some mammoth man-bird resurrected from thawing permafrost.

In answer, its feathered tail whipped out, splitting the air with a thunderous crack before flicking the ground in predatory warning.

I was dinner.

It lifted its chin, head partly hidden in the shadows of the trees. But fangs extended over a snarling mouth like jail bars dropping down.

Terror tripped along my spine, turned my bowels to water. I shook violently as a chill spread from the base of my neck.

It was looking at me. *Me.* Not Nereida. Because this demon had somehow detected my false soul, occupying this Ruhaven memory I had no business being in. That was why my chest felt like it was splitting down the middle.

Now, my punishment for stealing this dream would be living through my own death. Nereida's body would die, but I'd still be trapped, feeling its teeth shred me, until I was alone in a nothing void at the end of the memories. I'd never get to tell James the truth, never figure out why the Inquitate killed Willow.

When the beast let out a blistering howl, I shrank inside Nereida, trying to be as small as possible.

But he charged with his wings arched in spears, pounding clawed feet into Ruhaven, his heaving breath misting to gold, like he'd spotted the thief crouching in Nereida's mind and was now hell-bent on ridding her of it. My skull jittered on the ground. Yes, he'd cast me right out of this body, send me flying through the Gate like I deserved.

The monster thudded to his knees before me, muscled chest heaving deep breaths like he'd flown miles.

Eyes like Saturn locked on mine.

Let him kill me before he eats me, please.

Up close, his hair was blinding, his face terrifying. His wings were ghostly, massive, dappled-gray monstrosities that blocked out all light when he arched them above us.

Slowly, he slid taloned hands under my spine.

And I prepared to die. For Nereida to die. To feel the gut-tearing pain rip through the rest of her body when this monster tore her apart. This would be the end of my past life. Of this beautiful world.

But we didn't die.

No, we were *flying*.

CHAPTER 18

How Can I Tell You?

I burst from the Gate like a fish yanked from water, the lure still snagged in its gullet.

I was back. Back. Whole. My organs still in my body. The pain only a vague, warning whisper.

"Shhhh," Tye murmured. "You're alright now. I've got ya."

Shivering in my damp shirt, I squeezed my face into Tye's shoulder, breathing in the scents of smoke and campfire, relishing the rough plaid scraping against my cheek, the hands that stroked my back.

James ran a shaky hand over his drawn face. Pale and tired, he looked at Kaz. "Jayzus," he muttered.

Bryn woke slower than the rest, unfocused eyes blinking away the dream. Then he pushed to sitting, took in my sweaty face, the arm violently shaking around Tye. "*Where were you*?" Bryn demanded.

I sucked in a breath. "Why? Why does it matter? Is this what you wanted?" I asked, my breaking voice rising to hysterics. "For the beast to see me, for Ruhaven to judge—"

"*Rowan*," Bryn said sharply, but his face looked stricken. "I was speaking of Tye."

My jaw snapped shut just before I admitted everything.

Tye lifted his chin off my head to scowl at Bryn. "What the hell are you accusin' me of?"

"Rowan has quite obviously been in distress for some time. Why did you not anchor her?"

"Ya know, it ain't always that obvious for those new to the Gate, and this is your goddamn *fault* for making her go in. So don't ya go blaming me 'cause ya feel guilty now."

"*Lads*," James said, ending the argument with a single, exasperated word. Crouching, he grasped my clammy hand. "Roe, 'tis normal to struggle with the anchor if yer distracted like ye were." Concern radiated in the creases of his eyes.

He'd seen—of course—as Jamellian in the market. But did he know the beast had attacked me because of what I wasn't?

Fully awake now, Kazie lifted a lantern, her skin glowing in its gentle light. "That was wild, Roe. Wild!"

I massaged my sternum, trying to remove the stamp of pain left by the Gate. "Wait, what?"

She threw her arms out. "The market!"

For a moment, I forgot all about the pain that had burned my throat raw, my fear of being found out. "You—you were there?"

She cast her eyes to the sky. "Of *course*. Couldn't you recognize me?"

I nearly swallowed my own tongue. "You're not the mushroom woman with the…"

Laughing uproariously, Kaz said, "*Beretta?* No, that's silly, Roe. Horns, remember? You passed me when… Oh, never mind." She sniffed. "You never notice *anything*, Roe."

"Yera, I think she was a wee bit distracted," James defended me.

I rubbed the space between my eyebrows. It wasn't supposed be like this. I was supposed to encounter the Inquitate by now, or at least find some relationship between Willow and the other deaths. Instead, I was being attacked in the Gate, possibly by a mushroom woman, possibly by a demon bird.

"Oh—I—thanks," I said when Bryn handed me a wooden canister. Tea—and his, by the honeyed smell. "James, did you see if it—if it killed Nereida after Tye anchored me?"

Bryn's lips tightened into a thin line. Disappointed because Nereida was dead, or because I'd pretended to be her?

The line dipped into a frown.

"Drink, Rowan," he instructed briskly, rising with the cane. His leg quavered once before he found his footing, and he might have been a shade paler than usual, his seawater eyes stark in his face, like a heavy island on an overcast day.

I turned back to Kaz. "The beast, could it be an Inquitate?" Was that why it'd recognized me?

She scratched her nose ring. "The beast?"

Hadn't she just said she'd been in the market? "Yeah, the *beast*. You know…" I opened my arms wide in a flapping of wings, nearly knocking into Tye.

Understanding dawned on Kazie's heart-shaped face. "Ohhhh—the *beast*." Her full mouth curled into a wolfish grin. "That's O'Sahnazekiel."

"You *named* it?" I accused.

"That *is* his name," Kazie corrected with a laugh. "He's harmless."

"Kazie, he tried to *kill* me. And his *fangs*." I couldn't stop the shudder that rolled through me.

Kazie's lips contorted like she was trying to swallow a live eel. "Uh-huh," she managed at last.

James scowled at her beneath his glasses, while Tye smirked around a cigarette and Bryn did his best impression of an unimpressed rock. Not a flicker of worry about my near-death experience.

Something else occurred to me. "If the pain wasn't him, there was that female who fed Nereida these mushrooms… Could they have been poison?"

James turned his laugh into a hacking cough while Kazie danced around the clearing, collecting knapsacks and tea canisters. "Beretta's a darling, Roe! She'd never try to kill you."

If Kazie didn't tell me what had attacked me in the Gate soon, I'd hang her upside down by her striped glitter sneakers.

Some of my intention must have shown because James cleared his throat and asked, "Kaz, is it what I think it was?"

"Oh yeah." She straightened her polka-dot skirt with a huff. "Roe's Tether broke."

Everyone froze like chimes in a dead wind. Even the forest seemed to hold its breath.

"Well, not broke," Kazie amended with a careless shrug. "But, you know, like damaged or whatever."

The cigarette fell from Tye's lips.

"**Y**our Tether is your Drachaut. And Ruhaven and Drachaut are like people on opposite ends of a teeter-totter," Kazie explained, swirling her cocktail in the air. "It's all about balance."

I blinked at them under the glare of Naruka's kitchen light. "I don't get it," I said for the third time.

There was a collective groan.

Then James blew out a long sigh. "Alright Roe, listen so. I'll try to explain it another way."

While he fought with Kazie for a prop to do so, I let the wine burn away the worst of the memories.

At the stove, Bryn stirred a pot of bubbling tomato sauce. It was supposed to be my rotation tonight, but when I insisted I could still cook, he said, "Rowan, allow me to save us all from another surprise chicken casserole."

I'd forgotten they were vegetarian. Once.

At least Tye didn't mind. At the head of the table, he gulped down beer while pouring over the equestrian stats in the local newspaper.

"Here we are so," James said, stealing a euchre card in a muted-pink turtleneck that would have mortified any man in L'Ardoise. "Let's take this offensive leprechaun playing card, let's say it's the planet Tallah. And on one side," he tapped the top of the card, "is Ruhaven. And down here, ye find Drachaut." He flicked the bottom joker hard enough, the card fluttered into his spaghetti.

Kazie scooped it out and licked it.

"Drachaut—the other country," I clarified.

"Right!" she said, delighted with me. "When Tallah travels around our star," she dragged the card around the wine bottle, "it doesn't rotate, so one side—Ruhaven—always faces the star. The other side is Drachaut."

Tye slapped a palm over her moving card, and his petal-green eyes lifted to mine. "It's like this, darlin'. Two creatures are born together and die together—one Ruhaven for every Drachaut. Gravity, like I was tellin' ya before." He splayed his calloused fingers, and the joker winked under them. "They're Tethers."

"And mine…broke?"

"The connection between ye two did," James corrected. "They might be injured, or something's eating at the bond there."

Like my lies. "And if one dies?"

"So does the other," Tye finished.

James took the card from him, ripped it in half. "The breaking of the Tether is the first step."

Probably because I'd poisoned that bond.

I scooped up the cards, shuffled them. "So did the beast break my Tether?"

There was a collective groan from the table. Bryn stopped stirring.

"I've *told* ye, 'tis no beast that broke yer Tether," James scoffed.

Or maybe it doled out my punishment for reasons I couldn't admit to him. "Then what did?"

"Could be anything." Kazie shrugged. "But it totally won't happen again. One time deal. Now it's gotta be fixed before…" She snapped her fingers. *My death*, I assumed.

"If the beast didn't break the Tether, then why did he show up at the exact moment when I felt it?"

Bryn limped to the table, held out the wine. It took me a moment, then I lifted my glass.

"Rowan, I spoke to James, and the *beast man*—as you put it—is an Azekiel," Bryn said as merlot trickled from the bottle. "The species is Ruhaven, and therefore, will not hurt you. The Azekiels even bear the Mark of protection, so it likely lessened the pain rather than caused it."

Marks. Tethers. Inquitate. I wanted to pull out my journal and wipe the drool off my face with it. I was just an electrician. I was never going to figure all this out. I couldn't even stay in the Gate for more than fifteen minutes.

"What's Kazie's Mark?" I asked, forgetting what she'd said a month ago.

"I'm a Wykitome," she answered, sliding into her seat with a mountain of spaghetti. "A pattern detector."

I sipped the fruity wine. "Patterns of what?"

"Oh, just things," she said with an air of *if-you-really-have-to-ask*. Right—*that* was why I'd never asked.

"So Bryn's Mark is light, James and I are Kalistas who bond spirits—except not me, because my Mark isn't activated yet—Kazie is some pattern detector. Tye, you're what again…?"

He puffed out his chest and flexed a bicep. "Pure muscle, baby. But all the key stuff is in the right place, if that's what you're askin'."

James and Kazie rolled their eyes while I blushed scarlet.

Kazie held up a fork and said with her mouth full, "I think this is missing something."

"Burnt chicken?" Bryn supplied, not missing a beat.

She grinned so wide a noodle popped out. "That's it!"

I would *never* live that down. "Kaz, the next time you mention my cooking, I'm going to sneak into your room with a screwdriver." I picked up a fork to demonstrate. James's eyes widened. "And when I'm done, your light switch will spin the birdcage and your alarm clock will be my new pet."

Tye sliced me a grin. "Darling, you can feed me chicken any time."

"That's not what you said last week," Kaz retorted.

"Indeed not." The heavenly scent of roast basil hit me a second before Bryn slid a plate of spaghetti in front of me, then laid a cloth napkin on my lap. "No mushrooms," he promised. No, *teased*.

"Ha. What's her Mark? Beretta's?"

"She can talk to plants," Kazie answered matter-of-factly as Bryn straightened again.

"Probably convinced them to attack Nereida's Tether," I mused. Maybe they were all trying to get me to let go of the memory.

Kazie waved this away with a tired *pfft*. "Ruhavens don't attack each other. So O'Sahnazekiel's got fangs—so do you! And I've got a tail. I mean, I don't know what you're freaking—"

She broke off on a blood-curdling scream.

I leapt out of my chair, adrenaline flying. "*What*? What's wrong?"

Kazie lifted a trembling finger, jabbed it at the table. *Hissed*.

It took me five seconds to locate the crawling speck. "Oh, for the love of…" *Bang*. I slammed my palm on the newspaper, squashing the spider into a headline about fairy forts.

James tugged at his hair. "Ah sure, ye didn't need to kill it like!"

They were nuts, the lot of them.

So nuts that they'd think a flying, fanged beast had nothing to do with Nereida's broken Tether. That his arrival was just some coincidence.

I nudged the spaghetti aside, took out my notebook.

Drachaut—the land existing on the other side of the world and the name of the race that lives there. Not in the Ledger?

Tether—a thread, a connection, between Ruhaven and Drachaut. Then scratched out *connection* and replaced it with *lifeline*. Because if one died, so did the other. So it was someone to tie you to existence.

The dry wine curdled on my tongue. "What about Willow?"

James looked up from trying to find the dead spider to reassure Kaz. "Willow?"

I tucked my notebook away, shoved back my chair. "Yeah. What if one of us was a Drachaut? And the other came through the Gate with Nereida as her Tether?"

Then maybe, maybe I wasn't a total fraud. Maybe that was why I could see her memories.

The kitchen hiccuped on a beat of silence, a mosquito pinged off the lamp, then James shook his head. "Yera, I don't think so, Roe. First, 'tis only Ruhaven who come through the *Ledger*, and two, there's no entry for Willow—just yerself."

Or so he believed.

Looping my fingers in my belt, I paced the small kitchen, nearly knocking into Bryn's cane twice.

My Tether, something that bound me to life on Tallah, another person—no, a Drachaut. And seemingly unrelated, as no one had been born with a twin before.

It had to be Willow. Or rather, *I* had to be the Drachaut, but I didn't say that.

I stopped behind Tye. "But what if Willow was my Tether and got—well, pulled or something—and she came through and it just wasn't recorded?"

James folded his hands patiently. "Roe, there's no Drachaut here. And there's no missed recordings."

He said this like it was impossible for the *Ledger* to be wrong, and of course, it was in his world. This was the sacred book his life had been built on. He couldn't see any other possibilities beyond those weathered pages.

"Maybe they have a different book." That made perfect sense. The Ruhavens' book landed here, the Drachauts' somewhere else.

"No."

I rounded the table. "But you said there's never been a twin before either. Maybe there's an exception for the Drachaut too." I snapped my fingers as an idea came to me. "What if the Inquitate are infecting Drachaut and that's why Willow died?"

"Attacking." Bryn.

Tye lowered his newspaper with the spider's guts still clinging to it. "Infecting Drachaut?" he repeated skeptically. "Darlin', that's a little far-fetched, even for Ruhaven. And unless there's something Stornoway ain't telling us—he ain't Drachaut, and they targeted him."

The bubble burst.

"I'm trying to follow your logic. You tell me Ruhaven come through, that our souls are preserved, and that our souls are bound to these Drachaut. But you're somehow certain no Drachaut came through?"

Tye looked at me with pity. "That just ain't how it works."

"Well, how does it work? You don't really know how we come here, how the Gate works, you said that yourself, Tye."

Kazie rounded on me, a feat she managed even buried in a bowl of spaghetti. "Roe, okay look, here's the truth, okay? They're sacrificed. So they can't come through."

The wine smoked in my throat. "Sacrificed? To what? Why?" Nereida's Tether was *sacrificed*?

James sighed. "Ye see, when Ruhavens come through the Gate, there's got to be a trade. Everything's a balance, that's what we've always told ye. When they pass through the Gate, it's their Drachaut

~ 161 ~

that are sacrificed in the trade, and that's why 'tis only Ruhavens in the *Ledger*. One Drachaut is sacrificed to have our souls reborn here."

That was a *hell* of a thing to tell me now. "I don't know what to make of that."

James patted my hand in sympathy. "It doesn't matter, 'tis done. And yer making progress, Roe, asking the right questions."

I nodded half-heartedly. Big, fat questions was all I had, and only a vague connection between Willow in Paris one summer and Patrick four hours away in Marseille. Basically, I had nothing.

Then Bryn spoke. "You should investigate those who have experienced broken Tethers," he said as he circled the table, cane clicking on the linoleum. "Perhaps there is overlap. In the meantime, I expect that Nereida, Jamellian, and Kasmira will seek out her Tether in Drachaut, to fix what has been broken."

Tye turned, laid an arm over the back of his chair. "She oughta give Ruhaven a break for a little while."

I shivered when Bryn's mouth brushed my ear. "Surely, you are not so afraid of *one* little Azekiel," he said softly, then straightened. "Kazie and I will visit the Gate tomorrow at three. You will join us then."

Since I was hell-bent on Tethers having something to do with Willow and I, I pulled journals from any who'd experienced a broken Tether and suffered an Inquitate attack.

Patrick—broken Tether experienced on July 6, 1981

Oisín—broken Tether experienced on Feb 19, 1943

Anastasia—broken Tether experienced on Aug 2, 1963

I smoothed out the pages of Bryn's notebook, read his notes on Oisín.

Oisín Flannagan—died of a brain hemorrhage at 41 before he could make the Fall.

The Fall?

I flipped to the earlier pages of my notebook. Yes, I'd noted it next to Patrick's name. He'd been months away from making the Fall, but what was it? Some rite in Ruhaven, probably. Maybe it was the name for the rite they obtained their Mark in.

Anastasia Mikovich—Killed in 1963 in the USSR, number 1165 in the Ledger. *Another suspected brain aneurysm, but they could not get the medical documents at the time. Reported dead by her spouse, not a Ruhaven.*

Spouse. How would that work if she was visiting the Gate? *Hey honey, I'm just going to pop over to a fantastical world for a little while. I'll be back for dinner.*

I snorted and turned the page.

And suppose when they visited the Gate they had an... an *encounter*, like James and Essie. Would that be cheating? Everything *felt* real, so wouldn't it be as well?

Was Essie in the *Ledger*? James spent as much time as he could visiting the woman that his past life had loved. Wouldn't James want to find her here—reborn in the *Ledger*? They could visit Ruhaven together, talk about what they both lived. Or maybe she'd come through decades ago and they'd missed each other.

"...bring him back. Roe?"

I jerked my eyes from my notes. "What?"

Kazie rolled her shoulders. "I said, that's forty minutes. Can you anchor Bryn?"

Around us, the woods hummed with the soft chatter of Ireland. Tiny birds fluttered between branches that let in the faintest glow of afternoon light. And despite the visible sun, rain squeezed a path through the clouds and thundered on the vivid blue tarp that Bryn had strung above with clean, tidy knots.

"Is it time already?" I glanced at the man lying as quiet as death in the Gate. "Can't he go in for hours?"

Lounging against the tree across from me, Kaz lifted the sweater she was crocheting. Or maybe it was a scarf. "Yeah, but James is worried he'll get too obsessed again."

We were probably already past that point, but I nodded and crawled toward Bryn, eager to discover how to anchor someone.

He lay at the center of the meadow, entirely still but for the breeze stirring the hair around his brow. His cheeks were a bit rosy from the cold or the Gate, his parted lips equally pink.

"Where do I start?" I murmured.

"Take his hand."

I was about to ask Kazie if Bryn was okay with me touching him, but he *had* agreed to be my test dummy—my term. I eyed Bryn's still form. Would I see what light looked like?

More than just curious now, I picked up Bryn's limp wrist. He didn't stir, didn't even flinch, as if he were more than dreaming, as if his consciousness was somewhere else. His eyes remained closed, delicate eyelashes casting thick shadows over sculpted cheeks.

"*That's* holding his hand?" Kazie said dryly.

Rolling my eyes, I set his arm down again, slid my fingers through his, and grasped tightly when he couldn't squeeze back. His palm was surprisingly rough, not as smooth and unworked as it should have been. Must be all that Turner exam marking.

Kazie lowered her voice to a conspirator's murmur. "You need to get close to his ear and whisper his name."

I glanced at her. "I've never heard James call my name?"

"That's because you're in the Gate," she said primly. "Now, say '*Brynjar*' nice and sweet, like you're talking to your favorite garage tool."

I scowled at her. "You know, I can still dismantle that bird cage of yours. Or better yet, your alarm clock." She left it blaring every morning between six and seven.

She only *poo-poo'd* that.

Screwdriver. Birdcage. I'd do it, I swore to myself.

But I lowered onto my elbows. "*Brynjar*?" I murmured. Using his full name felt strangely intimate, but his left ear twitched at my voice.

Something tingled up my arm, a low pulse that wormed into the rest of my body, heating, teasing. "Kazie, is this right? It feels…" I felt myself blush. "Odd."

Her soft laugh carried behind me. "Oh, you're fine. Now, just lean over and give those gorgeous lips a big ol' kiss and—"

Oh, goddamn her.

I let out a string of curses that could have curled the ends of Bryn's golden hair. "Kazie, you don't even want to know what I'm going to do to your budgies," I threatened. "You'll be wishing for *chicken* casserole again."

Laughing, she ducked the branch I threw at her.

"Hello, Rowan."

I jolted at Bryn's low voice. Spun around.

He sat up, one knee bent, not a strand of hair out of place despite the wind, eyes twinkling like early morning mist on a lake. "Do you make a habit of seducing everyone in the Gate?" he drawled. "I am beginning to see why Tye does so enjoy your company."

I felt my shoulders slide to my ears.

"It's been ages since we had anyone new at the Gate," Kazie said, settling onto the blanket, impatient to be off to Ruhaven. "I have to get in my fun while I can."

Hilarious. "Thanks for that," I muttered. "I hope you gave Tye the same treatment."

Bryn caught the apple Kaz tossed him. "Yes, although Tye did not fall for her prank nearly as easily as you, Rowan."

I felt my face burn as he crunched into his apple, the juice wetting his lips. He offered the unbitten side of the Granny Smith to me, lifted a brow. "Are you hungry?"

I must have been staring like a dog in heat. "No, no thanks," I said, quickly adjusting the blankets, then looked up as Bryn kneeled beside me, mischief twinkling in his azure eyes.

"Would you prefer to be anchored the usual way?" he asked, taking another lazy bite of his apple. "Or shall I whisper your name like we are in bed?"

I was going to kill Kazie. Wrap her body in the hammock, then toss her and that alarm clock out the window.

"The usual way," I said through my teeth.

Bryn swallowed a long, slow bite. "As you wish."

And as Ruhaven swept us away, I forgot all about the looming beast.

✸⚙✦

I slipped through the dark, trickling void of my Prayama, through the cold tumble of the Gate, and when I arrived—

Alive. I was still alive.

And Nereida's pain was amazingly, blissfully gone.

Nothing threatened to tear us in two, the beast—or O'Sahnazekiel—didn't bare his teeth, and the only thing I felt was air trickling in through abnormally large lungs.

So Ruhaven hadn't rejected me after all. Relief washed over me, as thick and sticky as waking from a nightmare and realizing it'd been only that. But how long could I go on pretending? What happened when the Gate really did put its metaphorical foot down?

Maybe it didn't matter. Maybe it was worth the consequences. Everything I'd seen, lived, and experienced in Ruhaven was more exciting than anything that had ever happened to me in L'Ardoise. It might have been Willow's, but maybe, for a little while, it could be mine. And that wasn't such a bad thing.

Nereida nestled under a blanket as I waited for my eyes to come into full focus, for my mind to slide into hers like I was buttoning on jeans just a bit too tight.

At last my eyes blinked open and I watched the whirling gears feeding off the sky. Their quiet grinding filled the space between heaven and Ruhaven. Then Nereida tilted her head to the side.

I sucked in a breath.

For as gorgeous as Ruhaven was during the day, it had nothing on the night.

Fleshy trees burned, purple lanterns in a dark swamp. It was horribly beautiful, like the burning car I'd passed on the side of the road one night driving home. The trunks burned from the inside with violet flames that cast a tender glow around the woods. Sparks popped and fizzled out in the soil, filling the thick air with a smoked-vanilla scent.

On a deep exhale, I burrowed further under the blanket, enjoying the tickle of its soft feathers against my skin. This was why I'd returned—because for a short while, there was an unbridled wonder here I hadn't felt since Willow died.

Then Nereida sighed, shifted, the soft feathers brushing her bare shoulder, and I had a moment of terrifying clarity.

This was not a down blanket. It was feathers.

Wings, to be exact.

And I was naked. Dear god, I was *naked!*

Don't panic, don't panic. It might not be the beast. Maybe some *other* animal was about to eat me.

But—but that sense of recognition was tingling through her body, vibrating with awareness of the heat lying behind us. And if that wasn't enough, a sharp talon drew tiny circles on our waist.

Nereida huffed a throaty exhale, settling deeper under feathers.

I saw the massive dappled-gray wing clearly covering us—blackened at the tips and dusted with gold.

So the beast man had flown us to his bird lair. Maybe these fires were some ritual before dinner.

But it'd be okay because Bryn was watching, and I could trust him to yank me out before I lived through death. *I think.*

Seemingly unbothered, Nereida stretched our mouth into a long yawn. She sounded embarrassingly like a mewing cat.

I braced myself as she sniffed, pressed onto elbows, and began a slow roll that would bring us face to face with the beast.

A cocoon of feathers briefly shuttered the indigo night from view. They brushed Nereida's lips as she turned, butter-soft and tasting of misty clouds. Strong, too, with a hard bone running through the wing blade.

A shoulder came into view first, contoured with muscles larger than Tye's. The forearm looked like it'd been dipped in golden liquid and left out to dry. Four fingers and a thumb ended in talons of clear glass. And I knew by the intricate tattoos that this was the same demon who'd grabbed me on my first visit to the Gate.

I should have recognized him before.

More bronze tattoos trailed up his torso to a chest that swelled with muscle and polished stone skin.

What was coming out of his armpit? Hair? White hair? Or...*feathers*.

Feathers in his armpit.

On another exhausted sigh, Nereida plopped her cheek on his arm and I came face to face at last with the Azekiel.

O'Sahnazekiel.

For a heartbeat, I did nothing but stare.

Because he was like the trees—terrifying. And beautiful.

His head was longer than it should be with star-like freckles whispering over his nose, but his face was strong-boned with a solid chin and sweeping cheeks. His lips, a dusty rose, parted slightly on a quiet exhale, revealing a hint of the fangs I'd seen when he landed at the market. Five golden hoops decorated his pointed ears.

A long braid looped over his shoulders and wrapped down his back until it brushed his hips. Like his forearms, it was nearly liquid gold, the individual strands as thick as yarn.

I braced when his tail lifted, flicked—

And swatted a flying lizard away.

Nereida worked her hand loose, then reached fire-lit fingers toward him. But instead of attacking the beast with the blades she strapped at her wrists, the woman trailed the pad of our finger along his wide collarbone, caressing muscles strong enough to break us in half.

Because—because god, they weren't enemies. They were—were *lovers*.

As I mentally swore, the beast heaved a breath, tickling the jelly hair on my head.

I couldn't let James know, or Kazie, or especially Tye. But their past lives knew Nereida—what if they saw something in the memory?

Wait. No, it was worse than that. What if they saw Nereida—*me*—reacting while I lay in the clearing like James had with Essie?

I couldn't lie there moaning and sweating. God, no. I had to get out of here before—

The Azekiel's eyes winged open.

Holy god.

Molten irises gazed down at me. My pulse stuttered, stopped. The force of him was as physical as the hand sliding up my spine, but not nearly as tender.

Then his lips parted, and two fangs lengthened over full, wide lips.

It all happened too fast, the memory speeding along before I'd even had a chance to understand.

Nereida tilted her neck as those Saturn-ringed eyes locked on the vein I felt pulsing there. Breath whispered across my skin. My heart pounded, faster and faster as Nereida arched for him.

How long did I have left? Five minutes? Ten? Long enough to humiliate myself at the Gate with Bryn—

His teeth pierced my neck, drawing a low, husky moan from Nereida—*had anyone heard that?*—and a gentle tug pulled under my skin.

If embarrassment alone were enough to yank me back to earth, I'd have shot out of this memory like a rocket. But as it wasn't, I only lay there. Letting the Azekiel suck the—presumably—blood from my neck like some vampiric bird, his hand stroking my back as Nereida purred against him.

Suddenly, something cold trailed down my spine.

O'Sahnazekiel's talons? His tail? God only knew, but Nereida's moans had turned into hot pants. Worse, I wanted whatever this was as much as her when I *didn't*.

There was no way I wasn't putting on a performance at the Gate. I almost hoped Bryn didn't anchor me, so I could die of embarrassment quietly here. This was why they'd all been having a laugh at me yesterday, knowing the beast was her Ruhaven lover. God, that was almost worse than the teeth still at my neck.

The pressure on my spine increased until I squirmed in her mind. How did Nereida not feel this? My vertebrae felt like they were rearranging themselves, letting a line of energy drive straight through my body. Waves of power, of pleasure, vibrated in my blood. Fused my bones together.

Then I realized what it was.

Not the gentle hand of James or the sprinkling dust ball that was Kazie, but the solid, unshakeable command of a new anchor.

CHAPTER 19

Lost in a Dream

Wariness flickered in eyes washed up from the ocean, so blue they were like glass smoothed by waves over centuries.

Kneeling beside me, dirt coating his slacks, Bryn gripped my clammy hand in his own. Rain beaded on his bottom lip and darkened his hair to faded moonlight. I blinked back the haze and desire lingering from the Gate as my body screamed at me, confused about why it'd been interrupted.

It wasn't us! I shouted at it.

Kazie remained sprawled on the blanket to my left. Drool pooled at the corner of her mouth as breath fought a path through her nose, gurgling into a suspended snore.

Bryn squeezed my hand. "Would you have preferred me to leave you in the Gate?" The question held just enough of a challenge that I knew I'd been caught like James.

It wasn't my fault. I didn't want this. I *didn't.*

Heat crept into my cheeks and neck, hotter than the fires burning inside Ruhaven's trees. What a joke I must be to him. And now he'd gotten a front-row seat to me debasing myself with a mythical animal.

I yanked my hand away and sat up too quickly.

"You are still weak after the Gate, Rowan," Bryn noted. "You must build up more tolerance."

Maybe, but lack of Gate endurance wasn't what had my thighs shaking.

I loosed a shaky breath. *Speak, idiot.* "I'm fine," I said abruptly. "Fine." But I saw my fears written in every nonexistent line of his face. "You—you saw, didn't you?"

Bryn's mouth twitched. "I take it *the beast* did not eat you?"

I guess he thought if I was going to play pretend with another life then I deserved the consequences of it too.

"Bryn, if you tell anyone," I warned in a low whisper, "I'm leaving. I won't come back to the Gate. I'll finish the research in L'Ardoise. I don't care what you threaten me with."

He studied me, one hand on his knee, face impassive. "Very well, Rowan. Though I fail to understand why you are so embarrassed by your dreams." He rose and reached for a blanket, began unfolding it.

"I think it's obvious why I don't want to be watched with a bird man."

"An Azekiel," he corrected, and draped the throw over my shoulders. "You are shivering, Rowan."

Suspicious, I tugged the blanket around me, eyeing him as he unpacked cheesecloth-wrapped sandwiches, apples, and the canister of tea.

"No, thanks," I said when he sliced off a piece of a Granny Smith.

With a frown, he held out the sandwich instead.

I shook my head.

"Rowan," he said impatiently, "your blood sugar is low from the Gate. You remained for twenty minutes today. A new record."

I lifted my chin from my knees. Twenty minutes? Really? "I'm fine, I'm just cold."

He polished the apple on the corner of his shirt before tossing it in my lap. "Eat, Rowan."

Of course, not a hint of fatigue or stress worried his face after nearly an hour in the Gate. If anything, he looked healthier—his cheeks had more color, his shoulders were a little straighter.

I picked up the apple. Maybe, if I could anchor myself like Bryn, I wouldn't need to be watched while Nereida enjoyed the Azekiel. "How can you return without an anchor?"

Bryn settled back against a thick tree trunk covered in soft moss and draped his arms over both knees—casual, for him. "When I previously resided at Naruka," he answered after a moment, "I spent a vast majority of my time in the Gate. It allowed me to acquire a level of tolerance."

Vast majority—did that mean even more than the six hours he spent every day now? "Why?" I asked. "Why go in so much, especially if…" *It caused James to exile you.* "If it's so taxing?" I asked instead, and bit into the apple's taut skin, but when I thought of the teeth sinking into Nereida's throat, I lowered the fruit.

"Because, Rowan," he murmured in a wistful growl that tightened my belly, "I wanted what was in Ruhaven more than anything here."

I waited a beat. "And what was in Ruhaven?"

Shadows flickered over his pale face. "The truth," he said, then abruptly changed topics. "Has my research been helpful to you?"

I toyed with the apple. I'd figure out how to anchor myself then, or find another way. "Yes, thanks. There were three entries I found of Ruhavens who'd been killed by the Inquitate and also suffered from broken Tethers. One of them, Patrick, was in France at the time Willow visited. I thought maybe I'd look at him more."

Bryn propped an elbow on his knee, looked around thoughtfully. "I recall the pain of the broken Tether initially frightened Patrick away from the Gate." He paused as if considering it. "Which is why he moved to Marseille. I believe he took a rather large, orange tabby with him."

"That's right, it was in your notes. But you also mentioned something about the Fall? What's that?"

Bryn's eyes tightened. "Another Ruhaven legend. You need not worry over it now."

⚙✺

I n Naruka's ticking kitchen, with the remnants of last night's onion stew still lingering, I stared down James. Not too difficult, given we were the same height.

"I've *really* got to plaster today," I lied baldly.

"But it's Friday," James insisted for the tenth time, pointing to the calendar where a grinning pumpkin barely hid Father October's considerable sins. "Yer going to miss the market."

While it was true I needed to sand and plaster the drywall in the gate lodge, I might have exaggerated the urgency—and given that James had let Bryn repair his house with glue, I probably wouldn't be called on my lie.

But I did feel guilty.

Twice, I'd barely escaped having sex with O'Sahnazekiel—or *Sahn,* as I was now calling him—and only because, by some miracle, Bryn happened to be anchoring and pulled me out before I witnessed something biblically illegal.

Too close. It'd been far too close to someone else knowing exactly what Nereida was up to. And maybe a part of me—one I really wasn't proud of—wanted to experience some of what they shared…*alone.*

Still, while James might have given up pretending he wasn't with Essie, I couldn't live in the memories knowing whoever anchored might hear me moaning Sahn's name or whatever it was that Nereida growled. If Bryn wouldn't teach me to anchor, I'd come up with another idea.

I just needed to make peace with my arch-nemesis to do it.

James set down his wicker basket. "Well, if ye insist on staying here, then sure I'll have to stay meself," he bemoaned, doing a very good job of making me feel even guiltier than I was.

I looped my thumbs in my tool belt. "I know you and Bryn think the Inquitate will come back, but I've spent twenty-seven years without them. They haven't appeared since Oslo, and you can't follow me forever." Plus, I wasn't in the Ledger, so maybe it was just a mix up.

James wagged a finger. "I wouldn't be placing no bets on that." Which was saying something, considering he'd once put fifty on a horserace *replay*. But then, he'd had ten pints. "And sure, why would ye want to take the risk? Maybe it appears as someone else next time and ye haven't a clue."

"Doesn't Bryn go off by himself all the time?"

Nose twitching, he dropped his act. "Aye, but as ye've seen yerself, he's something of the Gate to protect him here."

That *glimmer*.

Except I didn't have a glimmer, couldn't anchor myself, so I'd have to use other skills.

"Ye know, if this is about falling behind with the gate lodge, ye don't need to keep working," James reminded me. "I've enough money from Ruhavens over the years, and those who send it from abroad."

Fixing Naruka was the only thing that eased my guilt for lying to James about who I was. At least, when he found me out, I'd be able to say I left Naruka with new shingles.

I adjusted the straps of my backpack, the weight of the contraption inside sitting heavily between my shoulder blades. "I can pull my own weight."

"Roe, ye should really—"

But I was already striding away, toward the gate lodge, where I had no intention of spending my day.

Once they were at the market, I'd head up to the Gate. I wouldn't overdo it, wouldn't take risks. Still, twenty minutes? I could stay in longer than that. Not so long that I wouldn't have time to do that plastering when I got back, but I needed to figure things out in the Gate—*alone*. Needed to figure out how I felt about the Azekiel without everyone watching me.

And on that thought, I bowled into Bryn.

Brushes scattered, white spirits burned a third nostril in my nose, and the palette he'd been holding flipped into a theatric arc, tumbling, tumbling, tumbling…

Splat.

I cringed when it landed paint-side down on the antique carpet.

James was going to kill me. The thing was probably some relic from a great aunt Ruhaven.

Stairs croaked before Kazie bounded through the lounge, leapt over the palette like a gazelle, and called a cheerful, "See ya later, Roe!"

One down, now just one more to—

I turned to Bryn. Winced.

Sprawled in the entranceway, a streak of paint marring his bleached-sugar sweater, he blinked up at me through thick eyelashes. Light from the stained-glass doors scattered over his bent form.

"Do you make a habit of stampeding through this door, Rowan? If so, I shall avoid it altogether."

God, I'd just flattened a cripple, and there were enough Jesus statues in this house to judge me for all eternity.

Fumbling for an apology, I bent and grabbed his elbow. "Are you alright?"

He reached for his cane and, bracing against it and me, righted himself in a doorway only a few inches taller than him. "I have survived worse. Why are you in such a hurry, Rowan?" Bryn asked as I briskly straightened his leather apron. *Stop touching him.* "Are you looking forward to the vintage tractor parade in town?"

I stepped abruptly away. "What?" Was this a joke about L'Ardoise or… "No, no, I'm not going to town today. I've got things to do here."

He limped away from me to peel the palette off the rug, studying the abstract design it left. "Not going?"

When I gave him the same excuse I'd fed James, Bryn cut me off. "We cannot leave you alone. If you wish to stay, then I will remain and paint a study of the lodge while you work."

I stabbed my clenched fingers in my pocket. "No."

Bryn looked at me with raised eyebrows as pale as his sweater. "No? Rowan, while you may believe the Inquitate are gone, I can assure you they will come back. You agreed not to take these risks."

I dug for patience and found the well bone-dry. "We can't always be together," I said, then rubbed my neck at how that sounded. "I mean, James, Kazie, and—"

"Until we find a cause, we will," he broke in, undeterred. "This is a reasonable precaution, Rowan. Surely, you do not find my presence… ghostly, as you described to James—so intrusive?"

Shame nipped at me.

But a new idea slowly began to form—one that would see him distracted and completely absorbed as he had been at the port. Luckily, it took Bryn at least a few hours to butcher a canvas.

"You're absolutely right," I said, switching my tone to what I hoped was repentant. "I wasn't thinking. But I'll just be disturbing your... your *process*, if you paint near the gate lodge."

Bryn capped a tube of paint. "That is quite alright."

"I mean, there'll be dust flying everywhere when I cut through the drywall. And it's loud too. Not conducive to painting."

He loosened the apron around his neck. "This does sound serious. I do hope you shall consider wearing goggles and ear protectors."

I ground my teeth. "I will. I do, and—"

"Not nearly enough," Bryn corrected, wiping his fingers on the rag in his front pocket. "I have been reading about your profession and small amounts of dust can cause blindness."

Profession. I almost laughed. But since he still wasn't getting the hint, I said, "It's just, well, why don't you try painting something with more color? Like the vegetable garden?" Or anything a comfortable half-mile from the cottage.

"You wish for me to paint James's garden?" He repeated like I'd said, "*I want you to paint the toilet seat*."

I handed him a blue tube—no, cobalt turquoise—and tugged at my ear. "Uh, yeah. The tomatoes looked nice. Pretty." Paintable? Did James even have tomatoes? After installing the chicken wire in August, I hadn't paid attention. "Maybe you should—*Oh*—I—"

Bryn snatched my wrist. "You have paint on your fingers, Rowan," he said, and wiped them with the end of his rag.

"Thanks," I murmured when he released me, my hand tingling from the solvent. "But for painting, I was thinking of something for the kitchen. James would like that."

Bryn picked up his easel, a half-smile playing on his lips. "As you wish then, Rowan. As long as you remain in Naruka's grounds."

I forced a smile that felt like I'd chomped on hay. "Of course."

When he offered his own sincere one back, I almost reconsidered. "Well, Rowan, I shall attempt this garden," he began, limping toward the kitchen with the satchel thumping his thigh, the cane stealing a free hand, and the easel under an armpit. "Perhaps we can take lunch together. Although I cannot cook the meat you prefer, Kazie tells me my sandwiches are quite edible. Does noon suit you?"

Lunch with Bryn? A quick glance at the apple clock told me I'd be back from the Gate by then. "Sure."

"Very well. Do consider the protective gear…"

I watched him duck under the doorway, nodded as he offered his painting gloves, and when he was well and truly set up in the garden, I stole away to the Gate.

Finally, I'd be able to see Ruhaven—*alone*.

In the cool, misty morning, I rolled out the blanket and toed off my shoes. Thanks to the socks that James kept misplacing in my room, I was wearing thick wooly ones today.

Then I unpacked the device that would bring me home.

Kazie's alarm clock.

It'd taken a few tweaks, but I'd rigged it to work on a battery, and added a built-in vibration that should wake me if the loud bell didn't.

I cranked the bronze knob. One hour. I could handle an hour.

Determined, I hugged the alarm to my ribs.

And awakened in Ruhaven.

N ereida batted silver eyelashes into a filmy lens with a distorted reflection that made recognition nearly impossible, and yet I saw eyes as silver as Sahn's were gold, framed by jelly-like eyebrows that matched the strands of gleaming hair.

I think I had freckles, too, so many they were a streak of glitter across my cheeks that had me smiling inwardly. Maybe there was something that connected Nereida and I, something that said this *was* my past life.

No—that was stupid thinking that would get me nowhere.

She gripped the frame of the glass, studying the odd, filmy lens that distorted our features. On her right hand, she wore a single band with twin half-moons braced on each side of an opal. Did they have moons in Ruhaven? At night, I'd been too distracted by the burning violet trees.

But as Nereida inspected the glass, I breathed in the heady scent of a rainforest in winter, and let my mind adjust.

I'd never get used to it—not just the sliding into another body, but the low beat of drums cascading over the lattice mountains, the wind blowing as thick as honey, the sweetness of lavender on my tongue, the sparkling pearls floating through the air, the—

AHHHH!

Nereida stumbled. Tripped. Fell.

An angel appeared from behind the glass, one fang curling over his lower lip, a dimple in his left cheek, and pure mischief in his pupilless eyes.

Sahn.

He puffed out his cheeks, fogging the lens before poking his head around with a grin. It was quick and wicked and not the least remorseful, but thankfully he wasn't naked. A single piece of material draped over one shoulder, fastened at his waist with a dark leather belt, and hung to his thighs. He curled bare, clawed feet into the pearly earth and fluffed his wings like an under-plucked turkey.

Playing with us—*again*.

Not to be outdone, Nereida ducked and palmed a heavy ball, then chucked it with such deadly aim that Sahn flung out his wings to dodge it.

His flapping blue-merle feathers sent a hoard of furry butterflies squawking indignantly. With an *oops* look, he held up clawed hands in surrender, his sensual lips moving, voice a teasing growl. Despite the language barrier, I heard loud and clear: *Is that your best shot?*

Whatever his flaws—like being part bird—they both had it bad for each other.

Nereida stalked toward the lens, shoved a cloudy arm through, and gripped the grinning Azekiel by his silky hair. The concave lens oozed around my arm, electrical pulses zapping into my veins like fireflies.

What a world this was—the sensations crawling up my translucent skin, Sahn's quick, feline smile, the air soaked with wintery vanilla warmth.

Laughing deeply, Sahn let me drag him through the lens, the goo sliding over his golden skin and clinging to his lengthening fangs.

Slow arousal curled in Nereida's belly.

Please, let the alarm clock work in time.

But maybe I could touch his feathers first, at least once. How did Nereida resist running her hands through them? They were all shades of gray except gray itself, like faded purples and greens and blues.

But before I could touch, he shook his golden head and flung gooey lens slime everywhere. His braid listed back and forth, sliding over a back carved with muscles while Nereida wiped a streak of slime from our cheek.

Then laughed.

The sound was like wooden bells—a chorus of chimes hanging in the woods, twenty notes of a scale that wasn't possible on earth.

Sahn might have been as transfixed as I was because his eyes warmed, and he gave her a slow, indulgent smile.

Then before I could blink—or she could—he was scooping me into his arms.

Wide lips lowered to mine. Nereida all but wilted at the first sweep of his tongue. Quick and playful, he tugged on my bottom lip with his fangs, each touch sending electric shocks tumbling through my belly.

On a moan, she threaded her fingers through his long braid.

When her legs circled his waist, two dappled wings shot out on either side. He moaned, long and low, the vibrations tumbling through our joined mouths. And his hands roamed over each inch of her, touching places I wasn't sure existed, the sensation like minty heat over my skin.

Her mouth found his neck, kissing the corded veins and muscle, the golden skin warm under her lips. He tasted like the sun, like pure, morning light. Gentle dew and rain, and a warming hope.

And I felt something else, something that couldn't—

Suddenly, a tinkling chorus of flutes assaulted my eardrums.

Panting, Sahn spun us around, my legs still around his waist, his wings cocooning us so I almost missed the tiny creature skipping by.

I squinted downwards, through thick feathers, and caught a pair of twirling, spiral horns.

She—and it was definitely a she—huffed an annoyed breath at me before skipping onwards, babbling music.

I grinned. Of course, of course I knew who this was.

In agreement, Sahn unraveled his wings, setting me softly on the floating pearl earth.

For the first time ever, I studied Kazie.

Horns was an understatement. Antlers sprouted from her head in a tangle of Medusa hair, like a thorny, overgrown maze, and extended well past her shoulders. They gleamed a polished black, the same color as her skin. Except, that wasn't right. It wasn't that her skin was *black,* but that it inhaled light—seemed to suck it in and become the void where it should have existed. White, pupilless eyes landed on Sahn and I in a face as empty as the rest of her form. Then she smiled—or rather, a set of pointy blue teeth emerged from the dark.

Nereida answered in that extra sense that said *hello.*

So this was Kazmira.

She stopped feet away from Sahn and I under the shadow of a blooming jelly mushroom.

Sahn tried to speak to her, but she waved him off, pointing instead to the mechanical forest growing from the sky. Nereida followed her finger.

These gears moved slower than the others, and rather than the clicks and chirps, they sounded like a cresting wave breaking against rock.

When I looked back at Kaz, she lifted a telescope and gazed at the gears. She murmured something, then pointed again. And again.

The ground rumbled under my feet.

Clink-clink-clink.

I scrambled back, bumping into Sahn before he caught me and shielded us from the spewing rocks as something massive speared through the earth.

Kazie let out a sweeping bark of laughter—like a hoard of chirping dolphins—and waved us away. *It's fine*, she seemed to say. *You're all a bunch of warts.*

Glittery dirt peeled away from the obstruction to reveal an enormous lens, identical to the smaller one I'd just been staring through.

Then another lens broke through the earth, and another, until finally, seven crooked metal arms surrounded us like spider legs. Each arm curled around an enormous lens that glinted in our star's purple light. Dirt streamed off the machines in sparkly waterfalls, but the lenses remained perfect, pristine glass.

Something pricked my neck.

What was that?

I tried to slap at it, and sighed philosophically when Nereida didn't move. It was probably Sahn trying to pick up where we'd left off.

Or did they have mosquitos here?

As it pinched me, I tried to soak in the details of this machine, amazed, as always, that it could look so similar to things back home, like something from an abandoned factory. Maybe a very rich, antique factory, but still it had cogs, pulleys, and smelled like oil and burnt metal shavings.

Kazie hopped off the telescope and cranked a dial on the base. It pivoted in answer, grinding toward the rock-lattice mountains.

Heat continued to crawl down my spine like a pinched nerve, but Nereida didn't react, nor did Sahn, who I saw was not behind me but beside me again. And he jumped whenever she stubbed her toe. Bryn was right about one thing—the male's Mark was definitely protection.

My shoulders wanted to squirm at the sensation between them, but I couldn't.

Was it my alarm clock going off? I should reassemble that thing into an egg timer.

But I didn't need to return yet. I'd lasted an hour, and my body and memory remained intact, alive, every sense firing awake. No, I was *stronger*.

I could taste the air and its sweetness for the first time. And Nereida's eyes not only zoomed, which no longer bothered me, but could detect the finest sparkle inside the veins running through the squid-like trees.

And the *sounds*. How could I have never noticed the music humming from the leaves? Even the gears were part of the symphony, a low base note accompanying the rest of the world. I'd needed to stay in longer to hear this. To *live* this and—

Something grabbed *inside* me.

A fist clenched my spine, no longer asking gently, but pulling with the force of a freight train.

This was no alarm clock.

I dug into Nereida, latching on to her as the power tried to wrench me away by the roots of the memory. Strong, it was so damn strong.

A headache stormed between my eyes as it pulled again, a wave sweeping me out to sea.

Before I was flung into the abyss.

CHAPTER 20

The Place Where Lost Things Go

Everything hurt. My brain. My *toes*. My skull. Something pounded between my eyeballs, something that wanted to escape my head.

Rowan?

Did I know that voice? Soft, lyrical, musical. Like the piano—that's what I'd first thought. A buzz under the veins that hummed even now, when every part of me hurt.

Rowan. ROE!

His voice echoed inside me, like the muscle that had yanked me out of Ruhaven, a fury that tugged me out with the force of a deep-sea current. This time, I hadn't seen the nothingness between worlds, the Prayama, I'd been thrown out of it with a fist on my spine.

And landed here.

Someone screamed again. No, not someone. *Him.*

A shudder swam through me. Bryn? I could feel him even in this numb state, like I could in every room. He'd know what was wrong—he knew everything. I just had to…

A moan slipped through my lips when I struggled to open my eyes.

Emerald leaves swirled into a crystalline blue sky. No—not a sky, Bryn's eyes.

Except it wasn't him, not really. Because for once, his face wasn't unemotional stone perfection. Deep grooves carved a *V* between his eyebrows, and a welt rose under his left eye.

"B—Br—?" I croaked, my voice scratching the length of my throat.

As I struggled to keep his face in focus, to keep my eyes on his perfect blue ones, something sparkled in the corner of my vision. Colors fractured and broke apart, like my sister had once told me they'd done when her retina had detached after she'd fallen in volleyball practice.

But my body was swollen and heavy from the Gate, my lips too numb to ask Bryn what was happening as the glimmer moved from the corner of my eye to surround us. Not just fractured colors, but an imaginary sky hovering just behind Bryn, with millions of tiny, golden stars winking in its depths.

I think Bryn was touching me, that even in this dizzying state, it was his cool fingers I felt on my neck, my shoulders. His voice whispering over the dull ache in my ears. His warm breath at my cold, cold cheek.

Was I dying? Had the Gate taken too much, just like James had warned? Or had it finally recognized me as the false Ruhaven and thrown me out?

The stars winked away. One by one, their gold light faded into the darkness, into the void of space, until they were nothing. Until I was.

⚙☀

I don't know if I slept, but I went somewhere.

It was like being a child again with Willow, lying next to her in the camping tent on a cold summer night, where the slight chill in the air somehow made the sleep all the better. The air tasted different then, like it did now, except I knew—somewhere—it was Bryn I felt, tasted.

Would he tell James that I'd snuck to the Gate? Maybe. Probably.

I drifted further, deeper. Floating, if not sleeping.

Distant *thwacks* of something being chopped echoed like a base tempo of a song I couldn't hear. The trees shimmied the next verse with the quiet, so quiet rustling of oak leaves.

In the cool shadows, I searched for Bryn again. And when his hand found mine, I slipped into sleep.

⚙☀

Slowly, I pried open my eyes. And stared into Bryn's.

"*Rowan*," he breathed.

Hands slid under my back, firm, warm, lifting me even as Ireland's greens swirled into pistachio ice cream. My stomach lurched, but I forced down the bile in my throat. How long had I been in the Gate? Had I awoken before? A vague memory of Bryn, of stars, poked through the fog in my brain.

"Head between your knees," Bryn insisted, pressing on my neck until I was forced to watch a ladybug crawl between my boots. "You slept for an hour, nearly enough for the effects to wear off."

Effects?

I ran my tongue over my lips, finding them dry and cracked, my throat rusty. Because I wasn't sure I could form words yet, I sucked muddy air through my nostrils and prayed to every Ruhaven god that I didn't throw up in front of Bryn.

He moved his hand from my neck to my forehead. "You do not have a fever," he murmured after a moment. "Or at least, not anymore."

Then it all came back to me—my escape to the Gate under Bryn's nose, the alarm clock I'd rigged, the numbing pain upon waking.

I craned my neck to look at him.

Bryn knelt in the dirt and weeds beside me, linen slacks ruined, the knees two soaked splotches like he'd fallen multiple times. The sleeves of his sweater were muddied to the elbows. Sweat and rain curled his hair, so it looped under each ear and framed the slope of his cheeks. A single bruise marred his otherwise pale, porcelain face.

I blinked at it. "What happened? Are you okay?"

His hand fell away. "You struck me with the alarm clock."

When? Why?

"Because I could not wake you quicker," he said when I asked. "It took me too long to notice you had stolen to the Gate. When you did not appear for lunch with me, I assumed you had been caught up in your work. But you were not in the gate lodge, not in your room, not in the garage or the woodshed."

Because I'd grabbed my knapsack and hiked directly to the Gate. And now he was here and...

"I thought perhaps you had gone for a walk, though I have never seen you do so," Bryn continued, voice scarily monotone. "But then I checked your room and I saw the empty hook above the dresser where you keep your rucksack. I arrived here as quickly as I was able, but the cane slowed me down—initially. I thought I may be too late, Rowan."

"Too late for what?" But I could see it in his eyes. The alarm clock hadn't worked, and I hadn't woken up in an hour. Stupid—that's what I was, and it was why I wasn't in the Ledger. "What time is it?"

For a moment, he looked like the portrait in his bedroom again, wild and windblown and dangerous. "What were you *thinking*?"

A bird chirped painfully near my ear.

"I—I—well—"

"Why did you not ask me to accompany you?" Bryn demanded, all earlier understanding gone—so much so that I wondered if I'd imagined the worry in his eyes, the hand that had lulled me to sleep. "You did this intentionally. Misleading James and I, and risking—risking yourself with this *foolishness*."

Because the real answer had a whisper of shame creeping into my cheeks, I flubbed a response. "I just wanted to visit the Gate alone, that's all." He'd never understand, not Bryn, who revered the Gate and everything in it.

"Rowan, do you not understand what may have happened?"

My pulse stuttered in my veins. "I—no, I didn't..."

"Did James not explain this?"

"He only said we needed an anchor."

"*Then perhaps you should have listened*," Bryn bit out, dragging the brass clock through the dirt. "And *this*." He flicked the bell, the sound thundering like a bullet through the woods. "This would have done nothing. Why, Rowan, why would you take such a risk?"

I firmed my lips, looked away. I hadn't asked him to watch over me, hadn't asked him to come here, even if I was grateful he had. If the Gate had taken me, it'd have been what I deserved for lying to it. Didn't Bryn know that? Hadn't he seen me from the very beginning and known what I was? Or more accurately, who I *wasn't*?

"Tell me now, or else I shall inform James of your suicide attempt today."

I swallowed at the harsh words, at the reality I hadn't wanted to acknowledge. "It wasn't that," I said quietly.

"If it was, I should never let you near the Gate again."

He forced me to meet his eyes, shifted so that our knees were nearly touching, the mud staining his now dry. "This was about the Azekiel," Bryn stated.

If I could be sure I wouldn't be sick, I'd walk home right now on my own. "No, it's not."

"You are lying to me again, Rowan."

How did he always know? From the moment I'd stood in his office, he'd looked at me and *known*. Who I was. Who I wasn't. Maybe the Mark of light gave him a gateway to truth.

I twisted a pile of loose ivy in my fist. "It's Roe."

He grabbed my hand, forced my fingers open until the prickly leaves fell loose. "Why is it that you are so ashamed of yourself?"

I stole my hand away, my skin now tingling like I'd grabbed a patch of nettles. Maybe I had. "I'm not. That's my name."

"You know what I am speaking of."

It must be nice to never doubt yourself. To be confident enough to let everyone and their uncle watch you in the Gate, to know the person you became in Ruhaven really *was* you.

"Rowan?" Bryn pressed, but without the bite.

I was failing at Naruka, Ruhaven, Willow, all of it, just like I'd failed at everything else.

"You do not wish to be with the Azekiel in the Gate," Bryn stated, voice utterly blank. "I understand, but I do not see why you have stolen to the Gate alone, have put yourself in danger, because of it."

"It's not that."

His fingers drummed softly into the earth. "You *do* wish to be with the Azekiel?" Bryn clarified.

"No—I mean, that's nothing to do with it."

The fingers paused, flattened. "Then what?"

His breath misted before me, Bryn's silence so potent that it felt like I was at a confessional, waiting for something or someone to grant me absolution.

"When Tye and I were anchoring at the Gate," I began in a small voice, "James was in Ruhaven with Essie." Of all the people to have to explain this to, why did it have to be *him*?

"Yes?" Another fog of breath hovered. Waited.

I stopped biting my cheek. "I mean *with* Essie."

A lowly potato bug crawled between flattened grass. It stopped an inch from Bryn's ring finger, then skittered in another direction.

"Rowan."

I didn't look up.

"Rowan."

When he covered my hand with his, I met his eyes. Torrents of rain, the breaking of icy snow in winter, a chill at midnight—that's what they were. What he was.

"You are embarrassed by how you may react in the Gate," Bryn clarified.

"Yes," I admitted. Like any sane person would be.

Blue eyes crinkled. "Rowan, James reacts as he does because he has spent over thirty years in the Gate. You, as such a beginner, shall react to a lesser extent," he said, mild amusement replacing his earlier bite.

But the hand that grasped mine was dizzyingly distracting. Bryn never touched me, never touched anyone if he could help it. Kazie might have launched herself at him, but he seemed to endure rather than enjoy it. He never shook hands, never hugged, never made a passing touch like Tye often did.

I stared at our joined hands like they could distract from the heat working into my ears. I'd never noticed the scars on his before. The slight dent on the knuckle of his thumb. The raised scar on the third knuckle. Even what looked like a rope burn that had healed poorly between his thumb and first finger. And still, he was beautiful. A pianist's hands without a piano.

"Rowan?" Bryn prompted.

I forced my gaze up. Talking about this while he was practically holding my hand wasn't helping. "But still, I'll *react*," I acknowledged lamely. "With the Azekiel."

He smiled slightly, then lifted his hand from mine and grabbed the knapsack, slid the canisters back in. "Yes, you will *still*," he confirmed. "Strong emotions always transmit, as your pain from the Tether did."

So there was no avoiding it.

Light rain began to pad softly around us, the drops sliding down Bryn's neck and disappearing under the collar of a shirt that was ruined from burrs when he'd hurried to the Gate. With a cane. I'd made a cripple chase me into the woods.

"Rowan," he said carefully, pivoting with the bag. "Perhaps you do not wish to speak of this to me, but I do understand how you feel about the irregular expressions of the Gate."

I nearly laughed. *Irregular expressions*. "What, because of all those fairy women?"

His eyes crinkled, just slightly. "I believe I have already told you there are no fairies—women or otherwise—in the Gate." Well, maybe that explained why I'd never seen a hair out of place, or a single heavy breath slip between Bryn's wide, perfect mouth. "And while there is no need to be embarrassed of your Azekiel, I may have an alternative."

My eyebrows shot up. "Really?" Then suspicion took hold. "What?"

He looked almost amused. "You know, Rowan, despite our unfortunate start in my office, I am not predisposed to disliking you."

It took me a second to unravel the words. "That's...good."

He shifted closer, his pale fingers digging into the black soil. "You are aware I can anchor myself, but I am also able to anchor both of us from *within* the Gate," he said, adding in a soft voice, "I would not need to wake up first."

"Anchor us both from the Gate?" Then he wouldn't see me here. No one would if we visited the Gate together. "How? Are you sure? What if we both end up lost in Ruhaven?"

Rain beaded on the tips of his eyelashes. "I am absolutely certain."

I worried my bottom lip. "But if you're wrong, I might cause both of us to get stuck."

"I would never risk you," he stated, so simply, it seemed like the absolute truth. "And I am certain it will work, as I have anchored us before. For it was not Tye who awoke you when your Tether broke, but myself."

"You—what? No, you didn't. You weren't there. You were in the Gate when Tye anchored me."

"Because I woke you from within the Gate, then anchored myself shortly after," he explained patiently. "So you see, I am quite capable of anchoring both of us should you prefer this solution. Or," he drawled, "you can continue to thwart my efforts of keeping you safe by pretending a suspicious level of interest in my painting subjects."

Caught red-handed, I winced. But why hadn't Bryn admitted it'd been him to anchor me? Maybe he didn't want Tye to know. Still, if he could anchor both of us, then my embarrassing, feathered problem was solved. "I'm sorry I lied to you about the vegetable patch painting."

"You should be, as I have never painted so terribly. Though, perhaps, it is because I exclusively paint nudes." I blinked, then his lips quirked. "That was a joke, Rowan. So tell me, would my proposition prevent any further alarm clock heists?"

I shook the image of Bryn painting nudes from my head and spun a finger in the dirt. "You definitely wouldn't need to wake up first?" And see me.

"No, we would be quite alone." His breath brushed my cheek. "Would you prefer that, Rowan?"

I felt myself flush at his suddenly teasing tone.

"I—I..." I shoved up before Bryn could stop me.

Oh no.

My stomach swam like a fishbowl, and I wasn't sure there wasn't a guppy floating around too. Bryn tried to steady me, but when my braid tick-tocked in a nauseating pendulum, I clapped a hand over my mouth, dived away, and ended up face-planting in a prickly fern.

Just. Great.

"Can you..." I shot out my index finger from the shrub in what I prayed was a direction far, far away. "Look—go—somewhere else, please? Anywhere else."

A twig snapped by my leg. Then Bryn was kneeling beside me, stroking my back like he had when I woke, and recalling some distracting story about how he'd once caught Kazie sneaking off to the Gate as well.

Please don't let him see me hurl yesterday's oysters.

But I relaxed into the firm strokes, each one easing some of the nausea, and sighed into the dirt as a slug crept by my nose.

When I peeked through the fern again, the sky had cleared to a powder blue with a few wispy clouds. A seagull soared by with a mighty *caw*.

Bryn's mouth curved into an easy smile. "Will you tell me what you saw in the Gate? Perhaps it will help distract you."

Nothing could be more distracting than Bryn, but I told him about the machine I'd encountered, then added, "Sahn stuck his head in the lens."

An interesting nickname. Amusement danced in the corners of Bryn's eyes. "Have you ever seen a sextant before?"

I coughed. "Uh, what? A sex ant?"

A quick chuckle escaped his wide lips. "Not a sex ant, a sex*tant*. A nautical instrument used for navigation at sea. It resembles what you are describing, except that it can be held in the palm of your hand. But in Ruhaven, what you saw is a *Florissant*—a machine that Ruhavens use to travel. Jamellian, Kazmira, and Nereida are likely configuring it to transport themselves to Drachaut to find your Tether."

I was still picturing a couple of ants crawling over each other. "Why?"

"Because they must repair the broken bond between you and your tethered Drachaut. With each minute, Nereida's life is depleting."

"So they need to find her—the tethered Drachaut—and figure out why she's injured?"

"I suspect so, yes."

I frowned into the dirt. How long did I have before Nereida's life ended? What would James do when I had no memories left to witness? "Will you tell James? About today?" *And doom me for eternity.*

"Only to cause him the same heart attack you inflicted upon me?" Bryn rubbed the golden stubble on his jaw. "I think not. No, I shall hold this over you until there is an appropriate time for leverage." But he smiled when he said it.

I released a sigh and lifted my sticky forehead. This was not the impression I wanted to leave, especially after Bryn had offered to anchor us both. I probably looked like one of those Irish badgers James kept shooing out of his garden.

Wait, what was that?

I shielded my eyes, squinting at something golden and rectangular shimmering under a fern.

I reached toward the object, found it cold, hard, and grooved. Thick ivy had grown over the thing, the sharp leaves pricking my hand when I tried to pry it from the dirt. It took me three tries, but when I did, I dragged the plaque toward me with dirt-encrusted nails.

Istilick mi liom, shakila, was engraved on the side coated in dirt. I'd seen this before, hadn't I? On some painting…

I flipped it over. On this side, a larger name was written in cursive trenches, the shiny gold reflecting an unblemished sky.

Mohammed Riulinimi…, I read, dusting off the dirt. *Mohammed. Mohammed Riulinimi.* Who was Mohammed, and why was a plaque dedicated to him buried here?

Then I noticed the others.

CHAPTER 21

Something There

Everywhere, the glittering plates poked above creeping ivy, beaded with dew and sparkling like a thief had split his sack of gold amongst the woods.

"Rowan?"

I pushed to my feet, brushing aside Bryn's offer of help. "What *are* these?" I asked, pointing to each in turn. How had I never noticed them before? "Is this some dedication?"

Bryn tried to reach for it, but I yanked it away. "What *is* it?" I insisted.

He shook his head. "A memorial."

A memorial? But I recognized these names—Ruhavens who'd visited Naruka. What would that—?

I dropped to the ground. No, *no*. The buzzing in my ears drowned out whatever Bryn was saying behind me. I stabbed my hands into the earth, digging through dark clay, slugs, and worms. *Snap.* I yanked at the roots, breaking them in my fist.

What would I do if I found something—something *human*?

Bryn's shadow fell over the hole I'd carved in the earth. "Rowan, stop this. These are sacred here."

Sacred. But he worshiped Ruhaven, existed inside that world for hours every day. Would there ever be a line he wouldn't cross for it?

"Why? What am I going to find?" I muttered just as my fingers scraped something smooth and clear. What was it, goddamn it? What was—

Not bone.

I nearly sagged with relief when I yanked out my treasure—a man's rusted spectacles. What were *these* doing buried here? And what an idiot I must have looked like right now, holding a pair of dirty glasses, my face probably still bone white. Had I honestly thought James would—

I jumped when Bryn's fingers curled around my shoulder. "You must rebury those, *now*."

Why? I twisted around, but was so off balance, I nearly decked Bryn with the glasses. "But what are these?" I asked, gesturing at the plaques. There must have been hundreds.

Bryn's face slipped into cold ice again. "If you cannot stomach a few undoubtedly entertaining rounds with an Azekiel, I doubt you are ready for this."

"I thought they were *irregular expressions*."

He set his jaw, his eyes going to unamused slits.

And there went any hope of him taking me to the Gate.

I resisted backing up when Bryn stepped forward, studying me from under dizzying eyelashes, his cane squelching in the mud.

I thrust the glasses between us, a barrier against my nerves. "Please, just tell me."

He exhaled, long, slow, like a wave cresting to shore, then curled his fingers around my hand holding the glasses. "This is a Token," he explained slowly. "Each Ruhaven chooses one to be buried for them before they make the Fall. This is what you have desecrated."

I clenched the glasses hard enough they would have cracked if Bryn hadn't stopped me. Since I'd first walked into his office, Bryn had held back information from me—from James too—when what he knew could have explained Maggie's death. "I'll desecrate the rest of what's buried here—scarves, hats, dentures, whatever—if you keep holding back."

His face soured, but still managed to look only as bad as a model who'd been given the least favorable design for the runway.

"I obviously cannot stop you from digging up our religious site like a child's sandbox." He rolled his shoulders, a bird adjusting its wings after landing. "James prefers to wait to reveal the Fall—wisely, I might add. However, I can tell you that the Fall is when a Ruhaven chooses to return home. Not to the memories, which can never be changed, but to be reborn as Ruhaven again. If we are in the Gate when our memories finish, then our souls can attempt the Fall."

The woods quieted—or my racing heart drowned everything else out. Had I heard wrong? Had he really said…

"Reborn in Ruhaven? That's…that's impossible. You don't believe that?"

But of course Bryn did. There was nothing of Ruhaven he didn't worship, if James had told him this was possible, he'd believe it.

"Yes, Rowan, I do. I have seen it. I witnessed Mohammed disappear at this very Gate, his soul returned to Ruhaven."

I backed away from him, the possibility of what he dangled left a cavernous hole that threatened to drown me. How would this even work? Did we go back in time? Did we transport? Did we remember who we were? Or were we reborn like now?

I blubbered out all my questions in a nonsensical loop, then landed on one. "If—if I did that, what happens to—to me?"

He reached for me again, grabbing my wrists, emotion banking in his eyes. "You are Nereida. Therefore, *you* will return to Ruhaven, but your life here would cease to be. You would not be Rowan, you would not remember who you were, no one would."

I stammered under him. I'd stop existing, and then—then I'd be someone else. Someone better, maybe someone like my sister.

"You do not need to make the Fall, Rowan," he said, softer now.

I stared blankly at the glittering graveyard. "They all... they all returned to Ruhaven?"

He closed the space between us, and the tingling in my wrists spread to the rest of my body. "In a manner, their souls returned, as yours would. You would become Nereida, though she would not remember you."

Was that why James had brought me here? Not to find the reason for the Inquitate, but because I could be Nereida. I could be James's sister— the real one.

Panicked, I shoved away from Bryn with the glasses still clenched in my fist, forcing him to fight for balance with his cane. "Rowan, this is why James did not wish to tell you yet. It is a great deal to understand and accept."

Air whistled in and out of my lungs. "What if I'd made the Fall on one of my trips in Ruhaven?" I'd die in the Gate, and never be able to say goodbye to Willow.

His voice was brisk now. "Breathe, Rowan, else the shock will take over and I shall not be able to carry you home. You will know before the Fall begins and the memories start to end. None of us wish for you to make this accidentally."

Yet that was exactly what could have happened.

"*Don't* you?" I accused, and chucked the glasses.

Bryn juggled the spectacles, annoyance riding high in his flushed cheekbones. "Have you no respect at all?"

Respect? When they didn't respect me enough to warn me? I ground my teeth. How could I expect them to when *I* was the one currently lying to everyone?

Shaking my head, I turned and walked quickly into the woods, away from Bryn, away from all of it.

⚙ ⚙

When the trees finally parted, Naruka's windows glittered with emerald reflections, and I heard the unmistakable sound of James's Ford farting up the lane. He drove with one arm out the window, a cigarette in his hand, switching between chatting and arguing with Kazie.

My lungs still ached from the rush down the mountain, from the shock of what might have happened to me. Why hadn't James told me? I could barely stomach the likely answer—that he'd wanted Nereida back, and it was just easier if I didn't know.

I watched as he pulled to a stop in Naruka's shadow, where the Ford's exhaust pipe shook like a scolding parent before settling into quiet disapproval.

Kazie popped out of the car first, shouting a quick hello to me as she flew past and into the house.

"Would ye stop visiting that Irish gift shop?" James yelled after her, slamming the Ford's door. In his soaked snowcap jacket and black rain boots, he looked like a dehydrated penguin. "Oh, Roe, how ye? Did yerself and Bryn go on up to the Gate? Where is he?" He squinted at the empty trail behind me.

How was I? Shaky, exhausted, and apparently one memory away from my soul tumbling through the Gate permanently.

"Got ya that Cork spiced beef ya like," Tye said, emerging with a bag of potatoes over one shoulder and a grocery bag cradled in his elbow. "As long as we're both still eatin' meat, we gotta splurge, huh?" The bag thunked against his back as he stopped and lifted his ball cap with his wrist. "You okay, kid? You're as pale as Stornoway."

I strode unsteadily toward the misty car that steamed fumes out its butt.

Did Tye know too? Had he planned to tell me? To warn me?

I planted my hands on the overheated hood, more for balance than anything. James looked at me curiously, crumbs dotting his jacket. I took a deep breath. "Were you ever planning to tell me about the Fall?" I asked quietly.

Shock registered on his handsome face.

Tye only arched a slow brow. "So, Stornoway spilled the beans," he drawled.

James cursed loudly and slapped the car. "Ah, for feck's sake."

Why didn't he want me to find out? Because he knew I wasn't Nereida? Or—or was it so he could exchange Roe-the-electrician for Nereida-the-sister like a Ruhaven slot machine?

I lifted my hands off the hood. "I found the plaques after I came back from the Gate. Why didn't you tell me, James?"

Tye answered, "Hun, do ya really think now was the best time to spring this on ya?" He shifted the bag of potatoes to his other arm. "You're just gettin' settled. Ain't no need to talk about the Fall this early."

James nodded as he dug for another smoke. "Roe, me mum taught me to space things out. Ye don't go throwing reincarnation at people after telling them about the Gate. I wanted to give ye a bit of time is all."

Relief whistled through my lungs. Was that really why he'd waited? "I could have handled it."

James let out a short laugh. "Oh, ye mean like when ye nearly stole me bloody car?"

"Or when ya thought that beast man was gonna kill ya?" Tye piled on.

"Or when ye wanted to avoid the Gate because yer Tether broke?"

Points unfortunately taken. I grabbed the smoke Tye held out. "But what if I'd made this Fall without knowing?"

"Ye think I'd let ye escape that easily?" James asked with a grin. "I'll explain things properly over tea like, or..." He broke off, scratching at his jaw and squinting at the spot Tye was now staring at. Then he let out a low chuckle.

I followed Tye's gaze.

Bryn limped from the shadows into Naruka's garden, sweat beading on his temples and hair plastered to the sides of his face. Mud spiraled up his cane in a crude art experiment.

I should have helped him walk back, should have stayed with him, just in case.

He stopped about ten feet away, bracing a hand on the hotel's stone walls to catch his breath. "Rowan, while you may enjoy the exercise, I am not a gazelle and do not take pleasure from bounding through the woods multiple times a day."

James nudged my side. "I'll say, I do quite like the state ye keep him in, Roe. Good for him."

Tye shoved past Bryn. "You ever think she's tired of all your hovering, Stornoway? You're worse than an old woman. Breathing down Roe's neck all the damn time like the Inquitate are gonna jump out of the shadows."

"Don't ye two get into it again," James warned.

"What happened last time?" I asked, but Tye only grunted as he booted open the tack room door.

Kazie came bounding out when he did, skipping in a loop around the house before grabbing another basket from the car, and shouting, "Hey, Bryn! Why do you have my alarm clock?" Then disappearing past me for the second time.

I stared at the clock in Bryn's fist, the one I'd left at the Gate, the one I'd forgotten about.

Slowly, I raised my gaze to Bryn's and caught faint amusement before he wiped it away.

"So James," I said, trying to draw his attention, "why don't you tell me all about the Fall now?"

But his eyes pinwheeled to the evidence of my self-guided trip to Ruhaven, his mouth gaping like the stuffed bass nailed above Naruka's fireplace. "Jayzus. Mary. And Joseph," he panted, fury widening his nostrils as I braced myself. "Tell me that's not what I think it is. Go on, tell me, Bryn."

His eyes twinkled before he threw me bodily to the wolves. "While I wish I could persuade you otherwise, James, I cannot."

Oh, you think that's funny?

Moderately.

James covered his face, inhaled, then dropped his hands and pointed a finger at me. "Rowan Tullum, ye will *not* tell me ye took a feckin' alarm clock to bring ye back. Oh, me feckin' word. Me mammy's rolling in her grave—circles! That's what ye've done to her. And Bryn, ye were supposed to be watching…" When Tye stepped out of the house, James trailed off before he could say *"after the Inquitate in Norway."* Instead, he settled with crossing himself.

Resting a hip on the car, I flicked up my hood as the rain started. "James, I swear I didn't know I needed a *person*."

He paced in circles before Naruka's crimson door, fumbling for another cigarette. "An alarm clock," he muttered. "Ye'll have me hair going feckin' gray before I'm forty, so ye will."

Bryn corrected dryly, "James, you *are* forty."

"Ah, go away with ye!"

I jumped when Tye planted his hands on either side of me, denting the car's hood. His hair was soaked to dark brown and curled under his ball cap. "Darlin', you don't have any goddamn idea what might have happened to ya," he growled, breath smelling of Irish coffee.

"I do know. I mean, I know *now*. I'm sorry."

In the corner of my eye, Bryn peeled himself off Naruka.

"Just because you wanted to go off on your merry own, ya go on up there without a fuckin' thought!" Except I *had* put a lot of thought into it—especially the clock. "You're supposed to be the one with sense around here, not with your head in the damn clouds. You might have died today for a bunch of fairy dreams."

I shrank under Tye's accusations. What if, because of his cane, Bryn hadn't made it in time? What if he hadn't been watching after me today?

I smoothed my palms on my shaking thighs. "Tye, I—"

Bryn grabbed Tye by the shoulder and yanked him away from me like a horse pulled back by its halter.

Tye stumbled, then jabbed him in the chest. "This is *your* damn fault, Stornoway."

"It's not," I said, shoving off the hood. "*I* went up there. I thought the clock would work."

"Then you're a goddamn idiot," Tye said flatly.

I winced.

James maneuvered between them, prying them apart with a hand on each shoulder. Then he turned on me. "Roe, I don't know what ye were bloody thinking. Ye know I'd take ye to the Gate meself, and there's a reason we've not been letting ye stay in as long. 'Tis not safe. But ye risk yerself, ye risk Nereida, ye risk me sister," he hounded me, on and on and on.

Sister. I only had one sister, and she was dead.

I curled my fingers in my jacket. "Stop it!" I shouted at him, unable to stand the tirade. Every favour he'd done for me, every stew he'd made, every walk to the Gate to show me Ruhaven, all the effort he'd gone to in bringing me here, had been for a lie. "I don't need you protecting me. I don't need Bryn following me. I don't need Tye critiquing my repairs. And most of all—I am *not* your goddamn sister."

James froze, his lips popping open like I'd slapped him, his pupils going wide and dark. A slow blush crept across his cheeks and nose. He lowered his voice until his accent had none of its up-and-down charm. "Well, if that's what ye think, Roe."

What I thought didn't matter, but what was true was that I wasn't who James wanted me to be. That woman had died of an aneurysm walking alone on a side street of L'Ardoise.

"James, it's not that I don't—"

He flipped up the hood of his jacket, spun on his heel, and strode briskly through the main entrance. The crimson doors slammed shut behind him.

I could actually taste my own foot in my mouth.

Tye stabbed his cigarette at Bryn's soaked woolen jacket. "Here we go again, Stornoway. Both of ya are too damn close to this." He ground the smoke under his heel and walked away.

Bryn and I stared at each other in the rain. His pale face beaded with wet rivers, his linen shirt now completely soaked through and clinging to muscle, the bluish vein at his neck disappearing under his collar.

"Rowan, you are getting wet," he said finally. *Go inside.*

And say what?

That even if I were James's sister, a few months in Ruhaven didn't replace a lifetime with Willow?

Bryn said nothing, only continued watching me through eerily blue eyes as the rain pounded harder and harder, cracking on the Ford's battered hood. I broke contact, then crossed my arms to pin my jacket tighter as I strode past him and into Naruka.

James was in the kitchen.

After months here, it was as welcoming as my mom's had once been, even if the occupier was angrily sorting teabags. The jacket he'd been wearing hung limply from the coat rack, a thin puddle gathering beneath it so the slow *drip-drip* fell in time with the clocks.

On the table, two dried-out sandwiches waited on wooden plates, a cup of tea in front of one, water for the other. Neither was touched.

And I'd left Bryn up in the woods. A Ruhaven wouldn't have done that. They'd have thought of how the trail would be slick with mud for a cripple, or of the Inquitate that might still be hunting him. They'd certainly have thought of James, who'd given up his life to help Ruhavens find Naruka, to show them that impossible dream up in the woods. A dream Willow might have wanted to return to, but I never would.

"James, I'm sorry that I said—"

"It might be," he cut in with his back to me, "that some of us take our past lives more seriously than ye, Roe. Might be offended by the way ye so flippantly throw that in our face."

I deserved that, but the coldness in his tone had my gut clenching. I couldn't possibly explain to him the mess I'd made for myself, or what it'd do to him if he knew the truth. What it was doing to me right now, to see the obvious pain I'd caused.

"I'm sorry," I said again, pausing under the priest calendar to rub my forehead. "I'm trying to... to figure all this out. It's not that I don't..."

How did I say this to him? I didn't have the words that Willow did, wasn't good with people like her.

But I liked James, liked his puppy-dog eyes and quick charm, liked how the simplest things made him happy—like when I glued a new rubber band around the oven door to keep the temperature constant. But I wasn't his sister. And he wasn't my brother.

His shoulders tensed. "Ye don't need to say it, Roe. Ye've made yerself clear." Tea trickled from a kettle in the shape of a polka-dot mushroom. "So I'll let that go and say only that I don't know what would possess ye to go to the Gate alone. I thought I made meself clear ye need an anchor. And yet for all yer sense, ye didn't listen. Why?"

I tapped the heel of my boot.

This was at least easier to explain, if a whole lot more embarrassing. Maybe he was comfortable with his public displays with Essie, but I would never be.

James swept his gaze over me. "*Well?*" he demanded when I remained mute.

Heat pricked the tips of my ears. *Just get it over with.* If I could tell Bryn, surely I could tell James. "It's just that when Nereida is… I mean, when she's with—"

"I will take Rowan to the Gate from now on."

I started at the sound of Bryn's voice from the doorway. His cane tapped softly on the linoleum as he stepped into the kitchen, angling himself between James and I.

Slowly, James set down his tea. "What's this about like?"

"I will anchor both of us. You know I am able."

Guilty relief lifted the weight on my shoulders. So he hadn't changed his mind.

James's brows knitted together—but he wasn't looking at me. "Ye think 'tis smart to be going to the Gate with Roe, to be in the memories with her?"

"It's safe," I answered immediately. "Bryn pulled me out before and I didn't realize it."

James made a noncommittal sound before sipping his tea. "I don't like it."

"It is not for you to decide," Bryn stated.

I glanced between the two. I was missing something, some unspoken challenge. But after moment, James said, "Alright so, if that's what ye want. But ye've made a right bollocks of the rest, telling Roe of the Fall. So ye'll make yerself scarce while I give her the answers ye've forced out of me too early."

Bryn hesitated, but this time, it was him who gave in. He turned and met my eyes, inclined his head, then strode out.

James leaned against the cupboard, face set in unreadable lines as he gripped his steaming tea.

I toed at a pebble I'd dragged in, glad he didn't look quite as angry. "You really think we just… disappear when the memories end?"

"Not think, sure, I know. I've witnessed it meself many a time and 'tis not something I'm likely to forget. It's something that we each choose when the memories end. I would have told ye eventually, of course, but ye were ready to leave Naruka only a month ago. I didn't think it was time."

He'd taken me to Norway, paid for my flight, the hotel room. Helped me find what must have killed Willow. But had it all been to get Nereida back?

"And you, will you make this Fall?" I asked.

He walked in a slow circle around the kitchen, studying the portraits, or maybe the clocks, seeming to need the time to settle himself. Automatically, he kicked the fridge as he passed, then straightened a fur rug thrown over the back of a chair.

"No," he admitted quietly. "Though how ye must believe that every bone in me body wants to. Though ye may not consider our relationships of much importance to ye, what with not wanting to be me sister and all, it so happens I do take them fairly seriously. So no, I won't be going back. I'll die a man here."

Why? Did he not believe in the Fall? I started toward him, stopped. "What is it, James? Why won't you go? If you believe it?"

He stiff-armed the chair, used it to support his weight as though he were an older man. "Don't ye understand yet, Roe?" He looked out the window, at the cliff jutting over Naruka. At the Gate which loomed over us all. "Didn't ye notice there's someone missing from the Gate?"

I frowned. Missing? "I…Willow?"

Annoyance flattened his lips. "No, not yer sister, Roe. Bloody hell, how blind can ye be?" He twisted away from the window, eyes swimming. "'Tis Essie who's missing from the *Ledger*. Don't ye understand what it's like for us, for me? Have ye no care at all for what it is to love Essie like I do, to see her every day in the Gate, to watch and love and hold her memory, yet to look at the *Ledger* and not find her name?" Eyes shimmering, he slapped a hand on the counter, fought back tears.

Even the clocks fell silent in the stillness of the kitchen.

Sticky shame washed through me.

Because no, I hadn't thought about Essie. She was just one more creature in the Gate, a character in a play that was as fictional as the Azekiel. "You wanted to find her here," I said hollowly.

He looked away from me, stared at the tiled backsplash above the sink.

Then realization struck, thick and consuming. "No, not just that. You thought she'd be *me*."

I could see it in his face—the truth written so plainly, I wondered how I hadn't seen it before. That's why he'd broken down in the forest. *Not for what I was, but who I wasn't.*

I wasn't Essie.

God, how could I be so blind? So *selfish*?

"Is there no one else she could be in the *Ledger*?" I asked quietly.

He shook his head, weary now as he gripped the counter, the tea forgotten. "No. There's no one, Roe. We've found the last, and anyone else is too old or young to have been her."

"But why not make the Fall then? Wouldn't you…" I was out of my depth. Emotionally. Theoretically. "Find her again?"

"No. Eight hundred years ago, one of two things happened to Essie. She either lived out her life, or she died and made the crossing here with me. As she's not in the *Ledger*, she would have passed away in Ruhaven some centuries ago. Only if we made the Fall together would our souls return. We can't. And I won't return without her."

I said nothing, just let the aching silence hang. How did I apologize for being what I wasn't? Never could be? Not Essie. Not the girl he'd grown up with as a child, not the woman he'd loved in the Gate later, with her round cheeks and curly hair. Not even his sister—I couldn't even offer James that.

In that moment, I felt smaller than the potato bug crawling up the chair leg.

"I wanted, so bloody badly, for someone to enter the Gate and look back at me through Essie's eyes," he admitted, fingers curling on the counter. "So badly. I hoped, that maybe—" his voice broke, "that maybe then, the woman I've known me whole life might finally know me as well. Might finally see me. *James*. Not Jamellian."

My throat went dry. He deserved that—to find Essie, to find someone who'd love him here. Not someone who'd thrown the fact of his sister in his face. "I'm… I'm so sorry. So sorry that I wasn't—"

"Ye know, Roe," he interrupted, voice so raw that I stopped talking at once to hear it, "I wanted ye to be Essie, 'tis true. But I never felt ye were, and I thought I should. So that day when I found out ye were me sister, it was when I knew for certain that Essie was dead." He rubbed his chin, fought for control. "But—but it was enough that I'd found me sister. It was enough. Until ye threw that back in me face today."

He strode out through the tack room, and quietly shut the door behind him.

⚙✦

I floated in the river of white milk where the bubbles floated up and up and up until they disappeared into the purple sky.

Here, I could lose myself again, forget what I'd done. I didn't want to think of James, of Essie, of the person I should be, but wasn't.

Kazie had voiced no questions when I asked her to take me to the Gate, to anchor me. I couldn't bring myself to ask Bryn.

So I kicked my feet, enjoying the feel of the thick warmth of the river as O'Sahnazekiel watched me with golden eyes from the beach.

He'd swam with me minutes ago, and now his braid hung in a wet swath past his waist, the end of it blackened like the wings that draped on the velvet, turquoise sand. Tattoos danced across half his naked body, caressing the inside of his thigh before wrapping around his left foot where talons dug into the sand.

I felt myself grin at him, beckon.

With a roll of his eyes—the motion like a planet circling the sun—he rose and stretched god-like wings. Their smoky depths spanned the width of the beach, casting the milk water and me in purple shadows, before he folded them gracefully behind him.

The length of him swung between his legs as he walked, and thankfully, I hadn't yet seen him use it. But a part of me wondered. And right now, miserable as I was, I might not care as much to see that side of him.

But Nereida only paddled toward the beach, watching with her zoomed vision the water rise over taut muscle, the tiny pulses of light gliding under his skin, as if his veins flowed with melted bronze.

When the river rose to his pebbled nipples and his braid floated, he grinned at me.

And a bubble burst in my face.

Nereida cursed and patted at the liquid streaming painlessly down her face. Just as she blinked it away, Sahn was there, scooping me up in his arms so that my feet kicked harmlessly in the water.

She pressed her hands to his cheeks, staring at him, saying something to him in that sense they used to greet each other, but this was something different, an invisible rope that strung from her chest to his. I *felt* him. Or some part of him.

She lifted her mouth to his as his fangs slid out.

And nipped his neck instead.

He let out a hoarse laugh when she jumped back, sending bubbles floating his way, this time bursting on whatever part of his braid had started to dry in the star's light.

He lifted his wings out of the river, held them above.

Don't you dare! she seemed to say.

With a devilish grin, he slammed them down.

The last I heard was Nereida's spluttered complaints as the wave smothered her.

CHAPTER 22

In Painter's Light

I was like the slugs that skidded over Naruka's mildew walls and dried out in the rare sun.

And now I'd upset—wounded—the one person who'd tried to help me from the moment I stepped foot in Ireland.

I'd smeared their entire belief system under my ugly shoes. Then I—this caused a line of embarrassment to flame up within me—I'd actually gone to Norway and accused a cripple of lying and maybe even injuring himself.

Slug? No, I was a speck of ant.

So I spent the next week avoiding the Gate, avoiding everyone, and cleaned the chimneys as my personal penance. My clothes were blackened with irreparable damage that I wore like a convict's chains.

At night, I slept fitfully, with dreams of Willow, James, and Essie all mixed up into one, with the grand finale of Nereida jumping off a massive cliff for the Fall.

What did I say to James? That I wished I *was* Essie for him? Or that I just wished I was someone for anyone, like I used to be for Willow?

Now I was no one. I wasn't even Nereida.

When the chimneys were so clean even Bryn would eat off them, I moved to the gutters. I'd roped in Tye to help me because I needed the reassurance there was at least one person who could still stand me here.

"Ya know, I kinda thought you'd have a lot more questions about the Fall," Tye mused as he grabbed a fistful of weeds.

Up on the roof, the wind slapped hot color into Tye's cheeks, and he somehow suited the rare blast of sun today, with his plaid jacket thick enough to withstand the October wind.

"I made a few notes. A number of journals mentioned it. I didn't know what it was before."

He squinted from the sun. "Look, you don't gotta worry about it now. It might be years away—twenty, thirty, could be tomorrow too. But the thing is, this is all normal for James and them. He grew up in the Gate. Ain't nothing that scares him when sometimes I think it oughta. Ya know?"

"Yeah," I said lamely. But James *was* scared—of not finding Essie.

Tye scratched his beard thoughtfully. "I saw someone make the Fall once, 'bout seven years ago. He heard the call at the end of the memories and up the mountain he went."

"Heard the call? What, like some dinner bell?"

Tye chuckled, deep and throaty, and tossed another handful of hogweed over his shoulder. "Something like that, yeah. I don't know what it sounds like, 'cause I ain't never been near the end."

"But if I go to the Gate when the memories end, what actually happens?"

Tye stabbed his glove into the eaves trough and ripped the weeds out by the roots. "Nothing," he said at last. "'Cause that's what happens to ya, Roe. You ain't you anymore. Your soul gets reborn some thousand years from now, or however long it takes your energy to get back to Tallah. And then you're what? Some fucker cleanin' toilets, maybe."

I smiled a little. "Ruhaven doesn't have toilets."

"Ya, don't I know it. But ya know what I'm saying. You ain't you. No memories, no 'hey, thanks, past life, for makin' that sacrifice.' You're just nothin'."

James didn't think so, though. He'd give it all up for a chance for Essie and him, if she was here.

What had Nereida thought before her soul made the crossing? Had she wondered who she might be reborn as, and whether they'd ever remember her? Was that why the memories existed at all? Maybe they were a kind of thank you to what had been, but then, why allow us to make the Fall?

"But what did you *see*?" I pressed. "During the Fall?"

Tye sighed long and deep. "I watched them disappear, watched Ruhaven steal them back," he said bitterly. "Their soul is stripped from their body, and through whatever damn connection exists between Tallah and here, it makes its way back. Then it's someone else with your soul."

"Isn't it mine still?" Or Willow's? Would it be hers that was sent back? If it took your soul?

"Technically, yeah, but who cares when ya won't remember who ya were?"

"Rowan?"

I didn't need Tye's annoyed sigh to tell me who stood below, but I slid my goggles over my head anyway, and glanced down.

Where the sunlight had given Tye a hearty glow, it had a different effect on Bryn. His skin appeared even paler than usual, his hair nearly white as the light simply melted off him.

Did he know about James and Essie? That James wanted me to be her?

"Are you certain it is safe to be up there?" Bryn asked, blinking back the light from his eyes. "The ladder is rotted, and the roof as well."

Tye guffawed beside me. "Don't ya ever get tired of cluckin' around here all the time, Stornoway? Go haunt the attic."

"I prefer other excitement." He held up a familiar paper bag. "Is this for me, Rowan?"

I scratched my cheek. "Yeah, I—I'm sorry about the Gate, and the lunch I missed."

Unbothered by what was likely the worst apology he'd ever heard, Bryn withdrew the sandwich until it hung limply from his hand. "You are not attempting some revenge by hiding chicken in it?"

Tye cocked his hip. "Why don't ya toss that on up here for the real men, huh?"

"I don't think real men turn into creatures in a Gate in the mountains," I said dryly, earning a small smile from Bryn.

"Indeed, Rowan. I came by to ask if you wished for me to anchor you from within the Gate, if you are ready now."

"What?" Tye barked, head whipping to me. "So just 'cause ya don't want us to hear a few moans, you're letting Stornoway—"

"Tye," Bryn interrupted as the wind stung my burning cheeks. "It is quite safe."

Tye's face went a shade of puce that the sun definitely hadn't given him. But whatever silent battle they were having was lost when Tye grumbled, "I don't like it." Like James, he seemed to give in to Bryn's demand.

I patted Tye's shoulder. "I'll be back for dinner."

"Yeah? As long as you ain't cookin' it, I'm happy. Otherwise, ya can just stay up in those woods a little longer."

I laughed as Bryn limped toward the forest.

Then Tye said quietly, "Roe, let's talk tonight, okay? Wanna talk to ya 'bout something."

My stomach lurched. Was this about what I'd said to James?

But I said, "Sure, Tye," with as much conviction as I could muster, and crawled down the ladder.

Somehow, I had to run to catch up. When the forest loomed, Bryn was already a pale shadow limping between the moss-covered trees. Weeks of rain had dragged up every critter hiding in the woods. Slugs oozed over the grass, worms peeked under logs, and spiders dried off their soaking webs. Willow would have hated it.

We walked in silence, with Bryn eating the sandwich I'd made him, not talking, not touching, until Bryn gripped my elbow and pulled me up the last step to the Gate.

"Thanks, I'm fine," I said quickly.

"Rowan, I was not raised to let you trip over rocks," he answered mildly, but released me. "Though it is preferential to be walking beside you and not chasing your shadow through the woods for once," he mused.

I huffed a reluctant laugh as the light over the Kerry hills draped over Bryn. It wouldn't set for hours, but it was low enough to turn the trees a dark black, twinkle off my eyelashes, and when it disappeared behind a tree, the world looked almost blue.

With a careful shrug, Bryn slid the knapsack he wouldn't let me carry off his shoulders and dropped it between the oaks. "Are you comfortable sharing a blanket?"

Sharing a—*oh*, for the Gate.

I scratched at my throat. "Sure, yeah."

I itched at my oversized wool sweater, wiped the dirt from my thrift-shop jeans. Then I stopped myself. This wasn't a date. Bryn was doing me a favor. And after I'd made him bound through the woods "*like a gazelle.*"

As he stooped to unroll a striped blanket, I said, "Um, thanks for doing this, anchoring us."

Bryn struck a match, lit the oil lantern, and strung it on the rope above. Candlelight flickered shadows over all the interesting shapes in his face. "I promised you I would," he said simply. "Have you and James come to terms with the truth of the *Ledger*?"

I kicked at a stick. So he had heard. "I don't know what I can say to him. I'm not her, and I can't make it so that I am. There's nothing else I can offer."

Bryn snapped the lantern shut. "You could be his sister, Rowan."

No. That I could never be—wasn't. But maybe I could understand what I hadn't before. "What exactly is a mate?" I asked, grabbing the other end of the tarp he'd unraveled, and tugging the rope through the two corner holes. The sky gave a flicker of warning, proving Bryn had been right to bring this for the rain.

He lifted his end, looping it around the trees, then adjusted the height when I couldn't reach as high. "There is no word for a mate here," he replied, tightening the cord in his fist. "But it is like a Tether, in that you are bound to another. Tallah is a planet which thrives on exchanges of energy—Tethers, the Gate, Marks—and a mate is yet another type of energy transfer, a binding," he explained, once we'd secured the tarp as a roof.

"But the difference is it's…" I searched for a word that didn't make my neck heat. "Romantic," I finished. Not like a Tether that most Ruhavens would never meet.

Bryn's mouth quirked. "Indeed. In the case of James, his mate is also his bonded spirit, his Mark."

I thought of the Azekiel. "Will Nereida's Mark be her mate as well?"

He rolled out another blanket. "As I understand, she does not have a bonded spirit yet, so it is theoretically possible. However, it need not be the case."

"Is it normal for mates, like James, to never marry? Never be with anyone but Essie?" Would I be expected to go along with this if Nereida fell in love with a blade of grass?

Bryn's hands clenched on the blanket. "Yes, that is to be expected," he said shortly.

I sank back on my haunches. That might explain why James wanted so desperately to find Essie here, if he truly believed this was some promise he couldn't break. Because while Ruhaven may have felt real, it wasn't *actually* real. "Why doesn't James find someone here? Instead of living in a dream?"

I flinched when Bryn's eyes flashed. "Is that all Ruhaven is to you, Rowan? A dream?" He pinned me with his gaze. *So this is how the dead moths in his office felt.* "Perhaps you do not need to visit the Gate at all then, if that is what you believe."

I forced myself to hold his stare. "What is it to you, Bryn?"

His lips prickled on an exhale, his breathing unsteady and quick. The wind tossed a strand of blond-gold over his left eye and I tensed, preparing for that sudden change I'd witnessed in Oslo.

But he drew himself together, draining the rush of energy like a squeezed sponge.

"It *was*," Bryn said evenly, "my life."

Then he shook the blanket and gestured for me to lie back.

I could see how Bryn might lose himself in Ruhaven. In its rolling drumbeat, in the milky lakes, in the thick spice of it. Seven years he'd spent here—not as long as James, but there was an unearthliness to him like a man touched by magic. Or Tallah.

When I rolled down, Bryn draped the blanket over me, tucking the corners under with unhurried and somehow intimate movements. Up close, his face was all angles and shadows, with that faint dusting of freckles like distant stars.

He tucked the blanket under my shoulders.

"Mummies were less secure," I joked.

"It is twelve degrees and we will be lying in the shade, unmoving," he reminded me, but there was a subtle authority in his voice, like the tone he'd used with James in the kitchen.

"Tye and James, they both seemed to—to back off when you said something about Ruhaven. Like in the kitchen about anchoring me, and then again on the roof. Why?" James, by everyone's admission, was the one in charge of Naruka and the Gate.

"Because, Rowan," Bryn said, sliding the blanket to my chin. I blinked up at him, trapped by his weight and the material, his breath fanning dizzyingly over my face. "I outrank them in Ruhaven."

When he pulled away, I let out a tiny breath. "Is that part of the Ruhaven rules?" I asked, toeing off my boots.

"Of a degree." When my feet popped out, Bryn eyed them warily. "Will your socks be warm enough?"

"Only because Kazie's been mixing up the laundry and giving me James's real wool ones."

He tilted his head, then bent to tug the blanket over my feet before lying back himself with a single throw.

"So when you anchor me, you'll be in the Gate, and you'll feel like you normally do?"

He turned his head, curled his lips. There was more than a bit of amusement in the look now. "And what do I feel like, Rowan?" Bryn murmured.

His voice shivered over me. What did he feel like? *A command, a promise.*

"Oh, just…" I shifted under the blanket, like the movement could dislodge the sudden charge in the air. "A pull."

"Then it shall feel the same."

I propped my head on my wrist. "What do *I* feel like?"

He mimicked my movement, turning so we were face to face. "You, Rowan? You feel like an old song. Now, will we attempt forty minutes? Since you were so ambitious with your alarm clock."

He could stay in a lot longer than that, but I nodded. "Bryn," I said hesitantly. "You said you had a theory before, in Oslo, about why the Inquitate targeted us—targeted you."

His eyes cooled to stone. "Yes. What of it, Rowan?"

I swallowed, shifting until I was staring up at the leaves. It was easier to talk to him like this. "You won't tell me what it is?"

His voice was crisp. "No."

"Why? It could help me figure out if Willow—"

"No. It is not relevant. And it is personal."

We weren't exactly friends, but what would make a theory too personal to share?

He exhaled a long, low breath. "I will assist you in finding out what happened to Willow, Rowan, but in this, I will not bend. It has no relevance to you."

That was a very Bryn way of saying "*Keep your nose out of my business.*"

I clasped my hands over my belly. Fine, I didn't need his theories. I had my own notes, and with this broken Tether, I might be getting somewhere.

I let my eyes close, tried to settle into the blanket.

Miles away, the neighbor's tractor *puff-puffed*, the farmer oblivious to what was about to take place. And beyond that, I might have heard the distant waves only in my imagination, lapping at the shore.

Bryn broke the silence. "What would you choose as your Token? If you were to make the Fall?"

"I wouldn't."

"But if you did?" he insisted.

"I don't know, drywall?"

Bryn's laugh was a low huff of breath beside me. "I will not allow James to bury drywall for you."

"Alright, what would you pick?"

"Your burnt casserole, as we can rest assured it will never decompose."

When I didn't muffle my laugh fast enough, he warned, "Careful, you may find yourself on a slippery slope to enjoying my company."

Was that what he wanted? "Oh, don't worry, I have excellent balance."

"That remains to be seen. Now then, shall we hold hands like you woke me before? Whisper in a sultry voice? Kiss in the dark?"

My heart gave an answering *thump*. "Go away."

"As you wish."

And when I fell through the Gate at last, there was a smile on my lips.

❀

R *owan?*

Only Willow called me Rowan. Was that her?

Something touched my cheek. Cool, gentle, then it was gone. "Rowan?"

I sucked in air, the first breath after being summoned through the darkness, through Ruhaven, and opened my eyes.

I saw endless seas. Seagulls cawed in sharp clacks, like they had all those years ago on Port Michaud beach with Willow.

I blinked rapidly. Not the Atlantic, not L'Ardoise, but Bryn. His hair, as perfect and golden as the Azekiel's, falling in silky waves over his forehead. Some of Ireland's green reflected into it, turning it brassy in places.

Another brush of my cheek.

The Gate. I was at the Gate.

Bryn smiled slightly. "There you are," he said, sliding an arm around my back and lifting me to sitting. The blanket fell away, and I shivered from the promised chill and the sweat drying on my spine.

They hadn't had sex—Nereida and the Azekiel—but it'd been close. Too close.

"Sorry," I mumbled. "The anchoring worked, I just..." *Was still burning up from Sahn.*

Bryn pressed a canister to my lips. "Water, Rowan."

I gave it a quick sniff. Not whiskey. I took it from him and drank greedily. Water—and a bit of honey.

He draped his coat over me, cozy and warm from his heat. "You must dress warmer and keep your boots on, even if you find it uncomfortable to sleep with them."

I nodded.

That hadn't been so bad. He'd anchored me like he said, and he hadn't witnessed my reaction to Nereida undressing Sahn. Maybe this could work.

"Do you wish to talk of it?" Bryn asked, not unkindly.

I searched his face, but there was no judgment, no hint of a joke somewhere. "No, I—well, thanks for anchoring me."

He smiled, crookedly this time. "Of course, Rowan." Then held out a hand.

O ver the next week, Bryn and I continued visiting the Gate together and I experienced the same near misses with the Azekiel. When I wasn't in Ruhaven, I repaired the gate lodge, or reviewed the journals of dead Ruhavens in the library.

And it was on one Thursday evening when I had my first breakthrough.

Sitting at the library's desk, I dragged a thin line across my notebook from my own name to Patrick's, the Ruhaven killed in Marseille, which I'd discovered was nowhere near Paris, where my sister had once visited.

But we'd both experienced broken Tethers.

My notes were a constellation of connections: broken tethers, intersections at Naruka, countries, friends, Ruhavens I'd heard about— a month's worth of scribbles and research.

Patrick Dubois I knew well now. Before he'd been killed, he'd enjoyed drinking wine on the south coast of France, visited Naruka often, and—above all—loved his orange tabby cat. Patrick was also a pattern detector like Kazie. James explained this to mean he could detect small reoccurring frequencies and larger groupings. Why did this matter? Prediction. And that was a powerful Mark.

Not like mine, which didn't exist, but anyway.

I tugged Patrick's journal toward me, one of many I'd laid out on the library desk, along with Bryn's extensive notes.

"So Patrick experiences a broken Tether in 1986, but he keeps visiting the Gate until 1987, when he relocates to Marseille," I said out loud to the empty room.

According to his last entries, he and another Ruhaven had been trying to locate his Tether—just like Jamellian and Kazmira were trying to do for Nereida. Connection? Both searching for their injured Drachaut? Or lured? Maybe someone wanted them to find their Tether, wanted them to go to Drachaut too.

I sipped my tea, let it simmer.

Levi, like Tye, had been recruited by Carmen, and had been missing ever since he left Naruka and returned home to Mexico. James had written to him over the years, but he'd never responded, and no other Ruhaven knew his location or whether he was alive or dead. Unlike Patrick, Levi hadn't been interested in Naruka and left after a few months, according to Bryn's records.

I tapped the notebook with the end of my pen, looked up from my notes. Through the foggy window, Bryn's flashlight played over his canvas where he stood painting the…well, I couldn't tell what it was. Maybe the barn.

It'd been nice of him to anchor me, and I could tell it was taxing. He always woke with sweat beading his pale temples, like a horse carting around a too-heavy load. But he never complained.

So I'd gotten him something at the thrift store in town this week, when Tye and I had gone in for groceries, and left it where Bryn was sure to notice it. A little joke, I hoped, he wouldn't be too offended by.

As I watched him, something appeared to his left. A woman. Barely there, her long, black hair hanging in a thick rope, bronze skin reflecting none of Naruka's lanterns. Willow?

My pulse skidded.

No, not Willow. *Me*.

Me standing next to Bryn, my hair completely still as the wind slapped at his apron.

Bryn!

I rose, reached toward the window—

And stopped. Blinked. My reflection stared at me in the misty glass, the apparition outside gone.

My heart thudded louder than the clocks that had suddenly chilled to silence.

As if sensing me, Bryn turned, a paintbrush in one hand, the end glowing a searing orange under the lanterns with a matching smear marring his borrowed jacket.

Our eyes met, hummed.

Are you quite alright, Rowan?

Of course.

I worried my bottom lip, Bryn's puzzled stare a burn I felt through the window. More than a month I'd been working with him and what had I discovered? Nothing. Maybe because the answer was more likely something we did to the Inquitate in the Gate that led them to kill us here—not some encounter, not something Willow had done or an Inquitate she had crossed in this life.

But why had Bryn believed that?

As I thought, I gravitated toward the *Ledger* at the apex of the library. Even the baroque chandelier, with all its medieval carvings and candles, paled next to the ancient book.

How many times had I stared at this one line? Mine. Willow's. Hoping that I'd been wrong, that one day I'd walk into this library and find I'd read the day incorrectly. Or maybe, the nearly duplicate line below was actually mine—the time was right, at least, a few minutes after midnight.

8 Iúil 1965 00:02 47.8344143, -110.6582699

Fort Benton, Montana. *Tye*.

I thumbed the spinner at my belt.

Behind the pristine glass, bog-covered pages revealed the locations of the Ruhavens that would be born this century. Each line was inscribed in deliberate strokes. Artwork lined the border in inky swirls of gold that should have never survived this long.

What did it mean that I could witness the memories without being in the book? Was I some abomination? Like an Inquitate, or a Drachaut that had slipped through, or something else entirely?

No one had ever been born with a twin before—that's what Bryn had said all those months ago. Was it pity then? A backup the Gate had created in case Willow died? Yet, in a way, there was another type of twin in the Ledger as well—a triplet, actually—like Tye, Bryn, and I.

7 Iúil 1965 23:52 63.519469 9.090167

Odda, Norway. *Bryn*.

What did it mean for us to cross so closely together? An anomaly, maybe.

I scanned the Ledger, noting the spacing of other births.

There were no doubles, quadruples, or other combinations—always triplets, or individuals born alone. Which meant those born together must have died at almost the same time, maybe because of some freak accident, but if that were true, then surely there'd be a few odd groups of Ruhavens together? Like a volcano erupting (if Ruhaven had volcanoes) or a disease…something.

Whatever the cause, Bryn, Tye, and I had died at the same time, which meant we were bound to meet in the memories eventually. The alternative being that we had coincidentally perished only minutes apart, without any knowledge of one another. But then, perhaps something—or someone—had caused that, executing each of us separately. That *seemed* far-fetched…

But this was Ruhaven, and I was living the memories of another realm—nothing was off the table.

Either we had met and died together, or something had killed us separately, at the same time. But wouldn't it make *more* sense that we *had* met, and that meeting—or something we'd done—had triggered the crossing here? Perhaps the same thing had triggered the Inquitate to target us.

Because the idea *felt* right, I flipped open my journal and pressed it to the glass, quickly jotting down my ideas next to where I'd noted Patrick's information. His birth was nearly a decade before mine, on the thirteenth of *Meán Fómhair*, which James explained was September in

Irish. Two others were born on the same date as well, with a similar time span as Tye, Bryn, and I, but…

Oh. *Oh.*

CHAPTER 23

Fair

Triplets. Patrick was a triplet. Just like Bryn, Tye and I—*Willow*—but what about the others…?

I swiped through my notebook until I found Ben Einhart, killed by the Inquitate—triplet. Levi, missing in Mexico—triplet. Maggie, a triplet with Carmen and another.

I ran through ten on my list, just to be sure, but each time, I found their triplet records in the *Ledger*. I slapped my notebook shut, then stood staring, breathing quickly, at the *Ledger*. This was it. Why though? *Why?*

If it was an energy transfer, maybe we emitted more energy. Drew them to us? Like a moth to a lightbulb?

No, that was stupid.

Something about dying together had triggered the Inquitate to attack us. Because too many had come through? Or were we corrupted? Maybe Bryn was wrong and we'd never done anything to them at all, maybe it'd been about maintaining some balance, like rooting out an infection.

But then—why had they targeted *me*? Because I was impersonating Willow? Was it just that simple? But they hadn't come after me until I'd visited the Gate. So was it something I wasn't supposed to see in the—

"Bryn!"

I nearly jumped as he appeared beside me, impossibly quiet, steadier than the pillars that held up the arching ceiling of the library. The leather apron was still secured snugly around his neck and waist. A smear of blue paint stood out on his collar.

"What have you discovered?" he asked quietly, as if he'd sensed the change. Maybe he had. Maybe his Mark of light let him sense the truth in things.

I took a breath, steadied, and flipped open my notebook. "I matched the rows with the notes you gave me. It's the triplets, Bryn. Something about us coming over together has caused these attacks."

His fist clenched and unclenched the cane, the movement flexing his shoulder. But all the color had fled his face.

"Bryn? What's wrong?"

He rearranged his features again, but there was something there, flickering behind his eyes. "Nothing, my Rowan," he murmured.

My?

"What are you—" But I broke off when he held out a hand for the notebook.

"If I could."

Nodding, I handed it to him, watched as he mimicked what I'd done only minutes ago, flipping through each page, his eyes darting between the deaths noted in my journal and the rows in the *Ledger*. His nose moved closer and closer as he did, until his light hair brushed the top pages. Hopefully, he didn't go too far back—I had some notes on him that weren't very flattering.

"What do you think?" I asked quietly.

His sucked in his bottom lip, let it out, and shook his head before handing the journal back. I slid it onto the mantelpiece.

"I think," he repeated slowly, "that I have been unforgivably incorrect in my assumptions."

"Your previous theory, you mean?" The one that had convinced him the Inquitate would never target me—because I was a lie. "How does knowing it's the triplets change things?"

His eyes tightened as he stared, hard, at the *Ledger*. Something clung to the air between him and the book, an invisible hum as if they recognized each other, or maybe the Gate just approved of him.

"Because," he answered at length, "knowing that the reason for our targeting is due to us crossing together eliminates any cause on Earth."

"Like who we might have known?"

"Or might have done, yes."

Or might have *done*? Was that what this was about? That he'd thought something we'd *done* had drawn the Inquitate to us? Had he thought Willow had caused this herself? That she deserved to be targeted?

Annoyance started to build, but deflated just as quickly. No, not just Willow. *Him.* Something he'd done—that's what he thought. Some mistake, some error, that had led the Inquitate to him.

When James had tried to contact Bryn, he'd ignored him. Then, when James had asked Bryn to return to Naruka, Bryn had said, *"What makes you believe I wish to return?"*

Not that he hadn't *wanted* to return, but that he'd thought he *shouldn't*. Because he'd done something.

He hadn't needed to document everything done by those killed from the Inquitate. He'd noted little things—a story about how Patrick had rescued the cat, Ben's love for the saxophone. Why bother? Unless they mattered. Unless something we did *here* mattered.

I stepped between Bryn and the *Ledger*, focused on those improbably blue eyes, his strong chin, the deep curve under his cheekbone, his slim nose, the enticing pulse at his neck.

It was an effort not to step back when his thick, golden lashes lowered to half-mast over eyes that felt like the only light in the room. My pulse gave a loud *thump,* then the left side of his mouth quirked, just slightly, in that lopsided tilt that caused a few wrinkles to appear at the corners of his eyes.

Ask your question, Rowan.

Sometimes, I could almost hear him. Part of the Gate, the illusion, the dream of it all. Maybe a glimmer.

"Did you think you did something to draw the Inquitate?" I finally asked.

He sucked in his bottom lip, let it out on a soft *pop.*

Yes. He swallowed. "Yes."

I hadn't expected him to admit it. What could he have possibly done, this man who did nothing but worship the Gate, paint, and read? "Bryn, you can tell me what—"

I felt my eyes widen when he grasped my wrist, the pads of his fingers cool and firm and rough. Then he released me, face blank.

"Rowan, I—I wish to tell you something. *Need,*" he corrected as a tingling sensation pulsed at my wrist. "*Need* to tell you something." He spoke so low that I leaned toward him to hear better. "When you arrived in Oslo, I—"

"What are ye two bloody doing in here?"

Fy Faen.

I spun as James burst into the library. Like Bryn, he had an apron tied around his waist, except James's was covered in flour and chunks of pastry and his sweater looked like it'd come out the other end of a compacter.

But before James could even make it across the library, Bryn filled him in on what I'd uncovered, giving me far more credit than I deserved for discovering what I should have seen months ago.

"I feckin' can't believe it like," James said when Bryn finished. "Let me see. Go on so and let me see."

I angled my journal toward him under the light. James swiped it from me and flipped through, glancing rapidly between it and the *Ledger*. "Roe, me love—"

I held my breath, bracing for the denial.

"—you're a bloody genius!" To my shock, he grabbed me in a crushing hug. "How the feck did I not notice this? Me mother, Levi—did ye check him?" He smacked a noisy kiss on my forehead.

"James, Christ," I swore, and blushed scarlet.

"Ah, so O'Sahnazekiel can kiss ye but I can't? Sure, I see how it is so."

Suspicion had my gaze shooting between Bryn and James. If Bryn hadn't committed some sin before to draw the Inquitate, he definitely had by telling James what was going on in the Gate. "So you know," I accused James as Bryn let out a low laugh.

He grinned wickedly. "Aye, I do, though ye can be sure Bryn's ever the gentleman. I've been watching Nereida and O'Sahnazekiel for years. Ye think I didn't pick up that they were together? Actually, I've a mind to give you a book on mating in Ruhaven."

I choked on my tongue.

Mouth pursed, James strolled through the bookcases. "Of course, sure. Ye wouldn't want any surprises, now would ye?"

Oh, god, please shut up, James. Please shut up right now. Not with Bryn—

"Ah, here it is." He tugged out a tome larger than anything that was written in this world. "Should cover the basics."

"I really don't think—"

"Now then," James said, pushing the book into my hands and nipping the journal. He flipped through my notes while I held *The Art of Mating* like it would catch fire. Hopefully, it would take me with it. "Jayzus, 'tis all here, isn't it? Me sister is bloody brilliant."

Sister.

Guilt gnawed at me. "James, I— About what I said outside that day…"

In that subtle way of his, Bryn excused himself, sliding around James until he was out of the library and closing the door quietly behind him.

"Roe, 'tis me who should be apologizing," James admitted when Bryn left, rubbing at the back of his head. "I don't know what came over me. Sure, we're so lost in the Gate sometimes and—"

"No, James, *I'm* sorry. I know what Essie is to you. I should have thought of her, and I wish...I know I'm not the sister you—"

He touched my shoulder. "No, Roe, ye are. Of course ye are. Would ye let me apologize for being an ejit? I know what Willow is to ye as well, I do, and I could see later how it must have seemed to ye. For me to be tellin' ye yer the same for me. Sure, 'tis only been a few months for yerself while I've known ye a lifetime. So...I'm sorry like."

My throat closed up. "Me too, James. Me too."

Seated at the kitchen table, James lowered his newspaper. Beside him, a stack of envelopes balanced precariously, each addressed to a different triplet. He glanced at our apple-shaped clock and frowned.

"Ya want more coffee, Roe?" Tye asked over the radio, already filling my mug, his shoulder-length hair loose and soaking up the bright morning.

I'd spent the better part of last night in the Gate, losing myself in the memory of Nereida, feeling the weight of the swords she practiced with—twin elbow blades as deadly as they were long. She might not have had any Mark, but she made up for it in skill. I'd never felt anyone move like her—like it wasn't swordplay but a dance, dipping and ducking the blows O'Sahnazekiel tried to land. Not that he'd have hurt her—something I realized after a few slipped through and I prepared for the memory to end.

"Will we leave in about ten so?" James asked after another glance at the clock. He'd spent the last week gathering addresses for the triplets.

Kazie laid a bangled hand on his arm. "Stop worrying. They've been fine for years—they'll survive a few weeks more."

I should have considered what this discovery would do to James after the immediate relief of *knowing* wore off.

Tye spread his hands. "I ain't ever seen an Inquitate, though, and I'm a triplet. I ain't sayin' you're wrong," he added when I frowned at him. "But you're gonna scare a lot of people with these letters, James. We oughta be sure."

But we *were* sure, as I'd explained to him last week. The pattern was clear—not a single Ruhaven had been targeted who hadn't been a triplet. James and Bryn had checked and verified every single one in the last century.

As Tye tossed other theories at him, James speared the butter and spread enough on his scone to earn him a fast track to type 2 diabetes. And if that didn't get him there, the spoonful of cream he added would.

I scooped half of it into my coffee, just in case.

"Get yer own like," James admonished, then asked Tye, "If it's not triplets, what else?"

"Maybe it's just us going on up there to the Gate?" Tye supplied.

I slid out my notebook, flipped to where I'd first written that theory of his down, crossed it out. "James, what about Levi? If he's not dead, we need to warn him. Did you find his new address?"

"No sure," he said around a raspberry scone that left him with a creamy mustache. "Tye, have ye had any luck contacting Carmen? She was his recruiter and might know where Levi's gone."

"I wrote her like ya wanted," Tye answered. "Be a few weeks still before we get an answer. But ya know how she is—don't want much to do with Naruka no more."

Why was that? "Did she have a—"

The kitchen door creaked open.

My pulse fluttered when Bryn limped through. A stupid response just because he'd been easier to be around these last weeks—playful, if I didn't know him better. Happier, maybe? It was hard to tell, but he'd seemed unburdened in a way he hadn't before. Which made me wonder just what he thought he'd done to draw the Inquitate before we'd discovered the triplet connection.

Still, I was enjoying the subtle change in him. Like right now—it was the first time I'd ever seen him in something as ordinary as *pajamas,* looking spectacularly un-Ruhaven-like in the striped bottoms and snug sweater. It was a side of him I wouldn't mind seeing more of.

Bryn cast around haplessly, like he'd forgotten he ever joined us for breakfast and didn't know where to sit or what to do. He looked a little windblown, too, with a faint sleep crease on his left cheek, and hazy eyes. Probably from all the late nights he'd spent in the library this last week, trying to find missing addresses for James.

I pushed out of my chair and grabbed a mug for him, filled it.

"Thank you, Rowan," Bryn said when I handed it to him, then he flashed such a blinding smile that my heart stuttered, flatlined, and restarted all in one beat. Yeah—*new* Bryn was definitely trouble for me. "Did you make this?"

"I—what? No, it's safe to drink."

He grinned, said, "A relief, I am sure," then motioned with the coffee to the bread box next to the fridge.

Oh, that. "Just something for James."

Bryn rubbed a thumb over the engraving. "A bow and arrow?"

I slid into the chair again. "I thought for him and Essie. My dad showed me a few tricks for carving. He can do much better."

"I find myself very envious of being able to create something both so artistic and functional," Bryn commented, opening and closing the box. "There is nothing to be done with my drawings but hang them on the wall, and I am certain James will allow no further to crowd his."

"Not unless ye do more nudes again," James said without missing a beat.

I bit back a grin as Bryn asked, "Have you eaten, Rowan?"

I lifted my now-creamy cup of coffee.

"If I am to take you to the Gate today, I expect you not to be in danger of fainting on me. Certainly, I will be unable to carry you home on one leg."

"I'll eat a pastry on the way."

Across the table, Kazie flipped a page of her novel, and the cover's impressive cleavage captured James and Tye's brief attention. She sucked her coffee through a spiral straw as she read. "Tye," she said when it drew spluttering air. "You sure you wanna go back home if the Inquitate are following triplets?"

My good mood took a nose dive when I remembered that he'd decided to take a few weeks in L'Ardoise.

"Gotta," he said. "The guys who took over my lease in L'Ardoise are causin' issues. One dude won't pay, the other's gone and blown out the bathroom floor with a burst pipe. Gotta sort it out, is all."

The only reason he had to sort that out was because he'd rented a place while he tried to convince me to move to Naruka.

"Tye, maybe you should let someone else deal with that," I tried, "until we figure out more about the Inquitate."

"Ya think I'm gonna fall for a damn illusion?"

"It's not as simple as—"

"Folks, I got things to take care of." He spread his hands on a copy of *Horse Riders Weekly*. "Ya think there ain't some risk every time I get on a stallion's back? Ya'll would have me never leave this house if it was up to ya. Live a little." He lifted the magazine and said over its cover, "And I *don't* mean in the Gate."

As Kazie argued with him and James weighed in with suggestions, Bryn slid a plate in front of me. Cheese wedges, diced cucumbers, sliced cherry tomatoes, and toothpick-speared olives were arranged in a pretty medallion. A fork and knife followed on a triangle napkin, equally pretty. Like he cared, maybe more than cared, like all those trips to the Gate together had mattered.

Bryn said from above me, "Why, Rowan, are you smiling?"

Tye lifted his coffee. "'Cause she's wonderin' who the hell eats *olives* for breakfast."

James shook his head and muttered, "Continental Europeans."

I looked up at Bryn, his face a rare mixture of amusement and uncertainty. "Thanks."

He smiled then, a real one, the kind he'd entered the kitchen with that could grab my breath and walk away with it. "You are quite welcome, Rowan," he said, and nipped a tomato.

The chair beside me was drawn back, then Bryn slid into it, unpacking a book from his satchel and setting it next to his coffee.

I sampled a cucumber—salted and surprisingly good at nine in the morning—and asked Tye, "Do you want me to come with you to the farm?"

James shot a careful look my way as Tye waved the suggestion off. "No, darlin', you stay here and enjoy dancing with the fairies."

"There are no fairies." Bryn.

When I peeked a glance at him, he was intensely focused on his book—a book, I realized a moment later, that I recognized.

"What are ye grinning about now?" James asked me.

I schooled my face. "Nothing. Did you find the address for Levi?"

James rose with a plate in one hand, some jam on the tip of his nose. "Not yet. Bryn, did ye have any luck yerself?" He paused when he caught sight of the book Bryn was reading, snorted. "*The Handy Handyman*," he read with amusement. "Does this mean one of ye is finally going to fix me car's feckin' spark plugs?"

Bryn's smile was quick and devilish. "I believe this novelty was a carefully placed gift from Rowan," he said, watching me under the shelter of thick lashes. "Am I correct?"

It was indecent to look so good this early in the morning.

"Consider it a trade for the socks I keep finding," I said drolly. After months of thick, wool socks turning up in my room, I'd finally realized they weren't misplaced laundry from Kazie.

Bright humor danced in Bryn's eyes. "Rowan, if someone is leaving you socks, I am entirely unaware of it."

I draped an arm over the back of my chair while my heart clamored. "*Are* you?"

He mimicked my movement, bringing us face to face under the light of the morning sun, whose warmth tingled my spine and turned the tips of Bryn's ears a pearly pink. I could count all the barely distinguishable freckles on his slim nose and high-boned cheeks. "Truly, I am mystified. However, should you uncover the culprit, I hope you at least wear the things, for whomever is leaving them must be tired of looking at such freezing feet all the time."

God, he was beautiful. "So it *was* for my benefit."

"Naturally, as this is for mine, no doubt," Bryn replied, lifting the dog-eared manual. "I found it hidden in my bookcase next to *Romantic Nudes*, and as you intended, it rather stood out."

I tucked my tongue in my cheek. "You need to learn, Bryn."

He sketched a slow eyebrow and leaned in. "I think my nudes are rather tasteful."

I huffed a rough laugh. "You know what I mean. The sink was leaking for months because you installed the male part wrong."

Across the table, Tye turned the page of his magazine. "Forget how a dick works, Stornoway?"

Christ, Tye.

Ignoring him, Bryn bumped his knee against mine. "Do you make a habit of sneaking into my room?" he asked, lowering his voice.

"Only as much as you do mine."

"Then quite. But if so, I shall need to leave out my own recommendations for you. Tell me, Rowan, do you share Kazie's interests in books?"

My eyes whizzed to the novel she sat smirking behind, and the ample cleavage on it.

Coffee slid down my throat like melted chocolate. *Say something.* "I, um. I really don't think—" I broke off on a startled gasp.

Bryn's irises burned pure, glittering gold.

"Rowan?" As the half-smile on his face wilted, I stared stupidly into his suddenly very normal, very blue eyes. "Are you well?"

"Your—your eyes," I stammered. "They were…"

Puzzled, he touched my shoulder. "Yes, Rowan?"

"*Gold*," I breathed, glancing around the table.

Tye looked unimpressed, Kazie still smirked, and James cast his eyes to the ceiling. Hadn't they seen it too? Or was I imagining things again?

A series of emotions passed across Bryn's face before his eyes softened, his lips curving slowly.

Was I staring at his mouth?

"Is that a—a glimmer?" I asked quietly. Though his eyes hadn't shot gold in Oslo.

Tye barked a humourless laugh, but it was James who drawled, "Oh, I don't think I'd call it that."

"I wonder," Tye said, voice sharp, "how your little trips to the Gate are going, Stornoway?"

Bryn's hand tightened briefly before sliding off my shoulder. "Quite fine," he answered crisply. "I am able to anchor Rowan from within the Gate."

"I just bet," Tye scoffed.

"What's that mean?" I said. "Did you see his eyes?"

Tye rose and polished off his coffee. "I gotta say I'm surprised is all. Ya know, that he's got any *strength* left to pull ya out, what with everything goin' on in Ruhaven."

My mind went blank. "Do you know each other?"

"*Tye*," James warned.

Tye brushed him away. "Nope. I ain't ever met Stornoway. But I told ya we kicked him out before 'cause he got too far in. Well, I'm seein' that all over again, ain't I?"

"Do not say one word further," Bryn warned, voice laced with that faint command. Was this the rank Bryn had mentioned? How could they actually obey some rules from Ruhaven?

But Tye continued, coming around the table and planting his fists on the duck placemats. "It's goddamn true," Tye challenged as Bryn met his stare. "You're obsessed, and draggin' Roe into it as well. She ain't even eatin' meat anymore and it's only been a few months. It's your fault, forcin' her into the Gate, making her believe that the life in there is worth as much as this is."

Bryn reached for his cane. "It is. It is my life. And yours."

Tye straightened with a look of disgust. "Life. Is that what ya call it? When you're just in there fuckin' your mate all the time."

Something froze inside me, slowed, almost like I was slipping through the Gate. Mate? *Mate*? The word ping-ponged in the empty space in my chest, a ribbed triage before my brain could take it out and process it.

The linoleum turned a dark crimson when Bryn's coffee slipped off the table.

He had a *mate*?

But that meant—for someone like Bryn—that meant no one *here*. So that hadn't been flirting, it'd been...Bryn not *disliking* me. Of course I'd read too much into it. Too much into the casual touches when really, he had this woman in the Gate.

If I'd lost my appetite before, it was in smoking ruins now.

Cane in hand, Bryn rose slowly to face Tye, cutting off James's attempt at defusing the sudden tension. "As usual, you are absurdly crude."

My heart sunk—*not a denial.*

Tye picked at a thumbnail. "Only sayin' the truth. You ever heard of that little thing? The truth, I mean?"

Bryn lowered his voice to a whispered threat. "You would disobey this law?"

Tye scoffed. "Stornoway, you're really gonna stand there and lecture *me* about Ruhaven's laws? Or did I get things wrong when I heard how much you were enjoying yourself in Norway?"

Every muscle in Bryn's body pulled tight.

"Oh, guess that bit of truth hurts, too, huh?" Tye taunted, and even Kazie let her novel flop down as the kitchen chilled a degree.

"It was *you* who exiled me," Bryn said in a low voice. "*You* who forced me out, who forced me to choose, and now you would…" His head whipped to the door, nostrils flaring.

"Bryn?" I murmured in the clocks' rhythmic chattering.

"Someone is here," he stated flatly. "In Naruka."

CHAPTER 24

Mariner Boy

Everyone went dead quiet.

Tick. Tick-tock.

Someone was in Naruka. In our house, with the library and the paintings and…

Crash.

"Ye let me deal with this now," James warned as both Tye and Kazie edged past him out the kitchen.

I rose, most of my breakfast uneaten.

Bryn clasped my hand. "Rowan, wait."

Tiny jolts of energy shot up my arm as his fingers curled to my pulse, pressed there lightly. Despite the intruder, it was suddenly just us in the kitchen. Us and the clocks and the coffee pooling at my feet.

I looked away, heart hammering as he kept my hand in his. Had he visited the Gate every day for *her*?

But, of course, I couldn't ask that.

Yet he had a mate, and he'd said nothing while expecting me to tell him everything I saw in the Gate.

"Let me go," I said quietly.

His throat bobbed once, then he did.

I turned, letting the kitchen doors whisk closed behind me as I entered the roaring warmth of the lounge.

And for a moment, forgot all about Bryn and his mate.

"Jayzus, that's me twelve poems of Enniskerry," James cursed as a book soared through the air with unnerving accuracy. "Ye absolute feckin' ejit."

Across the room, in front of the pool table, stood a man who looked vaguely familiar. Greasy hair, a square, cut-off jaw, and a set of very large ears. A vein throbbed at his temple and sweat dripped down the thick column of his neck onto a fur-collared jean jacket.

The man from the bar, I realized after a heartbeat.

Kazie pointed a glittery nail at him. "Colm, don't you *dare* touch another thing."

He swiped a lamp, threw it.

She didn't even move, just pursed her lips at the heap that landed five feet to her left. "Carmen liked that lamp. So, guess I'm glad it's gone," she singsonged.

To my left, Tye stalked toward Colm with his shoulders back, fists clenched. Colm was about to end up face-first in Simona's dung.

"Easy, Tye," James warned. "We don't need the Gardaí at the door like."

I didn't know what the local cops would make of a library full of centuries of stories about winged people and soul energy. James would probably find himself at the wrong pyre of an Irish witch trial.

"What, ya wanna let him destroy the rest of the damn place?" Tye barked, then jabbed a finger at me before pointing to the door. "Roe, get on out of here."

Colm followed Tye's finger, ball-bearing eyes narrowing on me. "So yer still here, are ye? Haven't they told ye their fairy tales that had Lana going crazy?" He tossed a chair out of his way. "Yer gonna be next, ye hear me? They took Lana, buried her body up there. I know they did. Too many going missing," he spat, and lunged for the fire poker.

Everyone sucked in a breath, backing up when he brandished it.

I bumped into something hard and warm.

Bryn's fingers curled over my shoulder, thumb grazing my neck. "Rowan, you should return to the kitchen," he murmured, voice vibrating against my back.

Like hell I was leaving James out here with Colm and a fire poker. Bryn couldn't do anything with his cane, James was too soft to kill a tiny spider, and Kazie was afraid of spiders.

We all looked at Tye.

Colm tossed another book across the room but kept the poker extended. "Tell me where Lana is," he demanded as Tye edged around him.

"We buried her in Simona's barn," Tye mocked.

"*Tye!*" James exclaimed, pulling at his hair. "Would ye stop baiting him like!"

He grinned as Colm rounded on us.

"She left, you idiot," Kazie hissed. "Probably couldn't stand the sight of your ugly mug."

This time, the book that sailed for her only nearly missed.

I reached for the screwdriver in my tool belt, palming the flathead instrument like it'd be some help against a three-foot iron rod. Nereida could use this though—she could throw a dagger a hundred feet, would have probably pinned this guy to the wall with it.

James held out his hands pleadingly. "Colm, ye know someone in her family passed away. She had to leave quickly."

"That's feckin' bullshit. She came to me the night before she went missing, raving about what you all have going on here," Colm shouted. "Said you gave her drugs—"

That sounded familiar.

"—and ye made her hallucinate. Then the next day, poof—she's gone," Colm said, snapping the fingers that weren't holding the poker. "Just tell me the feckin' truth. Tell me where she is."

In a move like water, Bryn slipped in front of me.

But the action drew Colm's attention, and his hazel eyes fixed on my new bodyguard. "Who the hell are ye?"

With the screwdriver clenched in my fist, I tried to step around again, but Bryn backed up, pressing me between the wall and the hard line of him. Not a bad place to be under another circumstance.

We can arrange such.

I rose on my tiptoes, met Tye's eyes over Bryn's shoulder. *Do something*, I mouthed, then tried to pass Bryn the screwdriver under his arm.

"Rowan, I am not planning on replacing a lightbulb," he said mildly, boxing me in like Colm wasn't bearing down on us both.

"Only you would think you need a screwdriver to replace a lightbulb."

Bryn's response was to flatten me against the wall. "How I do enjoy your wit, Rowan. However, perhaps this is best left to me."

Well, if it was, Colm was about to turn us both into a Ruhaven skewer.

"Lad, ye'd better leave now," James warned, sliding to Kazie and grasping her outstretched hand.

The room quieted, all but for the slowly ticking clocks and the sound of Colm's heavy breathing as he advanced with the poker on Bryn.

Then he stopped. His eyes widened, so much that the underside of his eyelids pulsed a sickly red. He backed up a step, mouth popping open, then another, until the chesterfield caught him behind the knees and he toppled over. His face went sheet white.

I gripped Bryn's shoulder, felt the muscle ripple underneath.

And then I knew—a glimmer. He'd shown Colm a glimmer.

A shudder rolled down my spine at the memory of what Bryn had shown me in that room in Oslo—a ripple of something underneath the surface that was terrifying not in the image, but in the knowledge that something *other* existed.

"You're crazy," Colm mumbled as Tye grabbed him by the collar, but he didn't have to do much, as Colm was tripping over his heels to get out.

Tye kicked open the main doors and tossed Colm bodily through the sunlit gap. Simona's annoyed baying groaned through before Tye shut the doors, locked them. "Well, ain't that fun," he said, dusting his hands.

When Bryn stepped away from me, James demanded, "What the bleedin' hell did ye do that for? Ye think 'tis not bad enough he's got the idea we're a bunch of witches up here, now ye've got to show him Evil Bryn too!"

I choked on a laugh. *Evil Bryn.*

Kazie ducked around James to pick up his book. The breath wheezed out of him when she slapped him in the stomach. "I never liked these poems, too stuffy. *English*," she said to me with a flick of her hair. "Better to read something in Ruhaven, and plus, it's all men. Really, James."

They were crazy. All of them.

I narrowed my eyes at Bryn, who was eyeing me thoughtfully. *And especially you.*

Me, my Rowan?

"James, aren't you going to call the police?" I pressed as he righted the furniture.

"What— Bring the Gardaí here? Reading me journals and looking at me paintings? No, we'll let him walk it off so. Best this whole thing goes away, though I've not an idea for how to make it so."

❀

Since absolutely nothing fazed Tye, including a half drunk Irishman barging into Naruka, he asked me to help him clean out the stalls to make room for the tractor he'd rented. He wanted to get the fields turned before he headed back to L'Ardoise to straighten things out with the renters.

So I spent the next week helping him as much as I could. Unlike James, Bryn, or Kazie, we didn't talk about Ruhaven, but the various games we were missing back home. Hockey was starting up again and so was football, but with the time difference, the only matches we caught were on Sunday evenings.

And as promised, Tye had booked us two tickets to a hurling match on Saturday.

"Do you play any sports?" I asked Bryn as we made our usual morning walk to the Gate. Burnt leaves crunched under our feet.

"Rowan, I confess I have never found any appeal in chasing an inflatable ball." *Well, when you put it that way.* "But before my leg, I enjoyed glacier walking in the fjords near my home in Odda, though I would not consider that a sport."

It was the most Bryn of responses. "Not really a team sport, I'm guessing."

"On the contrary. It requires a great deal of teamwork."

Silence descended, so thick and heavy that I said, lamely, "So you aren't from Oslo?"

He tugged his cane out of a dense patch of mud. "No, I grew up in Odda, where I worked on my mother's ship, then attended art school in Trondheim, and after my exile, found work in the capital."

"Mother's *ship*? What were you doing there—painting?"

Amusement danced in the corners of Bryn's eyes. "I am sure my mother would have found that preferable to my working as one of the crew."

My eyes widened so far in their sockets my eyeballs would have toppled out if they weren't attached at the corneas. "You were a *sailor*?"

"You sound surprised."

I scanned his pleated trousers, tailored sweater, and cashmere scarf. "But they're... And you're...you're..."

His lopsided grin was the work of a god who knew precisely what she was doing. "I am what, Rowan?"

I swallowed the hum in my throat. "Just you." Amusement flickered. "So I guess you're a knot expert."

His face barely changed. "I am sure I could tie a boat without it floating away."

I was picking up his rhythm now. "You're kind of funny."

Over the next half hour, I discovered ten varieties of fish I'd never eaten—and two I definitely never would. According to his mother, Bryn had almost sunk her ship twice, but he was sure she exaggerated the second attempt. When the boat's chef quit, he'd taken over the cooking for a week, which ended in half the crew having food poisoning.

"I am particularly partial to your energy theory," he said when we reached the Gate and the conversation changed to the Inquitate. "Everything in Tallah is about balance. That is why there is Ruhaven and Drachaut, why mates exist. For all, there must be an equal and opposite."

Mates. Was Bryn about to see his now? Did he want nothing more than this conversation to be over so he could be with her?

Bryn paused mid-unrolling a blanket, looked at me. "Are you well, Rowan?"

"Yeah, fine."

Because I wanted to avoid even thinking about mates, I stuffed myself into a blanket that even Bryn couldn't claim wasn't warm enough and gladly sunk into Ruhaven. Later, after I'd met up with Jamellian and Kazmira, who were still figuring out how to get us to Drachaut, Bryn woke me with coffee and lunch.

And so the week continued, with Bryn hoping to encounter the Inquitate in the Gate, and me worrying that Colm would come back to Naruka—but there was no sign of him. There was no Gardaí at our door, either. So however much he was certain James had buried Lana out back, it wasn't enough to report it.

What if, instead of moving away, she'd actually made the Fall? That'd explain why she broke things off with Colm.

Would her portrait have *"made the Fall"* next to her name like a sticker you earned, or would there just be a plaque up by the Gate?

I looped my thumbs in my pockets and did a slow walk of the lounge. It was a jolt to realize I knew some of these faces, had passed them every day and never looked.

There was Mohammed, smiling in a polished frame and wearing the glasses that I'd dug up, then Amelia, Ben, and a few others I'd come across in Bryn's notes. My lips twitched when I found Patrick's photo.

An orange tabby with one green eye, one blue, posed in his lap— Hermès, according to his diary. Beside it, a painting of a Ruhaven on an Irish hunt was so realistic, I could smell the sweat on the horse's neck.

Another portrait drew my attention. Noticeably smaller than the rest, it had the faded look of an era just discovering color. But I knew the stern lips of the lady would be crimson, her eyes a piercing gray.

Carmen.

Tye said she'd grown up with James's mother, which would make her at least fifty. No, sixty. But neither the photograph nor the woman in person looked anywhere near that. Despite *1983* scribbled on the bottom, her skin was as unblemished as Bryn's, but tighter, like a wet sheet clipped over marble.

I pulled out my notepad, added questions about her age to my notes. "Hello, Rowan."

My heart skidded at the voice, at the accent that sketched images of colorful villages in a Norwegian countryside, and I willed it to relax.

I rather enjoy your reaction.

I turned to see Bryn lounging against the kitchen's doorjamb, a leather bag slung over one shoulder and bunching the otherwise-ironed fabric. Heat from the fire ruffled hair that had grown past his ears since he'd arrived.

"I was worried about you this morning," he said.

"Worried? Why?"

"Besides my terminal fear you shall fall off our roof? You visited the market with James, where Colm may frequent."

"I guess I should drag you with me everywhere then, just so you can show Colm your…" I wiggled my fingers, "*glimmer.*"

With a smile, Bryn crossed to me, his cane thumping steadily on a rug worn by time, coffee spills, and Kazie. "I must admit, it does sound less intimidating when you say it like that," he said archly, then grinned when I let out a small laugh.

"Actually, I was thinking about Colm and Lana, how James said she left…"

Bryn kept pace with me as I inspected the portraits. "Yes?"

"Just that, well, she didn't make the Fall, did she? And her moving is just some, I don't know, euphemism?"

This time, his grin was a wide smile that lit up his eyes. "Like sending the dog to a farm in the country, is it?"

"Something like that," I muttered, stepping in front of Carmen's portrait again.

"You may rest assured we did not send Lana 'up the farm.'" He glanced at the portrait of Carmen, then my notes, his eyes tightening as he skimmed over the meager lines. "If Lana had made the Fall," he continued, the air of humor gone, "Colm would not remember her. Because we were never meant to be here, Rowan. When Ruhaven claims us back, we evaporate from the memories of everyone who knew us."

I studied him. He wasn't joking. "Evaporate?" I repeated.

He tucked his hands into his pockets, studying me in turn. "From all but Ruhavens' memories, yes. For everyone else, you will become a name forgotten, an old story—something that happened to a friend, not to themselves—an unoccupied space where your mother once thought you existed." The room chilled a degree. "Should you choose to accept the call," he added.

Who *would*? When everything that made someone would become nothing—not only their body gone, but not a single mark of them upon anyone's memory.

"Would you?" I asked.

He brushed my hand, the touch like wind on sea-sprayed skin. "That will depend, but I have time yet. The Gate calls to you before the end. Then you have but a few weeks to make the Fall. Something, perhaps, you shall witness of another first. It is an indescribable experience," he said, pausing. "To be there when it happens."

Outside, the chimes picked up their tempo, hollow tones mixing with the drone of cows.

"Some have seen visions," Bryn continued, "others have spoken to the dead, and when we watched Mohammed Fall, James told me he witnessed his entire life pass. He believes it is Ruhaven speaking to us. That she is asking something."

"It sounds like a religious experience," I said hesitantly.

"One could consider it such."

Because a strange silence had fallen, I shifted us back to Lana. "So Lana didn't make the Fall because Colm wouldn't have remembered her."

"Precisely. It was Levi who showed her the Gate, and she became quite inconsolable afterward, choosing to leave promptly. That very night, I presume, though apparently not before telling Colm enough to raise his suspicions."

Hadn't I tried the same? Taken James's car, made a run for it.

"Levi—you listed him as missing." I opened my notebook, scanned the dates. "And he's Lana's triplet."

"That is correct." Bryn nipped my notebook from me, quicker than a bird on a worm.

"Hey!"

He looked either amused or disgusted as he flipped through it. "Rowan, it occurred to me when you discovered the triplets that these notes resemble a detective's of a crime scene. Where is your daily entry on Ruhaven?"

I swiped for the journal, but he lifted it out of reach. *God, please, don't let Bryn see my notes on him.*

Why? What shall I find, my Rowan? he seemed to say.

What an ass you were.

Ah, "were." We are progressing.

"Bryn, would you—" I dove and missed again, but Bryn snagged me before I could rip the frame off the wall for balance. "I *am* writing about Ruhaven. Right there," I insisted when he held the journal out of reach.

"Shall I learn of your entertaining adventures with the Azekiel?" He tilted his head back, spreading the shadowed pages above him, then frowned. "Do not tell me you have only this paltry entry? Surely, he is treating you better."

I felt the vein under my eye twitch. "*Bryn*," I ground out. "Please, would you just—"

"Ah, this one must be from the day you thought a *clock* could return you from Ruhaven." He spared me a glance that held a touch of humor and warning. "It says only that you beheld a—and I quote you now, Rowan—'large metal contraption.'" He closed the journal with a snap and held it out. "Certainly, one does not imagine the portrait of beauty that is Ruhaven from this."

As if I had any right to record a life that wasn't even mine, to commit the fraud to writing.

"Tell me something," Bryn continued, limping to a card table, where he withdrew a notepad from his shoulder bag and laid it on the marble top. "Why did you decide to move to Naruka? Was Tye so very convincing?"

I frowned at his tone. "Why are you asking?"

"Morbidly curious."

"I'd prefer you just morbid."

This earned me a lopsided grin that replaced the bite in his words. "I do not think so." He withdrew a blade from his pocket, then turned it to his pencil, shaving off thin wooden strips into a tiny cup. "Are you always so taciturn on this subject?"

Taciturn. "Isn't English your second language?"

"Third," he said, his eyes catching the twinkle of the lanterns. "Well, Rowan?"

"I wanted a change, that's all."

"A change? Someone does not live their entire life in a town of a few thousand and suddenly move without cause to Ireland. Why did you?"

"I already told you." He studied my face, and because I didn't like what he might see, I stared hard at the pictures of those who'd traveled here before me. "What did you say you did in the Gate last? Some research on the gears, or—"

"No, Rowan," Bryn said firmly. "Tell me this, or perhaps, next time I shall let Kazie or James have the pleasure of anchoring while you are being made love to by a *'feathered beast man.'*"

I whirled, and caught the wicked humor in his eyes before he blinked it away. "We're not doing—*that*—yet. And please don't call it that."

Bryn propped his chin on fingers that would make a piano beg to be played by them. "Do you prefer something more descriptive? I can be inventive."

I bet he could. "No."

"Then tell me of why you left L'Ardoise."

I wanted to give the same answer, but his stare killed the words before they could wet my tongue.

Why did I leave?

Yes, Rowan.

I stuffed my hands in my pockets, staring at the portrait of Mohammed, the man whose glasses I'd crushed in my ungrateful fist. What had convinced him to come here? Had he worked long days on a farm like Kazie and dreamed of something better?

Or had he been like me?

It had been hard to work in the shop with my father after Willow died, then to sit down for Sunday dinner with my parents, to see that empty chair and feel what they hadn't wanted to say aloud. That it shouldn't have been Willow.

Rowan?

I blinked, my throat suddenly tight and aching, my chest no better. "Let James take me to the Gate again, then," I said and made for the stairs.

Rising, Bryn grasped my arm as I passed. "Rowan, I did not intend to—"

"*There* ya are." My head snapped up at Tye's voice. "Thought ya might still be at the Gate." He rolled out his neck, spared a glance at Bryn. "Ya ready?"

"For?"

"Date night," he said, grabbing my jacket. "We got a game to catch."

Bryn's eyes flashed hot before he dropped my arm.

CHAPTER 25

Cherry Wine

T he Ford's heater belched engine breath into my shivering hands, but my vigorous rubbing did more to warm them than the car.

Ireland's favorite game had not been spared from the endless rain. Even the wind had sided with the opposing team when it ripped my umbrella from my frozen hands and tossed it to them.

"I liked hurling, but it's really nothing like baseball," I decided, plucking my soaked jacket away from my breasts.

"Darlin', that's 'cause ain't nothin' like baseball." Tye grinned from the driver's seat, offering a smile with teeth whiter than the Irish players' thighs. I eyed his dry hoodie enviously. "But I'm glad to get ya away from Naruka for a bit. James has got even me on edge tryin' to reach all the triplets." Tye turned up the volume on the radio's sports recap. "Ya know he's got a hundred bucks on this game? That man must get some thrill out of losin' his money."

I chuckled as we swung through Capolinn. Strung between pubs, rows of red-and-white triangles for the local team fluttered in the wind. "Tye, what if the Inquitate come after you in L'Ardoise?" I angled toward the cracked window, hoping the icy cold would dispel the reek of cigarettes I'd unleashed with the heater—the car's cruel revenge for not fixing its spark plugs yet.

Tye scratched his eyebrow with the hand holding his cigarette. "I'm only worried 'bout you, hun."

Yet I still hadn't told him about what happened in Oslo. "Why do you think we came through the Gate together?"

"Since I can't see Stornoway and I bein' all that friendly, I gotta imagine we were forced into it." Frosted green eyes slid sideways at me. "*You* and Stornoway are lookin' pretty friendly right now though."

So I *was* staring after Bryn so obviously even Tye picked it up.

"He's been easier to talk to since we figured out the Inquitate pattern," I said carefully.

Tye just shook his head as we bumped up a narrow road leading away from Capolinn. The overgrown brambles that should have been brilliant green during the day were now sharp silhouettes guarding the curving corners.

"Look," Tye said as he slowed around one. "I gotta tell ya somethin' about him, since I do feel like you're getting close, and 'cause that guy would throw ya over quicker than a cat on a hot tin roof."

My stomach lurched. "What is it?"

Tye twisted the steering wheel between tanned hands. "Ya know how he was exiled before?"

"He didn't say why, and neither did James."

"That's 'cause they don't want ya to know. Don't want ya to know just what the Gate can do to ya." He went quiet for a moment, letting the spluttering engine fill the silence. "But me? I think you should know the realities of what we're doin' here, you get me?"

I chewed on my lip. "Yeah. Yeah, I get you, Tye."

He sighed, lifted his ball cap, let it flatten his hair again. "Did Stornoway ever tell ya how James recruited him?"

I frowned into the side mirror, where rain dissolved my face into a thousand reflections. "James said he offered him a commission for painting portraits. How does that relate to his exile?"

Tye turned down the radio. "Everything relates, Roe. Because Naruka, Ruhaven, it's about takin' who ya were and breakin' it. The people who leave? Like Lana? Those are the ones that didn't wanna break."

That was a strange way of putting it. "I don't think I'm breaking."

"No, but ya will. That's what the question of the Fall does to ya, and why James don't like tellin' folks too early. But anyway…" He stared hard at the windshield, then banged his fist on the dashboard when the wipers stuck. "You may not think it, but Stornoway actually had a life before all of this. A struggling artist—and there ain't no other kind, way I see it—but he had this college sweetheart, too, nice lookin' woman. He ever tell ya about her?"

I didn't want to know that. Didn't want to ever *think* of him like that. "No."

"Well, when Stornoway moved here, he kept the girlfriend for a while, even after Ruhaven. A lot of folks think they can keep both lives—before Ruhaven and after—but ya can't. That's what Ruhaven steals from ya.

"Now, ya know Stornoway's got a mate, and I suppose you know what that means for Ruhavens too. That girlfriend didn't stand a chance. After a few good romps with his Ruhaven lady, Stornoway was waving goodbye to that sweet Norwegian."

I could picture the kind of woman waiting for him in Norway, someone who'd look at his picture every day and think how lucky she was. Wondering, hoping he'd come back soon.

Tye swirled his cigarette at me. "Nothin' is ever good enough for Stornoway. He's like a stallion whinin' for the mare in the next farm. Got a nice girl here, but he had to find his Ruhaven *love,* his *mate.* So he started recruitin', lookin' for her in the *Ledger.*"

"Like James," I murmured.

"Like James," Tye agreed, tapping his cigarette on the steering wheel. "And Bryn found her."

My heart sunk—a stupid, foolish reaction. "He found her here," I said hollowly, knowing what that would mean to him, to find someone here he obviously loved in the Gate. How would she feel? Would she know how lucky she was to have *Bryn* look at her? Want her? The idea made me sick.

"He did," Tye said. "He found her in the *Ledger,* but they ain't ever met. She was killed by the Inquitate."

The words dangled between us in the car, mingled with the radio in some weird parody, and everything in me turned to ice. His mate was dead. The one I'd just—just *envied.* Here I was, posing as someone in the *Ledger,* and I was jealous of a dead woman. As if I had any *right.*

I sucked in my cheeks and stared hard out the window. I'd wondered, before, why Bryn had been researching the Inquitate before he'd been infected. This was why. Not for him, not for the other Ruhavens, but for *her.* Because she'd been one of those victims.

"Who was she?" I asked quietly. And which of the lives that I'd read, that he'd so carefully assembled notes for, had belonged to his mate? Had I asked him about her? Had I cared?

"Dunno, but you think James took it bad with Essie?" Tye shook his head. "That ain't nothin' compared to Stornoway. Guy was a fuckin' mess. Stopped goin' to the Gate for a while, then we couldn't get him away from the damn thing. He's goin' in there, livin', talkin', fuckin' this woman that don't even exist, won't ever be here."

How could anyone live like that? Knowing every interaction you had—every kiss, every touch—was with a woman who died twice over—in the memories, and again here. "What happened?"

Tye sucked in his cheeks on an inhale, blew it out. "I remember it was early April, 'cause the sheep had just finished lambing. The place is waterlogged—ya know how it is—fog everywhere, mist as thick as the smoke off this cigarette. James, Kazie, and me, we're all goin' about our business 'round Naruka. Ya know someone used to keep this place maintained before ya." He jabbed a thumb at his chest. "And I suppose none of us really noticed that Stornoway was missin'."

The warm lanterns of Naruka flickered through the dark trees.

"Kazie came 'round first, askin' 'bout Stornoway. Well, I wasn't keepin' tabs on the man, told her to check his room. She says no, he ain't there. I tell her check the woods then, probably paintin'. So she went lookin' for him.

"But he wasn't paintin', he wasn't in the woods, wasn't researchin'. Now Kazie, ya know how sensitive she is, she starts gettin' worried, and when James comes back from the market, she gets him in a state. Pretty soon, we realize no one's seen him since last evening when he gone and left for the Gate. That wasn't unusual, ya know, 'cause he could anchor himself."

Someone had left the wrought iron gate open, the lantern beside it lit, so Tye drove through without pause.

"Once we figured it out, where he likely was, well, I ain't ever seen James scale that mountain so fast. He flew up, Kaz on his tail, and me followin'. All I could think was that it was just like Stornoway—selfish. That man never thought of anythin' but himself."

I rolled down the window, needing the sharp ping of rain on my face.

"The mud slowed us some, Kazie kept trippin', but eventually, we made it to the Gate." He squeezed his knuckles on the wheel. "Kazie screamed. Ear-splittin', like a chicken under an axe. First I thought, maybe, thought the Inquitate had shown up. Then I saw him."

Tye let the image of Bryn at the Gate conjure itself before words ever could. I'd been sick and gaunt after a few hours—he'd have been in the Gate for nearly twenty-four.

"His clothes were soaked. I remember that first," Tye intoned, and his eyes had that glassy, faraway look of someone caught in the hooks of a memory. "And his hair was…" he wiped at his forehead, "soaked. It was longer then, nearly as long as yours, so he looked like a mermaid yanked up from the river. You ever smelled death, Roe?"

I dug my fingernails into the seat. "Willow didn't— I don't—"

"Then ya haven't," Tye cut me off. "Sweet, burnin' rubber. That's what it smells like. That's what the Gate does to ya. Kazie was sick, threw up in the bushes while James tried to hold it together," he said, voice as flat as his eyes. "Stornoway—he didn't look right at all. Skin all waxy, lips so gray ya can barely see 'em, and rain had pooled in his mouth like one of those bird fountains James has."

Sick dread spread like oil in my chest.

"When I saw Stornoway that day…" Tye rubbed his jaw. "Well, it changed things for me. James hauled him up, screamin' at the guy to come back. I ain't ever seen anythin' like it. We couldn't wake him up.

"It took both of us—Kaz was too distraught—to drag his limp body out of the Gate. But finally, when we got him 'bout thirty feet away, he came 'round. James started weepin'. I ain't seen a grown man cry since my daddy found out my sister was movin' to New York. But Stornoway, he don't apologize for what he's done, for bein' so damn foolish. Instead, he starts *screamin'* at us. Blamin' us for tearin' him away from his mate, 'cause she's alive in the Gate and he was gonna join her. Sick fuck."

How could he want someone that much? Even James wouldn't offer himself to the Gate like that. Did it make Bryn crazy, or in love? Was there a difference?

"That's what the Gate does to ya. Ya forget what's real, what matters. Stornoway had no intention of wakin' from the Gate. He went in to die that day."

I squeezed my lips together. He'd done that, for his mate, because he'd cared more for her, more for Ruhaven, than I had for anything. Even for Willow, I wouldn't have had the courage to waste away in the Gate, to offer everything I was to Ruhaven.

But Bryn would have sacrificed his life and friends in Norway, his years studying for a PhD in art history, his hobbies like glacier walking and painting boats in the port.

God, I'd been stupid, selfish. Only thinking about what Ruhaven meant to me, instead of realizing what it might mean to Bryn. What it'd done to him, what it must have been like to face the memories of a mate he knew was as lost as James's.

"So that's why you exiled Bryn," I said hollowly, "because of what he tried to do."

Tye grunted and switched to the stick, clunking the Granada into park. "That's right, Roe, for his own damn good."

What if Bryn tried to remain in the Gate again? He had been so busy watching me when *I* should have been protecting *him*.

Shaking, I climbed out of the car, following Tye's flashlight as it danced over the weeds and raspberry bushes picked clean by birds.

"Ya won't say anythin'?" Tye confirmed.

I shook my head as I stepped into the tack room that still smelled of saddle cleaner and toed off my soaked boots. Though everything in me screamed to go to Bryn, to tell him—I don't know—*something* that showed I understood some minuscule part of why he'd done it. That I wasn't just some selfish woman, that I understood the gift he'd given me by forcing me to see Ruhaven.

I'd thought he'd done it to punish me at first, to make me witness a life that didn't belong to me. But maybe it hadn't been a punishment at all, but a gift—a chance to live a different life, a chance to *be* someone again, a chance to matter. Bryn had given me that, even after what he'd lost.

The sound of ticking clocks floating in from the kitchen, as steadying as Bryn's own presence.

"Roe?"

Tye stepped under the light. His warm cheeks glowed, his dark hair looking soft as butterscotch. "The Gate, well, it means different things for different people, ya know? Made me realize how important life is here, how all those dreams and fantasies only make this more real." He ran a hand down my wet braid. "That's why I brought ya here, 'cause ya didn't see that. You were so broken after Willow. I knew this place could put ya together again." His eyes crinkled. "Wasn't I right?"

Right? Maybe. I couldn't stop thinking about Bryn. "I guess I never thanked you."

He stepped closer, ducking the lightbulb. "Guess I didn't always go about things the right way either, huh?" His tone was light, teasing, but those green eyes darkened to smoky rings.

I braced a stiff hand on his shoulder. "No, probably kissing me at the Gate wasn't the right way."

His lips parted, the bottom one pink under the light. "I've been thinkin' 'bout that," he said, voice dropping an octave. "Thinkin' I'd like to make up for it." A faint dimple popped under a scruff of beard.

My heart hammered a sharp tune. I hadn't thought of Tye like that in months. "Oh. Well. I—I think we're even."

"Naw," Tye said softly, pulling me into him, "'cause, hun, I never did really kiss ya back then."

Everything played out in slow motion—the intent in his eyes, the hand tightening in my jacket, the feel of the leftover rain sliding down my neck. But all I could think about was the image of Bryn up in the

Gate, lying in the rain alone. Waiting for Ruhaven to claim him for a mate he'd never see.

I shouldn't do this.

Even if I'd wanted Tye since that first hot dog he bought me at the park, and now here he was, his full lips a hair's breadth away.

Our mouths met before I could decide—firm, soft, a question. He tasted like sunny warmth and ball games, of comfort and home and cinnamon, exactly like I'd always imagined. And I'd imagined *a lot*.

To hell with it.

I opened under him, exploring his mouth as the lightbulb hummed above us and the moths beat their last breaths against it. When had I last kissed anyone? There was that awkward mess outside the bar, then there was...

Sahn. That was who I'd kissed last.

Tye murmured against my lips, his mouth and hands far more skilled than mine, drawing out every latent desire the Azekiel had burned into me over the past months before I'd woken on the cusp of them about to "*make love*"—as Bryn had said. Each smoldering look Sahn had thrown at Nereida that punched me in the gut. The feel of Sahn's broad muscles that I imagined were Tye's now as I gripped him.

The dim lightbulb swung overhead, revealing the heat in Tye's eyes with every pass, like a wolf's orbs flickering in the woods. We slapped into the kitchen door, pulling at each other's clothes. Tye cursed my soaked jacket under his breath.

If I didn't release all the burning tension Sahn had built up, I'd implode. What if Tye wanted to go back to his room? I'd have to creep past James to get upstairs, and Kazie's budgies would be squawking across the hall, and then Bryn shared a wall with...

Slipping on rolling onions, I grabbed on to Tye.

Mistaking it for enthusiasm, he shoved my jacket off, inched his hot fingers under my sweater, and I nearly sighed from their warmth alone. Then they were sliding over my flat belly, heating a path up my torso, undoing my bra.

I groaned as he kneaded my breasts. Yes, this was what I needed. To be touched again, finally, to be—

A gasp flew from me when a sharp pain pinched my heart, like a fine needle had slipped between my ribs and scored bone. I jerked hard enough to wrench Tye's fingers away.

"What—what was that?" I panted, bra hanging loose.

Tye's eyebrows pulled together. "Roe, darlin'? What's wrong?"

I grabbed at my shirt, still feeling the phantom pain. Some side effect of Ruhaven? Or another illusion?

"I—I don't know."

The pain began to abate, smoothing out like an ironed wrinkle, but it'd been a bucket of cold water on my arousal.

When Tye reached for me again, I gripped his wrist, stopped him. "Tye, we're in the tack room."

"So? You wanna go to mine?"

Yes. No. Yes. Maybe.

Tye's heavy breathing filled the dark. "This is 'bout Stornoway, ain't it?" He zipped up his jacket abruptly. "He's got you twisted around him, takin' ya to the Gate, gettin' ya obsessed about the Inquitate."

Wait, what? "It's not about him." *It might be about him.*

Tye held out his hands. "Then what do ya want, Roe? I thought you liked that day in the Gate, before, well ya know. I knew it wasn't the time after, so I gave ya some space. I've been givin' ya space."

I rubbed my forehead. Hell. This conversation was probably long overdue. "Tye, I—I did. Want this, before, I mean. But now?" I kicked the bag of onions. "I think, not now," I admitted.

Tye let out a gusty sigh. "Guess the Gate complicates everythin', huh?"

I peeked at him from under my loose bangs. "Yeah. Yeah, I guess it does."

He fixed my shirt, tugged lightly on my braid. "That's alright, darlin'. I tried. Probably, I should've tried back in L'Ardoise, but that's how things go." He tipped up my chin, pressed his lips softly to mine. "Let's go on inside." Hot light flooded the tack room as Tye stepped into the kitchen, likely illuminating my heated cheeks. "Comin', hun?" He held open the door.

"I'll join you in a minute."

"Suit yourself," Tye replied, and, whistling, strode through the kitchen.

When I was sure he was gone, I stepped inside the house, closed the door behind me.

I was in trouble.

Because only an idiot turned down a sweaty round with Tye Cannon.

I stared at the portrait of Bryn hanging on a yellow wall, knowing full well that my indecision was his fault, had been from the first day I'd set eyes on that Polaroid in guest room three.

I peeled off my wet jacket and tossed it over the clothesline.

Bryn had a woman in the Gate— *Female*? A ball of light?—one he'd tried to die for, and I needed to start respecting that. Maybe he'd kind of flirted—and that was a big maybe—but no one worshipped the Gate and its rules like Bryn. A mate in Ruhaven meant no woman here. Period. End of story.

I blew out a breath, eyeing the warm, peanut-brown sweater slung on the kitchen chair where I normally sat. Bryn's.

Before I could think better of it, I was sliding into its soft, buttery heat. It smelled like him, like spiced snow and a very faint whiff of paint thinner. I needed to talk to him, needed to explain that I understood what he lived through every day—memories of a dead mate, like James.

I hugged the sweater to my chest as I strode into the lounge with all the confidence of someone who'd been getting undressed on a bag of onions five minutes ago.

The scent of buttered popcorn hit me first.

Kazie and James lay on opposite ends of the sofa, their feet overlapping, a cup of tea in their hands. Her hair was a massive beehive poking from under the blanket. Tye claimed a couch, spreading his knees and arms wide.

On the TV, a black-and-white ship thundered through stormy seas—*Mutiny on the Bounty*. I forced worries of Bryn, of what he'd done and might do again, to the back of my mind.

"How far are you?" I asked roughly.

Kazie pounded the remote three times before the men froze mid-oar. "Too far," she stated, so abruptly I scrunched my eyes at her. Something wrong?

Tye patted the space beside him. "I'll fill ya in. They're out at sea, there's a mutiny. There ya go."

As I sat next to Tye, Kazie avoided my gaze, sliding further under the blanket and smashing at the remote until roaring men filled the lounge again.

James sighed and kept his eyes glued to the television.

"James," I said, "is everything okay with—"

A sharp wrenching tore through the hallway.

Twisting, I glanced down the carpeted corridor where lanterns set the portraits aglow and light spilled from under the washroom door.

Was Bryn sick? Food poisoning? Too long in the Gate? "What's wrong with him?"

Kazie grumbled into the blanket.

"He's fine," James said, and cranked up the volume until a volley of shouts drowned out the next round of heaving.

"I didn't accidentally cook chicken again, did I?"

Popcorn kernels crunched between Tye's teeth. "It ain't the damn food, Roe. Stornoway's in the Gate too often. Obsessed, that's what he is."

So my embarrassment at being caught with the Azekiel had caused this, put stress on him pulling both of us out. Or was it that he wanted to be with his woman in the Gate as often as possible?

I started to get up when the bathroom door creaked open. Light spread onto the checkered carpet, blasting a rectangle on the opposing wall.

Bryn limped out, hand shaking on his cane, sleeves rolled up to his elbows, cheeks as sharp as glass under the lanterns.

"Bryn?" I whispered.

His hollow gaze snapped to mine, and the air between us wavered like two wrong notes trying to synchronize.

"Tye, yer playing a dangerous game like," James warned under his breath. "Even I wouldn't be placing no bets on ye."

What game?

Clunk.

Bryn emerged from the shadows, his flushed nose the only dash of color in a face gone bone white. Dark markings decorated his taut forearm and disappeared under the bunched fabric.

Tattoos?

I tried to catch his eye, to see if he'd make light of something that obviously didn't suit him, but he hastily yanked down both sleeves like I'd annoyed him by looking.

Clunk.

His cane echoed on the hardwood floor until the rug deadened it. He came around the pool table, trailing a finger on the felt and polished wood as he approached. Sweat glistened in the dip of his collarbone.

James paused the TV.

"Are you okay?" I asked, but there was a look on his face, one I hadn't seen since Norway, that had my hand shaking on the sofa.

Saying nothing, Bryn approached our huddle of couches until his breath was a winter's gasp away. Firelight flickered in the shallows of his cheeks. Shadows swam in irises as dark and still as a lake. He didn't look so much like an art major from Norway but something sucked out of Ruhaven.

I pinched the sweater I wore, his sweater. "Sorry, I borrowed this."

"I know. I left it for you," he said curtly.

Accusation weighed heavily in those eyes of searing blue, and the guilt that had settled in my gut since I kissed Tye now became a stone around my neck. It didn't make sense. *This* didn't make sense.

Tye kicked his boots on the coffee table and asked, "Get a little indigestion there, Stornoway?"

James groaned softly.

Kazie cursed.

"Have you no respect at all?" Bryn addressed Tye in a voice like rough ice.

"Maybe you oughta remember which world we're livin' in," Tye warned when Bryn's nostrils flared. "And in which one ya only have one leg."

"What's gotten into you?" I demanded of Tye.

"I'm just statin' facts to your boyfriend here."

As my cheeks burned, Bryn finally looked at me, then down, his searing gaze narrowing on my breasts with a force somehow more physical than Tye's fingers. Heat flashed through me, quick and hot and ripe.

His eyes flickered, met mine.

I gulped air, hardly able to breathe when he was staring at me like that. But then he just turned.

And walked away.

CHAPTER 26

No Other Love

I tried not to think about Bryn. I failed, but I tried. And I kept trying until Kazie eventually insisted we all visit the Gate together for *Yizoumithou*—or, as she called it, Ruhaven's birthday. I might have insisted that Bryn and I visit alone, but he hadn't spoken to me since Tye left last week. Bryn had offered to anchor, but not from inside the Gate, as he needed to anchor a group. Or maybe that'd been an excuse.

Over the hillside of Ruhaven, thousands of glittery balloons drifted into the liquid night. They swayed with the call of drums that boomed from somewhere deep in the distant mountains. I could just make out the dragons stretching their wings under moons glowing like purple lava.

Whatever the reason for the color, nothing had ever been so beautiful.

In the memory, Nereida danced toward Sahn, whose wild mane of gold fell in loose waves today and threaded into a circlet so that he looked like a dark, golden prince. As he swirled, his loose robe spun in a wide, colorful arc, revealing dusty-rose nipples and tattoos of gears crawling up his abs.

My body hummed at the sight. Or, Nereida's did. But I'd probably have a similar reaction if I wasn't thinking about Bryn.

I couldn't stop replaying the look on his face when he'd stepped from the washroom.

Should I talk to him? He'd barely said two words on the hike here. Tell him I regretted kissing Tye? He didn't care. How I felt every pulsing inch of him, even across the room? That was fanciful at best. Idiotic at worse. And embarrassing to hear it even in my own thoughts.

No, I had nothing to say, nothing to apologize for.

But I *should* talk to him about his mate—which I would have if he hadn't been ignoring me for the better part of a week. All the more reason to get over my embarrassment of visiting the Gate with James and Kazie.

But did I have to enter the memories in the middle of them dancing?

Sahn's wing brushed my shoulder as he caught me, talons circling my waist. All his movements were familiar now, comforting. Loving. We spun in circles, laughing, screaming, as the violet fires scorching up the tree trunks became a swirling blaze—a sign of midnight in Ruhaven.

Jamellian and Essie danced beside us, her face glowing with life. Did James imagine it was real, that he was holding her here? Or was this memory everything he needed?

It couldn't be, as much as James tried to pretend otherwise. He'd wanted Essie to be born in the *Ledger*.

And what about Sahn?

When Nereida leapt into his arms, he caught me with a sideways smile that had my heart somersaulting.

Was Sahn in the *Ledger*?

Was I supposed to ask James? Surely, he would have told me if the Azekiel existed, if they'd met.

And what then?

He wouldn't be the male in this dream, twirling me through hot pebbled sand, kissing my neck and lips—he'd be someone else. Someone new and different and not the winged demon I'd grown to know.

I smiled inside Nereida, wishing I could pause the memory a little bit, just to taste the wet snow in the air, to dance with Sahn until I could forget who I was—or who I wasn't.

And it was kind of nice, holding him like this, feeling my body move in ways I knew would never be possible with my muscles on Earth.

But everything passed too quickly. The memory moved at its own pace, and Nereida darted to look at the next thing before I'd even glanced at it. It was both annoying and exhilarating, being out of control on a merry-go-round.

But at the moment, her attention was all for Sahn.

When he gazed at her—at *me*—the power beneath it buckled my knees. He looked at her like he felt everything she could, like he saw right through her to me. Like I existed entirely separate from Nereida, from Ruhaven, from anything else. Like he knew exactly who I was, even if I didn't.

Then his muscles bunched, his back rippled, and he launched us into the air.

It would have been nice to see more of James and Essie, but Sahn swept us up with the indigo sparks, his wings billowing and glowing with the radiance of the fires below as we climbed. When we peaked above the trees, they caught the wind with a thunderous boom louder than the drums.

Flying.

My heart wanted to burst. It was miraculous, my favorite part of the memories, this impossible freedom—feeling the air whip by my ears, the world a mesmerizing blur below. Dodging the gears that cranked in the sky, peeking at their intricate designs a moment before clouds covered them, seeing our shadows drape across the tops of trees when we slowed to a glide. Even the *taste* of the sky up here. Almost like Bryn, that cold wildness, no—*escape*. That's what it was. The taste of escape.

Sahn's voice rumbled low in my ear. His hand curled around my waist to stroke my stomach's silver skin. Nereida practically purred under his touch, a sound that would have made me burn crimson if anyone heard.

But what if Bryn had? He was anchoring right now. He would hear every moan she made—through me.

No, no, I wouldn't be embarrassed. Not in this world, because I wasn't Roe right now, I was Nereida.

Flying. Living. Escaping.

And Nereida was never embarrassed.

Sahn billowed his wings so the steep angle of them brought us to a sudden descent. I hitched forward in his arms, but he held me to his chest. Even as we drifted on stuttering currents thicker than water, he never let go.

The tops of the burning trees came into view again.

Purple smoke drifted upward like the northern lights, a sight so beautiful it twisted something in my chest—to know I'd never see this on Earth, to know that eventually, someday, the memory would end.

But Nereida stretched out a hand, letting the burning indigo leaves tickle our fingertips—furry, warm, and soft. Nothing like the prickly vines back home.

With a low laugh, Sahn flipped us in midair. I glimpsed the sky and the gears licking purple dust before we landed amidst the blossoms with a soft *whoosh*, slipping from tree to tree.

His wings cocooned us, wonderfully soft and comforting. Beautiful too. As gray as the twisted storms of Ireland and blackened at the ends.

The descent felt like a decadent carnival ride, like sliding down a rollercoaster on a bed of feathers.

Too soon, Sahn unraveled his wings, dropping me into a silk netting strung between the trees. Nereida stretched like a cat, enjoying the feel of her flexing muscles while I watched the moths flutter around us, their glow flickering off Sahn's golden skin.

He smiled, slow and wide, revealing glistening fangs. I knew that look—that hunger.

And I didn't need the book James gave me to figure out what would come next. It wasn't supposed to be too unlike humans. Still, no man from L'Ardoise had burning planets for eyes.

Slowly, Sahn ran his clawed hands up my bare legs, watched as Nereida arched at his touch, as she smiled at him. Then he lifted my silvery hand to his mouth, sucked each finger between his lips until desire filled me to bursting.

I waited for the anchor to yank me home as it always did, but none came.

Where was Bryn? He always had some instinct to anchor me before things went too far, and now he could see me, *hear* me. But maybe I didn't care—not today.

I'd danced, laughed, and ate with Sahn for months in the Gate. The angel had swam with me in milk lakes under thundering ivory waterfalls. He'd slept with Nereida beneath the smoked-vanilla skies with his wing over her shoulder. I'd watched them live their romance on a planet light-years away.

That's why James waited for Essie. He wanted a love experienced in the soul rather than in things. Experienced right *here*, in this space that used to be hollow under my heart.

I didn't want to wake up this time.

As Sahn pressed my palm to his face, a trail of gold encircled us. Something from the forest? Another creature? Nereida barely glanced at it, her eyes completely focused on the male leveraging himself above.

Arousal quivered in my gut when his fangs slowly extended and firelight glittered off their smooth bone.

Because I couldn't distance myself anymore, couldn't keep Nereida and me apart, when Sahn's breath caressed her neck, I felt every hot whisper of it as if it were me under him and not her.

I sucked in a breath when he bit down softly—a mating ritual, the book explained.

He groaned against my skin, the humming vibration skittering in my bones, in my soul. She writhed, clasping him harder, urging him to take more.

It was weird and wonderful and horrifyingly arousing.

And I wanted it all. Wanted to forget everything but this. Wanted to be no one but *her*.

With a growl, Sahn tore off whatever I'd been wearing, the scrap of material landing in a broken spiderweb. His dappled wings whipped wide, knocking into the rose-blooming trees and tiny firelights. Our legs tangled in the vine netting.

I never took my eyes off his—the longing in them, the desire, the hope, a blue flame at the center of a fire. And something else, too, a tempered sadness that didn't quite fit the moment.

But Nereida didn't notice as she threaded her fingers into his golden hair, urging him to her breasts with a soft exhale. He bent, nuzzling the translucent peaks with his eyes on me, the clouds spinning under her skin like they were as thrilled as I was to be touched like this again. Not quick floundering in the tack room or the rough, quick hands of men back home, but tenderly loved, where each touch was deliberate, teasing, arousing, like every piece of him was focused on *her*. Like only Nereida existed.

I wanted that. Even if it was a memory, even if it wasn't *me* he wanted.

His tongue flicked my hardened nipple, wrenching a moan from my lips as my world darkened to the twin golden lights in his eyes, watching me with an uncomplicated adoration, in a way no man in L'Ardoise ever had.

He stroked my breasts, talons scraping down my torso until I would've refused to leave Ruhaven. Not by Bryn. Not by anyone.

I tore at his heavy clothing.

Sensuous tattoos rippled along his muscled body, disappearing under the pants he still wore.

She tugged at the rope over his groin.

My heart pounded in a wild, erratic rhythm, too fast to be mistaken as Nereida's. The air around us glittered, vibrated with the new gravity forming in the hammock of silk leaves.

Sahn's burning eyes locked on mine. Held.

Rowan.

Then he drove into her.

Into *me*.

S omewhere in their rolling, mating, biting, and thrusting, I'd been
reborn.

My bones were melted and reshaped from diamonds, my blood
drained and replaced with the liquid gold of Sahn's eyes, and my heart
restarted by Ruhaven.

I wanted to feel his dew-dampened feathers over my skin again, the
caress of his hands—talons.

Why had I been so afraid of him?

I'd missed months of being worshipped by an angel and spent my
days bitter and half-aroused instead.

Sleepy and sated, I breathed in the damp soil, my body as boneless
as the chicken I couldn't stomach anymore. Rain thundered on the roof
of—

I pried open an eye. An *umbrella*?

When had I been pulled from the Gate?

The rough weave of the blanket itched my overly sensitive skin. My
entire body tingled with awareness, like each pore I didn't know I had
was singing "Hallelujah."

Groggily, I rubbed at my eyelids, squeezed my eyes, then blinked
them open again.

Someone was kneeling over me with skin as light and milky as the
river that ran through Ruhaven.

His eyes were twin pools of gold, molten metal.

Desire punched through me.

Bryn's lips parted on a shaky exhale, cold and crisp and wild.

Drops of rain clung to his eyelashes, dripped off his upper lip and
glistened in his faint beard. One caught the light, trickling a line down
his smooth throat before disappearing under his collar. His high
cheekbones were no longer ghostly pale, but pink with flushed color.

But his gaze, that burning gold fire, held on to mine more fiercely
than the storm prowling above.

When he didn't move, I whispered, "Bryn?"

Slowly, very slowly, he reached toward me. I went completely still
as he cupped my face, my heart speeding up like I was in the Gate again.
His lips curved in time with the thumb he stroked over my cheek—the
first smile I'd seen since that night after the game.

"Hello, Rowan," he said, voice rough.

I'd missed him this last week. Missed the teasing and the walks to
the Gate and the *fullness* of being with him.

Too soon, Bryn pulled away, shifting the umbrella and nestling it
into the crook of my elbow. He waited until my fumbling hand replaced
his own.

When he started to get up, I caught the sleeve of his rain jacket. "Bryn. Did you—did you see me here?" With the Azekiel, moaning in the Gate as my heart threatened to burst from my ribs? I had to know. Had to know if he…

Bryn's golden eyes softened as he lifted my hand from his jacket, his fingers calloused and tender as he raised mine to his mouth.

Warm breath whispered over my skin. *What was…oh.*

He kissed my knuckles. Gently, softly. Each and every one.

I said his name cluelessly, a bird chirping for its mate in the woods. This was Bryn. *Bryn*! He didn't kiss knuckles, and he didn't smile like that, and he never *looked* at me like that.

But after each knuckle tingled from his lips, Bryn lifted his head and curled my hand around the umbrella. "Do not be embarrassed, Rowan. You are very lovely," he murmured. "I must wake the others now."

Yet seeing him here, crouched above me, the rain smoothing his silky hair to his cheeks, it brought back the story Tye had told, of when Bryn had come up here to the Gate another night.

It was irrational and stupid the fear that gripped me—to know I'd been that close to missing him.

"Bryn," I said, almost begged, "don't leave."

He frowned slightly. "Of course not, Rowan." Then slipped out from under the umbrella, the rain gluing his cashmere sweater to the firm body beneath. He knelt carefully beside Kazie, gently rousing her from Ruhaven.

I angled my watch once my heart rate had leveled.

One hour.

It was the only time I'd been allowed to remain in the Gate as long as everyone else.

⚙✹

L ast night, in my pale room at Naruka, I dreamed of Sahn. But it hadn't been his face watching me as he'd plunged into me over and over. It'd been Bryn's.

Bryn, with his golden eyes and crooked smile. Bryn, murmuring soft words in my ear, whose fangs grazed my pulse. Bryn, who loved me as Sahn did Nereida. Waking up had been a slow, dawning disappointment, because none of that was possible. Not for a Ruhaven with a mate—that much had been clear from the book James lent me.

I blinked away the memory when Kazie yawned loudly. She lay sprawled on the chesterfield across from me in the lounge and scratched at a cat-eared hat. A tray of tea and biscuits sat between us, courtesy of

James, who'd taken pity on Kazie after I'd forced her to read another journal.

October had disappeared overnight, replaced by its eager sister, November. Like a new boss, she'd made some immediate changes—dropping four degrees, adding buckets of rain, and throwing in a bit of hail to assert her dominance.

Even with the woodstove, the wind tore through Naruka, rattling her ancient pipes into a chorus of ghostly songs. The storm circling over the west of Ireland would hit late tonight.

I sipped my over-steeped tea to ward off the cold and scrawled a few hesitant notes into my journal. I'd been steadily reviewing the journals from the triplets, searching for any pattern between them, anything that might point to why the Inquitate targeted those born in threes—and, ultimately, maybe why they'd gone after Willow.

But it was hard to concentrate.

In the week since Yizomithou, I'd been with Sahn twice more, and each time was better than the last. Bryn continued to anchor me, but if he noticed anything, he hadn't said so, and he hadn't kissed my hand again either.

I shoved that away and reread the same paragraph in Levi's journal for the fifth time. He was one of the triplets born with Patrick and Lana. Had that meant anything to Levi? Had he felt some obligation, like Tye had, to show Lana the Gate?

"Kaz, it's the feckin' Garda. Colm must have been on to them," James said, sticking his head through the doorway with a phone pressed to his chest.

Kazie examined her nails. "Human men," she huffed. "They can't keep away. It's the perfume."

I lifted a brow. She might have been joking. Though, the bubblegum scent she wore *was* unforgettable. I'd tried.

"Sure look," James said, "I'm telling them Lana went to Spain. Is that right?"

She shrugged. "Who knows? Not Ruhaven."

James just rolled his eyes and disappeared into the kitchen.

What would happen if the Garda raided Naruka? Could that happen in Ireland? Would they show up with a warrant to search our library?

The journals spread on my lap suddenly felt like bricks.

"Speaking of men," Kazie said, crunching on a biscuit. "Having fun at the Gate?"

I gulped my scalding tea. "Uh, what?"

Kazie fluffed her hair. "Like, did you ruffle any feathers?" She wiggled her eyebrows as I scowled. "Twist any tails? Bite any—"

I cut her off. "I really don't want to discuss this." Think, dream, fantasize—apparently, yes. But not discuss. "Is there anything in Lana's journal?"

She stretched out her cotton-striped legs, the bells on her toes jingling. "The only feathers Lana ruffled were Colm's."

Yes, it'd been a very good idea not to ask Kaz to anchor me. "I'm serious."

"Lana was, too, before she abandoned Naruka. Though I think she could have done a lot better in the Gate."

I folded my book. "What exactly happened between her and Colm? They were dating here, I take it, before Levi showed Lana the Gate."

"Yeah, but Levi thought James was dragging it out too long," Kazie supplied, already growing bored. "Maybe he felt some connection to her, you know, because she was his triplet. So when James was at the market, Levi took Lana up to see the Gate. She freaked out—kinda like you!" Kazie giggled and mimed a woman barreling out the front doors. "Think she wanted to just forget everything."

"And Levi?" He could be dead right now, or sipping piña coladas on a beach while his old address enjoyed increasingly worried mail from James.

"Maybe the experience with Lana freaked him out, 'cause he left a few months later to Mexico, like you know." An address that had never responded to a single letter from James.

As I thought about it, opening his journal again, Kazie chatted about Ruhaven—Kazmira was still adjusting the Florissant for us to travel to Drachaut—but actually, she might able to help me on something.

"Kazie," I interrupted, "Levi did see Ruhaven, right?"

She tilted her head at me, cheek bulging with a cookie. "Yeah, sure, a few times. But you know how it takes so long to stay in for any *real* length of time."

So he hadn't seen much. That could explain it, but…

"Listen to this." I flattened the page and read the English translation. "'Today, we walked for miles under Ruhaven's beautiful blue skies.'" I paused and looked up. "But they're not blue. They're indigo."

"So? All that means is his writing is dull. 'Beautiful skies'? I mean, there's about four hundred gears spinning up there and the dude can't think of *anything* else? But you know how guys are." She took care of the entire male species with a wave of one glittery hand. "And that dude was really into sports—football," she said, like it was a sad illness she was sorry to tell me of. "What's the original language?"

"Spanish."

Kazie nodded sagely. "Probably mistranslated. Even Levi wasn't that much of a dud. Check with Bryn, I think he speaks it."

Norwegian, English, Spanish, Ruhaven—Bryn made my one language feel like a sin.

So, Levi was here for years before Willow's death. Then why did nothing in these words remind me of Ruhaven? Of the smoked-vanilla nights, or the velvet trees' soft fur?

Maybe Levi had been as dull as Kazie predicted.

Or maybe he hadn't been in Ruhaven at all.

CHAPTER 27

Sybil

"Ye hungry, Roe? There's some of Kazie's stew left," James said.

So that's what this was.

I frowned into the moaning fridge. "I think it's gone off." But when I lifted my head, James's eyes narrowed on a spot below me. With a curse, he marched across the kitchen, swiped a magnet from the fridge door, and held it at arm's length. "If this is another…" He slid his glasses down a fraction. "*May the wind always be at your back, may the sun…* Ah jayzus!"

Disgusted, he tossed Kazie's latest tourist knickknack on the table under the calendar, then scrubbed his lenses as if to remove the poem burned into them. "What am I going to do with all this shite?"

I wiped my boots on the *Céad Míle Fáilte* mat below the sink. "At least she hasn't replaced the clock yet," I offered with amusement. The kitchen's boring, sliced-apple clock *tick-tocked* a hearty agreement.

"Me mum would be rollin' in her bloody grave," James warned, nicking the whiskey. If that were true, his mom would be turning faster than a cement truck by this point.

He adjusted the volume on the radio before sinking onto a kitchen chair, whiskey in one hand, his calendar in the other. "I forgot to tell ye, Tye left a message with the post office this morning from L'Ardoise and passed something on to ye I've no intention of repeating, though I'm sure it'll keep Capolinn entertained for many o' night. We'll just assume ye got the gist."

I winced. God, hopefully this was just his usual flirting. I couldn't juggle him and the Azekiel even if I wanted to. "Sorry, James. We're not…"

He waved me off. "Ah, I know like," he said, "but actually, ye know, I've been meaning to talk to ye about that, about Ruhaven, I mean." James shut his calendar with a deliberate flip and interlaced his thumbs over its twelve naked priests.

"Did something happen?"

He scratched one flaring nostril, a dad about to explain how periods worked. Or worse. "It's just I didn't think ye'd been *dancing* before."

Jesus, it *was* worse. I would have stuck my head back in the fridge if Kazie's stew hadn't permeated the thing.

"Yizmithou?" I tried for casual and landed on its distant cousin, twice-removed. "Yeah. Dancing. Fun." The Azekiel and I, naked and tangled in the purple vines, his fangs piercing my skin, pumping into Nereida.

I plucked my shirt from my sticky ribs and, cracking the tack room door, inhaled the soapy air.

"Listen like, it must be a bit strange to be with the Azekiel," James persisted like it was his sworn duty to have my face catch fire, "especially after ye thought he'd eat ye. But 'tis nothin' to be ashamed of. That's why I gave ye the book. Well, ye know how Essie and I are. But sure, if ye need to talk about it—maybe ye'd rather Kazie. Still, thought I'd offer, all the same."

Mortified, I turned my back to him, waving my sweaty shirt like a flag. Let some Ruhaven god strike me down now. "James, you wouldn't be trying to give me the birds and the bees talk about Ruhaven would you? Because that book was *more* than enough."

He swallowed an ice-rattling gulp of whiskey. "Sure, 'tis more like the dragons and the druids, but ye know yerself."

I certainly did, and glared at him until I could light the woodstove with my cheeks. "James, let's never—"

Kazie burst into the kitchen, the door no more than an inconvenient obstacle and one whose hinges I'd have to replace later. But I'd never been happier to see her.

Except then the other cause of my heated cheeks limped in on her heels. He dwarfed her in height, made Kazie seem like a tiny pixie in his shadow, but all I could think of was how he'd looked in my dream—nuzzling my breasts, leaning over me, not the unemotional marble he usually wore but with the fire I'd briefly seen.

When he turned those darkening eyes on me, and something flickered over his face, I wasn't sure my dream of him wasn't seared on my flushed forehead. Did he care that Sahn and I were having sex in the Gate? Of course he didn't.

I glanced at Kazie when she snipped the air with scissors, then tossed her mane of curls, spiraled a chair into a pirouette, and gestured at Bryn. "We're having a little salon day."

This was even weirder than Ruhaven.

His gaze cut to her. "We are absolutely not. Kazie descended upon me while I was searching for mailing addresses for James." His voice tightened slightly, but he lowered reluctantly into a chair. "Kazie is quite terrified I shall let my hair grow long again."

"Well, it looks good now. Short, I mean. I like it. Not like, just—it's fine. It's hair." Why was my mouth still moving? One kiss on my hand and I was stuttering like a schoolgirl—Willow would be mortified for me.

Bryn tilted his head at me, faint amusement playing on his lips. "By all means then, I shall keep it short. Actually, Rowan, would you assist in this? I wish to discuss with you my recent findings in the library."

Assist? That could only mean he wanted to avoid the mohawk Kazie would give him.

Yes, but I also have things to discuss with you. If Nereida can wield daggers, I am certain you shall manage scissors.

I huffed a resigned breath. I could almost hear his answer.

Without waiting, Kazie tossed the scissors at me, and only through sheer luck did I avoid them landing in my shoe. As she hustled out of the kitchen, calling out plans of the bar she'd chosen tonight, she dragged James with her.

Bang.

The door rattled behind them, leaving Bryn and I alone.

While I positioned myself with the scissors behind Bryn, he carefully removed an envelope from his wool jacket and set it on the placemat. A colorful stamp adorned the right corner and the writing on the front was blocky and familiar, written with all capitals.

"I discovered this letter in the closet of the room Carmen uses when she stays here," he explained, sliding the contents from the torn edge of the envelope. "This was addressed to her." When he unfolded the letter, I leaned over his shoulder to read, then dropped my hand when his muscles tensed. "In Spanish, the letter describes meeting a man named 'Parth', though I do not know who that may be, and a cantina that he, Parth, and Carmen visited." Bryn flipped the envelope. "The letter was postmarked in 1986."

"Who sent it?" I measured the ends of his hair and didn't think at all about his warm lips on my knuckles. Of the way he'd looked hovering over me in my dreams. Of how much I liked touching him, liked the goosebumps on his neck, the pale dusting of beard along his jaw.

Mate. He had a mate.

Bryn brushed a curling lock off the letter. "I do not know as he went only by his Ruhaven name, which is unfamiliar to me." Bryn tapped the return address. "Puerto Escondido, a town approximately six hours from Oaxaca, Mexico."

I paused and studied the writing again. "*Levi,*" I realized. I hadn't found anything on him besides the one journal. But this was him. His letter to Carmen from abroad, but Puerto Escondido wasn't the address he'd left us with.

Bryn's ear twitched. "I believe so, yes."

"What year did you say?"

"1986."

Six years ago. But if James had marked him missing since 1986, then he'd been alive for at least some of that period and writing to Carmen, of all people.

I mulled it over. "So he leaves Naruka after a few months of visiting the Gate, giving James an address that was always a dead end. Maybe, like Lana, he wanted to break all ties with Naruka."

Another hair fluttered over Bryn's ear and down his shoulder. He brushed it off. "It may be the case. Yet he wrote three times to Carmen over the following years, the last being this one in 1986."

My blood hummed, and not just from Bryn this time. I came around to his front, measured the locks where they ended on each side of his temple. "So," I said as his eyelashes fluttered. "Levi leaves a fake address and cuts off all contact except with Carmen. Because she was his recruiter?"

"Possibly. But Carmen went to some effort to hide these letters. I suspect there were more."

"So she wanted to keep their connection private," I mused. "And he must want the same if he gave a fake address and continued writing. Why?"

Finished with the haircut, I briskly dusted Bryn's shoulders, sending strays fluttering over his neck. I bent to blow them away. *No, too intimate.*

"I think you're good," I said, sliding onto a stool. And if he wasn't, he'd have to be, because I couldn't keep touching him.

"Thanks," Bryn said roughly. "It is possible that Levi moved without notifying James of the updated address."

"It may be nothing," I said as Bryn slid a sketchbook from his bag. "Tye said Carmen wanted space. If Levi felt the same way—and it seems like he did—then it would make sense for them to bond over that. But his journal is sort of odd as well."

"How so?" Bryn sharpened a pencil. "Will you hold that pose for a few minutes?"

Pose? I started to pull my propped fist away from my jaw, stopped. "Oh, sure. I guess his journal just sounded off, but it might be the translation. I'll show you later."

Bryn nodded, and as I settled into the oven's lingering warmth, the light scratching of paper filled the kitchen. "How did you get into art after working on a ship?"

"Oddly enough, I was inspired by the illustrations on Norwegian sardine cans."

A quick laugh escaped me before I could reel it in. "Really?"

He grinned. "I know, it sounds quite silly. While I intended to pursue illustration, I eventually found I enjoyed trying to capture things as they are. With all the subtle nuances of light." His eyes traced my mouth with an intensity that tingled my lips. "To paint something is to really look at it for the first time."

"But your paintings are so abstract," I murmured.

He lifted a brow. "Do you think? Perhaps you should stand further back. My instructor used to say, 'Be able to draw the invisible ear.' It was not until many years later that I understood what she meant." Before I could ask, he switched subjects. "Do you still wish for me to anchor you, or are you more comfortable now?"

Was Bryn worried about being sick again? "Um, if you're okay to keep anchoring me. I mean, if it's not making you ill."

His eyebrows knitted. "Ill?"

I shouldn't have said anything. "Never mind."

"No, tell me."

He moved on to my eyes so that there was no looking away now, and I was suddenly intensely aware of every eyebrow I had never plucked. "The night you were sick, after the movie," I said cautiously. "Tye said you were in the Gate too much. Because of me."

His face didn't change, but his voice was equally careful when he said, "No, Rowan, my being ill was not due to anchoring you."

"Oh." The word hung awkwardly between us.

Then Bryn lowered his eyes, releasing me from their hold. The left side of his mouth pulled up, nearly hidden in the shadows of the overhead light. "I only wondered," he murmured into his page, "about anchoring, as you did appear to awake a bit more...flushed, recently. Perhaps you are adjusting after all?"

Bryn was *not* doing this to me. Heat tumbled through me until even my toes were on fire. He wasn't supposed to see, even if he *knew*.

"Well, I— It's just that. I mean, I am, but not—"

"I do so enjoy rattling you, Rowan," Bryn interrupted with a grin. "Though you must not make it so easy. No, do not look away, else you shall end up with your nose in your forehead." And judging by the amount of time he lingered on it, either it was hard to draw or crooked.

"What do you look like in Ruhaven?" I asked. "You've never explained— Are you just a ball of light? Or do you have other features…" I mimed curling antlers.

"Ears? Antennas? Ah, horns. I must disappoint you, I do not. Though I only saw myself for the first time three years ago. As you know, reflective surfaces are fairly uncommon." Bryn peeked over the notebook, eyes alight. "What would you wish me to look like, Rowan?"

He wasn't so bad right now. "I'd take two arms and legs. But not one of those meaty dwarfs." I scrunched up my nose in imitation.

"So shallow?" Bryn teased, his tone light, playful.

I waved that away. "Don't worry, I look like a bug."

He bit his cheek. "Will I add an antenna to this drawing then?"

God, I hoped not. I shook my head vigorously.

"Six legs?"

"Two." I frowned and lifted out of my chair. "Can I see?"

He scribbled something. "Only if you are happy to be ear-less."

"I thought they were invisible," I joked, and tilted the sketch toward me.

Bryn had captured my freckles with a delicacy they didn't deserve, but given me the bug eyes I'd lamented—a pretty close approximation to the ones I'd seen distorted in the lens.

"You're very good," I murmured.

"Do you think?" He flipped back a page, then another, skimming the silky paper under my fingertips. "Perhaps you'd like to see my nudes?"

Heat crept up my neck. "Uh, no." *Yes.* "You're just trying to rile me."

But god, he should be able to say "nudes" without my heart stuttering like an overheated engine.

A smile played over his lips. "Is that what I am doing, Rowan? Riling you?"

The sound of slicing paper cut through the kitchen. "No, I mean, you know what—Wait, is that *me?*"

I stared, mortified, at the two page spread. At what was undoubtedly me—sprawled belly down on the couch in shaded charcoal, my braid hanging over the edge.

Bryn ran a finger over the drawing. "I believe I did remind you not to work all day in the damp cellar. You were rather exhausted, and if I recall correctly, developed a chest cold shortly thereafter."

That'd been months ago, weeks after Bryn arrived. "It wasn't from the cellar," I corrected.

"If you say so." He grinned and dragged another page over, then another.

A spread of quick-drawn sketches saw me in numerous unflattering poses. On a ladder attaching the eavestrough to the gate lodge, reading the Ford's manual in the kitchen, studying journals in the library, drinking a coffee in Capolinn.

"*Bryn*."

He looked up, eyes a warm honey-blue. "Yes, my Rowan?"

I tried to grab the book.

Without so much as blinking, he caught my hand in his, flattened it palm down into the page. "Would you like to keep these?" he asked softly, thumb skimming my wrist.

My heart thumped audibly. "I—well, it practically seems like my property anyway."

His eyelashes lowered, gaze latching on to the pulse stuttering at my throat before gliding back up. The low-hanging bulb swung shadows into his face, highlighting his slim nose, his golden eyelashes. "I shall trade you, if you like."

"For what?" I flipped our hold, gripped the edge of the book.

"Come find out," he suggested, holding on to the spine.

I pulled.

Bryn smiled crookedly, blindingly, then tugged—hard.

I tumbled forward, my knee knocking between his as I shot out an arm for balance. Ended up gripping his shoulder. "Sorry, I..."

His hand snaked out, wrapped around the braid dangling over my shoulder. Tugged lightly. But enough that I fell into him another inch, knee sliding over his lap. His thighs flexed in response.

Everything in me started to hum at the nearness of *him*. At the faint taste of sea and wind. At the minty tingles at the base of my scalp from where he kept my braid taut.

Then Bryn lifted his chin from the sketchbook still between us.

And when his eyes met mine, they were a burning, molten gold.

CHAPTER 28

The Northwest Passage

I froze, my fingers curling embarrassingly deeper into his shirt, into the muscle flexing underneath. And all the while, his irises whispered sparks over porcelain white cheeks.

"Bryn?" I whispered. "Your—your eyes—"

They lowered to my lips, so intense, I could almost taste him on mine. "Yes, my Rowan?" he breathed. He slid his hand from my braid to cup my neck, long fingers threading through my hair. More shivers burst out wherever they touched, until it was all I could do not to vibrate. It wasn't supposed to be like this. He was supposed to be cold and hard and brittle—or I wished he was, for my sake.

His thumb skimmed the length of my throat. "Does it embarrass you to be my muse?" Bryn murmured.

My heart pounded so loud, I couldn't hear my own lie. "No."

His mouth lifted, his wide lips glistening gold with the sparks from his eyes. The ones I should be saying something about right now. The ones that taunted my dreams.

I wet my lips.

"*Rowan*." Bryn's voice wasn't teasing anymore. It was dark, rough, a ripple of thunder at night.

The hand on my neck tightened in question. But there was no escaping now, not my trilling pulse, not the blood rushing to my head, not the roar dulling my ears, not the parted lips waiting for my answer, and not the two golden planets rapt on me.

I tasted his breath, tasted winter, tasted Ruhaven. And wanted.

Outside, the winds stopped whistling, the magpies fell silent.

His hand squeezed again, gently, as his eyes burned into a thick, melted pool that filled his irises, glowed over his sharp cheekbones.

He was like a god.

A god because he wasn't from here, but Ruhaven. Where he had a mate, one he was supposed to be faithful to. The one he was supposed to be with, even now. The one he'd climbed to the Gate for years ago because she had died at the Inquitate's hand. Because he cared that much for a woman in a dream.

"Bryn, your eyes…" I said, hating myself, hating him for putting me here. "They're *gold*."

The notebook slipped.

Its spine clattered to the floor, bouncing in a one-two jig that snapped the bridge between us.

I pried my hand off him, slid my knee from the lap I'd been all but straddling, and pushed away on knees weaker than my resolve.

I wanted to be the one he waited for in the Gate. Who brought a glow to his face at the mention of returning to Ruhaven. Who he'd given up his life for. Who he woke up every morning at five to visit. The woman that—right now—I hated.

"Rowan," Bryn said, and my belly tightened at the strain in his voice. "I need to tell you something. I—"

James barged in, flat cap in hand, vest half buttoned. "Right so. I'm ready for a pint meself now." He froze, gaze ping-ponging between us as a slow grin spread.

Bryn's irises snapped to an ocean blue.

"Well, Roe," James said with worrying charm. "I see O'Sahnazekiel's not keeping ye nearly as entertained as I thought."

He barely avoided the clementine I chucked at him.

⚙☀

I wouldn't look at him. No.

Because if I did, my face would heat up worse than it already was— which was bad enough with the Ford's spluttering heater.

When I rolled down the window, it jammed with five inches to go. Was everyone not sweating in this car?

I chanced a look at Bryn. His mouth twitched into a sideways smile.

"Are you well, Rowan?" he asked, his voice a near purr in my ear. *Yeah, not helping.*

When I tried the window again, Bryn huffed a laugh, reached across me, and wrestled it down. I tried to ignore the hand he braced on my thigh—and failed. "If that helps at all, do let me know," he added, then drew back.

Did he not regret what happened? Should I ask about his mate? No, better not.

I let the brisk wind bat away my arousal until James parked the Ford across from An Béal Bocht, one of the fifteen pubs in a town with a population of a couple thousand. And nothing, absolutely nothing, seemed better than about six shots of straight whiskey right now.

James held the door for us as we entered, Kazie leading. Candlelight stroked the oak-paneled walls, the light dim enough that even the most grizzled Irish fisherman would pass as handsome—which meant Bryn rose to the level of god-like.

The fireplaces blazed with applewood coal, drawing everyone to its flame and turning the pub into a low hive of conversation, laughter, drums, fiddles, and flutes.

But in the bar's stifling heat, Bryn was simmering ice at my back.

I shoved a hand through my hair—found my braid still loose from when he'd grabbed it. Desire stirred in my belly when I pictured his face again, the hand urging me closer, the all-encompassing *look* of him. Like he wanted me. All of me. *Roe.*

For once, he'd been absolutely clear.

I inhaled a steadying breath. Or I was turning an awkward mess into something it wasn't because I'd been in the Gate too often with Sahn instead of working.

After Willow died, making house calls and repairs had grounded me, not rolling under indigo skies with a feathered monster. Tomorrow, I'd fix Naruka's banister. Nothing leveled the hormones like a railing replacement.

Kazie nudged me and pointed. "Whoa, Colm spotted. Stay away, far away."

I glanced at the man leaning against the bar and felt Bryn stiffen behind me. Colm's mouth pursed around a smoke, his forehead furrowed in conversation. The man next to him belted out a laugh, but neither noticed us.

James put a hand on my shoulder. "I don't want any trouble with him tonight. One rumor gets out in a town like this and I'll be swimming in them for years. Bad enough I've had the Garda call me, so we'd best stay together."

I eyed the bar's fire poker ruefully.

James looped an arm over Kazie's shoulder. "Will we find a table, so? Leave these two lovebirds to get the drinks?"

Thanks for that, James.

Thoughts of Colm disappeared in the time it took to drag my hands down my face. But when the crowd swallowed James and Kaz, I had no choice but to pivot to the bar. And Bryn.

His crooked smile was a flash of teeth in the low lights. Had I really opened my big fat mouth and ruined any chance of those lips on mine? Yes, yes, I had.

"Is it Beamish, then?"

What? Oh. Drinks. If Bryn wasn't suffering from the lingering arousal of a kiss that didn't happen, then I shouldn't be either. I muttered a half-hearted agreement to the beer I'd already forgotten.

He ordered and said nothing while the bartender suspended time to pour a single stout.

Say something, you idiot. What, though? My brain had emptied of everything except *him*. What were we talking about before the non-kiss? Levi. *Ask him about Levi. Casual, though, like I'm not drowning in my personal theatrical play of what should have happened.*

"About the kitchen—"

"Bryn, I wanted to ask—"

I froze. Wait, what was he going to say about the kitchen?

Bryn smiled, and gestured for me to proceed.

No, no, go back to the kitchen.

"I, uh." God, this was even worse. "About Levi," I said lamely, and his brows winged up. *Yeah, this isn't what I want to talk about either.* I cleared my throat. Where the hell was that pint? "I meant to ask you about a translation for his journal."

He reached toward me, ran a tender thumb down my braid, then dropped his hand. "I believe I somewhat recall you mentioning his journal in the kitchen. Distantly." His mouth slid into a sideways grin again.

I would have to take that pint and roll it over my forehead.

"I—well—Kazie said you could speak Spanish." This was the worst after-almost-kiss talk anyone had ever come up with. "And I thought you could help with a few words." Because I was plucking at my scarf, I tugged out my journal from the pocket of Willow's jacket and angled it under the bar lights.

He moved to stand beside me, his scent filling my nostrils like I was on the deck of a boat. "These lines, is it?"

I swallowed, nodded, and held my breath as he scanned the few paragraphs along with my scribbled notes.

How many drinks would it take to end up right back in that kitchen again? Four? Five?

"No, that is all fairly correctly translated," he said, breaking through my imagination. "Blue skies, the smell of cinnamon—canela. You note that these are not the colors or smells of Ruhaven, and I agree. So Levi appears to have lied about more than just his address."

The stouts finally materialized, dripping with foam and cold sweat that had my mouth watering. "But we still don't know why," I said as we gathered them up and fought our way through the crowd to Kazie and James, Bryn a head taller than any man, even with his cane.

Sitting a short distance away from the band, they squabbled like young siblings, loud enough to compete with the traditional Irish music blaring in my left ear. One of the musicians, an old man with a bag under his elbow, squealed into pipes with all the delicacy of a car accident.

I slid into a miniature stuffless-stool while Bryn took the one beside me. He struggled to get comfortable, needing to stretch his crippled leg under Kazie with the pub so packed.

"James, I forgot to tell you, I saw Jamellian yesterday with Essie, practicing with your bow and arrow," I said, pushing a pint towards him. "You seem to have gotten better. Or, at least, Essie thought so."

His mouth twitched around the foamy head of the stout. "I'd better be. The woman has me training day and night." He held up his fingers like they could blister here.

Kazie added, "I've seen him too. He's still terrible. Essie giggles at everything."

James poked her. "Watch yerself." She rolled her eyes. "Yera, I did see we're closer to using the Florissant though. Might be we find yer Tether soon, Roe, once Kazmira's done adjusting the instrument."

Yes, Nereida had been poked, prodded, and pulled, and not just by Sahn. Kazmira had needed to take samples from her, including cutting off a jelly hair strand. I'd gagged when it started wriggling in Kazie's hand. My hair looked like someone had shoved stars into clear jelly and rolled it into long, putty threads. Willow would have paid a fortune for it.

I waited until the piper finished his solo. "And then what? After the Florissant?"

"Then," Kazie toasted, "we'll be in Drachaut! I hear it's freezing since it faces away from the star."

I shivered on my stool. Drachaut. What would it be like? And if I met my Tether, would I recognize it as *me*? Was that why Willow and I were the first twins allowed through the Gate? Because I'd been her Tether in Ruhaven—or no, Drachaut—and it'd allowed me to come through? Maybe our connection there was as strong as it was here.

As I contemplated over my beer, Bryn told James and Kazie about the letter he'd found.

James peered at Bryn speculatively. "That's—well, I guess 'tis still possible he's dead, but at least he was alive then. I wonder why he wrote to Carmen and not meself?" Something I'd ask Tye about when he was back.

Kazie pushed James's drink toward him. "Let's not talk about all that tonight," she said, then set James off with a reminder of the Englishman he'd gotten into a fight with two years ago at this bar. "What was it about again? Trees?"

"It was, as I recall, a vigorous argument about Irish oak," Bryn drawled.

James skewered the air. "That was it, ye've a good memory. They feckin' steal our oak, build their—"

Pints sloshed when Kazie slapped the table. "Not the Irish oak again," she whined, then mimicked James's accent. "*They built their parliament, they stole the bloody North*, something, something, *Cromwell*. If Ruhaven can live in peace with Drachaut, you can manage the English!"

When James flicked her, Kazie jumped like she'd been stung. "Just so ye know, the Drachaut never terrorized Ruhaven for a thousand bloody years," he grumbled, draining the pint.

We finished another round, then another, until Kazie strolled over with the fourth. That was the precise number for James to pop to his feet and belt out a surprisingly on-key tune. My cheeks hurt from grinning at them, from listening to Kazie explain how Bryn had convinced her to move to Ireland, then James's embellished tale of carrying Tye home from the bar, how Bryn had gifted the budgies to Kazie.

I kept my eyes on Bryn—on the rare joy that had laugh lines forming at the corners of his eyes, that loosened his stiff collar, that lifted his high cheeks on a coral wave.

I wanted to be a part of them. Nereida. A Ruhaven. To have James tell some story about me stealing his car in ten years.

And I wanted it bad enough to keep living this lie.

CHAPTER 29

You are the Moon

W hen the uilleann pipes began to resemble music, I knew I'd drunk too many pints.

"I thought they'd just spelled 'man' wrong," I defended myself after entering the wrong washroom. "James was mortified."

"Mná isn't misspelled! It's Irish for women." Kazie snorted bubbles into her pint.

The bartender slid his beady eyes our way, then roamed to the brightly lit taps and poured the next stout.

Someone slung an arm over my shoulder.

"Jayzus, Mary, and Joseph, Roe," James slurred in my ear. "Ye feckin' want to warn me next time ye barge into the jax? Give me some time to do up me pants like."

Too drunk to be embarrassed, I cast my eyes to the ceiling plastered with fiddles and fishing gear and passed him his drink. "Oh, now you're sensitive. After months of moaning in the Gate with Essie."

He barked a laugh, looking like a hiccuping turtle with the oversized sweater. "I think I prefer ye with a few pints. Now, where's Bryn? Ah, for the love of…"

As he ambled away, Kazie slid a sly look my way. "*So*, is sex with the Azekiel as great as I'm picturing?"

At least she'd called it sex this time and not *feather dusting*.

"Stop picturing it. It's weird enough that I'm living it." I glanced around the bar. "And where *is* Bryn?"

Kazie propped an elbow on the slippery counter, fist squishing her silky cheek. "Guy went to get food. You know how he can't eat anything here."

Yeah, but alone, and after what happened in Oslo?

When I started to rise off the stool, Kazie touched my shoulder. "Don't worry, Roe. He specifically told me to stay with you because of the Inquitate."

But didn't bother to tell me why he was leaving? "You know what happened in Norway."

She brushed that away, her seven rings glittering under the bar lights. "He knows how to avoid the Inquitate—saved himself, remember?"

"Saved? Kazie, he lost a leg." I drained my pint. "I'm not leaving him alone," I insisted over her protests, and turned, elbowing through the bar. What was he thinking? Bryn might have been Ruhaven's golden child, but he was as susceptible as any triplet. Surviving one attack didn't mean he'd be immune from the next.

I stepped on five different feet on my way outside and got half a pint dumped on my shoe, but eventually, I inhaled the smoke-free air of a blistery night.

I'd never get used to this weather. The cold seeped into my bones, settled under my skin, and the constant rain was about the only thing I could still be certain of.

Under a threatening sheet of that rain, a Gypsy horse *clip-clopped* home, partiers stumbled with curry chips, and a pharmacy's cross blazed a monster green. Ripe vomit flowed toward the sewer in a stream of piss and rain.

I braced a hand on the wall as I searched for Bryn. Kazie was right about one thing—there was nothing around here for him to eat. He didn't like chips, hot dogs, or hamburgers, and although he could stomach seafood, he wouldn't want it fried in a vat of grease.

What was he *thinking*?

Probably, *"Oh, I'm Bryn, the glimmer-blessed Ruhaven who can do no wrong,"* but I couldn't bring myself to be properly upset as I aimed toward an Italian takeaway down the street.

He'd forced me to return to Naruka on the condition—*condition!*—that we stay together. But does he? No. I'd throw that in his pretty face—yes, I would. His pretty, gorgeous, beautiful face, with his hair like spun gold and his eyes like burning fire.

God, I was drunk.

"Your eyes are gold," I mimicked my idiotic words under my breath. Gold. Rainbow. Fairy lights. Who cared? But no, I couldn't just shut up and kiss the god in the shabby kitchen.

Rowan, you must return to the bar. Now.

Swaying on my feet, I paused on the sidewalk. Wow, I was so drunk I was hallucinating Bryn's voice. I even got the accent right, and that faint touch of snobbery that was—

Rowan!

I pressed a hand to my forehead, except it was more of a slap that had me wincing. The streets crested in a sprawling mess, empty of everything but puddles, while the predicted storm hammered the roads, drenching my hair and plastering it to my cheeks.

"Hey!" someone shouted.

Bryn?

Blinking away the rain, I pivoted toward the voice. Through the dark, a man jogged toward me on the cobblestone road, his black hair a wet mass under the street lanterns, a smoke bobbing in his lips, his shoelaces untied and dragging in puddles.

James? I took a step toward him. Stopped.

Oh, hell.

"Wait!" Colm yelled as I threw up my hood and spun. The sidewalk wobbled like a river on a hammock, listing back and forth, the distant lights of restaurants turning into a messy blur.

Should have stayed in the pub. Should have stayed in the damn pub.

I pumped arms that felt numb. Why had I drank so much? How was I going to convince Bryn of anything when I was this drunk? I should have just talked to him, asked him about his mate and why he—

I swore as my toe snagged on the uneven sidewalk. *This is why we don't lay cobblestones anymore.* My knee whacked off stones lit with red light from the flashing exit sign inside The Cod Father, the smell of fried fish still lingering. Distant footsteps pounded, their sharp cracks ratcheting up my growing headache.

I hauled myself up by a lamppost, started to run.

Something snagged my jacket.

I tumbled backward, splashing into a puddle with cold rain pelting my face. My hood fell away and my braid sprung loose. Above me, an oil lantern glowed yellow, blocking out the stars that freckled the blackened sky. The wind cracked a line of red triangles strung over the empty street. I had to get up, had to get back to the bar to warn James and Kazie.

Cradling my side, I pressed an elbow into what I hoped was just water.

Then Colm appeared.

He looked worse than I'd last seen him, like the months missing Lana had taken their toll. Or Tye had done a lot more damage than I'd thought when he'd thrown him out.

A scrawny mustache perched on an upper lip that was almost nonexistent, and his left eyebrow winked with a gold piercing. He reeked of the spilled beer that stained his fur-collared jean jacket and shoes. Kneeling beside me, he blew out a long stream of smoke that singed my nose. "Yer going to tell me where Lana is," he said coolly, "and what they did to her."

I struggled to hold back the fear fighting through the haze of whiskey and beer. There was no Tye this time, no Bryn to stand in front of me, and I didn't have any of Nereida's fighting talent.

I reached for my tool belt. *Idiot, you're not wearing one.* I curled my fingers into a fist instead. *Aim for the throat,* that's what Willow had once taught me.

"Colm, I—I don't know Lana. About Lana," I tried.

He gripped the collar of my jacket, Willow's jacket. His breath rolled over me, and I forgot my plan to punch him and grabbed at his hands instead. They were slick with rain, hot, sweaty.

"Ye know, I sent another lad up there once," he said, baring uneven teeth. "No vacancies. That's what James told him. Now ye tell me what that's about."

Even *Kazie* was saner than this man.

But instead of getting away from Colm, I was stuck trying to peel his sticky fingers off me when Nereida wouldn't have allowed this. She could hit a moving target a hundred meters away, could stand toe to toe with an Azekiel who dwarfed her in size.

I wrestled with his hands, fighting to sit up in the puddle.

Colm's face became a blur, his words even more distorted. *Lana, and Naruka, and James…* All my thoughts and movements were a second too late, like I was controlling them from afar.

James would be so embarrassed that a Ruhaven was getting beat up by Colm. Wasn't I supposed to have some glimmer too?

I was so drunk, I screwed up my face as if I could summon the illusion like Bryn. Nothing.

Time stretched seconds into hours, but with the idea of James's disappointment hovering over me, I wrenched Colm's hands off me at last and started to rise.

In slow motion, he cocked back an arm to stop me and—

The blow connected with my jaw.

I heard it, felt it, but I didn't feel the pain right away, like my body was too shocked to send the signal to my brain.

I started to sway, dry-eyed, as a slow, tingling numbness spread over the left side of my face. Capolinn's squished townhouses tilted before I smacked into a lamppost, my left ear ringing. My face *throbbed* as awareness returned. With the ground wobbling, I wrapped my fingers around the pole's cold metal, but my knees buckled and I slid squeakily to the ground. My knees crunched on broken glass.

Someone shouted. At me?

I couldn't make sense of anything. But it was Colm who loomed above, framed by a backdrop of streetlights. My hands shook as his eyes darkened to twin threats, his words lost in the roaring pain in my left ear.

Was my eardrum broken? Had he hit me with a bottle? A hand couldn't hurt this much.

I pressed my palm to my cheek, felt the heat build there despite the rain, the lump pushing against my skin. My jaw might have had a pulse of its own, but the skin wasn't broken, and the pain wasn't debilitating enough that I should be sitting here, waiting for more.

When I started to rise, Colm swatted at me in a way meant to be more humiliating than painful. I held out a hand, trying to ward off the next blow, but only hit myself when he didn't stop. *God, do* something. *Do something.*

"Your demon boyfriend's not here now," Colm taunted. "What kind of voodoo are you guys doing up there? That's why Lana ran, isn't it?"

His words evaporated in the freezing downpour between us.

Cradling my jaw, I searched for a weapon within reach. A paper cup fought against the pull of rain gurgling into a drain. Ten feet away, a pint glass rested against a closed pub. I could grab that, maybe, or just run.

I crawled toward it, palms chafing on the rough stones and shattered beer bottles, my calves swimming in puddles.

Colm shoved me back with one careless push.

It wasn't supposed to be like this.

Nereida had never been this weak. She'd never lain on the pavement with ugly liquids leaking down the street. And I was supposed to be her? No, not a vein in my body could have run with the same blood, and certainly not my soul. I didn't need a missing line in a *Ledger* to tell me I wasn't Nereida.

Colm twisted his hold on my sister's jacket. It tightened, a noose around my neck, until I stared at the whites of his eyes.

For a moment, I was in L'Ardoise again, in a puddle outside my parents' house. They'd told me not to come back for a while, and didn't need to say what I already knew—that I was only a poor reminder of what had been. They weren't wrong. I was tired of myself too, of waking up and seeing no one and nothing but Willow in the mirror.

"Now, ye tell me what's going on and—" Colm broke off on a choked cry.

A whirl of spun moonlight broke the night.

Blinding, brilliant, impossible. A comet falling from the asteroid belt, searing my eyes with its heat. I squeezed them shut. Sent a prayer to Ruhaven—to whatever god existed—that I didn't melt into the pavement and die right here.

But the heat disappeared as quickly as it came, a cloud banking on an August day. I blinked through the cooling rain.

Colm stumbled away from me, his eyes wide and reflecting the sparking light of the man stalking toward him—a burning light of a man. Corded rivers carved his neck, his back heaved with strain. Gold pulsed from his skin like the boundaries of Earth were only a suggestion.

Some demon from the Gate.

I scrambled back just as his fist snapped out, grabbing Colm by the scruff of his jacket and crushing him against the storefront. Glass cracked in a spiderweb around Colm's head. His face drained of all color like it had when Bryn showed him a glimmer—even the flush of alcohol fled.

A growl rumbled low in the demon's chest as he bent, whispered something in Colm's ear, then rapped him against the wall, again and again. *Crack.* The *closed* sign wobbled on the door. *Crack.* An advertisement jostled, plummeted, and joined the broken beer bottles at the demon's boots.

Ignoring the pain in my jaw, I shoved to my feet with the aid of the post. I had to get to Bryn, to warn him. It couldn't be an Inquitate, though, because Colm wouldn't be able to see it. Something else then.

I wasn't going to stay to find out.

The ground spun as I tried to locate the distant lights of the restaurants. I needed to get to James and Kazie before the demon descended upon them next, or it created such mayhem that we'd never be able to return to the Gate.

I started toward the pub as another growl sliced through the air.

Then the demon froze.

I stopped, worried it might hear my boots splashing drunkenly through the puddles. And it did.

Very slowly, it started to turn its head.

Holy god.

I staggered. The breath in my lungs simply dried up. My mouth opened on a ragged gasp despite the ache in my jaw.

Because standing before me, under the lamplights on a street in Capolinn, a monster gleamed—one with the haunting eyes of a Ruhaven.

This was no glimmer.

"*Bryn?*" I croaked.

Except it wasn't him, not really. Planets spun in sockets that should have held his eyes, and his face shimmered with crackling moonlight. More light spread from his feet, pooling in thick, golden puddles until it blended with the rain. Even from here, I felt the heat of him as if I stood feet from a roaring fire.

No cane. He had no cane, stood fully for the first time.

I started to tremble before him, worse than I had when he'd confronted me in the hotel in Oslo. Somehow, here, it was even more real—a nightmare, a dream, all spread out before me in a hideously mocking reality.

Because this was Bryn. And it was truth. And it was terrifying.

"Stay there, Rowan," he ordered.

I couldn't move if I wanted to.

"Are you—are you okay?" I asked, my knees beginning to shake from the alcohol or the shock.

The light around him sputtered.

He stepped toward me, dropping Colm in a heap. Bryn's left leg, the crippled leg, vibrated under him, the calf jerking as he tried to walk.

Whatever had caused this—whatever had turned him into a burning god—was gone.

I started toward him.

Wind whipped my hair into my face, blinding me as I saw Bryn stumble, fall.

Then I was there, awkwardly catching his weight, wrapping my arms around his waist as the light from him flickered out.

We stumbled backward together, trying to find our balance without his cane.

Bryn shot out an arm, grabbing on to a green telephone box and, wrapped around each other, we thumped into the corner of it and the wall.

Just then, I didn't care that Colm was lying unconscious feet away, or that I'd seen Bryn blaze into a god, or that he'd lied about not running that day in Oslo.

I simply pressed my nose to Bryn's neck, and breathed.

He cradled the back of my head, holding me against him, murmuring words I couldn't yet process. But his voice, his warmth, his scent, it pushed away the cold ache inside.

I closed my eyes, letting the rain pummel me while he skimmed shaking fingers over my shoulders, up my neck, until he reached my jaw. Then they slowed, prodding the place that still ached, his cool touch as soft as O'Sahnazekiel's feathers and ice on the throbbing heat.

He lowered his mouth to my cheek, inhaling much like I had, and suddenly, I was very aware of him. Of us. Of the shape of his body against mine. Of the rain dripping down his cheeks and lips. Of the slow pulse of his heart.

Distantly, a car's tires splattered through the rain, a whiff of diesel following a few seconds behind.

When I opened my eyes again, I met his vivid Ruhaven blue. No trace of the spinning planets, no lightning crackling over his skin, no light pouring in puddles. Had it all been an illusion? His hair was soaked to a light brown, hanging in spirals over his cheeks. Under his jacket, his collar hung wide from where Colm had torn it, exposing a hint of tattoos.

But then I saw that he wasn't fine, not at all. "Bryn, you need the hospital."

He blinked rapidly, his lips nearly blue, his crippled leg shaking between us. "No, but I think, perhaps, that I have overexerted myself. I need James."

I started to pull away. "I'll get him."

"No," Bryn said quickly, tightening his hold. "He is close, nearly here."

What? I squinted through the sheets of rain, where the murky streets glowed with the ochre haze of streetlamps. A lone figure barreled down the sidewalk. Rain forced his head down, and his jacket cracked behind him in sharp whips. "How did you know?"

But then James shouted, drowning out Bryn's answer, and slid to a wet stop before us. He took one look at Bryn through his honey-brown eyes and said with little surprise, "Ah, for feck's sake. I sure hope that bad Italian was worth it."

So James had seen this before, this transformation. Not just a glimmer, a hint of something under the skin, but a living, breathing, walking god.

"I've got him," I insisted when James started to take Bryn's weight.

"He's three stones on ye."

"And you're nearly the same weight as me," I said, keeping my arm around Bryn.

But he disengaged himself when James reached for his elbow, and I felt the rejection like a blow. Because *I* was the reason he was like this, because I wasn't Nereida. "We should leave," Bryn said, "before Colm wakes up. And Rowan must ice her jaw."

Both James and I glanced at the man I'd forgotten about, sprawled in front of a poster advertising a cod special.

"Jayzus, did ye feckin' do that? He's not dead, is he?"

"Unconscious," Bryn coughed.

"Jayzus," James said again, but with a touch of admiration. "Alright, out of the way, Roe, I'll take him from here."

Bryn stumbled forward, leg almost giving out, but James righted him with surprising strength. "Ye know this isn't what I consider keeping a low profile in town, ye bollocks," James berated him. "I've got Mary at the post office wondering why I'm sending feckin' mail to Russia, and that nosy farmer next door who's making our little neighbor wall shorter each day. Now suppose Colm brings the bloody Garda to me door?" James turned to me. "Kazie's pulling the car around. Get in and I'll get yer man here."

Kazie. The car. Bar. Naruka.

"But I—"

"*Roe, get into the feckin' car!*" James shouted.

CHAPTER 30

Light of Love

S awdust coated my goggles and billowed up my nostrils. I pushed the pine two-by-six into the flattop grind blade until the garage filled with a high-pitched squeal of protest. In the corner, a cast iron stove glowed with coal and warded off the leftover storm. When the wood fell apart like a split banana, I switched off the saw, watched the heat of the wood stove blow the dust of sweet-scented pine in silence.

I hated that smell. The smell of clipped answers with my father in the shop, arguing about different jobs because everything I did and said annoyed him in the end. The smell of how much he hated seeing me— that's what it was.

It'd been two days since the incident outside An Béal Bocht.

An incident that I had caused.

I was *supposed* to be a Ruhaven. But I'd lied, I'd pretended, and because of that, Bryn had needed to summon an unholy ability to walk again. Now, he was bedridden, exhausted, and on *crutches*.

Shame filled me, thick and ripe and suffocating.

James had offered no explanation for Bryn's transformation, for how he could stand in the middle of Capolinn like a burning god.

There were a lot of things they didn't tell me.

How Bryn was able to summon his Mark? No answer. What exactly a ball of light was? Nothing. Where Bryn and Tye were exactly in Ruhaven? Silence. What the supposed rules of Ruhaven were? Well, for that, James dropped a book in my lap.

But I knew why they hadn't explained things, why even now, they wouldn't tell me what I'd seen, what Bryn had become—they'd begun to suspect what I'd known all along.

"Roe?" James's fuzzy form strode in, a whip of rain on his heels.

I snapped off the goggles. His zigzag-patterned orange sweater threatened to bring my two-day hangover recovery back to square one, as did the butter wafting off the plate he held.

I hefted the next sheet of pine, already embarrassed that he was bringing me scones when I was the one who'd caused all of this.

My tone was brisker than I intended when I said, "What do you want?"

He pushed a scone and two white pills onto my workbench, knocking screws, wrenches, and bolts askew in a loud, rickety dance. His brows lifted at the rose perched on the windowsill that Kazie had left. "Ye know, that's the only flower that exists in Ruhaven *and* here."

"That's nice," I said shortly, and busied myself by arranging the wood cuts, their edges still warm from the blade.

James scoured his eyebrows into fuzzy pipe cleaners. "I know yer mad that I've not explained what happened at An Béal Bocht, but 'tis for Bryn to tell ye. Now, ye need to ice that jaw, but the aspirin should help."

But I wanted to feel the pain, because it reminded me of the lie I was. Of what I was pretending to be every time I slipped through the Gate and awakened as Nereida.

I tugged the goggles down and flicked on the table saw. As the blade warmed up, I said, "I don't need you playing nurse Jamellian." But apparently, I did need Bryn to embody a planetary evolution to protect me from one delusional human.

James threw up his hands in dismay. "Ah, come on, Roe, I—"

BZZZZZZZZZ.

The saw screamed over James's protests, spitting sawdust as it gobbled the pine sheet.

He cut in when the blade slowed. "Listen like, I'm sorry for snapping at ye that night." He ran a hand through his tousled hair. "Have ye gone to see Bryn yet?"

"No. Why would I?" I stifled the thrum of guilt in my belly. "I don't deserve to know what happened, right?" Not Nereida, not a real Ruhaven. An imposter.

"Roe, don't ye be like this."

"Watch the miter saw," I barked, sending James scooting away from the hot blade.

Recovered, he stalked to eye level with me and planted his palms on the table saw I'd luckily turned off. "Ye know Roe, Bryn shouldn't have been able to do what ye saw. He's in the Gate every morning, every evening. It's too much."

And what, exactly, *had* I seen?

But James was right—I was asking too much of Bryn, just because I was too weak to anchor myself.

Still, I wasn't the only reason he visited the Gate. Where did I fit in with this mate of his? I'd had the last two days to gnaw the bone of that argument to death, and didn't enjoy the teeth marks I'd left. Would we kiss in the kitchen next time, then hike to the Gate to enjoy someone else?

James barely ducked the stack of planks I swung over my shoulder. "Maybe if I keep going in, I'll be able to transform into magic too," I said dryly. "Should make the next bar fight easier."

"Don't ye be getting cross with me now. Bryn told ye to stay at the pub. What if ye'd left and the Inquitate appeared again? Ye want Tye to kill me?"

I booted the garage door open and winced at the raging Atlantic wind. "Guess you'd have to get someone else to replace your banister."

My tool belt clanged annoyance with each step on the gravel path to Naruka. They *knew* it wasn't me in that *Ledger*. God, I was so stupid—stupid for believing, for hoping, for wanting it to have been me, even for a second.

I entered Naruka to the woodstove pumping a hot breath in the kitchen, a blessing against the otherwise freezing house. "Pub night" was written in purple marker below November's priest of the month—a naked Father covered in an unseasonable amount of maple syrup.

Balancing the planks, I maneuvered through the kitchen, knocking into the overhead light as Jesus judged me.

James's brisk clomps followed me into the lounge. "Roe, just what are ye doing?"

"Fixing your rotten banister before Kazie tries to tie another hammock to it."

Bang. I tossed the planks at the foot of the stairs, loud enough to wake Bryn and any Ruhavens alive, dead, or Fallen.

James stomped up the first three steps and spun around. Afternoon light haloed his hair as he frowned under the end of his crooked nose. "What the bleedin' hell is going on with ye? 'Tis me who should be pissed at ye and not the other way around."

"Nothing is going on with me. Bleeding or otherwise. And you're in the way." I hefted the first cut, the jagged edge biting into my palm.

He jumped a step higher and spread his arms, blocking me. "When we agreed not to tell Tye about the Inquitate in Oslo, ye promised to stick together. Then ye went off on yer own. I don't see why ye'd do that."

As if Bryn didn't go off by himself all the time.

"Get out of the way," I warned.

James gripped the end of the two-by-four and wrenched it from my grasp with strength that didn't belong to his waif body. He tossed it over the railing with a bang. "Why are ye so mad at me? 'Tis me who should be ringing yer ear, ye know. Ye'll hurt yerself and me sister."

"Nereida," I muttered, fisting my hands to keep them from shaking. "Except you *know* I'm not her. Don't you, James?" Knew I'd been lying to him for months.

His eyes widened. "Roe, me love, I've not a bloody clue what yer on about."

It wasn't too late to take it back, but I pushed onward, needed to get it all out now before I became a coward again. "Yeah, you *do*. It's why you won't tell me what happened," I said, forcing anger into my voice to bat away the pain. "*Willow's* Nereida. You know it, Bryn knows it. God, Kazie and Tye probably figured it out months ago."

Everyone had known, surely, but they'd let me have my humiliating delusions.

"What?" James stilled, brows knitting as if he didn't know. Then he said, very slowly, "Roe, yer reborn as me sister, ye live her memories. How in the world can ye think it'd be yer twin? 'Tis not how it works like."

For a moment, I held on to the words, wrapped them tightly in a bundle of hope that I never dared hold on to for long, then let them go.

It was time to stop pretending. Even if it meant James wouldn't look at me the same, even if it meant they forced me from Naruka.

Spinning on my heel, I stalked to the library, tool belt jingling. I'd show James exactly how it worked.

Slivers of swan-gray light crawled through the murky windows that nobody bothered cleaning, and with the fireplace untended, the temperature dropped at least two degrees.

I gestured at the *Ledger*, at the bog-encrusted pages spread like a bearded merchant showing their wares, at the line I'd stared at again and again, wondering if there was any chance it was wrong.

But it was exhausting to lie to myself. To know for months that it had never been me in the book, in Ruhaven. That all its glory and promise and dreams were meant for a woman who'd always deserved them more than I ever had.

"We were born minutes apart, James. Willow before midnight, me after. It's not *me* written here, it's *her*."

My words cracked in the suddenly minuscule library.

Willow. Always Willow.

Hot needles stung my eyes, and the rows of coordinates, dates, and times blurred. Hundreds of Ruhavens. But not me, never me. I was a poor replacement for Willow. A throwaway the Gate begrudgingly accepted as a consolation prize. Maybe that's what Kazie had been trying to tell me all those months ago—that there was some transference that allowed me to witness the memories in Willow's stead.

James slipped off his glasses as if his short-sightedness would reveal the truth. "Roe, ye listen to me now," he said, voice low and soft as he walked to me. "I don't know where ye've been keeping this, but yer wrong. Ye think I don't recognize me own sister?"

When he reached for my hand, I pulled away.

I wanted to believe him—God, did I want to, but I didn't want to lie anymore. "Of course it's Willow." I wiped at my eyes, hating that I was crying over a dream that wasn't even mine.

"Roe, whatever ye might think, whatever ye believed of yer birth, I know in me soul that 'tis yerself that Ruhaven wanted. She doesn't make mistakes, so I'd take her word over any time ye think ye may or may not be born. 'Tis proof enough that ye can see the memories."

I had to smother the spark of hope his words ignited. "But there's never been twins, has there?" I said softly. "You don't really know if it's me, or if Ruhaven accepts me because I'm close enough."

James just shook his head. "'Tis only yerself who doesn't know, love."

I shifted deliberately away from the *Ledger*. James stood with his hands in his pockets, opened his mouth to say more—

"Why didn't you recruit her first?" I blurted out. It wasn't fair to James, I knew that, but the possibility had been eating at me for *months*. That it could have been Willow standing here right now, alive, living in Ruhaven, if only he'd gotten there sooner. "If you'd gone to L'Ardoise years ago, maybe you'd have found her before the Inquitate."

He closed his mouth, looking stricken. I shouldn't have said that, shouldn't have—

"Roe, we *did*," James whispered.

The words landed like a blow. "What? *What*!"

He looked around helplessly, dragging a hand down his face. "Roe, I—I made a mistake at first. Yer records are very restricted, 'twas nearly impossible to locate them. So when I found a woman—Willow—who was born nearly a match to the time, well, I had Bryn try to recruit her. Three years ago."

James's words died on the roar in my ears.

Bryn had gone to retrieve Willow. That's why he'd known from the moment he saw me in his office what I was—a dream-sucking thief living off someone else's memories. Enjoying their past life that had done things I'd never even aspire to. Worse, I was a cheat. What else could I call it when I slept with Nereida's boyfriend? He probably knew. Even in the memory, I bet some part of Sahn knew I was a fraud.

Crack.

I glanced over as the library door swung open and banged off the wall.

Bryn ducked under the doorway, breath wheezing through his nostrils, a rare beard darkening his angular chin. For the first time since I'd known him, he was in jeans, not slacks, as if even his clothes were tired. Instead of his cane, twin crutches dug grooves in his armpits.

I should have gone to him, helped him, done something. But I couldn't stand to look and see my failure written in the hollows of his cheeks, in the shadows under his eyes. Mortifying—that's what it was, to see my own shame reflected back at me. I lifted my chin, like the act could save me from the judgment I deserved.

His eyes flicked down my body as if he could see the purple bruises on my knees and the side of my thigh.

"James, get out," Bryn said like cut steel.

I held my breath, waiting for James to shout at him too.

But after a quarter note of silence, he inclined his head and strode out, shutting the door behind him with a soft click. The library shuddered in the silence, the pews of bookcases waiting in the dusty window light. But with the *Ledger* beside me, it felt like there were still three of us in the room.

Bryn and I stared at each other, his eyes lingering on the bruise at my jaw.

On a shaky inhale, he thumped a path to an armchair by the fire, and its tired leather cracked under his weight.

"I'm sorry," I muttered, dragging my sleeve across my eyes, my runny nose, then winced as I bumped my jaw. Sorry I hadn't visited him, sorry that I'd lied to him, to everyone, sorry that I wasn't Willow. Sorry that he'd almost kissed a fraud.

His wide mouth dipped into a frown. "My Rowan, I do not know what you feel the need to apologize for. However, it does appear I owe you some answers." He laid the crutches alongside the chair, braced his hands on his knees, and grunted at even that small effort.

"You tried to recruit my sister," I said hollowly. "Why didn't you tell me?"

He stared at his hands, face a mask of emotion. Anger? Sadness? It was so hard to tell with him.

Then he looked up at me. Regret. That was it. "Because I failed, Rowan. I believed she to be you, and I was too late. She was dead when I arrived to recruit her. So I returned."

Returned to Naruka while my life was destroyed. I didn't know why that part upset me. What else was he supposed to do? Stay and comfort a grieving sister? I wasn't anything to him, until I was.

"But you came back when James realized I might see Ruhaven in her place."

His face registered surprise. "Of course not, Rowan. You have always been Nereida. It was me who mistook Willow as you. It is difficult to recruit, to locate the documents and photos needed to find the correct Ruhaven. There was never a twin before, Rowan. It should not have been possible. So we did not check. *I* did not check."

He loosed a breath. "In 1989, James located what he believed to be the 1274th entry in Ruhaven's *Ledger*. As I was living in Naruka at the time, I was tasked with retrieving this Ruhaven." He interlaced his hands under his chin, elbows digging into his knees. "I left shortly after for L'Ardoise in hopes of returning with her here, and showing this woman the *Ledger*."

Would I have passed him on the street in L'Ardoise? Would he have stopped for Mrs. Baker's blueberry scones? Something so mundane for him that it'd be like an angel having coffee.

"However, shortly after I arrived, I learned of Willow's death," Bryn murmured around his folded hands. "I believed I had been too late, Rowan."

Hadn't he?

Behind the dusty glass, Ruhaven's *Ledger* spread its pages, baring its decree—one row for the person born at 23:58. Not two.

"You didn't know Willow had a twin." Wouldn't have mattered, anyway.

He coughed, chest rattling with strain. "No, and I did not consider this, as a Ruhaven has never been born with one before. After I discovered Willow was dead, I returned to Naruka and began my research of the Inquitate. Six months later, James forced me to leave."

I turned slowly. "If he forced you out, why were you in L'Ardoise almost a year ago to recruit *me*?" That timeline never made sense, and he'd never given me an answer.

Bryn's wide mouth tightened into a white line. "I had difficulty accepting the death of what I had believed to be the 1274th Ruhaven. Years later, when James discovered Willow had been a twin, he rang me in Norway as a favor. I returned to L'Ardoise that same week to see for myself. And I did—I saw you, Rowan. I knew you to be a Ruhaven, and I should never have given up. Even after the Inquitate."

I looped my fingers in my tool belt, the soft leather a last birthday gift from Willow, and reconciled myself with what I had known to be true since I first believed in the *Ledger*—that I had stolen her memories in Ruhaven.

That was why she was the only Inquitate death that didn't make sense. Every single one had been a Ruhaven, had either met their recruiter or seen the Gate. She'd been killed because she was Nereida, and now maybe with her death, it jumped to me. Another type of energy transfer.

We were twins, not just sisters, and didn't that mean we shared something more fundamental? Enough that when she died, whatever part of her soul had been destined for Ruhaven became mine.

The chair croaked. "Rowan?" Bryn's voice softened. "Please, please don't cry."

I wiped at the warmth gathering in the corners of my eyes. Why wouldn't I be? Of everyone, Bryn would understand what Nereida had come to mean to me.

I inhaled against the rope binding my chest. "I've stolen Nereida from Willow," I admitted and, standing before the *Ledger*, it felt like a confession.

The silence of the library thundered in my ears. The journals, papers, and paintings blinked at me in judgment. The *Ledger* most of all.

I turned at Bryn's hiss of pain to see him reaching for his crutches, then collapsed back almost immediately. "If you need help, I'll—"

"No," he said abruptly, then repeated softer, "No. Rowan, you have not stolen anything. You *are* Nereida. That has never been in doubt, not since I first saw you in L'Ardoise. What it is about Willow that should make her Nereida instead of you?"

"Besides her birth?"

"I do not believe birth times are not subject to mistakes."

Was that possible? Of course, but—but—did *he* believe there'd been a mistake? Why should that matter to me so much? That Bryn might look at me, and think I belonged.

My eyes darted to him. Would he still think there'd been a mistake if he knew Willow?

"My sister was a musical prodigy," I said, and of course, my first thought made no sense. But somehow, that piano had come to represent everything I'd loved and envied in one person.

Bryn waited with that impossible patience, one that had been nearly frightening in its quiet quality when I'd first met him. Now, it was a kind of gentle encouragement to what I didn't want to admit even to myself.

"We were identical, we shared the same blood, the same DNA—maybe the same soul—yet one of us had come out right, and one of us wrong. That's what my parents told me, what I'd always known. I just knew it more after she died, when it became so obvious how lacking I was when her talent couldn't cover us both."

Willow had been someone more like Bryn, someone who'd stand out in a crowd of ordinary people.

"You'd like her—everyone did. She taught me piano, but I wasn't like her—gifted, driven. She'd never have dropped out of college because she knew herself—knew what she wanted—and had that rare gift of being selfish about it."

"Why did you drop out?"

"At the time, I told myself it was because our parents didn't have money for both of us. But really—really it was a *relief*. To just give up. I hadn't found some calling, nothing in the writing or reading or drawing or music ever spoke to me. I always wanted what Willow had—a purpose. A reason for being right where she was, never doubting it. She graduated with honors in music, but that didn't matter. It was just a piece of paper to say what she already knew. Me? I wanted the paper. Needed it. Something that could tell me what I was supposed to do. A label. I'm this thing. How pathetic is that?" I finished, tired and exhausted with myself.

"So you think you do not belong to Ruhaven because you are not as accomplished a musician as your twin? I do not need to tell you that who we are is not a skill."

Maybe. But at the core, I'd never deserved to be Nereida, never deserved any of this. Never deserved Bryn.

"I never felt her die," I admitted. "My own twin. That night, when she was walking home alone in L'Ardoise, when the Inquitate killed her. I slept. I *slept*."

That's how deep our connection had gone. Something to sleep through. Something to forget.

Outside, the storm broke so the sun heated the skin between my shoulder blades, caressed the back of my ears, stroked sunny fingertips up my neck.

Rowan.

Something as light as a fishing line snagged around my ribs, under my heart. Tugged. Then it was gone, and I stared across the room into Bryn's lightning-flecked eyes.

He gestured to the floor in front of him, patting his chair. "Would you sit here a moment? I wish to show you something and I cannot stand."

"Show me what?"

"Come, Rowan. Please."

I was so exhausted I didn't argue this time, just stepped between the teacup chairs, around the books James hadn't put away, and the tray of tea and half-eaten biscuits beside them. I shouldn't be talking about Willow, I should be forcing Bryn to tell me what I saw in Cappolin, what had left him so drained.

Bryn tilted his head back when I stopped in front of him, and golden eyelashes framed washed-out eyes that were far too dim in his pale face.

He widened his knees and patted the floor between them. "Sit."

Between his legs? When I hesitated, he offered a weak smile. "I promise not to attempt to kiss you again."

Images of the kitchen flooded my mind—his lips, the journal, the golden eyes.

He held out a hand. Waited.

Sunlight danced over the soft skin of his palm, pooled in it like water, like it had when he'd stopped Colm, when he'd strode through the streets of Capolinn as some miracle—*mine.*

I slid my hand into his, felt the connection zing up my arm, met his eyes.

He only smiled and squeezed lightly.

I let him steady me as I lowered to the embroidered rug. Didn't flinch when he scooped my braid over my shoulder and leaned forward, hair shielding his eyes from the sun. "Can you look towards the window, so your back is to me?"

I did as he asked, twisting between his calves, my fingers brushing the flowers unraveling under his suede boots. The afternoon sun glowed through the clouds, rendering the window sash invisible in the tangerine burst of it, and everywhere the light brushed, the wood floor glowed a vibrant orange.

He shifted until his legs framed my body. "I want to try something," Bryn whispered into my ear, voice like spice in the desert. "I am going to cover your eyes with my hands."

Trusting him, I nodded. His fingers shadowed my eyelids, a balm against their prickling heat. Energy pulsed under his fingertips like a circuit grounding itself through me.

As I struggled not to fidget, he spoke from behind, murmuring in a language I didn't know.

"Bryn, what...?"

And then something amazing happened.

Visions began to dance under the weight of his fingers. A world of indigo light and shimmering songs whispered in their place.

He was showing me his...his memories.

I flew as him over Ruhaven where the trees tumbled in a rainbow of colors. Volcanic wind lapped at my nose and tickled other ligaments I couldn't identify.

A female called to me from the woods below. Her voice carried like the chimes of Ruhaven in a melody of well-rounded tones, but laced with something else as well, like the aftertaste of ice cream and honey. We banked left, then plummeted through wet leaves that harmlessly whipped our body.

It was strange to feel this strong, to see Nereida-sized branches snap in half as we spun through the trees and his muscles barely strained at all.

We landed with a thump on Ruhaven's soft earth, the impact harder than I was used to in this body.

The female scanned him from head to toe with a fanged smile that was a quick one-two punch. I'd never met a creature like her, a little whimsical and lithe, like she might bound away at the slightest provocation, but I couldn't tell if I was seeing her through my eyes or his. There was what I knew I should feel—revulsion at the enormous eyeballs, terror at the gangly length—but I only saw beauty.

She wore a thin iridescent dress half off her shoulder, its folds sweeping over a body taller and thinner than proportions were supposed to be. Her skin was like Nereida's, with flickering translucency that hinted at a skeleton while clouds swam beneath the surface. She moved like a ballerina except faster. Her toes—clawed—dragged along the pearly soil as she approached, her heels lifted, her arms splayed as if to turn in a pirouette.

But it was her face I couldn't look away from—or rather, that Bryn couldn't.

Her hair was glittering silver. No, more like melted metal carved into strands that ran in a sparklingly waterfall to her waist.

Her face was long, thin as the rest of her, with ears that speared up and resembled a butterfly's wings. Sparkling freckles ran in a line over her cheeks and nose, then continued in a swirl down the left side of her neck and over her collarbone. A single tattoo, or some kind of marking I couldn't make out without Nereida's zooming sight, decorated the woman's left shoulder.

Metallic eyelashes blinked slowly at me, revealing an eyelid of a matching color. They should be revolting, but I stared at the moonlit irises like the answers to the universe were written in them.

The female lifted a hand, stroking something invisible in the air. Then darted away.

In the dream, my heart thrummed like a struck harp, should have burst from my chest on a flock of birds and disappeared into the lavender sky.

The woman had to be the mate Tye had mentioned, the reason Bryn visited the Gate so often, the reason he'd walked to the Gate and nearly ended everything two years ago.

This was *his* truth Bryn was showing me. So I would know why we couldn't go back to the kitchen, couldn't make that mistake again.

Bryn followed her through the woods where the indigo sky cast her sparkling hair in vivid hues, through trees that glowed even brighter, over the pearls that stirred beneath our feet, and when we burst through the forest at last, a sprawling land awaited.

Ruhaven.

A mountainous range so vast it hurt to behold the depth of it. The world was an artform in and of itself, like a painter had created it in her perfect vision. With mountains carved in the shape of lattices, flowing white water that streaked from one end of the world to the other, the clinging purple mist that descended upon everything.

As he chased after the woman, I could feel Bryn's love. A devotion that was as fundamental to his makeup as bones, skin, or teeth—an organ more vital than a heart. An unending faith that explained why he'd been driven to the Gate after losing her here.

I didn't know how long I floated in the peaceful vision, but eventually, Bryn's words slowed, and the last fell from his lips like a Christmas ornament from a tree.

Then the library and its dusty tomes replaced the dream that had, for a moment, felt as real as Ruhaven.

Bryn rested his hands on my shoulders, his breath warming the back of my neck. I leaned into him on a sigh.

And his lips brushed the soft space below my ear. *Oh.*

He whispered against my neck, "I lied about the kiss."

CHAPTER 31

Dead Sea

I told myself wearing a tool belt made it more official. Halfway up Naruka's staircase, the tray wobbled in my clenched fists, the china rattling louder than the hotel's pipes. Sugar cubes tumbled out of the miniature bowl. He didn't take sugar. The overflowing pitcher of milk spilled with each creaky step. He didn't take milk, either.

This was worse than when my mom made Willow and I play dress-up. I was only missing the frilly apron and tea towel.

When I passed a shuttered clock, I prayed something would fly out so I could blame shock when I tossed everything over the new stair rail.

Maybe I'd get Kazie to bring this tray up to Bryn instead.

"Oh, for feck's sake, Roe, it'll go cold by the time ye resign yerself to this." James fisted his hips, scowling at me from the bottom of the stairs. "Or else it'll be dinner and I'll have to bloody cook something else. What are ye up to, like? Go on. Go on!"

I swallowed, unbearably grateful he hadn't turned me out after yesterday. That he accepted I could see the memories, that he hadn't mentioned the *Ledger*.

"James, I look ridiculous."

"Now that ye certainly do, standing in the staircase for ten minutes like an eejit." With a huff, James tossed a tea towel over his shoulder and marched into the kitchen.

He was right, I should get this over with. Preferably before I started sweating.

Resigned, I plodded up the staircase. It was perfectly normal to bring someone tea when they were sick. It wasn't weird. And it certainly wasn't after whatever had happened in the library. Of course not. He'd shared a memory—through some Ruhaven magic—and that was that.

I paused outside his door. The hallway was filled with daylight's brittle sincerity from the mid-floor window, showing every dusty frame and torn section of wallpaper on a house that hadn't seen a décor update in a century.

I hitched up my tool belt. I was stalling again.

Maybe I didn't know how Bryn had shown me his memories, but I knew why. Ruhaven was sacred, whether I was Nereida or not, and that's why he'd shown me his mate. I'd been too embarrassed to be caught with Sahn, but Bryn hadn't balked from letting me see his own experience in Ruhaven—memories that were intimate, loving, sensual.

I held my breath.

Pushed open the door.

And loosed an exhale when I saw he was asleep, lying under a pressed linen quilt in the crisp, dewy room. Sunlight glittered over blond hair spread on a starched pillow, casting long shadows where his thick eyelashes remained closed. Across his chest, an open book rose and fell with his breaths. He looked like an angel tucked into bed.

I winced as my work boots echoed on the flooring.

The area under the window glowed with soft, wintery light that cast the floorboards in a pale ochre, crawled up the lime-washed walls, and bleached the wool blankets at the end of the four-poster bed.

"Hello, Rowan."

My pulse spiked, but I turned slowly with the tray.

Twilight eyes met mine, lighting with amusement before he set his book on the nightstand, sat up. "Why, Rowan, I was certain that would startle you. Have I lost my touch?"

When his lips curled, all my thoughts leapt out the window and dangled there for a few healthy seconds before I reeled them back in. "Maybe you're not as scary as I first thought."

"Or perhaps Ruhaven suits you."

Did it? Or was he trying to convince me I was Nereida again?

"James wanted me to bring you up something," I explained, standing like a support beam in the middle of his room. "Don't worry, I didn't bake it."

"If I suspected there was any chance of that, I may well have pretended to remain asleep."

I pursed my lips at his weak grin. "I may not be able to cook like James, but I can rewire your entire room so you really feel like you're in Ruhaven."

He let out a coughing chuckle. "Indeed. Though the chance of your extended stay in my room may not be the threat you so intend."

I sucked in my bottom lip. Didn't know what to say to that, other than to wish the butterflies in my stomach took a sleeping pill.

He smiled at my awkwardness and started to rise.

"No, I'll bring it. I…"

The sheet slipped from his shoulders, baring skin as pale and perfect as the rest of him, except for faded tattoos curling over his left shoulder. And he was *muscled*. Not bulging, like Tye, who attracted stares at the L'Ardoise beach last summer, but leaner, slimmer, with hard dips disappearing under—

He yanked the quilt up. "Rowan," Bryn said while I stared like an angsty teenager. "Will you turn around for a moment?"

Caught red-handed and glassy-eyed, no doubt.

I swiveled with the tray. Was the rest of Bryn naked too? "That's uh, not a pirate tattoo, is it?"

Bryn's quick laugh turned into a cough. "Naturally, it is the lost map of El Dorado."

Funny, but I'd seen them before on his arms, and the Bryn I knew would never get tattoos. Had he had a bit of a wild youth? I bit back a grin. Bryn on the streets of Oslo with his tattoos was quite the picture.

"Were you a teenager when you got them done?"

"No, I received them after I was exiled." There was a soft bite to his tone.

I didn't want to remind him of what he'd done to be exiled but… "Do you regret getting them?"

"Never."

Did they cover his entire body? Just where… *No, stop thinking about that*.

"You may look now."

I blanked my face before I did.

Bryn sat upright against the headrest, a long-sleeved shirt covering all the porcelain skin I'd glimpsed and—unfortunately—wearing pants. "Do you want to place the tray here, Rowan?" he said, patting the mattress.

Rounding the bed, I slid the milk, sugar, and scalding tea onto the smooth quilt.

Bryn reached for the teapot. "I assume, because you were given two cups, that James wishes for me to explain things."

Like with the tray, he patted the space beside him.

I must have looked like a confused mule because he added, "There is also a rocking chair if you find the bed too forthright."

I pulled my shoulders back at the faint amusement in his voice. "No, no." Then I bent, awkwardly pulling at my shoelaces.

I could rewire a house, replace a railing, make intricate cuts with a jigsaw—if James ever bought me one—but I couldn't serve tea. Or get my damn boots off.

I was sweating by the time I untied the third string.

"You may leave them on, if you wish."

His bemused comment only rattled me more. "I know how to untie laces, Bryn." One would think, anyway.

While I struggled, he sipped his tea and continued reading his book. I rolled my eyes behind his back.

When I eventually toed off my work boots, I lined their muddy soles on his clean rug and slid beside him, careful not to upturn the tray—just what I needed to do, spill an entire pot of Barry's Tea on these pressed linen sheets the first time I'm in bed with him. *You're not in bed*! But the idea had my neck heating as our shoulders bumped.

Then I stared at my feet, at the pink toes poking through the holes in my socks. Mortifying.

I started to switch to cross-legged when Bryn reached out and snagged my foot. "Do you find yourself in need of socks still, Rowan?"

I pried my embarrassment away from him and stuffed my toes firmly under me. "Maybe I'm waiting on the sock fairies. They've been very generous."

Bryn replied in a nearly inaudible purr, "If I see them in Ruhaven, perhaps I shall tell them to leave a pair under your pillow."

He handed me a cup of tea, then a plate of biscuits from the tray while I scanned his room like the loose papers were more interesting than Ruhaven. He'd drawn these sketches before he'd been exiled, and I could imagine him hunched over the whitewashed desk by the window, drawing his fantasies and living his dream of Ruhaven even when he wasn't in the Gate. Did he lie here at night and look at them?

My eyes trailed to the bookcase stuffed with novels and medical texts and art history books like it had been when I first arrived. The desk drawer where I'd first seen a photo of him.

I started at the memory. At how I'd stood here, inspecting the forgotten things of a man I didn't know, a man who'd eventually become... become a lot more to me. And the ring that had been amongst the clutter.

Had it been his mated ring? Had Bryn taken it off before he left because she was killed by the Inquitate? Or had it been something else—the symbol of Ruhaven and his life here, slipped off and packed away before James exiled him, because he'd needed that clean split.

Maybe it'd just been a ring, a family heirloom, a trinket from the market, something of no significance.

"What *are* you thinking, Rowan?"

I burnt my mouth on the tea. "I—I— Do you read a lot?" I asked stupidly with a mountain of evidence staring me in the face.

"I previously enjoyed adventure novels, but now I find my time consumed by *The Handy Handyman*," he answered easily. "Quite a tome you have given me."

He settled back into the cushions, sipped his tea through lips that were the palest shade of red, darkened only by the over-steeped brew. Even in bed, he didn't quite look relaxed, more like a grown-up doll that had been arranged just so.

"I am sorry I did not explain things," he said after a moment. "I had not experienced such a change before that night, or not to that extent."

I held my breath. "It happened in Oslo, didn't it?"

He nodded. "Yes, when you saw the Inquitate, for a moment, I could walk again as well."

"You weren't just standing close by, or got lucky, or whatever you told me in the hotel room." I wet my lips at the memory of him standing over me, of the sight of his leg, of the power that had rippled from him, of Ruhaven. "Why did you lie?"

He stared up at the lantern swinging inside the four-poster bed, seemed to struggle to find words. "Because, Rowan, I was unsure of how much to reveal to you then, of me."

"Because you didn't trust me."

"No, because you could hurt me."

My brows knit. Hurt him? Did he think that if I knew he was weakened afterward, I'd—what?—take out my frustration on him? Was that what he thought of me?

Of course not, Rowan.

"I believe," he continued as my worries spiraled, "that it is a manifestation of my Mark from Ruhaven."

Yet nobody but Bryn had ever shown a glimmer of themselves. Not even James.

"What exactly *is* your power? Running?"

Bryn's face broke into a wide grin. "No, not running, Rowan. And you may rest assured I am not an underground dwarf either," he added, dancing around my question.

"Is it sharing memories then, like you did yesterday?"

The teacup clinked softly in his palm when he shook his head. "No. For that, I used a connection in Ruhaven. I was not certain it would work, but I am glad that it did."

So he wouldn't tell me what his Mark actually was—because it was clearly more than just *light*. Light didn't explain his sudden strength, how he could stand without the cane.

The bed's curtains billowed like a ship's sails, tossing their crisp, Atlantic scent so the room tasted of summer nights back home.

Bryn drained his tea, set it down. "Will you tell me of your last time in the Gate? My voice is leaving me, and I enjoy hearing you speak."

And that was the biggest lie ever, because compared to his melodic accent, mine was an axe on brick.

But I shuffled through the recent memories. Since I wasn't going to describe the mid-flight sex I'd had with Sahn, I searched for an alternative. When I found it, I settled into pillows as crisp as snow and relayed an elaborate game I'd witnessed.

Bryn's laugh was like quiet waves when I described Nereida jumping off a tree to land on a balloon. She'd punctured it and ended face down in mushrooms, but Ruhaven was as soft and squishy as the balls, and falling never hurt.

"Willow would have loved it," I added wistfully, before I realized I'd spoken aloud. I wasn't prioritizing her enough, not keeping the goal of finding why the Inquitate killed her first and foremost. And the reason was the man next to me. "I'm thinking that when Tye's back, I'll see if he knows Carmen's address. I want to write to her about Levi, see if he knew something. Maybe it's why she left."

Bryn stiffened ever so slightly beside me. "And what else will you ask Tye when he returns?"

I knew what he was asking. "Absolutely nothing." I didn't want Tye, hadn't since he'd shown me the Gate, not really. "I thought he was a friend in L'Ardoise, a good friend, and maybe he was, but it was always to get me to come here," I admitted to the sketches on the wall. "And, I guess, I'll never know if any of that was real. If he was real. If we were."

Bryn had gone completely still, so much that I glanced over to check if he hadn't lapsed into sleep at my monologue. But no, his eyes stared like mine had, unblinking, at the desk drawer.

I probably shouldn't talk about Tye, not after we'd almost...well.

"What's Odda like? The town you said you're from."

He cleared his throat. "It stands at the mouth of a fjord, a fishing village where I first worked at the port, but it is very small."

His description of his fishing village and the locals was as soothing as the tea had been. I imagined the younger version of himself, gangly and uncoordinated, shy and funny, a boy without the weight of Ruhaven.

When he finished telling me about his most embarrassing story in school, silence hung comfortably between us.

Rowan?

I blinked open my eyes, and even with overcast skies, the light in this room was as pure as snow. "Yes?"

The bed squeaked when Bryn set the tray on the floor.

I sat up. "I'll go, sorry I'm—"

"No." He reached for my wrist.

I glanced at the rough fingers curling around a pulse that must be nearly audible. He rotated my hand face up, and, with his thumb still warm from the tea, began to map each line of my palm, slowly, delicately, until I nearly purred.

"I know it is not appropriate to ask while you are on my bed," he began as my heart sat up and begged. "Though it is likely no surprise to you that I am rather poor at expressing myself. I intended to ask you the evening you cut my hair in the kitchen, except you were so close, and, well, I suppose I forgot all about my good intentions." He drifted into silence while I said nothing, could say nothing. "But—but I fear I have made a rather poor impression since we met, and perhaps more recently you have begun to forgive that, and so I should ask you now, while I am more agreeable to you, if I may take you to dinner?"

Dinner? A date? Was that what he meant? There wasn't some weird Norwegian translation that—

"There is a place on the Kerry islands I have wanted to show you. A tiny restaurant on the seafront with live music and a pianist next Wednesday. I thought you might enjoy that. With me."

Definitely a date. I tried to pretend like my every cell wasn't singing at the fingers stroking up my arm, whispering over the crease at my elbow as he slid under my sleeve.

Say something, idiot. Tell this Ruhaven god you'll sing a damn tune yourself if it means you're going on a date together.

His fingers skimmed down my arm to link our hands. The act jolted me enough to remember why I'd ruined things in the kitchen.

I glanced at the desk drawer. Had he left her here? Did that release him from whatever rule James clung to? Or maybe I was getting ahead of things.

Bryn followed my gaze, tensed. "The ring," he said quietly. "I did not realize you knew I had one. I could no longer wear it."

I was a jolt to realize he'd nearly plucked the thought from me.

"Because you had to let go of Ruhaven." After James exiled him. After he'd nearly died.

"No. Because I broke its promise."

I met his sincere eyes. Its promise? "And what's that?"

"To protect. To love. To be faithful." He lifted our joined hands to his mouth, brushed his lips over my knuckles. Each touch of him sent whispers down my spine. "But Rowan, I will not break that promise again. Will you come to the islands with me next week?"

His eyelashes lowered to slits of blue, watching me while he kissed the tips of my fingers. Each and every one.

My insides went molten. "*Yes*," I breathed.

⚙ ☀

It took Bryn a week to recover.

And while he did, I visited the Gate with James and Kazie each morning, always swapping who went into Ruhaven first and with whom. I made them swear to stay at least twenty feet away so they couldn't see me, even if they could still hear me with Sahn. Although James swore I didn't react to the Azekiel, Kazie wasn't as good at lying.

But if I waited for Bryn to take me himself, I'd lose some of my Gate endurance, and I'd just started feeling comfortable with the full hour inside.

Nereida continued dancing and sword fighting while they waited for the Florissant to be configured. I had hoped the Inquitate might appear while we were still in Ruhaven, but it seemed more and more likely that we'd meet them in Drachaut. Yesterday, Nereida had tried James's bow and arrow, much to the relief of Jamellian, who really did have blisters on his fingers, though Essie hadn't been as accommodating for me in moving the rock used for target practice. I think she wanted James to feel better.

After our morning trips to Ruhaven, I worked on the gate lodge until lunch, then spent my evenings researching the Inquitate or reading the history of Tallah, which James and his family had steadily compiled over centuries. The library was more than just a collection of journals, and held encyclopedias of Marks, mates, and every other term in Ruhaven I hadn't yet discovered.

I pulled a book down dedicated to Azekiels and found Bryn had been—of course—right about their Marks being protection. Then I researched Kalistas, the Mark that James and I both had. According to the book, Nereida hadn't yet bonded with a spirit because she hadn't gone through the rite.

"You mentioned that before," I said to James as we sat huddled on a library couch. "What is it?"

"Yera, just something all Ruhavens go through to unlock their Marks. A wee bit like moving through adolescence."

I set the book aside. "What was yours?"

"Finding Essie," he answered with a grin. "But if yer wanting the story on that, I'll need a pint or two."

When I rose to get him just that, I asked, "Shouldn't Tye be back by now?"

Kazie replied, "He sent a postcard saying he'd be a week later. Should be in on Monday, or is it Tuesday?" She shrugged. "Time difference."

The roommate situation must have been worse than I thought—that, or his old manager who owned the farm dragged him into working some job.

The next day after a vegetarian full Irish, James, Kazie, and I visited Ruhaven again while Bryn stayed behind. Except this time, even Kazie kept her distance while James was in the Gate, because as he'd warned us both, "It's Essie and me's anniversary and I don't give a shite."

We waited until the last minute to yank him from the Gate.

And it must have been good, since he spent the rest of the day cleaning Naruka for the first time while jiggling—his dancing resembled a plastic bag caught in the wind—to seventies music on ear-splitting volume.

But it was on a Tuesday when Bryn came down the stairs with a *tap-tap-tap,* not from the crutches but the cane.

And when he stepped into the kitchen and looked at me, I knew one thing.

We were going to the Gate.

CHAPTER 32

Darkness I Feel

L ying at the Gate, I floated through the currents, into the empty
nothingness that always greeted me for a few breaths before
Ruhaven emerged. Months ago, it would have taken minutes for
my mind to merge with Nereida's, to feel the flow of energy through
her and the awareness spread to my limbs, yet now she slid on like a
second skin.

But this time, when I opened my eyes, I was not in Ruhaven.

I knew it instinctually—maybe Nereida's own thoughts had rolled
into me, but I could feel it too. This was not another part of Ruhaven,
not the wild avalanche of forests or the twisted mountains that grew like
a lattice wall, nor some other part of that world I hadn't discovered.

The ground *pop-popped* under my heels as I walked through a land
that was too bright, like sun blazing off icy roads in the morning. And
the smell was wrong too—like burned lemons and alcohol.

The world stretched for miles under the blinding light, reminding me
of the prairies in western Canada I'd never seen but truckers told stories
about. How it felt to drive over days of flat landscapes until the Rocky
Mountains were a mirage that never seemed any closer.

Head back, and for once in as much awe as myself, Nereida's gaze
soared over the impossible ice that cracked and fizzled where gears
should have turned.

Even after everything I'd seen in Ruhaven, watching the slow roll of
ice across the sky was breathtaking.

Then she lowered her chin, and I saw the ground was…glass.

Fields and fields of broken—no, not glass, *mirrors*. Thousands of them.

Her head whipped to the left, the right, ears quirking as she stepped around a stalagmite at least twenty meters thick to our left. My feet pleaded with us to return to the soft, pearly stones of Ruhaven. I winced, glanced down, and nearly jumped at my broken reflection glimmering in a thousand shards.

Shattered. Cold. Sharp.

But then she yanked her eyes up again and ducked under the opening of a cave dripping with gunpowder-green jelly. It clung to the rigid walls of the interior tunnel and puddled on the floor so that our bare feet made a bloody sticking sound when she walked.

Inside, the deep thumps of settling ice and the *drip-drip-drip* of melting glaciers blended into a disturbing harmony. A few centimeters beneath the walls, bluish veins pulsed with beads of light at uneven frequencies.

Was this Drachaut? Had we made it at last? But then where were James, Essie, Kazie?

I ducked a row of pearly ice drops strung like necklaces from the ceiling, following the tunnel until it opened into a dome-shaped cavern with a window at its center so a perfect circle of light was painted upon the floor. It was even colder inside the cavern, except that wasn't quite the right word. She didn't feel temperature, not in the way I did, but instead the air was either thicker or thinner, and in the cave, the particles spread out so each passed individually through my nose.

Nereida scented the air, and more bitter lemon assaulted me. Hopefully, she'd find whatever she was looking for and leave.

We passed under the beam of light, paused, sniffed again.

My blades slid out of their sheaths, the sharp glide a familiar tickle along the underside of my forearm. But this wasn't for some practice session with the Azekiel or a dance between her and James, because for the first time, I felt something from Nereida I'd never experienced before.

Fear.

It curdled in her blood, froze limbs that should have been loose for fighting, not the stiff and jittery movements of an amateur.

The chamber echoed with our heavy breathing, slower than a human's, but far too fast for Nereida. She only sounded like this when she was with Sahn. And where was he?

We surveyed the cavern. Five tunnels led out of the chamber, each pulsing with a different color vein.

I spun toward the orange tunnel a second before a stalactite plummeted in front of our nose. The wind of it had every silver jelly hair rising on my neck before it shattered on the ground.

Lowering to a crouch, she raised identical swords whose iron blades glistened under the golden light. Listened. Waited.

And then I heard it too.

Footsteps, growing louder with each moment, splashing through melted ice. The orange veins of the tunnel pulsed rapidly in time with the noise.

Nereida backed up a step, hands shaking.

Shaking—but she was never afraid, never nervous.

I braced automatically, in her body, in her mind, preparing for whatever had her blood running cold, what would be—by the growing noise—barreling through to us any minute.

Boom. Boom. *Boom*.

Nereida raised her swords, crossing them in an *X*, the sound like nails on a blackboard.

Boom. Boom. Boom

It had to be right there, right at the entrance to the pulsing tunnel where the footsteps became deafening, and the veiny lights had whipped into such a frenzy, there was almost no pause between each flicker, so the gateway glowed fiery orange.

Where was it? *Where was it?*

The sound pounded past the entrance, gaining speed. It should have been twenty feet from us, fifteen, ten…

My heartrate skyrocketed as Nereida swiped at thin air. *Invisible.* The damn thing was invisible.

The footsteps stopped, disappeared.

The cave descended into a chorus of dripping glaciers and Nereida's heavy breathing. She made an effort to steady it, but I could feel the panic choking her lungs, could see it in the blades that shook in her outstretched hands.

Something hot whispered across our neck.

She spun with her swords, plunged the left into invisible space, but I felt the tear of muscle, the thud of bone reverberating up the blade.

The thing howled, sending stalactites crashing around us.

And then it flickered into existence.

Diamond eyes pierced the night in a creature that should never exist. Bottled-blue scales rippled in waves over a muscled body that towered above Nereida. She yanked her sword out, stumbled back, and watched blue blood drip from the wound, staining the cloth hitched over his hips.

It pulled its gums back, exposing two rows of perfect teeth.

Then it struck.

Pain exploded in my wrist. The sword clattered from my grip, lodging tip down in the glass with a *crack*. Blood as silver and thick as my hair leaked from my arm before Nereida clutched it to her chest.

The demon heaved a rough laugh, circling us. She raised the remaining sword, holding it in a shaky fist, but the monster disappeared again so there was nothing to fight, nothing to attack.

Feet away, its growl rumbled through the cavern. Nereida glanced over our shoulder, eyeing the distance between her and the tunnel we'd entered.

Before she could make a move, it grabbed our throat. She raised her arm, slicing the remaining sword where the eyes had briefly hovered, but he knocked it away.

And hurled us backward.

A forest of broken ice smashed my cheekbone. My elbow collided at the same time, wrenching it from its socket, my back tearing open with painful awareness.

I grabbed a shard of glass as I bared my teeth, incisors digging into my bottom lip.

Nereida had no Mark, hadn't found her spirit, and this shard wouldn't do anything.

Glass broke a foot from my sprawled leg. I tasted the creature's breath before I felt it, rancid vinegar that stung each nostril and curled my lip.

It could kill me and I wouldn't even see it.

But something else pulled at me.

A tingling awareness spread from the base of my neck to my tailbone—a command that could seize my body with a strength stronger than Nereida.

Bryn.

Relief made my knees weak. *Yes, bring me home, please.*

His call drifted down my spine, fusing my bones, melting my blood, zinging my pulse into slow submission until I would be weightless enough to float from the memory. I closed my eyes at the soft pleasure, loosened my hold on Nereida, and waited to drift into the dark space before Naruka.

But something pulled back, fighting him. Fighting us.

I started sinking into Nereida again, feeling her broken leg and bleeding cheek, the dislocated shoulder that caused her pulse to pound around her armpit.

Then Nereida sniffed the air, head whipping left and right, scenting *him.*

Sahn.

Feathers flashing, he burst through the tunnel we'd entered with a growl that hurt my ears. Dark wings swept out and bumped into both ends of the cavern. His golden hair glistened under the single ray of light still illuminating the cavern as his gaze turned to me.

For a brief moment, when his eyes latched on to Nereida, a punch of recognition rolled through me. Then it was gone.

Bryn's call echoed along my spine again.

Light fingers grazed my skin, stroking, but that was all. There was no zinging pull, no lifting from the Gate that should have dragged me out of here.

Maybe I had to try harder.

I focused, reaching for the thread that dangled from the void, but it disappeared before I could grab on. The awareness in my spine loosened, died.

Nereida rose on shaky legs, and before Sahn could reach her, she stabbed out—striking true.

The demon flickered into existence, letting out a piercing howl at the blade wedged in its left side. Nereida yanked it back, causing cold, blue liquid to spurt from between his ribs and over our arm, before the dragon-like demon turned, its invisibility gone, and sprinted out one of the cave's tunnels.

Her labored breathing filled the silence before we dropped the blade, our knees giving way.

Then Sahn was there, smoky wings spread wide and blocking out even the sliver of light. In the darkness, his eyes spun like the rings of Saturn, the streak of freckles over his nose and cheeks nearly glowing. But his brow furrowed, two sparkling eyebrows pulling together as he inspected my shoulder, my cheek.

Every time I saw him was a tiny miracle.

The thought struck me out of nowhere.

He was hers, Nereida's, not just a lover or boyfriend or temporary fling. Not a man from L'Ardoise or a high school sweetheart. Not a sticky-fingered boy from the cinema. But as much a part of her as the hand he carefully inspected.

He drew our fingers together, and a tiny trail of wispy light spiraled up my arm—his Mark, his protection. Healing me like he had after the Tether broke.

My heart throbbed for him.

His eyes, those beautiful, exotic planets, latched on to mine as he looked at her—no, looked at *me*. Past Nereida, through her mind and the memories and the translucent skin, through her silvery blood and every cell and fiber that made up her being, to the human posing as her.

To me.

I wilted under his gaze. He'd know—even in the memories, he'd know. There wasn't a part of Nereida he didn't see, didn't feel, and though Sahn might have died centuries ago, this piece of him had remained.

The figment of memory was alive enough to know the truth.

But in that moment, with his irises burning a familiar fire, with the thread of gold whirling between us, god, how I wanted to be this woman.

Then his eyes winked out.

The world winked out.

And I was nothing.

No, no, I was *in* nothing, flung into the place between worlds like Sahn's very memory had commanded it. He wouldn't want me to inhabit Nereida, even as a dream.

In my Prayama, I inhaled a chilly breath, crossed my arms. I couldn't see him or anything else in this place that was all my own, a sensory-deprivation chamber if it wasn't for the vague trickle of water.

Not even my feet made a sound as I stepped through the darkness, searching for an exit that would only come when Bryn anchored me. But that might be minutes or hours from now. I'd never made it to this place without someone dragging me into it, someone who was ready to pull me the rest of the way.

I sucked in another cold breath. Who knew how time passed while Bryn was enjoying the warm lakes of Ruhaven, or those fairy women as Tye had once teased.

But no, he'd been lying about that, hadn't he? Bryn had a mate and he wouldn't be with anyone else. That was one of the few laws I'd learned.

Was she kind? Pretty? Did her features look more humanoid than Nereida's? Was he attracted to her?

Stupid questions.

But he wasn't supposed to be with anyone here either, and yet he'd asked me to dinner.

Pondering it, I plodded through darkness, almost grateful for the cold because at least I could feel *something*.

Why couldn't I have seen a kitchen overflowing with stews and dirty dishes like James did? Instead, I got miles of darkness. Not even an ominous door like Tye told me he once saw, or Kazie's world in black and white.

For me—nothing.

I was more scared of water than the night, of wooden roller coasters and parties with thirty or more people, but not this. So what did Ruhaven have to—

Then I stopped.

What if this was the *Fall*? What if I hadn't been thrown out of Nereida's body and anchored to this place, but she'd...*died?*

My pulse skittered up my invisible legs. That would make sense. It'd make complete sense. Because there'd been no anchoring call, no Bryn to latch on to—besides that brief moment when I'd thought...but no, it hadn't been—and then I'd appeared here.

Because she'd died in Ruhaven?

Yet Bryn had said I'd *hear* something before the memories ended. Why hadn't I asked him what it sounded like? Maybe I'd heard it without realizing.

But I didn't want to make the Fall, didn't want to give up my life for Nereida, to be reborn again in Ruhaven. I'd be nothing, I wouldn't be me, it'd be like I never existed.

Who's to say Ruhaven would even want me?

She'd flip through my life and see a woman who'd been Willow's doppelgänger, clinging to her for every scrap of life.

Even in death, I'd stolen her memories.

Sahn had known, I'd seen it in his eyes—he'd looked right into my soul and seen *me*. An imposter.

What if Ruhaven had already made her decision? She could have seen, judged, and exiled me to this space.

Forever.

Cold fear choked the air from my lungs. There was nothing here, nothing, and soon I would be the same.

I sank to my knees as the truth of it bowled into me. This would be my punishment.

No, no, no.

This was some impossible horror—to be stuck here indefinitely, to live in *nothing*. A punishment for taking Nereida's memories.

Would anyone come?

Could Bryn even reach me if Ruhaven didn't allow it? What if I never slept, never even got that moment of reprieve? Or what if Bryn did come, but the minutes passed like months—or years?

No!

I slapped myself. Hard.

But my arm passed through where my face should have been, the momentum dragging me into a ground that didn't exist either.

I made the same mistake again when I tried to fidget with my braid. To touch *something*. But there was nothing, nothing but me and…and…

What was that?

My head snapped up, and I nearly wept at the pain of the whiplash.

But there *was* something here. Not Bryn, not an anchor lifting me out, but a—a light?

I forced my shaking legs under me, stood, squinted.

A light—though its flicker was as faint as a distant star. I took a deep breath, then started toward it.

The thing immediately grew brighter. But it might have been more a ribbon, swimming in nothingness, wiggling in the air.

I started running.

My feet made no sound, air didn't pass by my ears faster, my lungs didn't pant for breath.

Feet away, the light shone bright but showed no water, no ground, no end to the room. The only thing it revealed…was me.

Naked, shivering, but alive. Existing. Not nothing.

I barely recognized myself under its golden glow. It smoothed out my scars, shimmered over my skin so I veritably sparkled. And I could *feel* it. Not the warmth of L'Ardoise's sun but a tingling peppermint sensation.

Was it some other inhabitant?

Stretching out a hand, I murmured at the thing, my voice an embarrassing plea for it to come near, not to leave me here. The tips of my fingers lit up like moonbeams as I held my breath. *Just a little more…*

It winked out.

No, wait! I'll—

And burst to life on my toes. I yelped, jumping back as it flickered rapidly, almost like it was laughing.

It *was* sentient. Another creature like me, lost here.

I started to bend down, to coax it to stay, but it swam circles like a fish in a coy pond. Not wanting to scare it off, I straightened again, watching it through blinking eyes, praying that it stayed, that my body remained as alive as it felt.

So I stood perfectly still, and wherever its light touched, my body flashed into existence.

When it nestled at my feet, I was a pair of ankles with no legs and no belly.

What kind of creature *was* this? Something from Ruhaven? Or some animal that lived in this dark pit?

Then it slid over my toes, warming them a humming degree, so much that I actually sighed into the dark. And I *heard* it this time.

The light laughed again in that quick flicker, then dissolved into golden moonlight to lay glittering at my feet.

Friendly. Comforting.

Slowly, it started to rise, like fog off a lake in the early morning when the distant shore is nearly invisible and the water a perfect mirror.

My knees knocked together as it licked up the insides of my thighs, revealing each freckle and the muscles I'd earned from lugging wood and tools and coils of heavy wire.

It swirled playfully around my hips, tickling my stomach. I still had a faint tan line from last August when Tye wanted to spend every weekend at Port Michaud beach. Its touch became like the sun back then, a hot feather drawn sensuously across my body.

I must be losing my mind.

But grateful for the warmth, I uncrossed my arms, letting them dangle loosely at my sides. In answer, its silky touch brushed my fingertips before whispering soft kisses onto my palms.

I sucked in blissfully cold, sweet air, the first breath after a fresh snow when the wind tickles your nostrils, but it's pure and clean and intoxicating for a brief moment.

Maybe this *was* the Fall, and Ruhaven had accepted me after all.

The light brushed my belly button before sliding up my torso, causing me to vibrate with embarrassing anticipation. My nipples tightened to painful points, my breasts grew heavy, but it only brushed the underside of them before pressing a light kiss, like dappled sunlight, to the space between.

I nearly sighed when it moved on. Maybe I did, because it laughed again in that flickering tempo.

What if this was my spirit? Nereida might have one that James didn't know about. It had to be. I'd *never* been touched so intimately. Not by Tye. Not by any man I'd been with in L'Ardoise. Not even by Sahn.

James had said my spirit could be anything. I could pluck a substance off the table of elements, suck it from the air, or extract an emotion.

Whatever it was—my spirit, some apparition in this space—gave a gentle tug on my hair that had my head falling back.

I sighed as snowflakes melted over my eyelids, my cheeks, my tingling lips, the tips of my ears, my throat, until my whole body was a buzzing hive of awareness.

I think I was floating away from the trickling water, up and up and up. I was a balloon a child had released into the sky with no cares, no worries.

And no thoughts but the endless freedom above.

I sat up on a gulping inhale.

Cold whipped my neck and shoulders as soon as the blanket fell away. But I was alive. Alive. Not Fallen with the others. No Token had been buried for me, no plaque sat waiting in the woods for a future Ruhaven to stumble upon it and wonder.

I pressed a hand to my trembling lips. What *was* that thing?

Bryn would know. He always knew.

But when I twisted to ask him, I found him still asleep in the Gate, with his palm facing the sky that was now empty without mine.

Had I anchored myself? Finally?

I grinned and patted my forehead, finding it and my cheeks hot and sweaty from whatever lightning worm had found its way into my room.

Above me, the wax pooled in the glass lantern that swayed in a lazy pendulum. Crows, robins, and magpies filled the woods with squeaky chirping and rustled leaves when they snuck from branch to branch.

It was nice to sit here, to see him like this, so calm and unaware. Younger, somehow, with the tight planes of his face all relaxed.

I reached toward him and smoothed back the stray hairs clinging to eyelashes that sparkled with the dying light over Kerry's hills.

Should I anchor him? No, no, he might want to stay in longer, but…

Bending an elbow, I lowered to the ground beside him, shifted closer, my body loose and sleepy like I'd had sex with Sahn instead of letting myself be caressed by light.

I glanced at the cane lying by his side. This was his first time in the Gate after the incident outside An Béal Bocht—what if it'd drained him? What if the anchoring worked differently? Or—or what if he stayed in the Gate longer on purpose, like he had when James exiled him?

Worried now, I slid my hand into his, felt his fingers flex in response, strong, solid, that connection that ran straight through my core.

"Bryn?" I whispered in his ear.

Strays of glittering blond hair fluttered in the quickening winds as the sun struggled to stay above the hills. Even these pink and orange hues seemed to love him, coloring his angular nose and cheeks, flushing his skin. Light always found him wherever he was.

His eyelashes wavered in the breeze but didn't blink open.

I repeated his name again, squeezed his hand harder. He was probably fine, probably just wanted to stay in longer.

Closing my eyes, I pressed my palm to his cheek, fingers grazing the roughness there, feeling for the connection we needed to bring each other home. How had I ever thought an alarm clock could do this? Ludicrous. It was too intimate for anything but a friend, lover, brother.

Bryn was there, somewhere in Ruhaven, drifting, waiting for me. I slid my hand down his cheek, his neck, over his chest until I found his heart pumping steadily against my palm.

I let myself sink into it, into him, under the current of the Gate that wavered like the surface of a vast ocean, feeling the cold leach into my skin as I pushed through the veil of that world.

A faint golden light pulsed once, twice, barely visible beneath the sea's currents. I swam toward it. None of this was real, not the feeling of icy water over my skin or the pressing darkness, nothing except the light. Except Bryn.

Arm extended, I stretched toward the gold, piercing the comfort of my own mind and reaching—

Pop.

A sharp sticking sound echoed in my ear a moment before the sea faded, the dark disappeared, and I stood in…an apartment?

I spun around at a burst of laughter.

Two women passed outside a window with the blind drawn to half-mast. Not an apartment, but some tiny cottage with unevenly whitewashed walls and a box of purple flowers—pansies? Tulips? James would know—on the windowsill. Wood popped in a fireplace opposite a lumpy, straw-stuffed couch. But the cushions arranged in various blues and purples all read a bit fussy, as did the matching glass vase over the stove, and the straw rug on a sloping, stone floor.

Then, I heard something that dragged up a thousand memories, of the hours spent listening to Willow play the same chords, practice the same song.

I turned slowly.

And stared.

The piano was a rich streak of bronze against the rigid bone white of the cottage, the only warmth in the accents of cool blues. But it was not Willow playing it.

Bryn hunched over the upright, fingers flying, his hands managing a scale I'd always struggled with, the chords thundering in the tiny cottage. Could he play in real life? Or was it only possible in this dream?

When my gaze landed on his neck, he straightened. Shifted.

Unyielding blue eyes collided with mine.

"Hello, Rowan."

My heart beat as loud as the swaying metronome on the piano. "Bryn?"

The pedal snapped up and the notes died on a humming melody as he rose unaccompanied. It was strange seeing him without the cane he used every day, as much a part of him as the light he drew like a magnet.

So this was his place between worlds, and I knew that if I were to open the porthole door behind me, I'd see the cusp of Oslo's port.

I scanned the pieces of his life scattered in the old cottage—the stones glued in a frame behind him, the model boat in the tiny kitchenette, the blackboard with a list of to-dos written in handwriting that wasn't his. There was none of his artwork, his sketches of Ruhaven.

I met his guarded eyes again. "This is your Prayama?"

"It is."

I didn't know what I'd expected, but... "I came back without you, without an anchor, or I guess I anchored myself. Then I saw you there. I just wanted to make sure you weren't stuck."

He tucked his hands in his pockets. "Rowan, you did not anchor yourself. I did."

"No, you tried to anchor me," I said absently, unable to stop myself from inspecting every inch of what his life had been, perhaps a bit desperate for some piece of him he'd never revealed. "But I couldn't answer you. I was in a cavern and— Anyway, it doesn't matter."

I itched to look around, to climb the twisted iron staircase that led to the loft, to see how he lived and what books sat beside his nightstand. Why did he need this place if he could anchor himself? Was it rude to look around?

"Rowan, that was me calling you," he said softly.

I stepped toward the magazine tented on the couch, but this wasn't one of the "Ten Steps of Drawing a Nose" I'd seen him reading before. It was a guide on fall fashion—mint green was in this year. "I know, but I couldn't answer," I explained, glancing over my shoulder as I reached for the magazine.

"No, not in the cave. In the darkness, in your *Prayama*," he said, then added with a quirk of his lips, "I was the light."

Why would Bryn be reading a book on— Wait, what?

I stared at him. "Sorry, what did you say?"

The quirk melted. "The light, Rowan. I was the light."

The magazine fell from my fingertips. The light? Not *the* light? *Wait...*

But the truth was written in his burning, golden eyes.

Oh god, I was stupid.

Light. His Mark was *light*.

He'd been the sparkling ribbon twirling on the ground that I'd let stroke me, caress me, kiss me while I purred like a depraved fool. I should have remembered, I should have known. Even in this imaginary room, my face swelled with heat.

It wasn't supposed to be *real*. It certainly wasn't supposed to be *Bryn*. I'd been *naked* and he'd—he'd— That'd been *his* touch.

Or maybe, maybe it'd just been in my head, and it hadn't been *real*.

He swayed elegant fingers over the keys, caressing the dust on their ivory tops. "Rowan, I think it is time we return now."

CHAPTER 33

One Day, You Finally Knew

"Bryn?" I whispered.

He knelt over me, the aging sun silhouetting his face. In the shadow, his freckles seemed more pronounced than ever, all those tiny imperfections I'd once counted. But here he was, more beautiful than anything in Ruhaven, and glowing as if visiting the Gate had filled him with a new source of life. Ruhaven's golden child.

"Yes, my Rowan?" His breath fanned my face, a cool caress of winter and mint and wildness.

I licked my lips. "Why?" I might have been asking why I'd forgotten he was light, or why he'd felt the need to anchor me like that, or why I'd never felt anything like him before.

He shifted, sliding onto an elbow to free his other hand and cup the side of my face. I went very still as my blood started to hum. Could he sense that? Hear me? I didn't know what to feel—embarrassment, worry, arousal. Though the last I certainly felt, with his thigh pressing against mine as we lay here together, like we had a hundred times before.

"Why?" he murmured, and my skin tingled where his calloused fingers brushed, softly, carefully, his thumb sliding over the dent in my chin. His eyes watched mine, as if waiting for a sign to stop.

But I'd never tell him no, because this was the Bryn from my dreams, when he was briefly unguarded, wild, reckless, and mine.

When I pressed my cheek into his palm, he said quietly, "I enjoy these stolen moments with you. Watching you wake, seeing the endearing flush to your cheeks. The brief, foggy silver of your eyes when you wake that I have never told you of. The freckles on your cheeks that stand out more starkly when you are tired." His thumb rested there for a moment while my chest rose and fell on shallow breaths. "Or do you mean why did I anchor you in such a manner?"

Such a manner. That manner would give me at least a month's worth of dreams.

"Yes." It was all I could manage.

"You were distracted while under attack, as you were when your Tether broke." He offered me a hesitant smile. "I could not wake you as normal."

No, that had certainly not been the *normal* way.

The wind tickled goosebumps from the porcelain skin under his collar. "I forgot you were light," I admitted. Silky, sensuous, embarrassing light. Was I fantasizing about *light*?

His lips twitched, his eyes warming in liquid amusement. "I apologize. I could not speak in that form to explain."

I nodded like it made perfect sense, like I hadn't wilted under him, like I hadn't been ready to give up my very existence just to stay a few minutes longer under that touch. "Right." The word sounded forced, so I tried again. "It's nothing. I mean, it's fine. You don't have a body, or— or *sight*, so…"

He stroked a knuckle over my trembling jaw, up my cheek, over my lips, lingering there as his eyes smoked to gold. "Yes, Rowan, I saw you," he answered, low and husky.

I swallowed so hard I think we both heard it. I couldn't *concentrate* when his irises were *gold*—it was like trying to think in front of Zeus.

"Why are your eyes doing that?" I whispered against his fingertips, fighting the desire to circle my tongue around one. Just to see what he'd do, what line he'd draw.

Faint amusement flickered over his face. "My Rowan, I think you know why."

I did know why. "A manifestation of the Gate?" *Just admit it.*

He studied me carefully. "If you prefer to think of it as that, then yes."

Anything else would only make me combust further. "So that's— that's what you look like in Ruhaven? You're…"

He brushed a distracting knuckle along my collarbone, still hovering over me and braced on one elbow. Anyone passing by would think we were lovers in a park.

"You're some form of light," I finished on a shiver.

"Not quite." Bryn searched my face, like he was waiting for *me* to explain how he'd manifested as light in my own room, of how he could embody it even here. "Rowan…"

I reached toward him hesitantly, catching a lock of his hair. "Yes?" I smiled as the strand fluttered between my fingers, as soft and silky as Sahn's feathers.

Bryn clasped my hand, stopping me. "Rowan, we must talk."

Something staggered in my chest, like my heart had been skipping along and suddenly snagged its foot. Talk? Had he changed his mind? Come to his senses? Remembered he had a mate? My eyes darted to his right ring finger, as if I'd see the golden band confirming my worries. But it was empty.

Carefully, with my hands in his, he pulled me to kneeling. But he didn't rise, didn't reach for the tea or the sandwiches we'd packed.

I wrung my now-empty hands. "Bryn, if this is about your Prayama—I'm sorry. I thought you were stuck. I didn't mean to just…appear."

"No, Rowan," he said, not unkindly, and when the quilt slid off my shoulders, he tugged it up, tucked it in. "This is not about you seeing my Prayama." He settled in front of me, our knees almost touching. The gold that had lit his irises had all but faded to a rusty blue.

"Then what, Bryn?"

He undid the top button of his sweater, the collar brushing the faint golden stubble at his throat. "Something I should have explained when we met in Oslo."

Oslo—how far away that seemed now. Had he felt what I did then? That terrifying connection? No, I'd only annoyed him, insulted him. I could see how I'd have offended him, knowing what I did now about his connection with Ruhaven.

As he had in the library, I reached out, took his hand. Even that simple connection caused something to flow between us—that energy Kazie was always talking about, like his recognized mine. But he didn't smile or acknowledge it in any way, only kept his steady gaze on me, unblinking.

"Rowan," Bryn said, voice deep, "these past months have been the most fulfilling of my life, and the most difficult for me."

I knew that, knew what it meant to be back in the Gate. How difficult it must have been for him to see his mate there and know she was dead here. That all he had of her was a memory.

Should I admit I knew what he'd tried to do in this very spot? Of how much of a struggle returning to the Gate would be? Of how I saw the longing in his eyes each time he did?

Instead, I squeezed his hand. "I understand."

No, you do not.

I blinked, sure I'd heard him this time. Inside me, not just a feeling, but actual—

You did.

I dropped his hand. "Bryn?"

He smiled a little, a crooked lift of the left side of his lips, the only time I ever saw a wrinkle on his porcelain face. "Yes, Rowan, I can speak to you…" *Like this.*

Dear god, he could read my thoughts. My *thoughts*!

No, only loose inclinations.

Close enough!

"Is this your—your Mark?" I stuttered, trying to wrap my thoughts in a vice-like grip.

Bryn grabbed my hand again, held it tightly. "No, Rowan. This is not my Mark, but a connection between us in the Gate."

But then he knew how I felt and—and he knew what I was thinking now. And all the things I'd ever thought about him. But no, it was "inclinations" and not thoughts. But my inclinations had been even *worse*.

I shook off his hand, jumped up. And swayed.

Bryn rose impossibly fast, steadying me by my elbow before reaching for his cane.

"Bryn, I—this Mark of yours. Or, what did you say? A connection? It's…" *Making me want to throw up.* Christ, did he hear that too? Did I *incline* to throw up?

He should have told me. Way before now, so I could have a chance to get a grip on all my ridiculous fantasies which— No, stop thinking. Stop *thinking*!

I stopped pacing when Bryn gripped my shoulders, forced me to meet his eyes. "Rowan, you need not worry so. I have not always enabled this connection. Though I apologize for telling you of this now—"

"I can see why you waited. It's—"

"—but it is not that which I needed to tell you."

That drew me up short. "What? Why? What else can you do?"

His thumbs smoothed circles over my shoulders. *Do not worry overmuch of this,* he reassured me, his voice sliding like slowly freezing water in my mind. *I do not hear your words as you do mine.*

Are you sure?

I braced a hand on his chest. As soon as I did, that same grounding energy flowed through my fingers. His breath quickened, his heartbeat filling my palm, my own eardrums, echoing in my veins. An entire hive of bees seemed to have taken up permanent residence in my chest.

He glided a hand over my spine, stopped at the small of my back, drew me in.

I looked up through fluttering eyelashes, watching as his irises darkened to another, almost familiar color. When his hand moved to cup the base of my neck, my lips tingled in anticipation.

"Whatever else there is, tell me later," I whispered. Not just because I wanted him, wanted that rare, unguarded closeness, but because I felt that approaching before-and-after moment Tye had talked about months ago.

Bryn smiled softly, wide and perfect under the sunset hues, his skin a canvas to everything I'd never noticed before—the flickering purple shadows cast by the leaves, the near-crimson glow of the tips of his ears, the lightness of his bottom lip next to the top.

Sometimes, things were better closer than afar.

How I wish it could wait, he admitted.

The wind picked up, raising goosebumps along his jaw. He pinched a strand of my hair and tucked it behind my ear. Inhaled. "James was not fully truthful when he told you my Mark was light."

I curled my fingers into Bryn's shirt. "You looked like light in my Prayama."

He stroked the back of my neck, twisting fingers in my hair, each touch perfectly tuned to what I didn't know I liked. "Light is a part of me. What you saw in your Prayama was a form that I may at times take, an embodiment of my Mark. But it is not how I normally appear."

I toyed with the soft cashmere of his sweater, imagined plucking the pearly button open, seeing what that map of El Dorado really looked like. "You're not a dwarf, are you?" I joked.

His hand tightened on my neck, not amused, not playing. "Rowan, you do not understand what it is to have lived for so many years in the Gate. What it can do to you, what it can take from you."

How close he'd come to dying right here, right where we were standing, in the Gate that had driven him to it.

I released the button, had to take a breath. "I know. I know what it did to you."

He caught my wrist, brought it to his lips. "No, you do not," he said against my pulse.

My fingers curled reflexively, trying to capture the warm breath gliding over my skin.

"Because you do not yet understand that I have waited years for you." He nuzzled my hand, breathing in, the gesture strangely tender.

Waited for *me*? But those words didn't make any sense, not in that arrangement. Waiting for me to what? For what?

"Bryn, I don't understand."

Bending, he cupped my face in his hands, touched his cool forehead to mine, our noses almost brushing. He inhaled shakily.

"Years, Rowan," he breathed. "Years of imagining how you would look, how you would speak, how we would be together. Years of searching for you. Of praying that I shall find you in this world. To share with you every whispered secret from the years in Ruhaven, to live the memories together as we have done. To find the connection I have missed."

I started to shake. In that moment, I think there was a tiny, far-off part of my mind that knew what he meant, that understood exactly what caused his voice to tremble.

But the Roe of the present couldn't accept it. No—*wouldn't a*ccept it.

"What connection?" I asked weakly.

The hands on each side of my face tilted my head back so I couldn't look away. Couldn't look at anything but *him*.

Bryn brushed my nose with his. Tender, playful, affectionate.

"Since I saw you in L'Ardoise, I have never been truly alone," he whispered. "I thought of you every day in Oslo, I have wondered silly things of you, Rowan. Like what time you wake in the morning, whether you prefer to sleep on cold nights or warm, if you take sugar in your coffee. When I walk into a room, I imagine what you shall make of it. I wonder how you would speak with my friends, whether you would enjoy hiking in Norway, which flowers you like or if you like them at all. And sometimes... sometimes I wonder whether you ever think of the man you met so briefly in L'Ardoise."

I—I couldn't even remember meeting him.

"Why?" I whispered, though I knew the answer, knew what I hadn't wanted to accept, to admit, knew what flickered between us was no random chemistry.

"Because there is no piece of my soul that does not have yours written upon it."

My pulse hiccuped when he dropped his lips to my jaw, kissed the bruise still fading there, his touch like snowflakes on my skin before he brushed the tender shell of my ear.

"And because, my Rowan, I am the Azekiel."

CHAPTER 34

The Greatest Bastard

I trembled as he whispered soft, gentle endearments I couldn't hear over the roar in my ears.

"You can't be," I insisted, though every rapid beat of my heart screamed it was the truth.

His hands tangled in my hair, tilting my head back until I had no choice but to meet those impossible eyes again—gold and liquid and endless. "But I am, Rowan. Of course I am. You know this."

My mouth felt like it was full of lead. "No, no. James would have *told* me. And you…you wouldn't have…"

His eyes tightened, almost imperceptibly, in a man too beautiful for Naruka.

No.

I pushed against his chest, lightly, but it was enough to have him drop his hands, for the gold to cool to blue. "I am sorry," he said softly. *Yes, I am O'Sahnazekiel. It is why I can anchor you and only you, why I could share my memory with you, why I can speak to you like this.*

I shook my head vigorously. "But he's…" A winged beast that I've been sleeping with for months. "And you're—you *can't*."

It couldn't be true. It *couldn't*. Because then every touch and kiss I'd shared with Sahn was really with—with…Bryn.

And then, well, that would mean that he'd known exactly what I was living through. He wouldn't have just taken me to the Gate, and let me…*with* me, while he was there, watching—no—*participating*.

I stifled a sob.

Bryn's hand shook on the cane.

He'd watched Nereida—watched me. Had seen my most intimate moments with the creature in my past life.

He'd lived it.

God, he'd lived it *with* me!

Someone was screaming in my head; it might have been me.

And I'd *thanked* him. Thanked him for anchoring me, for slipping through the Gate and watching every sordid thing Sahn and I had done—no, that Bryn and I had done. Together. And now, now I was like his Ruhaven pet he could take out and play with.

"Rowan, do not cry, please," Bryn whispered, emotion thickening his voice as his thumbs wiped away my tears. "I am sorry I did not tell you before when—"

"Don't *touch* me." I shoved at his chest.

Bryn slowly pulled back, unguarded eyes blinking in confusion.

Behind him, the sun dipped between the Kerry hills, its arms gripping the edge for the last bit of light. I was freezing and sweating and boiling in his coat. I threw it off me, tossing it with the backpack.

"You're Sahn," I repeated, for myself. For him.

He swallowed. "Yes. Yes, Rowan."

The wind tossed the silky strands I'd brushed away back into his eyes. He was Sahn. I was Nereida. I repeated the words over and over, waiting for them to settle into some semblance of truth.

But it made sense. It made perfect sense

It's why he'd hated me when we met. He was looking for Nereida, but he hadn't found her in L'Ardoise, he'd found me instead, and he hadn't wanted—hadn't wanted what he saw.

I did, Rowan, how I did.

"Stop that!" My shout drained more color from his face. "How long were you going to keep this from me?"

"I—I thought you would recognize me, Rowan, as I did you. When you didn't, it was difficult to find the appropriate time, but I have been trying to tell you." He dragged a hand through his perfect locks.

"Trying to tell me?" I echoed, aghast. "You *never* told me, you never said anything. You didn't even *like* me."

His brows winged up. "You know that is not true. And I attempted to show you instead—in the library."

I dragged a hand over my lips. The library? What had he shown me in the library? Something of Ruhaven, of his own memory of—of the woman who'd leapt through the woods, the one he'd chased after.

My tongue felt numb. "That—that was Nereida?"

His eyes softened. "That was *you.* "

Bryn stooped to pick up the blanket, folding it over one arm. Once, I'd have thought he was indifferent. Now I knew he needed the brisk movements to think over his lies.

"Rowan, the first time you met me in the Gate—met Sahn—you feared him, you thought he hurt you. Do you remember how you reacted when we woke from the Gate?"

I'd called him a beast. He had been. He was.

"I had planned to tell you," Bryn explained quickly, "but I was nervous at how you may react and was uncertain how far you and O'Sahnazekiel had…progressed."

"Had sex," I interrupted. He'd wondered if I'd had sex with his memory yet. Because that's what he'd been doing with mine. Before. Now.

"Yes," he agreed, a man who must have thought nothing of it after being with her for years. "So I waited for the correct opportunity, and to visit Ruhaven myself and determine your understanding of O'Sahnazekiel. As it was, they were parted for the duration of your initial visits and you had not yet encountered him."

Liar. He was a liar, just like Tye. Manipulating me so he could enjoy Nereida in peace and quiet.

"You forced me into the Gate," I bit out.

He let out a shaky breath. "Yes. Yes, I needed you to understand. Tye insisted I tell you, but—"

The breath left my lungs. "He *knows*?"

Bryn looked taken aback. "Yes, of course, Rowan. They all know. I asked them to allow me to explain things in my own time."

No wonder James had protested when Bryn told him he was taking me to the Gate.

They'd let Bryn humiliate me for months.

No—*I* had let Bryn humiliate me, and I'd thanked him for doing it.

I covered my burning face with my hands, sucked in a ragged breath. "You've made such a fool out of me," I whispered behind them, wanting to carve each memory from my brain. "Did you get some kind of cheap thrill from having sex with me in the Gate?"

He jerked back like I'd hit him. "It was *never* about that, Rowan."

I pressed the heels of my hands to my eyes, fighting for control of *something*. "So you don't enjoy their *mating*?"

A muscle twitched in his elegant jaw. "I will not apologize for that."

Tears burned but didn't fall; I didn't let them. Bryn believed I was Nereida, and who—I thought bitterly—would know better?

I dragged the knapsack toward me, shoved the tea canister in, the sandwiches he'd made for us, the bar of chocolate. "Then what *do* you want to apologize for?" I demanded, and it was hard to confront him, to stand in the eye of a storm and know how small you were.

I didn't have golden eyes, couldn't anchor myself, wasn't Ruhaven's chosen one. Until this moment, I didn't even think I was Nereida. "Because, Bryn? You'd better think of something."

He paced the clearing—nervous, if I didn't know better—rustling dead leaves under the weight of his cane. "Rowan, I thought it would be easier if I kept my identity from you. I thought it would give us a chance to know each other without the complication of Ruhaven."

I wouldn't break down, not again, not like I'd done with Colm. I slapped a frozen leaf and faced Bryn. All the times I'd lain with Sahn circled in my mind like crows over carrion. "You think you've made it easier by humiliating me?"

Bryn ducked the swinging lantern, the only light between the bent oak trees. "That was never my intention," he said carefully as we circled the altar of blankets and candles. "I had lived in Ruhaven for so long myself, and you were so very new. I could hardly place my years of burden on you as well. Could not confess my own desires to someone who despised the Gate."

"You forced me into it!" Forced me to make that bargain. "You manipulated me from the beginning." Had *any* of it been because he honestly believed I'd find answers for Willow in the Gate? Or had it been for *him*? So that he could play with...with whatever I was.

The last bit of color started to leech from his face. "I—Rowan, I was desperate. And then, when you met me at last, you *feared* O'Sahnazekiel."

"So this is my fault?" Unbelievable.

"No, of course not, but I..." He rubbed the back of his neck, looked almost embarrassed if I didn't know better. "I admit I did not anticipate this reaction."

My breath huffed to curdled smoke as I gaped at him.

So Bryn thought I'd be *happy* to hear he was Sahn, happy that the man I was about to go on a date with had been secretly lying to me for months, had been sleeping with me in Ruhaven, had been mocking me with it?

My fingernails dug into my palm. "You thought I'd be happy to know you've witnessed every intimacy I've shared with Sahn? That I'd be happy to find out I've had zero privacy? You offered to take me to the Gate, to anchor me because you wouldn't see. But all this time, you've—you haven't just seen, you've been living it with me!"

Bastard.

Disgusted, I hefted the knapsack and spun on my heel.

I'd taken only two steps before Bryn snagged it and forced me around. But it wasn't anger that hollowed his eyes and shook the hand he curled on my shoulder. It was fear.

I tilted my head back, met the shadows flickering across his face in the candlelight. If I felt sympathy for a man who'd once lost himself in Ruhaven, who'd been exiled from Naruka, who'd waited for Nereida, I pushed it aside.

His voice was rough, urgent. "Rowan, I thought you would understand. That day in the kitchen, you understood what James had been through with Essie. Why will you not afford me the same understanding?"

I had to resist breathing him in, the scent of him, the overwhelming vulnerability he so rarely showed.

All I could think of was the sacrifice he'd nearly made. For Nereida. For Willow.

I lifted my chin. "You want to talk about James? Let me tell you something about James—he'd *never* have done what you did."

Bryn flinched, and I had to shove down every instinct that screamed at me to reach for him, to take it back.

"You lied, Bryn. You lied to me from the beginning. This wasn't for my benefit, but for *yours*. Because for one second, you might not have control over Nereida."

He shook his head disbelievingly. "No, Rowan, it was for *us*. Why do you always believe the worst of me?"

I stabbed my finger at him. "You don't get to turn this around now. You wanted another version of Nereida and instead you got this one. So you tried to manipulate the situation. That's why you say '*my* Rowan,' isn't it? You think Nereida belongs to *you*." My voice wavered. "Well she *doesn't*. She's supposed to belong to me."

Couldn't he understand what it did to me to have him believe there might be a possibility it was my birth in the *Ledger*? To have Bryn stand in the library and tell me he believed Nereida was *me*? To be such a coward that his opinion alone was enough to put aside my doubts, however briefly? Only to learn I was just the closest thing left to Nereida after Willow died. That it'd been *her* meant for him. *Her* he'd tried to die for.

"I know that," he said softly. "'*My Rowan*' is what O'Sahnazekiel calls Nereida. *Finita Nereida*. My Nereida."

Fuck.

The tears I swore I wouldn't shed burned my cheeks, salted my lips. All the memories between Sahn and I were a lie—Sahn's bark of laughter under the indigo skies, the time the flying lizard had nestled in his hair, the mud he'd accidentally landed in, soaking us both and staining his wings.

I'd thought I'd known him. I thought he'd been *mine*. But he was as much mine as I was Nereida.

"You've stolen Sahn from me." But what right did I have to complain when I'd stolen Nereida from Willow?

Confusion tightened Bryn's forehead as I backed away. "Rowan, I *am* Sahn. I do not understand you."

He'd made all the decisions for us. Decided what I needed to know and when he'd tell me—why? Was I just the stupid repair woman? Not a sophisticated art history major who took people out to piano bars, not well traveled with five spoken languages or however many he knew. I didn't dress like him, didn't iron my jeans or layer my shirts or—

An itchy suspicion slithered between my shoulder blades.

I stared at his cashmere sweater, the color of pale oatmeal in the dim woods. In all the days he'd spent at Naruka, he'd never once worn a T-shirt. Even when the sun peeked out, and every Irish man, woman, and child would lie in Capolinn's park to soak up the heat, he was always fully dressed. He never even rolled up his sleeves, not when he was milking Simona, not when he cooked or washed dishes, not when he chopped firewood, never. Not because he was shy or conservative as I'd first thought, and not because he was cold—the man was from Norway, so Naruka wouldn't bother him—but because he was hiding something.

The evidence had been staring me in the face when I brought him tea that day in his room. A map to El Dorado, he'd joked.

I met Bryn's wary eyes. "Take off your shirt," I ordered.

Annoyance creased the corners of his mouth. Oh, he didn't like that, didn't like it at all. Too bad—I'd take control of something between us, starting now.

Crossing my arms, I spread my legs in a stance Tye would have approved of. "Now, Bryn."

His look narrowed in warning. "I have told you the truth, Rowan. Why do you persist?"

I whipped out a hand and fisted his sweater so hard, his lips popped open in surprise. He'd been waiting for Nereida, he said.

Well, I'd give him Nereida.

"*Persist*? You haven't seen *persist* yet. Now, either you take this off, or I'll rip it off," I warned, my voice like mulled ice. "Pick one."

He curled his fingers around my fist. "You have made your point, Rowan. I—"

"I don't think so." I tightened my grip, stretching up on my tiptoes so my mouth was a painful few inches away from his. "And don't think you've got any moral high ground after your stunt in the Gate. Maybe you got used to violating my memories with Nereida, but you had no right to see me naked."

Our breath fogged between us in the crisp glade.

But his face stayed carefully blank. "Rowan, it was far past the hour mark. I could not wait any longer for you to respond to my anchor's call. If I had not lifted you out of that room, you would still be in the Gate. You know that it was not me who rendered you naked in the place between worlds."

Naked. The memory of it still burned in my gut.

"No, but you did… *something*. You didn't need to touch me like that."

His blue eyes flickered before warming to liquid honey. God, he wasn't actually... "Don't even *think* of showing me that gold, Bryn."

A muscle twitched in his jaw. "It is hardly within my control. But as I explained, you were not answering my call. I needed you relaxed, calm, so that I could lift you from the Gate. I did not have the strength to do so otherwise."

Because he'd had to rescue me from Colm.

"And *that* was the only way?" I challenged, though it grated to know how transparent I was. "To touch me? I didn't know it was *you*, Bryn."

Some of the tightness left his face, and his bottom lip shined with the mist creeping in. "It was not my intention to offend you."

He probably thought it was just another form of flattery, or maybe he'd rolled naked with Nereida for so long that there was no difference between her and me.

I yanked on his sweater. "I said take this off. Or do you want me to ruin your thousand-dollar shirt?"

With one hand, he carefully loosened my grip. "Very well, Rowan. If this is how you wish to begin things with us." His cane thumped to the earth.

"Us?" I nearly gaped. The actual nerve of him. "There will be no us, Bryn. Take off your shirt. Off!"

The look he threw me could have curdled milk, but he shed the wool sweater and gripped the bottom of his shirt beneath, gathering the layers in a white-knuckled fist. They shook violently, and for a moment, I wondered if I'd embarrassed him. Then I remembered I didn't care.

I held my breath as he peeled up his sweater.

Muscled lines crisscrossed and disappeared under the band of his jeans. The brewing storm licked skin paler than moonlight, carved from the same marble as his face. Delicate amber hair trailed a path up a lean torso, taut and firm with abs he shouldn't have. Goosebumps prickled his skin as the moon took ownership of the skies.

My pulse became a swarm of bees in my ear.

He lifted the sweater over his head, barely disturbing his hair, before he slid the cashmere off his arms and squeezed the shirt at his side, tendons straining.

With his skin exposed, he'd laid bare what I'd suspected.

The tattoos were not bronze, as O'Sahnazekiel's were, not engraved metal poured into a cast, but they were the same gears that intimately mapped the Azekiel. Thorns twisted through the cogs. Roses bloomed in dark ink.

A dream brought alive. And another lie.

"Why?" I asked weakly. *Why carve yourself with the image of Sahn* after *you were exiled?*

Winter heat rippled off him. "To remind me."

I couldn't stop myself from looking, from admiring the markings spiraling up his forearm, over his left shoulder and pec, drifting down his abs and a corded hip, where they disappeared under his pants and—

I jerked my gaze up when he shifted.

Smoked gold irises stared back. "Will that suffice, Rowan, or do you wish to see the rest?"

It was a challenge. And a threat.

But I didn't look away as I closed the distance between us, keeping my eyes on his until I stood a foot away. Until I could see the trail of delicate hair down the center of his chest and his nipples pebbled with cold.

He sucked in a breath when I trailed my fingertips over the tattooed vines on his bicep, followed every swirling gear and rose I'd mapped with my tongue on Sahn. I didn't even need to look.

I skimmed his pec until my fingernail scraped the gear framing his nipple.

"Rowan," Bryn growled, his low voice turning my knees to jelly. "What is it you want?"

I wanted to hear him say my name like that many, many times. So I thumbed his nipple, watching his irises shoot gold with pleasure at each tug.

And swiped his sweater.

Surprise flickered the gold into blue.

"What do I want, Bryn?" I repeated as my blood hummed for him. "I want to not be made a fool of." I stuffed the sweater in my backpack. "You can wear all your lies if you're cold. I'll meet you at Naruka."

He didn't reach for me as I spun around and left him half-naked at the Gate.

CHAPTER 35

About Today

Bryn was Sahn.

The three words hammered at the memories I tried to box up on my hike back to Naruka.

Three weeks ago, when he and I had visited Ruhaven together, I'd swam naked with Sahn in a milk lake. Had made love on its lavender sand shore. Watched Sahn's eyes burn into a golden flame when he slid inside Nereida.

Bryn had not only seen that, he'd *lived* it. Lived it all while lying next to me on the damp soil under the swaying lantern and autumn birds.

Yet he'd felt every ounce of pleasure Sahn had given me, knew exactly how much I enjoyed it. All while I'd pretended nothing had happened.

He said he'd been *waiting* for me. But it hadn't been me he wanted at all—it'd been Nereida. Every look and touch between us had been meant for a silver-haired female in Ruhaven.

In the kitchen, I clenched the scalding mug of tea James had fixed for me.

Was I just some physical body Bryn could pretend with? Then he didn't have to break his *rules*.

Planting my elbows on the table, I tried to concentrate on the car manual I'd fished out to settle me. I'd thought about going upstairs, huddling in my room while I burned off the worst of my fears, but this was the only room with the stove on—and maybe I wanted to wait until Bryn returned safely. *I shouldn't have left him up there alone.*

The storm pounding the window thundered in agreement.

I couldn't even be happy that Tye was back. He'd gotten in while Bryn was lying to me at the Gate and greeted my sudden return with a bottle of nice French wine I didn't know L'Ardoise had and a smile that had wilted at my expression.

But Tye, James, Kazie—they'd all lied too. I swore I wouldn't be softened, not even by the barley stew James left out for me on the stove.

I turned my glare on Tye.

He rested against the counter, wearing a plaid shirt with what looked like stray bits of orange fur on the sleeve, and strumming a four-chord progression on a Rickenbacker guitar that drilled a hole in the center of my head. A hole I would have gladly thrown the guitar and Tye into.

James arched an eyebrow when my stare landed on him. He opened his mouth, drawing back a bow of questions, then snorted through his nose and returned to reading *Ruhaven in the 70s*.

Grumbling to myself, I flattened my manual and read the steps on how to replace spark plugs for the fifth time.

The low kitchen light swung in a tiny pendulum, flickering over the faded diagram. How would I disconnect a battery whose wires had rusted into it? I glanced at James. The answer wouldn't be in a book about the great seventies revolution of Ruhaven.

This was what I should focus on. This and Willow. I'd gotten sidetracked by Sahn, started to believe that for a moment, I might be meant for Ruhaven. Because Bryn had wanted me to be her, to be Nereida in Willow's place. Maybe I would—maybe I'd take her back from him, make her, make Nereida, my own again—just like Willow would have done.

And she'd be as pissed at him as I was.

Lightning flashed outside, blinding us for a heartbeat before the sky slurped it up again. Kazie let a whoop of excitement, then adjusted her telescope by the window. What could she even see in this weather?

Across the table, James lowered his book and sighed like an old dog. "Roe, ye didn't feckin' kill him, did ye?"

Now, there was an idea. Maybe Nereida would come to her senses and take care of that for me.

I licked my finger and flipped to page 203 on battery removal. "No."

Tye chewed on the guitar pick. "Darlin', ya know I'd help you bury him."

The idea mollified me slightly.

Thunder roared from the Atlantic, rippling over Naruka's dark-turquoise fields and smacking into the bay window. Bryn would be walking—limping—back in that storm. Without a shirt. *Tock*.

We were definitely not going to the islands anymore.

I felt Bryn long before I saw the candle flicker in the tack room, heard the soft thump of his cane up the concrete steps, or the jingle of the skeleton key in the lock.

Click.

The door creaked open, a frigid wind on its heels.

Tye let out a low whistle as Bryn ducked into the kitchen. His accusing stare landed on mine. I yanked my shoulders back, staring defiantly at him.

Are you quite pleased now? he growled in my mind.

I'd be pleased when he showed some actual regret. *Not even close.*

The rain had drenched his hair to a muddy brown and plastered it to his reddened neck. Fat drops dripped off his nose, brow, and chin. Soaked jeans clung to his thighs, and goosebumps covered a chest whipped raw by Naruka's thorny brambles. His shoulders shook with cold.

I still wanted to lick every dripping inch of him.

Thick, juicy waves of emotion rolled inside me—embarrassment, arousal, fear, humiliation, love. I wanted to thread my fingers through his blond hair and drag his lips to mine, then strip him naked and parade him through the streets of Capolinn so he'd know the humiliation I felt.

But Bryn's face was a portrait of self-restraint as he swiped his sweater from the clothesline.

James gawked, his glasses skittering down his thin nose. "Bryn? What the bloody hell did she do to ye?"

Not enough, not *nearly* enough.

I hid my face behind the manual and said, "Don't you mean *O'Sahnazekiel*?"

The kitchen went dead silent. Even the clock shut up. When Bryn limped to the woodstove, I could have measured the tension in the room with my voltage meter.

Tye slid off the counter and crossed his impressive arms. "Well, Stornoway, guess ya finally admitted you got a dick. Sure fooled me though."

Oh, he had a dick.

James shot out of his chair, palms slapping the Guinness placemat. "*Lads,*" he growled, conveying warning, exasperation, and amusement with one impressive syllable. But I wasn't going to forget he'd lied to me too.

"You told me he was *light,*" I accused James.

He fidgeted with the placement. "He is, it wasn't a lie. But he didn't want ye to know and I didn't feel comfortable pretending I didn't know him. Light is one of an Azekiel's forms. Which ye'd know if ye ever read that feckin' book I left ye."

So he'd *tried* to tell me. What had Bryn said before? That he outranked the others in Ruhaven—*that* was why they'd listened. I turned my glare on him, his tattooed back rippling as he dragged a towel through his hair. A gear ended at the curve of his lower back where the tops of his hips brushed his belt.

Tye planted a boot on the sheepskin bench, bent forward, resting his forearm on his thigh. He peered under his ball cap at the cause of my ire, but Bryn wasn't looking at anything but me now. Had there ever been anything between us, or had it just been a Nereida-shaped lie?

"Didn't your undercover operation go well, Stornoway?" Tye drawled. "Guess Roe's not too happy to find you've been bonein' her in the Gate and lyin' about it—and James says *I* don't know women."

Bryn shoved off the wall.

I slapped the manual shut. "*You* lied to me too," I said, raising my voice to Tye. He'd let Bryn sleep with me in the Gate for months, right under my clueless nose.

Kazie spun on the stool, watching the commotion with the horrified exhilaration of a car crash rubbernecker.

Tye squirreled a finger into his knee. "Now listen, I never wanted to keep that from ya, but it was Stornoway's call."

My voice dropped to a growl. "That's bullshit, Tye. Ruhaven rules don't tell you to lie to me."

He raised his eyebrows at James before dropping them on me again. "Well, that ain't for me to say. But damn, girl, there's a paintin' of you in the library. I never thought it'd take this long."

Me? He'd painted *me?* No. Not me—*Nereida*—and now I felt even dumber, if possible, and suddenly ridiculously jealous of a woman he shouldn't even know about.

Bryn clenched the towel in his fist, the top button of his pants undone when they'd simply given way to rain. *Stop looking there. Stop thinking about him.*

"There is much you do not see, Rowan," Bryn clipped out.

He had no right to look at me like that, not when he'd been manipulating me for months. There could have been something between us, but he'd ruined it because he was as selfish as human men.

Kazie piped up. "Don't worry, Roe, Bryn's a terrible painter. You're much prettier than that portrait."

Talk about not only missing the point, but driving right by it at ninety miles an hour. "It's not the prettiness I care about, Kaz." Then I turned on Bryn. "I care that he's been using me."

Bryn twisted the towel and tossed it on the stove. "Rowan, I will not talk to you about this here," he said, like I was a woman with bad manners arguing in front of the guests.

Well, he had no idea just how poorly I'd been raised. I wasn't going to take this from him, not from Tye, not from James. Whatever rank Bryn had in Ruhaven didn't entitle him to manipulate me here.

I stabbed my finger into the Ford's manual. "You've had months to talk about it. Instead, you made a *joke* out of me."

His chest heaved, muscles rippling under his frozen skin, reminding me just what he could turn into when pushed. I didn't care. Let him burst into light, into the Azekiel, and when he did, I'd show him what Nereida was made of.

James rose, a tea towel over his shoulder as he refilled the blackened kettle. "Listen, I know yer upset, Roe, but when Bryn asked us to say nothing, it made sense like." He shoved a glass whistle in the shape of a magpie into the end and clacked it on the stove. "And ye were with Tye."

What? "I was *not*."

Stuffing a cigarette between his lips, Tye shrugged off my annoyance. "Roe, darlin', I do so recall my hands full of you right here in that tack room."

I had a brief, exhilarating vision of whipping Tye with his own guitar strings. But as I rounded the table, a growl ripped from Bryn's throat.

Everyone looked at him. Cold fury rumbled under his skin, in his eyes.

So Bryn didn't like his Nereida body bag being with other men. It nearly made me want to run naked into Capolinn's fifteen pubs, including that one with the priests.

Bryn leveled his gaze at me. *Try it.*

Maybe I will. Maybe I'd bring them right back here and see what he made of Nereida's stunt double doing the— Wait.

He looked away.

"No, that's not—that's not why he was..." I trailed off. No, it was ridiculous. Ridiculous. He hadn't seen, hadn't heard, but had he—*felt* me? I swallowed, hard. "Why Bryn was sick after the night we went to the game?"

Tye's laugh was low, rough, and long. "I told ya he was obsessed with the Gate. Can't smell meat, can't eat meat, can't stomach his reincarnated girlfriend enjoyin' my very skilled hands, if I do say so."

When he wiggled his fingers, Bryn looked ready to rip them off.

James elbowed between everyone. "Tye, ye feckin' stop that now. And Roe," he waved his hands as if I were Tye's prize thoroughbred preparing to bolt, "do ye forget how terrified ye were? Ye called O'Sahnazekiel beast man for a month. Sure, it wasn't going to be me who told ye it was this git here." James jerked his chin at Bryn. "He didn't want ye to know, and 'twas business between him and yerself like." He lifted a googly-eyed canister and withdrew a teabag.

"Why?" I pressed, curling my hand on the table. James had shown me the Gate, endured my barrage of questions, and even forgiven me for suspecting he killed and buried Ruhavens beneath those plaques. But when he could have saved me from this embarrassment, he'd said nothing.

James gave my shoulder a reassuring squeeze. "Ruhaven rules. Sure, it seemed ye had enough on yer plate anyway, what with the Tether breaking and yer research on the Inquitate. To be fair to ye, it was a lot for anyone to take in."

Tye coughed. "Seems ya took him *in* just fine though."

James groaned, Kazie chortled, and humiliation scorched a raw line from my head to my toes. It was a miracle the old floor didn't catch fire.

Crash.

Glass exploded a foot from Tye's head. Colored shards scattered on the floor in what was left of the kettle's whistle.

Kazie covered her ears as Tye gritted out, "Take a fuckin' joke, Stornoway."

I spun around. Bryn's eyes flashed, showing a glimmer of the man I'd seen after An Béal Bocht. Not a monster at all—*Sahn*. Because it was the Azekiel's protection that had saved me after the bar. *That* was Bryn's mark. Protection.

He yanked a sweater over his flushed skin. "You push too far, Tye."

"You wanna go a round again, Stornoway?" Tye dusted porcelain flakes off his sleeve. "Why don't ya stop chuckin' pretty birds at me and I'll show ya just how far I can push."

At that point, I'd be happy if they both got a few good shots in, but James jumped between them, interrupting my fantasy as his waving hands knocked into the kitchen fixture. Bryn ducked the light's swinging loop.

"Must be a bitch to be so useless," Tye taunted Bryn over James's shoulder. "Gotta throw Christmas ornaments instead of actually defendin' your Gate girlfriend, and when you're some ugly beast in Ruhaven too."

I glanced at Bryn, then at his crippled leg shaking from the walk I'd made him do in the storm alone. When he escaped into Ruhaven, he'd experience Sahn running, swimming, and flying—among other things. Living like Bryn could never do here.

Do not look at me like that.

I jerked my gaze to his just as Tye advanced and James shouted, "Lads. Lads. *Lads!*" The kettle enunciated each word with a howl of steam. "Ye've already destroyed me mum's favorite whistle, I'll not have ye ruin the place like last time."

Kazie skidded into the mix, a ballerina in a jungle. "Boys, boys. I can fix this." She twirled her finger in the air before bringing it down on Tye's chest. "You're an asshole," she declared with some affection. "And Bryn, you probably shouldn't have made us lie to Roe for months." At least somebody had my back, even if it was a tiny woman in a leprechaun suit. "And Roe?"

What, me? Why was I part of *his* lies?

Her cobalt-lined eyes softened. "Bryn's been waiting for you for years. And I mean *years*. It messed with him, really bad. And now you're here, and yeah, okay, maybe he didn't go about it right, but cut the guy some slack."

I would only if I could cut it from Tye's guitar string.

Bryn drew himself in like a textbook snapped shut. So I'd get no answers as usual. He'd tell me what he wanted me to know and when he wanted me to know it.

He deliberately stepped away from Tye, who shot him a suggestion behind James's back. "James, Kazie, we have other things to discuss besides our private business," Bryn said in a way that made me want to walk up and shake him. "You should be aware we are in Drachaut now. O'Sahnazekiel and Nereida were ambushed—Kazmira, Essie, and Jamellian too. I met you outside the cavern before finding Rowan."

Bryn's quiet words defused the atmosphere like a plug yanked from the wall.

"Essie—is she alright?" James asked immediately.

"She is fine."

"Drachaut attacked us?" Kazie clarified.

"Just one. Rowan's Tether."

James nodded. "I was wondering when we'd meet him."

I tuned him out. Tuned them all out.

That beast was my *Tether*?

But it wasn't...that wasn't me, wasn't *Willow*. It was just some demon with blue scales. It meant nothing. *He* meant nothing. I'd felt no recognition.

"—I suppose they'll need to figure out why this Drachaut severed its Tether, but right now, I've got to go see for meself, make sure Essie's alright. Who can anchor me?"

Tye fluffed his ball cap over brown locks. "I'll anchor. Are ya gonna be okay, Roe?"

"What?"

Tye shot a look at Bryn, whose frozen skin was still getting its color back.

"Fine. I'm fine, go. The Tether doesn't have anything to do with me." Never did.

Tye frowned after me, but left quietly once James and Kazie had bundled into coats.

When the door closed behind them, Bryn released a long breath. "We need to talk."

"I agree."

He looked taken aback as I strode past the woodstove, the heat licking up my calves. I fisted the kettle, poured hot water into the teapot James had readied but hadn't used. Turned. "I want you to tell me something."

He hesitated, then took a shaky step to the bench, sat. "Anything, Rowan."

I let the warmth of the tea seep through my fingers. "When I came to you in Oslo and asked you about Willow, I hadn't planned to come back to Naruka. I was going to get answers and leave. But you swore she'd been a victim of the Inquitate."

"Yes."

I took a breath. "You told me then, that you believed the answers to why the Inquitate attacked us were in the Gate. That the only way for me to find out why Willow was targeted was to relive the memories, to find out what we'd done that had caused this."

"Yes, that is what I said."

I squeezed the teacup so hard that black liquid spilled over my fingers, trickled down my wrist. "Did you say that because you believed it, or because you wanted Nereida?"

The kitchen clock ticked rapidly before puttering out.

Bryn sucked in his cheeks. "I did not believe the answers to the Inquitate would be found in the Gate, though Kazie and James did. I believed the reason we were attacked was due to something we had done here. You proved me incorrect when you discovered the triplet connection."

I let the words soak into my bones, nestle there, and get comfortable, because I'd need to remember this when just looking at him threatened my resolve.

"Bryn?"

"Yes, Rowan?"

THE MINOR FALL

"James was right to kick you out."

CHAPTER 36

Mid Air

A week later, the Gate in Naruka sucked me back home, tearing me away from Sahn's body, his butter-soft wings, and his rough, low moans.

But I couldn't even enjoy him. Just the *thought* of knowing it was Bryn biting me, hearing me, driving himself into what was *my* memory and *never* his…

He'd stolen more than Sahn; he'd stolen Nereida too.

James patted my shoulder. "There ye are, Roe, yer back now," he murmured, setting a mug of tea on the blanket.

I murmured a thanks, then turned to watch the man rousing by my side. Color blossomed on cheekbones formed in a mountain slide. *He was as aroused as I was.* How had Bryn hidden it this entire time?

His eyes fluttered open.

Lust boiled in his golden irises, a star collapsing in on itself. Worse, it punched molten desire in my gut. But that wasn't my fault—any attraction I felt was because of Nereida.

Then he blinked, and the star cooled to a white dwarf.

I shoved up so abruptly, I knocked over the tea. The quilt tangled in my boots as Kazie and Tye stirred.

Bryn coughed, rolled over to his side, and tugged the blanket up. *Don't look down, don't look down.*

A wise choice.

You son of a—

"Rowan, I refuse to apologize for a memory," he said steadily, and nothing in the smooth tone would have anyone believing he'd just woken from plowing himself into Nereida. At least James had anchored him before he could finish.

"What about lying? Do you want to apologize for that?" I *wished* it was just the lying that burned my gut, that left me sleepless every night.

He leveled his stare at me. "I assumed my walking home half-naked in a hurricane was sufficient for you."

Ignoring me, he pushed to sitting as the wind ruffled the loose hairs around his brow. I'd trimmed his hair in the kitchen, joking about what Nereida looked like while Bryn pretended not to know. He hadn't guessed at drawing her eyes. He'd *known*.

"*Sufficient* would have been admitting who you were months ago."

As James woke Kazie, she tuned in to the show—for once more entertained by what was outside Ruhaven rather than in it.

"Rowan, now is not the time for this discussion," Bryn chastised me. I'd cared for him, and he didn't even have the decency to grovel.

"Not the time?" I accidentally kicked the mug of tea, sending it pinwheeling into his boots. I winced when it soaked his pant leg to a dark brown. "How about four months ago when we met in Oslo? Or when you so *generously* offered to anchor me?"

Bryn's nostrils flared in his perfect, beautiful nose, and it gave me a perverse delight to know each word of mine might finally hammer through his glass shield. "I was witnessing it regardless," he stated.

How dare *you.* I summoned all my anger and funneled it at him. *Are you getting my loose inclinations now?*

Yes, I believe I am.

James scrubbed at his eyebrows, reducing them to shaved ferrets before throwing up a prayer to the skies. Bryn had better hope they were listening because I was warming to the idea of Tye's body-burying services.

"For feck's sake, yer both driving me bloody mad," James yelled. "I'll put ye in a feckin' room and lock the door so I will."

Tye rose, hefted his backpack, and put a restraining hand on my shoulder. "C'mon, Roe, let's walk on back to Naruka. Stornoway here's just pinin' because he knows the only piece of ya he'll get is in a dream."

The comment immediately lifted my spirits.

Bryn heaved himself off the ground, annoyance sharpening the planes of his face. "Rowan, let us talk in Naruka."

Talking wouldn't undo his mistake. Just like talking hadn't brought Willow back. I was all out of talking.

"Tye, I swear I can't do it anymore," I said when we were out of earshot. "Just knowing it's him while I'm in there, knowing he can feel…" I swiped at air. "I can't."

Tye grunted, navigating the swampy path feet ahead. I hopped from stone to stone behind him, so distracted that I missed and got an ankle-full of mud.

"I think it'll be good for ya to take a break," Tye agreed. "I always thought ya were in too much, so if this is what it takes to get a bit of perspective, it's a good thing."

I stabbed my hands into my pockets when we'd cleared the worst of the puddle. "You could have told me."

"We've been over this, Roe. You ain't gonna make me explain it again?"

"Rules," I muttered under my breath, and tugged my jacket closed.

"That's right. Now I don't make 'em, but I do set store by 'em. Didn't agree with 'em either, but there ya go." His Guinness-brown hair bounced under his ball cap, then he flicked a grin at me. "Look, can't say I'd be in the Gate either if I was bouncin' on Stornoway."

I stepped beside him when the path widened. "I think I'm just going to focus on the Inquitate connection here. We're in Drachaut now, so maybe we picked up something."

"Drachaut ain't a disease," he said, annoyed.

"Well, I'm running out of ideas for why these triplets matter. And I'm worried I won't know until we watch ourselves make the crossing, see why we went over together."

Tye started to answer, stopped when the bird calls rose to a raucous, then resumed, "Ya won't actually get to watch the crossin', so unless someone else is there watchin' for you…"

"Like Jamellian?" I asked. "If James is there, he can tell me what happened."

Tye pulled out a smoke, offered it. "No?" He stuck it between his lips. "Ya aren't thinkin' 'bout makin' this Fall?"

I'd given it about as much thought as my own death. "Well, maybe if I hear the call on my deathbed…"

"It ain't gonna work like that. You're gonna hear it well before."

"How soon? How do you know?"

"'Cause I do," he stated, cutting off all conversation. "Look, Roe, I worry 'bout Stornoway tryin' to influence you on this."

I jumped another puddle. "Why?"

Tye hung his head. "Goddamn, Roe, you don't seem to have a clue the kinda mess you're walkin' into. I warned ya before that Stornoway ain't right, why we exiled him. That man's been living with Nereida for years in the Gate, pinin' over a dead memory. It messes ya up. You start thinkin' it's real."

"That's why Bryn asked me out, isn't it? For Nereida." I waited for Tye to deny it, to tell me no, there was something about me Bryn did like.

But Tye only let out a long sigh.

Of course there wasn't. Because we weren't living in Ruhaven, we were here where things like being a college dropout mattered and doctorates were important. The simple fact was that if Bryn and I had passed each other in L'Ardoise, he'd think I was as worthless as the rest.

"I'm sorry, Roe," Tye said quietly.

I pinched my nose, willed back the emotion I had no right to feel. I'd cry for Willow—*that* I'd earned—but I wouldn't cry for this.

"This whole business ain't healthy, if ya ask me," Tye continued. "Be better off if none of 'em had anyone they wanted to find in the Gate. Some days, I worry we ain't just better off forgettin' about all of this."

"Do you have someone in Ruhaven?" I asked.

His dimple flashed. "A girlfriend? Thank sweet baby Jesus I do not. I got enough women in my life to drive me crazy. Don't need to be seeing them in Ruhaven too."

Did he? I'd never seen anyone come by, but maybe that was where he went on weekends sometimes.

"But I bet Stornoway wouldn't mind a real woman to lose himself in after years of delusions, huh?"

Well, he wasn't going to get her.

"**R**oe, me love, it's been weeks like. Can ye tell me just how long ye plan on punishing Bryn?" James begged.

I pivoted on the ladder where I stood insulating the lounge windows. "Until his tattoos wilt off?"

James let out an aggrieved sigh. "Fine, so, just fine. Yer not visiting the Gate, Bryn's in a foul mood, Tye's never been happier, Kazie's obsessed with Drachaut, and then ye've poor me in the middle of it all! Have ye no pity, Roe?" He clasped his hands together.

"None."

"Ah, for the love of—"

"I'm sorry Bryn lied, James. I'm sorry he manipulated me in the worst way. And I'm sorry you're in the middle of that. But staying out of the Gate has been good for me, I think. I discovered that each of the Ruhavens who experienced broken Tethers all travelled to Drachaut afterwards, and the memories ended shortly after. None of them made the Fall, though." *Or were prevented from it.* "And Levi wrote about broken Tethers, but I don't think he experienced it himself."

James sipped his tea in loud intervals. "Well, I suppose that's something like. Levi…what the devil is with that lad? Leaving me some bogus address, and after I drag him here—"

"But it wasn't you, it was Carmen who brought him, right?"

He toasted me. "That's right, yeah, still all the same. I bloody helped him get settled, had his picture taken. I still put it up, so I did, even though he wanted nothing of Ruhaven."

I paused mid-spray of the insulation foam. "Where?"

James twisted around, shielding his eyes as he looked upstairs. "Outside Kazie's room, I think." He frowned into his tea. "Ye sure ye won't talk to Bryn?"

No, I was apparently just that petty. "Enjoy the market, James."

He grumbled something that sounded a lot like "*Yer worse than me in-laws,*" before calling after Kazie.

I continued spraying foam, watching out the window until James, Kaz, and Tye climbed into the seesawing Ford. As it burped out the lane, it passed Bryn, who was engrossed in demolishing a canvas.

However much I'd been avoiding the Gate, Bryn made up for it by going in double.

Was it worse that he was living the memory with me—or *without* me? Like every minute he was in there enjoying Nereida was another betrayal.

It was time to get past it, time to put whatever I'd felt for him aside and focus on Willow, fixing Naruka, and the Inquitate. With this in mind, I hummed determinedly along to the cassette James had left playing while I sprayed the window. A few lines of foam around these windows should stop the gusts from sneaking through, and stop James from having to wear half his wardrobe to stay warm.

Singing to myself, I hiked one foot up the next rung, reaching with the spray can for the top trim of the—

"I believe I have never heard quite such an interesting version of 'Dancing Queen'."

I jumped at the sound of *his* voice and sprayed a foam line straight down the windowpane.

Bryn grabbed my calf as I teetered half off the ladder. How had he gotten inside so fast? When I gathered my footing again, I eyed him warily.

He'd tied his leather apron—skinned from the finest Norwegian reindeer—in a snug knot around his waist, fastened the neck strap under his collar, and rolled the sleeves of his old shirt past his elbows. A smear of white paint nearly disappeared against his tattooed forearm.

Bryn smiled hesitantly up at me. "While Kazie, James, and Tye are in town, I was instructed to remain on duty for any alarm clock heists."

I tugged my foot away. "Don't worry, I'm not going back to the Gate."

Bryn sucked patience through two perfect nostrils. "Rowan, I misunderstood the extent of your embarrassment in this regard. I told you I do not express myself well." And yet he had five languages to do it in. "I have apologized—*profusely*—for my handling of this situation. Still, I do not understand why you persist in your anger. You *know* what Nereida is to me."

Yeah—a dream that wasn't me. "I understand exactly what she is to you, which is why you don't need me."

When I lifted the spray can to the window again, he grabbed my arm, stopped me. "Rowan, you cannot avoid the Gate forever."

I tugged my wrist away. "You're going in enough for both us."

He scanned my face. "Does it upset you?"

Yes. "No." It was like he was cheating on me *with* me.

"I shall stop if you prefer."

Annoyed with myself, I shook the can vigorously, the plastic pea ball going *clank-clank-clank*. "No. One of us should be watching in case the Inquitate appear again."

Bryn took a step closer, his shadow blocking out the light of the chandeliers. "Then you are truly resolute in your determination to avoid both myself and the Gate?"

I pressed my hands to his chest, then dropped them when I felt the connection *zing* up my wrists. "Don't ask me to return. You don't need me, and I can't stomach it anymore."

"You cannot stomach *me*, you mean."

I rubbed the space between my brows. "No, Bryn, I can't stomach what *I'm* not."

Bryn's fingers circled my wrists, capturing them. "What is it you believe you are not? I told you the truth at the Gate, that I have waited for *you*. For you, my Rowan."

Maybe some part of him believed that, believed that he'd have wanted an electrician in L'Ardoise, but I knew the truth—I was nothing but a warm body to house a dead dream.

"If I could fix this," he said softly, "I would. If I could return and tell you earlier, I would."

If only it was the lie that kept me up at night. But he'd used me, used my sister, to chase his own desires, even if the Inquitate had been in the Gate in the end, *he* hadn't believed it.

I pulled away, shutting my toolbox with a snap. "Sometimes, there's no fixing things. Enjoy the Gate, enjoy Nereida, just do it without me."

"I wish to—"

"I can't *do* this anymore, Bryn," I said, raising my voice. "Can't be what I'm not. Can't pretend for you. Go paint a flower or something."

My boots cracking on the rungs were the only sound in the lounge beside Bryn's unsteady breathing.

Then he said, very softly, "Have you no sympathy at all, Rowan? No sympathy for a man who lost himself in the Gate for you? Who spent years loving a woman he believed may only ever exist in a dream? Then, when he finds her at last, he is crippled by the Inquitate. And now, is too weak, too crippled, to do anything while she is insulted and belittled because of his mistake. Am I truly so loathsome to you?"

The air hummed in silence as his words hit their mark—right in my gut, where he'd intended.

No, no, he wasn't loathsome. He should be, I should feel that, but I couldn't. Even if all of it had been some twisted lie, one I'd perpetrated as much as he had.

But when I turned to apologize, Bryn was gone; I hadn't even heard his cane leave.

A strange feeling settled over me, one I couldn't shake long after I'd finished sealing the window and the rest in the lounge.

With Bryn still on my mind, I packed up my tools in a house that had gone quiet, and glanced at my watch. 2:47. James would be another hour still, enough time to hunt for the portrait before I pulled up the linoleum in the kitchen.

With my toolbox in hand, I climbed the creaky steps, carefully scanning the framed pictures, reading each name tag before moving to the next. There were so many. How did James keep track? Probably the same way he knew where every journal, book, and discography on Ruhaven was—obsession.

I smiled to myself, working my way through the hundreds of portraits ranging from tiny, palm-sized displays to a massive painting. Maybe I should just wait for James to come back.

Thinking this, I glanced at my watch again, but found it frozen on the same time as last. It had been Willow's once, long enough ago I'd replaced the batteries more often than made sense. But with no shortage of clocks, I dropped my wrist and checked the cuckoo clock by a photo of a pigtailed Ruhaven.

2:47.

I frowned at the time, at the minute hand frozen in the same position at my wrist.

I tapped the glass, then rechecked both times, waited, but the clock remained frozen at 2:47.

A little tingle started at the base of my neck as I turned to glance at the clock behind me.

2:47.

The house froze in a sticky, eerie silence, missing the everyday drone of its clocks.

My heart thumped twice, hard. Why would they be dead? What could possibly make them stop now? Was this another gift of Bryn's? Some manifestation of his Mark he hadn't told me about?

Or was it another's?

I yanked a bird-shaped clock off the wall and swapped its batteries for fresh ones in my toolbox, but the clock remained dead, unmoving.

I backed away slowly, my jacket catching a hard-edged frame as I bumped into the wall behind me.

What did it mean? I wished for James, for Bryn, for my sister who would have been shouting a hundred possibilities at me.

Pinching my lips between my fingers, I shook my head at the silent wall, the house that had gone so still, not even a curtain swayed.

Because time had stopped? That sounded ridiculous. Maybe one of our Marks was battery control, for all I knew, but the idea made a weak laugh hiccup from my throat. *Battery control.*

Energy, though, that was something, wasn't it? Souls were energy, energy was conserved, souls were reborn.

In a closed system, just like a circuit, you couldn't have any energy that didn't already exist. Everything in a circuit—resistors, lightbulbs—all consumed the sum of the energy flowing through. So how did the Inquitate come over at all?

I stepped towards the wall of clocks and picture frames. Was time a form of energy? In a way, yeah. A form of wave energy that could be manipulated like any other. By who? Was it one of our Marks? But which... *oh.*

I dropped my toolbox, and the sound shuddered through the hall, as if Naruka herself had flinched.

It wasn't a manipulation of energy, but an *imbalance.*

Slowly, my lips trembling, I glanced down the stairs and out the window now sealed with foam.

But only a dark circle of trampled grass remained where Bryn's easel had been.

CHAPTER 37

Samhradh Samhradh

I raced through the woods.

Fat raindrops slapped my cheeks, branches whipped my palms, nettles stung my ankles. The river, bursting from the storm, howled a bone-chilling song as it carved a swarthy path through the grove. Thick fog oozed between the trees, making all but the nearest invisible, and those that I did see were only smears of gray against a boiled-egg canvas.

Bryn was missing.

He wasn't in the woodshed, the gate lodge, or the vegetable garden where I'd once tricked him into painting. He wasn't in the tack room, his own room, or the mud room.

Naruka had tried to warn me—those clocks had stopped twenty minutes ago. But I'd been too lost in my head, and now my own heart was shouting at me.

Had he gone to the Gate? Fallen on the way? Seen an illusion of the Inquitate? And because I refused to believe the latter, I charged up the mountain path.

It was hard to run with my thoughts shouting at me, reminding me of my last words to him. So I allowed them one brief replay of the man who'd listened to my stories of Willow, who'd sketched me so tenderly my skin tingled, who'd been by my side from the moment he arrived from Oslo, who'd taught me how to live in the Gate.

Then I pushed it all down, deep into the monster that nestled in my gut for it to spit back at me later.

I needed to focus and find him—and he was probably fine. The clocks might not mean anything, but just the *thought*, just the *idea* that he might—might— and with one leg, he couldn't—

No, stop, focus.

The path to the Gate was barely visible in the rolling fog, yet it had become so well-worn over the last months that not a leaf dared inch across.

When I got to the bridge, I dove across the rotted boards, ignored the clacking under my feet, ignored the bitter taste in the back of my throat and the water sloshing up and over the sides.

Then I was out the other end, shoes soaked and my legs already tiring. I pushed up the slippery hill, up to the Gate, where I was sure Bryn would be. The Gate was his life, and I'd insulted him, swore at him, told him to leave. Where else would he go?

Am I truly so loathsome to you?

No. God, no. Never.

Nettles whipped my ankles as I struggled up the steep incline, slipped, and tumbled back a few feet before regaining my footing. I hadn't changed into boots before I careened out of Naruka and now I was losing time.

I have waited years for you.

Couldn't I have been more understanding? I knew what James had gone through, how much he'd hoped I'd be Essie, but I couldn't forgive Bryn?

Scaling the first bend, I lunged from rock to rock without slowing, using the branches worn by centuries of Ruhavens to propel myself up. My lungs strained for breath, the tightness unbearable with the adrenaline petering out.

Yet the forest was eerily quiet.

The chirping blackbirds and starlings and magpies and robins were so familiar, I hardly noticed the silence before. But now, only the slurping river echoed behind me. That, and the patter of rain on thick leaves, the wind creaking the branches before the next storm hit.

Higher up, the path widened, letting in the bone-white light of the sky so that what should be green twinkled a bleached blue.

Bryn had stopped Colm for me. Maybe he'd done it for Nereida, but I owed him better than this. He'd met his own nightmare while trying to find me in L'Ardoise, then been crippled for it.

Were they here again now? Was that what the clocks meant? Or was I losing my goddamn mind in a reckless panic?

As my thighs shook with exhaustion, I stopped dead. And all the fear, all the anxiety, all the worry dissolved as I spotted his easel perched on the jutting edge of a rock.

I breathed in, out. Painting. He'd gone painting, that was all. Just as I'd told him to, up in the woods where there were flowers or whatever I'd stupidly shouted at him.

Dizzying relief had my voice trembling when I called out, "Bryn? *Bryn?*"

One eye on his easel, I started up the rocks, slower this time, and allowed myself one belly breath before I rounded toward the spot where his easel sat. *He was fine. He was fine.* I drew back curtains of vines and thorny bushes with shriveled black berries that hadn't been picked in time by the birds.

The trees grew sparse as I approached the edge, the river thundering ever louder below.

Then I burst through at last, into the open air and the mountains that rolled into the sea and disappeared in a blue fog.

On the edge of the rock sat Bryn's easel, wood-framed, with three tripod legs extended and a metal toolbox for paints. The tray was pulled out and the faint puddles on the palette told me he'd been vigorously mixing color.

But Bryn wasn't here.

Maybe he was taking a break, eating a sandwich he'd packed or searching for another location to paint. The rain-drenched bluebell on the easel *did* look finished, and might have been his best work yet if it weren't for the drops of rain smearing it.

I called his name as I approached. My boots squelched in the tall grass, unflattened by a painter's boots, as if he'd only set up his station moments before wandering off. Paint tubes floated in an inch of water, with the cadmium red leaking a bloody stream down the palette.

I curled my fingers around the easel, half for support, half to peer around it and over the ledge.

The cliff descended into boulders covered in yellow moss and sprouting twisted trees from between them. Couch grass flickered in the heavy winds that lifted the back leg of the easel an inch off the ground. Far below, the river swam in a thundering mess.

I peeled away my shaking fingers and wiped the smeared paint on my jeans.

There were no flowers here, bluebells or otherwise.

My chest tightened as I stared at the painting, at the clever brushwork that had rendered a flower almost nauseatingly beautiful.

Where was the burn of paint thinner? Usually, I could smell the turpentine, but now there was nothing. Maybe the rain had washed away the scent.

I wiped a hand over my trembling throat. "Bryn?" I croaked.

The woods remained silent but for the river below me and my furiously beating heart.

I had to move, had to make a choice. Up to the Gate? Or back to Naruka? Even after what I'd said, would he have left me at Naruka, gone to the Gate alone?

Down. I'd go down.

I started to turn, to retrace my steps through the now-flattened grass, when something golden caught my eye.

My muscles seized with a fresh jolt of adrenaline as I gripped the easel, peering over the edge again.

I squinted through the trees, seeing little except the burnished leaves fading in the blinds of fog, branches that twisted like a witch's gnarled fingers, the river a few meters below, the overgrown shoreline and—

Bryn.

Fear kicked me square in the stomach. I clenched the easel, then stumbled forward before I realized I'd never make it down this slope.

Backtracking, I flew through the woods and around the bend, hopping rocks to reach him.

It was easier going down, easier when I knew what waited for me at the bottom, on the twisted bank of the river.

I rounded the last bend, frantically searching for the body I'd seen half in the water, drenched and shaking and clinging to the shore.

Relief flooded me when I spotted him.

I tripped over something—a branch, a trunk, whatever—but dropped beside him in the puddling mud. Had he slipped? Fallen? And where was his cane?

Bryn lifted his head. "Roe?"

I drew in a ragged breath, a razor blade scraped over my lungs. "Hold on, hold on," I said, and gripped him under the soaked armpits of his jacket. "Sorry, I—I thought…" No, that was for later.

His face was so white, his lips blue. He must have slipped on his painting break, but how long had he been here?

I shifted, dug my heels in, and heaved. Freezing water spurted from his clothes like a sponge, but he slid only an inch. "Can you grab that branch?" I asked as his teeth chattered.

"Roe?" Bryn said again, calm though, deadly calm, like we weren't slipping in mud on a riverbank with him shivering from exhaustion.

With sudden renewed strength, he pushed up onto a forearm and slid a hand behind my neck. I frowned, awkwardly tugging at his jacket to urge him to push with me but he didn't move.

His hands on my neck were like burning ice, his eyes a washed-out blue in skin the color of bone. The painter's clothes he'd worn earlier were gone, replaced by a t-shirt.

Did he want my confession now? "I'm sorry," I said quickly. "For telling you to leave. I didn't mean it."

"That's okay," he murmured, pulling me toward him, pulling my mouth toward him.

My heart scattered. Here? Now? He was still half in the water. "Wait, wait…"

I curled my fingers in his jacket, unwilling to push him away, but I couldn't kiss him *now*.

His lips parted, his breath like warm cinnamon as his hand tightened on my neck. I sucked in a quick gulp of air—it was all I could manage.

Our mouths met, his freezing from the river, mine hot from running. Even his tongue was cold as it thrust between my lips, and I nearly pulled back at the sudden intrusion, the urgency of the kiss.

He devoured my mouth, gripping my neck so hard I couldn't pull back. Where had this come from? It was more like being eaten than being kissed.

But he wouldn't *stop*.

"Bryn, wait," I mumbled through teeth and tongue. He groaned against me, but when his mouth dropped to my neck, I shoved him—hard.

It was enough to have him pull back a fraction, to look up, and I saw my own blood staining his lips.

Concerned blue eyes frowned at me. "What?"

"What the hell *was* that?" I demanded, rubbing a hand over my mouth to erase the kiss. "One minute I think you're dead, then you're in the river, and—and —"

Blue eyes.

Blue. Shouldn't they be gold? Or maybe I wasn't what he wanted anymore. Not Nereida, but—but that hadn't stopped the change before.

I started to inch away.

Bryn's eyes went flat. "I don't think so," he growled, and tightened his grip, no longer friendly, no longer a question. And then I knew real fear.

It was thick and numbing and slid in my gut like oil.

I grabbed at his hand, tried to wrench it away as he slid from the river, effortlessly, without favoring his left leg.

His grin was a horrible, bloody grimace when he rose and dragged me toward the shore.

I pitched forward, palms squelching into mud, acorns, and river roots as the shoreline dipped to the rapids. Yellowed foam gathered at the jutting rocks like saliva at a dog's mouth.

No, no, not the water.

"In you go," Bryn chirped. "And I do know *exactly* how much you fear it. I know all about you, Nereida. Knew you would come here looking for O'Sahnazekiel. You're a shit kisser, you know that? I'm gonna save him from that and your whining. *Willow, Willow, Willow,"* he sing-songed.

It wasn't Bryn, it wasn't him, and yet it still hurt to hear the words in his voice, from his wide lips.

But as he wrenched me toward the rapids, I dug in to the hogweed and rocks with every muscle in my body, stabbing my toes into any root or crevice that would anchor me. Sharp pain burst through my scalp when he gave one vicious yank on my hair that brought me eye to eye with my terrified reflection.

Tears blurred my vision. *Not like this. God, not like this.* There would be no Willow to pull me out this time.

My lungs burned like they were already underwater. Would I pass out first? Would I choke to death? Would I—

Bitter spray flew into my face, freezing my nose and cheeks. I sucked in a breath, preparing for Bryn to shove me under.

The fist in my hair tightened, then the *thing* whispered in my ear, "Do you know what I showed O'Sahnazekiel before I took his leg?"

My horrified face stared back at me. Show him? What did he mean? Or was this—was *this* what had attacked Bryn in L'Ardoise? Crippled him and ruined his leg, had turned it into the mess I'd seen in the Oslo hotel room?

An Inquitate.

I had to warn Bryn, had to... but what if it'd already found him? What if I'd driven him straight to them? My fault. Because I'd been selfish, stupid—

As the Inquitate shoved me forward, my reflection wavered.

Feathered wings flowed under the rushing current, not angelic and dappled gray like in Ruhaven, but twisted, broken. The hair that should have been brilliantly gold was a lifeless gray and shorn to the scalp. The eyes—the beautiful eyes that looked at Nereida like two spinning planets—were gone.

I was screaming when the Inquitate shoved my head underwater.

Icy runoff straight from the Kerry mountains shocked my system. My breath bubbled out on a long, high-pitched scream that flooded my mouth with the taste of dirt and diesel. This would be how I died, with my body floating next to Sahn's. I'd die like Willow had, my brain exploded into a mess worse than Bryn's leg, and some doctor would eventually circle the scan of my corpse and write *cause unknown*.

Everything that was me in that scan—the frontal lobe and whatever else made up my worries and hopes and skills and dreams—would become nothing. *I* would be nothing. Nothing but a black-and-white image in a binder like the one Bryn had handed me.

Would I be buried here? Or in L'Ardoise? Would my parents care? Would anyone? Would Bryn?

I squeezed my eyes shut. Was Willow waiting for me?

I didn't want to be nothing, didn't want to die here with the Inquitate's fingers twisting in my hair, holding my head under as I choked on the water.

If I died, James might come home from the market to find the Inquitate waiting for him at Naruka, Kazie might never see Ruhaven again, and Tye would suffer because I hadn't told him about Oslo, and he'd never understood how close the danger was. And Bryn—was he still alive?

I stabbed my hands into the riverbed, into every weed and slug that had once terrified me, as I stared at the vision of O'Sahanzekiel, broken and bloody on the bottom of the river.

The Inquitate yanked hard on my hair, dragging me up through the current a second before my head broke the surface. *God, the taste of air.* I sucked it in like a trout. Gagged. Liquid spurt out of my mouth and nose. Awful and burning, but the storms of Ireland had never tasted so good.

Distantly, through my waterlogged ears, someone was screaming. James? Bryn? What was real? And how did I know?

A hot breath blew in my ear. "I said, don't you want to know what I showed him?" the thing asked in Bryn's voice.

I fought the hands at my hair, arching away from the river.

It shook me again. "Ask me," he demanded. "Ask me what I showed him before I took his leg."

"Did you kill my sister?" I had to know—had to know if this *thing* was what had ruined my life, had taken hers. "Did you—"

This time, a startled cry left my lips when he yanked on my hair. *"Ask me what I showed him!"*

I swallowed shards of glass. "What—what did you show him?" I said to the Inquitate, some abomination born from the Gate.

It slid its slug-like tongue down my neck, cool, slick, slow. "I showed him *Nereida*," it hissed, and now it no longer sounded like Bryn, and the fingers no longer felt like his hands. The breath rolling over me was the stench of rancid acid, worms, rot.

I started to turn and face it.

"*ROWAN!*"

Bryn? *Bryn!*

His voice rang through me, echoing in my pulse like he'd struck me with a bell, and with it came an unexplainable relief. *Alive, he was alive.* Or was he just an illusion?

A sudden force yanked me back.

My jaw hit the earth, my brain rattling in its skull. The Inquitate reached for me, grabbed empty air as I was dragged through the trees by an invisible rope.

Leaves scratched my cheeks, my knees banged into roots as I careened through mud and brambles and acres of clovers that turned into a flattened trail in my wake.

I dropped face down in a bundle of sharp ivy, like whatever had dragged me had grown too tired to lug my body further. My breath huffed out in a trembling cloud as I shivered from shock, from the river, from the feel of Bryn's icy lips on mine. I searched for the rope at my waist, but found nothing as I expected.

But something had grabbed me.

There might be two of them—two Inquitate—and the other had pulled me away for whatever game they were playing now. That scream I'd heard could be it too—it could all be an illusion. The forest, the river, the feel of the ivy beneath me.

I squeezed my eyes shut.

No, *look*. Nereida would—she wouldn't sit in a pile of weeds and wait for the Inquitate to kill her.

I sucked in a breath, and my wits, and rolled over.

Vines hung from twisted branches, spiderwebs glistened on leaves that faded into a blank sky, but there were no terrifying illusions of Bryn.

I loosed a breath that turned into a hacking cough of river water. Then cocked my ear and listened.

The woods were still silent, as still as the clocks had been. No bees hummed, no birds chirped or rustled the trees. Wind slapped my frozen cheeks, but I didn't *hear* it.

I rose slowly on leaden legs.

Blankets of fog enveloped the trees. Empty, silent. I reached for the branch at my feet, clenched my fingers around its soggy bark. The sound of it dragging through leaves was louder than a whistling axe in the woods.

I gripped the stick with both hands. Lifted it.

"*Rowan!*"

Froze.

Bryn?

Or was it the Inquitate, hoping to lure me to him?

"Rowan, *please.*" His voice was almost pleading, and that was never like Bryn. He quietly demanded, he subtly ordered, but he never begged. Even his anchoring call was a silent command straight through my gut.

I jerked as something tugged my ribs again. It *was* real. Not just a feeling but a familiar force.

Rowan, finita Rowan. Please, I cannot live through this again.

I dropped the stick. Could they speak to me like Bryn? But then, it'd called me *Roe* before. Not Rowan, as Bryn did, and if it knew…

Something golden glowed in the distance, a shimmer against the mist.

Oh god. Bryn.

I flew toward it and his echoing shouts, through the muffled rain beating on the treetops, bracing myself on new saplings as my knees gave out.

Ahead, the same golden light that had lifted me from the Gate flickered like two ships firing volleys in a stormy sea, then winked out. I kept my eyes glued to where I'd seen it last. My boots squishing in the moss were the only sound in the woods, reverberating through the trees. *Boom, boom, boom.*

I passed over the trail to the Gate, slapping hard dirt for a brief moment before plunging into the soaked carpet of the woods.

Then I saw him.

It *was* Bryn this time, so obvious that the Inquitate's replica was no more than a poor painting next to the man. His hair glowed in the evening sun, his eyes burned a fierce blue.

Panting heavily, he leaned against a tree barely twenty yards from me, wearing the same rolled-up shirt he'd painted in. Rain or fog had soaked it to transparency, revealing every shadowed gear of Sahn.

But he didn't turn or blink when I desperately called his name. He just stood there, trembling against the birch tree, eyes fixed in horror on something invisible between the leaves.

I batted aside branches, spurs, and the thorny brambles that ripped at my legs like piranhas. If we were together—if we stayed together— the Inquitate could only conjure one vision.

But why couldn't he summon his Mark, the one that had leaked through on the night of An Béal Bocht? The Mark of protection. He'd been able to walk again, but now he clutched the tree for support, his leg quivering as something I couldn't see flooded his vision.

Bryn! Bryn! Bryn!

I screamed his name as I ran, but he never turned. Was it Nereida he saw? Was it my soul who drowned him? He stared unseeingly, like an angel waiting for the final blow. Rain trickled over the taut veins in his neck. Ivy spilled over his shoulders.

Then he convulsed.

An imaginary shock sent his head ricocheting into the trunk behind him. His eyes jittered in his skull.

No! I was only yards away, my own incompetency slowing me down. Because I hadn't been eating right, hadn't any Mark from Nereida to use here, and my quick spike of adrenaline had bottomed out long ago.

I hurtled over a stack of trees abandoned by old loggers and dropped a meter down the other side, the impact zinging up my ankles. Where was O'Sahnazekiel? Why wouldn't he protect Bryn?

That's when it clicked. Him running out of the Oslo pub, anchoring me when the Tether broke, the dream of him healing me after I'd stolen to the Gate, the imaginary force dragging me from the river.

Because it wasn't *Bryn* that Sahn protected. It was Nereida.

A yard away, I dove on him.

I crushed myself to Bryn's shaking frame, buried my face into his neck like I had that night outside An Béal Bocht, and inhaled the smell of night and winter, of something at the bottom of a lake. Not terrifying, as I'd first thought, but wild and exhilarating in the unknowing that awaited.

He didn't react as I tried to block whatever he saw, didn't move at all.

O'Sahnazekiel's Mark had never been protection for himself, but for others, for Nereida. It had allowed Bryn to walk so he could reach me after An Béal Bocht, and I was taking a wild gamble that it'd do something against the Inquitate too.

If they attacked me, if I was threatened. Just like Sahn had for Nereida.

Then, everything happened at once.

The claws of the Inquitate reached through my skin, its skeleton fingers curling around my bones like it was measuring the meat on a chicken. It grabbed hold.

And twisted.

Pain like I hadn't felt since the broken Tether ripped through my spine, wrenching a cry from my lips that I barely recognized. *Was it eating me?* Eating my spine and—

Bryn came to life.

CHAPTER 38

No Memories of Tomorrow

H is body burned beneath mine, porcelain skin glowing to gold, lightning skittering over his skin in a pulsing rhythm. The fog shone with it, revered it. The air behind him rippled for wings that didn't exist in this world.

And my blood sang.

It was like Nereida recognized some part of Sahn and called to him, a song as clear as the thunder rolling overhead. Here was the only piece of him I could hold on to. Not in a dream or a memory, but flesh and blood and real. The truth of it fizzled in my lungs, burying deep under my heart in the place I thought there'd only been space for Willow.

Bryn?

His eyes shot wide a second before he yanked me against him, spinning me around until my spine hit the trunk and his body blocked mine.

Something exploded against us, against him.

I gasped.

A million firelights winked in a perfect, protective dome, blocking out the fog and the evening sky. I couldn't hear the howling wind or the roaring river. The only light was from the flickering stars in the tiny world Bryn had created. Impossible. Magic. The same one I'd seen when he'd rescued me from my trip with the alarm clock.

Slowly, his eyes blinked open.

God. It was him.

Sahn stared back at me, let out two heavy, misted breaths.

Then, on a long groan, he dropped his head onto my shoulder. When I looped my arms around the warm heat of his neck, he skimmed his nose down my throat in a feather-soft touch, and all the while, the shield rippled around us. Its gentle lights were just bright enough to cast Bryn's face in midnight hues, the tips of his eyelashes into burnished amber. Indigo splashed the top of his shoulders as if the sky and stars above us were from Ruhaven and not Earth at all.

Pulling back, I grabbed his face in my hands, searched for any sign of the pain that had sent him convulsing into the tree. "Are you hurt? Are you—"

He pried my hands away. "No, Rowan. Not like before." Relief flooded my veins, but when I made to leave, Bryn boxed me in. "We must stay within this shield, as long as it is active, there is a threat outside." Then the Inquitate were still here, beyond the shield of stars that obscured the forest. "I do not know why they appear yet again. It seems they will not stop following us until one of our triplet is dead."

"James? Is he okay? Kazie? Tye?"

Bryn's eyes clouded briefly, then he said, "I do not believe they are under threat."

How could he know that? Just how far did his Mark extend? And why hadn't he told me about how his protection works?

"I'm sorry about what I said in Naruka," I said hurriedly. "I don't want you to go back to Odda."

"No, Rowan. No, I would never leave," he whispered, breath warm against my frozen skin. "You asked me not to before, when you awoke from the Gate."

The first time I'd slept with the Azekiel, when Bryn had hovered over me, eyes a burning gold.

His hands moved over my shoulders, my arms, my neck, then paused when they grazed my swollen lips.

I closed my eyes. "Bryn, it—the Inquitate—it said it was the one that hurt you. That it appeared as Nereida to you in L'Ardoise."

Something flashed behind his eyes. Pain? Embarrassment? "Yes, that is true." He drew back just an inch, but I felt the distance, more than just physical.

I slid my hands down his shoulders, braced my palms on his chest. "What happened in L'Ardoise?"

"Why were you in the woods, Rowan?"

I frowned at the sharp clip in his voice. "I—what? The clocks stopped. I thought the Inquitate had you."

His gaze darted to my lips again. *Show me,* he repeated.

"Show you what?" I asked aloud.

His thumb brushed my mouth. *This*. The words were a gentle caress in my mind, like feathers again, brushing a soft space between my eyes, relaxing. *Show me what happened*. He trailed his hand to my eyelids, waited for me to flutter them closed, then laid his fingertips overtop. *As I did before, except you shall give me a memory instead*.

Nerves jumped as I remembered sliding down the hill, thinking it'd been him drowning. Of every second of bone-chilling terror.

Then his hands warmed, and the memory replayed—my panic, its teeth biting my tongue, the shock of the water, and then the Inquitate's admission.

He dropped his hand, face unreadable.

"Why won't you tell me what happened to you?" I asked. "In L'Ardoise?"

But Bryn looked away, monitoring the stars swirling in the walls of the shield that even now kept the Inquitate out.

I gripped his chin, pulled him back. "You tell me nothing," I said quietly. "You kept your identity from me, you didn't tell me why you wanted me to visit the Gate. I don't really know you."

His eyes flashed. "Everything you need to know of me is in the Gate."

That didn't make any sense. "You're not Sahn. You have a life here. You grew up in Odda, you have a mother who captained a ship, you went to school for art, you enjoyed glacier walking, you had a pretty apartment with tulips."

He planted his palms against the bark, framing me with his body again. "Rowan, I tell you what I believe you are prepared to understand. Consider how you might have felt if you had known it was me in the Gate with you. Would you have visited?"

Not in a million years. "I can decide what I need to know."

He studied me coolly. "Very well, Rowan. Yes, the Inquitate showed me Nereida, and if I had known what I do today, I likely would have seen through the illusion immediately."

"Why?"

"The Inquitate show you something you desire. I do not know if it is always the case, or even always a person, but after you saw Willow, I assumed it must be."

I blushed to know I'd just shown Bryn a memory of them appearing as *him*.

He glanced at the shield, checking that it was intact. "I was running in the park outside L'Ardoise," he continued briskly, but at least he was telling me *something*. "I used to make a habit of doing so—running, I mean—and I quite enjoyed the landscape in your town. It reminded me of the west of Norway. But it was while I was jogging through the pine trees that she—it—stepped into my path."

Nereida. An Inquitate.

"She glowed like a fallen star and was surprisingly taller than me. I had never seen her but as O'Sahnazekiel. Now, she stood before me amongst the changing leaves, and I could barely utter a coherent word. She said, 'Hello, Brynjar,' in English, and it was strange to hear her speak it from lips that had only known Ruhaven. While I was staring at her, immersed, besotted, in awe—something else was eating away at my leg. Dissolving the bone and muscle."

His face had gone white, but he pushed on. "I was able to escape because I remembered you, as I had seen you in L'Ardoise and knew you to be Nereida. When I recalled this, the illusion began to dissolve. Then I felt what they had done to my leg. Someone called for an ambulance, believing I must have been run over by a car. After they stabilized me, I flew home to recover, to learn to walk again."

I should have been there, should have *known*. He'd been only a few miles away, suffering from the Inquitate, and I hadn't helped him.

He gently pried my hands from his shirt, dropped them. "You still do not recall meeting me in L'Ardoise?"

I sucked in my lips. "I think, maybe. I…"

His eyes cooled to clear ice. "No," he said softly. "After everything, you still do not."

"If you would just—Bryn!"

I screamed when something grabbed him through the shield, the starry dome bursting as Bryn fell backwards.

I lunged for him.

And was hauled off my feet.

"Goddamn it, Roe," a familiar voice cursed as it crushed me to a body that smelled of leather and soap and pine. "You ain't got any goddamn idea what a scare you gave me." Tye dropped me on my feet and whirled. "And you!" Tye jabbed a finger at Bryn's sprawled form, the paintbrushes from his pocket now littering the forest. "Fuckin' neckin' out here in the woods with the Inquitate everywhere."

Then he hadn't seen what Bryn could conjure.

I fisted Tye's leather jacket. "No, Bryn *stopped* them."

Tye wiped at his forehead, disbelief darkening his eyes. "*Stopped them*? Like he stopped Colm? Yeah, James told me all about that." He whirled back to Bryn, watching as he searched for a makeshift cane. "From what I hear, he was wanderin' the streets lookin' for a carrot or somethin' 'cause he's so far in the Gate he can't eat nothin'. Convenient, Stornoway, that you're off dilly-dallyin' while Roe's gettin' the shit kicked out of her by Colm. Now here we go again. Funny how you're always just a little too late, ain't it?"

Bryn tried to stand by planting a gnarled oak branch in the mud, but when I started to reach for him, Tye blocked me.

I elbowed Tye. "Would you stop? The Inquitate were—"

Like a dog struggling to keep up, James burst through the trees with Kazie on his heels. I closed my eyes for a moment, just took a breath, then another. *James was okay.*

When I opened them again, I saw that his jeans were drenched, his eyes wild and worried, and the relentless rain had finally tamed his unruly hair. "I feckin' come back, Kazie's yelling about clocks, ye two are gone. I thought ye were both dead!"

"The clocks *stopped*!" she squealed, her voice tinged with a manic excitement only slightly less crazed than her skirt. But god, I wanted to hug every stupid feather of it.

James glanced between us, then turned to Bryn and tackled him. Bryn swore as James wrapped him in a fierce hug. Kazie joined the fray, diving on top and crushing them into a bush of shriveled blackberries. They spoke over each other, pelting Bryn with questions as he lay sprawled under their weight.

"C'mon, Roe," Tye said, tugging me toward Naruka, his face devoid of humor. "You're gonna tell me everythin'."

⚙☀

S calding water pummeled life into my bones.
I planted my hands on the tiles, groaning as the shower spray cascaded over my shoulders, dripped off my breasts, and plastered my waist-length hair into a dark curtain.

I tried to wash away the twisted memories the Inquitate had conjured, and how close I'd been to losing Bryn.

He'd looked beaten. Mentally. Physically. And he'd been quiet on the way home, even as Tye tossed questions out in a rapid-fire assault. But Bryn had admitted nothing. Not the shield that had appeared to protect me, not the river I thought I'd drowned in.

Why had the Inquitate appeared again? And *why* did they need to root out the triplets? Was it related to mates? I'd found two others who were both mates and had suffered aneurysms, but the rest either weren't mated or never discovered they were. Had they been killed before they could? *Stupid.* What did the Inquitate care?

I wilted against the stall door. Dead ends—that's all I had, and now they were on our doorstep.

When even the water didn't help, I turned off the taps and stuffed my arms into the housecoat Kazie had left for me, my limbs moving like worms through dirt. Then I slipped on the matching dog slippers and strode out. If their drooling tongues dragged on the floor, I pretended not to notice.

In the main hall, Naruka's roaring fireplace stole some of the fear even the water hadn't been able to wash away. The apple coal burned to bright jewels, and logs the size of tree trunks sent five-foot flames scorching up the chimney. Everything from the paintings to the television to the glass tables was soaked in the smoky, golden light.

Kazie sprawled on a velvet teal chair near the fireplace, a biscuit halfway to her lips and wearing her hair in a poofy bun with jeweled pineapples dangling off the scrunchy.

Bryn slouched in a matching loveseat by the fire, his leg propped on a tattered footstool. He wore the simple, cotton pants he preferred sleeping in, with the bow of their drawstring half undone. Tattooed gears disappeared under the cuff of a gray T-shirt. For Bryn, it was a wardrobe in disarray.

I didn't want the hot shower, didn't want the warmth of the fireplace, had only the inexplicable urge to climb into his lap and wrap my arms around his neck.

I turned my focus on Tye. He leaned on the kitchen doorjamb, arms crossed, with a steady gaze that saw through me. Tye hadn't bothered with a shower or changing after the forest, as if the mud smearing his clothes proved a point.

Behind him, James tossed open the kitchen door.

"I can't feckin' believe this like." He crossed the room, draped himself on the velvet sofa beside me, and rubbed at his eyebrows until they resembled Irish moss. "In all me years, 'tis never been this bad. I've called who I could to warn them. But Jayzus, when I came home and didn't hear those feckin' clocks, me bloody heart stopped altogether."

I leaned forward. "Did you know they would stop for the Inquitate?"

James shook his head. "No, sure, but me mum was superstitious, and she told me once she put them up to protect us, never said why. Now I know. Aye, now I know."

But they hadn't protected her.

Tye rolled his shoulders in the kitchen doorway. "Maggie kept a lot of things to herself."

Bryn leaned forward, his damp hair hanging in silky trails over his eyes. "She did, indeed. This is why we must speak to Carmen, Tye."

"Carmen?" Tye barked. "What's she got to do with this?"

Bryn pulled an envelope from his pocket. "I believe she has *everything* to do with this. I have found earlier letters from her to Maggie."

"Goddamn, Stornoway, you're some snoop." Yeah, and pretty good at it.

James set down his tea. "What's this about letters from Auntie Carmen?"

Bryn thumbed one open, tossed it to James. "I found these hidden amongst your mother's old things. Carmen believed the Inquitate were created from Drachaut during the original Fall from Tallah."

Because, like a circuit, they'd needed an existing energy to be created? No, an existing *soul*—the Drachaut.

James blew out a breath. "That's some theory, like. But sure that's all it is. And what would Carmen know of it when she's not even been at the bloody Gate in years?"

Kazie nodded around a biscuit. "But it kind of makes sense doesn't it? Everything's energy," she reiterated, voice pitching up. "Mates. Tethers. The Gate. It's all about balance. If our souls get to make the journey here, it makes sense there's something that happens to the sacrificed Drachaut."

An Inquitate for a Drachaut's soul.

"Yes, that is what Carmen believed," Bryn agreed, shifting so his loose shirt showed a hint of taut torso.

Tye banged a fist against the wall before shoving off it. He paced in front of the kitchen doorway, his shadow blocking the light every few seconds. "She never told me nothin' 'bout the Inquitate," he growled, then yanked out a baseball from his pocket. "And Maggie? If she knew the whole time, why didn't she say nothin'? Instead, she ends up damn well killed with the rest." He tossed the ball in the kitchen, where it *ka-plunked* against the metal fridge, then strode toward Bryn.

I started to get up.

Stay there.

"Maggie's death is not her fault, but that of the Inquitate," Bryn warned in a low voice.

Tye brushed past me. "Ya know, I don't believe a word you got to say, Stornoway. So you let me see that letter now."

Saying nothing, Bryn handed it to him.

Tye unfolded the paper, read it with a frown that puckered his chin and widened his nose. He let out a muttered oath before swinging toward the bar. "Stornoway ain't lyin' this time, anyway."

I uncrossed my legs, then recrossed them when cold whipped up my thin housecoat. "So Carmen gets a wild hunch that the Inquitate are created from Drachaut and writes to Maggie about it? No, Carmen knows something, or someone."

I chanced a look at James's furrowed brow.

"Tye, yer close with Carmen," James said. "Maybe ye know her better than I do now. Do ye know how she'd come across this?"

Tye poured a lick of James's preferred whiskey, swirled his glass, then tilted his head back and downed it. James winced. "Close? Wouldn't say so, no more than anyone is to their recruiter. As far as the energy thing goes, I don't know nothin' 'bout that. We didn't talk 'bout that stuff."

"She never mentioned the letters to me mum?"

Tye shook his head, seemed to consider pouring another glass before he stalked around the lounge. He'd always been intimidating, but in a different way than Bryn. Meaner, stronger. "She never mentioned none of these theories. She was my recruiter and I respected that, but we ain't pen pals."

James slipped a bottle of whiskey from his pocket and doctored his tea. "Ye know Carmen's a triplet too. Ye think she'd want to be with us, be worried about an attack like."

Not if she knew how to avoid one. And why wouldn't she? She knew how they were made—maybe she didn't have anything to fear.

Tye rested his elbows on the back of an empty chair. "I told ya, ever since y'all found the Inquitate were causin' aneurysms, she don't want much to do with this place. But the fact is, there's a connection between goin' to the Gate and the Inquitate, whether you wanna believe it or not."

James lifted a black eyebrow. "Between the Gate and the Inquitate?"

"Well, ya don't see humans dyin' from 'em, do ya?" Tye shot back as he prowled the room, jabbing at each of us. "Souls bein' transferred, Inquitate created from Drachaut voodoo, triplets are magical—y'all don't want to admit why we're bein' attacked. Of course it's the goddamn Gate. But that wouldn't suit none of ya 'cause you're addicted."

I felt my hackles rise. "This isn't James's fault."

James waved me back. "No, no, don't ye go defendin' me, Roe. Tye, if ye've something to say to me, then come out with it."

Tye scooped back his hair into a short ponytail. "Ya want the truth, James? Because I sure am tired of holdin' my tongue," he said, looking like a horse picking up speed for the finish line. "I risked bringin' Roe here only 'cause you were gonna solve this problem. But it's gettin' worse! Fuckin' Inquitate in our backyard and not one of you is takin' it seriously. Kazie's got her head in the clouds. You, James, are gone stupid over a walkin', talkin' rock—"

"Rock *spirit*," James hissed.

"—and Stornoway spends his days gettin' his dick stroked by a dream."

I choked on my tea.

James just steepled his fingers. "Alright so, I know yer concerned for Roe. I am meself. There's never been a Ruhaven targeted more than once, but I don't think ye should jump to—"

"More than *once*?" Tye snarled like a coyote sprung from a trap. *Goddamn it, James.*

I braced when Tye rounded on me, leaning into the pointed toes of his cowboy boots. "Roe, did you go on and lie to me?"

We stared at each other. If I admitted the truth, that Bryn and James had asked me to lie, they'd be in worse trouble than me. Tye was right to be angry—this affected him too. He didn't understand how close the Inquitate might be to him.

"I'm sorry, Tye," I said, thinking up excuses on the fly. "I was in Oslo when I saw one, and I didn't tell you because I didn't want to worry you."

He bent down until we were nose to nose. "Darlin', do I *look* worried?"

Bryn had better be worth this. "Uh, no, but I didn't know how you'd react when I saw them and—"

"It was *me* who asked Rowan not to tell you," Bryn stated.

In the fireplace, logs popped like dislocated bones.

Tye whirled on Bryn. "*You?*" he uttered—condemnation, trial, and executioner.

It was a testament to Bryn's stone exterior that he didn't wither under the living torrent that was Tye and only adjusted his injured leg on the footstool.

"In Oslo," Bryn continued evenly, but I heard the steel under it, honed and sharp, "Rowan was approached by an Inquitate. I intervened."

Intervened—a careful phrase for tackling me as I chased after Willow. I'd been in danger, and he'd been able to run because of O'Sahnazekiel's Mark.

As usual, Bryn left me in a state of confusion. He'd lied. He'd protected me. He'd been a friend. He'd made a mockery of me.

"Ya know, I went along with your bullshit with the Gate for James's sake. He tells me you've got some misplaced right to keep that from Roe, and I go along with it. When you drag her up there to anchor together 'cause she's too embarrassed to go with us, knowin' full well you're fuckin' her when she thinks you don't know nothin', I hold my tongue. For James," Tye continued, but Bryn's face had started to lose color.

My own stomach twisted, because not one of those words were a lie, even if I didn't like the way he said it.

Tye slipped bunched fists from his pockets. "Now I hear you've put her in danger? Made her lie about the Inquitate? Not even for James am I gonna swallow your bullshit anymore, Stornoway." He planted his hands on each side of Bryn, grasping the armrests in an almost exact parody of what Bryn had done to me in Oslo.

"The first is between Rowan and I," Bryn said, gaze level. "The second, because you could never deal with the realities of the Gate."

Palpable rage rippled under Tye's skin. "You ain't got no fuckin' idea what I know of the *realities* in the Gate," he warned, voice barely more than a whisper.

I could taste Tye's hate as much as feel it, a loathing that went beyond a lie about the Inquitate.

His grip tightened, stretching the jacket over a body that would flatten Bryn. Flames withered in the fireplace, eating the oxygen not consumed by the men staring at each other.

I started to rise off the couch.

"Rowan, sit *down*," Bryn ordered, never taking his eyes off Tye. When I ignored him, he added, "James, stop her."

Then all hell broke loose.

Tye reared back and kicked the footstool from under Bryn's crippled leg. It flew across the room, smashing into the wall the same time his heel hit the floor.

A low groan hissed between Bryn's teeth in a face gone sheet white.

"What the hell are you doing!" I screamed, but James caught me as I lunged for Tye.

"This ain't about you anymore, Roe," Tye said, looking ready to draw blood and taste it.

"Get away from him!"

I fought with James. The tea went flying, scalding my toes right through the stupid dog slippers as he muscled me onto the couch with Kazie's help, her inch-long nails pinching into my housecoat.

Tye hitched up his jeans, crouching to eye level with Bryn, who was only a shadow against the fire. "What the fuck were you doin' out in the woods, Stornoway?"

Had he been? Had that been real?

Tye's hand snaked out and gripped Bryn's foot by the ankle.

Bryn didn't look at me as he said, "James, take Rowan out of here."

This was bullshit. "The hell you are," I said, swearing at James for the first time since he'd shown me Naruka.

James gripped my arm, looking torn between jumping on Tye and wrestling me, then ended on the latter when he pinned me to the couch, a knee on the small of my back.

"James, I swear, I don't care how much Irish charm you lay on," I hissed into the musty fabric, "I won't forgive you for this."

"Ah, but ye've only seen half of me wiles. Ye think I run Naruka for nothing, so?"

Kazie patted my head. "It's not for us."

What kind of weird Ruhaven law were they following now? "Tye, if you hurt him, I'll use my pliers—the *rusty* ones—on your toes." He wouldn't really hurt him, would he?

Tye didn't spare me a glance. "You're a cheap date, Roe. One Inquitate attack and you've forgiven him already." Bryn flinched as Tye began to twist his ruined leg. "Not going to stop me, Stornoway?"

Sweat beaded on Bryn's temple, his arms straining on the chair. "No," he said through clenched teeth. "I neither can nor will stop you, as you know."

So he'd just sit there and let Tye hurt him?

Tye pulled his lips back, baring a perfect set of teeth. "Where the hell were you tonight, Stornoway?"

"It was my fault," I bit out. "I told Bryn to go away, to paint a flower. Insulted him."

Tye cocked his head with an incredulous look. "Roe, this man's got one fuckin' job. And it ain't to paint no dandelions." He flashed his teeth. "Stornoway, I'm startin' to wonder why you're so goddamn bad at it."

"You are right," Bryn said tightly, his breathing strained now as Tye twisted. "It *was* my fault. I should not have left Rowan alone."

Tye wrenched out another hissed grunt. "Ya know, that just makes me wonder why ya did. Weren't you supposed to be watchin' her, your precious Nereida?"

"Yes."

"Protecting her?"

"Yes."

Tye curled his lip, leaned closer, his knuckles whitening, squeezing, twisting. Then he said softly, voice a dull dagger, "I hope she's worth the pain."

"Kazie," Bryn hissed a second before she slapped a biscuit-scented hand over my eyes.

I didn't understand, not at first.

Then it dawned on me. *He was going to break his leg.*

I fought against James and Kazie, bracing for the sound of breaking bone just as I tore Kazie's hand away at last.

How bad was it? How bad—

Bryn panted, his chest heaving as Tye stood slowly and wiped his knuckles across his chin. "Next time, I'm gonna fuckin' do it," he warned, voice low.

Relief had my knees going weak.

"Bryn, are you—"

He shook his head, wouldn't meet my eyes.

Tye unzipped his breast pocket, pulled a smoke from the pack he stored there. "Ya know, Stornoway," he began, sliding a cigarette between his lips, "it's a damn coward who only fights when he knows he can win."

I cursed Tye with enough zeal to make Bryn's mother blush, but Tye only squared his shoulders and let my words pummel him as he puffed on the smoke.

"That's some mouth on ya, Roe. Pick that up on the job, huh? Wouldn't mind hearin' it a bit more often. Could use some truth around here." He flicked hot ash at Bryn.

"Tye," James spluttered, "ye've got no business threatening him like that."

"He's lyin' about something, and he better stay away from that Gate."

James's mouth gaped. "Ye'll demand no such thing. The Gate's a bloody blessing like."

"A blessing!" Tye picked up the cane Kazie had found in the woods. For a heartbeat, I thought he'd hit Bryn with it. Then he whirled on James and I.

Bryn shoved out of his chair.

Tye kicked his leg out from under him, sending Bryn sprawling into the rug.

"This is your goddamn blessin', James." Tye waved the cane under James's shell-shocked face. "*You* caused this, and you keepin' things from me almost got Roe killed today too. As for you, Stornoway." Bryn grunted as the cane caught him in the chest. "Get your dick out of Ruhaven."

CHAPTER 39

Tangerines

A week had passed since the threat to break Bryn's leg had nearly put James on heart medication. The incident had left us shaken and wary of another outburst, even after Tye apologized the following day. James, with his good nature, had chalked it up to Tye's overprotectiveness. And whiskey. But even Kazie now gave him a wide berth.

Maybe Tye was right and we'd cursed ourselves with the Gate. That it was the wanting of something this deeply that summoned the corruption of the Inquitate. They were everything Tye feared. An enemy he couldn't fight, bargain with, or threaten. For someone who spent their life facing problems head-on, he'd come up against the immovable.

And although I understood his fear, I'd never forgive him.

I didn't like to think that kind of cruelty existed in Tye, in anyone. He'd worked Bryn like the horses he broke. Pushing, threatening, intimidating, until the thing caved.

Except Bryn hadn't.

Outside the gate lodge, Kazie supervised my work. She wore an enormous pair of earmuffs shaped like kittens, with whiskers protruding from each side of her head. To combat the cold spell, she'd opted for her preferred seagull-feather jacket, likely handmade, and boots that rose to her knobby knees.

"Why are you reading *Beautiful Banshees* now?" I asked Kazie, dumping the cement mixture into the MDF molding I'd nailed together. "Wasn't *Maiden and her Hens* good enough for you?"

She lowered the romance novel. "Maid. Henchmen. We can't all be so well-loved in Ruhaven." Eyebrows wiggled. "When you going back, Roe? You know you're totally going to throw up again now that you've waited this long."

"Never." I yanked my Blue Jays cap over my eyes, blocking out the rare heat of the Irish sun. Even Naruka seemed to frown at the cloud-free sky, disappointed to find she was the only gray thing in sight.

"Oh c'mon, Roe, you can't hide forever. Don't you miss O'Sahnazekiel?"

"No," I lied. "Do *not*," I warned as she wiggled jazz fingers at the wet cement, "do that." I dumped another bag of concrete mix into a red pail. "Oh for—are you five?"

Giddy, she kicked off her boots and posed like one of Bryn's naked models in the wet cement. "Rowie, take a breather."

"Never call me that." I lifted my ball cap and wiped my forehead as she wiggled her toes. "Maybe we don't all want your sparkly pink nails in this..." I swept an arm at the gate lodge surrounded by sheep dung, "historical artifact."

Kazie shielded her eyes. "Uh-huh. You want to read this when I'm done?"

"Absolutely not. I've had my fill of fantasy men in the Gate. The next time you're at the library, why don't you get something useful? Like a book on changing oil so you can help me."

Kazie scrunched up her bubble nose. "Ew, that's what men are for."

I smoothed out the second concrete batch while Kazie eyed it like I was preparing her canvas. "Just think how 'ew' it'll be when you're stranded in the middle of a bog in the Ford, whining to me, hoping..."

Crack.

My attention snapped toward the sound of a whistling axe.

In the shadow of the woodshed, Bryn split kindling with efficient strokes. Glistening sweat traced a path along the nape of his neck, curling strands of golden hair. His cotton T-shirt bared a tapestry of tattoos and clung to every long, damp line before tucking neatly into snug jeans.

"...and there's no oil."

"No oil?" Kazie repeated, twisting in the cement. Her smile was as coy as a cat after enjoying its bowl of milk. "Does watching someone do manual labor always get you so hot and bothered? Because I'm worried about that oil change."

She yelped as I shoved her off the cement, leaving behind two Kazie-shaped impressions.

From the corner of my eye, Bryn turned and glanced at the noise. The sun ran tender fingers over his wide shoulders as we stared at each other.

"Is it really so bad what he did?" Kazie asked.

I planted my boot on the shovel. "Yes."

Kazie plopped back into the dew-licked grass she'd promised to cut a month ago. "Bryn just does what he thinks is best, you know. For you, and him."

"Yeah? Is that why he nearly let Tye break his leg?"

Kazie's eyes sharpened on me. "No. Don't you know him at all, Roe?"

I stabbed the screed into the ground. "Obviously not." That was probably my fault for focusing too much on Willow, on the Inquitate, and not enough on what it'd be like for him to return after exile.

"Ruhaven is everything to him. He lives by its law, and you're Nereida whether you want to be or not. He was supposed to protect you. He didn't."

"So that means he should have his leg broken?"

"Do you have to be so literal?" she huffed. "Bryn's been punishing himself for a lot of things, for a long time. Why don't you come to the Gate with us tonight?" she suggested, tone lightening. "Tye said he'd anchor; he still feels bad about what he said to James."

Though not, apparently, for what he'd done to Bryn.

Kazie floated her body into a grass angel. "Even if Tye is right—and we're like, drawing the Inquitate at the Gate—I'd still go in. Yeah, I'd still go in."

It was a declaration of love if I'd ever heard one. And now I knew exactly how much Kazie was willing to risk for Ruhaven.

But when the evening came around, and James packed the backpack with his tea, whiskey, and sandwiches, I stayed behind. I didn't want to wake next to Bryn, didn't want to feel the tension between him and Tye, didn't want to taste James's guilt.

So tonight, with its clear, cloudless sky, I climbed to the roof armed with the telescope I'd borrowed from James.

In L'Ardoise, Willow and I had sat on the roof of Mrs. Baker's, eating fries with too much vinegar and watching the stars, but I couldn't remember the sky being such a royal blue. Here, the silhouettes of the trees were black, the spotted buildings not lit up by stoves and candlelight were black, but the sky was not. It was a color straight from the ultramarine paint Bryn applied too liberally.

While a million starry lighthouses speckled the blue, only one glowed from a planet thousands of light-years away.

"Are you cleaning the chimney?" Bryn's voice cut through the night's buzzing crickets.

Far below my dangling boots, he watched me with an annoyance usually only found in cats. And occasionally Kazie when I forgot to water this plant or that.

His pinched cheeks were as sharp as the eyes scrutinizing me, and the freezing wind had slapped color into his face so that his blue eyes glowed like a doll's.

I held up what I'd borrowed from James. "Cleaning the chimney with a *telescope*?"

His voice was as cool as the night. "Perhaps, because I cannot think of any logical reason why you would be alone on the roof after we have so recently been attacked by the Inquitate."

I checked my watch quickly—still ticking. "I thought you were ignoring me now."

His jaw tightened. "Rowan, I will not have this conversation with you on the roof. Come down."

"No." This was the only clear night we'd gotten in weeks. "I'm looking for Ruhaven."

His eyes flickered. "Why?"

Because when the memories ended, this would be all I had left—the view of the planet I'd once visited, somewhere past the Milky Way.

"Because there's nothing else to do. I haven't found a reason the triplets matter, a reason Willow died, a reason I can live her memories. I want something real of Ruhaven," I admitted. "Not something that belongs to her. Not a dream. Not a memory. Something I can have *here*."

Bryn was silent for a moment. Then he said softly, his voice raw, "You have me, Rowan."

I looked away from him because god help me I did want that, want him. But that wasn't fair to either of us. So I steeled my voice and asked, "Why didn't you tell me about the protection?"

He braced a hand on the ladder, any brief softness gone. "Do you wish for answers now? I was under the impression you preferred to hurtle tea at me in the Gate."

That'd been an *accident*. "You could have trusted me with your Mark. I was terrified for you. I thought they were going to *kill* you. I couldn't think, couldn't do anything, and then I just happened to put it together. If you had just told me how the protection worked, then—"

"I did not *know*!"

I recoiled at his sudden burst of anger.

"You assume I have unhindered knowledge of how my protection works? Have you considered that until Norway, I was unaware there was any convalescence from my attack? When I saw you bolt out of the pub, I did not know I could run again and was as surprised, I expect, as you and James." His fist tightened on the ladder's rung. "Throwing yourself between me and the Inquitate was an incredibly foolish risk, for if it had been anyone but you who did so, they would be *dead*." His voice finished on an echo.

"Why?"

"Perhaps you will figure that out as well. Now, will you come down?"

I stared at the telescope in my hands. He was right—I *was* foolish. It'd been foolish to pretend I was Willow, foolish not to tell James from the beginning, foolish to think I could find a reason for what killed my sister.

"Rowan?"

I looked at him, at the loose strands of hair tickling the tops of his cheeks, and wished I'd never known the truth. "I'm staying up here until I find Ruhaven."

He blew exhausted impatience out his nostrils. "Very well, Rowan. If you wish to forever dwell on what I have repeatedly apologized for, far be it from me to dissuade you from your commitment."

I was in the middle of telling him exactly how much I wished to dwell—*had* dwelled, spun, slid under, rationalized, and cried over—when he turned and limped into Naruka.

I watched him disappear between the hotel's double doors, until his shadow blocked the glow from the stained-glass windows. It paused there, hovering in the hallway, then it was gone.

I kicked at the eavestrough. I needed to focus, get the gate lodge over with, figure out what Carmen knew about the Inquitate, find Levi.

Instead, I smoothed out the solar map on my lap and spent the next fifteen minutes trying to find the violet planet through light-years of silky sky.

When I finally located something close, and adjusted the focus dial, piano music drifted up the chimney.

Willow.

I rubbed at my throat. No, of course not. But for a moment, it had *felt* like her again, before Bryn's unique style echoed through. His trills and triplets were effortless, the rhythm flawless, and the asynchronous left hand varied its tempo as little as the man playing.

A thousand times better than I had ever been.

I'd had no talent for the thing, no inherent skill that would somehow materialize in the hours and hours I used to practice. To sit there, playing a scale for the hundredth time, while watching Willow skip ahead with less.

I hugged my knees to my chest, listening as the song crept toward its melody, winding its way to it like an Irish horse and buggy up Naruka's trail.

If there was anything to convince me it'd been Willow meant for Bryn, this was it. Both talented, both musical, both charismatic in their own way—two missing pieces of a puzzle I wasn't part of.

I'd thought, just for a moment, when James had shown me the Ledger... That there might have been some chance. But no, not even in an imaginary world light years away, was I worth remembering.

I clenched the telescope in my grip. I shouldn't be upset—I should be grateful the Gate had accepted a replacement. Grateful that it'd chosen Willow, that it'd seen how special she was from the beginning.

Bryn started the same song for the third time, some vaguely familiar melody he must have liked. Willow had such an ear for notes, she'd have heard the minor drop, the augmented seventh, then—

Wait. *Wait*...

I *knew* that song. Didn't I? I'm sure that I'd—

I stood abruptly. I did. I definitely did. It tasted like a smoky pub, sounded like an argument with the manager, felt like the low lights of the bar where I'd worked.

Because I *had* heard it before—played by a man I hadn't known on a rainy night in L'Ardoise. A night I'd forgotten about until this moment. A night exactly one year ago.

I cursed Bryn each rung down the ladder.

CHAPTER 40

After Many Miles

I let the music carry me out of the cold and into Naruka's stifling warmth, past portraits and paintings, and the bathroom Bryn had been sick in.

The notes grew louder, insistent, exotic.

Mocking.

How many things would Bryn keep from me? A man who'd decided since the day we met what I should know and when I should know it. Who'd left me standing in his office, ready to beg for any scrap of information about my dead twin. Only after the Inquitate had appeared had he decided that I should know about his research. But not before forcing me to commit to the Gate and Naruka. Not to help me find what happened to Willow, but for *him*.

I elbowed into the music room.

Candles flickered against the worn brick and every-color lights dangled around the window. Two musty-pine wreaths pinned back the curtains on each side, their needles littering the carpet beneath.

And in the middle of mirrors and portraits, of plants and tapestries, below a chandelier, sat Bryn. He hunched over the piano, hands gliding over keys, his skin glowing under the light of two candelabras. James's shellac had left a thick sheen on the piano, like a lady with too many layers of makeup.

Bryn didn't look up as I stepped from his shadow.

His stiffened fingers pounded keys, his thigh tightening with each stomp of the pedal as he rolled into the next verse, tattoos flexing on his forearm. He'd removed his jacket and scarf and draped them so precisely over a bird sculpture that no one would ever guess it wasn't designed for precisely that purpose.

I stared at the dusty-blond hair parted precisely down the middle and hiding his eyes. I was tired of being the electrician the book had made a mistake on. If it had, it was my mistake to do something with. I could make this life my own and to hell with whatever birth the monks had written in the *Ledger* all those centuries ago. I was here, for better or worse. It was *me* who could live the memories, and I wouldn't let anyone else use them against me.

"Did you enjoy making a fool out of me, Bryn?"

He fixed his gaze on the piano. Moonlight rolled over his carved nose like two halves of a mountain, one in shadow, one in silky, yellow light. "That was never my intention, Rowan. But I infer your comment to mean that you do now recall where we first met."

Infer. "I do."

He gave a quick jerk of the head that fell into perfect tempo with the music before reaching for his wine, his throat bobbing under an open collar as he drank. A hint of his collarbone gleamed in the light. The hemp bracelet Kazie had made him months ago hung loosely from his left wrist.

Bryn set the glass down, the clink of it rolling like thunder, and curled his fingers to the keys.

"You were working in the Blue Nose, fixing a circuit board behind the bar, when I walked in." His words were clipped, even, factual, like he wanted to keep all personal emotion out of it.

"And you sat down and played the piano," I finished.

"I needed an excuse to speak to you, to introduce myself, and to eventually convince you to come to Naruka," Bryn explained. "I knew you'd attended music college, and of course, I knew your sister had been a prodigy of a sort. I suspected the piano would attract your attention."

It had, but maybe not in the way he'd intended. I'd listened to him for a long while, imagining that's what I could have been, if I'd stayed in college, if I hadn't been afraid of always being second to Willow.

"So you saw me, saw some other version of Nereida, and thought I'd jump to Naruka for a song."

"Yes," he said boldly. His fingers, orange and pink from the glow of the candelabra, struck the notes pointedly, carrying from C major, F, G, A minor, and F again.

Ping. I jabbed a broken ivory key on the highest octave. I was tired of this, the cold wall of feigned politeness he shoved between us, the clipped words. "You didn't introduce yourself, didn't talk to me."

"You were at the bar," Bryn continued like I hadn't spoken, "wearing your tool belt with a roll of electrical tape bouncing off your left thigh, workman's boots with striped ochre laces—the left shoe in a loose bow, and a checkered Venetian-red shirt with half the hem tucked into your pants. Your hair was in a ponytail."

And I hadn't remembered him. Point taken.

"Bryn, you looked different. Your hair was in a braid like mine." No, like *Sahn's*. That'd been a year ago, when he was exiled, because he'd wanted to cling to the image of the Azekiel. Until he hadn't. "And you had a beard, a toque—"

"Yet I have never forgotten you, Rowan. Not the feel of your eyes, not the sound of your voice." Bryn coaxed the keys into the next melody, pausing on a whole note, and for the first time, lifted his twilight eyes to mine, eyes that had been too dark to see in the pub that night.

I took a deep breath. "Did you expect me to recognize you in Norway?"

Disappointment sliced his glass cheekbones. "No, Rowan. I expected you to recognize O'Sahnazekiel."

To recognize that ripple of something other in his bones, the aura I'd felt from him in that stifling office. But I hadn't. Because I hadn't seen the Gate yet? Because I wasn't Nereida? Had this all be some kind of test?

"Is that what this is about?" I pressed. "It is, isn't it? You wanted to get back at me. I didn't recognize you in Oslo, so you'd make a fool out of me here. Humiliate me. Are we even now?"

He stroked the keys into a raging chorus. "The fact that you believe that of me proves how little you understand of us."

I slapped his hand into the second octave, crunching out a high-pitched wail. "Stop talking to me like that."

Like a dam about to burst, frustration rippled over his face before he quickly smothered it. "The choices I made to keep details from you—of us, of O'Sahnazekiel—were for your benefit. Not mine."

The gall of him!

"For *my* benefit?" I repeated, my disbelief pitching up to match the piano's higher octaves. "You lied to me for *months*! You let me think I was safe with you while everyone else knew exactly what was happening, what you were doing. I was naïve and embarrassed and you preyed on that. You made them keep your secret. And worse, Tye had to watch me go with you, saying nothing, keeping your secret. *He,* at least, had the decency to—"

Bang.

Bryn slammed the keys.

"*Decency?*" he growled, eyes flashing with temper. "Rowan, should decency and that man ever meet, I expect the world to be at its end."

The pedal snapped up into ringing silence, the aftermath of a comet dropped into the ocean when the shoreline retreats into the sea.

I took a careful step back as he swiped his cane, shoved up. My pulse pounded at the intent darkening his eyes.

"Bryn, don't—"

My spine hit the wall.

He planted a hand on either side of my head, forcing me to meet those burning eyes despite the fear bleating in my lungs. Fear because his shadowed portrait held none of its usual restraint. His nostrils flared, his lips parted, and his eyes darkened bit by bit to the deep, burning gold of O'Sahnazekiel.

"You push too far, Rowan," Bryn warned in a voice I didn't recognize, like poured fire over velvet. "Have you considered that Tye knew what you were to me? When he kissed you in the tack room, he knew. When he unbuttoned your soaked jacket, he knew. When he shoved his fingers beneath your shirt, he knew what you were to me."

How did he *know* all that?

"Knew I was *what* to you, Bryn? Your past life's replacement girlfriend? Some bug-eyed reincarnation? Some silver—"

His growl cut me off. "My *mate*, Rowan. You are my mate."

A shudder rolled through me at the emotion thickening his voice, the utter desperation and longing and fear that pumped from him.

"I'm not your mate," I said, voice shaking. This was so much worse now, so much worse.

His eyes flared. "*You* are Nereida, whether you wish to accept it or not. I have always known what and who you are, I do not need the *Ledger* to know you are mine. So know this, Rowan. There is *nothing* I would not do for my mate, no lie I would not carry, no consequence I could not bear."

Pulse fluttering, I flattened my palm against his chest, his solid warmth beating under me. "Including living a lie with me for months?"

"*Yes*," Bryn hissed out. "And damn the consequences. Do you think this has been easy? To watch Tye with you? To have him call me while I am recovering in Norway and tell me of your mutual involvement?"

I blinked in shock. For the first time, I was completely at a loss. Tye and I? Surely he didn't mean the kiss at the Gate? "What?"

Bryn leaned closer, so close that every pulsing vibration of his body caressed mine. "While I was learning to walk again, Tye had taken over the task of recruiting you." A vein flicked at his temple. "But he did not call to tell me you were moving to Naruka, but to tell me how far you two had *progressed*."

Progressed? But it was the flash of hurt in Bryn's eyes that had me understanding. "Tye and I never—"

"Of which I understand now. Yet at that time, he informed me you *were* in such graphic detail as to leave no doubt. Despite knowing who you were to me, despite understanding the rules of Ruhaven. *You* I do not hold to the same account, but *him?*" Bryn bent, whispered darkly in my ear, "I will not repeat to you what he said. Suffice you understand that it was not *decent*."

He pulled back, jaw clenched. Tension echoed in every rigid line of his body, the set of his shoulders, the veins corded in his neck. "So I did not return to L'Ardoise, nor Naruka," Bryn snapped out the words as if to get them over with, "for many reasons that I have not shared, and yes, because I could not bear to see Tye touch you."

Because it should be me, Rowan, and only me, he said, and I couldn't stop my answering shiver.

"But then you came to Norway," Bryn threw out. "And I foolishly believed it was because you wished to find me. As your mate."

Because *he* had, in L'Ardoise. Because somehow before he'd ever seen me in the Gate, he'd recognized Nereida. Not in Willow, but in me. Because I was more than just the *Ledger* to him.

I clutched Bryn's trembling forearm, met his searing gaze. "How did you know?"

"Rowan, I would recognize you anywhere. In any form. In any place."

I closed my eyes, opened them. "Why didn't you tell me who you were?"

Flecks of candlelight bounced off his clenched jaw. Beautiful, even in the shadows. "Do you not think I have wanted to?" Bryn shifted his hand from the wall to my hair, his fingers shaking like mine. "You came to my office not to find your mate, but for answers to something you did not apparently believe in. Ruhaven was *my life*, Rowan, a life from which I was exiled from, and you disavowed all that I had come to value, all that I had sacrificed for it. So while every ounce of my Ruhaven soul was screaming at me to touch you, to confess all you had become to me, to share all I knew of Ruhaven, of us, I could not face having you smear it with your disbelief. Because from *that*, I knew I could not recover."

His eyes winked closed, taking their burning gold with them for a moment.

"But I could not give you up again either," he said, opening them again. "So yes, I manipulated you into visiting the Gate, in the hope that you, Nereida, would come to see me. I wished for a chance to know you, my Rowan, without the influence of our past. I decided I would wait. And though I woke from the Gate as torturously aroused as you— many, many times—you still did not see me as O'Sahnazekiel." My thighs quivered before the liquid gold swimming in his eyes. "So you see, my Rowan," Bryn said roughly, "it is *you* who have made a fool out of *me*."

The truth of that settled in me, somewhere deep in my gut. I hadn't seen him, hadn't seen the truth I so desperately wanted for myself. The one person who could be sure of who I was.

Everything in me tightened as Bryn leaned in.

He brushed his lips lightly, slowly, over the corner of my mouth. And the world seemed to pause.

I whispered his name, turned to meet the mouth I'd fantasized about for months. But he kept moving, skimming my jaw, traveling silkily along my neck until his hot breath at my ear melted my core. All around us, the candles flickered in burned stubs, replaced by moonlight that shimmered through the window and tangled in his blond locks.

"*Rowan*," he groaned, covering my body with his, closing the vibrating space between us until he was gloriously, perfectly pressed against me. I wanted to melt into him. Melt, as each point of connection shot hot sparks into my veins—his chest against my breasts, his hips pinning me to the brick wall, his teeth grazing my earlobe.

On his next breath, firm hands stroked down my arms and captured my wrists. "Now, I will admit the rest, so you shall be truly righteous in your anger at me," he murmured, accent as dark and sinful as the lips pressed to my ear. But he could have admitted anything just then for all I cared. "I anchored you not to embarrass you, but to ensure you did not experience something beyond your comfort level. This is why you did not live through O'Sahnazekiel and Nereida's mating for months. I intentionally woke us before things progressed."

That was why I'd always woken—

"*But then you returned with Tye in the tack room,*" Bryn accused, and I whimpered when he nipped at my ear. "And so I made a decision. I knew what would happen on the night of Yizomithou in Ruhaven. I wanted it. Badly. I could have pulled you out and waited, but I chose not to."

The night Sahn and Nereida had danced under the mountains, flown through the churning gears, and landed amongst the hammock. He was with me, that'd been *him* I'd felt watching me.

God, I was burning up.

He wove fingers in my hair and tugged, exposing my neck to his warm breaths.

"Bryn—why?" I pleaded, panted.

He inhaled against me and my skin buzzed from just the promise of more, the fire in my belly moving lower and lower. "Why did I prevent their mating before? Because you were uncomfortable with Sahn. Why did I not do so on Yizomithou?" The flick of his tongue had me angling my neck for more. Every lick and touch was pure fire on my skin. "Because I wanted you to understand, needed to be with you in any way I could, and Rowan..." His nose skimmed my throat. "I do not think you were very uncomfortable then."

"But you were anchoring that night," I managed. "You weren't there. In the Gate." With me while Sahn...

"Was I not?" Bryn challenged in a silken warning.

Teeth latched on to my fluttering pulse and bit softly, wringing a moan from my lips.

On Yizomithou? No, he was anchoring when Sahn's teeth sunk into my neck, pinning me in the tree canopy before he...

I jerked under Bryn's bite. "*You*—you were there. You saw—you saw..."

"Yes, my Rowan." He released me, licking languidly where his teeth pinched. "I entered Ruhaven after the three of you slipped through the Gate, intending to anchor myself in time to wake you." When his burning eyes lifted to mine, cold air grazed my dampened skin where he'd tasted. "I enjoyed watching you, Rowan, watching as O'Sahnazekiel took you for the first time. Enjoyed feeling your eyes on me. Because I was that desperate to have any part of you, even if only in a memory."

Me, not Nereida.

His gaze dipped to my lips like he could hear my pounding heart. "My Rowan," he breathed, stroking a thumb along my jaw. "Are you very upset with me?"

Gold leaked from his irises, sparkling over his cheekbones, lighting up each and every hidden freckle. "Furious," I whispered.

His eyes flashed molten, fire whipped by wind, a brilliant, burning eclipse before his eyelashes swept down over them.

He drew my wrists over my head.

And then, with my name a groan on his lips, he crushed his mouth to mine.

CHAPTER 41

Dearly Departed

*B*ryn. Swallowing my shocked gasp, he melded my lips with his. For once so unrestrained that a bolt of primal awareness shot through me. Firm and soft, demanding and somehow tender, he kissed me with the intensity of a man on his last borrowed hour. And I wanted every minute.

His tongue slid along my bottom lip, back and forth, a torturous path that had me arching against him. In answer, he bit down gently, teeth sinking into the softness like O'Sahnazekiel had, each tug summoning tiny sparks of pleasure. My hands curled reflexively where he kept them pinned against the wall.

"Bryn, you're killing me," I murmured between panted breaths.

"Certainly, we—we cannot have that."

In one stroke, he parted my lips, tongue flicking, teasing, tasting before sucking my own between his teeth. Everything inside me went molten at the raw possession. I opened for more, angling to meet him stroke for stroke, and his answering groan vibrated through to my toes. Familiar. Wild. Now. A thousand years ago.

When he released my wrists, I fisted his shirt on a breathless curse, dragging him flush against me. His hand shot out for the wall on a half-groan, half-laugh, and the sound was as sweet as the wine I still tasted on his lips.

I'd wanted him to want me instead of Nereida, but I hadn't seen O'Sahnazekiel. Sahn wasn't a memory or a dream. It was—as Bryn had once said—his life. Not separate from Bryn, not even a part of Bryn as Jamellian was to James, but essentially, irrevocably, him.

"I'm sorry," I panted. "Sorry I didn't see you, sorry I didn't recognize you, sorry I…"

He made a dark, low sound in the back of his throat as his hands gripped behind my thighs, lifting me. "Rowan, I cannot separate you from Nereida," he said when I wrapped my legs around him. "Will not."

We managed three steps without his cane before bumping into the piano. My back hit the fallboard, my hands the keys, and a booming octave of crushed notes echoed through the room.

Then his mouth was on mine again, swallowing my muffled moan, his hands tangling in my hair, wrapping what was left of my braid in his fist. He tugged my head back, delving deeper, a consuming need that threatened to take me with it.

I wanted my hands on him now, now, now. Wanted to feel every humming inch of him. Fumbling with his shirt, I managed to snap the snug button of his collar, baring pale, gold skin that glistened under the candlelight. I broke the kiss to lick my way to his neck, tasting the rough column of his throat, feeling him swallow against me, my hands tugging at all that silky hair. When my teeth found his flickering pulse, I bit softly.

"Maybe I didn't see Sahn when we met," I said against his feverish skin, "but that's only because I saw something I wanted more. I saw you, Bryn. Just you."

Rowan, I cannot lose you again, not ever.

He dragged my mouth back to his in a wild mating of tongue and teeth and lips. I bathed in every sound he made, each oath and breathless pant and whispered promise, and touched him like it was my last chance to do so. I was shaking when I slid my hands under his shirt, mesmerized by the feel of him, of the solid muscle, the sharp planes, the heart that beat fiercely beneath my palm.

My fingers dug into his shoulders when he tugged my collar open. Then his mouth replaced his hands. His tongue exploring the ridge of my shoulder, collarbone, licking, soothing all the sensitive areas I didn't know I had until I melted into him. Boneless, hot, needy.

I skimmed fingertips up his back, dipped them into the curve of his shoulder blades where O'Sahnazekiel's soft wings would have sprung.

Crack.

The fallboard splintered under his grip.

"Is that—"

"Old, it is old," he muttered, his breaths sliding under my blouse, tingling the tops of my breasts. My eyes fluttered closed when he slipped his tongue under the loosened fabric. His hands tightened on my waist, his thumbs whispering across my ribs. A simple touch like that shouldn't have caused a wave of pleasure to shimmer through me, and now I wanted my mouth over every inch of him. Wanted to start making up for everything right here, right now.

As if he'd heard the thought, Bryn tilted his head, gaze flicking up so he peered at me through beautiful, gold-flecked eyelashes.

Somewhere in the back of my mind, a roll of thunder whispered over a starless night. A memory, not mine, but his—of us. In the kitchen, the night we'd almost…

But this time, the journal didn't slip, and I didn't pull away. Instead, Bryn yanked me into him until the image of me straddled his lap and his lips met mine, his hand curling possessively around my neck.

Just one of the many versions I have imagined, Bryn teased, skimming the sensitive skin under my breasts.

My blood lit to fire. *What else?*

Ah, Rowan. Hand bunching in my shirt, he nipped at my neck, my pulse, teeth pinching just enough to draw pleasure without pain. "I should likely not admit how unashamedly I think of us."

"How unashamedly?"

His huff of breath tickled my throat.

But my vision blurred again, and this time, we were on the kitchen table, Bryn bent over me, naked, back rippling, hips pistoning—

The image winked out.

Bryn. My blood sang as thick waves of desire had the legs I wrapped around his waist weakening. He braced both hands on the piano and pressed his hips into me. My breath snagged in my throat, the keys thundering a disjointed melody as he settled against me.

"Is this what you want?" he asked in a voice I didn't recognize, but one that had a thrill tripping down my spine. He licked a hot line up my throat to nuzzle at my jaw, then my ear, and murmured against it. "For me to take you here, Rowan, on the piano?"

A hot punch of answering need rippled through me.

I hitched my leg up his hip. "I—"

Bang.

My answer died beneath a sudden noise from downstairs.

Bryn went still, chest rising and falling on thick, heavy breaths. I tugged at his shirt— Whatever part of the roof had collapsed would just have to wait—and dragged him back against me. I skimmed his lips, reveling in how soft that stern mouth could be. His tongue flicked mine, lingered.

When he hesitated, I murmured, "What is it?"

He drew back, cursing softly. "The others have returned from the Gate."

What? Now? I glanced at one of the three clocks. But James should have been another forty minutes at least.

"Bryn! Bryn!" Kazie's scream carried through the room, silencing our still heavy breaths.

All the soft wildness that had come into Bryn's face now fled, his eyes cooling to a warm, honey-brown. He grasped my shirt and quickly laced the one button he'd undone. Then he drew me off the piano, brushed my cheek. "We will have to continue this conversation later, Rowan. Stay here."

"Why?"

I was reaching for him when he turned toward the door.

Something is wrong with James.

⚙☀

My legs felt like stiff Jello as I hurried after Bryn, my body quivering from the overwhelming lack of him. The trail his tongue had left on my neck that felt like a scalding brand. The lingering touch from where his hands had gripped my wrists. Even my lips tingled from the taste of him, like they couldn't wait to feel his mouth once more.

But when Kazie screamed again, all my romantic thoughts fled like spooked deer. We rounded the corner, Bryn one step ahead, and blocking me from whatever had Kazie hysterical.

Rowan, please, do no look.

I leaned around him.

For a moment, my world went silent. Utterly, deathly silent.

In the harsh light of the kitchen, James hung limply between Kazie and Tye. Drool glistened in the corners of his mouth and dripped down his chin onto a crocheted scarf. With his glasses gone, broken blood vessels framed eyes as white as bone china. Kazie stumbled under his weight, tears marbling her dark skin as she and Tye maneuvered him through the cluttered kitchen.

James.

I stood, stunned, watching helplessly as the man who'd become my brother spasmed in pain, and every bone in his body seemed to protrude under his oversized sweater. He gasped, his eyes glossy and cloudy as a fish, like the pike Tye killed for his brother.

Then the world came rushing back, a first breath out of water, and I shifted around Bryn to take his weight from Kazie.

Ripe, bitter vomit frothed from James's mouth as Tye angled us toward the table. He thrust James on top, shoving aside the leftover potatoes, carrots, and peas from dinner.

I grabbed James's clammy hand. Shouts rang out behind me, but I couldn't look away from the anguish contorting his face.

"Where are you hurt? Did the Inquitate—"

"It's not the Inquitate, it's the fuckin' Gate," Tye bit out as James's neck snapped back. "He's seizing. Get the car, Kaz. Get the car!"

She rushed out on a stampede of heels.

Across from me, Bryn held James down by his shoulders, their gazes locked. Whatever passed between them had Bryn's face shutting down. He seemed to shrink into himself, his eyes blank as I squeezed James's wrist to stop the shaking.

"Bryn?"

He didn't react. Didn't move, even as James seized again and it took all my strength to hold him to the table.

Bryn!

His eyes whipped to me, breath rushing back as his lips parted. I felt him then, somewhere on the cusp of my mind, a caress between my eyes. Then it was gone and Bryn shifted his attention to Tye. "You know the hospital will do nothing for him."

"Why?" I lifted my voice over James's moans. "What's happened?"

"We're taking him anyway," Tye barked. "Don't be a fool just 'cause you're pissed at me. Roe, get blankets—he's freezin'."

The next ten minutes went by in a frantic blur.

James threw up twice more before we could get him calm enough to move, but by then, he was shivering so badly I'd needed to bundle him in three blankets before Bryn, Tye, and I could get him to the car. We ended up half-dragging, half-carrying him into it when Kazie backed the Ford up to Naruka's entrance.

She swapped with Tye, sliding into the back seat with James.

"Roe, I'll call ya from the hospital," Tye shouted out the window.

What? I wasn't staying here—this was my brother. "No you won't, I'm coming." I rounded the car as the spark plugs fired off like shotguns.

"Roe, I think you can count. There ain't room for all of us. You wanna leave Stornoway for the Inquitate, that's your business. I bet James wouldn't care for that, though."

Bryn pried open the passenger door as the car huffed into gear. "We will share the front." He tucked his cane under the seat, slid in, and patted his thigh. "Come, Rowan," he said amiably. "I will not bite."

Not even the slightest flicker of his eyes revealed he'd done precisely that only minutes ago. His lips were, in fact, still showing the evidence of my own aggression.

"I'll hurt your leg," I warned, but slid onto his lap. His thighs flexed before adjusting to my weight, then he slipped his arms around my waist as the Ford roared out of Naruka, holding me like we'd been together for years.

I turned in his lap, meeting his eyes.

My pulse leapt when they flickered to gold for a heartbeat before cooling to perfect, still water.

I couldn't think of us right now, not with James near death in the backseat. But it was hard to ignore the comfort of Bryn's hand stroking my loose braid. Of how close he was again, of how he'd felt pressed against me only moments ago, of all that he'd laid out that I'd yet to disassemble. All he'd admitted.

James let out a low moan in the backseat.

Guilty, I drew away. *What's wrong with him?*

But when Bryn didn't answer—maybe I'd thought at him wrong—I craned my neck to look into the back. James lay gaunt and pale, with sticky sweat greasing the strands of his dark hair. A smear of vomit Kazie hadn't yet wiped away stained his handmade sweater. With his head in her lap, she gently stroked his hair back.

"Did he catch something in the Gate?" I asked. "Some flu?"

She shook her head, curls bouncing. "No, Roe."

"Then what?" I looked around the car. "*Someone tell me what's wrong with my brother.*"

Tye stared straight out the windshield, and James—swallowed in blankets—only breathed heavily through his nose.

Bryn's fingers tightened around mine. "Rowan," he said softly. I knew that voice, the careful tone, the hitch before the words dropped, as if by holding it in, you could lessen the blow.

"Who's dead?" I asked flatly.

Bryn scooped my hair over my shoulder. "Essie. It is Essie, Rowan."

No. *No.* My throat squeezed shut.

James's childhood friend, the girl he'd needed when he was bullied, the woman who brought a smile to his face when he visited the Gate. Essie, with her bubbly cheeks and wide eyes, always laughing as Jamellian struggled with archery before cooing to him after.

It shouldn't have been her. James didn't ask for anything, didn't want anything but Essie, even knowing she'd never return, was never in the Ledger.

"How did it happen?" Bryn asked. And maybe it was only me who heard the slight hitch in his voice.

Tye answered after a beat. "I was anchorin' when I saw James's body arching off the ground—and not the good kind when he's having his fun with Essie, let me tell ya. Guy looked like he'd been possessed by the goddamn devil." He let out a heavy breath of smoke. "I pulled him and Kazie out right away."

"Roe?" Kazie whispered, for once so serious and desperate that I hardly recognized her voice.

I swiveled to face her in the back seat.

Her dark skin was as pale as I'd ever seen it. "Roe," she said again. "It wasn't a Drachaut that killed Essie. It was an Inquitate."

✦❋

An Inquitate had killed Essie. The words, their meaning, echoed in a place where I couldn't fully process it. What did they look like? Had they wanted something? Why had they attacked Essie? Was she linked to Willow? But I couldn't think of that now—no, for once, I couldn't put Willow first, even if everything in me was crying out to hike to the Gate and see exactly what had killed my sister.

Instead, I shoved aside those worries, focused on the only thing that mattered right now—James.

Fluorescent lines flickered over Capolinn's tiny emergency room. I didn't see where James would find relief from a pain born of the Gate in a place that reeked of cigarettes and floor cleaner, with a wooden reception like a confession box.

We waited for him impatiently, with Tye whipping through cigarettes and Kazie emptying the vending machine of chocolate bars before they let her join him.

And what could they possibly do? What effect did the Gate even have?

Enough that centuries later, there was this—this connection between Bryn and me.

My gaze drifted to where he stood by the exit. I took in the lean lines, the wrinkle in his shirt from where I'd grabbed it, the streetlights that transformed his skin into warm porcelain, the eyebrows knitted in concern.

He was the most beautiful man I'd ever seen.

And I was his mate.

I was Bryn's mate. Bryn's. The sailor, the artist, the Azekiel. The man who couldn't hang a shelf.

If the roles were reversed and it'd been me looking for Sahn for years, would I have told Bryn I was Nereida? To face that rejection? To know that each time he went to the Gate he'd be experiencing what should have been his memories with me? No. Never.

Tye snapped his fingers in front of my face. "So even with James lyin' in the hospital bed, y'all can't let go of Ruhaven."

Ashamed, guilty, I turned to face Tye, who stood wearing the leather jacket he hadn't buttoned in his hurry to get James here, his hair still darkened from rain. "It's not what you're thinking."

"Oh?" Tye pinched a smoke between his lips. Grunted. "So those marks on your damn neck ain't from Stornoway?" He cupped the end of his smoke, and the flick of the lighter echoed in the waiting room. *Of all the things to ask me about.* "Thought ya weren't gonna fall for his shit?"

"Don't start, Tye. Not now."

"No?"

"No."

"Well, maybe ya should have thought about that before you were neckin' in the damn car and with James cryin' in the back seat."

Annoyance washed over me, but I wouldn't dignify that with an answer. Not with James in the hospital, the Inquitate having just killed his mate. My eyes flicked to Bryn, his gaze still rapt on me.

Tye thumped a boot onto a chair. "So ya just go from hatin' the guy to forgiveness, huh?"

"Bryn explained things," I said shortly. Panted them, licked them.

"Explained you're his mate?" Tye scoffed. "So what?"

So what? How could he be this flippant? James was in an emergency room because of that bond. Something strong enough that just witnessing her death in a dream could trigger seizures.

I pushed off the chair, trying to loop my thumbs in the tool belt I wasn't wearing as I paced the hospital. Outside, a moth beat its wings on the light as a couple strode past. "Look at what just happened to James when Essie died. Being a mate, even here, it means something." I hadn't really thought of that before, of what it would mean to Bryn.

Tye snapped his leather jacket over a faded football shirt. "Listen to yourself, Roe. You're startin' to sound like Kaz these days." He inhaled a drag that shot the end of his smoke bright orange. "You think because you boned the guy in Ruhaven it means anythin' here? On another fuckin' planet?"

I stiffened at his abrupt tone. "Tye, I don't—"

"When I wanted ya in the tack room, should I have said, 'Sorry, Roe, but I hear your past life has a boyfriend. Maybe we should leave it off'? I don't need to tell ya how stupid that sounds, do I?"

He did make it sound stupid. "Look, Tye, I'm just trying to make sense of this."

"Make sense of this, Roe—you ain't Nereida and you don't belong to a guy she fucked a thousand years ago." Tye stabbed his cigarette at me, then at Bryn's bristling form. "The fact that I even need to say that out loud tells me you're already buyin' his bullshit."

Do you wish for me to intervene?

God, that's weird.

Do you think? I rather like hearing you.

When I smiled at Bryn, Tye released an annoyed grunt and swung toward the exit, boots clacking.

"Tye, wait."

He stopped with a palm on the glass door. "What?"

I strode toward him so Bryn wouldn't hear. It wasn't time for this conversation, but I had to know. "What did you say to Bryn when you phoned him in Norway? And why did you lie?"

Really, Rowan, you shall have to move farther than that.

How far?

Perhaps a block. Though even Tye will know better than to repeat his words.

Tye shook his head. "So he told ya. For the first, we'll say that's just between us men. The second I did because he's a prick. Stornoway never knew a good thing when he had it and he'd toss your ass away in a second."

"Why do you hate him so much? Just because of what he did at the Gate?"

Tye shoved the door, letting in the tepid Atlantic wind. "For what he risked when he did."

CHAPTER 42

Turning Page

"James? James, open up. *Please.*"

I rapped my knuckle on the door, repeating the same jig I'd heard him make countless times. By my third pass through the song, the bed creaked loudly and feet shuffled across the floor.

It'd been three days since Essie died. Three days since I'd seen James carried out of the hospital between Bryn and Tye. Three days that he'd been closed up in his room, not eating, not talking. He hadn't returned to Ruhaven, to the memory now forever missing something vital.

So when James opened the door at last, I was prepared. Or I thought I was.

I swallowed hard at the sight.

The gaunt cheeks, the hollow eyes and oily hair, the paleness of a man who'd been blessed with skin a few shades darker than my own. Yet now it was as worn and pink as the walls behind him. Wrinkles lined the corners of his eyes where there had been none before.

"James?"

His cracked lips moved, but no sound came out. He cleared his throat, a hard, rasping sound that caused his bony frame to shake. "What do ye want, Roe?" James asked, voice as dull and brittle as he looked.

I clenched the tray in my hands. "Bryn made soup. Better than mine. I thought you'd like to try—"

"No."

When James started to close the door, I caught it in my fist, nearly dropping the scalding soup on my feet. "James, I don't know what to do for you."

He plucked at the collar of his thin sweater, the material loose and ruffled like he'd done that a hundred times today. "Do?" Agony flickered behind his dark eyes. Strange, to see them without the glasses. "Nothing, Roe. There's nothing to be done."

I should know that better than anyone. Still, I pressed the toe of my boot to the door, stopping him when he made to close it again. "James, talk to me at least. Come downstairs, we can go for a walk, or—"

"Don't ye understand, Roe?" he choked out. "There's no moving on for me. I've nothing. I've *nothing*. No body to bury, no headstone to mourn at. I've nothing but a memory. How do ye grieve a bloody memory?" Fat tears rolled in dark tracks down his cheeks. "Where do ye bury dreams, Roe? Tell me!"

This time, when he went to close the door, I didn't stop him.

I n the week that followed, Naruka sank into a bitter void that mourned Essie's loss as much as James. It was like the house was a part of him, or maybe some part of Ruhaven, and its roots had reached into the earth and connected with the Gate. Every time a gust blew, the windows rattled worse than a jailer shaking their bars, and I'd had to replace five fuses that shouldn't have blown.

Because I hadn't wanted to leave James, Bryn had gone to the Gate for me, but he'd only returned to report that though he was with Nereida, there had been no appearance by an Inquitate. Whatever had happened with Essie, the Inquitate who killed her was gone, and so went any clues about why she'd been attacked. Whatever James might have witnessed, he kept it to himself.

He said little, ate even less, and spent most of his days reading the same newspaper or staring at the television. He wouldn't speak to anyone—including Kazie, and she tried singing, dancing, and reciting his favorite Irish poems. When she butchered a cream of mushroom stew so badly the house smelled for days, I expected James would at least complain, but he'd only wrinkled his nose and returned to his book.

If anyone should know what to say to him, it was me. Wasn't his loss as hard as losing Willow? Essie *was* real to him, even if he'd lived with her through someone else.

When my twin had died, I hadn't been able to talk about it; everything people said seemed cliched and tired. Like Ruhaven, my bond with Willow had been beyond description, and no words, poetry, or song would ever be enough to bring that to life.

So I stood in the kitchen doorway, the tray of tea I'd prepared wafting steam under my neck, and studied my brother.

He slouched on the chesterfield with the granny-square quilt drawn around his legs. The television's blue light did little to offset his puffy eyes. A pair of winged glasses lay on the coffee table, leaving his nose oddly delicate without them. He was like the dolls Willow once played with, looking sad with their dark saucer eyes and thick hair, as if they were upset she'd grown up and moved on to practical things.

How would it feel to visit the Gate without Essie?

I'd refused to leave L'Ardoise after Willow died. I'd wanted to feel her around me, as painful as it was. To wrap myself in every memory of us. And each time I'd walked into the Blue Nose, I could look at the piano and remember. Even if no one else did.

James lifted his eyes from the television to me.

"Do you remember when Essie convinced you to swim in that weird yellow marsh?" I asked.

He looked away again. "No."

"Because you weren't there," I continued anyway, setting the tray on the coffee table. "I was, though. The normally white waters were this awful bubbling goo because there'd been some ceremony for a dead tree—or something like that. But Essie, she convinced Jamellian that it was a new type of lake she'd found, that it would taste amazing, that she just had to get to the opposite shore. Then, when you jumped in, she laughed so hard her eyes bled these tiny little jewels."

James's lips twitched. "So that was why I'd gone yellow for a week. I wondered."

I set the tray on the coffee table's lace doily. Took out the sugar, milk, lemon.

"Sometimes," James said on a heavy breath. "Sometimes I wonder what it's all for. To live as we do, to love in the Gate, to bring Ruhavens here."

I poured the tea, letting the trickle of it fill what I couldn't with words. When I offered him the cup, he rolled his sleeves back three times, then took it.

"What happened, James?" I hadn't wanted to push on the details, but I needed James to fill in the blanks Kazie had left.

His nostrils widened on an inhale, held, then he seemed to just deflate into the cushions. "I know I owe it to ye, Roe, to tell ye about what happened. I just—"

I stopped him. "James, you don't owe me anything."

"Aye, I do. Ye've been looking for answers for yerself and Willow, and I want ye to have them." His throat worked. "When I was—when I was— *No*," he said when I tried to tell him it could wait. "Let me get this done. Essie and I were in Drachaut with Kazie, but yerself and Bryn were somewhere else. I think we might have been looking for ye, to find out whether ye'd discovered why the Tether broke, if it could be repaired." He took another breath, one that was painful to watch. "We encountered another Ruhaven, and we traveled together for some time. I didn't know. *We* didn't know.

"It turned on us, Roe—not a Ruhaven at all, but an Inquitate wearing the skin of one. It made to strike me when Essie stopped it. Then she—she—"

I gripped his hands, warmed them between mine. "James, I'm so sorry."

He squeezed out a breath. "I'd accepted that Essie wasn't in the *Ledger*, but I never thought she'd die before I did."

And he'd had to witness it.

"It's not fair. It's *never* fair."

"But in Ruhaven, things are supposed to be in balance, every action is to have an opposite reaction. That's why we've mates and Tethers and Marks." He held up our joined hands. "Connections. Energy. Ruhaven and Drachaut. 'Tis a closed system of energy. Entropy—'tis the only thing that changes it."

Yet Essie's death wasn't the only thing out of balance. Wasn't that exactly the issue with Bryn, Tye, and I coming over together? Maybe the Inquitate were trying to right some wrong.

I pulled the ratty blanket over my legs so it covered both of us, and let my head rest against James's shoulder. Kazie's voice floated in and out of the kitchen, bickering with Tye, but I ignored it as I asked, "How did you and Essie meet?"

James hesitated, then slid an arm around my shoulders. "I never told ye? Funny story, so it is." He chanced a sip of his tea and winced. "Ye know how Ruhavens have to complete a trial of a sort to earn our Marks?"

"Like puberty, you once said."

He chuckled lightly. "Aye, and so it is. When I was eleven, I got lost in the Faruthian Mountains. Sure, it dazzled me speechless at the time, what with the trees being pure marble. Our Mark, they become what we need when we need them most. I was a wee lad, starving and sick in the woods when Essie found me, and only a young girl herself. I like to say I saved her." Then James snorted around his biscuit. "Or how she explained it to me was…" In that soothing way of his, James spun a story of talking trees and riddles, ones only Essie had been able to solve, and a love that had grown up in the woods when he was a boy.

James lifted a thin finger. "Nereida never went through her trial, but maybe she would have if she hadn't passed through the Gate. There was time."

Would my spirit have been like James's? Something derived from Ruhaven's earth, an element, like soil or water or grass as I'd once joked.

"So," James said in the same tone he'd used in the kitchen to ask me about Sahn. "Have yerself and Bryn...resolved things, now?"

I felt the tips of my ears pinken. We hadn't resolved *that* yet, but maybe we were on the right path. "I think so."

James's chest swelled against me before a sigh followed in my ear. "I wish that langer had told ye earlier about O'Sahnazekiel, about all of it. Sure, if me Essie was here I would've confessed me sins on the first day. Begged her to take me any way she likes."

But Bryn hadn't done that. He hadn't fallen to his knees and begged, hadn't even appeared to like me at first. Just because he thought I was with Tye? How could that keep him from someone he'd supposedly spent years waiting for?

Or Tye was right, and Bryn never risked something he couldn't win.

"I guess that's not Bryn's style," I said at last.

James slid his gaze sideways. "Suppose not. *Although*," he drawled, "I can't say Essie ever did make me struggle home half-naked in a storm like."

Not my finest moment, but I snorted when he elbowed me playfully.

"Did ye know Bryn confronted me in Oslo?" James asked.

"Yeah, I was there for the warm welcome," I said dryly, thinking of the man who'd circled me in his office. And how much different he was now.

James chuckled, the first laugh I'd heard out of him in weeks. "No sure, at the bar before ye took off after that Inquitate. Bryn pulls me aside, explaining Tye called him, and told Bryn that he and you—" James paused, coughed. "Suppose Bryn wouldn't want me repeating the thing. But he was accusing me like, saying, 'Is this how ye let Ruhavens get recruited now?' Sure I didn't know what he was on about, for if Tye and yerself were together, it was news to me so it was. I told him that, and to stop being such a bloody bollocks."

Tye had so many tricks up his sleeve, he should just open a show. "I guess that's partly why Bryn hated me at first."

"Ah, Roe," James said, understanding me perfectly. Sympathy softened his face into melted butterscotch. "Ye know that's not true, and if ye think Bryn feels differently about ye than I do about Essie, yer wrong. He's been punishing himself, in a way, I think. Ruhaven broke him, Roe, living with the memories of friends ye'll never meet, a mate ye'll never know."

I gazed up at James. "You live with it—seeing Ruhavens come and go, saying goodbye when they make the Fall."

He plucked at a loose thread on the quilt. "Ah, but sure I've had Kazmira, O'Sahnazekiel, and then, eventually, I had me own sister."

Because emotion clogged my throat, I offered James the tea and biscuits he'd set down.

He sighed and lifted a cookie, rolling it between his thin fingers. "Trying to feed me now, Roe? Sure, I thought I'd never see the day. What'd ye call me before? Nurse Jamellian?" He bit into it. "Ye sure know how to wind me up."

I smiled and settled against him in the well-worn cushions.

Then James let out a gusty exhale.

I lifted a brow. "What is it?"

"Roe," he sighed, "ye make a feckin' shite cup of tea, ye know?"

CHAPTER 43

The Night We Met

"**J**ames should stay out of the Gate for now," Tye argued, heaving the saw to his side of the vociferous tree.

"What?"

Tye rolled his eyes. "Girl, if you go anymore doe-eyed thinkin' of Stornoway, you're gonna get caught in hunting season out here."

I schooled my face. "I'm fine." Sweaty, hot, sleepless, but fine. "You think James should…?"

Tye huffed a foggy breath. "Stay out of the Gate," he repeated, grinding the blade against the wet, sap-laden trunk. Behind the pine tree, green needles littered his checkered jacket. "With the Inquitate tracking us now, who knows what's gonna happen?"

I was quiet for a moment. "Ruhaven is the only thing James has of Essie. He needs to return."

"Ya think, huh? Just like how you're going back?" Tye taunted, calling out my dry spell. "Way I see it? That Gate just causes trouble for everyone. And you still ain't got any answers from it about Willow."

He wasn't wrong. "What do you think about the letters Bryn found from Carmen? About her thinking the Drachaut become Inquitate?"

He kicked the tree. Once. Twice. The sliced trunk clung on, its glistening leaves shuddering under the attack. "Darlin', I don't know nothin' 'bout that woman's theories. Maybe she's right, maybe she ain't. It's all over my head."

"Did you know her in the Gate?"

He pulled off his toque and hair the color of good Irish dirt flowed free. "Nope."

Hm. "Well, how did she come up with the theory?"

"Dunno."

Tye sunk to the frozen ground again and picked up the saw to claw through the last remaining strand of the tree. How was it winter already? Though it certainly didn't look like it. Here, the forest stayed as vividly beautiful as the summer, unaware it was supposed to cower in the face of the frozen season or that it was supposed to change at all.

"James says it's all about balance. Mates, Tethers, and yet we came over in a threesome."

A dimple winked in his cheek. "If Stornoway wasn't a part of it, you'd be gettin' me excited." Then he ripped the saw back so hard, I ended up with a mouthful of pine needles.

I spat them out. "Right, well. What if it's mates that come over in threes?"

Sweat beaded on Tye's reddened neck. "What, and you're the first to figure it out? Don't ya think we'd have noticed when all the triplets started tearin' up the sheets 'round here?"

If only. "Maybe the Inquitate killed them before they found each other."

"Why? 'Cause they got some vendetta against true love?"

Broken at last, the timber teetered on its axis and smashed into the earth. Crows clucked indignantly, their wings thrumming like fairies into the sky, becoming a black triangle against the heavy clouds as Tye shrugged on his gloves.

"I don't know," I said as he hoisted the tree. "But they almost killed Bryn before we met."

"Ya did meet, hun. And guess what? Ya didn't even remember."

Yeah, that shot landed. "So it's not about dividing up true love." I pushed on. "Maybe it's about the balance. Something about the lack of balance in the triplets. And they're trying to fix the scale. Or…"

I was forced to grab the other end when Tye started walking with the tree. "Let's get this back before Stornoway starts sweatin'."

I rolled my eyes. "Or maybe it's not about the scale. Maybe it's about what caused us to come over in the first place. Bryn and I are mates. What if we grabbed each other? Then you got caught up in it?"

"But I haven't even met you guys. As far as I can understand, I'm in the city of *Esmeralda*, nowhere near ya."

"But we must meet eventually if we're making the Fall together. What happens when we do? When we make the Fall, I mean?"

His shoulders straightened. "What? You already know what happens."

"No, I mean us. You. Bryn. If one of us makes the Fall, does it affect the others?"

"Don't see why it would."

"Well, if we came over at the same time, maybe we've got to go back at the same time too. Have any other triplets returned?"

Another shrug. "Ain't none I know of."

That was odd, though, wasn't it? "You mean, no triplet has ever made the Fall?"

I could tell he was getting annoyed. "Roe, ya want a history of which Ruhaven did what, ya gotta ask James."

How had I missed this? The one thing I'd put out of my mind—the Fall—might have some correlation as well. If no triplet ever made it, was it because they'd been killed before they heard the call? But then, there was always one survivor of each triplet at least, so why hadn't the remaining one made the Fall?

I needed to ask James, see if he—

But no, not now, not while he was recovering from Essie.

I let out a weary breath. "I hope James wants a Christmas tree."

"Just don't tell him ya cut it down. Or else he'll—*Stornoway*," Tye uttered on a low curse.

My heart all but jumped in my throat. Unfortunately, that was all it could do right now. With James mourning Essie, Bryn and I could hardly pick things up again—on the piano or otherwise.

In the shadows of Naruka, Bryn leaned against a thick oak, cane in his pale hand, the sky's gray light surrounding him in a halo. He wore a thick sweater the color of sweet Irish cream, with three burgundy buttons on the collar and the dark jeans I'd begun to enjoy on him. He looked like a mouthwatering pint of Guinness.

And his smile had the same effect.

Hello, Rowan, his voice caressed my mind.

"I brought her back alive," Tye said sourly. "You can breathe again now."

Bryn limped toward us, inspecting me as if he expected to find a part missing. When he didn't, he ran a hand along my braid, pulling lightly, playfully. "Indeed."

I'd never get used to him looking at me like that, but I'd better learn soon because my pulse would beat itself into an early heart attack.

Tye grunted and started moving with the tree again, forcing me to shuffle my feet and follow.

"How was the Gate this morning?" I asked Bryn, deciding to shoot the elephant in the room first. I still hadn't been back, not since—

"I still remain in Drachaut, though I did not see you," Bryn said, referring to Nereida. "I saw Jamellian." The way his lips tightened told me all I needed to know.

"You haven't seen the Inquiate again?"

He shook his head.

There was a moment where the only sounds were the pine needles swishing the ground and Tye's grunting sighs, then Bryn said, "O'Sahnazekiel has been spending more time with Kazmira."

Bryn slid his hand into mine, interlacing our fingers in that simple gesture, still so new that heat zinged up my arm.

As we walked, he asked me about the holiday traditions in L'Ardoise, of how Willow and I celebrated. *By rolling hot maple syrup in snow with a popsicle stick*, I told him, which resulted in many more questions.

What did he miss? Reindeer meat.

Would there be snow in L'Ardoise now? At least five feet.

Did it snow more in Norway or Canada? Definitely Canada.

He and Tye ignored each other until we stepped into the castle's peaty warmth and dropped the tree, then Tye veered straight to the kitchen.

I hesitated in the lounge, unwilling to let go of Bryn so soon.

He squeezed my hand. "Will we go upstairs?" My heart flipped. "James wished to speak to you when you returned." *Oh.*

"You didn't tell him I was chopping down one of his precious trees, did you?"

Bryn huffed a laugh. "I certainly did not."

He brushed his thumb over the back of my hand, a short smile on his lips.

Where did we go from here? With James bedridden, and the Inquitate threatening us both in and out of the Gate? It felt wrong to be with him when James had just lost Essie.

As I angled toward James's door, Bryn squeezed my hand. "Rowan, may we talk?" My pulse flickered once, like a candle after a puff of breath, as I faced him. "I admit, I have been uncertain of how to proceed after James's loss."

Though I felt the same, it hadn't stopped me from fantasizing about him, from replaying every minute in the music room, from wishing and wondering what would have happened. From imagining what it'd be like to be Bryn's.

I lifted my hand to cup his face, like he had once with me at the Gate. *Can I touch you?*

His eyes danced underneath heavy lashes. "Of course, Rowan."

My breathing was barely audible as I slowly traced a line over his Nordic-cut nose and the playful, sinful lips, mapping their preference to lift to the left side. When he parted them, I rubbed my thumb along the bottom, a shade fuller than the top. His mouth was just a bit too wide, endearingly so, the anomaly giving him an impossibly rare and bright smile.

When I dropped my hand, his own settled on my shoulders—warm, firm, strong—and he lowered his head so our noses touched. My skin all but hummed beneath his fingers.

"Do you know what it is to be mated?" Bryn asked quietly.

My gaze flicked to the closed door beside us. *James explained what it was for him and Essie.*

"It is different for each mated couple," Bryn said, voice barely above a whisper, his breath tingling my lips. "But should we *progress*…"

"Progress?" I swallowed. "You mean those irregular expressions?"

His quick grin was a thing of beauty. "Yes, my Rowan." He trailed his thumb over my bottom lip, back and forth, back and forth until my thighs weakened, until an ache built between them. "Then things here would be as they are for us in Ruhaven. That is why James wished to find Essie in the Ledger."

How could things be the same here? Sahn and Nereida had been with each other for years, decades.

Bryn drew away slightly. "We have not spoken of this enough, of what it—it would…" I wet my lips, my tongue flicking his thumb, tasting him. "…would mean," he finished, and his rough voice sparked something low in my belly. "Rowan, would you be amenable to returning to the Gate together? Until—until James is more recovered."

Was that what he'd prefer? Nereida? "I…"

You are not in competition. You are one and the same.

Maybe Bryn thought so, but I hadn't lived her life, hadn't lived in the Gate for years like him.

He ran his hands over my shoulders. "Would you prefer I remain here? To not visit the Gate while you adjust?"

Would he? Would he really give that up? Could I ask it with us so close to the Inquitate?

As I worried, I could feel his gaze like a baby feather dragged over my skin, tickling my cheeks and running down my nose. Then it rolled over my mouth, teasingly, sensuously.

"How are you *doing* that?" I murmured.

Magic. His wide mouth quirked up. *Or, perhaps, I am simply your mate.*

I flattened a hand on his chest. *Is it simple?*

He tilted my head back, a low exhale parting his lips. "If you wish it to be, Rowan."

God, when he switched like that—silky voice inside me to low and rough outside… Legs weak, I pressed a hand to the wall, bumped some portrait or knickknack, sending it swinging wildly on its tiny nail.

Bryn caught the frame, steadying it with an amused look at me.

And then I spotted him.

Not in the picture I'd nearly ripped off the wall, but the one next to it—in the wallet-sized photo with a glass covering and an anorexic frame.

The portrait I hadn't noticed once the clocks stopped that night.

Bryn followed my fixed gaze curiously, but stiffened slightly when he saw whom I stared at.

Levi's skin and hair matched mine, but he was Mexican, not First Nations. His mouth was a dot, a pucker of the lips that neither rested nor smiled. His nose was a fraction too large, his eyes too small and looking away from the camera.

But that wasn't what caused my skin to prickle, and for once, it wasn't Bryn either.

I could imagine how Levi's tiny lips would pop open on a laugh, knew his smile was long and thin like a sliced green bean.

Because I'd met him.

CHAPTER 44

Chocolate

The walls were as pink as the roses Kazie left around the house.

Bryn paced James's bedroom, impatience in the tight lines of his broad mouth and steel eyes. I'd never been in here before, not even to do repairs, and I could see why.

The room was an homage to Essie, to Ruhaven, to the land James would never make the Fall to. Standing here, it was impossible not to feel the bone-deep longing ringing from every sketch and photograph of people who'd visited Naruka over the years, of his mother, of Ruhaven, but mostly of his mate.

Essie—painted in cool colors in the monstrous daffodils, marbled skin glowing a bright lavender from Ruhaven's light. Essie—drawn with a toothy smile that would have scared me once. Essie—with her side profile showing a round nose and deep-set purple eyes.

While Bryn might have painted and hung a portrait of Nereida in the library, he'd never descended to this.

James slumped at a desk of colorful drawers with hand-painted knobs. He wore a thick sweater with a vase of cheerful sunflowers embroidered on the front. Their happy yellow seemed a mocking contrast to the bags under his eyes, and he'd either chosen it to cheer himself up or, by his stuffed snowman look, had layered on all the clothes he possessed to ward off the chill.

"The walls are pink," I repeated.

James steepled his fingers. "Beige," he corrected. "They're beige, Roe."

They were pink.

Bryn planted his hands on the windowsill and gazed at wild fields unfurling into the sea. "What was Levi doing in L'Ardoise, James?" Bryn demanded.

I'd seen him at the bakery, which I wouldn't—and shouldn't—have remembered, except he'd spoken to my sister. To Willow, while I'd ordered coffee for us. I'd thought he was trying to ask her out, so I'd taken my time with the coffee. But in the end, he'd left with only a bag of muffins.

James dragged off his glasses, rubbed at the marks on his nose, and laid them next to a Santa-embossed coffee mug. "I've not the faintest idea like. It doesn't make any bloody sense. I haven't seen or heard Levi in years."

He brushed back dark hair that framed a face drawn from the strain of Essie and the news Bryn had dumped in his lap. I hadn't wanted to bring this to James now, but Bryn had rolled over my protests and virtually stormed into James's bedroom. When James cursed impressively at both of us, I quickly realized he was extremely private about his space—and with the hundreds of Essies staring at me, I could see why.

The wicker chair squeaked as James adjusted himself. "And suppose Roe's mistaken? It may be Roe—not that I doubt ye—yer misremembering."

But I couldn't have known the razor smile of Levi's lips or the faint accent I knew he spoke with.

"She is not," Bryn said before I could protest.

I sank onto James's bed, finding it cloud-soft and piled with pillows. "He was there before Willow died, but I'm not sure when. Maybe Levi was working on finding Ruhavens in the *Ledger*?" I ventured, because the alternative was more insidious and I didn't think James could handle it right now.

James shook his shaggy hair. "Ye think he just got some whim up his arse to start recruiting? Ye didn't know Levi, Roe, but he didn't much fancy this place like. He heard me out sure, but after a month or so he was gone. We left on good terms well enough, or so I thought at the time, but sure now I find he's gone and given me a bogus address!" The insult brought the first sign of life to his face in days.

Bryn hiked a hip on the window ledge. With the sunlight at his back, he looked like my avenging angel without wings. "Levi left Naruka prior to the discovery of Willow or Rowan's location, which suggests either someone told Levi later of the location, or he copied the *Ledger* and began a search for Ruhavens on his own."

Did other people do that? What for?

James scratched at his jaw. "Yer man's hardly gonna waste his time trying to recruit. Sure it's not an easy task like."

Tye would no doubt agree with that. "Maybe he wasn't recruiting," I said quietly, and Bryn and James turned to stare at me. "Both the Inquitate and Levi were in L'Ardoise. What if he brought them there?"

James set his untouched coffee down slowly. "Yer not saying ye think Levi has something to do with the Inquitate killing Willow?"

I rubbed my lips, switched tactics. "Carmen's the only one he kept in contact with and she seems to know more about the Inquitate than any of us. She would have known Willow's location when you found her, right? She could have sent him."

James held up a hand. "That's a wee bit of an accusation there, Roe. This is just what got ye into trouble in Oslo, ye know, when ye accused Bryn of lying about his leg."

I fisted the old quilt. He was right, and I'd learned nothing, apparently.

"Rowan may have been wrong about my leg," Bryn put in, "but she was correct that I was hiding something. James, I do think we must consider that there is an uncomfortable connection between Carmen and Levi, and no discernible reason he should be in L'Ardoise prior to Willow's death."

James, unwilling to have doubt cast on his aunt, said quickly, "It might be she was wanting to help with recruiting again."

"If it's not nefarious, let's figure this out." I pushed off the bed, pacing a line on the oval rug. "Levi visits L'Ardoise because they discovered that Willow and I are there. We can probably assume he didn't want to take a holiday in a place with one motel. So why go? He's a triplet, just like Bryn and I. Maybe he discovered that pattern and wanted to warn us?"

Bryn followed my pacing, letting me sort it out.

I knew Levi, somewhat, had read his diaries, as false as I believed they were. So I forced myself to go through the steps, no different than walking through a job for the first time. "We need to go back to the beginning. It took two months for Levi to decide he wanted to leave Naruka—that's what you said. But that's a long time to live in a world you don't believe in. Do you remember the reason he gave you?"

James folded his hands on his stomach. "Just that he didn't want to live in a fantasy. Some don't, Roe."

"And yet his book didn't describe Ruhaven. *No*, I know he wasn't there," I said quickly when James looked ready to interrupt. "If there are only two countries and he wasn't in Ruhaven, then maybe he started in Drachaut, but he didn't describe that in his journal, didn't talk about mirror floors and glacier skies. Instead, he *pretended* to describe Ruhaven. Why?"

Bryn pushed off the windowsill. "Possibly because he did not wish anyone to know."

I nodded. Like voltage in a circuit, everything eventually had to add up. "Yeah. So he wanted you to *believe* he was in Ruhaven. Why is that?"

James appeared genuinely perplexed. "I've no idea. Sure, it wouldn't matter to me if he's in Drachaut or Ruhaven. We're in Drachaut ourselves now like."

And that was exactly the question. Why would it have mattered so much that he was in Drachaut?

Bryn stopped in front of the illustration of Essie on a violet-sand beach. "The only person we are aware of whom Levi remained in contact with is Carmen."

"People often remain close to those who did their recruiting," James agreed.

I snapped my fingers. "Exactly. Close enough that he'd lie if Carmen told him to?"

James threw up his arms. "About what so? Ye think she told him to make up some wee story in his diaries? For what feckin' purpose? She may have some strange ideas about the Inquitate, but she's no reason to bother with this. Yer all but accusing Levi and me aunt of planting false evidence, but why lie about where ye were in Tallah?"

That stopped me.

I looked at Bryn. *No, why lie about* who *you were?*

When our eyes met—a punch that rippled through me—he slowly inclined his head.

Determined, I crossed to James, flattened my hands on his desk, and drew a line with my finger from his glasses, to the coffee, to the journal. "Not where, James. *Who*. I think the *where* was incidental." My blood pumped in my ears, loud and clear. I could smell the truth of it because I'd lived it through Bryn. "I bet they knew each other in the Gate, knew who they *were* in the Gate. Carmen and Levi. *And she told him to lie*."

"Why?" James asked, wide-eyed.

"Because," Bryn answered, laying a hand on my shoulder. "Who they are, where they are, must lead to the Inquitate. That is how Carmen knew of the sacrifice made to create them."

What did it mean that Levi had been in L'Ardoise? Had Carmen sent him? And who were they to each other in the Gate—mates? Friends? Enemies?

What did who and what they were in the Gate have to do with the Inquitate?

A chocolate pinged me in the cheek.

"So ya really think Carmen wanted Levi to write a bunch of bullshit in a diary?" Tye asked, readying another candy.

I dug the chocolate out of the couch cushions. "I don't know, Tye, what do you think? You know her better."

"What do I think?" He shrugged and propped his bicep over the back of the sofa. Tye had swapped his leather jacket for a soot-gray hoodie. The boots, as always, were leather, blackened, and dirty. "I think it's Christmas, Roe, and I wouldn't mind one damn day without talk of Ruhaven, Carmen, Levi, or any Inquitate. Chocolate?"

Before I could shake my head, he sent another crisp mint soaring over the coffee table.

Christmas in Naruka would have suited Willow down to every baked scone, apple tart, and candy cane, though she'd have recoiled at the vivid lime grass.

Our fireplace roared, its flames licking life into a house that had been too quiet after Essie. In an effort to liven up the place, Kazie had strung popcorn—buttered, by the smell of it—across each lamp and frame, and its scent mingled with the room's cocktail of blue spruce, orange peels, and chocolate mint.

The Christmas tree Tye and I had dragged back was wedged next to the television. Like the billiard table, the tree wore a thrift shop's worth of ornaments, from a tiny hand-carved rocking horse to molding orange slices. Six feet up, a red nutcracker gnashed its teeth, a concession James had not made willingly, as he'd been adamant it was a sign of support for the British.

I glanced up as the kitchen's farmhouse door inched open, the sounds of "O Holy Night" crackling from the radio, and beside it, a naked Father Christmas used a Santa hat to cover his unholy night.

James paused in the doorway, wearing his leprechaun apron with a tea towel flung over one shoulder, his glasses reflecting the flickering embers of the morning fire. Then, like a broken toy come to life, he forced his lips into a plastic smile and stepped into the room.

"James, are you—"

"Fine, I'm fine sure. 'Tis a fine tree too."

Playing along, I nodded at the blue spruce. "Tye, what's a Montana ball cap doing on my tree?" It perched over the glowing angel at the top—probably some subtle dig at Bryn.

"*Your* tree?" Tye drawled. "I reckon it took two of us that day."

James brushed the flour from his slacks and squinted at the tree's disco ball lights. "Kazie did a lovely job decorating. Where'd ye get it?"

When Tye drew a zipper across his lips, James's eyes widened until the whites of them popped like ornaments. "Jayzus, Mary, and Joseph. Don't say ye feckin' cut this down in Naruka—sure these are protected historical woods, for reasons I'd say we all understand."

When the whistle sounded from the kitchen, James hurried after it, passing Kazie, who slid in wearing a sweater with glued-on candy canes and reindeer antlers that bounced in time with the music.

"I expect plants from everyone," she stated primly. "Or books! Anything else and I'll worry that you don't know me at all."

Check. And check. "Then prepare to weep when you open your first drill set," I lied.

Chuckling, Tye tossed another chocolate at me. "Wanna guess what I got ya?"

"A chainsaw."

"Nope. Might have used that with your casserole, though."

The candy landed between my breasts, but before I could grab it, a smooth, pale hand smothered it. I lifted my chin and braced for the kick of power, the jolt that only Bryn could summon.

I met dark, winter-blue eyes in a face carved in the Norwegian fjords, with angel-wing cheekbones sweeping like a waterfall and gold glinting in a beard he hadn't shaved since yesterday. Snow-blond hair hung in soft waves to his ears, more angelic than the Christmas angel hiding under Tye's ball cap.

He closed his grip around the candy, pinching it between two long, elegant fingers. "Hello, Rowan." His voice was as rich as Christmas morning.

Deliberately, he skimmed the candy between my breasts, trailing a path up my body. His eyes lingered on my mouth.

I parted my lips.

He waited a beat, watching me through burnished-gold eyelashes. Then he slipped the chocolate onto my tongue, trailing a finger along my bottom lip. "Do you wish to guess what your gift from me is?" he asked in a voice like rough silk.

As my mind launched into fantasies, Tye drawled, "The finest plucked flowers from the glowin' fields of Ruhaven, if I know him at all."

Bryn didn't take his eyes off me. Didn't so much as blink when a memory flashed between us. *Nereida and Sahn, naked, rolling in lavender.*

I swallowed audibly. How could he *do* that?

Then it was gone, and Bryn replied, "I have something else in mind."

What? Really? *Tonight*? No, no, he was winding me up again.

"So, ready for New Year's?" Kazie called.

With a smile, Bryn straightened and explained in a low voice, "Kazie and I are planning New Year's Eve, an old tradition of ours since I first brought her to Naruka." He rested his elbows on the back of my couch. "James insisted we continue despite things, and I have been informed I am in charge of music this year."

Tye rolled over and smacked life into a dead pillow. "Suppose we'll be dancin' to something' like 'Sonata in A Major' then."

Bryn's reply was dry as dust. "I am certain we can find a compromise between a country song titled 'Twelve of my Favorite Trucks' and classical piano."

I tucked my tongue in my cheek, laid a hand on Bryn's, and settled back to enjoy the easy banter between him and Kazie, of hearing the old stories of them together at Naruka. Even Tye joined in when he didn't have to speak directly to Bryn.

As Kazie was wrapping up a joke about Bryn and a bicycle he'd tried to fix, the reek of burned cheese and cereal blew through the kitchen door. "An Choigilteoir Bean," James announced with a forced zeal that didn't match the gelatinous egg smoking in a casserole dish. The breakfast recoiled at itself, eggs swaying when James clacked it onto the coffee table.

Tye stabbed an eager fork into the wobbling mess. "This is James's traditional Ruhaven special, darlin', and a lot better than that goat head Stornoway tried to sell us on one Christmas."

Kazie shuddered. "I'll never forget the eyeballs."

Bryn said, somewhat stiffly, "It is a *Norwegian* tradition."

Well, eyeballs were about the only thing James's abomination was missing. Before I could subject my mouth to it, Bryn said, "Perhaps we shall add some of the wine Tye bought from his recent trip."

Both James and I stared at him like he was crazy. "Ye'll do no such thing," James warned.

But there was a calculated look in Bryn's eye. *What do you know?*

He didn't answer, simply pushed deliberately off the couch and disappeared into the kitchen as Kazie said, "I wouldn't mind the wine."

In answer, Bryn returned a moment later, wine bottle in hand. He set the bottle down next to the egg dish, spun it so that its castle illustration faced Tye. "I admit, when I saw this bottle, I did not expect you to have such fine taste in wine."

Arms crossed, Tye leaned back with a sneer. "You'd know."

"I do," Bryn agreed amiably. "Which is how I know this is not a label you shall find in L'Ardoise, despite you claiming to have bought it on your *trip*."

Tye straightened on the couch.

"Indeed, when I was in town last week, I brought it to the local wine shop, much to the delight of the shopkeeper, Darrel. You know him, James."

Looking as mystified as me, James wiped at his brow. "Aye, I do."

"And Darrel was quite happy to tell me this wine is from a local vineyard in the northwest of France, La Château Belle."

And that was important because...

"You did not visit L'Ardoise, did you, Tye?" Bryn said.

What?

Kazie yanked at her hair. "What is going on *now*? It's *Christmas*."

Tye rose with deliberate slowness.

"Tye?" I said, but he didn't look at me.

Instead, he yanked out a cigarette, stuffed it between his lips. "You're a goddamn snoop, Stornoway. A goddamn snoop."

Now James rose as well. "Tye, what the bleedin' hell is going on?"

Bryn answered, "He never went to L'Ardoise. He had someone else to visit, someone who also resides in France."

Then everything tumbled into place.

I shoved off the couch. "You went to see *Carmen*?"

Everyone started shouting at once with the steaming mash of eggs spoiling in the middle of us all.

Kazie tossed a new ball of yarn that bounced off Tye's face. "What do you mean you were in *France*?" She chucked another. "You know I *love* France and you didn't bring me?" Another twisted ball went flying.

Tye ducked one, two, three until he looked like a yo-yo. "Christ, woman, if ya wanna go so bad, I'll drag you there by this yarn."

James held Kazie back before she threw another.

"Tye, we've been trying to reach her since she left, and you've *known* how to contact her this entire time?"

He jabbed the cigarette at me. "Don't you go accusin' me of somethin' I ain't likely to forgive. I didn't know Carmen's exact address or nothing—when she left, she told me how to find her. I flew over, met up with her usin' the directions she left. Had to talk to this guy *Philippe* at some French café with baguettes. Ya think I wanted to do that?" He looked actually disgusted at the memory.

James cut in. "Ye tell me straight now, Tye, what ye were doing talking to me aunt?"

"Tryin' to find answers for Roe, what do ya think? Stornoway spends his days snoopin' through other people's letters, convinced my old recruiter's got somethin' to do with the Inquitate. I don't believe it, but I go on and meet with her just in case."

"But why lie, like?" James pressed.

"I don't know what you all are on about half the damn time," Tye shot back. "Conspiracies, energy theories, bullshit. I helped in the way I knew how and I didn't want to be goin' over there in the first place. Lady's in fuckin' retirement, and you got me askin' her questions 'bout Inquitate 'cause Stornoway's got some bug up his ass."

That almost made sense.

"*And?*" I pressed, cutting James off. "If that's true, then what did she say? Did you ask her why she thought the Drachaut turned into Inquitate? Why Levi went to L'Ardoise?"

Tye lifted his shoulders, dropped them. "This was *before* Levi, Roe. I asked Carmen what she knew 'bout the Inquitate. She wasn't much happy with me comin' to her, bringin' this to her, ya know? But I did that for you. She wouldn't talk to no one else."

I forced my shoulders to relax. "Well, did she say *anything*?"

"Not a whole lot, as I damn well thought. She had a bunch of conspiracy stuff. And yeah, she brought up the whole Drachaut to Inquitate thing. I didn't take it seriously."

Bryn skimmed a hand over my hair.

You've been keeping secrets, I accused him.

I did not want to raise your suspicions of him if my own proved to be misplaced.

"Look," Tye continued with a wince, "she might have told me about the clocks. Thing is, I didn't believe her, not 'til we came home that day and found all two hundred of 'em stopped. Christ, Roe, I just thought the old woman was batty."

"And yet you visited her without telling me."

"For *you,*" Tye said, visibly annoyed. "I go on and haul my ass to mingle with the French—not easy, let me tell ya—just in case she's got answers 'bout Willow. And I didn't tell you 'cause Carmen don't want people knowin' her business, and I respect that. She did me a favor, that's all it was."

"You lied about going to L'Ardoise."

"I *did* go to L'Ardoise, ya paranoid broad," he said, somewhat affectionately. "I did have roommates to deal with, but I stopped in France on the way back. *Christ*, a man can't even scratch his balls 'round here without gettin' the side-eye from one of ya. And I don't even know what you're accusin' me of."

Some of the anger stuttered out of me. No, he hadn't done anything wrong, and it made sense why he hadn't told me. Tye was too loyal a person to betray Carmen.

But when Bryn tried another angle, James shouted, "Lads, I can't feckin' take this anymore. Tye, would ye sit down before ye threaten to break someone's leg again on bloody Christmas, as Kazie so pointed out." James's voice crescendoed with the caroling choir on the record player.

Tye settled pointedly back on the couch, Bryn on the seat beside me.

"Alright so," James continued as Kazie emerged from the tree with her arms full and muttering about Paris. "Let's open the rest of these bloody gifts and remember to be merry about it."

If merry was the simmering tension between Tye and Bryn, then we were well on our way to achieving that goal.

James tossed gifts unmercifully in our laps, and anyone who didn't smile and thank the next person got a stern frown in return. I opened a jigsaw from Tye, a cactus from Kazie that I pricked my thumb on—"*Duh, don't touch it*," she'd said while Bryn picked the yellow hairs out of my skin.

James unwrapped a crocheted sweater from Kazie, an aged bottle of whiskey from Tye, and a drawing of Essie from Bryn. The latter caused him to break into a fresh round of tears that dissolved any remaining tension.

When Kazie started unwrapping my present, she shook it hard enough that if it hadn't broken yet, it would have by now. After ripping away the newspaper with a vigor only dogs and the young possessed, she held up her new book with a smile of sheer delight.

James peeled off his glasses, foggy from crying, and peered skeptically at the cover. "*Merman and the Maiden*," he read.

"Banned in all twenty-six counties," I added.

James slapped the couch. "Thirty-two, excuse you like." He picked up his coffee, sipped, then spat it out. "Ah for—where are me glasses?" He thrust the mug at Kaz. "This is yers, and if ye put any more sugar in that, ye won't live to see Ruhaven."

Bryn's fingers brushed lightly over the nape of my neck.

Will you come with me to the Gate tonight?

Why?

There was a brief pause. *If you do not see O'Sahnazekiel soon, I fear one of us will require a similar book.*

I choked on my coffee just as James picked up the envelope I'd left for him and fanned the fireplace with it. "What'll this be, Roe? Me feckin' bill, I imagine?" If I was still charging him, it'd be five times the size.

But he ended up being pleasantly surprised to discover not a well-deserved and itemized bill, but a scone recipe I'd tracked down from his favorite café.

Bryn received a truly terrifying three-dimensional reindeer sweater from Kazie—which I immediately forced him to wear.

"What's this?" I asked her, opening a slim, hand-carved box with two elephants. Inside, hardened beans sat in smooth cups in four rows of ten.

"My mother made it for me."

I nearly dropped a bean. "Maybe I shouldn't…"

"Of course you should," she said briskly. "It's just a game. You'll like it."

"You don't want it?"

She paused, mid-cuddling the skein of Irish wool Bryn had given her. "I've already played it, and I don't need it anymore."

"But—"

"Ah, Rowan, you must truly want to see more of my poorly painted boats," Bryn interrupted.

With a last look at Kaz, I turned to watch him unclamp the portable easel I'd made for him. "I just thought with your leg, and having to carry the old one…" I blushed profusely when he pretended it was good.

But there was no gift under the tree from him, which only made me start to sweat that I'd misunderstood, that I shouldn't have gotten him anything. Maybe mates didn't give gifts.

It was in the middle of my burgeoning panic that Bryn looked at James and Kazie and they quietly left the room. Music filtered in from the kitchen—James turning his radio up.

"Rowan?"

I rubbed my knees. "Yeah?"

When Bryn laid his hand over mine, I glanced over. His mouth curled into that familiar, crooked grin. "Would you like your gift now?" He lifted a hand, wiggled his fingers. "A memory, Rowan. As I do know how you love flying."

And then, he showed me how Sahn and Nereida met.

✸✿

"Did ye make this?"
I stuck my hands in my pockets. "Yeah."

Behind Naruka, in the soft, springy earth that belonged only to Kerry, James and I stood shoulder to shoulder.

Pink wildflowers had sprung up early, their tangled stems twirling through logs washed up from the reservoir. Wet bramble leaves reflected the turquoise of the sky. By spring, the gnarled cherrywood tree we stood under would bloom with the pinks I'd seen when I first arrived.

James tugged up his slacks before kneeling at the headstone. He ran his thumb over the engraving of the bow and arrow, then the name, *Essie,* poorly chiseled in the stone.

"I suppose," he said at last, "this *is* where dreams go."

⚙❋

T hat evening, I returned to the Gate.

On a jutting cliff, I watched the fractured skies of Drachaut ripple like broken glass, crinkling on the horizon until it split the light into a prism of color across the land. Skyscraper stalagmites stretched from ground to sky, dripping like melted wax.

O'Sahnazekiel's golden skin warmed my shoulder. I leaned into him, into the dove-soft wings I'd missed, cocooning us from the thick smoke of Drachaut, his arm curling around my waist.

On my other side, Jamellian and Kazmira held hands, their legs dangling over the cliff's edge as we watched a star set in the distance. Essie, who should have been with us, was gone. Her loss was evident in each tight line of Jamellian's body. I turned to him, noting that his skin's vibrant purples had simmered out in a low boil, but his eyes, the same size as mine, widened at the beauty eating the land.

It wasn't Ruhaven.

But, in its own perfect way, Drachaut was beautiful. Because it was part of Tallah, this land I had grown from, skin and bones and silver hair.

Sahn grazed a talon along my forearm, causing the clouds under my skin to spin into new constellations. Then he lifted his finger under my chin, turning me to face him.

I gazed into irises of burning, melted gold.

He arched a dusty wing into a feathered wall until it was just Sahn and I in the shadow of it. He leaned forward, fangs glinting in the smoky night.

But when his wide mouth pressed gently across my lips, it was only Bryn I felt.

~ 412 ~

CHAPTER 45

You are Cold

Naruka had been beaten, rung out, and left to dry in the days after Christmas, and was now as hungover as the rest of us. I cradled my forehead, an elbow propped on the desk in the low-lit lounge, and struggled to focus on my notes.

"James insisted I bring the milk," Bryn said, setting a platter of tea on the desk. "Though I told him you would not take any."

"Oh, sorry. Here." I ushered my papers aside, knocking over pencils, maps, and my empty cup.

"Have you made any progress?" he asked once there was room to flip over two cups.

"Maybe," I replied as Bryn hovered over me, eyes dark under his brow, the faintest beard showing from the holidays. A white collar poked above a rust-colored sweater, and he'd rolled up its sleeves to reveal smooth, tattooed skin.

I forced my gaze back to the journal. "There's something I don't get about Levi. Why did he go around James to show Lana the Gate?"

"Perhaps for the same reason he went to L'Ardoise." Blond silk brushed the bridge of Bryn's nose when he lifted the pot, poured my tea. "Eat something, Rowan."

I propped my chin on my fist. "Well, from the records, she had a terrible first trip to the Gate."

"Some do. It can be traumatic, as you yourself learned."

"Yeah, but maybe he did it on purpose."

"What for?"

"To scare her? To get her to leave Naruka, just like she did?"

"But to what end?"

I blew out a breath. "Well, she was never targeted by the Inquitate. In fact, no one was who didn't plan to return to Naruka. Because all those killed abroad had plans to make the Fall."

Bryn carefully sliced the bread. "So you believe Levi may have attempted to save her? By scaring her away from Naruka?"

"Maybe that's what he was doing in L'Ardoise too."

Bryn's forehead furrowed. "It is highly unusual. And those who respect Naruka do not disobey James, do not work behind his back." He wiped the fork on a napkin. "Eat," Bryn ordered.

I stared, cross-eyed, at the perfectly assembled bread, cheese, and sliced grape he held to my lips.

How could he go from the man in the music room—panting, grinding his hips into me, growling at my throat—to *this*? I'd rather eat him than the bread.

Bryn arched a cherubic brow into hair still damp from his shower. Waited. He didn't need to speak, even in my head, for me to know he'd heard every burning thought I'd just had.

I swiped the cheese from him, stuffed it into my mouth. *There. That's what you get for listening in.*

His lips twitched as he planted his hands on the desk, leaned in. *Do you prefer me how I was in the music room?*

I looped a finger in his collar, pulled him forward. *Guess.*

His answering smile, wide and crooked, was a heart-stopping punch—and that was before his irises flashed to hot gold.

Lust curled my toes into the plush rug. Maybe we could sneak off now, find somewhere to—

"In the spirit of our seventies night theme," Kazie decreed, bounding in with an armful of clothes. A breadcrumb trail of shirts and a miserable-looking James followed. With a huff of breath, Bryn pulled away. "I've decided to liberate all of you from your dour attire. It's time to choose your New Year's outfit if you dare!"

Please don't let mine be the color of cranberry sauce and ending in knee-high sparkly socks.

I am not altogether opposed to the socks, should they be on you.

James sank into his rocker. "I don't dare."

That I could be believe—with his layers of sweaters and massive glasses, he looked like a well-fed owl.

I said to Bryn, "You chose seventies music?"

He limped to the sofa, stretched his legs over the armrest, and picked up the book he'd been reading earlier. The tea he'd been drinking sat on a coaster beside a vase of heady roses. "Yes, Rowan, you might say I was inspired after hearing you sing, though apparently Kazie does not favor your vocal renditions as much as myself."

She tossed a heap of clothes on him. "Bryn, you've got it bad if you think Roe's at all a good singer."

When he lowered the novel a fraction, twin blue eyes smoldered brighter than the hearth. "Indeed."

I draped an arm over the back of the chair, eyed the book that I recognized as the one I'd gotten Kazie for Christmas. "Looking for pointers?" I teased.

He turned a page with mock slowness. "I thought to familiarize myself with the basics, as it has been a while. However, I admit I simply do not recall fins being so popular." His mouth quirked up on an angle. "Do you have an opinion on the matter, my Rowan?"

Just how long had it been for him here? And who was the woman? Likely a porcelain-skinned, platinum-haired Norwegian—

Kazie smacked him lightly. "Stop winding Roe up."

He grinned, rubbing his hair, which only made the moonlit locks more attractive.

"I'm apparently more of a feathers woman," I said dryly.

His eyes twinkled. "How fortunate I find myself."

James heaved a massive sigh before removing his glasses and folding his book. "Ye two. I'm not at all sure I wouldn't rather ye go back to pretending ye didn't know each other in the Gate."

Though his tone was mild, the aim was true, and I guiltily looked away from Bryn.

"Here we are!" Kazie shouted, digging through the bundle of clothes she'd dropped on Bryn's lap. "I've got a cowboy vest or rainbow shirt or a…" He grunted as she punched into the pile. "Leprechaun blouse."

As I eyed up my choices of New Year's attire, Tye clomped down the staircase. An unlit cigarette teetered between his lips, and the thick metal zippers of his leather jacket jingled with each step.

"Heading out?" I asked.

He adjusted his ball cap. "For a bit. Game's on."

"Football?"

"Baseball." He strode toward the main doors as I frowned after him. *Baseball?* At this time of day?

"Wait, Tye," Kazie called, tossing the cowboy's vest at the hallway. "This'll be perfect."

He paused as the tassels of brown suede fluttered to his feet, then bent, picked up the leather, and turned with it bunched in a fist. "Ya know what?" His jaw twitched. "Ya'll can leave me out of your little send-off," he said, and tossed the vest at Kaz.

Send-off? But when I glanced at James, his brows were bunched in as much confusion as mine. "What are ye on about?" he demanded.

Tye jutted his chin at Kaz. "Ask her."

In the middle of the room, Kazie's jeweled eyes narrowed like a cat assessing a crow that kept outwitting it. "How'd you find out?" she asked, voice utterly flat, holding none of its earlier joy.

Find out *what*? But I caught Bryn tense on the couch, the veins in his arms flexing.

Tye clunked a lazy rhythm around the pool table, its low lighting throwing a green glow up to his jaw. When he stopped behind Kazie, she only lifted her delicate chin.

Setting his novel down, Bryn limped toward me.

Tye spoke in her ear, loud enough for us to hear but only a degree above a whisper. "Ya think I didn't notice that look in your eye after the Gate?" He bunched his fist on the top of the couch. "Why, I could see the excitement pourin' off ya."

What happened after the Gate? I asked again.

Silence.

James drew himself out of the rocker. "Tye, ye step away from her now."

Ignoring everyone, Kazie casually glided around the couch, picking up clothes and layering them over one arm. "You're right, Tye," she admitted. "So like, it might be that I didn't tell you all something. Only because I knew you'd freak out, and it *is* Christmas. Or was." She tossed a shirt at James as I stared, dumbfounded. "And James, I didn't tell you right away because I worried how you'd handle it right now. I want to celebrate. I don't want this to be a bad thing. You know?"

Celebrate *what*?

James sank into the chair just as Bryn said hollowly, "You have heard the call."

What call? Who called her?

Bryn, what's going on?

It was quiet on the other end before an image flashed of a man walking through the trail I recognized so well, surrounded by James, a woman in a velvet cape, and…Carmen?

And I understood.

Yes, Rowan. But even in my mind, his words were far away, exhausted, weary. *Kazie's memories will be coming to a rapid end, and so, too, will Kazie should she make the Fall.*

"The Fall might be a few weeks away. I've got time for a final party," she said, slipping a sparkly shirt over her shoulders and testing the size. "So you were right about that, Tye."

Curling his lip, he kicked at the clothes she'd left for him. "Ya wanna throw your life away, Kaz? Fine." He jabbed a finger at her. "But don't for one goddamn second think I'm gonna go to your end-of-life party like it's a rodeo."

"It definitely won't be a rodeo, but you don't need to do anything," Kazie retorted like she was talking to a child instead of a foaming bulldog. "I made this decision a while ago, and I know what kind of dream I'm chasing."

So that's what this New Year's thing was about, a weird funeral for floating away to Ruhaven and—

Bang.

Tye slapped the pool table with an open fist. The three ball quivered, then rolled quietly into the pocket where it clinked with the others. "Ya don't know a goddamn *thing* 'bout what there is after. Ya know why? 'Cause there ain't *nothin'*." Tye batted the words over the couch. "James, are ya really gonna stand by and let Kaz do this?"

"'Tis not my choice, Tye," James said from where he stood by the fireplace.

And he'd make the same choice if Essie were here.

Tye seethed. "Kaz, ya wanna watch a memory, live in dreamland, fine. But now ya hear a little tune," he swirled a finger around his ear, "and ya wanna head on up to the Gate, lie down, and die? That's what we're talkin' 'bout here—" He rolled over James's protests, face red, eyes dark. "No, no, you wanna make everythin' pretty. The Fall? It's real and it's ugly. You're gonna die, Kaz. It may be I'm the only goddamn one who'll tell ya the truth on that."

Was that what it was? Death? Or rebirth?

Bryn's hand found mine, squeezed.

James squinted at Tye. "I don't want Kazie to leave any more than yerself. But if she feckin' wants to return, 'tis no business of yers to say otherwise."

But if James was right, she wouldn't *be* anyone when she returned. Not even a figment of that life would remember a girl with frizzy hair and terrible outfits. Wouldn't be thankful for her sacrifice.

Tye anchored his fingers on the top of the couch. "'*No business to say otherwise*,'" he hurled the words back to James. "I bring Roe here, teach her 'bout the Gate, and you're gonna tell me it ain't my business?"

"Tye, don't throw me into this," I warned as Bryn tried to tug me behind him, but I stepped in front of him instead.

James sagged like a sack of potatoes. "Tye, ye've taken this so personal like."

Tye exploded. "Personal! You're goddamn *right* it's personal. Must be nice to all have your romp in Ruhaven together. Ya don't bother askin' where I am anymore. Haven't in a long time. I just watch each of ya carry on, laughin' together, talkin'. Meanwhile, I'm by myself, figuring things out. Then y'all decide you'll lie down and die like a bunch of dogs. Well, I ain't gonna fuckin' stand for it anymore!"

I recoiled at the outburst.

"Ye never wanted to talk about the Gate!" James challenged, pacing around the chair, journals scattering. "Sure, if I'd known, I'd hear everything. What's this about?"

What *was* this about? James was right—Tye *never* talked about the Gate. And now he was lonely?

Kazie stood her ground, and though James tried to help, she didn't need it. Raising her voice over both of them, she said, "James, you've got nothing to feel bad about, and Tye, you don't know a freaking thing about my life or what I've been through."

Here? Or in the Gate?

Here.

Tye loosened his jaw in a conscious effort to relax. "Kaz, ya might not've grown up with a lot, but this—"

"Nothing!" She cut him off at the knees, and though her curly hair wouldn't have come above his chest, her voice carried. "I've had nothing, I've *been* nothing. I've watched my friends work hard, meaningless jobs just so that *other* people can live *their* lives. People like you, Tye. So you can have things that don't mean anything."

When she stepped around the couch, Tye backed up. "Kaz, I ain't tryin' to tell ya how to live, I—"

"No, that's exactly what you're trying to do," she said flatly. "You know why you can't understand? Can't figure out why I'd choose the chance at Ruhaven over *this*?" She scanned him from head to toe before her glossy lips twisted in mocking disappointment. "Because you never wanted anything you couldn't buy."

It might have been the first time I'd ever seen Tye blush.

Bryn stepped in the middle of everyone, gestured for James to sit, Tye to calm down, me to wait. "Kazie," he said firmly, "let us speak about this."

"No, Bryn," she said as he limped to her. "I've made up my mind."

But he took her hand, gestured up the stairs. "That may be, but you shall hear me out at least."

She sucked in her bottom lip, looking between Bryn and James. And I knew exactly how it felt to try to argue with Bryn, to resist when he used that voice.

After a moment, Kazie shrugged her Tinkerbell shoulders. "Fine. For you, Bryn."

Bryn turned to James. "James?"

He rubbed his eyebrows. "Yera. 'Tis been too long since anyone last made the Fall. I've a list of things to go over, I..." He looked around, as if this checklist of *before-the-Fall* items would emerge. Then shook his head. "Let's talk, aye, let's talk first."

Rowan?

I need to talk to Tye, I said.

I do not think that is—

I'm not asking you.

Bryn's eyebrows drew together, but when Kazie tugged his hand, he seemed to let it go, let me go.

As they ascended, James's voice carried down the stairs, arguing with Kazie, but he wasn't against it. None of them were.

In a way, this was the conclusion of it all—the reason we were in that *Ledger*, the reason we were allowed to watch the memories.

When they disappeared upstairs, I rounded on Tye. "What is going *on* with you? First, you visit Carmen without telling me, then you're threatening to break Bryn's leg, and now you're losing it on Kazie."

"*Me?*" He shoved away from the couch. It clanged back and forth as he shook his head in the same motion. "You need a break if ya think I'm the crazy one here. She's gonna kill herself, Roe, and I ain't gonna stay 'round for this no more."

"Kill herself? Is that how you see it?"

"That's how it is. She's gonna walk to the Gate and let it steal her soul, her body, exchange it for some future Ruhaven who ain't gonna remember her. What the hell else would ya call that?"

"But we're reborn."

"*As someone else!*" he roared, and shoved his finger at the stairs. "You think who she's reborn as is gonna remember her? They ain't, and her sacrifice is gonna mean shit. You're as good as dead, Roe, if ya make the Fall."

"If that's what you believe, then why'd you bring me here?"

He inhaled, swallowing enough air to launch into the next tirade, then blew it out in a low oath and propped a hip on the pool table. Behind him, the table's lights cast a warm backdrop, a theatre's lighting before the show. "Maybe because I thought ya deserved more, but now I see Stornoway's got ya not knowin' up from down anymore, and one day, he's gonna talk you into makin' that Fall too. Ya ever think about that?"

I stopped midway reaching for the book Bryn had been reading. "What?"

Tye lifted his crystal glass of whiskey, saluted. "Don't you remember me tellin' ya how he almost died for Nereida?"

Dread and a kind of irrational fear filled my belly. "Yes. Yes, of course I do."

"Well, don't ya ever wonder why?"

I sunk into the couch, still warm from where Bryn had been reading. "What are you getting at?"

He set down the whiskey, came around the couch. "Girl, I wanted to protect ya from all this from the beginning. Why do ya think I didn't want Stornoway comin' back? It's true I don't like the look of him, sours my teeth to think what he'd throw away, but I did it for you. I knew he'd try to convince ya to make that Fall one day, and that day might be comin' a little sooner now."

I rubbed my temples. "Tye, Bryn doesn't want me to make the Fall."

He cocked his head, looking at me like a farmer considering which runt to put down—a mix of vague sympathy and resignation. "Damn, Roe, you're gonna break my little heart. But I guess we all like the pretty story, and we don't like the one who's gotta ruin it. Well, I don't mind being that guy, 'cause I tend to think you're better to kill 'em with the truth than let 'em dream with a lie. So I'll tell ya."

He ground out the last of his cigarette on the table's ashtray before settling back. The old couch squeaked indignantly from the added weight, the hole-addled blanket sliding off its back.

"Stornoway didn't try to kill himself because he thought Willow's death meant he had lost his chance to be with his mate *here*," Tye began. "He tried to kill himself because he thought he lost the only chance he had to go home to Ruhaven—*with* Nereida. Back when he thought Willow was you. Don't ya get it? If he made the Fall without the woman she was here, he'd go back alone, without her. That's why James didn't make the Fall, 'cause he never found Essie."

I hadn't thought of it like that. If Bryn wanted to return to Ruhaven, there was only *one* way to go back with his mate—if I made the Fall. "So if I heard the call," I said slowly, "I'd need to go to the Gate, let it exchange me for Nereida. Otherwise, she's only a memory."

Tye waved a silent finger at me. "Don't ya even *think* of lettin' him talk ya into makin' that Fall. You don't owe him nothin'. You're Roe, always have been, no matter how much ya want to be someone else. Not even Ruhaven can give ya that, as much as I gather you might want it. So who, I wonder, do ya think Stornoway would rather have—you or Nereida?"

Nereida. He'd rather Nereida. But I couldn't bring myself to say it aloud.

Tye didn't need me to. He just nodded, almost sadly. "*Now* you're finally listening to me. So you understand when I say you're the only thing standin' between Stornoway and Nereida."

I stared hard at the grandfather clock, the pendulum listing back and forth, back and forth.

"Because he can't have both," I said, understanding. "When the memories end, so does Nereida." The woman he'd tried to die for. "And I'm what's left." Unless I made the Fall—for her, for him.

"That's right, Roe, and he didn't spend years lookin' for Nereida's human body 'cause he wanted to get married and make some life with ya here. He wanted to trade you, pure and simple. Your soul for Nereida's rebirth. If you make the Fall, Nereida returns. If you don't, she dies in the memories. It's just that simple."

Because if I didn't walk up to the Gate when I heard the call, she'd never come back.

"Maybe. I mean, yes, he'd rather Nereida," I admitted, more for myself than Tye. "But Bryn wouldn't trick me, he wouldn't ask me to make the Fall, or force me if that's what you mean."

"There's a lot of ways to convince someone." Tye stamped out his latest cigarette and stood. "Look, ya wanna play the fool? That's for you to decide. I said my piece, it's up to you what ya wanna do with it. I'm only tellin' ya because I don't want you to throw your life away like Kazie will. To die for a dream that ain't even your own." He ducked and plucked one of the roses from the table's vase, twirled it thorns and all. "Ya got a blind spot when it comes to Stornoway. Always did."

I looked up at Tye, caught the hurt behind his eyes before he hid it.

CHAPTER 46

Something Stupid

I glanced across the club at Bryn, at the smooth, expressionless face under the bar lights that seemed completely unaware it was New Year's Eve.

The disco shirt Kazie had forced him into was pale pink, close cut, and highlighted the lean, muscled lines he usually kept hidden. He'd allowed himself to undo exactly one button, which was as casual as I'd seen him since the music room.

I swallowed my chilled stout without thinking.

Years ago, Bryn had walked up to the Gate—before the cane, before the Inquitate had ever attacked him—not to see the memories, but to join them. Because if he'd waited for the memories to end and made the Fall, he would be reborn into a world without Nereida.

Had Bryn wanted that fate for me?

What had he seen when I'd arrived in Oslo—Nereida? The potential of her? Or the woman he'd played the piano for in L'Ardoise?

"Roe, are ye alright?"

I offered James a smile that slid across my face like oil. "Yeah, fine. Just thinking about Kazie." I rolled my shoulders in the rainbow-hued blouse she'd picked for me. I'd thankfully vetoed the sequined dress, but I hadn't expected the jeans to be this tight and unforgiving.

James had put up only a token protest before donning the flowery blouse he now wore, unbuttoned at the collar, where he'd stuck his glasses at Kazie's suggestion. He looked good with his hair styled with a messy gel, and dark brandy eyes.

"Ye want to talk about it?" he pressed. "About Kazie making the Fall?"

What was there to say? She'd heard the call and now in a few weeks would be gone. No body. No nothing. Not even a memory for those who weren't Ruhaven.

But she was making the most of her "going-away party."

Beneath the hot spotlights, her sequins glittered under the disco ball, sweat beaded on her bare neck, and the scrappy dress showed off her deep-lavender skin. If my car had been iced over in L'Ardoise, I could have broken it with the back of her strappy heels. But no one would suspect her impending demise was around the corner.

Despite the threat of the Inquitate, Tye had not joined us for New Year's. James had thrown a fit, but Tye refused to leave Naruka, saying only that if we had the right to throw our lives to the Gate, then he had a right to take his chances tonight.

I leaned over the sticky bar table. "James, do you think Tye is right? Maybe we shouldn't go back, maybe this is wrong." And god, how I wanted to ask him about Bryn too. If anyone knew the truth, it'd be James. Which was exactly why I didn't ask.

"Why give us the memories, so? I've a mind to believe, as me mother did, that we were right to go back."

"But you won't."

James drank deeply from his pint before answering. "No, I won't." He fumbled for a cigarette, the bar already so full of smoke I didn't know where the cigarettes ended and the fog machine began.

"So that's it then. She's going to walk up there and let the Gate take her. She'll be another plaque."

"Ye make it sound as if it's not hard for me, but yer wrong," James stated, the smoke vibrating between his two fingers. "It's not easy watching ye all leave, to know I'll stay, to know I'll never see Ruhaven. And worse, to know that when the memories end for meself, what becomes of that world I'll only hear of from others."

I hadn't thought of that, and the reality of it drove a wedge right under my heart.

"James, I..."

"Ye know, I don't want to have to say goodbye to ye, to any of ye. And Roe, especially not to yerself." He looked up over a half-empty pint glass, eyes misty. "Don't ye think I wasn't happy to find me sister. I've been watching ye in the Gate for years, ye know. Grew up with ye as I did Essie. I'm very glad I got to meet ye here. And if ye do make the Fall, Roe, I'll miss ye."

I squeezed his hand. "James, I won't be leaving, so don't worry. You'll be stuck with me for a while yet."

What would James say if I told him Bryn wanted me to make the Fall for Nereida? Would he even see anything wrong with that? Maybe not. James would have done the same thing with Essie, wouldn't he? Walk hand-in-hand to the Gate one day to be reborn in Ruhaven and to hell with whoever they might have been here?

Kazie tucked a sweaty arm around my waist. "Aw, Roe," she slurred. "I don't want to end on what Tye said." She dragged a stool between James and me, her dress glittering in the busy club.

I swirled a finger in the sweat of my pint glass. What did I say to someone who thought they'd disappear in a few weeks? What did a person do before they expected to die?

"Are you—I don't know—going to see your parents?"

"They're dead, Roe." There was no inflection to her voice. "My life is here now, and soon, I'll start again."

"And you're ready to lose who you are?"

"No, I'm ready to be who I am." She tilted her mane of curls. "You're just letting Tye get to you. I've seen people take a lot bigger risks for a lot less. And sometimes, Roe," she paused and flicked a blueberry earring, "sometimes I'm just tired. We're all so busy chasing something that exists less than a dream ever did."

"And what's that?"

She grabbed James's pint with sparkly fingers and dragged it across the table. I didn't know if she realized it was empty or just needed something to hang on to. "I wish we'd talked more, Roe. But we'll have time after you make the Fall."

"I won't. What is it you're chasing, Kazie?"

She toasted me. "Magic."

"Well…"

"You know I practically lived at this library in Malawi," she began, "when I was a kid, and even after Bryn found me, I still had about ten books checked out. I think, living in those books, I think it was the happiest time of my life until I found Ruhaven. I used to think they were all real." She blinked her thick eyelashes at me. "One day I thought, who decided they weren't?"

Because life was real and the imagination wasn't? "And you think the answer is Ruhaven?"

"I know it is. I've always known. I feel it *here*." She pushed two fingers into the sequins over her breasts. "A longing, so bad it's a bruise on my heart. Do you understand that, Roe? Have you ever wanted anything so badly?"

Yes. Yes, I wanted Willow back so much it hurt every morning. "Yeah."

"It's so bad it gives me anxiety to be away from the Gate this long, because I'm worried it won't let me back every time I'm away, you know?"

That wasn't how I felt, though. Did Bryn?

"Tye said there's nothing of us to be reborn," I recalled. "You're giving your life away to a person who won't remember—or ever know—who Kazie was."

She lifted a brow and tapped her heart. "Did you forget O'Sahnazekiel?"

I stole a glance at Bryn, found his eyes still on mine. Swallowed. "No. No, I suppose not."

"I've been in love with Ruhaven since I stepped through that Gate. No one is going to stop me from going back. And I know it's what we're meant to do, else why write the *Ledger*?"

I was silent a moment. Why indeed? Not even Bryn had an answer for that.

Kazie grabbed James's cigarette from him over his protests, wedged it between her lips. "I want more than this world. More than the work and the little things we buy to pretend we're alive. I want the magic of the thing." She tapped the burning smoke to her bodice. "If you don't feel that, Roe, don't make the Fall."

Bryn could at least pretend to stumble with the cane. But in dancing, like everything, he was unnaturally talented.

Smoke and sweat flashed under disco lights when Bryn spun me in a quick circle, his cane a helpful prop. Unfortunately, a handful of bolts tossed into the air would have landed with better rhythm than me.

What would I do if he asked me to make the Fall? He'd wanted Nereida. Impossibly more than I had loved anyone or anything. Except Willow.

What if it'd been me looking not for O'Sahnazekiel, but Willow? And what if the one person standing between me and her was Bryn? Would I sacrifice him?

The space between us grew heavier, shorter, weighed with a history I couldn't understand—a history that had driven him to walk to the Gate and sacrifice his own life for a chance to be with a memory. And if Tye and James hadn't intervened, I'd have never heard the careful cadence of his words, never felt the collision of us when I walked into his office in Oslo, or listened to the colorful tales he spun of his hometown.

I'd never have known what it was to be held by someone who made my entire being vibrate like a struck piano, to feel that connection stretch across time, wind its way through a memory of another woman, and find a place in me.

How badly I wanted to be the woman Bryn waited for. Wanted to be worth waiting for.

He caught me around the waist when I tripped over his cane. "Rowan," he said in my ear, "you are shockingly uncoordinated for a woman who regularly climbs onto our roof."

"Before you get too cocky," I warned as he spun me, "remember you almost took down Naruka installing a shelf."

Bryn smiled widely, shifted, and pressed his teeth lightly to my neck. "How was I to know it was a load-bearing wall, my ever-so-talented Rowan?"

Laughing, I shivered in the smoky heat, Bryn's gentle pressure on my hand pulling me forward a step. One. Two. "Keep your eyes on me," he mouthed before asking for a turn. "You may find you will spin on a more relatively straight line. And I enjoy looking at you."

"Looking at me? Or watching my toes tie themselves in knots?"

He flattened my chest against his. "Both are highly enjoyable." His irises flashed gold, then died to blue.

Before I could worry about the locals seeing that bit of magic, I fell into his rhythm, spinning clumsily with my eyes on him like a sailor finding her lighthouse. Bryn's rare panting laughter zinged along my bones as he asked me to step in a bizarre pattern that confused my brain as much as my feet. Twice I kicked his cane, which echoed a bass line like a stomping foot. But through all the turns, spins, and missed side-steps, I locked my gaze on the rare, bright smile that belonged to O'Sahnazekiel.

He switched his grip, sliding his thigh between my legs as his hands landed on my hips, the air between us already going taut as his breath quickened in time with mine. Coolness blossomed on my neck when Bryn swept aside my loose hair.

His lips brushed my ear. "Rowan."

Yes, Bryn?

He smiled against me, rocking us in a slow back and forth. "Do you think of me when we are in the Gate?" His voice dropped an octave.

"In the Gate?"

"When you are with O'Sahnazekiel," he murmured. "Do you imagine it is me? Watching you?"

Everyone in this pub must be hearing my pulse skyrocket right now. "Why are you asking?"

"Perhaps because I wonder if you prefer *'feathered demons,'* as you once described him," he said with a sideways smile, "or me."

He was teasing me, I knew it, but I answered anyway. "You, Bryn."

He pulled me against him, hard, skimmed his nose along my jaw. "If we do not stop, my eyes shall soon attract the attention of every patron of this pub." He wasn't wrong, they were sparking under his lashes even now, but I wanted every piece of him he was willing to part with.

I lifted my mouth to his ear. "I don't care."

His gentle intake of breath was just barely audible. "Do you not?" He murmured, voice no longer steady. "Then tell me, my Rowan, when we wake from the Gate, do you wish I would touch you as O'Sahnazekiel does?"

I curled my fingers into his shirt. "*Yes.*"

He breathed against my neck, skimming the tip of his nose along the pulse beating rapidly there. When I met his eyes, they were a deep, gleaming gold.

"What do you wish to do?" he asked softly.

What did *I* want to do?

I wanted to get the first taxi home and peel his clothes from each lean muscle like I should have done instead of leaving him half-naked at the Gate. I wanted to pick up exactly where we left off on the piano. And mostly, I wanted to finally know Bryn.

"I'll tell James we're leaving."

⚙✸

I cranked open the window of the overheated cab. How fast would I extinguish that gold if I hung my head out?

Probably pretty fast.

Hey.

I turned and caught Bryn's teasing grin, though his eyes remained closed. With his left hand, he drew tiny circles on my knee until I wondered if I had some erogenous area there I didn't know about.

The cabbie, oblivious to the state of his passengers, continued his one-man conversation. "Did ye want the heater on, love? It's quite cold out there so it is."

If this car rose even a single degree right now, steam might shoot out my ears.

"I think we are quite fine, thank you," Bryn answered, keeping his eyelids shut tight.

But as the car climbed up the Kerry mountain, it wasn't just Bryn's thumb on my knee that had me heating up.

Bryn had been sleeping with Nereida for what— Six? Seven years? —and if he was like James, he hadn't been with anyone else since then.

That meant for the last six years, the only woman Bryn had been with was Nereida, and I happened to know she was much better at the whole thing than me.

I stole a glance at Bryn.

He rested against the back seat of the taxi with his eyelids closed, appearing entirely at peace other than the bronze leaking from under his thick eyelashes.

No, don't look at him. That had been a mistake—the man was indecently good-looking, which wasn't helping things. But still, I— *Jesus Christ, was this window broken*? I needed air.

I dragged it down a smoker's two inches before the cabbie gave me such a hard look that I wound it up again.

Bryn's thumb stopped its circling. The back seat softened as he leaned into me, his cool breath brushing my ear a second before his voice. "Rowan, we do not need to do this now. If you prefer to wait."

You're not reading my thoughts or something?

No indeed, Rowan, but I know when you are nervous.

Nervous—what else could I possibly feel? He'd sacrificed himself at the Gate just for the chance to be with Nereida when he'd thought I wasn't in the *Ledger*. And now? Well, it didn't make any sense—but some part of me felt like I needed to justify that.

Bryn gripped my hand as the car bumped up Naruka's drive. The dim light flickering in his bedroom window only heightened my nerves. He handed the cabbie a twenty—*keep the change*—before I could wiggle my fingers into my glued-on jeans.

As I helped him out of the taxi, he popped open the umbrella for us both, draping an arm across my shoulders as the rain thundered on our canopy.

Wheels crunched gravel, and then we were alone.

Together, we limped to the tack room, each step causing my heart to tango with a trapped bumblebee.

It'd taken me five minutes just to untie my boots that day in Bryn's room. He might have some fancy Norwegian buttons I'd get tangled over while his arousal leaked out his ears. He'd be praying for Nereida in the Gate before long.

I was jumpy by the time we ducked under the overhang where the rain thundered like wooden spoons smashing tin pots.

Click.

I turned when Bryn unlatched the door.

My knees buckled at the twin eyes of golden desire burning in the night. "Your eyes are still gold."

He cradled my jaw, slid his thumb over my mouth, between my lips. "What do you wish to do about it, Rowan?" His voice was gravel.

Oh, to hell with it.

I slapped the unlocked door at his back and shoved us through.

We tumbled into the kitchen. I'd probably end up injuring Bryn before we ever got to the bed, but he steadied both of us, his cane in one hand, me in the other. His irises burned like twin candles, lighting our way.

Then his mouth came down on mine, hard, fast, his fist bunched in my shirt. I parted for him, whimpering under the possessive sweep of his tongue as we bumped into chairs and countertops. Here was Bryn—brilliant, scorching lightning, heat, and wildness. A power straight from Ruhaven.

His cane clattered to the floor.

I yanked him against me, twining my hands around his neck, needing all of him.

When we hit the table, he grabbed my hips and lifted me onto it in one smooth motion. "I need you, Rowan. I have since I first saw you in L'Ardoise."

Covering his mouth with mine, I dragged him on top of me. Newspapers scattered, a vase of roses rolled, spun, whistled through the air, and cracked on the ground.

God, how I loved the shape of his lips, the way he teased with every kiss, the hard bites he left along my neck. Maybe here would be better than a room—it was certainly *now*, and I couldn't think of anything more critical.

"I want to know *you*, Bryn, not Sahn tonight." I just hoped I was enough too.

He captured my wrists, pinned them over my head. I groaned as the weight of him settled between my legs. "You already have me, my Rowan," he promised a second before his warm mouth devoured mine. His tongue swept in hungrily, swallowing my embarrassing moans, testing what was still new and undiscovered between us.

Panting, breathless, I murmured, "I *love* your mouth."

He licked a hot trail to the opening of my blouse until I was writhing against him. "This bodes well for us then, as it has not done very much yet."

Promise?

His answering laugh was like velvet in my mind.

Shaking my wrists free, I wrenched at his shirt buttons, kissed my way down the side of his throat, loving every whisper of skin and breath that tasted of Ruhaven. I started peeling his shirt off, needing to see him bared as he'd been at the Gate.

"Rowan," he said, and the slight waver in his voice had me hesitating. *I have not been with anyone since I saw you in L'Ardoise.*

I nodded as my eyes trailed over the sweat and rain dampening his chest. Why was he mentioning this now? I didn't want to ever think of him with anyone. So I tugged his shirt off his muscled shoulders, tossed it into a heap in the kitchen. Was I supposed to tell him when I'd been with someone last? Maybe this was a Norwegian custom or—

Oh.

All my thoughts died when I feasted on the sight of his bare torso.

Interlocked gears, woven together by vines from Ruhaven, twisted along his nipple, spiraling in a forest of dark tattoos over abs damp from the club. I ran my hands down his chest, around his pebbled nipples, over grooved abs that disappeared into his jeans. He waited as I memorized him, as I looked at the reminder he'd stamped on himself, at Sahn, at Ruhaven, at the promise of both he could give.

He jolted when I dipped my finger under the band of his jeans, over the hard edges of his hips.

His burning eyes found mine for a heartbeat.

Before I could reach the other blatant evidence of his arousal, he pulled me to sitting. "Rowan," he breathed against my neck. "Will we go to my room?"

Yes. His room, in his bed, with Bryn above me. And his golden eyes in the dark.

Half-naked already, he lifted me off the table, set me on my unsteady feet, and shot me a blinding grin when I wobbled.

Then his mouth was on mine again, warm, soft, and patient. His fingers tangled in my hair as we stumbled like teenagers through the kitchen, his cane long forgotten. He slapped the wall for balance, knocking into old paintings that would wind up with both of us in trouble if any one of those broke. The Jesus statue nearly toppled when he gripped the top of the doorjamb.

By the time we made it to the lounge, we were both breathless and laughing, eyeing the stairs with what must have been mirror expressions.

Too far. I grabbed Bryn and shoved him into the velvet chair by the fireplace.

He blinked at me through glittering eyes. "My Rowan, if the walls are quite thin, I should think the lounge will be even—" He broke off on a low curse as I straddled him, pressed myself to the rigid length straining under his jeans.

Rowan, he groaned.

"We'll go upstairs, soon," I murmured, swallowing his ragged breaths as I moved against him. "Just let me…" I needed to feel him under me, just a moment longer, before things became awkward and I tripped over my shoelaces.

Or didn't live up to Nereida.

I ran my hands over his shoulders, traced his tattoos with my tongue, bit into his soft nipple that tasted of melted ice. The house groaned long and loud in the winter storm. Fireworks exploded, their twinkling colors glowing through the window.

His fingers curled under my chin, tilting my mouth to meet his before his hands dipped into the opening of my blouse. His touch was soft and teasing at first, but my pulse skipped a beat when a button snapped open.

"Rowan," Bryn warned, "I believe you owe me one shirt."

The reminder of how I'd left him at the Gate had my toes curling into the chair.

Chill air brushed the swell of my breasts as he slowly undid each glittering button, somehow, without touching my burning skin beneath. When he finished them all, he tugged on my braid to raise my head.

Our eyes met.

It was the same punch from all those months ago, when I'd first stood in the doorway of his office and felt my knees give. Except this time, his fired gold.

Rowan, how desperately I want you.

My breathing hitched, but his eyes never left mine as he glided the shirt over my shoulders, his thumbs brushing my skin as he tugged one sleeve at a time. I shivered on his lap, pressed my palms to his chest for warmth, then lowered my eyes to his mouth when I couldn't hold his gaze.

He'd seen me before—I shouldn't be this nervous. But it was *Bryn*, and no one had ever looked at me like he did.

My bra's clasp snapped like a twig in the quiet. But when I tried to lean into Bryn, he held me firmly and slid the loosened straps over my arms.

A moment later, my bra joined the blouse on the rug, and I sat, naked from the waist up, on his lap. It was a strange thrill to be here with him like this, to be exposed in real life instead of the memory. But even as I felt my breasts peak in the crisp night air, he didn't look down.

"Rowan," Bryn whispered, hands circling my waist. "You need not be so nervous of me. I have known you for years."

I swallowed, nodded.

Then his eyes left mine with terrifying, exhilarating slowness, trailing jolts of electricity wherever they touched like he was sketching me in the kitchen again. Down my nose and lips, the hollow of my throat, the sharper bones in my collarbone, until my breasts throbbed to feel just his *gaze* on them too.

And then they did.

Goosebumps spread over my chest, the skin tightening, begging, almost like he'd brushed a cold silk cloth over me instead of the eyes flaring hotly on my breasts.

"Do you know what I thought when I saw you in the Gate?" Bryn asked, hands tightening below my ribs. "Naked and shivering in the place between worlds?"

I closed my eyes because him, his words, the memory, it all left me teetering on the edge of delirious arousal and nerves. "Why I was weirdly aroused by light?"

I felt his smile. "No, Rowan. I thought you were more beautiful than even Nereida." He skimmed a teasing knuckle along the underside of my breasts, just enough to have me leaning in, not enough to satisfy. "Did you enjoy how I touched you then?" His voice was rolling thunder in a storm.

A memory flashed of light dragging up my body, kissing my palms, threading through my hair, brushing my lips. *His* memory.

"You know I did," I whispered.

"Tell me, Rowan."

The man was maddening. "Yes, yes. It was better, better than even Sahn."

And like that day, I relaxed helplessly into the fingers that tugged my hair until I leaned back into his arms. The chair gave a quiet groan as he tilted forward.

"Rowan," he said, and this time, I felt his breath tease my nipple, taunting, arousing, the heat of him against the chill air driving me crazy. "I much prefer seeing you here, in my arms, than in a dream."

I clutched his shoulders, unable to move, to do anything other than beg for that touch again.

Then his mouth closed over me.

A whimper escaped my lips. Teeth scraped along my skin, his breath like fire against me, always tantalizingly close but too far. He cupped my other breast and brushed his thumb over my nipple. Soft, light touches that dragged his name from me.

While he played, his tongue circled over and over. And when at last he sucked me between his teeth, I melted to liquid honey in his arms.

It was better than Sahn.

Because this was Bryn, the man I'd lain with in the Gate for months, who hadn't given up on us when I'd accused him of the worst possible things, who'd nearly died up there before we ever met.

I tried to pretend the hand cupping my breasts, the mouth suckling them, wasn't making me vibrate. "You never did this when you lifted me out of the Gate," I managed, voice embarrassingly throaty.

He tugged lightly with his teeth, sending a bolt of pleasure through me. "I restrained myself. Through some reservoir of self-control that even I am startled by."

I grinned up at the ceiling.

Did you like when I showed you a memory before?

Yes, yes. And I didn't know if I was agreeing to the question or the mouth devouring me.

Slowly, Naruka's molded ceiling transformed into Ruhaven's night sky, where a million tiny gears floated and shimmered in a dizzying splash of stars. "Do you remember when I..." Bryn murmured.

And when the stars parted, Sahn and Nereida appeared in another memory, his angelic wings covering her in a lavender field. One of the memories we'd lived together. Laughing. Moaning. Rolling. Crying out when he drove into her, pinning Nereida into the lavender, then they flipped and she rose above him.

I dug my fingers into Bryn's shoulders, rocking against him as Nereida did with Sahn, and held him to me. With his mouth at my breasts, his hands curling around my back, the threads of gold glittered around us like the dream, like the ribbon that had lifted me from Ruhaven.

He swirled his tongue once, twice, licking me like ice cream. My body started to hum and beg in places I didn't know I had, and I imagined how it would feel to have *Bryn* looking at me at last and not just through Sahn's eyes.

The memory wavered in the ceiling.

Was he thinking of her now? Of the years he had wanted and hoped and given up for Nereida? All to find this one woman. Had he wanted to swap me for Nereida? To spend years trying to locate her soul in the *Ledger*, not to be with the woman she became, but to exchange her?

No. No, Tye was wrong.

Bryn released me with a soft sucking sound. A shudder wracked my spine when he blew teasingly on the damp trail over my breasts before his hot tongue licked its way upwards. He nuzzled my neck, kissed my birthmark with soft affection, but in question too.

When his eyes locked on mine at last, my knees trembled.

What is it, Rowan?

Nothing.

He searched my face. *There is something else, not merely nerves.* He pulled me against him, so his body warmed me immediately. *Tell me.*

Later.

No, now. His hands, gently stroking my hair, were at odds with the voice. But I didn't want to stop, didn't want to face these questions, didn't want to think about whatever Tye had tried to tell me.

Rowan, he demanded, and I knew he wouldn't continue now.

He waited, the silence stretching between us.

You were looking for Nereida in the Ledger, I began.

His brows drew together. "Yes."

"Why?" It was simpler to just ask, wasn't it? Would he lie? Could I handle it if he didn't?

His eyes flickered between blue and gold, a candle's flame caught in the wind. "Because she, *you,* are my mate. Please tell me what you are thinking, Rowan. I do not understand."

I felt the intensity of his stare in my toes. This was so hard to say, impossible to admit what I believed.

I want to know—to know if you wanted to find me for me. Or if you did it just to trade me for her. For Nereida. So I would make the Fall and you would have her back.

Gold extinguished. Proof before the admission fell from his damp lips. My ears hollowed on the emptiness of Narurka, the silence before the storm as the sky inhaled.

Even still, when his response tumbled through the void, the lack of denial had my stomach bottoming out.

Did Tye tell you that?

So it was true. He'd wanted to trade me. It really was that simple. This wasn't about me at all—I could be that—that *chair* for all I mattered.

Shaking, I crawled off Bryn. I scooped up my shirt, fumbling with the inside-out sleeve.

"Rowan, that was before I knew you," Bryn explained like there wasn't an invisible knife in my back. "I knew only Nereida. Loved only Nereida. But, of course, it is different now."

He looked at me with confused arousal, his moonlit hair mussed from where my fingers had held him against me, his lips reddened. The flickering fairy lights taunted the marks I'd bitten on his shoulder so that he looked like some sex-starved Greek god.

I started redressing with my bra first this time, tugging it over my sensitive skin. "You wanted to trade me," I repeated, voice hollow. "It's okay. I understand." Understood what Nereida was to him, and what I couldn't be.

"You are entirely mistaken," he said, sounding almost angry as he rose half-naked from the chair. "You continually think the worst of me in all cases. Shall I never earn your faith?"

I fumbled with the bra snap. All my clothes were too tight; I couldn't *breathe*.

In two strides, Bryn was there, and in one movement, he snapped the bra clasp closed, then gripped my wrists. "Rowan, look at me." He exhaled softly in the darkness. "Please."

I swore I felt a gentle tugging on my ribs before I glanced up.

Lanterns colored half of Bryn's face in their soft gold. The other half disappeared in cool, violet shadows. His skin glowed, sweaty and tattooed. I couldn't weather the storm on Bryn's face when he looked at me like that, as my own heart betrayed me with each pounding kick in my throat.

He squeezed my wrists. "Yes, I intended to make the Fall with the woman who Nereida became—no, do not pull away from me," he said firmly when I shoved at him. "I did not see this as a trade. I always intended to make the Fall and I assumed the woman who Nereida became would as well."

"Why didn't you tell me that's what you wanted?" Then, at least I could have prepared myself.

"Perhaps I should have, but I have not wanted to do so since I met you in L'Ardoise. When I saw you at The Blue Nose, when I felt…"

—*This connection between us*—

"—it changed things for me. I did not expect to recognize you as I did. And now—now, I no longer feel the same as I once did."

I struggled not to drown in the promise he dangled before me. So I nodded at the tattoos on his bare, sweaty chest. "You branded yourself with Ruhaven after you were exiled so you'd never forget. But if you don't make the Fall, you'll never see the memories again, never see Nereida."

And he'd never give that up.

Bryn flattened my hands against his heart, held them there until his eyes were a burning sun, melting my resolve. "I would give up far more for you," he promised, low and rough. "When we are in Ruhaven, I see only you in Nereida. When O'Sahnazekiel is with her, I imagine it is your dark hair, your brown eyes, your smile. My Rowan, how can you not see how deliriously in love with you I am?"

The words were a direct punch through my chest, which was all the more tender and vulnerable from the emotional beating it'd taken. Did he mean it? Surely he wouldn't say that so effortlessly if he felt even a fraction of what was burning me from the inside.

His eyes softened. "Is that what you needed to hear, Rowan? These words mean little when we are bound across eternity. When I have you, my mate, alive and whole and beautiful, a gift far better than Nereida a lifetime ago."

I wanted to believe him so badly, it caused my ribs to throb. He may not need the words, but I did. I always would.

"You say you didn't want to trade me after you saw me, but how can I believe that? You tried to die for Nereida and—" His eyes widened. "—And she's why you go to the Gate every morning, why you were exiled, and you spent years trying to find me to get her back. Now you want me to believe you'd change your mind because of one visit to a bar? For a college dropout fixing a fuse box, who doesn't even have a real Mark, who isn't in the *Ledg*—"

On a low curse, Bryn covered my mouth with his. "I love you, my Rowan," he said roughly as gold swirled around us. "And I will give you whichever words you require to believe it."

Even if I won't make the Fall?

Bang.

Naruka's main doors burst open.

CHAPTER 47

It Would Break Your Heart

T he gold that had briefly surrounded us fell away.

Bryn reversed our positions, his tall shadow blocking me from the man barging into the hotel. Desperate, embarrassed, I clasped at my gaping blouse.

What was I thinking, undressing in the lounge? Standing here with my shirt half open when anyone could come in. We should have been in his room, and now James or Kazie or—

Footsteps cracked on the wood floor louder than the thunder bellowing outside.

Of all the people right now.

Bryn backed us up. *Indeed.*

Tye's leather jacket sparkled black from the rain, his hair a muddy brown and curled into shaggy ringlets. Drops of the storm clung to his beard.

He stopped in the hallway with a *thunk-thunk* and shook like an Irish wolfhound, splattering the crimson walls with the poor weather. Salty, Atlantic air filled the room before the door banged shut behind him. Where had Tye been celebrating?

Bryn pressed me into the wall, shielding me from view.

Tye cocked an eyebrow. Looked Bryn up and down before letting out a low whistle. "Finally learn how to use your dick, Stornoway?"

Christ, Tye. I tried to make myself smaller as he peered around Bryn, earning him a low growl. But when Tye saw my face, his eyes went to slits. "Or maybe not. You ain't supposed to make 'em cry."

I hastily wiped at my cheeks as Bryn went still. "Tye, don't start something, not tonight," I warned.

Humming some Western song, he strode past us into the kitchen, hands in his pockets. "If ya wanted privacy, don't see why ya get undressed in a hotel lounge. Some might think you'd have more class than that, Stornoway. But not me."

Ignoring Tye, Bryn turned and buttoned my blouse for me, his hands surprisingly steady. Everything inside me ached for him to a painful degree.

And despite Tye, the tears, my accusations, his eyes still burned gold. *Crack.*

I flinched at the sudden noise from the kitchen.

"Least he won't be able to use one of his sticks now," Tye chortled as he moved out the door, drunkenly grim. "What a sentimental choice of wood too. You're welcome darlin'."

I frowned down at my blouse. What stick? What wood? If Tye was going to drink this much, he should have come out for Kazie's send-off.

Bryn's fingers stilled on the final button, hesitated, then slipped it through. *Tye is not himself. We should leave him be.* He picked up my hands, gathered them in his. *I think we should talk, Rowan, upstairs.*

I nodded, glancing around the lounge. "Your cane...?" Oh, in the kitchen. I felt the blush coming at the mess Tye must be staring at right now. "I'll get it."

Bryn tightened his grip. "No, let us go upstairs. I can manage with the railing and your help."

I gave a quick tug. "I'll be quick."

"No."

"Bryn, I'm getting your cane."

"He broke it, Rowan. Now let us go upstairs."

I stopped struggling. *What?*

It is quite fine. I shall obtain another one easily, but not now.

That's it. I shoved up my sleeves.

Bryn caught me around the waist, gave me a firm tug to the stairs.

"This is too far," I insisted.

"Then speak to him tomorrow if you like, but not tonight." He took my hand, gentler now. "Come with me?"

I glanced between the kitchen and Bryn, at the marks just fading from my hands on his pale, porcelain skin. Swallowed. "Okay. Upstairs."

Without his cane, I had to tuck an arm around him to navigate to the staircase, but he managed by hopping and using the backs of lounge chairs for support.

The clocks, a cuckoo and a grandfather, ticked a protective rhythm as we climbed to the first level. A window spanned the entire wall with soft, white curtains that were blue in the moonlight. Rain splattered the frosted glass in out-of-sync rolls.

On the floor below, Tye's tell-tale boots thumped into the lounge. I glanced down the stairs as Bryn murmured to keep walking. Tye scowled at me around a cigarette that stuck out of his mouth like a chunk of hay he'd forgotten.

What *had* gotten into him? I'd seen Tye drunk before, but there was an unguarded meanness in his eyes tonight.

"Gonna try to pick up where ya left off, Stornoway?" Tye called up the stairs.

"I can still use my pliers," I warned.

His eyes flashed hot before cooling to liquid green. "Fine, hun. You wanna let him lie to ya, get ya to make that Fall, and still sleep with him? Guess that's your business." He ground the cigarette out on the wallpaper, took a step up as he flicked it over his shoulder. "But Stornoway? I'm keeping an eye on you."

"Be sure that is all you keep your eye on," Bryn said crisply, leading me up to the second floor.

"Still mad about how I showed Roe the Gate?" Tye grinned toothily. "Knew that would piss ya off, you possessive freak. Or maybe you're still feelin' that time in the tack room."

"*Stop*," I warned as Bryn stumbled.

"Bet it's a lot easier when it's a memory you're fuckin', huh Stornoway?" Tye's lips puckered around the cigarette as I gaped at him. "Probably can't even get it up without picturin' Nereida."

"Don't talk to him like that."

Bryn's face remained admirably blank. "Tye, if you wish to know precisely how my Mark is activated, you are not very subtle." His Mark? What did his Mark have to do with it?

"Ya know, subtle never really looked that good on me." As if just remembering he had a new cigarette in his mouth, Tye cupped his hand around the end and clicked the lighter. "Darlin', don't ya ever wonder why Bryn left the Blue Nose that night he met ya?"

Bryn pressed a hand on my back, leading me up as Tye climbed.

"He was supposed to be bringin' ya back to Naruka, but he just leaves that night? If it were my long lost mate and I believed in that kinda thing, I'd be busy nailin' the hell out of her. But not Stornoway here. Nope, he just…" Tye fluttered his hand like a bird, "goes on home. Strange, ain't it? But maybe he got a little stage fright, huh? So does he come back the next day? Or the next?"

No, he hadn't. After that night I remembered meeting him, Bryn had gone home.

"*Tye*." Bryn's low growl was both a warning and a plea.

I stopped, resisted the tug Bryn gave me, and faced Tye. "You expected Bryn to see me while he was in the hospital?"

Tye wagged his finger in tempo with the grandfather clock's pendulum. "The Inquitate attacked a *month* after he met ya. But for a whole month, he said nothin', did nothin', went about his merry business in town never approachin' you—his mate. When he should have barely been able to stay away."

Was that true?

Bryn's face was carefully blank. "Let us speak privately. I will answer your questions then. Not like this, Rowan, not with Tye."

There was always something else.

The corridor stretched behind me. Candles flickered on the walls, wax swimming in their saucers.

Bryn steadied himself on the railing, but his eyes were tight, pained, and light-years away from their earlier gold.

Tye crested the steps and leaned a shoulder against the wallpaper, swaying a frame out of place. The sticky, cherry reek of his cigarette turned my already-weak stomach.

"What was Bryn doing in L'Ardoise for a month?" I asked him directly.

Tye's eyes tightened a fraction. "It ain't what he was doin', but what he wasn't doin'." Snapping his fingers, Tye summoned the answer. "Ya see, what Stornoway didn't tell ya is that he had a big, beautiful, expensive problem back in Norway he had to deal with first."

Bryn cursed Tye vehemently.

Tye puffed out a smoke ring. "Sticks and stones, Stornoway, and don't ya forget who's got both."

My heart swam in my chest, the answer so obvious I should have asked Bryn months ago. Because of course I knew—the answer had been behind a door in Oslo—but I'd been so distracted by Ruhaven that I'd—

"Darlin', what our little Romeo didn't tell ya was that he was *engaged*."

I stared blankly at Tye.

Engaged to what? I wanted to shout, even as it registered along a tiny circuit in my brain. Sticky shame filled the void left by arousal. It shouldn't matter. I hadn't known Bryn then, and yet my face burned with rejection, with embarrassment, with the image of him with an unnamed woman. Perfect and blonde and white as snow. Except I knew her, didn't I?

Turning slowly, I blinked at Bryn, at the truth scratching hot color into his cheekbones.

"You're *engaged*?" I didn't realize I'd shouted until my voice echoed back at me in the hallway.

Bryn stared at a painting like it'd open a portal to Ruhaven and take him through. "*Was*. I *was* engaged." Then he narrowed his eyes at Tye. "Are you quite satisfied now?"

Bryn had been planning to marry another woman. Had loved another woman. Had *wanted* another woman.

Tye wagged his finger. "You're the one who sets store by Ruhaven's rules, Stornoway. And as I understand it, you ain't *ever* supposed to be with someone here. Ain't that right, oh mated one?"

Wasn't I worth waiting for?

Rowan, please.

I walked in a daze toward my room, dragging my fingers along the peeling wallpaper, brushing over frames, candleholders, a thin cabinet covered in dust, while Bryn called my name.

Scenting blood, Tye continued in a low, taunting, relentless rhythm. "Stornoway, it was me who had to go to L'Ardoise because you were too busy fuckin' your fiancée."

I was going to be sick. Right here on the embroidered rug.

Bryn's growl snapped through the hallway, and for a moment, I could have sworn it was Sahn behind me.

Tye continued, unrepentant. "I brought Roe back while you were havin' a damn pity party over your leg, over your fiancé, over James exilin' you. Couldn't even pick up the damn phone. So I had to show her the Gate. Maybe you don't care for how I did it, but at least I was here, lookin' after *your* goddamn Gate girlfriend."

I wrestled with my doorknob. Was that how Bryn had gone back to normal? With a fiancée? It should have been me with him, me helping him walk again, me protecting him.

I shoved open the door, pushing Bryn away when he tried to follow.

"Rowan, let me explain," he insisted, catching the door as I slammed it behind me, eyes stark behind a loop of curling blond hair.

How could I admit I was upset that he hadn't waited for a memory? After I'd mocked James? How stupid I must have sounded to both of them.

Tye stalked toward us, exhaling a low tendril of smoke across Bryn's neck.

I backed into my room while Bryn stood at the threshold, palming my door. His chest, still naked, rose and fell on sharp breaths. His milk-white hair framed a face that looked nearer to his breaking point than I'd ever seen him.

Over Bryn's shoulder, Tye's eyes flickered to me for a heartbeat, almost in apology, I thought. Then he whispered, inches from Bryn's ear, so I could barely hear, "Now, Stornoway, do ya need me to…for ya too?"

Cold fury blanketed Bryn's face a second before he whipped around with a snarl.

Tye caught him by the throat, shoved him into my doorjamb, rattling paintings and photos as Bryn fought for balance, his crippled leg useless without the cane.

He dodged Tye's first punch, blocked the second, but as Bryn tried to pivot, his leg buckled and he smacked into the wall. A portrait shattered at his feet, then Tye was on him.

"Thought that would do it," Tye grunted, digging his elbow into Bryn's windpipe. "Ain't gonna burst into O'Sahnazekiel, though, are ya?"

Bryn's lips pulled back from his teeth. "You are lucky I cannot."

The hallway candles flickered over his face, casting it golden against Tye's shadows. Then Tye drew his fist back.

"No, Tye! Stop!"

Bryn gasped out a breath, slid a foot down the wall from the blow, unable to defend himself without O'Sahnazekiel.

"You and your goddamn lies all the time," Tye cursed. "Guess you're gonna keep relyin' on Ruhaven to—"

Blood spurted from Tye's nose.

Where the hell had that come from? Bryn? How?

Fat crimson drops spilled over Tye's lip and blended with the plaid jacket. He swore, pinching the bridge of his nose as Kazie's voice yelled up the stairs.

Then James stepped into view, his face full of contained outrage, his eyes flat and cold. "Don't ye *ever* talk to me sister like that," he panted, massaging his shaking fist. "Tye, I want ye out of here. As soon as ye can get yer things, I want ye gone. I'm so feckin' angry with ye."

Tye's smile was a bloody grimace. "I've been kicked by horses harder than that, James."

"Then yer bloody lucky I don't let Simona have a go at ye. I knew ye had it in for Bryn, but punching a cripple is a new feckin' low, even for yerself."

"He deserved it," Tye spat. "Lyin' to Roe, pretendin', hidin' his whole life. I come in tonight, see her cryin' for god's sake. What am I supposed to think?"

"It wasn't like that," I said quickly, "and you—you shouldn't have said any of that, Tye."

"Aye, I heard him, and so he'll start packing tonight," James said firmly. "I want ye gone in a week. That'll be enough time. And ye two stay away from each other," he added, nodding at Bryn.

Tye wiped his mouth on his sleeve. "If that's how you want it." He waited, looked at me, but I steeled my face. "Seems you do. So I'll go, and anyway, I don't need to watch you two let Kazie, let Roe, throw their lives away just so Stornoway can get a woman back in a fuckin' dream." He cast me one long, bloody glance before shoving past James.

Bryn stared after him, eyes burning.

James turned, speaking quietly to Bryn before looking at me. "Are ye alright, Roe?"

Not at all.

I gripped the door. "Fine, I—thanks, James." *Please go.* I needed to be alone before I collapsed in a heap.

He nodded and patted Bryn's bare shoulder. "He's sure got a way with timing," James said mildly. "I'll get him out and leave ye to it so." He threw one sympathetic look over his shoulder before striding out of view, his feet echoing down the stairs.

Bryn stared at me, the hallway candles flickering at his back as he filled my doorway, his hair nearly grazing the top. A welt rose on his left cheek from a blow I hadn't seen Tye land, and a bruise was already purpling on his ribs.

His nostrils flared once before he spoke, low and with seemingly little patience left. "Rowan, I am sorry I did not tell you about Abby. Now, may I come in?"

Abby. Not a roommate, as I'd thought when James and I knocked on her door in Oslo, but his fiancée, his future wife. She had been as perfect and serene as I had pictured for him—a coifed blonde premade and packaged in a Norwegian sweatshop.

I couldn't even be mad. "No, not tonight," I said on a long sigh, and just closed the door.

⊗✴

M y body ached, from brain to heart to wobbly knees. And because all my clothes were somehow both stiflingly hot and damp with sweat, I dragged off my blouse, the jeans, the wire bra I reserved for special occasions—which apparently included nights when I learned I'd been both Gate fodder and a backup to a fiancée—and tossed them in a heap on the floor.

With the moonlight to guide me, I strode naked to my dresser and pulled on old sweats and a scratchy wool sweater, inhaling the chill air, almost welcoming it when it settled my pulse.

I needed to *do* something. Fix something. Punch something—maybe Tye. Anything to prevent my mind from drawing up elaborate scenarios of Bryn and Abby to torture me with.

I slumped into my desk chair, clicked on the lamp.

Amber warmth flooded a room I'd spent little time in. My desk was the same raw wood as the dresser, with ivory knobs on its two drawers and a pink rose just beginning to wilt.

I rebraided my hair with quick strokes, like putting it back together could undo the night I'd had.

It really shouldn't have mattered that he'd had a fiancée.

Because it was about the lie.

That was why my gut was a block of ice. Not because I was thinking about Bryn proposing, of how it would look to have those eyes on me and hear whatever wonderful words his silk voice would promise.

As I'd done countless times before, I opened my journal and stared at the notes like the reason for Willow's death would magically reveal itself between the lines.

Would James force me to leave when the memories ended? Would Bryn even be interested anymore? It likely wouldn't take long for the memories of Nereida to fade, for Bryn to turn to me and wonder why he'd been interested in a repair worker.

I tensed as the hallway creaked, then relaxed again—just someone going to bed. There were no long-term plans with Bryn. Eventually, he'd grow bored watching a woman toil her life away in other people's houses.

Scribbling in the journal, I sketched the gate lodge kitchen I'd nearly finished. Made a list of materials I'd need. This, I could do, had always done when my life slipped from under me—the straightforward work of turning something broken into something fixed.

Crack.

I jumped when my doorknob clattered to the floor.

In its place, light flooded into the two-inch hole before a finger stabbed back the latch. I swiveled in my chair as the door swung open.

Bryn stepped through, a screwdriver in his left hand, a makeshift cane of driftwood in the other. A bruise swelled below his eye.

"Back to your old repairs?"

He bent, picked up the knob listing on the floor, his reflection glittering in its faded bronze. "It is good to know I can at least still dismantle a door." He set the doorknob in front of me. "I am sorry," Bryn began, keeping his voice low, "that I am unable to prevent Tye from saying what he did."

I'd deal with Tye, with how he'd spoken to Bryn.

"Don't be sorry that Tye told me the truth."

Bryn exhaled a weary breath, a rare sound, and glanced around the room. When his eyes landed on the spare chair by the dresser, he limped to fetch it.

I ignored the feel of him passing, stared intensely at the journal as if the lines weren't blurring. Why hadn't I been able to figure this out? The one thing I owed Willow was hiding amongst my notes—a secret for why the Inquitate attacked us both—but after months, I was no closer.

What did I really expect? I hadn't even figured out that Bryn was Sahn, couldn't put together the simple conclusion that the woman I'd met in his apartment was so obviously *not* a roommate. I just hadn't *thought* about it.

Then months later, when I'd discovered Bryn was Sahn—well, of course she couldn't have been anything more because he wasn't *allowed*.

But he had. And he did.

The chair legs scraped across the old wooden floor until Bryn stopped beside me, sat. He rested his hands on his knees. "Rowan, I told you once that you may lie to others, but not to me. You are upset about Abby, not that I kept her from you."

I flipped back a page, circled the notes I'd made yesterday about mates, about the theory of them crossing together.

Why wouldn't I be upset to know what he'd want if he had any choice? If he wasn't bound to this mate connection?

"She suits you," I said shortly.

When I started to get up, he grabbed my wrist.

I forced myself to meet his eyes, open, honest, a vivid blue under concerned brows.

"She did, once. We knew each other in college, in Trondheim, before I had ever met James or knew of Ruhaven or Nereida."

Worse—that was somehow worse. Now I was an eight-hundred-year-old duty that had stolen him from his childhood sweetheart. "I don't want to hear this."

"I suspect I would feel the same if I had learned you loved another," Bryn admitted.

Loved. I swallowed the bile in my throat. "And did you love her?"

"Yes." No hesitation.

Well then, he was right after all. "I guess the words don't mean anything."

Against my protests, Bryn grabbed both my hands and leaned forward until the lamp's amber glowed over his shoulders. "I said that because they cost nothing. They are cheap and free to give as I have given them before. But what I have sacrificed for you, Rowan, was not easy, and it did not come without a cost."

And I knew that cost.

I blinked down at our joined hands. I wouldn't have expected him to give up his fiancée, never wanted him to walk to the Gate and sacrifice himself—that wasn't love. That was duty, devotion, a commitment of the soul.

He angled his right hand. "When you sat on my bed and asked about the ring I keep stored in my bookcase, there were answers I should have likely given you then. But I was embarrassed about many, many things. When James exiled me from Naruka, I left the ring here. I did not want reminders of Nereida if I were to try to move on."

I stared at the empty ring finger where he'd once worn a symbol for Nereida. On the right hand, because only Drachaut wore it on the left. "So you did. Move on."

"No, but I tried," he admitted. "Let me tell you from the beginning, Rowan. Please."

He waited, breath barely audible.

There was always something else with Bryn—some secret, some lie, some half-truth that sucker punched me when I least expected it. Tonight wasn't supposed to end like this. We should have been falling asleep with each other by now. I should have known stupid, insignificant things like what his sheets felt like, whether they smelled like him, and if he slept on the right or left.

It shouldn't be this hard to be together. Wasn't that why there were mates? Two creatures destined across time, across worlds, like James and Essie. They never fought, never lied to each other, and...

I looked at Bryn.

James had never been unfaithful, even when there'd been no hope of finding Essie in the *Ledger*. No—even when she was *dead*, he'd remained faithful.

Bryn squeezed my hand. "Please, Rowan," he said quietly.

Like dragging a hammer up by a thread, I pulled the rational part of my thoughts forward. The ones that said he didn't owe me an explanation for why he'd needed to find something—anyone—after

James exiled him, who knew what Ruhaven was to him, and knew what leaving it had cost him. That loving someone wasn't a crime. That it was healthy, a sign of moving on, even if a much larger part of me hurt to think it. No—broke and shattered and *ached* to think it.

So I tried to shove all of it down, down, down. The image of Abby in the doorway of their pretty townhouse, of her glossy lips that would know exactly how it felt to be kissed by Bryn, her short platinum hair that I had to stop myself from wondering if he preferred.

"You don't need to explain," I said hollowly. "Tye told me how he—how James, Kazie, and him—found you at the Gate that day." The next words were like shards of glass in my throat. "I understand that you needed someone. After."

He closed his eyes. "I was ashamed of what I did," Bryn bit out. "Can you imagine how foolish I felt? For six months, I assumed you had died in L'Ardoise as Willow when I was but weeks away from finding you, that I had been too late. And so I gave up, thinking Nereida was lost, and all the while, you were there, alive. I might have passed you in L'Ardoise and never known. James was right to exile me. I know this even if I do not fully forgive him for it. I must have known it then, as well, for that is why I left the ring, why I so quickly fell into a life again with Abby."

Her name made my pulse leap.

"I was twenty-one when James visited me in Norway and convinced me to travel to Naruka. I was dating Abby at the time and we agreed to remain in a long-distance relationship while I completed my commission for James. Then I met Nereida on my third trip to the Gate, very briefly, as I could only remain for short periods. I did not understand their relationship in the beginning."

His lips curled, and for a moment, he looked impossibly young. "The first time we were intimate was quite a surprise. I felt like an inexperienced boy again. I did not have someone to pull me out before things escalated, as I did for you. Nereida and I would speak in one memory, and mate in the next. But it changed me. Not just the act of it, but the connection. Mates. James explained it to me."

Our knees bumped.

"He explained how things were for Essie," I clarified. It had to help having someone there who knew exactly what you were going through. And now James was alone on a New Year's he should have spent in the Gate.

"Yes, among other things. The ring, for instance, what it meant. As I continued to enter the Gate, I saw Nereida frequently and learned to speak Ruhaven so that I may understand what she said to

O'Sahnazekiel. Eventually, I fell in love with the memory of her, with Ruhaven, with the unending vastness of the dream, with the longing that made my nose burn and my heart hurt."

His winter's breath fluttered my eyelashes. "I ended my relationship with Abby. After living with Nereida, I understood what Abby and I had was what children do—fleeting infatuation. I no longer felt I was being faithful while lying with Nereida in the Gate."

I'd never thought of the life Bryn had given up before Ruhaven—relationships, careers, friends. Pity stirred in me for Abby, who'd been discarded for a dream Bryn would never see.

Releasing my hands, he slipped my braid over my shoulder, then eased off the elastic and began unraveling the twisted strands with forced slowness.

"When James exiled me, the woman I had spoken with for years was suddenly dead too. A woman I had made love to, protected, cared for, shared secrets with, sworn an oath to. It was all taken from me. I did not know who I was anymore without O'Sahnazekiel, without Nereida. Without Ruhaven.

"I returned to my mother's house in Odda and began sorting through old photographs and paintings and memories, as if they could tell me who I was, who I had been before Ruhaven. I needed these as much as you had once needed a degree."

I squeezed our joined hands.

"Being alone became difficult, so I moved to Oslo, where I could be around many, and found a position as a teaching assistant."

He paused, and I knew what was coming.

"I discovered Abby had gained work in the city as well. We met for coffee. She had always been a good friend and we had not spoken in years."

I thumbed the bruise Tye had left on his cheek. "You fell in love again."

"No. No, I wish that were the case, but rather, I was simply embarrassingly desperate. She was a lifeline to a world I once knew. There was no magic here, no gears in the sky, no Nereida. I had lived in the memories for so long that without them, I became depressed, lonely, and desperate. Abby provided a salvation. So I used her to help me forget and I hoped, with our old romance, I may eventually forget Nereida too."

Our noses were almost touching. "And did you?" I breathed.

With the braid undone, he threaded long fingers through my hair. "Never. But Abby and I began dating again, and because she was older now, she rightly did not wish to waste her time with me."

I could be an adult about this. "You proposed," I said, as though the word hadn't burrowed into my heart like a worm in a rotted apple.

His eyes softened. "Not quite. It was rather rushed and informal. She had a ring on order for me to propose with, but then James called..." He paused and thumbed his right ring finger. "He was upset when he heard. Those who have mates in Ruhaven do not marry here, ever—that is why we wear the ring. I think he has always acted the protective brother, even before he knew you."

I should be doing more to help him with Essie.

When I straightened, the oval mirror above my desk reflected a woman I didn't recognize. One with long, midnight hair framing irises that glowed silver instead of brown, my face paler than I'd ever remembered, my freckles dark pinpricks. A world away from Abby, but perhaps, in some ways, not so far from Nereida.

Bryn pushed off the chair and stepped around me until his reflection joined mine in the mirror. He rested his hands on my shoulders, watched me carefully through all-seeing eyes. "I am sorry, Rowan."

He had nothing to apologize for. "It's done. It's in the past."

"It may console humans to think of things as in the past, but for Ruhavens, it does not matter when. I was never supposed to take another."

I let my eyes flutter closed when his fingers massaged my shoulders, softening all the tension and aches of the evening, as Sahn had done before.

"I should have told you all of this," he said softly.

I opened one eye. "Why didn't you?"

"Because I was ashamed," he admitted, and I could tell, even without the connection between us, that the words cost him. "But I do not wish to hide it from you any longer."

You deserve to know who I am, and should we have grown up in Ruhaven together, you would have.

His hands traced up my neck, over my cheeks until they covered my eyes. "If you wish for the truth," he said hoarsely, "I can show you, though my memories are unpleasant."

CHAPTER 48

A Case of You

It was the antiseptic I smelled first, like a sharp vinegar in the nose. The light was too bright, and harsher than the fluorescent sconces in An Béal Bocht. Starched cotton brushed my fingers, and a very angry man cursed in Norwegian.

I opened my eyes. And recognized Abby immediately.

She swam before me, her hair delicately styled up, slouching puffy-eyed and red-nosed in the hospital's guest chair. She'd exchanged the pastel blazer for a lilac blouse and the suit pants for a high-waisted skirt. Stray hairs hung in ringlets around her trembling chin, but they seemed a fashion statement rather than the distress of a weeping woman.

Behind the dividing sheet, a man's rambling in Norwegian drowned out the regular beeps of machines. *He wasn't going to wait any longer! Three hours he'd been here and still no doctor, and what the hell was that on the TV?* Bryn tuned him out.

A piece of red tape overlapped a tattoo on the inside of his elbow. An IV snaked up the dark vein in his arm. A hardened cast covered his left leg, from ankle to knee to thigh. He would never walk on his own again. Never.

The thought banged in his mind, as painful as the tears spilling copiously down Abby's swollen lips. Even flushed and wet, her face was heartbreaking, with fat teardrops that decorated the corners of her eyes before puddling on her glossy bottom lip.

Bryn curled his fingers in the starched cotton sheet. This was his punishment. He knew it. After years of searching for Nereida, he'd been too late. Then, instead of finding what killed her, he'd tried to take his own life at the Gate. Worse, unforgivably, he'd been wrong, had acted so foolishly when Nereida was still alive.

Then, when James saved him, instead of seeking some redemption, he'd sunk lower and broken the only oath Ruhaven had ever asked of him. Because he'd been selfish, desperate, lost, he'd agreed to marry Abby despite James's warnings. He had broken every rule Ruhaven had ever blessed him with. Spat on the Gate herself.

Maybe the Inquitate came to claim your soul.

He'd never found a link between the attacks, but perhaps those who'd been killed had committed an unforgivable sin. James believed in that, as did the church he attended every Sunday in Capolinn—a church that would have condemned what Bryn had done. James had been right to exile him.

What if the Inquitate were not an enemy but a guardian against Ruhavens, like him, who would attempt the Fall when they hadn't deserved to? That made sense in an odd, twisted way.

Especially the timing.

Rowan had been Nereida; he'd known it as clearly as his own heartbeat. He'd planned to make the Fall with her, and the Inquitate—knowing this—had tried to stop him.

So as he lay there, propped at an awkward angle on a bed that was too small for him, he reminded himself that he deserved each and every thing that would be denied to him now. He would never sail again, never dance at night, never run in the streets of Odda, never feel the glaciers cracking under his boots, never hurry for anything, ever again. His life would be at a snail's miserable, sneaking pace.

Instead of returning to Rowan, he needed to stay here, rather than risk bringing the Inquitate to her too. She would be safe in L'Ardoise, having never broken any Ruhaven law.

For long moments, the only sound was of the man arguing with the nurse and Abby's soft tears. Then her voice broke. "I can't believe you're doing this to me again, Brynjar."

After everything, his promises had been as worthless as they were the first time. It was just another sin the Inquitate had punished him for. He'd known, as soon as he'd seen Rowan in the Blue Nose, that he'd have to end things with Abby. Even so, the decision had driven him insane in the weeks that followed. He dreaded making it, knew what kind of a man it made him.

"I am sorry." The words were as hollow as the nurse's platitudes to the man next door.

When Bryn reached for Abby's freckled hand, she yanked it back and shoved out of the chair. Pinprick heels clacked on the tile floor as she wiped at a crimson button nose. "If this is about your injury," she began, tissue shaking in her clenched fist, "it doesn't matter to me. We'll work through it. I'll stay home. We'll hire help."

He couldn't take it. He didn't deserve Abby or her kindness. This was the fourth time since he'd returned to Oslo that he'd tried to end their relationship. Each time, Abby convinced herself it was the effect of the injury rather than a decision he'd made in L'Ardoise.

"I know, Abby. It is not about my leg," Bryn said hollowly, a cassette being rewound again and again.

She firmed her coral lips. "Then why, Brynjar? You're not thinking clearly now. It's not the time for these decisions."

He plucked at the thin sheets. "I am, I—" He swallowed against his raw throat but didn't reach for the water. "I am very sorry. Very sorry, Abby."

She lowered the tissue. "What will I tell my parents?"

He closed his eyes, wanting to throw up. "I will speak to them. To your father." At this rate, the Inquitate would likely return to finish him off.

"And what will you *say*?" Her voice teetered on a high tightrope. "Why are you doing this to me, Brynjar? Why! You are not thinking right."

His breath rattled out in a long exhale. "I met someone," he admitted to the pulsing beeps of the hospital.

Abby's lips parted, and her eyes grew round, disbelieving. "No," she breathed, ample chest heaving. "What are you saying? I don't believe you."

He swallowed glass, then cobbled together half-lies and truths. "In L'Ardoise, before my accident, I met a woman."

Abby wilted. "Are you saying—are you saying that you were with her? You?"

In a way, he thought. "Yes," Bryn whispered, and even the raspy man next door stopped shouting at the nurse.

Slap.

Bryn barely flinched at the blow she'd landed. Didn't stop the next.

"How dare you, Brynjar," Abby cursed, fumbling with her velvet clutch.

Her hand shook as she pushed back the curtain. "Don't talk to my parents. Don't ever speak to me again."

As he listened to her heels fade on the tiled floor, he wiped at the tear sliding down his cheek. He would never, he vowed, return to Naruka. Never see Ruhaven again. Never see his mate.

It was no less, and no more, than he deserved.

And in doing so, he'd prevent the Inquitate from finding the other Ruhavens, from finding Rowan.

When I felt the tug at my wrist, I didn't answer. I floated in the memory, in the grief and regret, in the desolation that had become Bryn's world. When my heart broke, I didn't know if it was for him or because I was him, but at last I let go.

And swayed in a dark, silver pool.

At some point in the night, I woke. I drifted between dreams and life, where sleep lapped at me like the gentle waves of a dark lake. I recognized the cool, hard pillow under my head, the patchy quilt tickling my throat, the faint scent of roses.

I was in my bed.

I didn't remember ever waking long enough to make it here. Had Bryn carried me? I reached for him instinctually, found the quilt smooth and warm beside me. My lips were dry when I whispered his name into the cold, empty room.

When only pittering rain on the window answered, I melted into the sheets.

And dreamed of the woman who'd loved Bryn.

I woke the next morning, certain it'd all been a dream.

In the quiet of my room, I slipped on jeans and a cotton sweater, socks, and another sweater because the hotel was always cold unless I was working. I stood in front of the mirror as I braided my hair into a long tail at my back, then slapped my cheeks for some color.

I needed to talk to Bryn.

And say what, I didn't know. Something, some measure of understanding of what he'd shown me, and why he'd kept it. To deal with what had scraped me raw last night, what I could forgive but not forget.

I took a breath, then another, and slipped out of my room.

When I stood in front of Bryn's, I didn't hesitate this time—I knocked softly, then let myself in.

And just looked at him.

Naked, he slept on his stomach, the sheets bunched at his waist despite the chill, an arm slung over the side of the bed, a hand beneath his cheek on the stark pillow, mouth slightly parted. A breeze stirred his gold eyelashes and mussed hair.

My heart gave a solid thump.

Sunlight peeked through the wispy curtains of his bed, leaving spots of bright yellow against sheets that looked purple in the shadows. A shaft of it struck one side of his face, highlighting the mottled bruise Tye had left.

He breathed in absolute stillness, his back barely rising.

Bryn?

Eyelashes fluttered, then one wary blue eye peeked through. *Rowan.* Even his voice was careful, hesitant, probably unsure of whether I was still harboring a grudge from last night.

He shifted slightly, trying to cover himself, but I reached him before he could, laid a hand on his.

His eyes flicked up to me in question.

Saying nothing, I came around the bed. When I passed the desk, I saw his open sketchbook, the pages dotted with different faces— Nereida, James, my own. Then I slid quietly onto the bed, atop the quilt as I had when we'd sat here together drinking tea after An Béal Bocht. The pillow was as crisp as snow against my cheek.

I stroked my hand over his spine, the dip in his lower back, tracing the ridge of his hips. Goosebumps broke out wherever I touched, but after a moment, he relaxed into the pillow with a quiet exhale.

"I wonder, sometimes, what you see when you look at these," I said, gliding my index finger over a gear at the base of his spine.

"What do you mean?" Bryn asked softly.

"I guess I wonder if you see him. Sahn."

His throat worked against the pillow. "Yes. O'Sahnazekiel, Ruhaven, my life for too many years here." *What do you see, Rowan?*

I paused at his shoulders, then massaged the space where wings once sprouted. He let out a muffled groan.

"I just see you, Bryn. I've always seen you. Even after you admitted you were Sahn, it didn't change anything. I mean, it didn't make me want you more, or differently. It still doesn't." I trailed my fingertips over his ribs now, over the twisted tattoos that must have hurt to have the needle touch bone.

After the memories he'd shared, there was something I needed to tell him. Something I'd put together a while ago. Maybe the only thing I'd gotten right.

Bryn?

Yes, Rowan?

"It's just—about what you thought, about Ruhaven not accepting you for the Fall," I said, remembering his guilt. "You should know that even if I hadn't found the triplet connection, the Gate would have taken you. Ruhaven would take you still."

His shoulders tightened. "Perhaps."

I smiled slightly. "Bryn, don't you know?"

He shifted so we were face to face, and the sheet fell a little further. "Know what, my Rowan?"

I'd thought of this for a while, of the things that slid through the Gate over the years from Ruhaven. Archery that had materialized in the bow and arrow here, the swords, the games they played, the dancing and music, the ring. Little pieces of another world that had traveled through the memories and been reborn again here. In inventions, in life, in culture.

And though Bryn may call himself an Azekiel, I knew what he was. What the legend of his race had come through as in our world.

"You're not an Azekiel," I whispered. "You're an angel."

⚙❋

The next day, James made breakfast for everyone for the first time since Essie died. He packed the table with flat pancakes and blueberries, whipped cream and chunks of butter, honey and almonds, sliced pears and shredded coconut.

Naruka had never been fed so well.

As we ate, Kazie updated us on her plans for the next week to get her "affairs in order." This was said with the casualness of someone happily planning their own funeral, a mother who didn't want you to have to fuss when she was gone. Since both of Kazie's parents had died years ago, she was writing to her aunt and five cousins.

What she planned to say, I didn't know.

Hello, I'm planning on dying in a dream and leaving you my feathered skirt and two budgies.

But without batting an eye, James dutifully mailed her letters the following day. I didn't know what would happen to her at the Fall, didn't want to think about what only reminded me of how close Bryn had been to the end.

So I tried to finish the gate lodge, letting the mundane work mellow my worries.

Stroke by stroke, I sawed through marble with the angle grinder, one of the few tools James had agreed to buy.

Wires dangled from the ceiling where light fixtures would eventually be installed. The cupboards were raw wood, simple, except for the antique knobs Kazie had found in a thrift shop. Next to Naruka, the place smelled too clean, lacking the underlying whiff of mold, cellar, and—of course—James's scones.

The cupboards had been misaligned in a few areas, so I'd worked a few shims in to level them. The grout might have been uneven at the start, but I'd learned quickly, and most of it was passable to the naked eye. My dad, well, he'd have picked out the misalignment by the stove, the sloping end where the tile didn't quite line up with the old stone wall.

I felt like an artist who'd spent five years on a mural only to realize it wasn't that good.

I plucked at my loose shirt. It was done. And thankfully, done was better than good. Even if done meant Kazie could now paint the cottage in wildfire pink.

Clunk. Clunk, clunk. Boots that could only belong to one man christened my cemented stairs.

Well, I'd been waiting for this, and he'd dodged me long enough.

I wiped my hands on the rag in my pocket, then groaned as I stood and granted my knees a break. I could all but feel the bruises blossoming on my calves.

Pushing aside the curtains James had hung, I studied Tye as he strutted under my overhang.

He didn't look like a man who'd been told to pack his things and leave within a week. There was a confident cockiness to his loose stride, like he owned the cottage, Naruka, and the land it sat on.

Was there any irony in him helping James exile Bryn and now finding himself banished? Probably not. Tye didn't do irony.

Under the woodshed, Bryn paused with the axe midway through the air and glanced over his shoulder, then dropped it with a bang when he spotted Tye. I could all but see him cursing as he swiped his cane and took two strides in my direction.

I waved at him through the window. *Bryn, wait there.*

I saw the minute he heard me. *You wish me to leave you with Tye? I've got it.*

Bryn frowned, but didn't follow as Tye strode through.

He was the only man I knew who could walk around in a short-sleeved shirt in January. His faded jeans hugged toned thighs and swept down to pointed Western boots. His face, I was pleased to see, was still healing from James's blow.

Spotting me leaning against the windowsill, he nodded and closed the door silently behind him.

"No smoking," I said sharply when he dragged a cigarette from his back pocket. I didn't need the place looking like the Ford's ceiling.

He paused with the smoke a few inches from his lips, lifted a brow. "So that's how you're gonna be, then."

I rolled my neck. Like Nereida, it was important to stay loose, relaxed. "Yeah, that's how I'm gonna be."

Tye's dimple had the nerve to make an appearance as he crossed to me. "Well darlin', I—"

My fist caught him dead in the gut.

Tye doubled over, air leaving him on a *whoosh* as I stepped back. "*That's* for the cane."

Yeah, that felt good. Maybe Nereida was on to something.

You need not defend me, Rowan.

He had it coming. And mind your own.

Tye coughed. The axe outside paused. Then he grinned under the ball cap. "Damn, Roe," he wheezed. "You sure pack a punch. Just tell me now how many more of those I got comin'."

Chin up, I strode to the new cupboards. "How many more times do you want to humiliate Bryn?" The coffee he had brought me earlier had cooled to one degree warmer than outside, but I drank it anyway. "And think about it, because all those memories of Nereida are starting to pay off."

But Tye just grinned and stretched out his neck. "Glad it was James who clocked me in the face and not you is all I'll say on that."

I studied him over the cup. "You must like getting punched."

"Just by you, hun."

"Aren't you supposed to be gone?"

Tye rubbed his beard, amusement dancing on his lips as he patted his pockets and frowned, as if just remembering I didn't want him smoking. So he cocked a hip on the deep windowsill and dragged off his ball cap. "Look, I wanna apologize for what I said on New Year's. I can't say I was myself. Fact is, I had too much to drink, wanted to rile Stornoway, and it all got a bit away from me."

More like it broke out of a burning barn and galloped across half of Ireland. "You broke his cane, Tye." The words I could eventually forgive, the truth I'd appreciated, but the cane—never.

Tye's jaw flexed, a quick up-down that looked like a facial sit-up. "You got me there, Roe. Maybe I let my emotions do a bit more talkin' than I should have. Didn't like the look of you when I walked in, didn't like all the things he'd kept from you either."

"Fine. When are you leaving?"

"Tomorrow morning," he said briskly. "That's what I came to tell ya. I figured my time was about done here anyway. What with Kazie makin' the Fall and all—I just can't watch that." He rose, crossed to the counter, and leaned his rigid forearms on the wood. He smelled like it, too, like fresh-cut pine and leather. "Will ya promise me you won't do it, Roe?"

I set my coffee down with a soft *clink*. "What? Make the Fall?"

"Yeah."

Even if I wanted to, Ruhaven would never accept Willow's replacement. "I promise."

Tye frowned, studying me through ivy-green eyes. "Well, I guess this is goodbye then, huh?"

Goodbye. The word settled over me like a stifling blanket. "Are you going back to L'Ardoise?"

He shifted closer. "Don't see anythin' else for me to do. I always liked workin' with horses, the farm. It's simple work, but simple is easy to understand. This?" He cast his eyes at the Gate hidden behind the looming cliff. "This ain't natural."

Well, there was no arguing that, but whether it was natural or not, it was real. "It always surprised me you'd believe in it."

Tye snorted. "Surprised myself, I suppose. But I know when my time is up, ya know? So tonight, I'm gonna finish packin', maybe take a last visit."

"What about Kazie's Fall?"

"I need a clean break." He made a cracking motion with his hands, then waved me over. "Look, I don't wanna make a big fuss out of this. So let me say my goodbyes now, before things get heavy."

He held his arms wide, waiting.

I met his flickering eyes. How far we'd come from L'Ardoise and the man who'd recruited me, helped me with the shop, given me Ruhaven. And yet, since Bryn, we'd not seen very much of each other.

When I crossed to him, Tye grabbed me in a fierce hug, hands tunneling into my hair. I patted his back, all but feeling Bryn's annoyance.

"Thanks for bringing me here. I probably should have said that months ago."

My hair muffled his answering grunt. "No problem, kid."

I closed my eyes, breathed him in. Leather and horse and farm. Comfort. I fought to hold on to this memory of him. Maybe Tye had been as much of a dream as Ruhaven had, because whoever he'd been in L'Ardoise, it'd been what I needed then—a firm hand, a shoulder to lean on, someone who didn't judge me. He'd been all of that, hadn't he? Even after I'd discovered Ruhaven.

When I'd been about to leave, to give it all up, Tye had looked me in the face and told me the truth—that I'd been nothing in L'Ardoise.

It'd hurt. God, it'd hurt. But it was truth.

"Come back with me, Roe," he whispered against my neck.

I felt Bryn bristle. The connection he'd created for us had to be getting stronger.

"I don't think so."

But Tye tightened his grip when I started to pull away. "What? You don't wanna see your folks? Your old friends? It'd be good for ya, Roe. I'll even let ya use my truck."

I huffed a laugh. "Your truck? Now that's an offer." But I still had Willow's.

"Ain't it?" Tye grinned, rubbing my arms. "C'mon, ya need a little time to clear your head from all this."

From Ruhaven, the Fall, from Bryn. I probably did.

"I'll think about it, Tye."

"Hun, that's not exactly how plane tickets work. But maybe I'll get ya one, knowin' you'll change your mind."

"No, Tye, thanks but—"

His hand closed around my wrist, twisting my arm and spinning me around until my spine slapped against his chest.

Whiskey breath tickled my neck. "Let me show ya somethin', Roe," he said, clamping an arm around my waist and inching my wrist up my back.

"You really do like getting punched," I said, fighting his hold.

"You're just gonna get me excited," he teased, but wrestled my arm up another few inches. "Hmm...let's just see if that's enough."

Tell him to stop, that I am coming.

This was to get at Bryn again? Why? I stomped my heel on Tye's toe. "Whatever you're planning, you're just going to piss off James." And Bryn, if the vibrations down the channel were any indication.

"Sorry, darlin', looks like it's gotta be a little higher. Deep breath now, there ya go."

Deep breath? What the hell was he—*oh.*

Fury ripped through the channel.

I gasped as pain flickered at the joint. "What are you *doing*?"

"One day," Tye murmured against my throat, "you're gonna have to make a decision." A shadow of wings passed behind the window. "'Cause he's gonna look you right in your pretty, smoky eyes and say anythin' to make you take the Fall. And when he does, I want ya to remember somethin'."

"That you broke my arm?" I gritted between my teeth, struggling to break free.

"That you're nothin' to him but a Stornoway-shaped doorbell."

The door slammed open.

But it wasn't Bryn who stood in the doorway. It was Sahn.

His eyes burned like an avenging angel—no, a guardian angel. Crackling thunder filled the room, booming as if coming from deep within his chest. And I knew now how Colm had felt, standing before Bryn that evening outside An Béal Bocht.

Terrified. Humbled. In awe.

Tye shoved me.

Tripping on the flooring, I cradled my elbow as I fell. *Goddamn it, Tye, goddamn—*

Bryn caught me, pulling me tightly against a shirt still damp from cutting wood. Lightning jumped off his skin, buzzing over mine in tiny electrical shocks.

Tye grinned cockily. "Five seconds from the woodshed. Not bad, Stornoway."

Bryn pried my arm away from me, inspected it with hands that glowed with light, then nudged me toward the door. "Go wait outside, Rowan."

What? Panic fluttered when I saw the look on his face. "He was only playing," I said, gripping the doorjamb.

Tye cracked his knuckles. "C'mon, Stornoway, you've only got so much time."

Time? For *what*?

Then I saw it in the flash of Bryn's otherworldly eyes.

Of course—he could walk again, could stand straight, had strength and power and magic bursting from his fingertips. "Don't—"

He spun back to Tye, moonlight rippling in thick waves over his body, lightning crackling at his feet. I all but saw Bryn's careful wall come crashing down, the bricks blown apart, crumbling on my floor.

Tye set his jaw, bracing for what he'd brought on himself.

But it was too late.

Lighting speared through the room, blinding me, shrieking with a shocking intensity before slamming into Tye.

Plaster rained down—thick, white chunks that turned his hair a brownish-gray. Oh, for the love of—

Bryn's fist collided with Tye's gut.

As he bent over, Bryn grabbed his hair with light-flecked fingers, wrenching his head up so that Tye was forced to look at him. Then Bryn leaned down, close enough that his mouth nearly touched Tye's ear.

"'*Fuck my mate,*' was it?" Bryn's whisper was like claws dragged over silk, the repeated words so crude it seemed impossible they'd come from his lips.

Tye grunted as his jaw was snapped sideways.

Jesus, Bryn was going to kill him.

I rushed across the room, grabbing Bryn around the waist. *Stop!* Heat sizzled into my palms.

But the channel was quiet on the other end.

Tye leaned away from the lightning crackling over his skin. "Don't worry 'bout me, darlin'."

Bryn shook me off, shoved his shoulder into Tye, and pinned his left wrist as sweat broke out at Tye's temples. "I have imagined for quite some time how I would repay you for the tack room," Bryn said quietly, deadly. "Do you wish to tell me which of these touched her? Or shall I guess?"

Tye grinned a dimple-less smirk. "All of them," he spat, blood dripping from his newly split lip.

"That will certainly make this easier."

"Tye, shut *up*."

"And she enjoyed each one," he added. "Ain't that right?"

I felt the blood drain out of my face.

Bryn snapped at Tye's throat. "Then I will start here," he decided, separating Tye's pinky.

Oh my god. "Bryn, don't! Don't!"

"Rowan, look away."

I grabbed his elbow, tried to wrench it off, but his muscles were like iron.

Snap.

Tye's face lost all color as his finger went limp. Bryn didn't even flinch, just grabbed the next—his ring finger this time. My stomach dropped to my feet.

"All of them, I believe you said?"

"Every. Single. One," Tye gritted between his teeth.

I'd throw up if I saw another finger break, if I had to watch Tye's pinky dangle like an overcooked noodle any longer.

I shoved at Bryn, wedging myself between his heaving form and Tye's whistling breath. Lightning nearly blinded me when I faced Bryn, gripping his shoulders. His skin was scorching. "Stop."

His face hardened. *Rowan, Tye has earned this and more.*

My shoulders cowed in the face of his fury, but I ordered my spine to straighten, even if my feet urged me to beat a track out the door. *He didn't do anything wrong in the tack room,* I said, and let my own annoyance move through the channel. *And neither did I.*

Bryn's lips peeled back, revealing two elongated fangs. *Tye is aware of the rules. You were not.* Veins like forked lightning flickered down his temples.

And if I was? I challenged.

His jaw flexed, but then I caught the light dulling in his eyes and pushed. "We're not in Ruhaven. We're here, and we can't afford to go to the emergency room. Someone will bring the Garda to James if Tye has ten broken fingers."

"At least."

I swallowed. "Right."

But his fangs retracted.

Tye swore as Bryn dropped his arm and stepped back, the light around us beginning to fade, the thunder a quiet rumble now. I moved out of the way of both of them.

Tye took a few breaths, wincing at his broken pinky. When he'd regained some color, some composure, he angled his wrist and tried for a shrug. "So that's fifteen from the wood lodge, and sixty for your glowy shit. Not bad, Stornoway." He cradled his finger and winced. "Guess ya don't remember that I never broke your leg that night, huh? That's true colors for ya. Don't ya forget it, Roe." Tye tapped his hat with his uninjured hand.

"You're *crazy*," I said when he left.

Bryn turned to face me, lifted a brow. "Do you think? This morning, I was an angel."

"That was before you threatened to remove all of Tye's fingers."

He stalked across the room. "I suppose that is fair. Though I admit, I was hoping to disprove your hypothesis in *other* ways."

"What—"

In one quick motion, Bryn had my back against the wall, a knee between my legs. He lowered his mouth to my throat. "*Guess*," he said, and licked a trail to my collarbone as my breath quickened into a new drumbeat. He inhaled against me. "Do you know what you smell of, my Rowan?"

"*Fear*?"

I felt him grin. "No, you smell of smoked amber and Ruhaven. You smell of dreams."

To hell with Tye, the lightning, the broken finger. We'd deal with that later.

I snuck my hands under his sweater. "Bryn?"

"Yes?"

"You ruined my wall," I said, grazing the band of his jeans.

"Indeed." He nipped my ear. "How shall I make it up to you?"

We could do this here, now, in the gate lodge, away from Naruka—the only reward for months of half-hearted renovations. "You know, the walls are a lot thicker in here."

He slipped a hand under my shirt, toyed playfully with my bra. "I am lucky to be in the company of a woman who is so educated on such matters." The clasp snapped, loosening the hold on my suddenly aching breasts. "Now, what was this about O'Sahnazekiel being an angel?"

He cupped me, thumbing my nipples as his tongue slid over my lips, between them.

James burst through the door.

"Oh, me poor suffering eyes," he cursed, draping a forearm over his glasses. "If yer gonna feel up me sister, can't ye do in a locked room?"

Bryn coughed a half-laugh, deftly reclasping my bra and straightening my shirt like a teenager caught fondling their sweetheart in the school corridor.

"We are quite decent," Bryn said, but his voice was still beautifully rough. "What is it?"

James dropped his arm, blew out a relieved breath. "This sure isn't the best time, but Kazie's, uh—well, she's decided to make the Fall sooner."

Bryn froze. "When?"

"Now like. *Now.*"

CHAPTER 49

The Foggy Dew

erns scratched at Kazie's bare legs, water squished in her low heels, and January numbed goose-pimpled arms. I shivered in sympathy. She'd threaded silk ribbons through her braids, a fairy walking to the Gate in the last chapter.

James offered her his coat, but she shook her head.

An hour earlier, James had burst into thick, blubbering sobs that fogged his glasses. Then Kazie had taken a walk with Bryn, the man who'd first shown her Ruhaven, and when she'd jumped into his arms, his quick, surprised laugh was a rare sound.

When she came to me, I hadn't known what to do. It was like saying goodbye to a friend who was enacting their funeral in a school play. My words felt hollow, like I was no better than an audience member congratulating a performer. So I promised to water her plants, feed her budgies, and take care of James. And tactfully declined her offer of moving into her room—it really was only a matter of time until the hammock caved in the roof.

But even as her eyes sparkled with tears, I hadn't been able to convince myself that she could leave us. The Inquitate I could explain as a hallucination, a brain defect we were born with, while the memories were a quirk in the oddity of space, and Bryn's ability to walk was a miracle.

But to drift up into the sky to be reborn?

It didn't have the aspect of truth to it. Where were the bright stage lights, the music from the hills, the recognition by the world that something impossible, something monstrous was about to happen?

Shouldn't the woods be screaming with the magic of it? Instead, my feet crunched in congealed pine needles and thorns.

Maybe they had it wrong.

Bryn limped at my side. The waterlogged bridge, as soft as Naruka's carpets, made barely a sound as we crossed. In the river's reflection loomed the rock where I'd imagined Bryn's easel the day the Inquitate had come.

When I reached for him, he tucked my hand in his. Any lingering arousal from the gate lodge was packed tightly away, miles from woods that breathed in quiet awareness of what was about to happen.

We entered the Gate together. Kazie rolled out the blanket and kneeled on its worn threads, fluffing her dress around frozen legs. Didn't she want to skydive, eat at a fancy restaurant, or buy something before being sucked into the universe?

What would I do if this were my last day? Finish the gate lodge? God, that was sad.

No, no. I looked at Bryn. Yes, I knew exactly what I would do.

He lifted the lantern from our bag, hung it on the tattered clothesline, and lit the candle inside as James wiped at his eyes. How was that string still intact? One day, the lantern would fall on our heads and I'd be right that something besides a human could wake us from Ruhaven.

Though there might not have been a momentous trumpeting to mark the passing, there was a calm hush, a quick pause of life that reminded me of the nights Willow had spent cross-legged with burning incense.

In tenth grade, she'd gone through a witch phase—short, luckily—and filled our shared room with piles of rocks, sand, and herbs. Dried flowers were strewn over our bunk bed. Plants were harvested and prepared. Our windowsill was transformed into a garden of crystals and rare stones. She prayed to the moon, mixed potions, and tried her hand at tarot readings.

One day, I'd turned to her and asked, "But Willow, is it real?"

"What do you mean?" she replied, genuinely perplexed.

I held up the book describing a potion to hex a relative. "I mean, do you really think this is going to curse Uncle Phil?"

She scratched at her knee-high striped purple stockings, and asked, "Does it matter?"

I turned to Bryn. Dew curled his hair behind a tall, slightly pointed ear as he blinked under long eyelashes.

"Rowan, James and I believe you should witness the Fall, as we have both seen it previously. If you were to decide to make this decision for yourself..." He trailed off. "James believes that if you were to decide as Kazie has, that it is important you understand the experience."

I searched his porcelain face that gave away nothing. *What do you want, Bryn?* Instead, I asked, "What will happen?"

He dropped the backpack as he'd done a hundred times before. "The Gate will claim Kazie when Kazmira dies in the memories."

I chanced a look at James, teary-eyed and gaunt, coal-black hair wilting under his flat cap. Could he handle losing Kazie so close to Essie?

"I'll anchor," I agreed after a moment. If anything were to happen to Kaz, I'd need to scorch my eyeballs with the truth of it.

I waited while James hugged her to his chest and spoke in her ear. He wouldn't make the Fall, which meant he would never meet Kazie again, not in this life or Ruhaven. How many times had James watched a Ruhaven make a choice he felt he never had?

Kazie undid her dream catcher necklace and clenched it in her fist over her heart. Her token.

Why was everyone acting so normal? Shouldn't there have been some ritual beyond a token in Kazie's palm? A funeral, a gift, a card?

Yet they laid next to her, James with tears in his eyes and Bryn with the soft delicacy of stone as he grasped her hand. He'd live the last memories with her, with Kazmira.

What happened if the Gate wanted him too? Could it scoop him up? What if they were wrong and the Fall could happen at any time?

I sank beside Bryn, clutched his arm. "Are you sure you're not going anywhere? There's no chance...?"

He propped himself on an elbow. "No, the Gate will not take me now."

But the Gate could claim someone at the end of the memories. What if Bryn slipped away, unaware he'd even made the Fall?

I tightened my grip. "Bryn, are you absolutely *sure*?"

His eyes softened. "Yes, my Rowan." *But just in case...*

He cupped my neck, slanted his mouth to mine. The kiss was light and gentle before his tongue slid in a soft question over my lips.

Too soon, he released me. His lips quirked, a tiny, lopsided smile that outed him as mortal after all. "I would hardly risk leaving after waiting so long to find you," he reminded me.

"C'mon, guys," Kazie called, looping her arm through Bryn's.

Reluctantly, I let him go.

They created a colorful chain under the barren branches of winter. Their eyes closed together, like a mother drawing a blanket across her children.

There was no fear in Kazie's dark face, no tension in the glossy set of her mouth.

"Kaz, are you going to be okay if nothing happens?"

Her lips crept up into that banana grin, a perfect half-circle. "Of course something will happen. I can't wait to see you in Ruhaven." She yawned. "Look after the budgies. Fred likes carrots. Bye, Roe. See you in…?"

"Kazie?" I said softly. "Kazie—" But her eyelashes fluttered once before the Gate claimed her.

I held my breath.

And waited like an idiot, like she'd poof into the air before my eyes.

Bryn's hand loosened in mine as he joined her. His toes rolled out, his lips—still damp from our kiss—parted. James's bony shoulders relaxed into the quilt. He no longer uttered embarrassing noises or other indications of his time in Ruhaven. Not with Essie gone.

But Kazie did not wither and disappear. Her braids sprawled in a medusa halo, her skin puckering from the cold as she replayed her last memories.

The woods quieted, listening as the Gate made its decision.

How could she know Ruhaven would take her back? What if it was like Bryn thought and it judged you, like a St. Peter's Gate to Tallah?

People didn't just float away.

But people also didn't see memories from another planet, meet their brothers from hundreds of years ago, or find their mates who gladly broke off engagements for them.

As a breeze ruffled Bryn's hair, I brushed aside the scattered locks. His forehead was cool and unstrained, asleep in a world he loved, watching the last moments in Drachaut for Kazie.

What could have happened that would have brought Bryn, Tye, and me through the Gate together?

I shivered as fog squeezed between the bare oaks and birch trees like pudding pushed through a strainer. But with the sudden lack of wind, I unwound my scarf from my sweaty neck and twisted it into a ball.

I checked my watch. Fifteen minutes.

What would I tell Kazie if she woke and her soul was not in Ruhaven, but this world she'd never loved?

Even in the Gate, she kept her fingers tightly fisted on the dream catcher resting on the folds of her dress. Folds that pooled and dripped over her body.

I rubbed my eyes, tired from the last few days. Between the bomb Tye had detonated on me and Bryn's memories, I could barely keep my thoughts straight. And now Kazie was—

I squinted at her dress again.

But it *was* dripping. It pooled on her stomach and spread into the weave of the quilt.

I scrubbed at my face. It wasn't supposed to melt. *She* wasn't supposed to melt. James would have told me if the Fall caused her clothes to bleed off her *body*.

Or was it an illusion? *Inquitate?*

I shot to my feet.

Bare patches of dark skin rippled under material that was no more than thick water so that she looked like a woman plucked from the river, like the sea-sprayed statue at the head of a boat.

I jumped away from the floral dress running in rivers over the blanket. Her belly button piercing—a ceramic lemon—poked through the thinning material that dripped off her breasts. Another tattoo, this one of a blindfolded woman, smiled at me on the side of her thigh. But unlike the clothes, Kazie remained untouched. Her dark, naked skin perfectly matched the evening folding itself into the skies.

Dropping to my knees, I splashed in the pool of her dress. "Kazie, wake up! Wake up!" I grabbed at her and ended up planting my hand through her knee.

I held up my shaking fingers, now coated in the fondue of her dress. *Jesus Christ.*

Kazie's naked body wavered.

Right in front of me, in the middle of the Irish oaks and yellow moss, her entire existence faltered like a cut umbilical cord.

My breath stuck in my throat. The drumbeat at my temples whipped into a frenzy.

Then, with each blink, she dematerialized further.

Blink. Her feet whispered away. Her kneecaps dissolved. Her beautiful beaded braids scattered like fleeing ants. Her hips and torso wavered, a mirage in the desert, before they, too, were gone.

And when her face slipped away, the only thing left were the fingers grasping a dream catcher.

Then they evaporated too.

Only the deerskin-wrapped necklace, with its beaded threads, lay still upon the quilt.

I stared, unblinking, at the space between James and Bryn—a street with an empty lot, whose overgrown yard was the only indication of the house that was once there.

She'd...she'd...

I pressed shaking hands to the rough blanket. *Dry.* There was nothing left of her. No color, no liquid, no dress. No Kazie. Nothing but a flimsy piece of jewelry.

I scratched at the blanket, tore at it, my breath burning. There had to be something left. I yanked so hard that James and Bryn spilled off the edge. Yet all evidence of her—of everything that had been Kazie—was gone.

Kneeling in her empty lot, I bundled my knees to my chest.

Despite everything I'd seen, it felt like the first time Tye had taken me up here and forced me to witness what I'd thought had been a dream. When the world had shifted under me and brought with it that mind-numbing *terror* to know you weren't alone in the world. That there was more, so much more, and your existence meant nothing.

Then my head snapped up at a distant voice.

"Istilick mi liom, shakila."

The hairs on the inside of my ears pricked with awareness. Everything became a dull roar inside my head.

"Istilick mi liom, shakila," it repeated.

Willow?

Her voice. My sister's. One I'd never forget, no matter how many years separated us.

"Istilick mi liom, shakila! Istilick mi liom, shakila!" she yelled, urgent now.

I ran trembling fingers down my cheeks. My breath came out in rapid pants.

"Willow!" I called hoarsely, voice lost in the rustling leaves.

"Istilick mi liom, shakila."

Something flickered between the trees.

Heart pounding, I jumped to my feet, lunged toward the path—

"Rowan." Bryn snagged me around the waist, his warm breath at my neck as he squeezed me to him.

"Bryn, I—she's—was there and then—"

He smoothed back my hair, folded me against his warm heartbeat. "I know. She has returned to Ruhaven. It is a shock to see it for the first time," he said, mistaking my stuttering.

Was it her? Was it Willow? Or an Inquitate? Should I tell Bryn? I reached out a hand—to call her back, to beckon, I didn't know. Then I remembered—he'd spoken of this before, the illusions of the Fall. That he believed it was Ruhaven speaking to us.

Through Willow?

James let out a low wail as he woke.

Istilick mi liom, shakila, Willow had said, and hadn't I heard those words before?

No. Not heard. *Seen.* Engraved in the plaques around the Gate, the ones that even now glittered invisibly.

James and Bryn spoke quickly under their breaths, words I couldn't process, couldn't hear, just a low rumble against my chest as I replayed Willow's voice again and again, as I pictured Kazie melting into the earth, as I fought to understand what that meant for me now.

As I shook, Bryn murmured in my ear, soft words that soothed the wrong shock. "She is in Ruhaven now," he repeated, rocking us like boats listing in a port. "She has gone home."

Yes, Kazie was in Ruhaven.

And somehow, somehow, it made perfect sense. She was exactly where she was supposed to be. Where she was meant to be. Where she deserved to be. A puzzle piece slid into the empty slot I hadn't seen.

James ran spindly fingers over the bumps in the quilt where Kazie had lain, picked up the dream catcher. "I didn't see the end in the Gate," he said heavily. "Did ye?"

Bryn's hair tickled my ears when he shook his head. "No. No, I was with Nereida, with Rowan."

I clutched his wool jacket. "She—her clothes," I stuttered, voice raspy in my throat. "They melted." Before I heard Willow.

Bryn grasped my hand. "Yes, it is Ruhaven taking only her soul." His throat worked, bobbing under the collar of his jacket as James knelt on one knee and skewered the ground with a shovel I hadn't noticed. "James will bury her token now."

Her token. Nothing more than a metal plate buried in soil and worms, waiting for the next Ruhaven to vomit in a shrub and discover them.

When the hole was deep enough, James gently lowered the necklace and set it between the glittering plaques. After scooping soil, he withdrew a metal rectangle from his coat pocket and nestled the gilded plate on the makeshift grave.

I glanced at Bryn. He knelt solemnly in the dirt, eyes dry and a little vacant, but not shocked, not surprised, not a drop of remorse that I could see on his pale, pale face.

Did he, even now, want our plaques to be buried amongst this graveyard?

James drew a deep inhale before a song left his lips. Not in Ruhaven, but in Irish.

I pulled away from Bryn to lean over James's shoulder. Kazie's bronze bar glittered green under the leaves, the grooves of the name catching flickering lights.

"*Istilick mi liom, shakila,*" I read aloud. The first time I had, it'd been Bryn with me here at the Gate. When he'd told me of the Fall. "What does it mean?"

James wiped at his eyes. "*And in the end, the beginning.*"

"What?"

"It is a Ruhaven blessing," Bryn explained quietly. "For those who have made the Fall. A chance to begin again."

I swallowed against the sudden harsh constriction in my throat. "You're sure?"

"Yes, of course." The corners of his lips dipped. "What is it?"

Sick and anxious, I rubbed at my throat, willing my voice to stay even. "Nothing. Nothing, I'm fine."

⚙☀

"Rowan!" Bryn's voice trailed me through the forest. "Please wait for me. I cannot keep up with you."

Not with one leg, and for once, I was eternally grateful for it.

Willow had called to me from the Gate. From Ruhaven. From that dark, naked room. *Why?*

There could only be one reason, even if I didn't want to accept it, even if everything in me was screaming in denial at what must have been so obvious from the beginning. And now I was dangling on a precipice of numbing possibility.

I ducked branches automatically, having memorized their crooked curves from all the hikes to this Gate. I stepped over logs and onto moss that squished half a foot before my boots met solid ground.

And in the end, the beginning.

It was all so horribly clear now.

The end for me. The beginning for her.

Because after everything, after the months of living as Nereida, I'd never really escaped the truth. And now that the Gate had given me this gift, had allowed me to witness what was never mine, it was asking for its sacrifice.

It wanted Nereida back. It wanted Willow.

This was what it had come to—and of *course* it had. The reason for it all, the meaning of my name in that *Ledger*. Because I had always been on borrowed time, a borrowed life, one that the Gate needed me to return now. Because watching the memories hadn't come without a cost, and the cost was to return Willow to Ruhaven. That was why I'd been allowed to witness her past life. If there was enough of Willow's soul in me to watch the dream, then there was enough to bring her back too.

I blinked away the burn behind my eyes. James had nearly convinced me that it'd been my birth in the *Ledger*, and then Bryn had seemed so certain, but it'd all been a delusion. Mine. And delusions came with a price.

Had I really thought I could pretend that I was someone else? That the Gate wouldn't come and extract something from me? And who was I to deny it now? No one. I'd never *been* anyone.

I never had dreams like Willow, never finished college, never wanted anything in my whole life. I was something that materialized between the gaps in Willow's life, springing up like flowers in the cracks on a grave.

And now I expected the Gate to—to accept me? As a replacement? No. I hadn't done anything *worth* accepting.

A cobweb hanging between two glistening birch trees broke across my face before I could bat it away.

I was the only Ruhaven ever born a twin, a twin whose soul was as intricately bound to my own as Nereida's Tether. And *souls* were what Ruhaven accepted—that's what Kazie had said before it'd taken her own.

If Willow's soul was bound to mine, then some *piece* of her—and I didn't know which piece—but some piece of her *had* to come back with me.

When Naruka loomed into view, light guttered in her windows as if she were looking down at our numbers and wondering why one was missing. Smoke puffed from her chimney, staining the royal sky with pewter soot.

How long did I have before Naruka was mourning me too? Years? Months?

I stumbled through the tack room and barreled into the kitchen.

But pulled up short when I caught sight of Tye leaning against the stove, a bandaged hand gripping the counter.

"She's gone then," he said without emotion.

Was she? Or was Kazie right now running through Ruhaven as Willow might be? And how long did I have before the Gate asked me to sacrifice myself like Kazie? "What?"

Tye's eyes hardened to cool, emerald stones, his lips moving in some indistinguishable pattern. My thighs felt numb, my mind empty, my fingers fought to undo the suddenly unfamiliar shape and form of buttons.

Two steps brought him toe to toe with me. He grasped my trembling hands. "What is it?" he asked firmly.

I couldn't *breathe*. My shoulders tightened on a wave as I fought air into lungs that had shriveled to raisins. "How long do we have?" I managed at last. "I mean," I said, struggling for another noseful of air. "How long do *I* have? Before the call? Like Kazie?"

Tye's eyes went to wide discs of green. "What the hell are ya talkin' about?"

What was I talking about? Making the Fall? Was I prepared to cast myself away like that? For Willow? When I had—when I had—

Tye's hands tightened on my wrists, and he gave me one good shake, hard enough that the words tumbled out. "The Fall," I managed, collecting myself. "When will I hear the call? Is it years? Months?" My voice strained into a whisper. "*Weeks*?"

Tye shook his head in disgust and released me. "You ain't got long," he said abruptly.

Not long. Not long to live at Naruka, not long to be *me*, whatever that was, and not long to be with Bryn.

"How do you know?" Did Kazie? Did everyone? Had I missed some crucial piece about when the Fall would happen?

The clock *tick-tocked* on the wall.

Tye didn't look at me. "I know in the same way that Stornoway knows. We ain't got a lot of time, and your time's comin' up."

Bryn knew? *How?* But when I asked, Tye only shook his head. "I always knew he'd manipulate ya into it." But his voice wasn't angry, it was weary, resigned. Defeated. Something I'd never heard from Tye, not once, not even when Bryn broke his finger. "You're gonna make the Fall."

Was I? Was I really saying that? Committing it? Promising it? What did it mean to turn away from something Ruhaven asked from you? No—not Ruhaven, *Willow*. Could I ignore my sister's own request for me to save her, to sacrifice myself at the Gate? One soul for another.

"Listen," Tye said quietly. "I don't know how long we got—you got, before the call comes, but when it does, ya only got weeks to make it on up to that Gate. Before ya do, ya better make sure there ain't nothin' here ya wanna hold on to. Nothin' here ya wanna do before ya leave. Ya know what I'm sayin'?"

No, because I couldn't begin to comprehend what my own death would mean, when it seemed as unrealistic as Kazie disappearing into the earth.

"—I bought you that plane ticket." Tye's words leaked into my ears again. "I said I would, and it's leavin' tomorrow. If I mean anythin' to ya, you'll come back with me. Have a think about all of this away from Naruka. Away from Stornoway."

Go back to L'Ardoise? A last goodbye? Would my parents want to see me? Or would they be glad to never have the reminder again of what they'd lost?

"I've seen people just like you," Tye continued. "They get all caught up in it. They see someone make the Fall, they lose their mind for a bit, think it's callin' 'em or somethin'. Roe, please, I'm damn near beggin' ya. If you could just take a week, remember where you're from. Don't rush into this."

Because everything that was me would be buried under a plaque in the Gate. I didn't even know what my token would be—maybe drywall, after all.

I nodded without thinking, and Tye said, "That's good now. You go on upstairs and pack. I'll come get ya in the mornin' and we'll sort this out. You're gonna be okay, Roe. It's all gonna be okay."

CHAPTER 50

Turtles All the Way Down

I n the ticking silence of my bedroom, I emptied the dresser at random, oblivious to what I packed as my suitcase went from empty to swollen. When tears burned my eyes, I wiped them quickly away, as disgusted with myself as the Gate must be. I should be happy it was giving me this gift, not upset about the cost.

A rapid knock shook the door.

Before I could answer, Bryn opened it on a loud squeak.

The window's blue moonlight highlighted the strain around his wide mouth as he thumped into the room, turned, and scraped the bolt into the latch.

How would I ever give him up? But then, maybe it'd be like he first wanted—he'd have Nereida back, just not me.

Bryn's gaze crawled over my suitcase, the heaps of clothes on my dresser, the socks I hadn't packed. He peeled off his jacket, laid it across my desk chair, then unwound his scarf and repeated the motion. His eyes—flat, cold, and icy blue—met mine. Held.

"I assume you are in a state of shock," he said.

Was I? Is that why my legs felt numb, why there was a burning dread eating away at my stomach lining? Why I couldn't bear to look at Bryn and realize I'd never be able to give him up?

"Because I fail to understand why you would otherwise leave with Tye at such a time," he said when I remained mute.

I walked mechanically across the room, tugged open my drawer, and dragged out a handful of socks.

"Tye bought me a plane ticket," I said tonelessly.

"And that is all it takes for you to *leave* with him? Tye, who very nearly broke your arm."

Why was I holding socks? "He wouldn't have."

Bryn shook his head, then limped with loud footfalls to my window and brushed aside the dangling curtains. The dusky twilight silhouetted him in purple lines, his back warm and lit by the lamp. A leaf he hadn't noticed from the Gate still clung to the hem of his sweater.

Headlights glared through my window—Tye leaving with the Ford.

"He told me you are considering making the Fall."

I fumbled with the socks as Bryn turned from the window, the twilight fading to crystalline black. His face was so utterly blank, so completely unreadable, that my gut twisted into a thousand knots.

"Isn't it—isn't it what you wanted?" I asked weakly.

He looked at me with disbelief. "Of course not. While I had once believed we would make the Fall together, I no longer feel the same, as I made clear in the lounge. If we did so now, we would not remember each other. We would be reborn again, would spend centuries apart, unaware of who or what we once were. Is that what you truly want? To forget me? To forget us?"

No. *Never*. But it wasn't me making this decision.

My voice, when I spoke, wasn't at all steady. "Seeing Kazie like that, it just—it put things into perspective," I lied.

Bryn, his face still a mask of stone, walked slowly to the end of my bed, his cane and suede boots burying themselves in the fur rug Kazie had recently replaced. Above, the wicker lampshade swayed from an imaginary breeze.

"Perspective," Bryn repeated, blinking at me, but his eyes weren't golden now. "Is that what you call it when you so casually, so effortlessly, decide you will eventually end everything you are to me?"

Now I caught it, the emotion he didn't want to show—shock, pain, fear.

Bryn gripped the iron railing of the bed and squeezed so hard I worried it'd snap in his fist. "I do not understand you, Rowan. Only a few nights ago, you accused me of wanting to trade your soul. You cried in my arms at the idea of it. Yet now you are prepared to meet that end, should Ruhaven beckon tomorrow?" His voice broke, nearly undid me.

Tell me why, he demanded as if he couldn't bring himself to speak.

"It's Willow," I blurted out. "I think, if our *souls* are what's collected from Ruhaven, and she was my twin, then there must be some piece of her that would come through too." Enough of her in me that I'd been able to witness the memories these last months on her behalf.

The railing groaned beneath Bryn's hand. "You think it shall return her to Ruhaven."

"Yes."

"Because you still believe her to be Nereida."

"Yes," I said quietly, though it wasn't a question.

"Goddamn you, Rowan," he cursed softly. "What of us? In your world, how long shall we have? Weeks? Months? Is that enough for you? Will you be so satisfied to have a year together before you toss our fates to the arms of Ruhaven again?"

Decades wouldn't be enough. I wanted a life with Bryn, wanted to see him grow old, wanted to learn every minuscule detail of the life he'd lived before we met, wanted him to point out all the streets of Odda he used to run through. But I couldn't admit any of that, because then I'd never be able to make this sacrifice.

"Isn't that what you believe in?" I said to hide how the words ate at me. "Your whole world is Ruhaven. I thought you would be glad to go back."

"*Glad*?" He spun around, his eyes and nose dotted with bright color that should have shamed me. "Glad that I shall never know *you* again? That, after spending years searching for you, I shall need to wait centuries once more? Do I mean *nothing* to you? When I showed you my worst memories, ones I do not wish to recall myself, did my sacrifices mean nothing?"

I wet my lips. God, it wasn't like that, but every word he threw at me was breaking through my resolve. "You know that's not true. You know what I felt."

"Do I?" Bryn choked out. "Rowan, I feel that I bare every piece of my soul, and you do nothing but look at the odd picture it makes."

My throat tightened. "Bryn, I know what you gave up. I see it every time you look at me. But this—it isn't about you and me. I can't let myself think of that."

"'*Let yourself think of that*'?" he repeated, very slowly, his hand shaking on his cane. "Of me. Let yourself think of *me*, you mean. I do not know how much you believe I can withstand. I learn you not only plan to one day make the Fall without discussion, but you are packing to leave with a man whom James has banned from Naruka. Who threatened to break my leg, who routinely seeks to embarrass and denigrate me before you, who stood in that gate lodge and threatened you this morning."

I opened my mouth. Closed it again. He was right, and I didn't deserve him, never had—Nereida did. "I'm sorry. I'm *sorry*, Bryn, but you've never lost anyone. You don't understand what Willow was to me, what I owe her—" I broke off when all color drained from his face.

"I lost you. I lost *you!*" he shouted. *"Fy faen,* Rowan, do you not understand what that did to me? To stand over your sister's grave in L'Ardoise and believe it was—that I was—" He cursed his breaking voice, fought for precious control as I stood there, a second from dissolving into the floor.

Bryn rubbed a hand over his mouth. "To believe that I had been but weeks from knowing you. To believe that my mate was waiting to be found and I had failed in this simple task. That I had let her die alone, that she should never know of Ruhaven." He took a steadying breath. "I made mistakes, Rowan, with us, from the moment you appeared in my office. I did not seek you out after my attack because I believed the Inquitate were following me, that they would come again, and I did not want you hurt because of that.

"I did it to punish myself, for I was not supposed to fail you, to attempt to end my life in the Gate, and never, ever to take another, as I did. This was the law, and I broke it. And I was punished. You may have found the triplet connection, but I know that whatever the reason, Ruhaven does not forgive, does not forget."

Was that what all this was about? Guilt because he'd tried to move on? Guilt because he couldn't stop something he had no control over?

I took a step toward him. "Bryn, it wasn't your *fault*."

His eyes guttered. "It was, yes. I *chose* to die at the Gate, and would have had James and Tye not dragged me out. I *chose* to take a coward's path and resume my relationship with Abby, despite the laws."

I shook my head, all that I could manage. I could barely *think* of him with her. Except that was a lie, wasn't it? I'd thought about her all too much, about just what kind of woman it'd take to have someone like Bryn break Ruhaven's laws.

He waited. "But you are leaving," he stated, circling us to the beginning.

Not to L'Ardoise. That wasn't what he meant now.

I laid a hand on the suitcase Willow had covered in stickers. My chest ached for him, for us, for her. "Willow and I were born together," I explained softly.

"Rowan, so were *we*," Bryn promised, voice raw.

I felt it in each grinding bone in my body. "You taught me about Ruhaven's rules," I reminded him. "*You* told me that Ruhaven speaks to us at the Gate. Now she has and she's asked me to—*Bryn!*"

He wrenched the suitcase from me and tossed it against the wall. Lime paint poofed in a cloud of dust. The luggage clunked to the floor and sprung open, socks tumbling out. "That's *Willow's*."

He grabbed both my arms before I could duck and right the bag.

I braced for the next avalanche of words, the argument I knew I wouldn't be able to resist, because he was right, I knew that, and he deserved better than this, than me, and always had.

I pressed my hands to his chest, stared up into eyes of bottomless blue. "Bryn, I'm so sorry that I—"

Breath *whooshed* out of my lungs as he crushed me to him. His arms slid around me, cradled my head, held me against his beating heart that had become my own metronome.

I squeezed my eyes shut, stroked his quivering shoulders, in the dip between them. I wouldn't be strong enough to choose Willow over him.

But Bryn peeled back, raw emotion swimming beneath his pearl skin. "I am terrified of losing you," he breathed. "If you choose to make the Fall, I would follow you, but I do not wish to wait centuries ever again."

He dropped his cane.

Then very slowly, he lowered to the floor, one hand braced on my bed, until he kneeled on the rug at my feet. The bedside lamp divided his face into shadow and light, a fallen angel, and for once, I was looking down at him, at the frozen blue of unguarded eyes.

He grasped my right hand. "Rowan, do you know why Kazie made the Fall?"

I tried to tug him up, but he didn't rise. "Because she loved Ruhaven," I said at last.

He licked his bottom lip, nodded. "Yes, she loved the wild freedom, the magic, but mostly she loved who she was. She loved Kazmira. It was who she always wanted to be," he breathed, his gaze unflinching, even as his hand shook around mine. "But I only wanted you."

My heart leapt into my throat. "Bryn, if…"

"I did not want to ask before," he said quickly, a whisper in the quiet room. "I have always believed the Fall was your decision to make, without influence, without the pressure of what had once existed between us. What I believe still does."

He squeezed my hand. "When I met Nereida, I found my mate, my missing soul, in a woman I believed I would never know but for a memory. Then, against all odds, the *Ledger* returned you to me. When I saw you for the first time, the connection between us was as alive and vital as it was in Ruhaven.

"Since that night, I have seen you in every woman, felt you in every touch, heard you in every song. My only wish is to be to you what O'Sahnazekiel is to Nereida. I am sorry, Rowan, for the mistakes I have made, for the promise I broke, but I would ask you anyway, would beg you. Please stay with me. Stay so that we will not forget each other—as we certainly will if we return to Ruhaven—and because, Rowan, I cannot bear to lose you again so soon."

I couldn't stop my tears. He'd never spoken like this, never. "Bryn, I don't want to leave. I swear I don't, but—" I broke off, glanced down when he held out his other hand.

And slowly unfurled his fingers.

My heart stopped—the pulse just gave way entirely to complete, humming silence.

It was not the simple metal band I'd found in his room, but a delicate, thin, gold circlet with an opal stone and twin moons.

"This is yours," he said, thumbing the ring in his palm. "I had it made after we met. The one Nereida wears."

Mine. My ring, because…

I sunk heavily onto the bed.

Moonlight glinted off the stone he held, still waiting for an answer. Or was he? Was this a—a proposal? We'd never talked about what mates meant, other than the book James gave me. Or was this some acceptance of what had been in Ruhaven? But both meant the same thing—a reason to stay.

Still on his knees, his lips quirked into a hesitant smile—one I'd always loved. "Rowan?" Bryn wiped away the tears burning my cheeks. I didn't even know what I was crying for— Him? Me? Willow? The Fall?

I couldn't answer. Didn't know what it was he wanted. "I—I—I—" My breath was coming in quick, ugly gasps now. I pressed a hand to my chest, willing my lungs to expand properly again. "Bryn, this is…is…*overwhelming*."

His smile fell like a flower wilting in a storm.

I had never felt so small, so utterly inadequate, not even when James stood in his kitchen and admitted he hoped I'd be Essie.

Bryn's fingers closed back over the ring, set it on the nightstand. "Why?" His voice cracked on the single word.

I wiped my sweaty palms on the old quilt. I didn't have an answer for him. There was a kind of dead buzzing in my ears, like a part of me was floating a few inches away, as shocked as I was.

"I don't know what it means," I said lamely as Bryn rose. He used the nightstand, the bed, for support, until his shadow blanketed me in cool purples.

He reached a hand toward me, stroked the length of my jaw with one knuckle. "What it means, Rowan, is that which we already are."

I looked up at him, surprised to see the whisper of warmth in his irises.

This bond between us is the same that exists between Nereida and Sahn.

He trailed his hand down my arm, circled my wrist in long fingers, and brought my palm to his heart. He squeezed his eyes shut, breath shuddering between his soft lips. Something warm tingled on my fingertips, but when I tried to pull back, he held firm. "Rowan, trust me."

Whatever it was heated and spread between my fingers until tiny, golden threads blossomed over my wrist.

I'd seen this when he'd kissed me, had thought it was a hallucination or some piece of his Mark appearing. Yet here it was again, swirling up my arm like fireflies in the dark, light as spiderwebs, pulsing with quiet music.

I jerked my gaze to his, in awe, in surprise. "How are you doing this? What is it?"

He grasped my hand tighter. "Our bond, Rowan, the one that exists even here, that has survived centuries." Had I seen it with Nereida and Sahn?

My skin tingled under it, nearly burning with an internal heat. Panic leapt into my throat when I tried to tug my arm free, but it stayed glued to Bryn's chest.

"Something's wrong," I said, urgent now as the golden thread crept slowly over my shoulder.

Bryn slid a knee onto the bed as I fell back. "You need to trust me. Trust *us*," he said thickly.

"I don't... It's too much. I can't, not now. Not with Kazie, and Tye, and the ring and..." And your fiancée I was only just accepting.

Then the lamp winked out, and the only light in the room was the glittering thread that matched Bryn's golden eyes.

"Make it stop," I insisted, but it came out as more of a gasp.

The silky chain he'd summoned slithered over my collarbone, its heat like prickling sparks as it wound around my neck. I tried to yank at it with my free hand, as the burn turned to blister—because it *wasn't me*. Because Bryn was trying to summon a bond that was for him and *Nereida,* for Willow, not for me. Just like the Gate had warned.

He caught my wrist, pinned it, the bed's old springs groaning under his weight. "Trust me," he begged. "I can show you Nereida, Sahn, our life together. Please, Rowan, I—"

"Bryn!" I shouted at him, and this time, he froze, confusion flickering over his face where he kneeled over me.

But the thread slipped under my shirt, settled between my breasts on a throbbing pulse, sticking like moths to a lightbulb, bleating wings burning up in the light.

The headache brewing behind my eyes twisted my thoughts into balloon animals that *pop-pop-popped*.

Memories flashed in rapid-fire behind my eyelids, not steady visions like Bryn had shown me before. He wanted me to trust him, but there were always more secrets. The ring. Abby. Sahn.

Now he'd try to prevent me from saving Willow. And that I'd never allow.

"Rowan? *Rowan?*" Bryn's normally confident voice became worried, pleading.

The golden thread plucked my heart like it was a fiddle instead of an organ that belonged to me. I blinked away the flashes of seizing memories, patted weakly at my breasts. "It hurts."

His porcelain face wavered as I struggled to hold on to it, to him. "No, it is not supposed to..." He let go of my hand, but the tangled thread he'd summoned clung to us, bound us.

His voice grew distant, underwater below the deep, murky depths I'd feared. The memories of the last few days spread into a puddle in my mind. Kazie. Willow. The Fall. Abby. Tye. James.

My ears filled with the jumbled conversations of people speaking in…Norwegian.

The growing pain in my skull threw itself against the vision, a crashing wave trying to keep the memory at bay. I cried out, felt rather than heard him call my name, but I was slipping into foreign images that tumbled like rocks down a hill, burying me beneath them.

And in Bryn's memories, we were not in Ruhaven.

So it was not Nereida who smiled at me in the woods, who made Bryn's heart burst out of his chest, but Abby, the woman he'd loved enough to propose to. To want to marry. Not Nereida, and not me.

Across the sea of memories, Bryn called to me, but the water drowning my mind gobbled up his words.

Images flashed by like a roll of exposed film.

I was in a cafeteria with burnt cabbage stew and young students sitting around long, wooden tables. Bryn's college in Trondheim.

Beside me—beside Bryn—sat Abby, with kind eyes not old enough to crinkle, spreading a textbook with sun-dipped fingernails and a matching butterscotch hair clip. The kind of woman who would know all about Picasso.

Was there something else he wanted me to know about them? Something that would show why I should stay? Of all the times to push this on me...

I twisted in the vision, reaching for anything to pull me out of the memory. I caught the twinkle of the thread and leapt for it, grasping the wretched thing in both hands. And tugged. Hard.

Far away, above the murky, dark water, I heard Bryn gasp. The sound rolled in my eardrums a second before new scenes tumbled like marbles on a sheet of glass.

Smash. Smash. Smash.

Coconut-scented hair swung in a scrunchie. I caught the silky strands in my fist, lightly tugging the woman around. Abby's lips parted in surprise before my mouth—*Bryn's* mouth—smacked her cherry-Cola lips.

I recoiled at the memory, at the lust curling in Bryn's gut.

"Don't show me this," I pleaded to nothing but the endless dark water, the gold thread still in my fist. I tried to pull myself out, but the rope slipped from my grip.

The memories came with the flood of a broken dam in a storm. Stale coffee and cardamom buns wafted in a café. Abby grinned over a latte, a dimple ripening one cheek before she laughed in tiny, tinkering bells.

Compared to Abby's perfection, my smile belonged to a lopsided ogre.

"Bryn. Please." My voice was rusted steel. *Don't show me her, not her.* Wasn't it enough to know he'd been engaged? Had wanted to spend his life with this perfect woman?

Then colored lights flashed, and Abby's ponytail whipped fruity shampoo in my face, her toothy smile gleaming as Bryn spun her in tight circles, her feet twirling in a perfect line.

Where he'd learned to dance. In Oslo, with his fiancée, before his injury from the Inquitate.

I was drowning without the benefit of water. Where was that rope? I looked down, found it wrapped around my fist again.

Pinching the glittering rope between my knees and elbows, I struggled to climb out of this hell.

Ping.

A thread snapped loose. Then another. The rope strained under my weight as I swayed, a branch creaking in the storm.

I braced for it to snap.

But then, with a handful of strands left, the rope slackened and I tumbled down. Wind hollowed my ears as the golden vines tangled around my limbs.

Crack.

My stomach slapped into a sticky syrup. *God,* the pain.

"Bryn," I called weakly as water began to cover my lips, my eyes. "Bryn?" But he was gone. And I was alone. Like the room between worlds, where nothing existed but the dark and the water.

I sucked in a breath before my body sank beneath the waves.

Deeper.

And deeper.

And deeper.

And then, Bryn was—was—

No, no, no! I thrashed in the teeth of the memory, but couldn't escape. Couldn't escape what broke every rule of Ruhaven.

Before, I was drowning.

Now, I was dead. Dead and hollow and empty at last. Drifting in thick, bitter syrup while the sharp talons of the memory shredded into my corpse.

When gold sparks fractured on the surface, I closed my eyes.

And floated to the bottom.

CHAPTER 51

To the Bone

At the bottom of the pool, the visions stopped.

The noose of golden thread disappeared, and my lungs no longer strained for air. The truck on my chest had driven off to run over someone else. I didn't breathe at all. It was quite nice, peaceful even, to feel nothing.

Far above me, light sprinkled along the water's surface, but I was safe down here, lying on the sandy floor of my mind where the liquid was a perfect turquoise blue. I curled my hands into warm flour, the powder slipping between the cracks in my fingers. Maybe I had made the Fall after all and now I would sleep and wait for Willow.

Rowan.

I shied away from the painful voice. No, I wanted just Willow. Willow, who would lay down and make flour angels with me like we had when we were children.

But in the perfect, still water, I remembered she was dead, missing from my life forever, a memory better than Ruhaven, a door closed, an ache that had crept between my ribs and never left.

In the cool darkness, firm hands lifted me from the soft bed, cradling my limp body against a scent I recognized. I didn't want to go. Didn't want these hands touching me.

I pushed him away, but he ignored my protest and carried me from the warm seabed.

I always find you, Bryn repeated, over and over against my temple, waves inside a seashell.

I wanted to crawl into the toilet and flush myself down with the vomit. Yet that still wouldn't be enough to forget everything I'd seen.

Bryn held my hair back with shaking hands—the same hands that had stroked Abby's perfect, pale skin.

I gripped the freezing toilet bowl and heaved.

There couldn't be anything left inside me.

This round didn't burn as much, had subsided to low-acid water that stained my cheeks with only more humiliation.

"Go away," I croaked when he pressed a cold cloth to my forehead. As if it could wash away what he'd forced me to watch.

I didn't want him touching me. Didn't want him anywhere near me ever again. I flushed the toilet to drown out his answer, watched the last of my stomach contents swirl down a rusted hole, and tried to shove him away again.

Kneeling beside me, Bryn's voice was barely audible. "Rowan, I—I am so sorry."

Sorry. The apology settled over me, a blanket on my bed of sick exhaustion. Sorry for what? That he'd forced me to watch what would become my never-ending nightmare?

I didn't want to look at him. I didn't want his apologies. I wanted to curl into a ball until I became a stain the tiles eventually absorbed. Or vomit all over the ironed sweater of a man who fit perfectly with Abby—two china angels my mother would have stored in her cabinet and polished each Sunday.

"Rowan, please forgive me. I—"

"Will you fucking *go*, or do you want to leave me with absolutely no dignity at all?"

I wiped my stinging eyes as I remembered his words, kneeling before me, looking at me like Kazie looked at Ruhaven, asking me to stay with him, showing me the ring.

Then he'd pulled the golden thread from his body and...

I floundered for the toilet again, dry heaving over it until my stomach was empty of even water now.

I couldn't look at him, so I spoke to the porcelain toilet lid, voice flat. "I said get out, Bryn."

But he sank to the floor in front of me, a candle melting to wax. His eyes were two circles of red-rimmed pain in a face the color of washed bone. The water I'd spilled slid over his knees, turning his slacks a dark brown against the white tiles. He fluttered his hands to my face, then back to his lap when I flinched.

"I heard you." His voice broke. "I heard you pleading with me, begging me. 'I'll stay,' you said, as if I were not fighting to reach you, as if I would *ever* wish you to see what is *my* shame." He brushed a sticky strand of hair off my forehead before I could shove him away. "It was my fault. I meant to show you our bond only." He grabbed my clammy hands. "I tried to hold the thread, but when you pulled, it would have broken if I had not let go." His eyes burned with tears that didn't fall. "I am terribly sorry."

No. No, I wouldn't accept his apology, not this time.

I struggled to my feet, brushing aside his offer of help as I twisted the rusted tap and dunked my head into arctic water that was only one degree warmer than the ice in my belly. But it steadied me. After rinsing my mouth, I wiped my face and exhaled slow, uneven breaths in the mirror.

Bruises tugged at my eyes, my pale lips all but matched my skin, and still, all I could think about was Abby. I would never be her, but was that what he'd preferred?

I stared down at my chest.

Then balled my hand into a fist and punched the mirror with all the blistering accuracy Nereida had taught me.

The shards cracked under my knuckles, which ripped open at the seams and turned the bowl of water into a pink lake.

Bryn grabbed my hand before I'd even pulled it back, spinning me around and pinning my back to the sink. I slapped at his chest, cursed him as he fought to hold me steady.

When he yanked the towel off the rack and tried to wrap my fist in it, I swiped it away, hurtled it into the next room. "Stop it. *Stop it!*" I screamed at him.

Face stricken, the breath rattled out of his chest. "Rowan, I do not know what to do."

I shoved at his chest. "I didn't want *you*. Want *this*." I'd never be enough. Never. Not for the Gate, and not for him.

He caught me as I crumpled. "Rowan, I am sorry, so sorry."

I didn't want him, didn't want to hear the soft murmurs in my ear in the same voice that had whispered to Abby.

I shoved out of his hold, tripping over the bathroom doorway as my stomach heaved. But I had to get out of there, had to breathe after being drowned.

The suitcase I'd packed lay open against the wall. The lamp, glowing on my nightstand, scattered light over my mess of a quilt.

How had I gotten to the bathroom? And when had I woken up?

"I carried you," Bryn said, his eyes stark on the bed. "It appears that O'Sahnazekiel's Mark extends to protecting you from me as well."

I looked him dead in the eye and hissed, *"Good."*

I started moving around my room mechanically, grabbing Willow's jacket, punching my fist through its sleeve, wrapping Kazie's scarf around my neck. And if I imagined punching Abby's perfect, serene face, that was only natural. Healthy even.

Concern clouded Bryn's face as he followed my progression. "Are you cold, Rowan?" He knelt and lifted my sweater off the rug. "You were sweating in—in the memory. I took your jumper off. And your hand is still bleeding."

I wiped it deliberately on my jeans, then zipped my coat into my scarf, snagging the wool. "I'm taking a walk," I said shortly, and pivoted.

"I will come with you," Bryn called, but I was out the door, taking the creaking stairs two at a time as I rushed to fresh air like a fish flip-flopping on the boat, hoping to launch itself overboard. The frames shook as I rounded the staircase, Bryn on my heels, the clocks humming louder than a night full of crickets.

I landed with a thud on the bottom floor, shoved my way into the kitchen.

James glanced up from the table, bafflement flickering in his swollen eyes. "Roe?" He asked hesitantly, voice tired and drawn.

I shot past him, stabbed my feet into impossibly small, double-knotted boots. The stove-cooked air was stifling, but not as bad as that room.

"Where ye going like?" he asked, face tear-stained from Kazie—whom I should have been mourning, but instead, I was fixated on a woman miles and miles away.

"A walk," I retorted, managing at last to get my heel into the boot.

"What do ye mean like? It's bloody midnight and the Inquitate are about." He rose carefully, shoulders hunched under an oversized sweater. The act seemed to drain the last of his energy. "Roe?"

"Ask Bryn," I said crisply.

As I wrenched open the door, I heard James yell, "What the bleedin' hell have ye done to me sister now?"

Then I bolted.

It was a mild night, warm from the recent rain, but my body didn't know what temperature it wanted to be. I was freezing, boiling, sweating, shaking as I walked briskly along the path through stubs of raspberry bushes that wouldn't bud for months yet. My boots sunk into the sodden earth, and it only took a few steps for the Irish gloom to drench my feet.

I gulped the air that tasted of soil. Needed it to settle me.

The surrounding fields and navy sky were as simple as they were ordinary, uncomplicated by Ruhaven and a mate who'd wanted to spend his life with another woman. I needed to breathe without him for a little while. Until something cracked the memories that wouldn't stop playing.

Because all I could see was Abby—sweet, angelic Abby. And all I could feel was Bryn touching her, tasting her awful cherry lipstick.

I stumbled, gripped the rotted fence post before I fell, and stared at my hand clutching the post. It was far darker than Abby's, with a scar on my pinky from when I'd caught it in a car jack. Lines crisscrossed my knuckles from solvents and years of scrubbing off hard grease, and unlike the manicured fingers that had dug into Bryn's bicep, my nails were short and unpainted.

Had he wanted that? Had he seen me and regretted?

It wasn't *her* fault. She'd only loved a man I was unhealthily attracted to, not a criminal act, even if I wanted to try and convict her for it.

I tore my hand away and started forward. I wasn't Abby, wasn't anything like her, and if Bryn didn't like that, then he could—

Something snagged me around my waist. No, not something—the gold thread he'd summoned before. Gritting my teeth, I shoved forward against it and—

My legs were knocked out from under me.

I splattered into the mud, cold soil flinging up my thighs and squishing my palms. So I would be left with no dignity at all tonight.

As I struggled, the rope slithered under my ribs, wound around my arms and tightened on my wrists. I yanked against it, tried to crawl, to get away.

Then it flipped me, wrenching a strangled cry from my lips.

A terrifying, golden thread floated above. What had Bryn said ? *A bond*—no, it was an abomination. One that bound my wrists and pinned me in Naruka's field. I wouldn't watch those memories again, couldn't endure another second of Bryn and that perfect woman.

As my breath tripped in my throat, I followed the comet tail of the thread that led back to Naruka, winding its way to the tack room where—

Bryn.

My breath died in my lungs. The golden thread pulsed from his heart to his outstretched hand, coiling around his long fingers like a pet snake.

Bryn's stark eyes met mine. Then slowly, he curled his index finger. *You wouldn't* dare—

The loop on my ribs moved, tugged, demanded.

I gasped against the intrusion, slapping myself like I was beating out a fire. He'd put me through this again? I swiped at the floating thread, but my fingers passed through it.

I would dare, yes, because despite what I have done, you are still my mate and I will never let the Inquitate have you.

"Stop this," I warned as Bryn limped toward me, his breath frosting into dark clouds. He wore only a long-sleeve collared shirt as it began to rain. Thick drops pinged my cheeks like bugs on a windshield.

In the glow of the thread, his sallow face shone with the light of an avenging angel. "You can control it as well," he said softly. "As it is *our* mating bond, not mine." He planted his feet, glanced down at me, eyes twin jewels in the dark.

He'd actually use this Ruhaven monstrosity to keep me here? To stand over me and talk about a bond that *he'd* betrayed.

I glared at his angelic face with all the nauseous fury I felt. "I remember now when I felt this pull before," I said, straining against the bond. "The day the Inquitate attacked, it tugged me away. I thought it was the Inquitate. Not a bond you've lied about, manipulated."

Bryn released his cane, letting it *whoosh* into the rosemary bush, and slowly crouched to eye level with me. His voice was unrepentant. "Rowan, if I were not injured then, I would have dragged you back to Naruka by this thread. I do not regret it. I do not regret trying to protect you as I am now."

The rope skirted under my breasts like his hands, as seductive as it was threatening, which meant I was losing my mind. "Is that what you call showing me you and Abby? *Protecting* me?"

His eyes hollowed. "No. What I did was unforgivable."

That might be the first true thing he'd said. "Then let me go."

Do you plan to run off into the night to the Inquitate?

"No," I gritted out, and by the flash in his eyes, we probably both knew I was lying. But Bryn nodded and the bond disappeared.

As if driven by its own outrage, my hand pulled back and slapped him hard across the cheek. "*That's* for the memory."

The blow left a harsh imprint of red color behind, but Bryn hardly flinched, hardly registered it at all, like he'd known it was coming. Just like he'd known when Abby hit him in the hospital.

"You may strike me," he said with no inflection, "as I deserved that and more, but I will not let you run to the Inquitate."

What I did was none of his business, including if I needed to take three laps of the forest to burn off what he'd done.

Scrambling up, I leapt into a sprint.

He snagged my ankle.

My jaw met the soaked grass, bounced. He had no *right* to do this. I kicked out and crunched something solid. *Good*—he should know some puny fraction of how I felt right then. His hand closed around my arm, and we struggled like we had in Norway all those months ago. But I was better now, better from all those days spent in the Gate learning how to fight as Nereida.

Cursing, he flipped me over. Burning eyes met mine, his hair a drenched mess as the wind picked up. He sucked in cheekbones sharper than the cliff jutting against the sky. "Rowan," he repeated my name as I pounded on his thighs.

I didn't want to look at him. To look and wonder if he regretted it was me and not someone like Abby. I was like a decision he'd been forced into. Tears blurred my vision. I didn't want to feel this tearing rip through my chest again. I wanted Willow, who'd have understood exactly how I felt before she punched Bryn.

But the fantasy disappeared as quickly as it came. There was no Willow; there was only me and Bryn, and the problem between us was as ugly as I'd ever been thrown into.

"Rowan, I am *sorry*."

I bucked under him, but he held on, his hunched form blocking the heavy rain.

"I made a mistake, with her, with the thread tonight. Can you not forgive me?"

Forgive? How could I when what hurt me was so fundamental and raw, it burned my throat to have to admit it.

"You *enjoyed* her." I snarled the accusation, even as some part of me knew it was unfair. But that voice was distant and weak and stupid. And my fingers itched to give him the pain I felt. "You enjoyed—"

When I reared back to slap him again, he pinned both my wrists with one hand, temper replacing the sympathy on his face.

"Goddamn you, Rowan. I thought you were *dead*," he heaved, rain lashing his back as he trembled, a mountain before the avalanche. He laid a hand on his heart. "I was your mate, and I was supposed to protect you. Yet I wondered, loathed, that it may have been me who brought the Inquitate to your doorstep. Then, when I could no longer deal with the possibility of your death, it nearly took my life too."

As the truth of it twisted in my gut, Bryn released one of my wrists.

"Do you wish to get even with me?" He flattened his free hand between my breasts. "Would you like me to pull such a memory from you? To hurt me as I have you? Because nothing would be worse than believing you dead."

We stared at each other, shaking, vibrating, with the rain flooding the ground, soaking our clothes.

Do it, I wanted to shout, *do it so a tiny fragment of what I feel will stab you too.* But I said nothing as my chest rose and fell beneath the pressure of Bryn's palm.

He blinked away the raindrops gathering on the tips of his lashes. "As you wish, then," he said quietly.

In the dark, a faint glow rose between my breasts and seeped through his fingers. He'd do it then, watch something that would become a nightmare for years.

The tiny thread pulled gently from between my ribs, a soft tugging, not painful yet, but as it grew stronger, my memories shifted and rearranged themselves.

I was eleven and running from Simon, both of us young and awkward, playing hide and seek in the woods in L'Ardoise. The memory was more vital than my own, as if Bryn had brought it to life by pulling it from me. I could smell the thick sap of the pine and the wild freedom that ran like a river in my blood. Every twig was a sword, every snake a dragon.

I'd forgotten how silly I was then.

A swinging bridge came into view, leading to the waterfront where the forest melted into sand and docks. My little feet jumped across, barefoot and leaping over the planks with a wild exhilaration to escape the boy chasing me. I wanted to scream at myself to be careful. Didn't I see the slippery old wood? The bridge was rotted, unsafe, slimy with mold and rain, the ropes frayed. I should have plummeted through it.

But I didn't, and at the end of the bridge, the boy jumped into my path.

I screamed a young girl's scream—like a balloon losing air—and leapt away from Simon's hand, but he snagged my backpack.

Got you, Simon teased, spinning me around. Then my heart leapt from something else entirely. Not fear, but a girl's silly romance for the prince in her kingdom.

The kiss was sloppy and quick.

I'd forgotten about that. Forgotten how it felt to have my first kiss, still too young to know why I should want it. The foolish grin on Simon's face dissolved, and another image switched in on a memory conveyor belt.

This one was more recent with the hard, unforgiving edges of adult life. There were no soft smiles and sloppy kisses, no tender innocence and make believe. No romance, no imagination, no magic. The memory wavered—or maybe Bryn did, as one drunk night in college slowly materialized.

Do it, I wanted to shout at him. But I felt Bryn then, his fear, his shame, and I couldn't.

When I pried Bryn's shaking hand off me, the memory winked out. I could live with Abby, but I wouldn't make him live with this.

A storm raged behind Bryn's unyielding blue eyes. His breath came in ragged, harsh pants that fanned my face. "What do you want from me, Rowan?" he demanded. "What do you *want!*"

I twisted in his grip, but he held firm. What did I want? I'd followed Willow around for years trying to figure that out, hoping that something she did or loved or wanted would eventually rub off on me, like a hot piece of flint sparking off a rock. Then, eventually, I'd realized I just wanted to be her.

But mostly, I thought now, with a chest-caving realization, I wanted to do it over again.

I wanted to be someone better. To be the little girl in the woods with her life ahead of her, with a thousand chances to do something different. I wanted to choose to finish college, to try harder on every exam, to try out for the volleyball team—or *any* team—and to have, just for *once*, have reached for something, anything. To do something worth recording.

"I want to do it over again."

Bryn's grip loosened on my wrists. "What?"

I balled my now-free hands into fists, drilled them into his chest. "You don't understand. You looked at the Ledger for the first time and you saw what you expected."

He searched my face. "Which is what, Rowan?"

"Who you were, the truth, some destiny that belonged to you," I said. "But when I moved here with Tye, it was the first decision I'd ever made because I—I *wanted* something. A chance to start fresh, to be something other than Willow's sister, maybe to find something I loved. I'd never even left L'Ardoise before." I wiped my nose, feeling as pathetic as my words. "Then, when James showed me the Gate, when he explained who he thought I was, when he pointed to the *Ledger*, to say it was *my* birth written there, I…"

Tears flowed down my cheeks, thick and humiliating, but I pushed on. "I believed him. Until I saw—until I saw it was Willow's birth. Not even here in Ireland, not even in Ruhaven, could I escape all that she'd been. It was as if the Ledger had known, before I'd ever had a chance to fail at anything, that I wasn't worth recording, and never worth bringing home.

"And then, to find out you'd gone to Willow—? To think that it might have been her here with you, instead of me? That when it comes right down to it, even *you* would choose her, Bryn." I knuckled the tears away. "If I'd ever been more than just a shadow of Willow, then you wouldn't have been with Abby, and the *Ledger* would have chosen me. But it didn't. Like it knew, even before we were born, that there was *nothing* of me worth remembering."

His face went white as he clasped my cheeks. "God, Rowan, if you knew what it did to me to find you here? If you knew how I felt every time I look upon you. You were *always* someone to me."

I inhaled a shaky breath. "But I want to be someone to myself," I whispered.

Very slowly, Bryn laid his forehead against mine, the heat of him smothering the bite of cold, despite the rain dripping off the tips of his ears. When he laid his lips at my temple, I didn't resist. I couldn't anymore. There was nothing left.

I swallowed the rain sliding over my lips.

"Bryn, it was—you and Abby, it was vile," I choked out.

"I know." He closed his eyes. "I could not endure it should you have shown me the same."

Rain slid into my ear, muffling his unsteady breaths, but I had to say the rest, had to tell him what I'd known in the marrow of my bones, what had gnawed at me in the awful pit of that memory.

"It was vile, because whatever was written in the *Ledger*, you're supposed to be *mine*." I swallowed the burning in my throat and turned to face his ravaged eyes. "I know that. More than I know anything, more than I know myself. I don't care which birth time is listed on line 1274, I don't care that it was Willow's. I don't care if it's not me in the *Ledger*, because there is *nothing* that will ever convince me I don't love you, Bryn. Because I do recognize you, and I've been waiting for you too. I won't share you, not even with a memory. I know I'm not allowed to feel like that but I do, because you're *my* dream—and I'll swear on everything I have left that you're *mine*."

His breathing hitched, his lips parted.

The world swam above, the one we couldn't undo, with all the permanency of planets and gravity.

"Yes, Rowan, I am."

It was a prayer, a promise, an oath.

And suddenly, there were no barriers between us, because what simmered in his eyes was love stripped raw, whittled down to its bones, flayed to an inch of its life. The thread flashed in the night, wrapping us together. A connection between worlds.

"Rowan," he growled, a warning as much as anything else, "you are also mine." Hands tightened on my wrists.

And with four words, I threw everything we were into the space between us. "Then make me yours."

Bryn's irises fired to the burning stars of O'Sahnazekiel. Brighter and richer than the moon, blazing like Sahn's on the night of Yizomithou. I drew in his breath like it was mine. Because it was, *he* was, and damn the *Ledger*.

My pulse leapt as Bryn grabbed my jacket in his fist. Buttons snapped, cotton ripped. Freezing rain soaked through my thin shirt, tightening my nipples, but even as I shivered, the rapid pummel of it brought me alive.

I wriggled a hand free—or Bryn let me—and ripped at his collar, hungry to feel his muscles under my fingers, to see the tattoos spiraling their way to cut hips. When I pulled his shirt apart, pale skin glittered with the moon's silver and the thread's golden light. I ran my free hand over each rain-slicked inch as I watched him, watched his eyes on me as they had always been, even in the Gate.

"Rowan, with every breath I took, I betrayed my promise to her." He was panting, growling, his eyes so brilliantly gold they burned like the sun, like the thread that weaved between our bodies. "I dreamed of Nereida then." My shirt tore straight down the middle, and I blinked in shock at the claws on his fingertips, claws he couldn't possibly have. Another slice, and my bra sprung open. "And now, now I dream of you."

Cold rain raked my breasts before his scalding touch covered them. I moaned, fisting his hair, melting his mouth to mine, tasting frosted mornings and Irish rain, a thousand memories at once. He shoved my arms over my head, ran claws down my bare torso, teasing the band of my jeans, the thread circling my waist.

"Let me touch you," I begged as he locked my wrists in one hand.

But he only smothered my words, claiming my mouth with his as his free hand glided over my jeans, between my legs. Cupped me.

I arched into him as his tongue stroked me in time with his fingers, gentle, coaxing. God, how I wanted these clothes off, to feel him against me, in me.

"I promise I am yours," Bryn rasped, pressing his lips to my throat. He dragged my neck to the side, sunk his teeth lightly into my pulse before devouring. I closed my eyes, holding on to those words like a buoy in the sea.

Rain soothed wherever his scalding mouth touched, and it was everywhere. He lapped at me with a hungry frenzy, teeth nipping, scraping, biting, growling against my breast. I cried out when his tongue lashed my nipple. Bucked when his hand stroked through my jeans. And still, I couldn't get enough.

Wings blocked out the stars. I was losing my mind, hallucinating, drowning in him. I tunneled my fingers into his soaked hair, wanting to drag his perfect mouth back to mine, but he lapped at my breasts until I couldn't feel the rain anymore.

Lust. Need. Desire. I swallowed it all—a direct injection into my heart that threw it into a frenzied creature as Bryn's lips murmured against my belly, sliding lower, lower. I couldn't hear him over the blood roaring in my ears, the lick of the thread weaving through my body, the fire erupting from my center.

"I can feel you, Rowan." His voice was a rough murmur below my belly button. He lifted his darkened gaze, held mine between the swell of my breasts. I wanted to melt in those burning rings. "Through the thread."

Then he must know I was a breath away from combusting under him.

Rain slicking his hair to his cheeks, he ducked his head. When I felt his tongue slide under the band of my jeans, I thought I was melting into the soil. Then his hand slid up from between my legs and gripped the button separating me from him.

Bryn knelt, bowed over me, shoulders quivering. And just looking at him like that, soaked and shaking, with his own desire straining against the pants I hadn't slipped off him, stretched my arousal to the point of pain.

But he didn't move further, and the waiting was like being sliced in two. The thread snagged my wrists, tugged them above my head. But still, he didn't move.

I was crying now. The rain mixed with my tears and the desire that flayed me raw with everything that had happened today—the Fall, Kazie leaving, Abby, the memories. I wanted to forget it all, for him to take it away.

"Rowan," he murmured in the night. He pinned my hips with a shaking hand, drew a ragged breath that flexed the stiff muscles of his back. Burning eyes lifted, peeked up at me over my stomach. Just the sight of him undid me—the thick lashes beaded with rain, the desire heating his cheeks, the lick of moonlight that turned his hair silver. I wanted a thousand nights like this, in the rain and mud and cold, when there was nothing between us.

"We should not," he ground out. "Not now. Not after..."

Don't even say it.

He dropped his forehead to my belly, his breath warming my skin. "I want you, Rowan." Bryn's low groan stroked the burn inside me. "You can feel how much I do, through the thread."

It swamped me, a sweet, golden emotion so intense I barely recognized it. More than desire, more than love—devotion.

"Bryn, please. *Please.*" *I don't care about the thread, about what happened.*

He let out a low oath. *Rowan...*

I whimpered when his fingers curled in my jeans. If he stopped again, I'd explode like a shooting star and join the others in the sky.

But he didn't.

CHAPTER 52

Paper Airplane

Bryn yanked my jeans down.

Grass tickled my skin, rain pelted my thighs. It should have dissolved into steam on contact, but only beaded on my moonlit legs. Then his mouth was on my inner thigh, licking away the rain, his eyes locked on mine. And just that look of him, the way his burning embers stared at me—

Slowly, tortuously, he kissed a path toward the burning ache between my legs, and when his hot breaths panted over me at last, I tugged against the thread binding my wrists. It held firm.

He nuzzled my thigh. "I want to taste you," he murmured.

There was a sharp ripping sound. Biting rain stung the building heat as what was left of my underwear was tossed to the wind.

With my jeans tangled around my boots, I trembled before him. I could feel his eyes on me, could hear his shaky breaths that mirrored mine as rain pounded between us.

Then Bryn lowered to the ground, hands circling my waist, tilting me toward him. "I have imagined this a hundred times since we met," he warned.

"*Bryn*," I panted.

"No, a thousand," he corrected. "Or perhaps, indecently more."

"Stop teasing," I begged on an oath.

His lips quirked, and then, with a long, low groan, his mouth found me at last.

And my world imploded.

The sky swam as another memory flooded the stars. Norway. With its threaded waterfalls tangling in cliffs too high to believe unless you were Bryn standing below. It thundered to resolution in otherwise still water, roaring...

The stars winked to life as the vision faded, as Bryn struggled to reel the memory in. But I didn't fear it or what it might show me. Didn't fear us.

A low growl ripped through the night before his tongue flicked out, slid down my center. Devoured.

I bucked against him.

Bryn pinned my hips, setting into me with a wildness I'd always craved from him. His tongue was pure fire, stroking a hot path that carved me in two, circling until my mind blanked, until all I could see was *him* and his golden eyes watching me.

Then he slid his tongue down me, *into* me.

I moaned his name, to the Gate that loomed above the distant cliff, to the gods in Ruhaven I didn't know if we had.

As Bryn tasted me, filled me, the thread slowly unwound from my wrists. It flickered over my body like writhing light, its glow casting my skin in sparkling hues, its touch as sensual as it'd been when he lifted me from the Gate.

I gripped the earth as it stroked my body, the light indistinguishable from Bryn's own touch. It tugged at my nipples when he replaced his mouth with his fingers. One, two, they sank into me, gloriously deep as he felt me for the first time. As I felt him, felt his groan vibrating between my thighs.

"Look at me, my Rowan," Bryn commanded, voice like gravel.

I lifted my head, and my eyes locked on to his simmering golden ones as he curled his fingers. This was Bryn. Sahn. A thousand years ago. Now.

"You're better than the Gate," I choked out.

And when his mouth quirked up in that crooked smile that had scattered my brain from the very first moment, I felt the first tremors of the orgasm.

I reached for him, caught his hand in mine. Our fingers linked, locked.

Let go, Rowan, he ordered.

His name was on my lips when the pleasure ripped through me in thick, rolling waves that unraveled my being. As his eyes flared to white gold, I didn't look away. I held on to him when every nerve in my body sang and my soul melted and the stars swam in my blood. When memories of Ruhaven danced in my vision. When, for a moment, I wondered how I had ever doubted who I was.

It wouldn't stop under his demands.

And my body answered, as helpless against Bryn as I was. He slid his tongue into me again, driving me up and over the next wave while his thumb circled. *You are mine in any life.* My heart was trilling so hard—for him, for the fear of losing him I couldn't keep at bay. *Here or Ruhaven.* He stayed with me when I came again. *Where makes no difference...*

I floated for a while. Up in the stars like I had when Bryn had wrapped the light around me in the dark waiting room of the Gate. I didn't want to ever come back down. I wanted to float in this magic, in the mindlessness, a place that existed so fully, I wondered how I could ever doubt it.

But eventually, I descended like a balloon deflating under the cold and pressure.

His lips curled when I landed.

As I lay there, boneless and somehow still burning for him, Bryn moved to hover over me, his ragged breaths exhaling to mist. And when his warm body covered mine at last and his hips pressed into me, I was ready for him.

He planted his elbows on each side of my head, loosing a shuddering breath when I hitched a leg over his waist.

I needed him. Wanted him. Had to know there wouldn't be that space between us ever again. I locked my ankles around his back, shifting until the rigid length of him was pressed against me. He ground his hips in long, tortuous strokes that had me reaching for his pants.

But when I did, he caught my wrist. Brought it to his lips.

"Rowan," he said against my burning skin. "I think, perhaps not tonight."

No? Was he saying no? My haze-addled brain couldn't make sense of it when he was over me like this, when his irises continued to burn. "You don't *look* like you want to stop," I teased.

"Because I do not," he said between his teeth. "I want to take you until you are mine in every life. But not here, not now."

I ran my hands over his torso. I could touch him for days, could lick every square inch of skin and still need more. "Do you want to go inside?" I asked hesitantly.

The rain had slowed to a light mist, but his wet hair swung as he shook his head. "Yes, but not in the way you mean."

I started to sit up. "What's wrong?"

He dragged my mouth to his, kissing me hard enough that my worry disappeared, and when he held me against his still-beating heart, I suddenly realized we were out in the garden covered in dirt and rain.

"I think we are overwhelmed, both of us, and I do not wish for this to be our first night. Not after what I did, and not now that we have a shared thread."

My blood cooled enough to focus on him. "A shared thread?" I glanced at the tendrils of the ribbon dancing around us.

He stroked a thumb over my jaw, a smile in his eyes. "It means the bond between us is felt through both of us now, all our—our emotions are heightened. As they are for Nereida and O'Sahnazekiel. It is overwhelming—too overwhelming, I think, to continue when we are only becoming aware of it."

Now he wanted to be cautious? "We'll be fine," I murmured against the thumb tracing my lips. But the image of Abby danced on the cusp of my mind.

"Perhaps, but we have time." Though his voice was calm, the gold had barely dimmed. "I am quite certain you would regret it if James were to find us in his garden." He dipped his head, licked my throat. "Naked and covered in mud."

"I don't care." And for once, I really didn't.

Bryn's rough chuckle zipped along my bones. Then, with a low sigh, he sank back on his knees, his mouth a sensual slice that stretched into a mind-scrambling grin. All I could imagine was how it'd looked as a crooked smirk between my legs, how his tongue had...

I swallowed deeply. *How long do you want to wait?*

His eyes lighted. *Ah, my Rowan enjoys me after all.*

I grinned. *Tomorrow?*

Perhaps.

I studied the shirt I'd torn through, the marks my nails had left over his neck and chest, then met his gaze. "Tomorrow," I said firmly. *Then it's my turn.*

His eyes flared on my lips. *I shall be well and truly yours.*

A humming second passed. Two. Three. Then Bryn let out a low sigh. Kneeling, naked from the waist up, he reached down and struggled to button pants over a bulge in direct conflict with his decision.

"Eyes up here, Rowan," Bryn drawled with such amusement that I felt myself blush, then grinned helplessly.

Hoping to keep him with me, I pawed at the glittering thread still hovering around us. "Bryn, when I figure out how to—" I lunged like a cat on an infrared light, "—use this, you're not going to like it."

He snatched my wrists, leaned forward, and murmured in my ear, "But, my Rowan, I fear I shall like it *very* much."

God. "Bryn, you're not helping things."

He chuckled, low and dark, before reeling the thread into his chest, spooling it into the world where it lived. Holding it for both of us. When it was tucked away, he dragged my arms through his shirt, buttoning the ruined thing over my breasts.

Chest bare and grass-stained, he said with a faint smile, "Will we just tell James you tripped over these?"

I followed his gaze to the tangled, muddied laces of my boots. He lifted one onto his lap and tied it in a swift bow, the gesture oddly tender. He switched to the other boot.

While he tightened and tied, I let my eyes feast on every inch of him. "Bryn?"

"Yes, my Rowan?"

"We're going to continue this conversation."

"I would hardly let you go otherwise." His grin was a quick slice of the moon as he helped me to my wobbly feet. "Come, Rowan, we have time. Time enough for me to do this right."

I hoped we did.

✦ ✹

B ryn and I stumbled like drunks, arms around each other's waists, following the guiding light under the tack room door until Bryn shoved it open and pulled me through.

I blinked as my eyes adjusted to the kitchen's flickering candles.

And found James staring at Bryn, mouth open, eyes still red-rimmed from Kazie but coated in shock. I glanced over.

Mud ran down Bryn's bare chest, rain darkened his hair, and grass stains coated his elbows and chin from when he'd—well.

I crossed my arms over my braless state, but Bryn was already blocking me.

James braced his hands on his hips. "What in the bloody hell did ye do to me sister?" he demanded, peering around Bryn.

As the stitching of my jeans rubbed against every naked inch of me, I realized there was a scrap of black material hanging somewhere in the vegetable patch right now. "I tripped," I said with a grin.

"So ye didn't want to be caught in the Gate with Sahn, but ye'll roll around in me daffodils before they're even bloomed?"

I felt the blush build.

Then Bryn burst into laughter. Great, shaking bursts that rolled through the kitchen and had James looking on helplessly.

"Well, go on so," he said, whipping the tea towel toward the stairs. "I'd just as soon prefer not to know."

I muffled my laugh as I hugged the shirt and aimed toward the exit. "I'm going to shower," I called to Bryn.

But when his eyes lit and he started to follow, James said, "Now, ye'll hold on just a minute. I'll have a word or two with ye first."

Bryn drawled, "James, I believe I am far too old for this conversation."

"Ye know, ye'd think that and yet ye bring me sister in here covered in mud and yerself half-naked."

I cast Bryn a pitying look over my shoulder. But the hot water—something I was immensely grateful for fixing right now—beckoned.

His eyes twinkled at me. "I will see you in my room, Rowan."

It wasn't a question.

"**L**ove, you're in my pants."

Rolling over, I nestled into sun-kissed bedsheets. It couldn't be past six. Seven at the latest. The mattress squeaked, bouncing my head off the pillow as someone hurtled themselves onto the bed.

I pried open an eyelid and scowled at Willow's unruly face. "Go away."

She grinned a cat's smile. "I said, you're in my pants."

I sunk further under the comforter. "Nope."

She whipped the covers off so fast I had to choke back a scream from the frigid air. "How much did you take last night anyway?"

I lunged for the sheet she held out of reach. "Who puts magic mushrooms in peanut butter?"

"Who eats another person's peanut butter sandwich?" she accused, and won the quick tug of war.

I couldn't help but laugh. "Willow, please, god, just let me sleep, and I will never eat another of your disgusting, mushroom-covered peanut butter sandwiches ever again."

"Or take my pants."

I giggled. "But they're my favorite pants."

"Roe."

"Roe, wake up!"

I bolted upright, the remnants of the dream falling away like pastry flakes. Where the hell was I? *When* was I? Outside a frosted window, morning peaked in an orange clementine over the sea.

Bryn's room.

Last night returned to me in a flood of memories. Kazie was gone. The Fall. Bryn had shown me a ring, then Abby...

Bryn was right to wait. Even after we'd come up to his room, he'd only wanted to sleep. So we'd slipped into his bed together, the crisp cotton sheets a cool comfort against his warm body, his sleepy breaths stirring my hair like a night breeze.

I rubbed my eyes. Squinted at the bulky shadow sitting on the bed. "Bryn?"

"Just me darlin'." Tye.

I slid a hand beside me, a fading warmth heating my palm. Why was Tye here on my bed—Bryn's bed?

"Where's Bryn?" I asked, dragging the quilt with me as I sat up.

Tye offered a lazy shrug. "Ironin' his shirts? Roe, we gotta go."

"Go?" I repeated as Tye fumbled with the lamp—*click*—and low light blinded me. "Don't ya remember we gotta flight to catch? Two tickets. Leaves at noon. We better get a move on." My suitcase *thunk-thunked* by the bed. "Saw you packed already, that's good. Get yourself up, and let's get goin'."

Flight. Home. The Fall.

Willow. I'd wanted to make the Fall for Willow. But after last night...

I closed my eyes. "Tye, I don't think I can go now."

The bed wobbled as he parked himself on the edge. "Darling, I bought the tickets. You're going. It's one god damn week. If ya can't leave Stornoway for seven days, you've got a problem."

That, I definitely had.

Bryn had asked me to stay with him. Not to make the Fall. There'd been a ring and...and where was it now? In my room still?

Maybe I could use the week in L'Ardoise to figure out what Willow had asked of me. I could talk to Tye about it. He might not want me to make the Fall, but he'd always listened.

But then Bryn and I couldn't— No, no, that was stupid. My hormones were growing legs at this point. It was one week. *One*. Bryn and I could pick things up when I returned, when I knew what I wanted.

One more week.

It felt like a month.

"Okay, but Bryn—"

"Made it this long and ya know what? I bet he'll live without ya for a couple days."

And he must be okay with it if he'd given Tye a chance to talk to me like this. Maybe Bryn wanted to make up for how he'd reacted yesterday.

I tossed the blankets off like Willow had and swung my legs over the bed. The hemp rug scratched the soles of my freezing feet. It was strange to wake to the quiet chirping outside Bryn's window instead of Kazie's blaring alarm clock.

"Let me get dressed then, and—" I dropped the quilt as Tye gripped my shoulder.

"What's this?" he demanded of the circular stamp.

"A birthmark." I swatted at him. "What's wrong?"

He only tilted me under the lamp, lowering his nose close enough that his hot breath skittered under my collar. "That ain't no birthmark, darlin'. It's from the *Ledger*. It's—"

Tye's arm was knocked away.

"*Get out.*" Bryn stepped in front of me, temper radiating from each taut line of his body.

So he hadn't let Tye in, hadn't known or thought about L'Ardoise.

When I started to rise, Bryn laid a hand on my shoulder but kept his eyes on the intruder. "Tye, you should not even be in Naruka, never mind in my room with my—"

"Your *what*, Stornoway? Your mate?" Tye mocked.

"*Yes*," I answered for Bryn.

"So now he's got ya believin' that bullshit too." A muscle twitched in his jaw. "I heard what ya did yesterday, Stornoway. James filled me in. It's always about you, ain't it? Anythin' to convince Roe to stay. *Selfish*, that's what ya are. And a manipulative bastard." Tye shot out an arm, swatting Bryn's makeshift cane away. It clanged off the floor, rolling until it banged into the woodstove.

I sprang to my feet, grabbed Bryn before he fell. "Tye, get out."

Tye clenched his jaw, then straightened. His lips relaxed into a tiny smile. "Fine. I'll just meet ya at the car, *darlin'*."

Bryn went rigid in my arms.

Oh, hell. *Tye.* "Bryn, I—"

He pulled away, gaze darting to the suitcase Tye hefted. When he lifted his eyes to me, they were blank, empty. "You would leave now? After last night? And when the Inquitate may at any point approach you again?"

I fumbled the explanation that had made perfect sense in my head.

"Damn, Stornoway, you ain't that good in bed. And of the two of us," Tye reminded him leisurely, "I ain't the one that let Roe follow the Inquitate into the goddamn woods. Let's go." Tye jiggled the suitcase and stomped out of the room.

I turned slowly, and met Bryn's burning, accusatory eyes. "It really is just a few days," I said weakly. "Tye bought the ticket already, and…"

He ripped his arm from my grasp. "Rowan, we both know this is not about a simple visit to L'Ardoise. You wish to say goodbye to your friends, to your parents, in case you hear the call and do not have the time to again."

The room chilled a degree.

I'd forgotten about the thread. He'd know exactly what I was feeling now. "Bryn, it's not— You don't understand. I *heard* Willow. At the Gate, I swear, and I…"

He turned his back to me and swiped the cane off the floor. "I cannot lose you twice. Not after Nereida," Bryn said shortly. "If you wish to make the Fall, then we cannot continue."

My throat tightened. Words swelled and died on the tip of my tongue. How could a few months with Bryn replace a lifetime with Willow? It couldn't. It *shouldn't*.

How could he say this after last night? He'd waited for us, but he couldn't let me figure this out? "You don't know when the call—"

"It is not long enough," he said crisply, staring out the window. "I want it all, Rowan. So leave, because Tye is right—you are safer with him than I."

Liar.

"You're forgetting this thread goes both ways," I said, drawing a sharp breath. "You didn't want to wait last night because of Abby or the thread. You wanted to wait because you want me to choose you over Willow."

But a lifetime with Willow couldn't be replaced this easily. Even if Bryn had thrown the ring at me, the memories, even after last night. It wasn't enough.

Maybe I wanted it all, too, just not the same all as Bryn.

Ruhaven was giving Willow a chance to come back as Nereida, as who she was meant to be, even if that meant I wouldn't exist.

He paused in front of the window, a dark silhouette against its light. "No. I want you to leave."

The words echoed off the hollow floorboards. But Bryn worshipped the Gate, and *he'd* been the one to tell me what it meant to have Ruhaven speak to you.

"Bryn, you aren't listening to me. I *heard* Willow at the Gate. She told me to make the Fall, for her, and—"

"*I. Do. Not. Care.*"

I gaped at him.

You don't care?

He tossed his sweater over the bedpost. Turned his back to me.

If he didn't understand this, didn't understand Willow, thought whatever this was could ever replace her…? "That's why I came to you in Oslo. That's why I'm here. Now you don't care? I don't believe you."

His face was stone. "I care about Willow as much as you care of me, Rowan. Get out."

I planted my feet. "I'm not leaving you, not like this."

"You know what I think?" he said quietly. "I think this is not about Willow at all. This is about you not wanting to accept who you are. You will never be Willow, Rowan. Not in any life. Not even Ruhaven can give you that."

A cold, suffocating heat crept into my lungs, into my heart.

He lifted a hand.

The thread flickered, grabbing me like it had before, except this time, there was none of the gentle caress. It snagged my ribs, yanking me back. Hard. Like it had at the river.

I tumbled, tripped over the rug, banging my elbow off the doorframe.

He didn't look up. Only stared out the window, at the boats cutting through the sea miles from shore. At the sky that was nearly green now with dawn, and the mulled clouds threatening to smother it.

The thread pulled again, and I slid over rough wood, my sweatpants snagging on a splinter. A hole ripped down the side before I twisted to my hands and knees, shoved up.

Another tug and I was in the hallway.

I jumped as something burned my bare feet, then looked down.

A teapot lay on its side, dripping boiling water in a dark stain across the carpet runner. Honey oozed in golden waves. Squashed grapes escaped across the hall like lost children. James's soft scones were arranged on a broken china plate, the jam oozing over the edge, the cream a white smear on the coral napkin.

Bryn's door slammed shut.

"Roe, darlin'," Tye yelled from below. "It's three damn hours to Shannon Airport."

A grape popped under my heel.

I stepped over shards of teacups, sliced pears, and sugar cubes that neither Bryn nor I preferred.

In my room, I dressed in silence, the fields of Ireland stretching before me until they disappeared beneath the orange hues of a sun just pushing over the clouds, when the rays burst and drenched the hills in a color more beige than green.

When I was dressed in Willow's jean jacket, with her scarf fastened around my neck and the steel-toed boots I'd first worn here, I walked back into the hallway. Locked my door.

Each step downstairs tightened the invisible string between Bryn and I until I half expected to feel the snap of the band.

And when I clambered in the car and Tye kicked the engine to life, the new spark plugs turned over without a whimper.

CHAPTER 53

Empty Chairs

L'Ardoise, Cape Breton Island

I do not care.

I slapped the pedal down. Well, if Bryn didn't care, neither did I. Didn't matter that the heat pumping out of Willow's truck was drying my tears into sticky tracks on my cheeks.

Because snot didn't dry as quick as tears, I wiped my face on my shoulder. Goddamn Bryn.

I squeezed the wheel of a truck that was basically on palliative care, because Willow had begged me to keep the thing running year after year. I might not be as handy with cars as I was with homes, but the core of the vehicle was fine. It was the little things that broke. The little things I could fix.

I eased back on the brake, letting the truck I'd adopted come to an easy stop. I glanced left, right. Only the barren, snowy roads of L'Ardoise's countryside stared back.

Slowly, I pressed the gas, feeling the tires spin before the tread caught the icy sleet and yanked me forward. A mini piano swung from her rearview mirror, like the one Bryn and I had first kissed on.

The plane ride two days ago had been a sleepless nightmare, only made moderately better by Tye's silence for once.

I don't care.

I don't care about Willow, about your twin.

This is about you not wanting to accept who you are.

I cracked open my window, sucked in the empty and brittle air.

The truck roared down highway seven, the eight pistons firing smoothly despite the months away. It nearly purred compared to James's Ford.

I swung a wide right onto Devil's Glen Lane.

It followed L'Ardoise's river, the iced-over water barely distinguishable from the land. The only indication of the bank were the sparse bits of dead shrubs poking from the snow like an old man's wiry hair. I passed a faded sign warning to stay off the ice, but it was covered in snow and lost in the haze of satin trees.

The truck bumped over the last bend, knocking my hands off the frozen steering wheel. I'd forgotten gloves, and the heater did nothing but complain that I'd abandoned it. I'd gotten it ready for storage before I left, but you couldn't leave something for half a year and expect it to remain unchanged.

Finally, Tye's old farmhouse loomed dark against the sky, the place he'd spent months in L'Ardoise during recruitment.

I dropped the truck into a clanging third gear, gently applied the brake, but the driveway had been shoveled to a thin velvet white and the tires barely skidded.

The house was more barn than residence, with aged paneled-walls and peeling red paint. A chair blocked a portion of the deck that had caved in. Crows circled a chimney that melted a puddle in the snowy roof. A lamp turned the curtains pink.

I switched off the engine.

Birds scattered when I slammed the driver's door, then followed the trail of footprints to where his roommates' boots were lined up outside the entrance.

I kicked the snow off my heels, slid the key Tye had given me into the shiny lock, and nudged open the door. Familiar whistles of a hockey game carried into a dated paneled hallway.

"Tye?"

Puddles of melted snow and the reek of yesterday's pepperoni pizza led to the kitchen, where horses galloped on an out-of-date tile backsplash. A harsh blue light—a clean light—swept through the window, over the sink, and bleached the space of color. Everything was cold, drafty, almost gray compared to Naruka's rundown warmth. It wasn't cluttered either, not with Irish knickknacks that James would have scoffed at, or magnets holding this week's list of groceries.

I glanced at the cow-spotted clock on the wall—four past one. Tye should be back home by now, but...

Meow.

I nearly jumped at the fat orange tabby currently licking himself clean in areas I did not want to see.

Tossing the truck's keys on the counter, I turned toward the living room to find Tye when he stepped through the doorway, a beer in one hand.

"You're back early," he drawled.

"My parents weren't home," I lied—I was still working up the courage to face their reluctance of me.

Tye tugged off his hat and chucked it with the keys. "You look a little beat up, Roe. You over the jet lag yet?"

"I'm fine." I jerked my chin toward the low voices from the living room. "Your roommates?"

"They're catchin' the Boston game."

"Oh." I angled my head, but Tye blocked my line of sight.

He frowned around the beer. "You wanna talk about what Stornoway did?"

I felt myself blush scarlet. Talk? It was all I could do not to think about it. Had replayed it a few hundred times since I'd left. "What he did? I—well, I—"

"Jesus, not that, kid," Tye scoffed. "James told me ya pulled some memories from him you ain't supposed to see."

My blood cooled. "No. I mean, yes. But no, I don't want to talk about it." Or think about it, ever.

"Bastard," Tye muttered. "You needed this week, Roe."

I scrubbed my face. Yeah, I did, especially because Bryn's last words had upset me more than the looming possibility that I wouldn't have much time before the Gate asked me to make the same sacrifice as Kazie.

I paced the kitchen, trying not to look at the cupboards hanging at lopsided angles and the phone loose on the wall. Maybe I should call Bryn? No. No, he'd been in the wrong, absolutely wrong, even if I hadn't stopped thinking about us in the garden.

"He asked me to stay, Tye," I said quietly. "Bryn never wanted me to make the Fall. Never intended to trade me for Nereida like you said." And after all my worries that he did, I'd thrown his confession in his face. Then accused him of not understanding me when the Gate wanted me to make the same sacrifice for Willow.

God, maybe *I* was wrong.

Tye scoffed. "He's just playin' ya, darlin'. He'd say anythin' to get ya to that Gate with him."

Except he hadn't, Tye had been wrong on that account.

I shrugged out of my jacket, tossed it over the back of the chair. "He wasn't playing."

Tye grunted, then turned to drop two slices of bread into the toaster.

No, Bryn hadn't been lying when he'd held the opal ring in his palm and looked at me with such hope that if there was a St. Peter of the Gate, he'd point his gnarled finger in the other direction when I came knocking. That's what Bryn had been worried about—that Ruhaven would reject him for what he'd done.

"Tye, if we make the Fall, who do we return as?"

His eyes narrowed. "Ya don't need to worry 'bout it."

"I want to worry about it. You said I needed to come back to L'Ardoise to get some space, to think about things. You're not even giving me the chance to—"

He shushed me. "Alright, alright, alright. Who do you return as? No one. Next."

"I mean, am I still a Kalista? Will I look like Nereida, or could I come back as Essie, or grass, or something?"

"You ain't gonna come back at all. It's Nereida who'll come back. And yeah, she'll come back as a Kalista again. Will she look the same? Dunno, can't imagine she will, 'cause her old body died."

"Will she remember me?"

Tye formed his lips into a tight *O* to pop out, "Nope."

"And Sahn, he'll be there?"

"If Stornoway makes the Fall, yeah." He lit his smoke on the toaster. Bryn had said he'd make the Fall if I went, but I hadn't thought about what that'd mean for *him*. Only for Willow—always—it was only Willow that I thought about.

"But he won't remember me either."

Tye cast me a pitying look. "Might be he remembers Nereida—but you? Nope," he said as the cat jumped off the kitchen chair.

Yet he'd loved Nereida for seven years before he ever set eyes on me. And suddenly, the weight of the last days dragged on me, tugging at my shoulders and the space between my eyes. I was so tired of this, of all of it, and mostly I was tired of myself. There were questions I needed answers to, yet I'd asked all the wrong ones.

"You said in the kitchen, back at Naruka, that it wouldn't be long until I heard the call. How do you know? And how long do I have?"

"Maybe a week."

A—a *week*? "But how can you know that?" And how could I only have a week of this life left? How could the Gate ask me to give up everything with so little warning? How could I ask Bryn to?

The left side of Tye's mouth lifted in a dimple-less smile. "I know that 'cause I've been watchin' Nereida in the Gate for some time."

I felt the crease between my brows deepen. "I haven't seen you," I said automatically, baffled. "I thought you were in the Faruthian Mountains?"

Meowwwwww. The cat flicked up his tail and wound between Tye's legs.

"I was for a little while, back about five years ago. Not anymore. Not since they had to use me to get to Nereida. That's how I knew we'd be makin' the Fall soon."

The sleepless nights must be starting to catch up with me. "Who's *they*? And what do you mean 'get to Nereida'?"

"'*They*' are the Inquitate."

I slowly lowered the hands I'd been scrubbing over my face. "You've seen the Inquitate in Ruhaven? And you never told me?"

"That ain't what I said."

Meowwww.

My gaze shot to the cat again, its back arching with a lazy yawn before stalking a floating piece of dust. It pounced, skidding on the tile floor, then scared itself stupid.

The toast popped out of the toaster with ringing clarity. *I knew that cat.*

My heart trilled, a bee with one wing left buzzing in circles. The saliva in my mouth dried to dirt.

"I…"

The *cat.*

I jerked when it brushed a bushy tail up my calf before sauntering between Tye's legs and rubbing its calico fur on his jeans. Tye bent down, scrubbed it absently with one hand, his cigarette in the other, then straightened.

I rubbed my throat, swallowed.

"Hermès?" I called quietly, voice hoarse.

The ears twitched in my direction, then it turned, licked a lazy paw.

And two bicolored eyes met mine.

Oh no.

I took a step back, then another. My spine bumped the hard rim of the kitchen table. An empty beer bottle fell over, rolling, rolling, rolling until it hit the floor with a loud *crack*.

Tye watched me. "Somethin' wrong, Roe?" Smoke drifted from the end of his cigarette, obscuring his face.

The panic bleating in my heart grew louder, nearly audible, as something pounded on the still-blossoming thread between Bryn and me. I pressed my palm to it, felt the heat of the connection brush my fingertips.

"No, no, nothing's wrong," I murmured.

But something was very, very wrong. And I didn't need Bryn's panic—which I could somehow feel even here—to tell me that.

Because this was not Tye's cat. It was Patrick's.

The little tabby with the bicolored eyes he'd loved enough to pose with in the photo that hung in the lounge, to bring with him from Naruka to Marseille, where he'd lived for six months before the Inquitate had found him.

"I think, maybe, I'll try to see my parents after all," I said, my tongue tasting like cardboard in my mouth. "They might be home now." I made a show of glancing at the clock. *Four past one.* "Yeah, I think maybe they'll be home now and we'll get dinner or something. Catch up, like you said. Maybe go out." I was rambling. I knew it, Tye knew it.

Why the hell was the cat here?

There was no explanation. No possible explanation for Tye to have Patrick's cat in a farmhouse in L'Ardoise, not unless he'd been in Marseille, when the Inquitate had—

My head snapped up. *Four past one.*

Oh no. *No.*

Bryn's panic was an alarm in my head, but I didn't know if it was his fear or mine that flowed in an icy trail along my spine.

The Inquitate were here.

I gripped the edge of the table as Tye continued to stare at me. In the next room, the game clicked off, the faint blue glow from the TV retreating.

"Roe?" Tye said, voice quiet. "What ya thinkin' 'bout?"

An eerie calm settled over me, softening the tightness in my shoulders when I realized a reassuring truth—James and Bryn weren't here. Now, they would know through the thread to be safe, enough that they'd escape whatever happened next.

I lifted my chin. "I forgot something in the truck," I told Tye.

He scratched at his nose. "Oh yeah? What's that?"

"Cigarettes."

"You don't smoke anymore."

"I started."

His eyes never left mine as he slowly pulled out a pack from his pocket, held it out in the kitchen between us. The thread gave a hard flicker. "Then take one."

I stared at it, then him.

A little smirk tilted the lips under his beard, twitched his nose. "Don't ya want the smoke, darlin'?"

I backed up another step, sliding around the table and chairs. "Thanks, but I've got something I need to do." Like keep the Inquitate away from James and Bryn. When my spine bumped the wall, I flattened my quivering hand against the peeling wallpaper.

And glanced at the clock again.

Tye tracked the movement, his slow grin terrifying.

"Roe?" he said softly. "I don't think you forgot no cigarette."

I steeled myself. "No," I said, surprisingly calm. "I didn't."

Suddenly, a lot of things made sense at once. Not just my impending death, but the months Tye had spent provoking Bryn—and learning his trigger. When it worked, and when it didn't. He'd even timed it. *Five seconds from the woodshed*, he'd mocked.

Because he'd needed to know how far Bryn could be away from me when I was threatened and still turn into Sahn. But what did *I* matter? Or maybe this was about Nereida—or Willow.

You are disconcertingly curious of my trigger, Tye.

Not just curious, as Bryn had said, but planning, preparing.

I pivoted toward the door.

"I don't think ya wanna do that, Roe."

I couldn't stop my shudder at the warning delivered through flat eyes.

"Do ya know why the clocks stop?" Tye asked conversationally. "No? It's 'cause the Inquitate are so damn wrong, so corrupt, that even time is revolted by them. That's why Tallah don't want them anywhere near. Too imbalanced."

His words hit me like the thump of a closed coffin.

"What do you *want* from me?"

Tye stabbed his cigarette in the sink, let the sharp fizzle of it fill the kitchen as he tilted his head. "Ya know, I think I've been pretty damn clear about that, Roe. I wanted ya to stay right fuckin' here and not make the Fall. But you didn't wanna listen to me."

I took a deep breath that stretched the tightness in my chest. If I could control my nerves, I could face this, I could handle whatever was about to come. But the frozen clock over the counter was like trying to ignore a dead man swinging on a rope.

"I won't make the Fall," I lied. "I was thinking about it, that's all." If the Inquitate were here, then James and Bryn were safe, and that was all that mattered.

"That's why I knew I had to get ya out of there. Away from Naruka. And—no, don't go takin' another step," he warned when I inched toward the door.

Maybe it was better to stay and get answers that Bryn might hear through the thread.

"Why don't you want me to make the Fall?"

Tye pulled the toast away from his lips with a crunching sound. "Haven't ya figured it out yet? Goddamn, Roe, this ain't rocket science. Even I can keep up faster."

"Well, it looks like I can't, so why don't you tell me?" And explain in explicit detail why the Inquitate are here so James and Bryn will know how to prepare themselves.

His bottom lip protruded while his mouth contemplated. Then he huffed a breath, but the sound was more resignation, dismissal. "I know you're gonna see me as the bad guy here and I'm gonna accept that, because eventually, you're gonna know the truth. That I was the only goddamn one wantin' to keep you alive."

Is that what he thought this was? Dragging me to L'Ardoise, to a house where the Inquitate must be nearby? Or was he one now? But he sounded too much like himself, with that drawl and scowl that no illusion could imitate.

He crossed the kitchen with a lazy ease, like the cat watching from the corner. The vibrations of his boots hummed up my calves.

I flattened my spine as Tye neared, stopped, stared, his breath a cocktail of toast and beer. He narrowed eyes both greener and sharper than blades of grass. "Don't ya recognize me?"

Recognize him? Was he an Inquitate after all?

His dimple blinked in and out, then Tye squirreled a finger into his ribs. "Ya got me pretty good right here. Don't ya remember?"

"Tye, I didn't punch you there. I…"

Then it hit me, and I felt the blood drain out of my face. He was right—I *was* stupid.

It wasn't in the gate lodge that I 'got him.' Not *here* on this planet at all.

In the Gate.

But then—that would mean…no. It wasn't possible—James had made that clear all those months ago in the kitchen.

Not possible.

Because they didn't come through the Gate. Were never in the book.

Tye nodded as the haunting realization must have settled over my face. "Now ya understand, don't ya?" he whispered, breath stirring my hair.

The panic under my ribs had grown to a full-blown assault. And now—now I understood why.

"You're a—you're a—a—"

Tye finished the sentence for me. "*Drachaut.*"

The word dangled between us on imaginary wires.

The pounding in my chest grew louder, like I had two hearts instead of one, and maybe I did, because someone was screaming at me, inside me.

"Does James know? If James—"

Tye's fist crunched through drywall.

Dust rained down on my shoulders. The cat hissed, bounded off the counter with a thump, and took off into the living room.

"Forget James. Forget Naruka. Forget Stornoway for one goddamn second. Look at *me*, Roe."

Breath whistled through Tye's nose, his eyes went to twin green slits, sweat beaded on his upper lip.

Behind him, the clock remained frozen.

My voice shook. "I am, Tye. I am."

"Good." He bared his teeth. "You understand who I am now?"

"Yes," I whispered.

"Say it, darlin'. I want to hear it from your pretty lips."

I stared at the clock.

"You're my Tether."

CHAPTER 54

Mise En Abyme

T he hot air of his chuckle warmed my neck. "Yeah, that's right, kid. Ya stabbed me straight through the ribs. That was a nice little surprise when I returned to the Gate."

Back in a cave in Drachaut, back when I'd thought maybe *I'd* been the Tether, or at least Willow had. And Tye had the nerve to accuse Bryn of lying about who *he* was in the Gate.

That's why Tye was never with us, because he was never in Ruhaven, he was in Drachaut waiting for his Tether to find him. For *me* to find him.

I wrangled my nerves together, so much that if they'd been Tye's herd of sheep, they would have lined up and walked in a straight line to the fields. "I never took you for someone with scales," I said to hide my fear.

"No, suppose ya preferred the golden feathered boys, huh?" Tye shoved abruptly away and swiped his beer. The jacket strained as he paced in rapid circles, boots clacking on the tiled floor. "You were right about the Drachaut coming through the Gate, Roe. Ain't nobody else figured it out. I talked James out of it years ago when he got a hair up his ass that some might actually survive."

Then he'd stood right there in the kitchen and lied to me over a plate of spaghetti that night. More, he'd lied to James, lied to Kazie, lied to every Ruhaven who had ever lived at Naruka.

"Willow, was she—"

Tye rounded on me. "Hell no. She wasn't no Drachaut, and neither are you. Of course, the only time ya even think of us is when ya think your sister's involved. But you go on and look at me every day and don't see what's right in front of ya." He wiggled fingers over his ruddy face.

He was right. I'd only seen the man I'd been infatuated with—the easy-going charm, the slow accent. Not the Drachaut living with us, pretending to be one of us.

"You're Drachaut," I repeated, as if the words could sink through my ears and register with my brain. "But you're in the *Ledger*. The Drachaut are supposed to be sacrificed to create Ruhavens."

"Oh no, she's right. They're tossing Ruhavens through the Gate on purpose to create Inquitate."

They? "Who's they?"

"The Inquitate. Keep up, Roe." He stabbed the sandwich at me. "But it's Ruhaven they send through, 'cause they need their Drachaut to get sacrificed to make the crossin'. Ya get me? One goes in, the other gets killed. There's always a cost, Roe. Life's full of them."

Then wouldn't Tye have been sacrificed?

"You're saying that when Nereida went through the Gate, she pulled her Drachaut with her." Because they were bound, like a teeter-totter, as Kazie had explained once. "How are you here, then? Shouldn't you be an Inquitate if you're my Tether?"

My *Tether*.

"Ain't you forgettin' somethin'? You didn't come here alone, did ya? Triplets, darlin'. Hell, you were the one who figured out that pattern. I thought for sure you'd see right through me. When ya didn't, well, once Bryn found those letters from Carmen, I was just waitin' for one of ya to look at me and wonder. Guess ya were too caught up in whatever romantic games Bryn likes to play."

His name had the thread fluttering in my chest. "What is it about the triplets that means you—a Drachaut—came through the Gate, and were written in the *Ledger*, instead of becoming an Inquitate?"

Tye rummaged through the bread and pulled out four slices. "I'll explain it like this. There's a place where we can make the crossin'. I don't know how we get there or why we do it, but the Inquitate want us to. So Stornoway—O'Sahnazekiel—he's this slice of bread here, okay?" Tye dragged off the top slice. "He steps into the Gate, makes the crossin' first." He tossed the bread at my feet. "Two things happen next, but the order matters. The first thing is his own Tether gets pulled into the Gate. Their bond is immediate." He lifted the next slice of bread. "So his Drachaut gets forced into the Gate at the same time, and what happens to that Drachaut?"

"They get sacrificed for the crossing," I answered hollowly. "Turned into Inquitate."

Tye crushed the slice in his hand. "I'd like somethin' more dramatic than stale bread," he said conversationally. "But there ya are, ya get the point. This one's dead." He rubbed his fingers together, crumbling it into bits that dusted the floor. "And its soul now powers the Gate."

"If the soul powers the Gate, why does it become an Inquitate?"

"Because energy is always conserved. That's the rule. Nothin' lost. And nothin' gained. Then…" He carefully slid off the third slice, dangled it between us. "Who do ya suppose this is?"

He waited.

"Your mate," he said when I remained silent. "For Ruhavens, it's as strong as a Tether, and when Stornoway went through, he pulled ya with him seconds later." The third slice landed at my feet on top of the first. "That's your fine ass—the bread, I mean," Tye added, then weighed the last in his palm. "Now, who do ya think this guy is?"

"You," I answered hollowly. "I pulled you."

"You got it. You pulled your own Tether, which was me, but the Gate was already open so I didn't need to die and become Inquitate too."

I repeated his explanation. "You're saying for every triplet, four went through originally. One died and became Inquitate, two Ruhavens made the crossing, and one Drachaut came with them. But—but it's not just you. I mean, you're in the *Ledger*. You're Drachaut, but there are other triplets. Are each of them…is there one Drachaut in each triplet?"

"Give the little lady a prize," Tye said, tossing everything into the garbage with a *clang*. "It sure wasn't easy for Carmen to figure all this out and now I'm just givin' it to ya for free."

"How did she…" I broke off at the sound of clicking heels.

They echoed on the floorboards like marbles, sharp, painful. Hairs rose on the back of my neck as Tye looked into the other room, his face blank.

Something pinched my lungs, and I stumbled back a step, flattened my palm over the light buzzing between my breasts.

Carmen stepped into the kitchen.

Her perfume was a sharp tang, spicy apple, floral death. She was as sophisticated as Abby in a crimson suit with matching pinprick heels and black stockings. But where Abby was soft and curvy, this woman was all edges, from the harsh slice of her cheekbones, to the starched blazer collar, to the ironed pencil skirt. Eyes of crystal-blue glass took my measure. Her lips drew back into a deflated slit of unimpressed power beneath a bony nose.

She eyed me with some amusement. "How nice to meet you again, *Nereida*."

I stepped toward the door.

And knew, without the clock to warn me, without the bleating in my chest, that I was standing before someone more powerful than Bryn. Someone who didn't need protection for their Mark to be activated. Someone who radiated the curse of the Inquitate with each breath.

Now she was here, in L'Ardoise, in Tye's little farmhouse.

A triplet, like him, like me, which would make her...

"A Drachaut." Carmen answered my thought with a razor smile.

Could she read my mind? Or was the internal grinding of my brain that clear? She'd warned Maggie of what became of the Drachaut because she *was* them. And now she was here, watching me—why? *Why?*

The gnawing under my heart rose to a fervor. I panted against the pressure of it, against the fear curdling my blood that might have been mine or Bryn's.

But I couldn't afford to feel any of that, not if Ruhaven had asked me to make the Fall for Willow. Was that why the Drachaut were here? Because they didn't want Willow to come back?

Then one word rang through. Not in my own voice, my own thoughts...but Bryn's.

Run.

I didn't hesitate this time, not with the power pulsing off Carmen as palpable as claws down my skin.

I twisted toward the door.

Slow. Too slow.

Knees weak, I slapped off the corner wall, tripped over the shoe rack. My feet skidded in the snow that had melted to mushy puddles of salt and water since I'd entered. I needed a damn *Mark*, something that would allow me to escape them long enough to make it back to Ruhaven.

Tye bellowed my name while Carmen remained silent, which was somehow worse.

The frozen doorknob, a complex mystery I couldn't figure out, slipped in my sweaty hand as boots pounded behind me.

I twisted. Pulled.

The old door banged into the wall and icy, sweet air froze the sweat on my temples as I lunged outside.

"Roe, stop. *STOP!*"

Tye's hoarse yelling followed me as I plunged over the stairs, skidded on a patch of black ice, and burst into a cold sprint. Without my jacket, the cold burned the sweat under my armpits into icy awareness of my own panic. What did they want? Why was I here? Why were *they* here, in a cabin in the backwoods of my hometown? Did they want control of the Gate? Or did they want to stop Willow from returning?

The landscape spread for miles, a blank canvas for barren trees to grow. A five-foot snowbank all but smothered what was left of the rotted fence around the property.

I'd get out of there, find a telephone, call—what the hell was Naruka's number? And could the Drachaut find me anywhere?

And those were all useless thoughts. I needed to escape—*now.*

Skidding in the snow, I threw open the door of Willow's blue pickup. I'd burn this thing out of here and wouldn't stop until I was at the airport, where even the Drachaut wouldn't kill me in public. But the Inquitate? How did I stop them? *Just don't fall for any illusions of your sister.* That was easy, but—

I stared at the ignition

The keys. The fucking *keys*.

On the counter, on the...

Voices hollered, boots crunched snow, and someone burst out of the house. I leapt away from the truck.

Rowan, the farm next door.

That was a *mile* away, across a field as barren as the rest of this town. I'd never outrun Tye, maybe I should turn and face them when—

Now, Rowan!

Bryn's voice rang out with all the power of his anchor's call.

Arms pumping, I took off down the laneway, leaving the clear, shoveled path and tearing into calf-deep snow. The forest enveloped me, the empty branches letting in sparse light that glittered on snow brighter than the sky. It was nearly as blinding as the mirrors in Drachaut, except the shadows of trees scraped stark blue shadows on what should have been white.

My stinging breaths turned into panicked mist as I dove through the stubby forest like Willow and I had when we were kids. A mile away, far across the river, a red barn jutted out of the landscape.

I angled toward it, crunching through layers of hard snow that held for a second before breaking. Each step was a cracking strike in woods that had been silent. Branches frozen together by ice broke, pine cones crinkled, even the hardened leaves cracked.

Then a second set of footsteps joined mine.

Tye?

Not wanting to slow down and check, I jumped a log, snapping sticks and plunging into ever deeper mounds of congealed snow. My thighs ached with the effort of plowing through, of suddenly finding myself knee-deep, and I could only hope it was as hard for the person behind me.

The trees began to thin, bowing out to the stretch of serene, flat snow whose only disturbance was a single track of deer prints.

The river.

I knew I'd left the safety of the woods when my boots smacked into hard, unyielding ice. Each step sent a shock up my heel and into my thighs. The frigid wind burned an icy path across my cheeks.

Only the snow kept my boots from slipping as I bolted for the farmer's cottage on the opposite side. And then what, Bryn?

Bang on his door with Tye on my heels? And what if it was empty?

Rowan, do not stop. Not for anything.

There was something in his voice, even through the thread, that made me want to turn around and look. Something that would have me giving up the race to the farmhouse for what was behind.

But I didn't stop. I sprinted across the river, taking the largest strides as I could without slipping on the ice.

The labored breathing behind me grew closer and closer, but it didn't sound like Tye. The feet were too light, too quick, too quiet. Was it Carmen? An Inquitate?

An audience of twisted, dead trees watched me struggle to outrun them.

"Nereida!"

Ignore him.

Ignore *who?* No, don't look, keep going.

I was halfway across the river now, the farmhouse looming like a red savior, the chimney puffing a hot breath that dissolved into the sky. An overturned canoe sat with a mound of snow on their beach. Could they see me, whoever was home?

"Don't you want…" a winded voice huffed, far enough away that I might yet outrun them. "Want to know what I showed her?" A man's voice. Not Tye's.

Showed who? Showed what?

Keep moving. Please.

Okay, Bryn, okay.

I pumped my arms, pushed forward. A tire swung from a creaking branch on the waterfront property. The rope was knotted, probably something kids climbed every summer.

So close. I could feel the heat of the fireplace that would scorch my face when I banged straight through the door. Imagined the shocked looks on the family huddled around their hearth.

"Your sister, Rowan," the man panted behind me. "Don't you want to know what I showed Willow?"

Willow?

I tripped, stumbled, but caught myself before I careened into the ice. What did he mean? Show *what* to her? How did he know Willow? And who was he?

The questions pounded at me as loud as my heart rate.

"When I was—in…"

Do not listen to him. You will make it, Rowan. I am coming for you now. I am…

"…and I saw her…"

Bryn was trying to shout over him, to block out whatever the man behind me was trying to say. The wind nearly gobbled up the words.

"I knew what she was," the man shouted. "*Ruhaven.*"

Yes, she was, and she was the best of both of us.

The thread flared in my chest, light blinking bright enough that it reflected off the snow. Bryn trying to get my attention, to distract me.

"I ended it. Ended her."

My legs slowed before I registered the action. There was a pounding in my head, pressing my skull together. My breath died in my throat, my blood cooled to ice.

It was him.

No, Rowan, do not turn around, do not—

He was *dead*.

Skidding to a stop, I whirled on the ice. One of us would end here, now. I didn't care if he was Inquitate or Drachaut or another damn Ruhaven.

But when I saw what—*who*—he was, I froze.

For a second, I could only stare at the tanned skin, the narrowed eyes, the lips no more than a thin slice under a hooked nose. A fur collar fell back in the wind, the bulky jacket hindering him more than my thin sweater. Snowflakes clung to the gnarled end of his beard and wet the tips of his black, shoulder-length hair. His jeans were soaked to the knees from tracking me through the woods.

I'd been looking for him for months, reading his diary for months.

Levi.

He slammed into me with the force of a charging car as Bryn screamed my name. I careened onto the river's surface, smashing into it and sliding ten feet. The clouds passed in a blur that was only broken up by a triangle of geese soaring across. My palms burned from the cold pain, my knees ached with the impact of hitting something harder than concrete.

Then Levi loomed over me, blocking the geese and the sky. A faint mustache sprinkled his upper lip and glistened with the snot that ran from his crooked nose and into his mouth. He sniffed loudly, then grabbed my sweater by the scruff.

I gripped his wrists.

"I thought that might stop you," he hissed.

Him. Here. Because he hadn't been in L'Ardoise to warn Willow, but to kill her. And I'd been reading the diary of my sister's killer for months. But why was he claiming to have done it when it was the Inquitate?

"Why are you—"

My words ended on a hard slap across the face.

Salty blood slid from my burst lip, but I welcomed it, needed it to focus, needed the numbing pain in my left cheek to remind me why I'd stayed at Naruka in the first place.

To find why they'd targeted Willow, to find this man.

Between us, the glow of the thread lit up Levi's neck and chin like a flashlight. But that was all my bond with Bryn could do. I didn't have a Mark, had nothing but my fists and the skills I'd learned through muscle memory in the Gate.

"That was *my* Inquitate," he shouted, rapping my head against the ice. He ground his knuckles deeper into my skin, using Kazie's sweater to burn a line across my neck in warning. "We control them, you know? Yes."

Controlled them? How? All of them? No. No, *my Inquitate*—that's what he'd said.

I brought up my knee, tried to buck him off, but my boots slipped on the ice.

"She was supposed to be you," Levi said in my ear. "Stupid James. We waited for years for him to locate you so we could prevent you from returning to Ruhaven, from making the Fall. So I waited, yes?"

I leaned away from his hot breath, the mouth that nearly kissed my neck.

"And we find it's this Willow girl. So I move to L'Ardoise, and I find her one evening. Alone, because it's easier."

I swallowed the bile in the back of my throat, firmed my jaw. And when I finally spoke, my voice didn't tremble. Didn't crack with the grief digging rivers in my throat. Didn't so much as hint at the roiling monster burning in my gut. "Tell me what you showed her."

He sighed against my throat, eased back. "I show her—"

I swung out.

This time, I didn't miss. Because I'd been listening in Ruhaven, memorizing every blow Nereida landed, the weaving dance she did when she fought, the arc of her blades.

Fists flying, I caught him square across the jaw. My knuckles sang—a sweet, biting song—with the blow that sent him lurching off me. I'd kill him now. Inquitate. Drachaut. It didn't matter, and I could feel something stirring under my skin at the thought of hurting him. Of what he'd done to Willow.

I trapped his ankle with mine and bucked, swung again. My palm collided with his jaw. Not enough to injure, but it had him off balance. That was all I needed.

I swung my right leg up and over, rolling him to the side as I scrambled on top. Not with the same finesse as Nereida, but it was enough.

Bryn's voice was only a dull roar in my ears now.

My first blow crunched into his jaw, snapping it shut.

He looked stunned, as if I'd actually hurt him.

Why had he killed Willow? She had nothing to *do* with this, and he'd taken *everything* from her. Everything she'd wanted to be, everything she was.

The second blow sent his head snapping back. Silver sparkled in the corners of my eyes, nearly blinding my vision.

Every joke she'd told, every friend she'd made, the hours and days and years she'd spent at the piano. All that she'd loved was stuffed into a hole in the ground.

He'd killed my twin.

But I'd bring Willow home, and neither Levi, nor Tye, nor Bryn would stop me.

Then the silver wasn't just in my eyes, but sparking around me, a shimmering smoke that was at once nothing and everything. Not the bond between Bryn and I, but something else.

Didn't matter. Not now.

I slammed Levi's head into the ice as I screamed at him. I was crying, begging, cursing. He lifted his elbows to block the attack but my blows landed—elbows, fists, one after the other in a deadly dance like Nereida. His skull cracked into the ice, rebounding off it with each hit. Blood dribbled down his chin.

I'd never felt like this—powerful, strong, my pulse *singing* for the fight I shouldn't be winning. My hands moved inhumanly fast, nearly disconnected from my body. My left punch disappeared mid-throw, reappeared a foot to the right like space had eaten it up and spat it out.

Chaotic, random, *impossible*.

I stopped when I saw what was wrapped around my fist—a silver smoke, like the liquified remnants of a million tiny stars.

It is your Mark, Rowan.

But I didn't have one—a spirit. Nereida hadn't gone through the rite.

Then my fist whipped down, nearly driven by its own rage, and blood gushed from Levi's nose, spilling into a red puddle on the ice. It stained my knuckles, then his neck when I ground them into him.

I choked off his air, gritted my teeth. "Why did you want to kill Nereida?"

"You're a Ruhaven. A triplet. And you'll kill us if you go back."

What? *Kill us?* Kill who?

I shook him when he tried to elbow me off. "What do you mean? Tell me. Tell me!"

But before he could answer, something golden grew in the distance—a light that was so familiar, I eased my grip, lifted my head, and squinted at the unmistakable glow spreading over the snow like spilled honey.

I went completely still.

He was massive—as tall as the barren maple trees, with lilac-gray feathers dusting the snow. They stretched the width of the river when he unfurled them in one sweeping arc. The ice cracked under his footsteps, louder than thunder.

I couldn't look away.

His hair was pure threaded gold, too painful to look at with human eyes, and brighter than the ball of sun setting behind him. Each gear tattoo rotated slowly until his bare chest and arms were a moving machine.

Sahn.

I stared in awe, in horror, in shock, as the god from Ruhaven strode across L'Ardoise's barren river.

Before my world went black.

CHAPTER 55

Wildfire

Hot rage bubbled in my chest.

I should have known the angel walking on the ice wasn't Bryn. Even now, I was still falling for the Inquitate illusions, and Tye had spun such a beautiful rendition of the Azekiel that I'd missed my one chance to get revenge.

The cold, burning heat of it still tingled in the knuckles that had collided with Levi's face, because for a moment, there'd been a glimmer of something *other*. My Mark? It didn't make sense.

I grunted as Tye muscled me up the second floor of the farmhouse, his sweaty grip hot on my wrist. Water damage stained the peeling chicken wallpaper, like a wet teabag had been squeezed against it. Each step up brought musty, hot air, and the reek of thick mildew.

How had I been reading my sister's killer's journal for months and not known? The triplets. Levi. It'd all been right there, in front of my Bryn-crossed eyes. And I'd missed it because I'd been distracted by him, by Sahn, by the lure of Ruhaven. Of what I hoped I could have been.

I pretended to trip before Tye hauled me against him with one arm, my heels smacking into the stairs.

"I told ya you're too far in the Gate," he warned, his breath at my ear a mix of beer and sweat. "One little illusion of your Azekiel and ya forget everythin'. Ya know why? 'Cause you're a love struck fool, Roe."

Yes, but not enough, apparently, to choose Bryn.

"You're lucky I got to ya before Carmen," Tye added when I remained mute.

He'd known. This whole time, he'd known—about Levi, the Inquitate, Carmen, all of it. How far back did it all go? Were Bryn and James in danger, even now?

I grabbed for the railing before Tye ripped my hand away. "No ya don't. Up ya go."

I tried to summon whatever power I'd so briefly had and make him pay for every lie, every misleading trail he'd sent me down, and mostly, for how he'd stood by and let Levi destroy the best thing in my life.

That rage burned so hot and deep, I wondered how that brief, impossible power didn't burst from me in flames.

"Consider yourself lucky I called the dogs off Stornoway."

My chest cracked with fear. "You—you—"

"Easy, girl," Tye cooed, like he wasn't dragging my body up the last flight. "Ya play things right with me and that don't gotta change."

It took everything I had to tamp the fear down, to shove my sick and sweaty nerves into that box I'd kept so tight. To not wonder why the thread between us had gone completely quiet. Because Bryn was everything I hadn't been, could never be, everything Ruhaven deserved. Like Willow had been.

We crested the top landing with Tye holding my arm against my back, a parody of how he'd threatened me that day in the gate lodge.

"Why?" I asked, swallowing the ice in my throat. "Why did you let them kill her? She didn't do anything, wouldn't have done anything to you. She wanted to be a musician, wanted to—"

"Ya think I had any part in hurtin', Willow?" Tye booted open an iron door and shoved me inside. "What do ya fuckin' take me for?"

I'd taken him for someone I could trust. Instead, he'd betrayed not only me but James, too, in every way possible.

"But you knew about Willow, and…"

I stared, wide-eyed, at the attic.

A mattress sprawled in stark relief under a barred window, the flower bedspread wilted and torn. Plastic insulation dangled from an unfinished ceiling, and water damage soaked a dirty trail into a bathroom with one toilet, a shower. At the peak of the angled room, I could just stand without ducking.

"Carmen and Levi, they thought Willow was you, just like James did. So they needed to stop ya before you could hurt us. But I ain't never held with Carmen's choices on that."

When Tye prodded me in the back, I dragged my feet over plywood boards. There was a metal card table with a vase, two chairs, and a faded painting of a lake basin hung above a lit fireplace with a single bucket of dried wood. Beside the bed, the window wallowed in a gray haze that led to dead witch's broom trees.

The closest neighbor, an abandoned tree fort, was coated with a layer of snow. On the opposite bank, the farmhouse Bryn had urged me to escape to was dark. There was no smoke from its chimney, nor hazy light glowing through the windows.

My knees shook, the adrenaline having long since nose-dived, and being knocked unconscious had my body hanging to the unsteady cliff of oblivion.

"Roe."

I sank onto the bed. Springs squealed, my breath fogged into cold mist.

"Roe."

I lifted my gaze to Tye's, and for a moment, he looked as foreign as the room. His face was a study in contrasts, the left side licked with yellow flame, the right as blue as the frozen snow outside. Faint wrinkles fanned out from the corners of his eyes, but his mouth was tight and drawn.

He loosened a button of his collar. "I didn't want it to be this way," he said to the crackling logs. "It's why I did what I could to keep ya from the Fall, from being manipulated by Stornoway into makin' it."

Except Bryn had wanted me to stay here. Despite everything, he'd chosen the electrician from L'Ardoise.

And I'd chosen Willow.

"What am I doing here, Tye?"

He closed the door, locked it. "Ya know what the problem is with you Ruhaven?" he said, strolling to the fireplace, hands in his pockets. "Ya only think of yourselves. Me, me, me. And if it's not about you or Stornoway, it's Willow."

If I'd thought of her more, I wouldn't be in this situation.

Tye grabbed a log from the basket, breaking it into kindling over his knee. *Crack. Crack-crack.*

And if I'd spent more time researching the Drachaut, looking at those triplets, I'd have answers for her. If, just for once, I could be *good* at something, at this, I wouldn't have put James in danger too. Wouldn't have Tye threatening to send Levi after Bryn.

"Tell me what Levi did to Willow." My voice was cold, unrecognizable even to me, and I gripped the lamp beside the bed.

Tye's eyes flashed with impatience. "Darlin', if I gotta hear that woman's goddamn name *one* more time, I ain't gonna be happy."

Fuck. Him.

I exploded off the bed.

"Goddamn it!" Tye ducked the vase's whistling dive before it smashed into the wall, the handle rolling on a separate path from the body. "You're lucky I'm too much of a gentleman to throw that back at ya. Ya deserve it, let me tell ya."

"Then throw it." Better to start a fight here, now, and maybe I'd be able to escape in the mayhem.

"Look who finally found her spine," Tye mocked, lifting a smoke to his lips and crossing his legs. "But there's a lot ya don't know, Roe, darlin'. Like how Stornoway and Kazie have been meetin' in the Gate, their past lives colludin' over just how to get yours to make the original crossin' over here. It's why all three of us ended up gettin' reborn in the Ledger. Fuckin' Stornoway, always up to his tricks, ain't he?"

My head whipped to Tye. Bryn had *known* why we'd been reborn here? No, not just known, Tye was saying that Bryn—*Sahn*—had *wanted* Nereida to be in that Ledger. For what purpose? Why? And why would Bryn keep that from me? Never mind what role Kazie might have played.

We are really going to have a conversation when I'm back, I said down the thread to Bryn, though the words landed in emptiness. *If I'm back.*

"That's right, darlin'. They both knew the end of the memories was gettin' closer, knew that when Kazie passed through, ya only had days. So now, here's what's gonna happen," Tye said with a short nod. "You're gonna stay in this room 'til Bryn, you, and me, all hear the call together—like a nice little happy family. When two weeks pass after that and ya miss the Fall, I'll let ya go."

My heart sunk. I wouldn't make it to Ruhaven for Willow, would never make the Fall, would never bring her back.

"I'll give ya this, Roe, ya really had Stornoway over a barrel," Tye continued as my thoughts spun and escape plans hatched. "I was nearly whistlin' at how ya left him in that room. He tries to Romeo himself at the Gate, then he tosses his very, *very* attractive—sorry, Roe—fiancée away just for your mere existence. And when all he asks is that ya stay here with him, live a good long life just like I'm tryin' to do, you throw your delusions of Willow in his face. I bet he'd like to strangle her dead memory just as much as I would myself."

I pressed a hand to my gut. "You've been lying to me, saying he was controlling, crazy, that he was—"

Tye waved me off. "Well yeah, Roe, and that ain't a lie either. He *did* want ya to make the Fall. How was I gonna know he changed his mind?"

"You told me he was a liar." But it's *you.*

Tye kicked the bucket of wood. "He *is* a liar. He lied to ya about being your mate, he lied to ya about the bond, he lied to ya about just how far he'd go to get Nereida back. You ain't never seen him for what he was. Like that day in the woods—it wasn't him that saved ya, it was *me*."

I squeezed the edge of the windowsill. "You're delusional."

"I was keeping the Drachaut away from ya for months. But that day, Levi went around my back, he was lookin' for Bryn to finish what he started back in L'Ardoise. But then he found you and thought he'd take care of ya for me."

Why? Just because I was a triplet?

Tye paced up and down the small attic, needing to hunch to avoid clipping his head on the beams. He ran his fingers over the insulation behind clear plastic, stabbing through the odd holes. "I used my own Inquitate to get rid of him, and I didn't much like doing it, Roe. I hate those things." He curled his lip.

Yet Tye didn't have any problem with summoning his Inquitate on the ice out there.

"Do ya know how much I had to fight with Carmen and Levi to leave ya alone? They were worried you'd make the Fall. I had to convince 'em otherwise, so I kept a close eye on ya, just in case. And when I couldn't, I trusted Stornoway to do so. Then you go and piss him off so much he must have been too far away not to feel the Inquitate right away."

I had. I'd belittled him, insulted him, humiliated him. Called him names it made me blush to think of.

"And Oslo?" I asked, throat rough. "Was that Levi too?"

Tye's fingers tightened on an overhead beam. "Carmen. Like I said, they wanted to get rid of any risk to me. So when you went to Norway, she saw an opportunity. Then I find ya kept it from me. I coulda throttled ya. You're goddamn lucky Stornoway never left your side again."

What risk was I to Tye? What risk was Bryn? Why did it matter if we made the Fall?

"Fuck, Roe," he cursed when I asked. "The same thing that happened when ya made the crossin' here. You're gonna pull Bryn *and* me. You'd go on and steal my life—my very fine life—right out from under my nose. I might be on the beach drinkin' a beer one day and suddenly find myself disappearin', my soul gettin' torn through worlds to be reborn as someone I don't know and don't care to know. You'd do that to me."

Then this wasn't about me going back for Willow, it was about *Tye* going back. *That's* why they'd killed the triplets. To prevent any of us from pulling them through, ending their lives here. And Willow had been killed for the threat they thought she represented, that she'd return to Naruka one day and make the Fall, dragging Tye with her.

The overhead bulb quivered in a circle. "It's a damn stupid idea anyway," Tye added. "Throwing your life away here. You're killin' yourself and just not callin' it what it is."

If that's how he felt, then why had he brought me to Naruka to begin with? He could have left me in L'Ardoise, or easier, had the Inquitate kill me like Willow.

"Don't look at me like that," Tye warned under his breath. "I never killed no one. And I ain't gonna apologize for wantin' to stay in a world you despise so much."

My breath wheezed through my nostrils as if all the oxygen up here had been sucked into the fireplace. "I had to make that choice," I said through my teeth. "For *Willow*. I don't want to leave Bryn—"

Tye slammed his hand on the card table. "I told ya, I don't want to hear her name no more. Your twin's life ain't worth more than my own. And if ya think Stornoway's gonna come save ya here, you're wrong. If he really wants ya and not Nereida, he'll let me take care of his dirty work by keepin' ya here. If he doesn't, if he wants Nereida back, then he'll show up, 'cause he'll never go back without her." Tye hefted the door. "This ain't such a bad deal, Roe. And one day? You're gonna thank me. 'Cause I knew what you didn't—Ruhaven? She ain't no fuckin' dream."

He slammed the door.

CHAPTER 56

Dead Sea

J ump.
Jump!
Nereida waved hurriedly at Sahn as she pointed to the jutting edge
of the cliff. My stomach pitched at the unending drop below, the
distance too phenomenal for my human eyes to bear. Yet even as I
thought it, her pupils dilated until she focused on a tiny bird floating on
the surface of the milk waters below.

Sahn gestured to the surrounding mountains, pointed at the path
down. No, we'll walk, he seemed to say.

I stared at him, soaking in the details of his gilded hair, the cloth
draped across one shoulder and wrapped at the waist, the feathers that
fluttered in Ruhaven's warm breeze. The best friend I'd discovered in
the Gate.

And one I'd never meet again. Not if the memories were ending.
How could it all come so quickly to this shuddering stop? I hadn't had
enough time. To know Sahn, to know Bryn, to live in a world more
impossible than life.

I wouldn't be able to say goodbye to the land I'd been born from,
wouldn't be able to kiss Sahn or hear his rolling laughter one more time.
It was like losing Willow again, but slower, a death dragged out over
weeks.

She would never return either. Never know Ruhaven or Tallah, the
smells of the world, the cliffs that peeked over mist.

Sahn snapped my attention back to the dream. He was yelling at me,
Don't jump, don't jump.

But I backed up, talons digging into the bone rock. A wild, reckless exhilaration filled my lungs. I could do this. I had to do this.

My muscles bunched, the tendons in my legs straining as I started toward the edge. One stride, then another, I was a bird with invisible wings. Maybe in the next life I'd have them.

The cliff gave way to miles of empty blues, of faded mountains and the roaring white lake below. I braced, feeling the ground for the last time, then leapt.

And fell.

I woke to the sound of rain trickling down the attic's window.

How long had it been? Three days? Four? Were Bryn and James still safe? Would I feel it if they weren't? But then, I hadn't even felt Willow die, hadn't felt Levi's Inquitate end her life.

I needed Tye to come back so I could get any remaining answers out of him. But he seemed to be done with me now. I was like bread in the oven—waiting to rise, or for the Fall to pass.

How long would it take to hear the call? And what would it sound like? I could imagine what Kazie would say—*hopefully nothing like your singing, Roe*. Why hadn't I asked her what she'd heard? Why hadn't I visited Ruhaven with every waking breath? I took for granted that I'd have years, when I'd only had months.

I pried open a groggy eye.

And shot off the bed.

It wasn't rain I'd heard trickling on the windowpane, but tea being poured by a hand inching out of a candy-apple red suit. The only color in this attic room. What was *she* doing here?

Maybe Tye wasn't feeling so sympathetic anymore.

Well, neither was I.

Holding my breath, I stretched out an arm and slid the wire from the overhead light I'd disassembled off the nightstand.

"Roe." Carmen's voice carried through the room, authoritative, brisk, and quietly disappointed. "At any point, including this very moment, I may order my Inquitate to show you a never-ending nightmare that would have you ending yourself before I could. Put the wire down."

I tightened my grip on the weapon.

Her Inquitate—because they all controlled one. I'd find out how, then I would hope that the thread communicated everything to Bryn for me.

Carmen sat at the metal card table, the vase righted and returned to its original place in the center. But there was a tray there now as well, like Bryn had brought up the stairs the day I left.

I rose slowly, the wire in my fist. Could I see the Inquitate if it wasn't an illusion? Did it always appear as someone else? And how long did it take to attack?

Her skin glowed nearly blue in the morning light. It was painful to look at, harsh and edgy, tight, like you could slice yourself on her forehead. Her shoes were black and polished, in a style that belonged to a dead era, or nuns.

Then she looked at me.

For a moment, the image of her wavered, something else replacing the skin almost as fine as Bryn's. It sagged under the jowl, wrinkled at the brow, folded at the neck.

I dropped the cable.

Carmen's lips spread into a thin, bloody line as she moved a bony finger through the air, stroking an invisible pet. "Have a seat, Nereida." She crossed her ankles, tucking them neatly away as she folded manicured hands. "I expect you have questions for me."

The pot of tea steamed on a lace doily. "What's this?"

"Diplomacy," she answered, tapping the cup across from her. "Do sit. I have agreed not to harm you for Tye's sake."

So Tye hadn't decided I was better off dead.

I walked carefully around the bed, ducking the slanted rafters. She didn't flinch or tense when I stopped a meter away. Not worried I could hurt her like I did Levi?

I slid into the hard seat and studied her.

James's aunt appeared as unlined as her portrait, without a single wrinkle around the eyes to indicate she'd experienced a second of life. Her lips were thin, but they didn't pucker, and her forehead allowed only a single, faded crease between her brows.

I sniffed at the tea she'd poured for me. It smelled like a dead rose. "Were you ever in France?" I asked, or had Tye been lying about visiting her there?

She lifted a biscuit as thin as her nose. "Yes, of course. I own a pied-à-terre on the east coast. I prefer to stay near to Naruka, to save other Drachaut."

Saving them. Was that how she saw it? Kill a Ruhaven to prevent a Drachaut from inadvertently returning via the Fall. Didn't they *want* to go back? Maybe not all, maybe not even most, but surely *some* found the same lure in Drachaut as we found in Ruhaven.

Carmen lowered her nose. "You don't think of this as saving."

"Do you think that's how Patrick sees it? Do you think he's in his grave right now feeling very saved?"

"As a triplet, he would have killed one of us, and he did plan to make the Fall. You know this, as it was in his diaries Tye informs me you read." She smoothed the non-existent lines of her knee-length skirt with nails of the same color. "So I save Drachaut, yes. What would you call it when we are destroyed, when our lives here are stolen without warning, when we fade from existence for a Ruhaven's misplaced dream?"

I didn't have an answer for her. "So you kill the triplets." Killed my sister.

Delicate nostrils flared on an impatient breath. "If James intends to recruit them, then yes. The Inquitate make things simple. We control them, and the deaths appear accidental—indeed, are accidental—as the attack is an illusion."

An illusion they control. "What about Bryn's leg?"

"His leg? Oh. O'Sahnazekiel. That was mere overindulgence on Levi's part. If he had simply killed him quicker, then this mess could have been avoided."

Bile rose in my throat. "Did he overindulge on my twin too?"

Carmen reached for another biscuit but she didn't eat this one either, only twirled it until crumbs soiled the tea. "No, precisely the opposite. I think you can understand how that was strictly preservation. When it was reported that James had discovered your location at last— mistakenly, I later learned, Maggie's son was never as bright as her—I had Levi remove Willow before she could put Tye's life in danger. Little did I know she had a twin. In my years at Naruka, I have never encountered such." She looked both perplexed and delighted at the idea.

I reached for the tea I hadn't touched.

Carmen lifted a candy-red nail, tilted it back and forth at me. "I will have you convulsing on this dirty floor should a drop of that hot tea touch me," she warned.

How long did I have before that? Long enough to grab the teapot, dump it into her pristine lap, and bolt out the door? Long enough to get past Levi? To make it to the Gate? Was I prepared to arrive at Naruka with the Drachaut on my heels?

"And consider this," Carmen added after a slow blink. "Tye has convinced me that Brynjar is not currently a problem. As his existence only threatens Tye, I have allowed him to live, though it makes me uncomfortable. I don't like being uncomfortable."

"Bryn has *nothing* to do with this." *And if you touch him, I will find my Mark again, and no illusion will stop me from what I'll do to you.*

"He most certainly does, and I suggest you use the information you already have to draw your own conclusions." She set her mouth to the stain of matte red lipstick on the teacup. Paused. "But should you provoke me, I may at any point change my decision on Brynjar. It must be difficult to walk to the Gate with one leg. I can only imagine how hard it shall be with none."

I eased my hand off the tea—for now.

"Good girl. Now eat." She tapped the biscuit.

I grabbed one and bit into crumbly sewage.

Carmen nodded. "You know, Maggie doted on James. She knew what a soft heart he has, so she kept most everything from him. He'd have never stomached what she put the Drachaut through."

It was hard to swallow the sodden crumbs. "He doesn't know about the Drachaut, that the Fall would pull you as well," I deduced. James would have never stomached that consequence.

Her laugh was a dry cough, a vacuum choking on a sock. "Of course not. Maggie spent her life hiding the unsavory parts of Ruhaven from him, the consequences of what it means to go to the Gate, to view the memories. We grew up together, Maggie and I."

"But you were Drachaut." How had Carmen visited the Gate for years and neither Maggie nor James realized there were Drachaut in the Ledger?

She set down the tea with a knobbly knuckle. "Yes, but I did not understand it. I lived in Drachaut, as some Ruhaven do, and so I was like the ugly duckling, forever fancying itself a swan amongst the fowl, only to find I was something far more hideous. That was how I lived, day after day." She glanced out the window, where the snowy fields reflected in her clouded eyes.

Hideous? Was that how she saw the Drachaut? "But you recruited anyway. You found Tye."

"Yes, even the Drachaut want company, want the familiar. I consider it my job to protect them." Turning from the window, she tilted her head at me like a crow surprised to find the mouse asking questions. "I remember the year I discovered who I was, as there was some trouble up North—weapons smuggling—but then they were always blaming the British for this or that." She made some vague sounds. "I was twenty-two at the time. Maggie and I were in the Gate together, and when we woke, she asked me, as she always did, about what I experienced. My name was Ariqutaque in the Gate, and she was a vociferous reader, so I often returned with more detail about the history of Tallah that I'd gathered from these books. But on that day, something different happened. I met my Tether." She lifted a silver eyebrow, each individual hair groomed to submission. "I believe you met your own Tether, Partheon, in the Gate?"

"Who?"

Disapproval shone on her waxy skin. "Tye."

That was his name—the demon I'd stabbed. "Yes."

"I told Maggie I'd met mine and described the creature to her. She told her mother—a truly insufferable woman—and naturally enough, the old bat pulled out the texts, rifled through until she found a creature of a matching breed. It was an Azekiel. And all Azekiels are Ruhaven, which would make me…"

"A Drachaut," I finished.

"Until then, they had been unaware of any coming through the Ledger. So her mother forbade we inform anyone. And slowly, Maggie—my friend since we were twelve—began to distance herself from me. That is what a Ruhaven is."

There was no way James had known about this.

"What happened to Maggie?" I asked quietly.

Carmen planted knobby hands on the table, leaned in until her breath reeked worse than the tea.

I met her eyes.

"I think you understand, Nereida, that I do not mind getting my hands dirty when it is needed." She leaned back with a tiny smile, and added, "You should be aware that Drachaut, unlike you Ruhaven, do not need the Gate to call them to make the Fall. At any point, I may decide to right some old wrongs. Be sure, for your own sake, that I do not feel compelled to."

❋✹

Carmen had killed James's mother, had ordered Willow's death. Levi's Inquitate had killed my twin. Tye had lied to me since we met. James had been deceived by everyone, even his own mother.

Holding a bracket of the broken door latch, I fought to loosen the second bolt on the barred window. Either the screws were frozen solid, or my fingers were, but the damn thing wouldn't budge. An hour ago, I'd gotten it to crank a full inch, and I was really hoping I hadn't hallucinated that.

I needed to escape *now* and warn James about Carmen, because I wasn't sure how much Bryn could hear when the thread between us had been dead for days.

Luckily, the attic was only one flight up, short enough that if I eased myself out the window with the cable I'd pried from the light switch, I might not break a leg on the fall—which would make running through the woods afterwards very difficult.

Why couldn't my Mark—as Bryn had thought the thing on the ice had been—materialize *now*? Not that I could chaotically punch my way through these bars, but I wouldn't say no to a fire Mark, if that was even possible.

Wait.

I eyed the lighter on my nightstand, the one Tye had left next to a pack of cigarettes. It'd be stupid, but maybe I could—

A sudden blast of noise had me shooting out an arm and gripping the frozen bars of my window just to hold myself upright.

Music stabbed into my eardrum at a head-splitting volume, like I was standing at the front of a concert with my ears glued to the speaker. I squeezed my temples, wincing as the notes pounded into my skull.

I fell to my knees as it ratcheted up even higher. Each note buzzed in my bones, wove an unknown melody behind my eyes, plucked my skin alive with the imaginary strings of a harp.

The thread flickered for the first time in days, glowing as bright as Bryn's golden eyes. Warmth seeped into my ribs, heating my body from the inside out like I was hugging a hot water bottle to my chest. Could Bryn feel this too? The soaring notes that were tearing me in half?

Then it stopped.

Silence exploded as deafening as the music, ringing a long, empty cry, like a wave rippling through the sea until it died on the shore.

I knew what this was, as certain as I knew Bryn was my mate.

Kneeling, I waited for the ringing to stop, for my world to right itself on its axis again. Then I heard something else.

Willow.

She was repeating those words over and over again, like she'd done at the Gate. Like Ruhaven had—because it hadn't forgotten what I owed it. Even trapped in this attic, it wanted me to make the Fall. To give back what it'd lent me for a short while.

And now I had only two weeks before Willow was gone forever.

※

4 days after the call

I curled my fingers around the cold edge of the toilet, breathing through my nose as rust dripped into a bowl that was still less revolting than the eggs.

Tye's work boots skidded into view, the tips of them coated in snow. "Look at what Ruhaven's done to ya," he admonished. "You're as bad as Stornoway. Can't stomach eggs anymore? There ain't even a word for that."

The last time I'd thrown up like this, Bryn had been beside me, trying to get me to drink something, apologizing for what had been both of our mistakes. I hadn't trusted the bond he was showing me then, had been full of suspicion—that's why I'd pulled those memories out.

I flushed the toilet, wiped my mouth. "Why do you hate him?"

"Stornoway? Besides the obvious, that he's a self-entitled prick?"

No, he'd put everyone else ahead of himself. Had stayed in Norway just to keep the Inquitate away from us, believing they were pursuing him.

"Roe, that guy never knew a good thing when he had it," Tye said from above me. "Gets to play angel man in Ruhaven but he's still not happy, still needs that witch, Nereida—no offence, Roe—and loses his goddamn mind when he can't have everythin'. Then he goes up to the Gate to kill himself. It ain't right."

And even knowing Bryn tried to die for Nereida, I'd chosen Willow.

Tye crouched down, puckered his lips into a whistle, and blew out the high-pitched tones of the call I couldn't stop hearing. The call of Ruhaven. Or was it Tallah?

"Stop that."

The whistling died on a smirk. "Why, Roe? You're hearin' it in your head every day anyway. Gettin' hard to ignore, ain't it? Damn thing nearly keeps me up at night. But we only got ten more days of this."

I rose, brushed off the hand Tye steadied on my elbow, and shoved out of the bathroom. "Why do you keep bringing me what you know I can't eat?"

"Other than to punish ya for tryin' to light the attic on fire?"

My eyes flicked to the blackened roof boards. I'd gotten a sizeable amount of smoke started before the lighter ran out.

"Not bad, darlin'." Tye moved to the window, tilted the blinds, shrugged. "I give ya the eggs 'cause I like to remind ya."

"Of what you're keeping me from?" From Ruhaven, from saving Willow.

Tye lifted a brow. "Of what it can do to ya." He eased open the window, letting in the snow and sap of L'Ardoise in winter. I used to love that smell—now I couldn't remember why. "Seein' Stornoway there that day, lyin' near-dead and waxy and hollow, well, I didn't know what it might've done to me. He wasn't just riskin' his own life, he was riskin' mine as well."

"Because you thought he was your Tether."

"I did. I mean, I knew it could have been the other triplet, but the way that everythin' about the man ground against me like a fuckin' cheese grater—right from the beginnin', ya know?—I thought, fuck, it's just gotta be him." His eyes darkened on me. "But I sure am glad it wasn't. As soon as I met ya, I thought there was somethin' there."

"There wasn't. There isn't," I said as I inched toward the door. The lightbulb swung between us, blinding his view briefly.

Tye wagged a finger. "Don't know that I recall ya feelin' that way when we were in the tack room, darlin'."

I almost sprinted for the bathroom again. "That was a mistake."

Tye blew a kiss. "If ya wanna pretend. But like I said, I hated Stornoway, so when I got a chance to rip him up, I took it. And knowin' he could do nothin' without revealin' his little charade? Well, I slept like a baby that night after the tack room."

Bryn had known Tye was sabotaging us from the beginning and said nothing, not even when I'd pushed him to the brink.

"You should have just left me in L'Ardoise," I said. "Told James I was a lost cause." Why *hadn't* he? For the last few days, when I wasn't trying to pry the bars off the window or set fire to the roof, I'd turned the question over in my mind.

Tye had spent six months in L'Ardoise, and at any time he could have permanently disabled me with his Inquitate, or told James that I wouldn't move to Naruka. After all, not every Ruhaven did or could move. James might have persisted because he'd thought I'd been his mate or sister back then, but Tye could have talked him out of it.

Yet Tye had brought me to Naruka and shown me the Gate himself. Not only that, but he'd argued with me when I'd wanted to leave, had called L'Ardoise a nothing town, had insisted I keep visiting the Gate.

If he'd feared that I might make the Fall one day, then why bother with any of it?

Tye turned from the window, crossed his arms. "I thought about leavin' ya," he agreed, his voice gone contemplative. "It'd been six months and James was wonderin' what was takin' so long. But I needed to stay at Naruka and he wouldn't've let me recruit again if I messed this one up." He tossed an extra quilt on the bed. "One of us needed to know who James was tryin' to contact. Who might be goin' through the Gate, just in case. I didn't mind it so much there. Carmen, she hated everythin' and everyone. But I liked James, liked you, Roe. I just had to make sure ya didn't make the Fall."

Tye scraped out the chair that Carmen had sat in less than a week ago. He looked up at me under wavy locks, his petal-green eyes as sincere as the day we met at the ballgame.

I lunged for the door. Locked.

"Do I look bone fuckin' stupid, Roe?" Tye said when I cursed. "That's your problem, darlin'. Ya always underestimated me."

I let go of the door, turned, and stared at Tye in his tired Wrangler jeans and plaid jacket, the fur brushing a squared jaw I'd once found attractive. I worked my tongue around the anger tightening my cheeks, then clamped down, hard, on the words I wanted to shout at him, but the wintery frost of L'Ardoise cooled the bitterness that wouldn't help me.

"Soon you'll be outta here, Roe. Think how happy Stornoway'll be. Lots of time left to spend with him."

And what of Willow?

Tye tossed a pack of cards on the table. "Ya wanna play? Not enough for euchre again, but I reckon we can figure somethin' out."

When I said nothing, he sighed and started dealing anyway.

But I was done being something he could play with.

My bare feet froze on the floorboards as I crossed to him. Took a seat. He folded the cards in his big hands and dealt them slowly, face down.

He'd let them kill Willow. He'd manipulated James. He'd threatened Bryn.

I turned a card over, then another.

"That ain't how this is supposed to work, Roe."

Levi was responsible for crippling Bryn. "No?" I flicked the cards at him. "I don't think you've got much more to hide."

A muscle twitched in his jaw. "If that's the way you wanna play this."

"That's the game I like." The cards landed around his boots, rested on his thighs, stuck out of his pocket. "Tell me, Tye, when you watched me scrambling around for months looking for signs of the Inquitate, did you have a good laugh to yourself?"

He dusted his jacket. "You forget it was me who put ya on that path?"

And why *had* he? "But you tried to convince us the Gate called the Inquitate."

"It is the reason, ain't it? Maggie was killin' us for that thing. I wanted ya to understand why."

"Where's Levi really been?"

Tye's fist curled on the edge of the table. "Right. Here. Levi took over this place for me, and when I came back a few months ago, I helped him get it ready." He nodded at the barred window. "Just in case."

I emptied the rest of the pack. "In case you needed to imprison Ruhavens?"

"Just you, darlin', 'cause I'm a gentleman like that." He dug out a lighter. "Afterwards, I needed to talk to Carmen in France and explain the plan I had in case ya got *stupid* and decided to make the Fall. Killin' folks with the Inquitate was never my way."

Now he wanted to play the hero?

"No, just because you didn't want to go back, your way was to let them kill Willow."

Down came Tye's fist. Coffee soared off the table, splattering the wall and blending with the water damage. The mug clattered across the floor, the broken handle flinging in the opposite direction.

"*Just because I don't wanna to go back?*" he hollered, shoving to his feet. "You would kill me, Roe. That's what ya'd do to me if ya made the Fall. And you wanna stand there and be righteous?"

I held my nose as I swiped the tray off the ground and chucked a slippery egg at his hard jaw. Tye ducked, then caught the next.

"You're killing Willow by keeping me here." I could feel it inside me, had since Kazie left—a drawing, aching thing ready to escape, like if I disobeyed the Gate, it'd take its punishment anyway. "I heard her when Kazie made the Fall. That's why I want to go back. Ruhaven told me to. Willow told me—"

"That's why you wanna go back?" he roared, and swiped the tray from me, flung it across the room where it clanged against the rafters. His fist whipped out, grabbing me by my sweater. "Darlin', right now, I'm the only goddamn thing between you and the worst illusion you'll ever see," Tye warned in a low voice. "I could make you watch the skin peel from O'Sahnazekiel's bones, and it'd be as real as smellin' the blood yourself. Or maybe I'll show ya what Bryn looks like from the inside out, and maybe it won't be no fuckin' illusion either."

My belly turned to ice. "If you *ever* touch him again I'll—"

"Oh, now ya wanna pretend you give a shit?" Tye sneered. "After the way ya treated him? You left with me and there ain't no takin' that back, honey."

"I love Bryn."

"Bullshit!" His face swelled to the color of Carmen's suit. "You love Willow. And that's the only goddamn thing you ever did love, Roe. He ruins his life over and over for ya while you just spit in his face. Every one of us is makin' sacrifices for you, but do ya see any of that? No. Ya don't see what I'm doin', and you sure as hell never loved Stornoway."

"You're a liar, Tye, a manipulator, a cheat, a user, a—"

He twisted my sweater, choking off my air. "No, I'm your goddamn salvation." Then he leaned in and whispered, "Eat the fuckin' eggs, Roe."

CHAPTER 57

The Last Unicorn

Day 9

In the dream, I floated on a lake of milk with the heavy liquid cradling my limbs.

Above, the trees glimmered with shimmering purple fur that rustled in the wind. I knew this lake—I'd seen it the first time I met James in the Gate, and then later, Sahn and I had swam together before making love on the sparkling shore.

Soon, these memories would be all we had of Ruhaven. Would Bryn make the Fall without me? If he didn't, would he wake up every morning and wish he'd Fallen when he'd had the chance?

Then a crisp breeze swept under my nose, something caught in the night's tide. I smiled in the water, recognizing the scent immediately.

O'Sahnazekiel.

I'd forget him soon, forget all of this once it really was no more than a memory.

I searched for him on the overgrown beach, where a rainforest of color spilled onto lavender sand, the foliage curling into tentacles that dipped into the water like a hundred octopuses gathered at the shore. Toothy butterflies the size of shoeboxes fluttered in the breeze. And all around us, the grinding of the gears could be heard.

But there he was. On the edge of the beach, Sahn lounged in a perfect imitation of the Gate's memories—dappled-gray wings with the color and softness of a stallion's coat, hair like golden smoke, velvet tail nestled in the sand, eyes glinting like metallic paint. A milky bubble burst on the side of his marbled torso, dripped.

He was naked. Gloriously, superbly naked.

I lifted my gaze and found his golden eyes rapt on me. A heated smile played across his face as bright and sweet as the indigo morning cresting behind us, the leaves glowing bright purple with the brilliance of it.

Feeling boneless and relaxed, I splashed lazily from the ivory water and into Ruhaven's hot winds. If this was the last time I saw him, I wouldn't waste it.

His gaze raked my naked form, roving over the milk that slid off my breasts, lingering at the heat already building between my legs.

For the first time when he spoke, it was in English and not Ruhaven.

His tail twitched in the sand. "I have been looking for you, my Rowan."

His voice, his smoldering gaze, my name on his tongue—it was a direct gut punch, even in the dream.

I took my time walking to him, not wanting anything to prompt the lucid dream from suddenly ending and ruining the mirror image of Sahn—the male who was so beautiful, it seemed ludicrous I'd ever been afraid.

He leaned forward, draped his arms over his knees, hiding nothing. *Please don't let me forget you.*

The corner of Sahn's mouth lifted in a lopsided grin, exposing a single fang. The gesture was all Bryn. "My Rowan, I certainly hope you do not," he said dryly, my mind having perfectly captured his light teasing.

Steps away from Sahn, he snagged my ankle and tumbled me into his arms, laughing as he rolled on top, smothering me against hard flesh. Yes, this was what I wanted. All I wanted.

I looped my arms around his neck as he slanted his mouth over mine. The kiss was hard and wild and thrilling, with his fangs nipping my tongue, my lips, his hands diving in my hair as he consumed me.

"Rowan," he murmured, sending a thrill buzzing under my skin, like my body delighted in his voice alone. His wings arched off the ground, feathers flexing and spraying and flicking hot sand over the legs I wrapped around his waist.

I brought my mouth to his sun-kissed neck, licking drops of the lake I'd dripped on him, whispering to his thundering pulse. I trailed my claws down his chest, my heart beating a wild rhythm that matched his own.

Then he drew back, stretched my arms over my head. "Rowan," Sahn repeated, his mouth quirking up. "It is *me*."

I tightened my legs, pulling him down. Sahn's tail whipped the ground, sending another wave of sand over us.

"Rowan, I—" He huffed a laugh as I nipped at his neck. "No. I mean to say, I have been looking for you."

Looking for me? I pulled away, frowned at the burning god who, for some reason, had decided to have a discussion now, of all times.

Rowan, this is not a dream. I am here.

I spluttered, a sound—I was sure—Nereida had never made before. "I...Bryn?" I choked out.

He grinned. "Yes, my Rowan." My name rolled in a slow, deep avalanche.

"You— You're here? I mean, where even is here? Am I dreaming?"

He smiled at me. "Somewhat. You are asleep, yes. I have created this bridge between us while you were unconscious."

"But...*how?*"

"Magic," Bryn teased, his long braid tickling the tops of my breasts. "Us. Me. You. Our thread." He punctuated each with a kiss while bubbles rose around us, the sand blinking in and out in the wild fog. "Instead of showing you a memory, I was able to create this space for us to speak."

"Even if I'm in L'Ardoise, and you're—"

"Rowan, if a million stars did not keep us apart, I do not think Tye will either."

Emotion swelled in my throat—regret, love, worry, but there was no time for any of that. "Are you safe? Is James? Is Naruka—"

"You are the only one in danger." He stroked a thumb down my cheek. "Do not worry of James or myself."

But that wasn't true, because I was the only one Tye had bothered to spare from the Inquitate.

"And this," I said quietly as a bubble burst on the shoreline. "Is this real?"

"As much as us."

I closed my eyes, not wanting to acknowledge the reality we'd left in his room. "How much do you know?" I asked softly.

The playful humor left his face as he pushed up to one elbow. "I heard nearly all before I was too weak to maintain the thread," Bryn answered, sliding his hands over my buzzing skin. "It exhausted my abilities to speak to you so far away. But I know of the Drachaut, of Tye, of Carmen, of what Levi did to Willow."

Yes, that'd been the last time I'd heard Bryn.

I tilted my cheek heavily against his palm. As his thumb moved over my lips, I said, *I'm sorry for leaving you.*

He sighed and drew me against him, resting his chin on my soft, jelly hair. His chest was a warm map of tattoos I knew as well as my own skin.

I closed my eyes, breathed in just him, a scent that was still Bryn, even when he wore the Azekiel's body. His arms tightened around me until the hold was so perfect, so complete, it seemed impossible to believe in things like the Drachaut or the Inquitate.

This must have been how Nereida felt, why she mated with Sahn so many years ago.

I rubbed my nose up and down the column of his neck, listening to every trip in his breathing. "Did you tell James about the Drachaut? About Carmen?"

Smoky wings circled around us, blocking out the light of the lavender sky. "Yes, I told him before I left," he replied, hand stroking so leisurely up my spine, I nearly purred.

Then his words registered. *Left.*

"Bryn," I said, stiffening. "Where are you? You're not—not *here*, are you?"

He huffed in my ear, tightened his arms before I could pull away. "I most certainly am. How else could I make such a bridge with you?"

"But the Inquitate, they're—"

He smothered my complaints with a sharp kiss. "I know. It is why I am not inside with you now. I cannot get past the Inquitate, not without them threatening you directly."

"Where *exactly* are you?"

"Outside Tye's farmhouse in what I believe must be an abandoned children's fort. I can see your window."

"You need to go, *now*."

His hands curled gently around my wrists when I shoved at him. "My Rowan, I am not going anywhere." He skimmed his nose along my neck, back and forth.

"You shouldn't have come," I said, even as I leaned into him. "I'm fine, and now James is alone."

"In this, James and I were of one mind. You may rest assured that should you somehow force me away, he will only send me back."

James. I owed him so much—*too* much.

"Did you hear the call?" I asked Bryn, and thumbed a tattooed gear over his shoulder. It was the first time I could move and touch, not as Nereida but as me. I lifted my eyes to his, let my fingers explore the curve of his cheeks, the slash of jaw, the fangs slipping ever so slowly over his bottom lip.

"It was as Kazie described to me." He nipped the hand I mapped his face with before his eyes turned serious. "Rowan, I know how we ended things, how this may appear to you. Please do not think that I wished for this to happen, for Tye to keep you from the Fall."

I'd *never* think that of him, and yet he'd known—hadn't he? That the Fall was coming, because somehow in the memories, Sahn was involved. But it wasn't the time to ask him now.

"I thought you'd given up. On this, us, me."

He touched his nose to mine. "I could no sooner part with you than my own soul."

He might have meant it romantically, but it was true, wasn't it? Our souls were so bound up that we'd traveled from Ruhaven together, had pulled each other.

I'm sorry I hurt you. With Tye, when I chose Willow, when I left.

His lips quirked, exposing a single fang. "Ah, does this mean my mate has at last forgiven me for hiding I was Sahn?" he teased quietly.

"Yes, which is why you need to return to Naruka before—" I broke off when his tongue circled under my ear, the texture like soft sandpaper.

And groaned when he lashed my pulse, cool as snow against the hollow of my throat. His hands slid from my shoulders to my breasts, as Sahn had a thousand times before, but this was Bryn and not a replay we had no control over.

He thumbed my nipples, moving in languid circles that somehow felt different than in Ruhaven. His heartbeat was as wild as mine, faster than the slow pulse of O'Sahnazekiel.

Fog crept into the jungle around us, spilling onto the sand as every nerve in my body focused on the palm pressing below my belly.

"Is it tomorrow?" I murmured.

"Yes, but Rowan," Bryn said, voice husky. "I do not know that I can hold this world together while we are like this."

I bit his lip. Sucked it into my mouth between Nereida's tiny fangs. "*Try.*"

His quick laugh died when I ground against him and found him hard, ready. Lightning sparked in his star-dropped eyes before his right eye flamed to melted gold. The left stayed an Irish Sea blue.

This was Bryn. And he was mine. In any life, like he'd said. That was the truth.

I curled my fingers around the solid length of him, stroked silky flesh. He inhaled sharply as if this touch were different than Nereida's, than all the memories.

I would miss the Fall, and the Gate would close forever. This would be the last time I could touch, taste, or hear Sahn, the male who had been my mate a thousand years before, and the truth behind Bryn.

He spread his wings wide, feathers nestling in the hot lavender sand as I stroked the blade of each wing, then he flipped us in one smooth motion, stretching over me.

Above us, the lavender trees dissolved into the sky. The world was disappearing already.

"I need you," I whispered, and locked my arms around him, anchoring Bryn, anchoring Sahn.

Breath rattled in his chest, echoing the breaking world around us. His back muscles rippled, wings sprouting from skin bunched under his shoulders. Sweat curled on his taut body. The tattooed gears marring his left bicep began to spin.

Gray angel wings arced wide, scattering any remaining sand, their beauty as staggering as him.

Burning stars, one blue, one gold, captured my gaze as he levered above. Fog scattered to gold dust, and the forest fell away, the sand melting into rivers. The dragons quieted, the phosphorescent trees dimmed, the wind froze, and music stopped.

Panting, I writhed against his hardness.

I do not think we shall have long, he warned roughly. *I am already losing control of this bridge.*

I gripped his hair. *Then make it count.*

Rowan. It was a curse, an oath.

My body lit with a pleasure that tingled from my toes to my head, a thousand memories spinning between us when he rocked his hips.

And the world exploded.

CHAPTER 58

The Wild Swans on the Lake

I gasped for air.

Ripping the covers off my burning body, I kicked at the sweaty sheet, then shivered as the rotating fan flung a dry breeze over me. The attic was empty.

I pressed a hand to my forehead and tried to ignore the throbbing ache between my legs. No, no, it hadn't been a dream. Couldn't have been.

I rolled over in bed, tried to get my bearings. Washed gray light spilled through the window, leaching the trodden rug and walls of color. The coffee Tye had brought me earlier sat on the card table, the bread beside it.

What had Bryn said? If he was nearby, could the Inquitate sense him?

I cursed inwardly. Instead of warning him, of telling Bryn everything I'd learned, I'd tried to—

Rowan?

I froze on the edge of the bed. He *was* here, it was him, and we'd—we'd almost, but not, and I was probably going to die if he wasn't inside me right this second and—

I truly feel the same.

I slapped a hand over my sweaty brow. *Bryn! You've got to stop doing that.*

Oh? I thought you were asking me to very much continuing doing that.

I smiled in the freezing, filthy attic. *My thoughts—stop listening to how obsessed I am with you.*

I felt him grin. No, I felt him *beam.*

When I have you under me again, I shall show you the meaning of the word. But for now, let me try to bring our world back. His voice slid like silk in my mind, a wolf prowling at the edges. *Can you lie on the bed again? It is easier to create the bridge when you are relaxed.*

I grinned to myself, and for a brief moment, all my earlier worries seemed far away. *Maybe you should have given us clothes, then.*

I am not altogether certain I regret the decision not to, although I do believe this is the first time I have been so aroused in a treehouse.

I huffed a laugh into the darkness. *You really are funny.*

If you witnessed the state I awoke in, you would not think so.

My toes curled in the rug, but, feeling giddy at the idea of seeing him again, I quickly laid on the bed, patted the damp sheets, and tried to force myself to relax.

When a light pulsed under my shirt, I gazed in wonder at the glow between my breasts, where golden heat drenched my skin in color and pushed at the window's empty light.

This was us, what Bryn had wanted me to understand before. Now I did.

Minutes drifted by.

I clasped my hands over my belly, my elbows splayed, and waited for the world to return as Bryn whispered on the cusp of my mind.

Close your eyes. It will help.

Another ten minutes passed.

I heard the waves before I saw them.

Then the ivory lake swam into view, vanilla-scented roses swayed on the shore, warm lavender melted between my toes, and the lattice mountains loomed in the color of worn, faded jeans.

Sahn—Bryn—clasped my wrist, his thumb squeezing my pulse. Down wings tickled the soft curve of my back as he sat beside me.

I lifted a brow. "I'm naked again?"

A fang worried his bottom lip. "I could not resist."

"*You're* not," I pointed out. A swath of material draped across his hips.

"I compromised." Then he tugged me into his lap.

"But you're so pretty naked."

"So O'Sahnazekiel is no longer the terrifying beast man you regaled us with during your first encounter? Prepared to eat and devour you and 'fly you to his nest,' I believe it was."

I laughed, the sound like music, like my throat was some wind instrument.

Bryn stroked my arm. "I believe I did warn you I would not be able to maintain this world," he reminded me with a lifted brow.

"I had to try."

"Certainly."

But we stared at each other, everything unspoken between us, the air zapping with enough energy I wondered if we shouldn't attempt it again.

Then I swallowed a laugh when his wings tossed lavender sand over us. We could wait. Soon, we would have years.

"Now, tell me what I cannot understand through the thread. Are they feeding you? You feel hungry, and I keep sensing cold ham. And eggs."

He looked so perplexed that I laughed. "I still can't eat meat. But I'm fine."

"And this?" He stroked my left cheek, unmarred in this world. "Does it still hurt from Levi?"

I cupped his hand. "No, it's fine. *I'm* fine. Are you sure James is safe? The Drachaut won't come for him, will they, if he's not a triplet?"

Bryn looked at me for a long minute, as if deciding something.

Then his fingers stroked lazily over my body—familiar, comfortable, because this was Nereida's body, and he'd lived with her for years. "No, he is safe and currently scouring his mother's history."

"They didn't think he knew about the Inquitate."

"It is true that Maggie did not always share her knowledge of Ruhaven. And now we learn that it was Carmen who killed her. I did not tell James, as he would be distraught. That will be for later, when you are safe, and we shall tell him together."

Together. Because that's what we'd have.

His cool breath whispered over my neck before teeth grazed my pulse. Distracting. Exhilarating. I forgot my next question as Bryn inched his way to my mouth.

"If they are keeping you from making the Fall because of Tye, then who am I Tethered to?" he asked.

"Your Tether is an Inquitate now. They think we fell together, that in Drachaut, you entered the Gate first and triggered a chain reaction."

"Because we are mated."

I nodded.

He studied the lapping shoreline for a moment. Winged goldfish *plop-plopped* in continuous loops. Wherever they landed, fist-sized bubbles floated up.

He stroked my hair, but it was an absent gesture now, automatic as his gaze grew unfocused. "We are the same, my Rowan. *Souls* are what are sent through the Gate, not people. Not beings. The soul, like energy, is conserved, even in death."

It was why Ruhaven had called me to make the Fall, because twins must share enough of a soul that I had a chance to bring her home with me.

Bryn remained silent, stroking my hair as he continued to watch the leaping fish and bubbles. Could I touch one of his wings now? I eyed their dappled perfection. Nereida never did, only fleetingly a few times. They were the most beautiful things I'd ever seen, something from a storybook.

"Do you think I could—"

A sudden pain ripped through my heart.

I clutched my ribs when they shuddered like cracking ice. *The thread.*

When I looked at Bryn, pain tightened the rippling cords at his neck, flared his nostrils.

"What's wrong? Are you…?"

Then his face went carefully blank, his eyes cooling to unreadable opaque. The sharp pinch in my chest disappeared.

"What was that?" I repeated. "I felt you, didn't I?"

His chest expanded on a slow inhale. "Nothing. I was only thinking of my Tether. Of their death."

Are you sure?

Yes, I apologize.

I rubbed at the memory of the ache—stronger than what I'd felt in his room before I left. "I guess it's strange to think they could be an Inquitate now and—"

I yelped when Bryn suddenly scooped me up, wings flaring.

"Come, Rowan," he said, his voice back to careful exuberance. "Let us swim."

"Swim? Now? Are you sure you're alright?"

He carried me into the milk lake where bubbles floated and burst into a shower of raindrops. Vanilla waves rippled away from his massive wings. "Yes. I cannot force Tye to give you up until the Fall has passed. When it does, I do not know whether I shall be able to maintain these illusions."

My toes dipped into the cold silk. "You mean the thread between us?" I patted the space on his chest where he'd pulled it from before. "We'll lose this?"

He covered my hand. "I hope not."

But I was only just understanding this, and him, and now that would be gone too?

I looped my arms around his neck as he lowered us into the lake. Above, the gears rotated in grinding slowness under skies ripped to life by stars. "When will I see you again?"

A flicker of sadness touched his lips, then they relaxed. "When will you no longer be able to make the Fall? Days, I expect."

Days then, until Willow would never be saved. Would remain like Ruhaven—a memory. *No, don't think of that.*

I focused on the angel blocking out the gears. On Bryn, who would remain, even when Ruhaven disappeared. "When the Drachaut let us go…" I murmured as milk lapped my cheeks, "I have some extravagant plans for us."

"Do you?" Delight lifted Bryn's voice. "I look forward to hearing of these, Rowan. In *extravagant* detail."

"Then come here." I dragged him into the water with me, whispering in his pointed ear.

His wings twitched, his tail swatted the water. "Careful, Rowan," he warned roughly. "It is likely you shall implode this world again if you continue."

On a laugh, I pushed away and watched as Bryn's gaze ate up each ivory drop that rolled down my breasts. "You do have it bad for Nereida," I chided, flicking the lake at him with my toes.

He caught my foot, massaging the sole as I floated languidly. The water was more buoyant than the sea. "Only you, my Rowan. As always, only you."

I hoped so, because soon, Nereida would be as much a memory as Sahn.

"I could live here forever like this," I admitted to the sky. "You and I in Ruhaven, if we remembered who we were."

"Would you, Rowan? Stay in Loch Luna? With me?"

He said it playfully, but there was a question in his eyes. Was he still wondering about what had been unanswered? The one that left a ring between us and the memories of Abby?

I dipped my chin into the water. "Even with the tail and fangs," I said seriously.

One pointed tooth slid out. "And the wings?"

Tugging my foot away, I flipped over and paddled toward him. His eyes stayed glued to me as I grabbed the backs of his thighs, lifting myself slowly out of the water, and dragging my tongue up his tightened belly. He grunted when I nipped his chest.

I gripped his neck, wrapping my legs around his waist again. "The wings were my favorite part," I whispered in his ear.

"Indeed?" His voice lifted. "Then I am exceedingly grateful I was not born a dwarf."

I chuckled against him before resting my head on his shoulder as he rocked us back and forth, humming quietly so his voice joined the chorus of babbles and flickering wings.

⚙ ☀

While we spoke, night had draped a thick curtain across Loch Luna. Trees glowed with an inner fire unique to Ruhaven, the light radiating up trunks as translucent as my own skin.

Sitting on the beach, he turned me so his chin could rest on my silver hair. I laid my hand over the arm he snaked under my breasts and relaxed into him, watching Ruhaven's tiny creatures splash in the loch.

The thread whispered circles around us, as real as it had been on our only night together.

"Rowan, you tried to tell me before you left Naruka that you'd heard Willow."

Before I'd abandoned him for Tye, for L'Ardoise. "Can we forget that morning?"

He stroked my cheek, and even with the claw, the gesture belonged wholly to Bryn. "I was not listening to you then, but I am now. What happened during the Fall? I know something did—beyond Kazie disappearing—for you shut down afterwards, suddenly deciding that you yourself must join her. I assumed it was the shock of experiencing the event, but later, I began to wonder if there was not something else…"

I squeezed my eyes shut, nodded. And told him.

When I finished, Bryn exhaled a shaky breath, a tree casting off snow from its winter branches. The arm around me tightened. "I believe you. That it was Ruhaven, that she called to you. That she did so because she—or some part of her, perhaps kept alive by the Gate—wishes you to make the Fall."

I blinked in surprise. "No hesitations? No worries it might have been an Inquitate or my own hallucination?"

He brushed the birthmark on my shoulder. "I wish I could tell you it was the case, but no, I believe it is exactly as you have supposed. When I laid at the Gate the evening before James and Tye found me, I heard Nereida."

My mouth went dry. "You did?"

"Yes. She spoke in Ruhaven, asking me to stay, not to leave like this. It may have been the first time I disobeyed her."

I squeezed his hand. "Why did you?"

"I thought it was my own fear manifesting, but I read accounts of others afterwards and spoke to James. We learned it is not an uncommon experience, that many Ruhavens who have witnessed a Fall, or become so lost in the Gate, have heard a voice of a loved one at the end."

I let out a slow exhale. "Do they come back or... I mean, is there something about the Gate that makes them alive again?"

His fingers stroked up the back of my neck. "No, Rowan. Nereida can no more speak to me here than Willow can."

"But what if—"

"It is Ruhaven," he explained gently. "I believe she has always protected her children. We are born from her, and if it was Willow you heard, who advised you to make the Fall, then you were asked by Ruhaven herself."

"What would you do?" I asked him.

"If I had stood at the Gate as you did, and heard Nereida call me home?"

"Yes," I whispered. "If she'd called you, if Ruhaven called you."

He crossed his arms under my breasts, hugged me to him. "It would be against Ruhaven's laws to disobey her. What would you do, Rowan," he said instead, but his voice wasn't teasing or playful, but deadly serious, "if you were not trapped here, if you had never left L'Ardoise, if I had supported your need to decide from the beginning? Would you have heeded the call?"

His breath, which had been stirring the hair by my ear, calmed to stillness.

Willow and I had loved each other for twenty-three years. Nothing, not Ruhaven, not even Bryn, could replace that. Willow would never have given up on me. She was the strongest person I ever knew, and I had no doubt that if she'd been standing before the Gate, hearing the call, she'd have met that destiny.

For me, for her.

Because Willow had never been afraid of the unknown, of remaking herself at every stage of her life. Never feared that she'd left something crucial behind, never worried she wouldn't find herself again. She seemed to nurture a limitless source of will, of rightness, that no matter how she fell, she'd find herself.

I took a breath. "I would have gone back for Willow."

I waited for the judgment to come, for Bryn to push me away, but then he only said, "I told you months ago that O'Sahnazekiel has been researching something in the Gate."

At the change of subject, I let out the breath I'd been holding. "I've never seen Sahn working on anything."

"This is because he was purposely keeping the project from Nereida. He began it while I was exiled in Norway, and I did not know the reason of it until recently. I did not tell you, because I did not want to believe it." He stroked a claw along the inside of my wrist. I could hear his heart beating rapidly—too fast for Sahn.

This was what Tye had tried to tell me. "He was researching the Fall," I said, and Bryn glanced at me, surprised.

"Yes. I believe that he not only knew what would occur with the Gate, but that he planned for it."

Bryn's exhale had goosebumps pricking my neck. Then Tye hadn't lied, and Sahn had purposely wanted me to make the crossing, and all the times he'd looked at me, and I'd wondered if he'd seen an imposter as Nereida, a part of him had not only known—but predicted? "Why? How?"

Another deep breath. "Because—because I believe he wished you to return. From here, to Ruhaven."

Me? No, Nereida. Bryn was saying Sahn wanted Nereida to make the Fall back. "I don't understand. If he knew we'd make the crossing, why would he also want Nereida to make the Fall back? Why not just stay in Ruhaven? Why go at all then, unless…"

"Unless there was something that would happen in the future, some eight hundred years later, that she was needed for."

"That's a hell of a gamble, Bryn." And one that had ended with me in a dirty attic in L'Ardoise, miles away from the dream Sahn might have once hoped for.

"I suspect it was not much of a gamble at all. You know that Kazie was a pattern detector. She and O'Sahnazekiel had planned for this very moment."

"For us to be trapped by the Inquitate, unable to make the Fall?"

"I do not believe that is the case," Bryn continued hollowly. "You see, despite knowing his wishes, I have resisted them at every turn. Even when you told me you wished to make the Fall, I attempted to dissuade you. Because I am selfish, Rowan, and I do not want to return you to Ruhaven, to Sahn, to a man I will not be and will not know."

My heart thumped, so loudly he must have heard. "I thought that's what you wanted."

He pressed his lips to my neck, my cheek, my ears, like he couldn't touch me enough. "Once. But not since I saw what was between us in L'Ardoise. I want you here, selfishly, to myself. That is why I reacted so poorly in my room before you left. And so now, for the first time, I find myself at odds with O'Sahnazekiel."

Whatever he thought, there was nothing we could do now, no possible way to escape the Drachaut. And even if we could, was I really prepared to look Bryn in the eye and choose the Gate, choose Willow, over him again?

No, I didn't have the guts for it, for what it'd do to him.

A lizard with butterfly wings *plopped* into the lake, swam deep, and disappeared into the crystal weeds.

"Rowan." His voice was muffled against my neck. "I want a memory from you. Not one that I pull from our thread, but one you give me."

I turned, my nose skimming his rough jaw. "One that I give you?"

"Yes." His voice was steady, firm now. "If we missed the Fall, what would you wish to do together, after Naruka? After Ruhaven?"

I could think of a thousand things to do in bed alone, but that probably wasn't what he meant. "Can we go to Norway?"

"Wherever you wish to be. Would you like me to find a tiny cottage for you to build and me to paint?"

I laughed deeply, picturing just that. "No, Bryn. I think—well, I think I don't ever want to fix, paint, or build anything ever again."

He nuzzled my throat. "Then what would you like? Perhaps a man who understands what a load-bearing wall is?" Bryn whispered, so seductively my toes curled.

"I—I'd like you to take me sailing. I want to see the fjords, to live on a boat for months, to see the lighthouse from your memories." And know what it was like to live that freedom. To taste the salt air and feel the boat swell on waves ten meters high. To listen to the fiddles play below deck, the songs sung over a drink, the brisk, salty air slap me in the face. To grip the soles of my boots when the boat rose, to see the bow of the ship carve through the mist of Norwegian fjords. To have nothing and no purpose but tomorrow.

I stared at the flickering lights over Loch Luna, the opaque liquid that light didn't penetrate, but it wasn't an endless pit to me anymore, it was the tiny room between life and dreams.

"I would like that," he murmured at last, voice soft as the milky waves. "What else?"

Encouraged, I nestled into his warmth. "Well, if I could eat meat with the memories finished, I really want to try that sausage and cabbage stew."

"The memory I showed you of Odda?" He huffed a laugh. "Then it certainly looks better than it tastes, for it is rather bland altogether. However, if your heart is set on it, I do know a family shop in Trondheim that is famous for its stews."

"I'd like to see that too—Trondheim, I mean. I want to walk up the steps to the college you went to, then I want to sail to Odda, and know the person you were before the fancy education, when you were working on the ship in the summer."

He nibbled my ear. "Oh, but my Rowan, what if you do not like me windblown and uncouth?"

I laughed against his chest, his teeth tickling my earlobe. "*You*, uncouth?"

"Perhaps you have already forgotten how close we were to trampling James's carefully planted daffodils," he teased.

"I don't think I'll ever forget," I said as everything inside me heated.

"Neither shall I, and I have replayed it many times, just to be certain of that fact," he promised, making me shiver. "What will we do after Odda?"

"If you aren't bored of me by then?" I teased, and he squeezed my waist. "We'll sail north until we hit the next country."

"The North Pole?"

I swept my silvery arm at a mass of toothless shrubs. "We'll take a left."

"Scotland, then."

As the fires steamed in translucent trees, Bryn and I sat wrapped in each other, his claw circling my belly, the rise and fall of his breath as gentle as the ripples in the loch while I told him every dream I'd never known I had.

"And then we could go somewhere hotter, like…" A warm drop fell on my shoulder.

I glanced up at the canopy of leaves, held out my palm. "Are you making it rain?" I asked, circling my hand in the air.

But when he shuddered, I pulled away, turning in his lap. "*Bryn?*"

I'd never seen O'Sahnazekiel cry.

Tears beaded in his eyes, tiny golden things that leaked out and over his cheeks. A single fang worried his bottom lip. Coral pink pushed away the normal gold sheen of his cheeks.

Something was very wrong.

I gripped his shoulders. "Did the Inquitate find you?" We must have been talking here for hours. Did time pass in the same way? "Bryn, tell me."

"No," he said softly as I smoothed away his tears. "No, I am quite fine."

"Obviously you're not," I insisted as his hands moved up and down my arms, circled my wrists.

His damp eyelashes fluttered closed.

And that's when I felt it.

A fissure ripped through my chest, a pain that could only come from the thread. I'd felt it hours ago, and now it felt like a dam burst, like he'd smothered it until this moment.

"Tell me," I pleaded, my voice a shuddering puddle. "What is it?"

He opened his eyes. "I fear I have been drawing out the inevitable," Bryn admitted, voice hoarse.

My chest sank. This was my fault—I'd let him stay here instead of insisting he return to Naruka with James. "Did the Drachaut find you?" I managed.

"No, it is not that." He took a ragged inhale. "The Drachaut believe that when I—when O'Sahnazekiel—passed through the Gate in Drachaut, that he carried Nereida with him through their mated thread." Bryn ran his hands over my shoulders, down my body and up again, mapping the dips and lines of it as I'd done with his. "I believe we may still have a few days left to make the Fall."

It must be just settling in for him, with the last few days to see Ruhaven now ending, that this would be all there was left. "I'm sorry," I said softly, wiping away his tears. I wanted to tell him he could go without me, that I'd understand, but I couldn't get my thick tongue to work.

He cupped the back of my neck, stared into my eyes. "While you may not be able to travel to the Gate, I can."

My heart stuttered. "If you—if that's what you want." He was going to leave then, now, while I was here with Tye, because he needed Ruhaven. I should have said it myself, for him to go.

Like I said, she'd take you, I said through the bridge, because I couldn't stomach the words.

You misunderstand me. Bryn shook his head. "I told you once that you are written upon my very bones. Do you think I would allow my soul to be separated from yours?"

I pressed our foreheads together, like he'd done the night he'd tackled me into the garden. "But if you're thinking of—of making the Fall, then that's what would happen." His soul to be taken by Ruhaven, mine to remain here as Tye intended. And then he'd be reborn as someone else, someone new, and I'd be Rowan. Not Rowan and Bryn. Not Rowan and Willow. Just Rowan.

"Do you recall what Tye told you, about triplets?" he breathed. "Eight hundred years ago, O'Sahnazekiel sacrificed himself in the crossing to bring Nereida here, and now, I will be able to do the same. For you, for Willow."

Realization rolled through me like thunder.

"This is what you wanted," he said softly, like his words weren't tearing me apart, like I wasn't even now staring at his lips and wondering if this was it. If this was all we would ever have. Just a dream.

Tears burned, swelled, and dropped until he was nothing but a blur. The bitter salt of them leaked into my lips that should have been kissing every piece of him.

He took my face in my hands, held me solidly as Sahn. "This is what you wanted, my Rowan. What Ruhaven wanted, and maybe, what Willow wanted too. We are still mated. The thread is as vital as it was in Ruhaven. It will work if I return to Naruka now."

I gripped the hands holding my cheeks, licked my lips. "Bryn, I heard Ruhaven, but we don't know if it meant Willow would make the Fall with me—"

"Is it not souls that make the Fall?"

"That's what James said, but—"

"And is Willow not part of your soul?"

I squeezed my jaw shut. *Yes.*

His eyes guttered. "Then I believe I know why Ruhaven called you home, why she did so as Willow, why O'Sahnazekiel made the crossing, why he needed you to return."

I met his starry eyes when they opened.

"Because," Bryn answered his own question, "there was something for you to bring back. Not just Nereida. *Willow.*"

He fisted my hair and pulled me to him, kissing me over my protests so I could barely draw air. There was only him and the golden thread spiraling around us, the hands that slipped over my body like it was Bryn touching me and not Sahn, pressing us together so our hearts beat in a wild tango that roared in my eardrums.

Not a kiss of passion. But a kiss goodbye.

This couldn't be happening. "We can't—you can't—"

"It is okay, my Rowan," he insisted between kisses. "I can give you this. Give *us* this. You told me you wished to do it all over again, and this is your chance. The only one."

But tears gathered, fell, in eyes of glistening blue and gold.

He flipped us in the sand. Covered my body with his again, demanding acceptance with each stroke and bite. Then his clothes were gone, and we were naked, pressed skin to skin to one another, because he didn't fear the world imploding.

Because he was leaving.

He was ravenous, his hands everywhere, even as I tried to take back what I'd chosen.

You wanted this at the Gate before I attempted to convince you otherwise, he said inside me, but even here, I could hear the pain.

That was before I knew it would take you too.

Your sacrifice is mine. I will not exist where your soul does not.

Tears leaked down my face. "But I'll never see you again. We'll never have Norway, we'll never be together here. You'll never be Bryn." And Bryn was who I'd wanted, who I'd loved. "I want you, not Sahn."

His smile was the saddest thing I'd ever seen. "Rowan, there was never any difference. We will have the memory. Memories were enough for Nereida and I. They will be enough for us."

I couldn't accept this, wouldn't. "Bryn, please. Not now, just wait."

"It may already be too late to—"

I cried out when a sudden pain struck my shoulder.

Bryn rose above me, fear darkening his golden eyes. *Rowan, what happened? What is it?*

Then something pinched my arm, yanked on it, on me. "I don't know. I—it feels like someone's grabbing me."

His dappled-gray wings whipped wide. "No. *No!*" Bryn grabbed me, tried to pin me to this world while his tears fell like rain on my cheeks.

But Sahn's perfect face wavered, the leaves behind him beginning to dissolve in pinpricks of light. My body jittered in the sand like it'd been struck by lightning.

"Don't let go, Bryn. Don't let—"

But then the world broke apart for a second time.

And when I woke, I met Tye's desperate face.

CHAPTER 59

Repeat Until Death

Day 10

I beat my fists against Tye's chest.

It felt like my ribs were being pried apart with a crowbar.

Bryn! I shouted, but the channel between us was dead.

The bed squealed like a stuck pig when Tye plunged a knee into its springs. "Roe!" he shouted, voice hoarse, face stark in the swift afternoon light. "Roe, Jesus Christ, wake up!"

He grunted when my punch connected, but held on. "Where's Bryn?" I demanded incoherently. "Where is he?"

Tye shook me roughly. "What the hell are you on about now?" He pushed away from me, stabbing a hand through his hair.

My breath panted out in the freezing room.

"You've been asleep for nearly twenty damn hours," Tye said.

Twenty hours? Was that how long it'd taken for me to convince Bryn to throw himself at the Gate? It'd take his soul and toss it to Ruhaven, but it was me the Gate was supposed to take. Me that should have traded my soul for Willow's. Never Bryn.

"You let the room get sloppy with cold. It's your own damn fault if you're freezin' up here, Roe. Twenty hours. What the hell's gotten into ya? And now you're beggin' after Stornoway. Can't ya make it two damn weeks?"

I reached inside me, struggling to grasp the thread, but it evaporated in my grip.

Because Bryn was suppressing it now.

The room swam as a sob burst from my throat.

Tye lurched to me. "Goddamn, I don't got time for this. Levi's missin', and you're havin' a nervous breakdown after two weeks without your boyfriend." He grabbed my shoulders, half-hugging, half-shaking me. "You've only got days to go. Days, and then ya can leave."

Days until I'd never know Bryn again. Until everything that made him was nothing. Until I killed him.

I shoved Tye. "Get away from me."

"Fine, Roe." Tye strode toward the door, paused. "But I'm gonna check on ya in a few hours. Don't ya be takin' no twenty-hour trips again."

I was crawling to the window before the door slammed.

My heart hammered in my ribs, a moth's wings bleating the light. I wedged the old glass up one painful inch at a time, the wood swollen, paint peeling, and propped it on my shoulders, then shoved my head into January's frozen light.

And frantically searched for the tree house he said he'd hid in.

Snow blinded the witch trees, banking into frosty mounds. Pines stood awkwardly between the barren twigs and congealed leaves. But in the crowded forest, the old fort was empty.

Day 11

Day 12

Day 13

M y throat felt like someone had dragged nails down the inside of it. I'd run out of things to blow my nose on yesterday. My stomach ached, my eyes burned, my entire body seemed to be rejecting what I shouldn't have allowed.

"Roe, darlin'?"

Had Bryn made the Fall? Had he taken Willow with him? Would I even know?

"Roe."

What had my last words been? Something insignificant and forgettable.

Selfish. That's what I was. Just like Tye had accused me of being.

"Are ya even listenin' to me?"

The ripe smell of leather soap stung my nose. Boots clacked across the hardwood floor, a jackhammer against my temples.

Someone crouched in front of me, their seaweed-green eyes a distant cousin of blue. Not like Bryn's, which were ice held up to the sky.

Tye swept his auburn hair into a short ponytail at his neck. "Ya got one day left, Roe. There ain't no need to be sittin' under this freezin' window, waitin' for the cold to steal a limb or two from ya. If ya ask me, you've needed these two weeks a hell of a lot more than I thought."

Bryn should have made it to the Gate by now.

I would never touch him again. We would never go to Norway together, never see Scotland. I would never take a left with him at the North Pole. I wouldn't hear his polite voice, or his soft groan when I licked his throat. I'd never hear him play the piano. Never learn how he'd become so skilled at it. I'd never see Odda. Never have cabbage stew.

"...think I'll go to Las Vegas," Tye said, drawing a smoke from his pack.

I would never go sailing. Never see the lighthouse in Bryn's memories, never run my hands through his cornsilk hair, never watch his eyes fire to gold.

"I always wanted to see the world, do a bit of travelin'. Think maybe now's my time to do it. Got a bit of money put away, what with workin' for Carmen. She's always had things taken care of, as far as that goes."

Las Vegas. That's what Tye had chosen over Ruhaven? That's why he'd helped Carmen kill us?

But was I any better? I'd sold Bryn for my twin.

A lit cigarette fell to the floor, rolled silently under the bed.

I'd never go fishing with Bryn, never—

Tye roared.

My gaze flew to his. Mouth open, he stumbled backward. Staring at me with eyes wide and wild, fear coating his face. Nostrils flaring.

"Tye, what—"

"No, no, NO!" The floor cracked when Tye dropped to his knees, a shaking hand reaching toward me.

I swatted at him, but my hands passed through.

My startled scream died in my throat when I saw what he was staring at.

Tye rubbed the tail of my braid between his fingers—a braid that was disappearing. In the cold light, like tiny firelights burning out of oxygen, the strands whisked away, one by one by one, floating in the breeze of the fan, dissolving into nothing.

Like Kazie had.

Slowly, I raised my shaking hands.

My fingers were translucent, the bones shining through like an x-ray until I could see clear through to Tye's enraged face.

Then Bryn had made it. He'd made it, and soon, I'd feel nothing, be nothing. All of this would go away. I'd go away, just like I wanted.

"What the hell have you done?" Tye growled, dropping my braid like it'd scalded him. His horrified eyes stared at me through my palm, through the finger that should have worn Bryn's ring.

I curled what was left of them into fists at my side.

Everything that was me, was Roe, was coming to a rapid, miserable end, finishing with as little fanfare as it began—in the shadow of Willow.

Tye shot to his feet.

"I'm sorry, Tye." They were the only words I could think of.

He whirled on me, eyes hot with fear and dread. "Sorry? You're sorry for killin' me? For somehow—some goddamn how—makin' the Fall after I spared you? After I made sure you'd have a fuckin' life here?" He launched his foot into the food tray, sending it pinwheeling across the room.

Then my feet disappeared.

The lack of them sent Tye into more outrage, but his voice was distant in my ears.

I hugged what was left of my knees to my chest. "Bryn's doing it for me."

Tye's face twisted into disbelief. "For you?" Then his voice lowered to a fast-talking growl. "When we left, Stornoway didn't know nothin' 'bout us being Tethered. 'Bout how it pulled us through the Gate. Roe, darlin'," he crouched to eye level with me. "What the hell have you fuckin' done?"

I'd sold Bryn. "I told him through our thread, and now he's—he's—
"

Tye clenched his jaw so hard, the veins bulged in his temple. "You're a damn fool, Roe. Ya know that? A damn, lovestruck fool." He lifted his hand, and for a moment, looked like he might strike me. I would have welcomed the physical pain. Instead, he stroked the hair from my face, his hand vibrating with barely restrained fury. "You just handed Stornoway the last thing he needed—permission."

I shook my head. "He didn't want to make the Fall. He never did."

"No, Roe." Tye's eyes cooled to jade stone. "That's been his plan from the beginnin'. Why I wanted to keep you two apart. Why I called him in Norway, said what I said 'bout you. 'Cause all you've ever been is a ticket home for Nereida."

Biting my cheeks, I lifted my chin. I wouldn't play this game with Tye anymore. I had nothing to explain, nothing to convince him of. I knew what the truth was—and that was Bryn.

Tye grinned, but it was all teeth. "You fell for every bit of it. Even when I warned ya. He's been manipulatin' you to make that Fall since ya met, and here I was, knowing the truth the whole time—that he never needed you. That as soon as he made the Fall, he'd yank ya with him. As Nereida. So I pushed him away, pushed James to exile him, to keep him away." Tye smoothed his thumb over my throat.

Disgusted, I looked away from him, staring hard at the unfinished attic wall.

"You wanna know the real bitch if it?" he said. "Carmen wanted me to get rid of ya, but I saw a sad woman in a lousy repair shop, and I couldn't do it. It'd be like stompin' on a little mouse—that's the way I saw it. Maybe 'cause you're my Tether, I dunno. But I didn't think ya deserved to die as Nereida. Or to be used like that."

I swallowed against his thumb. "You want me to be grateful you didn't kill me? Bryn's going to the Gate for Willow. For me."

Tye shoved me against the wood beam. "Bullshit! He's doin' it for himself. Because you were stupid enough to tell Stornoway he didn't need ya. I kept the connection between the three of us a secret to protect you. If Stornoway knew, he'd have thrown himself to the Fall without ever worryin' about whether you wanted to."

No, Bryn would never do that to me. Of the two of us, it'd been me who threw him away.

Bryn would be at the Gate now, facing what I should have had the courage to do. For the second time, he would stand before Ruhaven in judgment. For Willow, for me.

And maybe, for the belief that we were meant to return, that there was a reason we'd been written into the Ledger. That Ruhaven had called us home.

"Look what you've done to me. To us." Tye's hand trembled at my throat. "What kinda life am I gonna have in Drachaut?" He leaned in, pressed his hot lips to my forehead. Sweat beaded in the scruff of his throat. "I could finish this right here," he murmured, softly now. "Do what Carmen wanted me to all those years ago. What I should have done."

"It's too late," I managed. "And I know you won't."

Tye shifted closer, practically in my lap because my legs no longer existed. "Ya don't think I will?" he whispered.

"No. No, I don't," I managed, voice rough. "You think I don't see you, Tye, but I do. I did. Whatever you said about needing to stay at Naruka, about needing a Drachaut there, it's not true, not really."

He sneered. "Sure it is. We gotta keep tabs on you guys. Before ya kill us, just like you are now, like Carmen warned me ya would."

Something scurried beneath the bed, furry, quick, a little mouse come to watch my last breaths. But I focused on Tye. On the lily-green eyes that had looked at me all those months ago and told me I was nothing. On the lips that had lazily sneered about my hometown.

Because he'd wanted me to see Ruhaven. Even if it meant I'd learn about the Fall.

"You didn't have to bring me to Naruka, Tye. You could have left me in L'Ardoise, told James I wouldn't leave my family, had found another job, that I hated you." I swallowed, trying to work feeling into my throat before I lost it too. "But you didn't."

His eyes burned furiously. "I shoulda. Goddamn it, I shoulda."

"But you gave me a chance," I pushed. "The same one Bryn is giving me. And— And you saved the cat."

His eyes went wide. "What?"

"Patrick's cat. You brought him here when Levi killed him."

The hand tightened again. "So you think 'cause I saved a cat, I ain't gonna save myself now?"

He *should* save himself.

Because who was I? Who *was* I? Nothing—Tye had said so from the beginning, and maybe he'd seen that before anyone else. A little girl in a little town. A dumpster, he'd called it.

Because I'd been like L'Ardoise.

A void of indecision, like a cutout in a piece of paper, and I was the shape it left.

Not like Willow, who'd known from the first stroke of a piano key what she wanted. But she wasn't a skill or a degree. She wasn't the last concert in L'Ardoise, or any of her awards. She wasn't her friends, she wasn't her purse with the beads. She wasn't our old apartment with the magazine pages taped to the walls. She wasn't her favorite pillow with the tassels, she wasn't the same movie she'd watched over and over. She wasn't even just my sister.

She was Willow.

And that had always been enough. She hadn't stumbled upon the piano one day and suddenly recognized who she was. She didn't need anything to define her.

And that's what I wanted.

Because who was I? Really?

An electrician, a handiworker, Willow's sister, Bryn's mate. Line 1274 in the Ledger.

No, none of those things.

Maybe that's what Bryn had given me—a chance to be someone to myself, a chance to start over.

I lifted my chin, met the greenest eyes I'd ever seen, but they were already beginning to fade—like me. "Tye, you said before, when you first showed me Ruhaven, you said I didn't know who I was."

The frown between his brows deepened. "So?"

"Well, I think I know who I am now."

He bared his teeth. "Who, my fuckin' executioner? Is that it?"

"No, Tye," I said softly. "I'm Nereida."

CHAPTER 60

ℌallelujah

I groaned.

Something burned in my heart, in my chest, in my lungs, like a bone collector had rummaged through and plucked out all the best parts of me.

Dead. I was dead in that attic.

The pain was my soul being carved from this body, then washed and prepped for its journey home.

Had Bryn made it?

Had Willow?

Had I?

I squeezed my eyes harder and—wait. *My* eyes. These weren't my eyes.

I winged them open.

Water droplets collected on the tips of metallic eyelashes with such clarity that they appeared as gigantic bubbles. I looked past them to the electric teals, violent purples, radioactive blues. *This isn't right.* Everything sparkled, even the fine drops of mist in the air.

Slowly, I looked down.

My silver skin glistened from the rain and showed every curve of lean muscle. Strands of clear jelly hair pooled over my body and tangled in the grass. A diesel-scented breeze fluttered over my naked body, tightening my nipples, curling my claws into the supple earth.

Though the skin was unbroken, my chest burned with invisible pain. But I almost welcomed it, some last feeling before I didn't exist.

I flexed my fingers and felt them extend suddenly, whipping out too fast.

Because I was in control.

Not a memory, not an illusion, not a dream I'd slipped into. But *me*. My body, my thoughts. *My* lungs that rose and fell around the crack in my chest.

But this wasn't Ruhaven.

After three tries, I rolled to my hands and knees. Coughed.

The oaks looked different through these eyes—filthy, dirty, invisible black particles clinging to the bark.

I struggled to crawl. Ended up tunneling through soggy grass as easily as butter.

Ireland. I couldn't be Nereida in Ireland.

But I was.

Fear coiled in my heart, mixing with the pain that was steadily slicing it in two.

Then, a strange sound broke through my daze.

I lifted my head.

Another wheezing cry hiccuped into my left ear. It didn't register right—the decibels were off, the whole world was too sharp and muffled at the same time.

But I turned toward the sound, seeing the trees whip by because I'd moved too fast again.

My eyes landed on something wooly and dark, the fabric a dense thread with little specks that—

I zoomed out. Focused again.

James?

Another sob hurt my ears.

I couldn't focus, couldn't concentrate with my eyes latching on to every insignificant detail before jumping to the next.

"James?" My voice tinkered in the air, and I could swear I *saw* the sound of it.

He knelt at the Gate. His mouth moved quickly, a prayer mumbled under his breath. His shoulders shook. Dark tear tracks stained his face.

I called again, my voice distorted. Maybe he couldn't hear me in this octave.

I started toward him, off balance in this new body. My talons bit into cold dirt, burying themselves in the cutting ivy and velvet moss, sending a thousand tiny pulses to my brain.

"James, I'm here, and Tye, he…"

Wait. What was that? That *thing* he was staring at? My eyes flicked out, in, out, adjusted.

And finally landed on what lay sprawled before James, pale and naked on the frozen dirt.

My pulse thumped. Died.

And the pain in my heart gave way to something so much worse.

My hands shook violently, my elbows knocking together. Bile burned the back of my throat. Something in me was breaking, some piece of me I didn't know I had.

"Ye bloody buggering," James murmured, wiping at tears. But the words weren't for me. I didn't exist. Not here. Not anymore. "Ye fecking ejit, ye bloody, ye—ye…" He broke off, pressing the heel of his palms into his eyes and cursing violently.

And as he did, I stared at what had once been Bryn.

My Bryn.

He lay on his back, on the striped blanket he'd always rolled out for us, naked, but for scraps of pleated trousers, a linen shirt. They clung to his waxy skin like Ruhaven had started to pull him home, then spit him out.

His right hand rested in a fist over his chest. Shadows flickered blues over skin that looked like a cruel art sculpture. His hair, the only color left, stirred as the wind blew. The rain had left silver tears over goose-pimpled skin. Dark tattoos stood out in stark relief.

Snap.

The lantern crashed to pieces at my silvery knees. James glanced at it, but not me. Wax pooled between flattened clovers and stones. I crawled over the glass, dragging my heavy limbs through the warm liquid.

My bones felt numb. Even the aching pain in my chest had lowered to a distant throb. I couldn't feel my muscles. My ears were the inside of a seashell.

I choked on a sob.

Please, please, not *him*.

This wasn't possible. It wasn't. It couldn't be. Bryn never faltered, never doubted, was never wrong. He—he'd known everything about Ruhaven. Had worshipped the world as much as Nereida.

Ruhaven would never reject him. And he'd never let it.

And he'd never leave me.

When I finally reached Bryn, my body was empty of everything.

I could only stare. And stare, and stare. Time seemed to give up and go home. James was some distant memory. L'Ardoise nonexistent.

"Bryn?" I mumbled through tears. "*Bryn?*"

He stared at the shuddering leaves, frozen, alone—opaque eyes like an endless dead sea.

I tried to check for a heartbeat, to lay my cheek on his chest, but I only passed through.

A ghost. I was the ghost now. A ghost of Nereida. As inconsequential as I'd ever been.

And Bryn was dead.

But Ruhaven hadn't taken him.

I had.

For a moment, I just kneeled there. Time passed. James no longer sobbed. But something broke inside me, again and again, until the pieces of whatever had shattered were yanked out of me on a choking sob.

It was happening again.

God, this should have been *me*. Not Willow. Not Bryn. *Me* who lay here at the Gate, *me* who died by the Inquitate.

I wrapped my arms around my ribs as uncontrollable sobs wracked my body, the sound like crashing bells on marble. But James didn't look at me. He heard nothing. Saw nothing.

Because this was my punishment. For choosing Willow. For killing my own mate. For offering everything Bryn was to the Gate like he was garbage.

Clutching my ribs, I tried to hold on to Bryn, to grab his hand again, but my own passed through. Over and over and over.

Eventually, like he could bear my ghost's attempts no longer, James crawled to Bryn and reached toward the pale hand clenched over Bryn's chest. James turned Bryn's fist over, peeled up stiff fingers, and pried out the tiny thing in his grasp.

The opal ring shined pink in dawn's light on a circlet of meteor gold.

I hadn't noticed the fine detail before, the gold band carved in the shape and form of a twisted branch, when he'd been pouring his heart out to me on my bedroom floor. When I'd thrown it all back at him and chosen Willow.

"I'll bury this for ye anyway," James said stiffly.

While he dug a fresh hole, mist dribbled from the skies, uncaring of the Ruhavens huddled under the ancient oaks. The tractor trumpeted the fields, cows droned a constant hum. Rapeseed was replanted. Life, in Naruka, plowed on.

But my long ears twitched when I heard something behind me, sharp and heavy, like footsteps crunching in L'Ardoise's snow.

My blood went to ice. My eyes to James.

Back to me, tears fell as he dug with his hands. How long had it taken for me to appear here, as Nereida? Long enough for Carmen. For Tye. For Levi.

And every protective instinct kicked in.

I grabbed for James before I remembered I could do nothing.

But he didn't look at me, or the shadow slithering toward us and over Bryn's lifeless form.

I rose slowly, dragging Nereida's body up limb by limb to face the threat behind me. I could feel its slow breathing whisper across my neck.

My talons slid out. I barely felt the slight tearing of skin as they lengthened and bit into my palms. Teeth pricked my bottom lip. My blood began to pulse rapidly, not as fast as a human's, but a grizzly rousing from hibernation.

I dug my heel into the ground, spread my hands wide to block both James and Bryn.

And spun around.

Then stopped. Froze.

"Willow?" I croaked.

She—I—she was—

I stumbled back. Shuddered and jerked when my heel went straight through James's back.

Across the Gate, Willow crept toward me, a shadow amongst the bare trees, wearing the outfit she used to lounge in every Saturday morning—coveralls, a striped red-and-white top, and her patched jean jacket with a music note stitched on the breast pocket. With each step, a tiny, jeweled piano thumped against her neck—the one that now dangled from her truck's rearview mirror. The blonde hair she'd been buried with was gone, replaced by the long, dark mane that had always matched mine. Until it hadn't.

An Inquitate. And yet...

I bit my lip when my chin wobbled. My eyes burned, my lungs strained, my throat tightened until I was surprised I could draw any air at all.

Was she shorter? I'd always had to look up to her. But no, I was taller now—as Nereida.

"Rowan."

My legs vibrated. It was her voice. Her exact voice, with all the easy sway and lyrical sound that made you think if she wasn't a pianist, she should be. It was the voice on the recording of her introducing a rehearsal piece I'd listened to a thousand times over.

"Willow?" I said again, while a tiny person inside me screamed to run. To warn James. To confront this Inquitate before it defiled the Gate.

But my tongue seemed glued to the roof of my mouth, and her old scent of clarinet oil and books was so familiar that my throat swelled in recognition.

"Rowan? It's me," she said quietly. Her eyes bent in sympathy.

Warily, I circled the Gate, keeping my ghost between her and the Ruhavens behind me.

"You're an Inquitate," I told my sister, my wavering voice betraying my fear.

She stopped feet away, but her face held none of the joy I'd imagined when we met again. "Rowan, I'm so sorry. For Bryn. For leaving you. For wanting to leave L'Ardoise. For not being here with you."

God, I hadn't even known how badly I'd wanted to hear that. "*Stop.*"

She took another step forward. "Rowan, I've missed you so fucking much."

I blinked against the flood of tears, struggled to keep my hands lifted, ready. I wanted to grab her to me, just hold her for a second. Just once, even if it was an illusion, even if I didn't deserve it.

But I couldn't. For James, for Bryn.

"Which are you?" I croaked. "Levi's? Tye's? Carmen's?"

She seemed to struggle with her own tears—something I'd never seen from Willow. "Levi's dead," she said.

I raised my arms, hands balled into quivering fists. "You're a liar."

She shook her head, dark hair catching on the stitched patches of her jacket. "Bryn killed him. Four days ago," she said, wetting her lips, her mouth crinkling with all the lines it used to have.

Of course Bryn hadn't killed him. Not with a cane, not without Sahn.

I shoved my fingers through my hair, the slimy strands the only thing I could touch. Everything that made me was boiling from the inside out. My sister standing before me, my mate dead at my feet, James's muted cries a dead beat in my ear. And a part of me wanted it to all end.

"Rowan, I don't have long."

My gaze snapped back to Inquitate.

"Not nearly long enough to explain, to apologize," she continued, throat bobbing. "For everything." Deceptive tears welled in her midnight eyes.

We both watched James slowly rise, murmuring the prayer he'd offered Kazie, then lower the ring I'd rejected into the hole he'd dug.

That's when she moved.

"*Don't, don't, don't!*" I yelled, my hands passing through Willow as I lunged.

I splattered in the mud, in the weeds and ivy. "Please," I begged my twin.

Standing next to Bryn, her toes touching one open palm, she stared down at his naked body. His unseeing eyes bore into hers.

"Was it worth it?" she asked hollowly.

"I'll do whatever you want. Go wherever," I tried, rising to my knees. "But leave them. Don't—"

"Tallah trades in energy," she spoke over me, toying with the piano at her neck. "Bryn wanted to bring something to Ruhaven that wasn't there before. *Me*. He upset the balance, and Tallah made up for it. He knew it would."

My heart beat so wildly, I could barely hear her words. "If you just tell me what you want," I begged, "I'll—"

"Ruhaven gave him a choice." Her dark eyes were like the void, the empty space between worlds. Like my Prayama. "He chose. Me for him," she said. "For you, Rowan."

I pressed my hands to my eyes. *Lies*. He'd *never* have chosen to separate us, to die with our souls divided between Tallah and here.

Her hair, as black as her eyes, swirled in tendrils of dark smoke. Multi-colored veins pulsed at her temples. At her fingertips, the nails shone with twilight's last gasp of color. Her skin flickered in and out, stars winking in the night.

On hands and knees, I crawled to Bryn, arched over him, as if my ghost could protect his. "Please," I begged, tilting my head up at the illusion of Willow. "Not him."

Her low exhale was like an ancient forest taking its last breath. Then she lifted a hand, hovered it over us, her fingers flickering like a television caught between channels. There. Gone. Twirling. Still.

"I'm assuming you don't want someone else?" she asked, an eyebrow snaking up, the movement so like my sister that it jolted.

She sank into a crouch, gliding her hands through my head and over Bryn's sprawled form. I swatted at her fingers, the darkness that pooled at the tips. But I felt nothing. Could do nothing.

James sat beside all of us, watching through empty eyes. If they killed him, too, I couldn't—couldn't—

"Willow," I tried, my lips thick and numb. "Whatever you want, whatever *they* want, I'll do it. I'll shut down Naruka, stop Ruhavens from Falling."

The darkness seeped from her fingertips into Bryn's body. "I'm not an Inquitate, Rowan."

I folded over Bryn, through him, into the wet earth below. Clung to whatever there was left. "You're *not* my sister."

"No," she said, lifting opaque eyes—two black holes where light didn't penetrate. Where stars burned and died. "I'm your spirit. You passed the rite."

Silence rang. "What?"

"That's what Bryn gave us, what Ruhaven wanted, what Sahn waited eight hundred years for—a Mark that exists outside of laws and trades. Outside of Tallah. The entropic spirit. Entropy. Me. That's why we were the first twins in the *Ledger*—one of us was the spirit for the rite we never passed together in Ruhaven. But now you have, Rowan, by choosing me, choosing Ruhaven."

My heart hammered in my ribs. "Get *away* from us. Get—" I broke off when James flinched.

His mouth opened to gaping, the cigarette he'd been trying to light dropped from his shaking fingers. He started to rise, staggered, then fell to his knees, his eyes fixed on Bryn's body.

Willow stood, walking away from Bryn, toward my brother.

I started to crawl. "Wait, please."

The woods quieted, the leaves barely stirring, the normal hum of critters gone. The breaking dawn speared tangerine rays through the leaves. The light stopped when it struck Willow—no, it bent, twisted, and died.

But a flash of movement drew my attention from her.

To the man who'd been born of and from Ruhaven, lying in the middle of the Gate.

His gears were turning.

Oh god.

I was weeping, rocking, as the marks whirled on his skin. "Willow, what have you *done*?"

"I told you," she whispered. "I don't need to make a trade. I can bring O'Sahnazekiel with us, without an exchange. That is why O'Sahnazekiel wanted you to return with the spirit of entropy, because it is the only thing that can fight the Inquitate, the only energy not bound by the laws of balance." Willow stood behind James, her hands settling on his shoulders as she bent down, whispered something that had James's eyes widening behind thick glasses, his mouth parting in surprise.

She straightened and turned around, casting a glance over her shoulder. "Rowan," she said, and for a moment—just a moment—that old smile glimmered. "I'm really glad I didn't have to punch this one."

My chest caved in.

"No, no, wait—goddamn it, wait!"

But the mist swallowed her, a curtain of cream fog that collapsed in her wake. The sky, with its streaky pink hues and clementine golds crept through the canopy of leaves until Willow was only a vague scent in the air—bananas and clarinet oil and the crisp newness of sheet music.

James turned and looked over his shoulder like he could see my sister. Then he rose on legs that trembled as much as mine and took one hesitant step toward where she'd disappeared. And another.

But for once, I didn't go after her, because I'd never leave Bryn again.

His body glowed with a hundred tattoos, each burning gold and spinning. The cogs moved over his arm, down his torso, along his inner thigh, to the top of his right foot—like they had when Sahn rescued me in Drachaut, when he'd made love to me in the woods, when he'd teased me after I'd jumped at a butterfly.

My heart pounded—Nereida's heart pounded—a wild, reckless rhythm. And the pain in my chest dulled for the first time.

Bronze light bled through Bryn's eyelashes, trickled in thick drops over his cheeks, pooled at the corners of his wide mouth, and ran down his rough jaw to the shallow crevice of his shoulders.

It spilled out his mouth, bubbled up on a gasp. Our thread flared and flung itself out in a forked whip, snapping the earth like electricity searching to be grounded. Sparks shattered before floating up in an invisible vortex.

A cry broke the silence.

Eyes closed, Bryn arched off the ground, skin stretched tight, sweat beading on his forehead. Veins bulged under his neck and ran blue over his bare chest.

"Bryn, I'm sorry, I'm sorry, I'm sorry," I babbled, trying to hold him, to help, to ease.

Bryn rolled to his side, his body rippling like an invisible beast lurked beneath.

On a low growl, he dropped his forehead to the earth.

His back split in two, and dappled, silver wings whipped through the forest.

My mouth dropped open.

They sprouted in a rainbow of smoke—pure snow at the wing's blade, to dappled gray, to silky charcoal, to pink where the sunrise glowed through. The sky parted for them, the trees cowed. His feathers brushed leaves and ivy, branches snapped, even the hawthorn tree bowed and toppled over.

When I looked again, I barely recognized the Norwegian who'd wanted a home in Ruhaven, knowing in my soul, in my heart, that I was looking at Bryn for the last time.

He bunched his fingers, drove his fist into the earth.

I reached for his hand. And this time, mine didn't pass through. So I held on, our fingers linked, and swore every promise I should have made to him long ago.

I felt the ripple of it—of power, of the new and the reborn, of starting over.

His torso expanded, his shoulders broadened, the muscle knitted in his broken leg, the blackened skin smoothing out to the palest gold, his toes curled into talons deadlier than mine.

Crack. A velvet tail snapped the crisp air, feathers whistling on the end.

Drums bellowed from far-off mountains—the call of Ruhaven, a soaring chorus that vibrated in my very bones.

I stared and stared at him, even as the fangs lengthened, hoping to memorize each detail before he was gone. The soft crease of his eyes, the faint laugh line that hadn't had time to deepen, the angular nose that would twitch with amusement. The man I'd never see grow old.

And then it was done.

Bryn was gone.

Sahn panted into my palm, skin flickering like a lightbulb about to burst. The short, moonlit locks lengthened into a golden river that tangled with my silver hair. Light crackled and popped around us as he shifted to his hands and knees, head bowed, his back rippling with the effort of lifting his newly formed wings.

When he opened his eyes at last, I knew I hadn't lost him—the man who'd given up everything for Willow and I, for me.

"Rowan? God, Rowan?"

I cupped his face in my silvery hands, thumbing away the golden tears that leaked down his shimmering skin, pressing fleeting kisses over his cheeks before I wrapped my arms around him and buried my face in the crook of his neck, as if I could keep his shaking body tied to mine. But I knew we didn't have long now. I could feel it everywhere, nipping at my skin, the same feeling as when his own world had dissolved between us.

"I did not believe we would have this chance," he said, his words muffled against my neck.

"Of course we would," I whispered through my own tears, more certain than I'd been of anything before. "Because you were right—there's no place your soul could ever go that mine wouldn't follow."

I held on to him, held on to every piece of us that never was, and every piece that could have been. The mornings in Norway we might have had, the ship we'd have sailed, the scent of Bryn that had always been full of adventure and secrets. The whisper of his lips at my ear, the feel of his hands cradling my cheeks, the sound of his own promises, as if by mapping each piece of the man, I wouldn't forget. Wouldn't forget what we had, what was, what would yet be still.

And when the soaring notes slowed, the melody holding a fermata on the ringing, augmented chord of E major, at last, at long last...

I heard the minor fall.

ACKNOWLEDGEMENTS

First and foremost, to my husband, Declan—*thank you*.

Four years ago, while I was compelled to write this story, you kept life running: you kept me fed, kept the wheels on the car, the house clean, our bills paid, and got the dog to the vet. I don't know how either of us managed to juggle both my writing and painting, but I know few people are as lucky as I am to have someone like you. I want to especially thank you for giving my manuscript your "Irish sensitivity" read, though I still insist James would have said "like" a lot more.

To my sister, Rachelle—I don't know if this book makes up for how much I hated you when we were kids, but I definitely know paying for all those trips around Europe together did! You were my very first reader, and the only critic that mattered, which wasn't easy because you had to brace yourself every time I took umbrage at your feedback. But you hung in there, you persisted, you sent me audio recordings even though you risked an earful when you told me Bryn and Roe kissed too early, and ultimately, this book is better because of you.

To my best friend, Rachelle (pronounced 'Rachel'!), thank you for being not only one of my initial readers, but the only reviewer to leave the cutest little thoughtful notes on nearly every page. It was nearly as rewarding to read your feedback as it was to write the novel, and I'm so glad you loved Bryn as much as I did!

To Victoria—wow, I probably have a lot to thank you for—moral support, reading all my texts (and podcasts), inviting me to Bulgaria, volunteering to read the book of a first-time author, creating an entire cover at the last minute when my own designer quit suddenly, all the other graphic work you did, explaining what bleeds are, and generally being awesome.

To my editor, Jessica McKelden—thank you for your attention to detail, and for the fun and thoughtful comments you left throughout my manuscript.

To my friends in Ireland—thank you for listening to me explain this book again and again (and again). For nodding through every chapter breakdown, indulging every idea, and never once telling me to please, for the love of everything, stop talking about it.

And finally, to Roe, Bryn, James, Tye, and Kazie—thank you for being in my thoughts for the last four years, for coming to life on the page when I didn't think I could type another word, and for providing me with endless inspiration. I think it was hard to let this book go, because I didn't want you to end.

But that's okay, because we'll see each other soon in Ruhaven.

Bye, guys. *xoxo*

About the Author

Kayla is an award-winning oil painter and author living in Wicklow, Ireland, where the rugged landscapes and vibrant culture provide an authentic backdrop for her debut novel.

A lifelong reader of romance fantasy, Kayla has been writing stories since she was given her first computer, spending weekends huddled in her room, writing page after page of new worlds.

Now that she's *slightly* older (sigh), Kayla draws on her diverse interests and experiences to create authentic, unforgettable characters, and her artist's eye helps her craft vivid, atmospheric scenes.

Kayla has always been drawn to stories of soulmates and romance, and her own love story began in Florence, Italy, where she met her now-husband during one very interesting vacation (perhaps, eventually, there'll be a book on that too!).

Outside of writing, Kayla enjoys painting, playing the piano, and walking her dog, Storm, through Wicklow's beautiful forest trails, where she received much of her inspiration for *The Minor Fall*.

This is Kayla's first novel, but it won't be her last.

To get updates on the latest giveaways, new releases, and events, go to theminorfall.com. You can follow Kayla on social media at @kmmartellauthor.

9 781036 913106